THE WORKS OF
RABELAIS

THE WORKS OF
RABELAIS

TUDOR PUBLISHING COMPANY
New York

CONTENTS

BOOK I

BOOK II

BOOK III

BOOK IV

BOOK V

TO THE READERS

Good friends, my readers, who peruse this book,
Be not offended, whilst on it you look:
Denude yourselves of all deprav'd affection,
For it contains no badness nor infection:
'Tis true that it brings forth to you no birth
Of any value, but in point of mirth;
Thinking therefore how sorrow might your mind
Consume, I could no apter subject find;
    One inch of joy surmounts of grief a span;
    Because to laugh is proper to the man.

THE WORKS OF
RABELAIS

THE AUTHOR'S PROLOGUE

TO

THE FIRST BOOK

MOST noble and illustrious drinkers, and you thrice precious pockified blades (for to you and none else do I dedicate my writings), Alcibiades, in that dialogue of Plato's, which is entitled, "The Banquet," whilst he was setting forth the praises of his schoolmaster, Socrates (without all question the prince of philosophers), amongst other discourses to that purpose said, that he resembled the Sileni. Sileni of old were little boxes, like those we now may see in the shops of apothecaries, painted on the outside with wanton toyish figures, as harpies, satyrs, bridled geese, horned hares, saddled ducks, flying goats, thiller harts, and other such like counterfeited pictures, at pleasure, to excite people unto laughter, as Silenus himself, who was the foster-father of good Bacchus, was wont to do; but within those capricious caskets called Sileni, were carefully preserved and kept many rich and fine drugs, such as balm, ambergreese, amamon, musk, civet, with several kinds of precious stones, and other things of great price. Just such another thing was Socrates: for to have eyed his outside, and esteemed of him by his exterior appearance, you would not have given the peel of an onion for him, so deformed he was in body, and ridiculous in his gesture. He had a sharp pointed nose, with the look of a bull, and countenance of a fool; he was in his carriage simple, boorish in his apparel, in fortune poor, unhappy in his wives, unfit for all offices in the commonwealth, always laughing, tippling, and merry, carousing to every one, with continual jibes and jeers, the better by those means to conceal his divine knowledge. But opening this box, you would have found within it a heavenly and inestimable drug, a more than human understanding, an admirable virtue, matchless learning, invincible courage, inimitable sobriety, certain contentment of mind, perfect assurance, and an incredible disregard of all that for which men commonly do so much watch, run, sail, fight, travel, toil and turmoil themselves.

3

Whereunto (think ye?) doth this little flourish of a preamble tend; for so much as you, my good disciples, and some other jolly fools of ease and leisure, reading the pleasant titles of some books of our invention, as Gargantua, Pantagruel, Whippot, the Dignity of Codpieces, of Pease and Bacon, with a Commentary, &c., are too ready to judge, that there is nothing in them but jests, mockeries, lascivious discourse, and recreative lyes; because the outside (which is the Title) is usually, without any farther enquiry, entertained with scoffing and derision. But, truly, it is very unbeseeming to make so slight account of the works of men, seeing yourselves avouch that it is not the habit makes the monk; many being monasterially accoutred, who inwardly are nothing less than monachal; and that there are of those that wear Spanish cloaks, who have but little of the valour of Spaniards in them. Therefore is it, that you must open the book, and seriously consider of the matter treated in it, then shall you find that it containeth things of far higher value than the box did promise; that is to say, that the subject thereof is not so foolish, as by the title, at the first sight, it would appear to be.

And put the case, that in the literal sense you meet with matters that are light and ludicrous, and suitable enough to their inscriptions; yet must not you stop there, as at the melody of the charming syrens; but endeavour to interpret that in a sublimer sense, which, possibly, you might think was spoken in the jollity of heart. Did you ever pick the lock of a cupboard to steal a bottle of wine out of it? Tell me truly, and if you did, call to mind the countenance which then you had: or, did you ever see a dog with a marrow-bone in his mouth (the beast of all others, says Plato, lib. 2, de Republica, the most philosophical?) If you have seen him, you might have remarked with what caution and circumspectness he wards and watcheth it; with what care he keeps it; how fervently he holds it; how prudently he gobbets it; with what affection he breaks it; and with what diligence he sucks it. To what end all this? what moveth him to take all these pains? what are the hopes of his labour? what doth he expect to reap thereby? nothing but a little marrow. True it is, that this little is more savoury and delicious than the great quantities of other sorts of meat, because the marrow, as Galen testifieth, 3. *facult. nat. et* 11 *de usu partium,* is a nourishment most perfectly elaboured by nature.

In imitation of this dog, it becomes you to be wise, to smell, feel, and have in estimation, these fair, goodly books, stuffed with high conceptions, that seem easy and superficial, but are not so readily

4

fathomed; and then, like him, you must, by a sedulous lecture, and frequent meditation, break the bone, and suck out the substantial marrow; that is, my allegorical sense, or the things I to myself propose to be signified by these Pythagorical symbols; with assured hope, that in so doing, you will at last attain to be both very wise and very brave; for, in the perusal of this treatise, you shall find another kind of taste, and a doctrine of a more profound and abstruse consideration, which will disclose unto you the most glorious doctrine and dreadful mysteries, as well in what concerneth our religion, as matters of the public state, and life economical.

Do you believe, upon your conscience, that Homer, whilst he was couching his Iliads and Odysses, had any thought upon those Allegories, which Plutarch, Heraclides, Ponticus, Eustathius, Cornutus, squeezed out of him, and which Politian filched again from them? If that is your faith, you shall never be of my church; who hold that those mysteries were as little dreamed of by Homer, as the Gospel Sacraments were by Ovid, in his Metamorphosis; though a certain Gulligut Friar, and true Bacon-eater, would have undertaken to prove it, if perhaps, he had met with as very fools as himself, and, as the proverb says, "a lid worthy of such a kettle."

If you give any credit to him, why are you not as kind to these jovial new Chronicles of mine? albeit, when I did dictate them, I thought thereof no more than you, who possibly are drinking (the whilst) as I was: for, in the composing of this masterly book, I never lost nor bestowed any more, nor any other time, than what was appointed to serve me for taking of my bodily refection, that is, whilst I was eating and drinking.

And, indeed, that is the fittest and most proper hour, wherein to write these high matters and deep sciences, as Homer knew very well, the paragon of all philologues, and Ennius, the father of the Latin Poets (as Horace calls him) although a certain sneaking jobbernol objected that his verses savoured more of the wine than of the oil.

A certain addle-headed coxcomb saith the same of my books; but a turd for him. The fragrant odour of the wine; oh! how much more sparkling, warming, charming, celestial, and delicious it is, than of oil! and I will glory as much when it is said of me, that I have spent more on wine than oil, as did Demosthenes, when it was told him, that his expense on oil was greater than on wine.

I truly held it for an honour to be called and reputed a good fellow, a pleasant companion, or Merry-Andrew, for under this name

5

am I welcome in all choice companies of Pantagruelists. It was up-braided to Demosthenes, by an envious, surly knave, that his Orations did smell like the sarpler, or clout, that had stopped a musty oil vessel. Therefore, I pray, interpret you all my deeds and sayings, in the perfectest sense; reverence the cheese-like brain that feeds you with all these jolly maggots, and do what lies in you to keep me always merry. Be frolic now, my lads, cheer up your hearts, and joyfully read the rest, with all the ease of your body and comfort to your reins. But, hearken, Joltheads, O, Dickens take ye, off with your bumper, I will do you reason: pull away, Supernaculum.

RABELAIS'S WORKS

TREATING OF THE INESTIMABLE LIFE OF THE

GREAT GARGANTUA

CHAPTER I

OF THE GENEALOGY AND ANTIQUITY OF GARGANTUA

I MUST refer you to the great Chronicle of Pantagruel, for the knowledge of that genealogy and antiquity of race, by which Gargantua is descended unto us: in it you may understand more at large, how the giants were born in this world, and how from them, by a direct line, issued Gargantua, the father of Pantagruel. And do not take it ill, if for this time I pass by it, although the subject be such, that the oftener it were remembered, the more it would please your worships: according to the authority of Plato, in Philebo and Gorgias, and of Flaccus, who says, "That there is some kind of matters (such as these are, without doubt) which, the *frequentlier* they be *repeated,* still prove the more *delectable.*"

Would to God every one had as certain knowledge of his genealogy since the time of the ark of Noah, until this age. I think many are at this day emperors, kings, dukes, princes, and popes, on the earth, whose extraction is from some *porters* and *pardon-pedlars;* as, on the contrary, many are now poor wandering beggars, wretched and miserable mumpers, who are descended of the blood and lineage of great kings and emperors, occasioned (as I conceive it) by the revolution of kingdoms and empires,

From the Assyrians to the Medes;
From the Medes to the Persians;

From the Persians to the Macedonians;
From the Macedonians to the Romans;
From the Romans to the Greeks;
From the Greeks to the Franks.

And to give you some hints concerning myself, who speak unto you; I cannot think but I am come of the race of some rich king or prince in former times; for never yet saw you any man that had a greater desire to be a king, and to be rich, than I have; and to the end only, that I may make good cheer, do nothing, nor care for anything, and plentifully enrich my friends, and all honest and learned men: but herein do I comfort myself, that in the other world I shall be all this: yea, and greater too than at this present I dare wish: As for you, with the same or a better conceit, enjoy yourselves in your distresses, and drink fresh if you can come by it.

But to our matter again; I say, that by the especial care of Heaven, the antiquity and genealogy of Gargantua hath been reserved for our use, more full and perfect than any other except that of the Messias, whereof I mean not to speak; for it belongs not unto my province; and the devils (that is to say) the *false accusers,* and hypocritical *church vermin,* would be upon my jacket. This genealogy was found by John Andeau in a meadow, which he had near the pole-arch, under the Olive tree, as you go to Narsoy. Where, as they were casting up some ditches, the diggers, with their mattocks, struck against a great brazen tomb, unmeasurably long, for they could never find the end thereof, by reason that it entered too far within the sluices of Vienne. Opening this tomb, in a certain place thereof, sealed on the top with the mark of a goblet, about which was written in Hetrurian Letters *HIC BIBITUR,* they found nine flaggons set in such order as they use to rank their skittles in Gascony; of which that which was placed in the middle, had under it a big, greasy, great, grey, jolly, small, mouldy little pamphlet, smelling stronger, but no better than roses.

In that book, the said genealogy was found written all at length, in a Chancery hand, not in paper, not in parchment, nor in wax, but in the bark of an elm tree; yet so worn with the long tract of time, that hardly could three letters together be there perfectly discerned.

I, though unworthy, was sent for thither, and with much help of those spectacles, whereby the art of reading dim writings, and letters that do not clearly appear to the sight, is practised, as Aristotle teaches it; did translate the book, as you may see in your Pantagruelising,

8

that is to say, in drinking stiffly to your own heart's desire; and read-
the dreadful and horrific acts of Pantagruel. At the end of the book
there was a little treatise, intituled "The Antidoted Conundrums."
The rats and moths, or (that I may not lie) other wicked vermin had
nibbled off the beginning; the rest I have hereto subjoined, for the
reverence I bear to antiquity.

CHAPTER II

THE ANTIDOTED CONUNDRUMS, FOUND IN AN
MONUMENT.

———————————— The Cymbrians overcomer
Pass thr—— the air, to shun the dew of summer;
————At his coming great tubs were fill'd,
————Fresh butter down in showers distill'd.
————His grandam overwhelm'd; so hey
Aloud he cried,————
His whiskers all bewray'd, to make him madder,
So bang'd the pitcher, till they rear'd the ladder,

To lick his slipper some told was much better,
Than to gain *pardons,* and the merit greater.
In the meantime a crafty *chuff* approaches,
From the depth issued, where they fish for roaches;
Who said, "Good sirs, some of them let us save:
The eel is here, and in this hollow cave
You'll find, if that our looks on it demur,
A great waste in the bottom of his fur."

To read this chapter when he did begin,
Nothing but a *calf's horns* were found therein.
"I feel," quoth he, "the *mitre* which doth hold
My head so chill, it makes my brains take cold."
Being with the perfume of a *turnip* warm'd,
To stay by chimney hearths himself he arm'd,
Provided that a new *thill*-horse they made
Of every person of a hair-brain'd head.

9

And this continue shall from time to time,
Till Mars be fetter'd for an unknown crime.
Then shall one come who others will surpass,
Delightful, pleasing, matchless, full of grace.
Cheer up your hearts, approach to this repast,
All trusty friends of mine; for he's deceas'd,
Who would not for a world return again,
So highly shall time past be cried up then.

He who was made of *wax* shall lodge each member
Close by the hinges of a block of timber.
We then no more shall *master, master,* whoot,
The *swagger* who th' alarum bell holds out,
Could one seize on the *dagger* which he bears,
Heads would be free from tingling in the ears;
To baffle the whole storehouse of abuses;
And thus farewell Apollo and the Muses.

CHAPTER III

HOW GARGANTUA WAS CARRIED ELEVEN MONTHS IN HIS MOTHER'S BELLY

GRANGOUSIER was a good fellow in his time, and notable jester; he lover to drink neat, as much as any man that then was in the world, and would willingly eat salt meat: to this intent he was ordinarily well furnished with gammons of bacon, both of West-phalia, Mayence, and Bayonne; with store of dried neats' tongues, plenty of links, chitterlings, and puddings in their season; together with salt beef and mustard, a good deal of Botargos, great provision of sausages, not of Bolonia (for he feared the Lombard Boccone), but of Bigorre, Longaulnay, Brene, and Rouargue. In the vigour of his age he married Gargamelle, daughter to the king of the Parpaillons, a jolly pug, and well mouthed wench. These two did oftentimes do the two-backed beast together, joyfully rubbing their bacon against one another, in so far, that at last she became great with child of a fair son, and went with him unto the eleventh month, for so long, yea longer, may a woman carry her great belly; especially when it is some masterpiece of nature, and a person predestinated to the performance, in his due time, of great exploits, as Homer says, that the child, which Neptune begot upon the nymph, was born a whole year after the conception; that is, in the twelfth month; for as Aulus Gellius saith, Lib. 3, this long time was suitable to the majesty of Neptune; that in it the child might receive his form in perfection. For the like reason, Jupiter made the night, wherein he lay with Alcmena, last forty-eight hours; a shorter time not being sufficient for the forging of Hercules, who was to rid the world of its monsters, and its tyrants. My masters, the ancient Pantagruelists, have confirmed that which I say, and withal declared it to be not only possible, but also maintained the legitimacy of the infant, born of a woman in the eleventh month after the decease of her husband. There are many laws by means whereof the widows may, without danger, play at the close-buttock game with might and main, and as hard as they can for the space of the first two months after the decease of their husbands. I pray you, my good lusty springal lads, if you find any of these females, that are worth the pains of untying the cod-piece point, get up, and bring them to me; for if they happen within the third month to conceive, the child shall be heir to the deceased, and the mother shall pass for an honest woman.

When she is known to have conceived, thrust forward boldly, spare her not, whatever betide you, seeing the paunch is full. As Julia, the daughter of the Emperor Octavian, never prostituted herself to her belly-bumpers, but when she found herself with child; after the manner of ships that receive not their steersman till they have their ballast and lading.—And if any blame the women for that after pregnancy they still continue buxom, and push for more; whereas any beast, a cow or mare will kick and flaunce, and admit no farther courtship from the bull or stallion: the answer will be, these are beasts and know no better: but the other are women, and understand the glorious right they have to the pretty perquisite of a superfœtation, as Populia heretofore answered, according to the relation of Macrobius, Lib. 2. Saturnal. If the devil will not have them to bagge, he must wring hard the spigot, and stop the bung-hole.

CHAPTER IV

THE occasion and manner how Gargamelle was brought to bed, and delivered of her child, was thus: and if you do not believe it I wish your bum-gut may fall out. Her bum-gut indeed, or fundament escaped her in an afternoon, on the 3rd day of February, with having eaten at dinner too many godebillios: godebillios are the fat tripes of coiros; coiros are beeves fattened in the ox-stalls, and guimo meadows: guimo meadows are those that may be mowed twice a year; of those fat beeves they had killed three hundred sixty-seven thousand and fourteen, to be salted at Shrovetide; that in the entering of the spring they might have plenty of powdered beef, wherewith to season their mouths at the beginning of their meals, and to taste their wine the better.

They had abundance of tripes as you have heard, and they were so delicious that every one licked his fingers. But, as the devil would have it, there was no possibility of keeping them long sweet, and to let them stink was not so commendable or handsome; it was therefore concluded, that they should be all of them gulched up, without any waste. To this effect they invited all the burghers of Sainais, of Suillé, of the Roche Clermaud, of Vaugaudry, without omitting Coudray, Monpensier, the Gué de Vede, and other their neighbours; all stiff drinkers, brave fellows, and good players at nine-pins. The good man Grangousier took great pleasure in their company, and commanded there should be no want nor pinching for anything: nevertheless he bade his wife eat sparingly, because she was near her time, and that these tripes were no very commendable meat; they would fain (said he) be at the chewing of ordure, who eat the bag that contained it. Notwithstanding these admonitions, she did eat sixteen quarters, two bushels, three pecks, and a pipkin full. What a filthy deal of loblolly was here, to swell and wamble in her guts?

After dinner they all went tag-rag together to the willow-grove, where, on the green grass, to the sound of the merry flutes and pleasant bag-pipes, they danced so gallantly, that is was a sweet and heavenly sport to see them so frolic.

CHAPTER V

THEN did they fall upon the chat of the afternoon's collation; and forthwith began flaggons to go, gammons to trot, goblets to fly, great bowls to ting, glasses to ring, draw, reach, fill, mix, give it me without water, so my friend, so, whip me off this glass neatly, bring me hither some claret, a full weeping glass till it run over, a cessation and truce with thirst. Ha! thou false fever, wilt thou not be gone? By my figgins, godmother, I cannot as yet enter in the humour of being merry, nor drink so currently as I would; you have catched a cold, Gammer; yea, forsooth, sir; by the belly of Sanct Buff let us talk of our drink, I never drink but at my hours, like the pope's mule; and I never drink but in my breviary, like good father Gardian. Which was first, thirst or drinking? Thirst, for who in the time of innocence would have drunk without being a thirst? nay, sir, it was drinking; for *privatio præsupponit habitum*. I am learned you see, *Fæcundi calices quem non fecere disertum?* We poor innocents drink too much without thirst. Not I truly, who am a sinner, for I never drink without thirst, either present or future, to prevent it (as you know) I drink for the thirst to come; I drink eternally, this is to me an eternity of drinking, and drinking of an eternity. Let us sing, let us drink, now for a catch, dust it away, where is my nogging? what, it seems I do not drink but by proxy. Do you wet yourselves to dry, or do you dry to wet you? Pish, I understand not the rhetoric (theoric I should say), but I help myself somewhat by the practice.—Enough; I sup, I wet, I humect, I moisten my gullet, I drink, and all for fear of dying; drink always and you shall never die. If I drink not, I am aground, and lost. I am stark dead without drink, and my soul ready to fly into some marsh amongst frogs; the soul never dwells in a dry place.

O, you butlers, creators of new forms, make me of no drinker a drinker: a perennity and everlastingness of sprinkling and bedewing me through these my parched and sinewy bowels. He drinks in vain that feels not the pleasure of it: this entereth into my veins, the pissing tool shall have none of it. I would willingly wash the tripes of the calf which I reared this morning. I have pretty well now ballasted my stomach. If the papers of my bonds and bills could drink as well as I do, my creditors would have their hands full. Hold up your dagger-hand; that hand of yours spoils your nose. O how many other such will go in here before this go out; what, drink at so shallow a ford? It is enough to break both girths and breast-leather. This is called a cup of dissimulation. What difference is there between a bottle and a flaggon? great difference: the bottle is stopped with a stopple, and *Flaccon a vis.* Our fathers drank lustily, and emptied their cans; this is *bien chié chanté,* well cacked, well sung. Come, let us drink: will you send nothing to the river? Here is one going to wash the tripes. I drink no more than a sponge. I drink like a templar knight. And I *tanquam sponsus.* And I *sicut terra sine aqua.* Give me a synonymon for a gammon of bacon; it is the compulsory of drinkers; it is a pully; by a pully-rope wine is let down into a cellar, and by a gammon into the stomach. Ha, now boys hither; some drink, some drink; there is no trouble in it. *Respice personam; pone pro duo, bus non est in usu.* If I could get up as well as I can swallow down, I had been long ere now very high in the air. Thus became Tom Toss-pot rich; thus went in the Taylor's stitch; thus did Bacchus conquer India; thus philosophy, Melinda. A little rain allays a great deal of wind; long tippling breaks the thunder. But if there came such liquor from my buttock, would you not suck the udder? Here, page, fill, I prithee forget me not when it comes to my turn; and I will enter the *election* I have made of thee into the very *register* of my heart. Sup, Simon; pull away; there is somewhat in the pot. I appeal from thirst, and disclaim its jurisdiction. Page, sue out my appeal in form. This remnant in the bottom of the glass must follow its leader. I was wont heretofore to drink out all, but now I leave nothing. Make not such haste; we must carry all along with us. Hey-day, here are tripes fit for our sport; godebillios of the dun ox with the black streak. O, for God's sake, let us lash them soundly, yet thriftily. Drink, or I will. . . . No, no, drink, I beseech you; sparrows will not eat unless you bob them on the tail; nor can I drink if I be not fairly spoke to. Lagonædatera, there is not a cunniborow in all my body, where this wine doth not ferret out my thirst. Ho, this will bang it soundly; but this shall banish it utterly. Let us make proclamation by the sound of flaggons and bottles, that whoever hath lost his thirst come not hither to seek it. Long spits are to be voided without doors. The great God made the planets, and we make the platters neat. I have the word of the Gospel in my mouth, *Sitio.* The stone called Asbestos, is not more unquenchable than the thirst of my paternity. Appetite comes with eating, says Angeston;

16

but the thirst goes away with drinking. I have a remedy against thirst, quite contrary to that which is good against the biting of a mad dog: keep running after a dog and he will never bite you; drink always before the thirst, and it will never come upon you. There I catch you, I awake you. Argus had a hundred eyes for his sight; a butler should have (like Briarius) a hundred hands wherewith to fill us wine indefatigably. Ha, now lads, let us wet, it will be time to dry hereafter. White wine, here, wine boys, pour out all, *per le diable,* fill, I say, fill and fill till it be full. My tongue peels. *Lans tringue*: to thee, countryman, I drink to thee, good fellow. Comrade, to thee, lusty, lively, ha, la, la, that was drunk to some purpose, and bravely gulped over. O *lachryma Christi,* it is of the best grape; I faith, pure Greek, Greek. O the fine white wine! upon my conscience it is a kind of taffatas wine, him, him, it is of one ear, well wrought, and of good wool. Courage, comrade; up thy heart, Billy: we will not be beasted at this bout, for I have got one trick. *Ex hoc in hoc.* There is no enchantment nor charm there; everyone of you hath seen it: my prenticeship is out; I am a free man at this trade. I am an abbot. (Pshaw, I should say.) O, the drinkers, those that are a dry; O, poor thirsty souls! Good page, my friend, fill me here some, and crown the cup, I prithee, *à la cardinale; natura abhorret vacuum.* Would you say that a fly could drink in this? *A la mode de Bretagne.*—Clear off neat, *supernaculum,* swill it over heartily, no deceit in a brimmer; nectar and ambrosia.

CHAPTER VI

HOW GARGANTUA WAS BORN IN A STRANGE MANNER

WHILST they were on this discourse, and pleasant tattle of drinking, Gargamelle began to be a little unwell in her lower parts; whereupon Grangousier arose from off the grass, and fell to comfort her very honestly and kindly, suspecting that she was in travail, and told her that it was best for her to sit down upon the grass, under the willows, because she was like very shortly to see young feet; and that, therefore, it was convenient she should pluck up her spirits, and take a good heart at the new coming of her baby; saying to her withal, that although the pain was somewhat grievous to her, it would be but of short continuance; and that the succeeding joy would quickly

17

remove that sorrow, in such sort that she should not so much as remember it. "On with a sheep's courage," quoth he; "despatch this
boy, and we will speedily fall to work for the making of another."
"Ha!" said she, "so well as you speak at your own ease, you that are
men: well, then, in the name of God, I'll do my best, seeing you will
have it so; but would to God that it were cut off from you."—"What?"
said Grangousier. "Ha!" said she, "you are a good man indeed—
you understand it well enough." "What, my member?" said he.
"Udzookers, if it please you, that shall be done instantly; bid 'em
bring hither a knife." "Alas!" said she, "the Lord forbid; I pray
Jesus to forgive me; I did not say it from my heart: do it not any kind
of harm, neither more nor less, for my speaking: but I am like to have
work enough to-day, and all for your member; yet God bless both
you and it."

"Courage, courage," said he; "take you no care of the matter; let the
four foremost oxen do the work. I will yet go drink one whiff more,
and if, in the meantime, anything befall you, I will be so near that, at
the first whistling in your fist, I shall be with you." A little while
after, she began to groan, lament, and cry: then suddenly came the
midwives from all quarters, who, groping her below, found some
peloderies of a bad savour indeed: this they thought had been the
child; but it was her fundament that was slipped out with the mollifi-
cation of her *intestinum rectum,* which you call the bum-gut, and that
merely by eating of too many tripes, as we have shewed you before.
Whereupon an old, ugly trot in the company, who was reputed a
notable physician, and was come from Brispaille, near to St. Gnou,
threescore years before, made her so horrible a restrictive and binding
medicine, whereby all her arse-pipes were so oppilated, stopped, obstructed, and contracted, that you could hardly have opened and enlarged them with your teeth, which is a terrible thing to think upon,
seeing the devil at mass at St. Martin's was puzzled with the like
task, when with his teeth he lengthened out the parchment whereon
he wrote the tittle-tattle of two young mangy whores.

The effect of this was, that the *cotyledons* of her matrix were all
loosened above, through which the child sprung up and leaped, and
so entering into the *vena cava,* did climb by the *diaphragm* even above
her shoulders (where that vein divides itself into two), and, from
thence taking his way towards the left side, issued forth at her left
ear. As soon as he was born, he cried, not as other babes use to do,
"mies, mies, mies"; but, with a high, sturdy, and big voice, shouted

18

aloud, "Drink, drink, drink," as inviting all the world to drink with him. The noise hereof was so extremely great, that it was heard in both the countries at once, of Beauce and Bibarois. I doubt me that you do not thoroughly believe the truth of this strange nativity. Though you believe it not, I care not much. But an honest man, and of good judgment, believeth still what is told him, and that which he finds written.

Is this beyond our law, or our faith? against reason or the Holy Scripture? For my part, I find nothing in the sacred Bible that is against it; but tell me, if it had been the will of God, would you say that He could not do it? Grammercy; I beseech you never dumb-found or embarrass your heads with these idle conceits: for I tell you, nothing is impossible with God; and, if He pleased, all women hence-forth should bring forth their children at the ear. Was not Bacchus engendered out of the very thigh of Jupiter? Did not Roquetaillade come out at his mother's heel? and Crocmoush from the slipper of his nurse? Was not Minerva born of the brain, even through the ear of Jove? Adonis, of the bark of a myrrh-tree? and Castor and Pollux, of the doupe of that egg which was laid and hatched by Leda?—But you would wonder more, and with far greater amaze-ment, if I should now present you with that chapter of Pliny, wherein he treateth of strange births, and contrary to nature; and yet am not I so impudent a liar as he was. Read the seventh book of his Natural History, chap. 3, and trouble not my head any more about this.

CHAPTER VII

AFTER WHAT MANNER GARGANTUA HAD HIS NAME GIVEN HIM; AND HOW HE TIPPLED, BIBBED, AND CURRIED THE CAN

THE good man Grangousier, drinking and making merry with the rest, heard the horrible noise which his son had made as he entered into the light of this world, when he cried out, "Drink, drink, drink"; whereupon he said in French, "*Que* GRAND TU AS & *souple le gousier*"; that is to say, "How great and nimble a throat thou hast"; which the company hearing, said, that verily the child ought to be called Gargantua, because it was the first word that, after his birth, his father had spoke, in imitation, and at the example, of the ancient Hebrews; whereunto he condescended, and his mother was very well pleased therewith: in the meanwhile, to quiet the child, they gave him to drink a *tirelarigot,* that is, till his throat was like to crack with it; then was he carried to the font, and there baptized, according to the manner of good Christians.

Immediately thereafter were appointed for him seventeen thousand nine hundred and thirteen cows, of the towns of Pautille and Breemond, to furnish him with milk in ordinary; for it was impossible to find a nurse sufficient for him in all the country, considering the great quantity of milk that was requisite for his nourishment; although there were not wanting some doctors of the opinion of Scotus, who affirmed that his own mother gave him suck, and that she could draw out of her breasts one thousand four hundred two pipes and nine pails of milk at every time: which, indeed, is not probable; and this point hath been found duggishly scandalous and offensive to tender ears, for that it savoured a little of heresy. Thus was he handled for one year and ten months; after which time, by the advice of physicians, they began to carry him abroad, and then was made for him a fine little cart, drawn with oxen, of the invention of Jan Denio, wherein they led him hither and thither with great joy; and he was worth the seeing, for he was a fine boy, had a burly physiognomy, and almost ten chins; he cried very little, but beshit himself every hour; for, to speak truly of him, he was wonderfully phlegmatic in his posteriors, both by reason of his natural complexion, and the accidental disposition which had befallen him by his too much quaffing of the Septembral juice. Yet without a cause did not he sip one drop; for if he happened to be vexed, angry, displeased, or sorry; if he did fret, if he did weep, if he did cry, and what grievous quarter soever he kept, bring him some drink, he would be instantly pacified, come to his own temper, be in a good humour again, and as still and quiet as ever. One of his governesses told me (swearing by her fig) how he was so accustomed to this kind of way, that at the sound of pints and flaggons, he would on a sudden fall into an ecstasy, as if he had then tasted of the joys of Paradise; so that they, upon consideration of this his divine complexion, would every morning, to cheer him up, play with a knife upon the glasses, on the bottles with their stopples, and on the pottle-pots with their lids and covers, at the sound whereof he became gay, would leap for joy, would loll and rock himself in the cradle, then nod with his head, *monocordizing* his fingers, and *barytonizing* with his tail.

CHAPTER VIII

HOW THEY APPARELLED GARGANTUA

BEING of this age, his father ordained to have cloaths made to him in his own livery, which was white and blue. To work then went the tailors, and with great expedition were those cloaths made, cut, and sewed, according to the fashion that was then in vogue. I find by the ancient records, to be seen in the chamber of accompts at Montsoreau, that he was accoutred in manner as followeth:—To make him every shirt of his, were taken up nine hundred ells of Chateleraud linen, and two hundred for the gussets, in manner of cushions, which they put under his armpits; his shirt was not gathered nor plaited, for the plaiting of shirts was not found out till the seamstresses (when the point of their needles was broken) began to work and occupy with the tail.— There were taken up for his doublet eight hundred and thirteen ells of white satin, and for his codpiece points, fifteen hundred and nine dog skins and a half. Then was it that men began to tie their breeches to their doublets, and not their doublets to their breeches; for it is against nature, as hath most amply been shewed by Ockam, upon the *exponibles* of Master Hautechaussade.

For his breeches, were taken up eleven hundred and five ells and a third of white broad cloth. They were cut in form of pillars, chamfred, channeled, and pinked behind, that they might not overheat his reins; and were, within the panes, puffed out with the lining of as much blue damask as was needful; and remark, that he had very good knee-rollers, proportionable to the rest of his stature.

For his codpiece, was used sixteen ells and a quarter of the same cloth, and it was fashioned on the top like unto a triumphant arch, most gallantly fastened with two enamelled clasps, in each of which was set a great emerald as big as an orange; for, as says Orpheus, *Lib. de lapidibus,* and Pliny, *Lib. ultimo,* it hath an erective virtue and comfortative of the natural member. The ject, or outstanding of his codpiece, was of the length of a yard, jagged and pinked, and withal bagging, and strouting out with the blue damask lining, after the manner of his breeches: but had you seen the fair embroidery of the small needlework purl, and the curiously interlaced knots, by the goldsmith's art, set out and trimmed with rich diamonds, precious rubies, fine turquoises, costly emeralds, and Persian pearls, you would have compared it to a fair cornucopia, or horn of abundance, such as you see in antics, or as Rhea gave to the two nymphs, Amalthea and Ida, the nurses of Jupiter.

And like to that horn of abundance, it was still gallant, succulent, droppy, sappy, pithy, lively, always flourishing, always fructifying, full of juice, full of flower, full of fruit, and all manner of delight. Blessed lady! It would have done one good to have seen it: but I will tell you more of it in the book which I have made of the dignity of codpieces. One thing I will tell you, that as it was both long and large, so was it well furnished and provided within, nothing like unto the hypocritical codpieces of some fond wooers and wench courters, which are stuffed only with wind, to the great prejudice of the female sex.

For his shoes, were taken up four hundred and six ells of blue crimson velvet, and were very neatly cut by parallel lines, joined in uniform cylinders: for the soling of them were made use of eleven hundred hides of brown cows, shapen like the tail of a keeling.

For his coat, were taken up eighteen hundred ells of blue velvet, dyed in grain, embroidered in its borders with fair gilliflowers, in the middle decked with silver purl, intermixed with plaits of gold, and store of pearls, hereby showing that in his time he would prove an especial good fellow, and singular whip-can.

His girdle was made of three hundred ells and a half of silken serge, half white and half blue, if I mistake it not. His sword was not of Valentia, nor his dagger of Saragosa, for his father could not endure these *Hidalgos borrachos maranisados como diablos;* but he had a fair sword made of wood, and the dagger of boiled leather, as well painted and gilded as any man could wish.

His purse was made of the cod of an elephant, which was given him by Her Pracontal, proconsul of Lybia.

For his gown, were employed nine thousand six hundred ells, wanting two-thirds, of blue velvet, as before, all so diagonally purled, that by true perspective issued thence an unnamed colour, like that you see in the necks of turtle-doves or turkey cocks, which wonderfully rejoiceth the eyes of the beholders. For his bonnet, or cap, were taken up three hundred two ells and a quarter of white velvet, and the form thereof was wide and round, of the bigness of his head; for his father said, that the caps of the Marrabaise fashion, made like the cover of a pasty, would, one time or other, bring a mischief on those that wore them. For his plume, he wore a fair great blue feather, plucked from an Onocrotal of the country of Hircania the Wild, very prettily hanging down over his right ear: for the jewel or broach, which in his cap he carried, he had in a cake of gold, weighing three-score and eight marks, a fair piece of enamelled work, wherein were portrayed a man's body with two heads, looking towards one another; four arms, four feet, two arses, such as Plato, in Symposio, says was the mystical beginning of man's nature; and about it was written in Ionic letters, Ἀγάπη οὐ ζητεῖτὰ ἑαυτῆς.

To wear about his neck he had a golden chain, weighing twenty-five thousand and sixty-three marks of gold, the link thereof being made after the manner of great berries, amongst which were set in work green jaspers, engraven, and cut dragon-like, all environed with beams and sparks, as King Nicepsos of old was wont to wear them, and it reached down to the very bust of the rising of his belly, whereby he reaped great benefit all his life long, as the Greek physicians knew well enough. For his gloves, were put in work sixteen otters' skins, and three of Lougarous, or men-eating wolves, for the bordering of them: and of this stuff were they made, by the appointment of the Cabalists of Sanlouand. As for the rings which his father would have him to wear, to renew the ancient mark of nobility, he had on the fore-finger of his left hand a carbuncle as big as an ostrich's egg, enchased very daintily in gold of the fineness of a Turkey seraph. Upon the middle finger of the same hand, he had a ring made of four metals together, of the strongest fashion that ever was seen; so that the steel did not crush against the gold, nor the silver crush the copper. All this was made by Captain Chappuys, and Alcofribas, his operator. On the medical finger of his right hand, he had a ring made spire-ways, wherein was set a perfect baleau ruby, a pointed diamond, and a poison emerald of an inestimable value; for Hans-carvel, the king of Melinda's jeweller, esteemed them at the rate of threescore and nine millions eight hundred ninety-four thousand and eight French crowns of Berry, and at so much did the Jews of Augsburg prize them.

CHAPTER IX

THE COLOURS AND LIVERIES OF GARGANTUA

GARGANTUA'S colours were white and blue, as I have shewed you before, by which his father would give us to understand, that his son to him was a heavenly joy, for the *white* did signify gladness, pleasure, delight, and rejoicing, and the *blue* celestial things. I know well enough, that in reading this you laugh at the old toper, and hold this exposition of colours to be very extravagant, and utterly disagreeable to reason, because *white* is said to signify faith, and *blue* constancy. But, without moving, vexing, heating, or putting you in a chafe (for the weather is dangerous) answer me if it please you, for no other compulsory way of arguing will I use towards you, or any else; only now and then I will mention a word or two of my bottle.

What is it that induceth you? What stirs you up to believe, or who told you that white signifieth faith, and blue constancy? An old paltry book, say you, sold by the hawking pedlars and ballad-mongers, intituled, "The Blazon of Colours." Who made it? Whoever it was, he was wise in that he did not set his name to it; I know not what I should rather admire in him, his presumption or his folly. His presumption, for that he should without reason, without cause, or without any appearance of truth, have dared to prescribe by private authority, what things should be denoted and signified by the colour, which is the custom of tyrants who will have their will to bear sway instead of equity; and not of the wise and learned, who, with the evidence of reason satisfy their readers.

His folly and want of wit, in that he thought that, without any other demonstration or sufficient argument, the world would be pleased to make his blockish and ridiculous impositions the rule of their devices. In effect, according to the Proverb, *To shitten tails, turd never fails;* he hath found (it seems) some simple ninny in those rude times of old, when high bonnets were in fashion, who gave some trust to his writings, according to which they shaped their apophthegms and mottos, trapped and caparisoned their mules and sumpter-horses, apparelled their pages, quartered their breeches, bordered their gloves, fringed the curtains and valance of their beds, painted their ensigns, composed songs, and, which is worse, placed many deceitful jugglings, and unworthy base tricks clandestinely, amongst the chastest matrons. In the like darkness and mist of ignorance, are wrapped up these vain-glorious courtiers, and name-transposers, who going about in their *impresa's,* to signify *espoir,* have pourtrayed a *sphere:* birds' pens for *pins: L'Ancholie* for *melancholy:* A horned moon, or *crescent,* to shew the *increasing* of one's fortune: A *bench broken,* to signify *bankrupt: Non,* and a *corslet* for, *non dur habet,* otherwise *non durabit,* it shall not last: *Un lit sans ciel,* for *Un licentié;* which are equivocals so absurd and witless, so barbarous and clownish, that a fox's tail should be pinned at his back, and a fool's cap be given to every one that should henceforth offer, after the restitution of learning, to make use of any such fopperies in France.

By the same reasons (if reasons I should call them, and not ravings rather) might I cause *paint* a *painer,* to signify that I am in *pain:* a pot of *mustard,* that my heart is *much tardy;* one *pissing upwards* for a *bishop;* the bottom of a pair of *breeches* for a vessel full of *farthings* (*fart-hings*), a *codpiece* (as the English bears it) for the tail of a *cod-fish;* and a *dog's turd,* for the *dainty turret,* wherein lies the love of my sweetheart.

For otherwise did heretofore the sages of Egypt, when they wrote by letters, which they called hyeroglyphics, which none understood who were not skilled in the virtue, property, and nature of the things represented by them: of which Orus Apollo hath in Greek composed two books, and Polyphilus, in his Dream of Love, set down more. In France you have a taste of them, in the device or impresa of my Lord Admiral, which was carried before that time by Octavian Augustus. But my little skiff, amongst these unpleasant gulfs and shoals, will sail no further, therefore must I return to the port from whence I came; yet do I hope one day to write more at large of these things, and to shew, both by philosophical arguments and authorities, received and approved of, by and from all antiquity, what, and how many colours, there are in nature, and what may be signified by every one of them, if God save the mould of my cap, which is my best wine-pot, as my grandam used to say.

CHAPTER X

OF THAT WHICH IS SIGNIFIED BY THE COLOURS, WHITE AND BLUE

THE white, therefore, signifieth joy, solace, and gladness, and that not at random, but upon just and very good grounds; which you may perceive to be true, if, laying aside all prejudicate affections, you will but give ear to what presently I shall expound unto you.

Aristotle saith, That supposing two things, contrary in their kind, as good and evil, virtue and vice, heat and cold, white and black, pleasure and pain, joy and grief: and so of others, if you couple them

25

in such manner, that the contrary of one kind may agree in reason with the contrary of the other; it must follow, by consequence, that the other contrary must answer to the remnant opposite to that wherewith it is conferred: As for examples; virtue and vice are contrary in one kind, so are good and evil; if one of the contraries of the first kind be consonant to one of those of the second, as virtue and goodness, for it is clear that virtue is good, so shall the other two contraries (which are evil and vice) have the same connexion, for vice is evil.

This logical rule being understood, take these two contraries, joy and sadness; then these other two, white and black, for they are physically contrary: if so be, then, that black do signify grief, by good reason, then, should white import joy. Nor is this signification instituted by human imposition, but by the universal consent of the world received, which philosophers call *jus gentium,* the law of nations, or an uncontrollable right, of force in all countries whatsoever; for, you know well enough, that all people, and all languages and nations (except the ancient Syracusans, and certain Argives, who had cross and thwarting souls) when they mean outwardly to give evidence of their sorrow, go in black, and all mourning is done with black, which general consent is not without some argument and reason in nature, the which every man may by himself very suddenly comprehend, without the instruction of any; and this we call the Law of Nature: by virtue of the same natural instinct, we know that by white all the world hath understood joy, gladness, mirth, pleasure and delight.

In former times, the Thracians and Grecians did mark their good, propitious, and fortunate days, with white stones; and their sad, dismal, and unfortunate ones with black; is not the night mournful, sad, and melancholic; it is black and dark by the privation of light; doth not the light comfort all the world? and it is more white than anything else, which to prove I could direct you to the Book of Laurentius Valla against Bartolus, but an Evangelical testimony I hope will content you: Matt. 7, it is said, that at the transfiguration of our Lord, *Vestimenta ejus facta sunt alba sicut lux,* his apparel was made white like the light; by which lightsome whiteness He gave His three apostles to understand the idea and figure of the eternal joys; for by the light are all men comforted according to the word of the old woman, who although she had never a tooth in her head, was wont to say, *bona lux.* And Tobit, chap. 5, after he had lost his sight, when Raphael saluted him, answered, "What joy can I have, that do not see the light of Heaven?" In that colour did the angels testify the joy of the whole world, at the resurrection of our Saviour, John 20, and at His ascension, Acts 1. With the like colour of vesture did St. John the Evangelist, Apoc. 4, 7, "See the faithful cloathed in the heavenly and blessed Jerusalem."

Read the ancient, both Greek and Latin histories, and you shall find that the town of Alba (the first patron of Rome) was founded, and so named, by reason of a *white sow* that was seen there. You shall likewise find in those stories, that when any man, after he had vanquished his enemies, was, by decree of the senate, to enter into Rome triumphantly, he usually rode in a chariot drawn by white horses: White, in the Ovatian Triumph, was also the custom; for by no sign or colour would they so significantly express the joy of their coming as by the white. You shall there also find how Pericles, the general of the Athenians, would needs have that part of his army, unto whose lot befel the white *beans,* to spend the whole day in mirth, pleasure, and ease, whilst the rest were a fighting. A thousand other examples and places could I allege to this purpose, but that it is not here where I should do it.

By understanding hereof you may solve one problem, which Alexander Aphrodiseus hath accounted unanswerable, why the lion who, with his only cry and roaring, affrights all beasts, dreads and feareth only a white cock? for, as Proclus saith, *"libro de sacrificio et magia,"* it is because the presence, or the virtue of the sun, which is the organ and promptuary of all terrestrial and syderial light, doth more symbolise and agree with a white cock, as well in regard of that colour, as of his property and specifical quality, than with a lion. He saith furthermore, that devils have been often seen in the shape of lions, which, at the sight of a white cock, have presently vanished. This is the cause why the Galli (so are the Frenchmen called, because they are naturally white as milk, which the Greeks call Gala) do willingly wear in their caps white feathers; for, by nature they are of a candid disposition, merry, kind, gracious, and well-disposed, and for their cognizance and arms, have the whitest flower of any, the *flower de luce,* or *lily.*

If you demand how, by white, Nature would have us understand joy and gladness? I answer, that the analogy and conformity is thus, for as the white doth outwardly disperse and scatter the rays of the sight, whereby the optic spirits are manifestly dissolved, according to the opinion of Aristotle, in his Problems and Perspective Treatises;

27

as you may likewise perceive by experience, when you pass over mountains covered with snow, how you will complain that you cannot see well! as Xenophon writes to have happened to his men, and as Galen very largely declareth, *Lib.* 10, *de usu partium:* Just so the heart with excessive joy is inwardly dilated, and suffereth a manifest resolution of the vital spirits: which may go so far on, that it may thereby be deprived of its nourishment, and, by consequence, of life itself, by this *pericharie,* or extremity of gladness, as Galen saith, *lib.* 12, *method. lib.* 5, *de locis affectis, & lib.* 2 *de symptomatum causis.* And as it hath come to pass in former times (witness Marcus Tullius, *lib.* 1, *Quæst. Tuscul.* Verrius, Aristotle, Livius, in his relation of the battle of Cannæ, Plinius *lib.* 7, *cap.* 32 & 34, A. Gellius, *lib.* 3, *cap.* 15, and many other writers) of Diagoras, the Rhodian, Chilon, Sophocles, Dionysius, the Tyrant of Sicily, Philippides, Philemon, Polycrates, Philipion, M. Juventi, and others, who died with joy. And as Avican speaketh in 2 *Canon. & lib. de virib. cordis,* of the saffron, that it doth so rejoice the heart, that if you take of it excessively, it will, by an excessive resolution and dilatation, deprive it altogether of life. Here peruse Alex. Aphrodiseus, *lib.* 1, *probl. cap.* 19, and that for a cause: But what? it seems I am entered further into this point than I intended at the first: Here, therefore, will I strike sail, referring the rest to that book of mine which handleth this matter to the full. Meanwhile, in a word I will tell you that *blue* doth certainly signify heaven and heavenly things, by the very same tokens and *symbols* that *white* signifyeth joy and pleasure.

CHAPTER XI

OF THE YOUTHFUL AGE OF GARGANTUA

GARGANTUA, from three years upwards unto five, was brought up and instructed in all convenient discipline, by the commandment of his father; and spent that time like the other little children of the country; that is, in *drinking, eating, and sleeping; in eating, sleeping, and drinking; and in sleeping, drinking, and eating.*

He was continually wallowing. and rolling up and down in the mire and dirt; he blurred and sullied his nose with filth; he blotted and smutted his face with any kind of nasty stuff; he trod down his shoes in the heel, lay with his mouth open to catch gnats, and ran a hawking after the butterflies, the empire whereof belonged to his father. He pissed in his shoes, shit in his shirt, and wiped his nose on his sleeve; he did let his snot and snivel fall in his pottage, and dabbled, paddled, and slabbered everywhere. He would drink in his slipper, and ordinarily rub his belly against a panier: he would pick his teeth with a wooden shoe; wipe his breech with his finger, wash his hands in his broth, and comb his head with a broken ladle. He would sit down betwixt two stools, and his back to the ground; would cover himself with a wet sack, drink in his pottage, gnaw the bone he could not swallow, eat his cake without bread, bite laughing, and laugh biting, spit in the dish, fart in his fist, piss against the wind, and hide himself in the water for fear of rain: he would strike before the iron was hot, would blow in the dust till it filled his eyes; be often in the dumps: he would flay the fox, say the Apes *Paternoster,* would run at mutton, and turn the hogs to the hay: he would beat the dogs before the lion; put the plough before the oxen, and claw where it did not itch: He would leap before he looked; at *Midsummer-Moon* spend his *Michaelmas Rent,* and take misreckoning for good payment: By griping all, would hold fast nothing; and always eat his white bread first: he shoed the geese, tickled himself to make himself laugh, was cook-ruffian in the kitchen, would sing *Magnificat* at *Matins,* and found it was an enemy of God, would turn to account: he would eat cabbage, and shite cauliflowers; catch fish in a dish of milk, and make them all cripples: he would tear the paper, rase the records, then trust his heels for his security: he would pull at the kids' leather, or vomit up his dinner, then reckon without his host: he would beat the bushes without catching the birds; thought the moon was made of green cheese, and that everything was gold that glitters. He would sooner go to the mill than to the mass; took a bit in the morning to be better than nothing all day; would eat his cake and have his cake; and was better fed than taught; he always looked a given horse in the mouth; would tell a tale of a tub; throw the helm after the hatchet; when the steed was stolen would shut the stable-door, and bring his hogs to a fair market: by robbing Peter he paid Paul; he kept the moon from wolves, and was ready to catch larks if ever the heavens should fall: he did make of necessity virtue; of such bread such pottage; and cared as little for the peeled as for the shaven: every morning he did cast up his gorge; his father's little dogs eat out of the dish with him, and he with them: He would bite their ears, and they

29

would scratch his nose; would blow in their arses, and they would lick his chops.

But hearken, good fellows, may ye be sick of the mulligrubs with eating chopped hay, if now ye do not listen: this little leacher was always groping his nurses and governesses upside down, arsy versy, topsy turvy, *Harribourrquet,* with a *Yacco haic, hyck gio,* handling them very rudely in jumbling and tumbling them to keep them going for he had already began to exercise the tools, and put his codpiece in practice; which codpiece his governesses did every day deck up and adorn with fair nosegays, curious ribbons, sweet flowers, and fine silken tufts, and very pleasantly would pass their time in taking you know what between their fingers, and dandling it like a little baby; then did they burst out in laughing, when they saw it lift up its ears, as if the sport had liked them. One of them would call it her pillicock, her fiddle-diddle, her staff of love, her tickle-gizard, her gentle-titler. Another, her sugar-plumb, her kingo, her old rowley, her touch-tripe, her flap-dowdle. Another again, her branch of coral, her placket-racket, her Cyprian sceptre, her tit-bit, her bob-lady. And some of the other women would give these names—my Roger, my cockatoo, my nimble-wimble, bush-beater, claw-buttock, eves-dropper, pick-lock, pioneer, bully-ruffin, smell-smock, trouble-gusset, my lusty live sausage, my crimson chitterlin, rump-splitter, shove-devil, downright to it, stiff and stout, in and to, at her again, my cony-borrow-ferrit, wily-beguiley, my pretty rogue. "It belongs to me," said one; "it is mine," said the other; "what," quoth the third, "shall I have no share in it? By my faith I will cut it off then"; "ha! to cut it off," said the other, "would be a scurvy business; madam, is it your way to cut off little children's things? Were his cut off, he would be then master Bob." That he might play and sport himself, after the manner of the other little children of the country, they made him a goodly whirlygig of the wings of the windmill of Myrebalais.

CHAPTER XII

OF GARGANTUA'S WOODEN HORSES

AFTERWARDS, that he might be all his lifetime a good rider, they made for him a fair great horse of wood, which he did make leap, curvet, yerk out behind, and skip forwards all at a time, to pace, trot, rack, gallop, amble, to play the hobby, the hackney-gelding, go

the gait of the camel, and of the wild ass: he made him also change
his colour of hair, as the monks of Coultibo, according to the variety
of their holidays, use to do their cloaths, from bay, brown to sorrel,
dapple-grey, mouse-dun, deer-colour, roan, cow-colour, gingioline,
skued-colour, pie-balled, and the colour of the savage elk.

Himself of an huge big post made a hunting nag; and another for
daily service of the beam of a wine-press; and of a great oak made up
a mule with housing for his chamber. Besides these, he had ten or
twelve spare horses, and seven horses for post; and all these were
lodged in his own chamber, close by his bed-side. One day the lord
of Breadinbag came to visit Gargantua's father, in great bravery, and
with a gallant train; and at the same time, to see him, came likewise
the Duke of Friemeale, and the Earl of Wetgullet. The house truly,
for so many guests at once, was somewhat narrow, but especially the
stables. Whereupon the stewards and gentlemen of horse to the Lord
Breadinbag (to know if there were any other empty stables in the
house) came to Gargantua, then a little young lad, and secretly
asked him where the stables of the great horses were, thinking that
children would be ready to tell all. He led them up the great staircase of the castle, passing through the second hall into a broad great
gallery, by which they entered into a larger tower, and as they
were going up at another pair of stairs, said the gentlemen of horse
to the steward, "This child deceives us, for the stables are never on
the top of the house." "You may be mistaken," said the steward, "for
I know some places at Lyons, at the Basmette, at Chaisnon and elsewhere, which have their stables at the very tops of the houses, so it
may be that behind the houses there is a way to come to this ascent;
but I will question him further." Then said he to Gargantua, "My
pretty little boy, whither do you lead us?" "To the stable," said he,
"of my great horses; we are almost come to it, we have but these
stairs to go up at." Then leading them along another great hall, he
brought them into his chamber, and opening the door, said unto
them, "This is the stable that you asked for; this is my gennet, this
is my gelding, this is my course, and this is my pad"; and laid on
them with a great cudgel. "I will bestow upon you," said he, "this
Frizeland horse, I had him from Frankfort, yet will I give him you;
for he is a pretty little nag, and will go very well; with a cast of gose-
hawks, half a dozen spaniels, and a brace of greyhounds; thus are
you king of the hares and partridges for all this winter." "By St.
John," said they, "what a couple of puts has he made us? what

31

monkies?" "Hold, hold, gentlemen," said he, "you must shew your tails, ere you pass for monkies." Judge you now, whether they had most cause, either to hide their heads for shame, or to laugh for company. As they were going down again thus amazed, he asked them, "Will you have a whim-wham?" "What is that," said they? "It is," said he, "five turds to make you a muzzle." "To-day," said the steward, "though we happen to be roasted we shall not be burnt, for we are pretty well basted and larded in my opinion. O, my jolly dapper boy, thou hast given us a gudgeon; I hope to see thee pope before I die." "I think so," said he, "myself, and then shall you be a *puppy,* and this gentle Popinjeay pop into some office under me." "Well, well," said the gentleman of the horse. "But," said Gargantua, "guess how many stitches there are in my mother's smock?" "Sixteen," quoth the gentleman. "You do not speak gospel," said Gargantua, "for there is *sent* before, and *sent* behind, and you did reckon them ill, considering the two under holes." "When?" said the gentleman. "Even then," said Gargantua, "when they made a shovel of your nose to take up a quarter of dirt, and of your throat a funnel, wherewith to put it into another vessel, because the bottom of the old one was out." "Cocksbod," said the steward, "we have met with a prater. Farewell, master tatler, God keep you from harm, now your mouth is so mellow."

Thus going down in great haste, under the arch of the stairs, they let fall the great lever which he had put upon their backs; whereupon Gargantua said, "What a devil you are (it seems) but bad horsemen, that suffer your bilder to fail you, when you need him most. If you were to go from hence to Chausas, whether had you rather ride on a goose, or lead a sow in a leash?" "I had rather drink," said the gentleman of horse: with this they entered into the lower hall, where the company was, and, relating to them this new story, made them laugh like a swarm of flies.

CHAPTER XIII

HOW GARGANTUA'S WONDERFUL UNDERSTANDING BECAME KNOWN TO HIS FATHER GRANGOUSIER, BY THE INVENTION OF A TORCH-CUL OR WIPE-BREECH

ABOUT the end of the fifth year, Grangousier, returning from the conquest of the Canarians, went by the way to see his son

Gargantua; there was he filled with joy, as such a father might be at the sight of such a child of his. And whilst he kissed him and embraced him, he asked many childish questions of him. about divers matters, and drank very freely with him, and with his governesses, of whom in great earnest he asked, among other things, whether they had been careful to keep him clean and sweet? To this Gargantua answered, that he had taken such a course for that himself, that in all the country there was not to be found a cleanlier boy than he. "How is that?" said Grangousier. "I have," answered Gargantua, "by a long and curious experience, found out a means to wipe my bum, the most lordly, the most excellent, and the most convenient that ever was seen." "What is it?" said Grangousier: "how is it?"— "I will tell you by-and-by," said Gargantua. "Once I did wipe me with a gentlewoman's velvet mask, and found it to be good; for the softness of the silk was very voluptuous and pleasant to my funda-ment. Another time with one of their hoods, and in like manner that was comfortable: at another time with a lady's neck-kerchief, and after that I wiped me with some ear-pieces of hers made of crim-son satin; but there was such a number of golden spangles in them (turdy round things, a pox take them) that they fetched away all the skin off my tail with a vengeance. Now I wish St. Anthony's fire burn the bumgut of the goldsmith that made them, and of her that wore them. This hurt I cured by wiping myself with a page's cap, garnished with a feather after the Switzers fashion.

"Afterwards, in dunging behind a bush, I found a March-cat, and with it wiped my breech, but her claws were so sharp, that they scratched and exulcerated all my peritoneum. Of this I recovered the next morning thereafter, by wiping myself with my mother's gloves, of a most excellent perfume and scent of the Arabian Benin. After that, I wiped me with sage, with fennel, with anet, with marjoram, with roses, with gourd leaves, with beets, with colewort, with leaves of the vine-tree, with mallows, woolblade (which is a tail-scarlet), with lettuce, and with spinage leaves. (All this did very great good to my leg.) Then with wild mercury, with pursley, with nettles, with comfrey; but that gave me the bloody flux of Lombardy, which I healed by wiping me with my braguette. Then I wiped my tail in the sheets, in the coverlid, in the curtains, with a cushion, with arras hangings, with a green carpet, with a table-cloth, with a napkin, with a handkerchief, with a combing-cloth, in all which I found more pleasure than do the mangy dogs when you rub them." "Yea, but,"

said Grangousier, "which torchecul didst thou find to be the best?"
"I was coming to it," said Gargantua, "and by-and-by shall you hear
the *tu autem,* and know the whole mystery and knot of the matter.
I wiped myself with hay, with straw, with thatch-rushes, with flax,
with wool, with paper; but,

> "Tousiours laisse aux couillons esmorche,
> Qui son ord cul de papier torche."

> Who his foul tail with paper wipes,
> Shall at his ballocks leave some chips.

"What," said Grangousier, "my little rogue, hast thou been at the
wine-pot, that thou dost rhyme already?" "Yes, yes, my lord and
king," answered Gargantua, "I can rhyme out of measure; I can
rhyme and chime, and clink till I stink again. Hark what our privy
says to the skiters:—

> "Shittard
> Sguittard
> Crackard
>   Turdous,
> Thy bung
> Hath flung
> Some dung
>   On us.
> Filthard
> Cackard
> Stinkard,
>   St. Anthony fire thy arse-bone,
> If thy
> Ditty
> Toby
>   Thou do not wipe ere thou be gone.

"Will you have any more of it?" "Yes, yes," answered Grangousier.
Then said Gargantua

> "A ROUNDELAY
> A shiting, I found yesterday
> The tax I to my arse should pay;
> The bung-hole breathed so vile a funk,
> That one would wonder how I stunk:
> O had but then some brave Signor

Brought her to me I waited for,
 A shiting:
I would have cleft her water-gap,
And join'd it close to my flip-flap;
While she had with her fingers guarded
My foul nockandrow, all bemerded
 A shiting.

"Now say that I can do nothing. By the merdi, they are not of my making, but I heard them of this good old grandam that you see here, and ever since have retained them in the budget of my memory."

"Let us return to our business," said Grangousier. "What," said Gargantua, "to skite?" "No," said Grangousier, "but to wipe our tail." "But," said Gargantua, "will not you be content to pay a puncheon of Briton wine, if I do not blank and gravel you in this matter, and put you to a *non plus?*" "Yes, truly," said Grangousier.

"There is no need of wiping one's tail," said Gargantua, "but when it is foul; foul it cannot be, unless one have been a skiting; skite then we must before we wipe our tails." "O my pretty little waggish boy," said Grangousier, "what an excellent wit thou hast! I will make thee very shortly proceed doctor in the Belles Lettres, by G—, for thou hast more wit than age.

"Now, I prithee, go on in this bumfodder discourse; and, by my beard I swear, for one puncheon thou shall have threescore pipes, I mean of the good Breton wine, not that which grows in Britain, but in the good country of Verron." "Afterwards I wiped my bum," said Gargantua, "with a kerchief, with a pillow, with a pantoufle, with a pouch, with a pannier, but that was a wicked and unpleasant wipe-breech! then with a hat; of hats, note that some are shorn, and others shaggy, some velveted, others covered with taffities, and others with satin; the best of all these is the shaggy hat, for it makes a very neat abstertion of the *fecal* matter.

"Afterwards I wiped my tail with a hen, with a cock, with a pullet, with a calf's skin, with a hare, with a pigeon, with a cormorant, with an attorney's bag, with a montero, with a coif, with a falconer's lure; but to conclude, I say and maintain, that of all torcheculs, arse-wisps, bum-fodders, tail-napkins, bung-hole-cleansers and wipe-breeches, there is none in the world comparable to the neck of a goose, that is well downed, if you hold her head betwixt your legs: and believe me therein upon mine honour; for you will thereby feel in your nockhole a most wonderful pleasure, both in regard of the softness of the said down, and of the temperate heat of the goose; which is easily communicated to the bumgut and the rest of the intestines, in so far as to come even to the regions of the heart and brains.

"And think not, that the felicity of the heroes and demigods, in the Elysian fields, consisteth either in their Asphodele, Ambrosia, or Nectar, as our old women here use to say; but in this (according to my judgment) that they wipe their tails with the neck of a goose, holding her head betwixt their legs, and such is the opinion of Master John of Scotland."

CHAPTER XIV

HOW GARGANTUA WAS TAUGHT LATIN BY A SOPHISTER

THE good man Grangousier, having heard this discourse, was ravished with admiration, considering the high reach and marvellous understanding of his son Gargantua, and said to his governesses: "Philip, King of Macedon, knew the great wit of his son Alexander, by his skilful managing of a horse; for his horse Bucephalus was so fierce and unruly, that none durst adventure to ride him, after that he had given to his riders such devilish falls, breaking the neck of this man, the other man's leg, braining one, and cracking another's jaw-bone. This by Alexander being considered, one day in the Hippodrome (which was a place appointed for the breaking and managing of great horses), he perceived that the fury of the horse proceeded merely from the fear he had of his own shadow; whereupon getting on his back, he run him against the sun, so that the shadow fell behind, and by that means tamed the horse, and brought him to his hand. Whereby his father, perceiving his marvellous capacity and divine insight, caused him most carefully to be instructed by Aristotle, who at that time was highly renowned above all the philosophers of Greece. After the same manner, I tell you, that by this only discourse, which now I have here had before you with my son Gargantua, I know that his understanding doth participate of some divinity; and that if he be well taught, and have that education which is fitting, he will attain to a supreme degree of wisdom. Therefore will I commit him to some learned man, to have him indoctrinated according to his capacity, and will spare no cost."

Presently they appointed him a great sophister-doctor, called Master Tubal Holofernes, who taught him his A B C so well, that he could say it by heart backwards; and about this he was five years and three months.

Then read he to him, Donat, Le Facet, Theodolet, and Alanus in Parabolis. About this he was thirteen years six months and two weeks. But you must remark, that in the meantime he did learn to write in Gothic characters, and that he wrote all his books; for the art of printing was not then in use.

And did ordinarily carry a great pen and ink-horn, weighing above seven thousand quintals, the pen-case whereof was as big and as long as the great pillar of Enay; and the horn was hanged to it in great iron chains, it being of the wideness to hold a ton of merchandise.

After that was read unto him, the Book de Modis Significandi, with the Commentaries of Hurtbise, of Fasquin, of Tropditeux, of Gaulhault, of John Calf, of Billonio, of Berlinguandus, and a rabble of others; and herein he spent more than eighteen years and eleven months, and was so well versed therein, that to try masteries in school disputes with his condisciples, he would recite it by heart, backwards; and did sometimes prove on his fingers' ends to his mother, that *de Modis Significandi non erat Scientia*. Then was read to him the Compost, on which he spent sixteen years and two months. And at that very time, which was in the year 1420, his said Præcepter died of the pox.

Afterwards he got an old coughing fellow to teach him, named Master Jobelin Bridé, who read unto him, Hugutio, Hebrard, Grecism, the Doctrinal, the Pars, the Quid est, the Supplementum, Marmotretus, de Moribus in Mensa Servandis, Seneca de quatuor Virtutibus Cardinalibus, Passaventus cum Commento; and Dormi Securè, for the holidays, and other such like stuff; by reading whereof, he became as wise as any we ever since baked in an oven.

CHAPTER XV

HOW GARGANTUA WAS PUT UNDER OTHER SCHOOLMASTERS

AT the last his father perceived, that indeed he studied hard, and that although he spent all his time therein, yet for all that did he profit nothing; but, which is worse, grew thereby a fool, a sot, a dolt, and blockhead; whereof making a heavy complaint to Don Philip of Marays, viceroy of Papeligosse, he found that it were better for his son to learn nothing at all, than to be taught such like books, under such schoolmasters, because their knowledge was nothing but all trifle, and their wisdom foppery, serving only to bastardize good and noble spirits, and to corrupt the whole flower of youth. "That it is so, take," said he, "any young boy of this time, who hath only studied two years; if he have not a better judgment, a better discourse, and that expressed in better terms than your son, with a completer carriage and civility to all manner of persons, account me for ever hereafter a very clounch, and bacon-slicer of Brene." This pleased Grangousier very well, and he commanded that it should be done.

At night, at supper, the said Don Philip brought in a young page of his, of Ville-gouges, called Eudemon, so neat, so trim, so handsome in his apparel, so spruce, with his hair in so good order, and so sweet and comely in his behaviour, that he had the resemblance of a little angel more than of a human creature. Then he said to Grangousier, "Do you see this young boy? He is not as yet full twelve years old: let us try (if it like you) what difference there is betwixt the knowledge of the dunces Mateologian of old time, and the young lads that are now." The trial pleased Grangousier, and he commanded the page to begin. Then Eudemon, asking leave of the viceroy, his master, so to do, with his cap in his hand, a clear and open countenance, beautiful and ruddy lips, his eyes steady, and his looks fixed upon Gargantua, with a youthful modesty, standing up straight on his feet, began to commend him, first for his virtue and good manners; secondly, for his knowledge; thirdly, for his nobility; fourthly, for his bodily accomplishments: and in the fifth place, most sweetly exhorted him to reverence his father with all due observancy, who was so careful to have him well brought up; in the end, he prayed him, that he would vouchsafe to admit of him amongst the least of his servants; for other favour at that time desired he none of Heaven, but that he might do him some grateful and acceptable service. All this was by him delivered with such proper gestures, such distinct pronunciation, so pleasant a delivery, in such exquisite fine terms, and so good Latin, that he seemed rather a Gracchus, a Cicero, an Æmilius of the time past, than a youth of this age. But all the countenance that Gargantua kept was, that he fell to crying like a cow, and cast down his face, hiding it with his cap, nor could they possibly draw one word from him, no more than a fart from a dead ass.

Whereat his father was so grievously vexed, that he would have killed Master Jobelin, but the said Don Philip withheld him from it by fair persuasions, so that at length he pacified his wrath. Then Grangousier commanded he should be paid his wages, that they should whittle him up soundly, sophister like, and then give him to all the devils in hell. "At least," said he, "to-day, shall it not cost him much to his host if by chance he should die as drunk as an Englishman." Master Jobelin being gone out of the house, Grangousier consulted with the viceroy what schoolmaster they should choose for him, and it was betwixt them resolved, that Ponocrates, the tutor of Eudemon, should have the charge, and that they should go all together to Paris, to know what was the study of the young men of France at that time.

CHAPTER XVI

HOW GARGANTUA WAS SENT TO PARIS, AND OF THE HUGE GREAT MARE THAT HE RODE ON; HOW SHE DESTROYED THE OX-FLIES OF THE BEAUCE

IN the same season, Fayolles, the fourth king of Numidia, sent out of the country of Africk, to Grangousier, the most hideously great mare that ever was seen, and of the strangest form; for you know well enough how it is said, that Africk always is productive of some new thing. She was as big as six elephants, and had her feet cloven into toes like Julius Cæsar's horse, with slouch-hanking ears, like the goats in Languedoc, and a little horn on her buttock. She was of a burnt-sorrel hue, with a little mixture of dapple-grey spots; but, above all, she had a horrible tail; for it was little more or less than every whit as great as the steeple of Saint Mark beside Langes, and squared as that is, with tuffs and hair-pleats, wrought within one another, no otherwise than as the beards are upon the ears of corn.

If you wonder at this, wonder rather at the tails of the Scythian rams, which weighed above thirty pounds each, and of the Surian sheep, who need (if Tenaud says true) a little cart at their heels, to bear up their tails, they are so long and heavy. You country wenchers have no such tails. And she was brought by sea in three carricks and a brigantine unto the harbour of Olone in Thalmondois. When Grangousier saw her, "Here is," said he, "what is fit to carry my son to Paris. So now, in the name of God, all will be well; he will one

39

day be a great scholar: were it not for dunces, we should all be doctors." The next morning (after they had drunk, you must understand), they took their journey; Gargantua, his pedagogue Ponocrates,
and their equipage, and with them Eudemon, the young page; and
because the weather was fair and temperate, his father caused to be
made him a pair of dun-coloured boots; Babin calls them buskins.
Thus did they merrily pass their time in travelling on the highway,
always making good cheer, and were very pleasant till they came a
little above Orleans, in which place there was a forest of five and
thirty leagues long, and seventeen in breadth, or thereabouts. This
forest was most horribly fertile and copious in dorflies, hornets, and
wasps, so that it was a very purgatory for the poor mares, asses, and
horses: but Gargantua's mare did avenge herself handsomely of all the
outrages therein committed upon beasts of her quality, and that by a
trick whereof they had no suspicion; for as soon as ever they were entered into the said forest, and that the wasps had given the assault,
she drew out her tail, and therewith skirmishing, did so sweep them,
that she overthrew all the wood along and athwart, here and there,
this way and that way, longwise and sidewise, over and under, and
felled everywhere the wood with as much ease as a mower doth the
grass, in such sort, that never since hath there been there either wood
or wasp; for all the country was hereby reduced to a plain champagne
field—which Gargantua took great pleasure to behold, and said to his
company no more but this: *"Je trouve beau ce,"* I find this pretty;
whereupon that country hath been ever since that time called Beauce.
But all the breakfast the mare got that day was but a little yawning
and gaping, in memory whereof, the gentlemen of Beauce do as yet,
to this day, break their fast with gaping, which they find to be very
good, and do spit the better for it. At last they came to Paris, where
Gargantua refreshed himself two or three days, making very merry
with his folks, and inquiring what men of learning there were then
in the city, and what wine they drunk there.

CHAPTER XVII

HOW GARGANTUA PAID HIS BEVERAGE TO THE PARISIANS, AND HOW HE TOOK AWAY THE GREAT BELLS OF OUR LADY'S CHURCH

SOME few days after that they had refreshed themselves, he went to see the city, and was beheld of everybody there with great admiration: for the people of Paris are such fools, such puppies, and naturals, that a juggler, a carrier of indulgencies, a sumpter-horse, a mule with his bells, a blind fiddler in the middle of a cross lane, shall draw a greater confluence of people together than an evangelical preacher. And they pressed so hard upon him, that he was constrained to rest himself upon the steeple of our Lady's church; at which place, seeing so many about him, he said with a loud voice, "I believe that these buzzards will have me to pay them here my welcome hither, and my beverage: it is but good reason. I will now give them their wine, but it shall be only a *par ris,* that is in sport." Then smiling, he untied his goodly codpiece, and lugging out his Roger into the open air, he so bitterly all-to-be-pissed them, that he drowned two hundred and sixty thousand four hundred and eighteen, besides the women and little children.

Some, nevertheless, of the company escaped this piss-flood by mere speed of foot, who when they were at the higher end of the university, sweating, coughing, spitting, and out of breath, they began to swear and curse, some in good hot earnest, and others *par ris, carimari, carimara; golynoly, golynolo;* "ods-bodikins, we are washed *par ris,*" from whence that city hath been ever since called Paris; whose name formerly was Leucotia (as Strabo testifieth, lib. quarto), which in Greek is whiteness, because of the white thighs of the ladies of that place. And forasmuch as at this imposition of a new name, all the people that were there swore, every one by the Sancts of his parish, the Parisians, which are patched up of all nations, and all manner of men, are by nature good at swearing, and not a little domineering; whereupon Joanninus de Barrauco, *libro de copiositate reverentiarum,* thinks that they are called Parisians from the Greek, as one would say, bold talkers.

This done, he considered the great bells which were in the said steeple, and made them ring very harmoniously: which whilst he was

41

doing it came into his mind that they would serve very well for tingling tantans to hang about his mare's neck, when she should be sent back to his father (as he intended) loaded with Brie cheese and fresh herring; and, indeed, he forthwith carried them to his lodging. In the meanwhile there came a master beggar of the friars of St. Anthony, for some hog's purtenance; who, that he might be heard afar off, and to make the bacon shake in the very chimneys, had a mind to these bells, and made account to filch them away privily. Nevertheless, he left them behind him very honestly, not for that they were too hot, but that they were somewhat too heavy for his carriage. —This was not he of Bourg, for he was too good a friend of mine.

All the city was in a uproar, they being (as you know, upon any slight occasion) so ready to uproars and insurrections, that foreign nations wonder at the patience of the kings of France, who do not, by good justice, restrain them from such tumultuous courses, seeing the manifold inconveniences which thence arise from day to day. Would to God I knew the shop wherein are forged these divisions and factious combinations, that I might bring them to light in the confraternities of my parish. Believe for a truth, that the place wherein the people (gathered together) were thus sulfured, moiled, and bepissed, was called Nesle, where then was (but now is no more) the oracle of Lucetia. There was the case proposed, and the inconvenience shewed of carrying away the bells.

After all their *ergoes,* with their *pro* and *con,* it was concluded in Baralipton, that they should send the oldest and most sufficient of the faculty unto Gargantua, to signify to him the great and horrible prejudice they sustained by the want of those bells: and notwithstanding the good reasons given in by some of the university, why this charge was fitter for an orator than a sophister, there was chosen for this purpose our master Janotus de Bragmardo.

CHAPTER XVIII

HOW JANOTUS DE BRAGMARDO WAS SENT TO GARGANTUA
TO RECOVER THE GREAT BELLS

MASTER JANOTUS, with his hair cut round as a dish, his Liripoop on his head, after the old fashion; and having sufficiently antidoted his stomach with kitchen-cordials, and holy water of the cellar, conveyed himself to the lodging of Gargantua, driving before him three red-muzzled beadles, and dragging after him five or six artless masters, all thoroughly bedagled with the mire of the streets. At their entry, Ponocrates met them, who was afraid, seeing them so disguised, and thought they had been some maskers out of their wits; which moved him to inquire of one of the said artless masters of the company, what this mummery meant? It was answered him, that they desired to have their bells restored to them. As soon as Ponocrates heard that, he ran in all haste to carry the news unto Gargantua, that he might be ready to answer them, and speedily resolve what was to be done. Gargantua, being advertised hereof, called apart his preceptor Ponocrates, Philotimus steward of his house, Gymnastes his esquire, and Eudemon, and very summarily conferred with them, both of what he should do, and what answer he should give. They were all of the opinion that they should bring them to the can-office, and there make them drink like roysters, and line their jackets soundly. And that this cougher might not be puffed up with vain glory, by thinking the bells were restored at his request, they sent (whilst he was plying the pot) for the mayor of the town, the rector of the faculty, and the vicar of the church, unto whom they resolved to deliver the bells before the sophister had delivered his commission. After that, in their hearing, he should make his fine harangue, which was done, and they (Janotus and the rest) being come, the sophister was brought into a full hall, and began as followeth, in coughing.

CHAPTER XIX

THE HARANGUE OF MASTER JANOTUS DE BRAGMARDO FOR THE RECOVERY OF THE BELLS

HEM, hem, *gudday* Sir, *gudday & vobis,* my masters, it were but reason that you should restore to us our bells: for we have great need of them. *Hem, hem, aih fu hash,* we have oftentimes heretofore refused good money for them of those of London in Cahors, yea and of those of Bourdeaux in Brie, who would have bought them for the substantifick quality of the elementary complexon, which is intronisicated in the terrestreity of their quidditative nature, to extraneize the blasting mists and whirlwinds upon our vines; indeed not ours but these round about us. For if we lose the liquor of the grape, we lose

43

all, both sense and law. If you restore them to us at my request, I shall gain by it six baskets full of sausages, and a fine pair of breeches, which will do my legs a great deal of good, or else they will not keep their promise to me. Ho by gob, *Domine,* a pair of breeches is good, *& vir sapiens non abhorrebit eam.* Ha, ha, a pair of breeches is not so easily got, I have experience of it myself. Consider, *Domine,* I have been these eighteen days in metagrabolising this brave speech. *Reddite quœ sunt Cœsaris Cœsari: & quœ sunt Dei, Deo. Ibi jacet lepus.* By my faith, Domine, if you will sup with me in *Camera,* by Cox Body, *charitatis nos faciemus bonum cherubinum; ego occidit unum porcum & ego habet bonum vino*: but of good wine we cannot make bad Latin. Well *De parte Dei date nobis bellas nostras.* Hold, I give you in the name of the faculty, *a Sermones de Utino,* that *utinum* you would give us our bells. *Vultis etiam pardonos? Per diem vos habebitis, & nihil payabitis.*

O, Sir *Domine, Bellagivaminor nobis;* verily *est bonum urbis.* They are useful to everybody. If they fit your mare well, so do they do our faculty. *Quœ comparata est jumentis insipientibus, & similis facta est eis, Psalmo nescio quo.* Yet did I quote it in my note-book; *& est unum bonum* Achilles, a good defending argument, *hem, hem, hem, haickhash;* for I prove unto you that you should give me them. *Ego sic argumentor. Omnis bella (clocha) bellabilis in Bellerio bellando, bellans bellativo, bellare facit, bellabiliter bellantes. Parisius habet bellas; ergo gluc.* Ha, ha, ha, this is spoken to some purpose; it is *in Tertio Primœ,* in *Darii,* or elsewhere. By my soul, I have seen the time that I could play the devil in arguing, but now I am much failed; and henceforward want nothing but good wine, a good bed. my back to the fire, my belly to the table, and a good deep dish.

"*Hei Domine,* I beseech you, *in nomine Patris, Filii & Spiritus Sancti, Amen,* to restore unto us our bells; and God keep you from evil, and our lady from health; *Qui vivit & regnat per omnia secula seculorum, Amen. Hem, hashchehhawk sash qzrchremhemhash* [*coughing*]. *Verum enim vero, quandoquidem, dubio procul, œdepol, quoniam, ità certè, meus Deus Filius:* A town without bells is like a blind man without a staff, an ass without a crupper, and a cow without cymbals; therefore be assured, until you have restored them unto us, we will never leave crying after you, like a blind man that hath lost his staff, braying like an ass without a crupper, and making a noise like a cow without cymbals. A certain Latinisator, dwelling near the hospital, said once, producing the authority of one Taponus, I lye, it was Pontanus the secular poet, who wished those bells had been made of feathers, and the clapper a fox-tail, to the end they might have begot a chronicle in the bowels of his brain, when he was about the composing of his carmini-formal lines: But *Nac petetin petetac, tic, torche Lorgne,* more the deponent saith not. He was declared an heretic. We make them as of wax. *Valete & plaudite, Calepinus recensui."*

CHAPTER XX

HOW THE SOPHISTER CARRIED AWAY HIS CLOTH, AND HOW HE HAD A SUIT IN LAW AGAINST THE OTHER MASTERS

THE sophister had no sooner ended, but Ponocrates and Eudemon burst out a laughing so heartily, that they had almost split with it, and given up the ghost, even just as Crassus did, seeing a lubberly ass eat thistles; and as Philemon, who, seeing an ass eat those figs which were provided for his own dinner, died with force of laughing. Together with them Master Janotus fell a laughing too as fast as he could, in which mood of laughing they continued so long that their eyes did water by the vehement concussion of the substance of the brain, by which these lachrymal humidities, being pressed out, glided through the optic nerves; and so to the full represented Democritus *Heraclitising,* and Heraclitus *Democritising.*

When they had done laughing, Gargantua consulted with the prime of his retinue what should be done. There Ponocrates was of opinion, that they should make this fair orator drink again, and seeing he had shewed them more pastime, and made them laugh more than a natural fool could have done, that they should give him ten baskets full of sausages, mentioned in his jolly harangue, with a pair of breeches, three hundred great billets for the fire, five and twenty hogsheads of wine, a good large down bed, and a deep capacious dish, which he said were necessary for his old age.

All this was done as they did appoint; only Gargantua doubting that they could not quickly find out breeches fit for his wearing, because he knew not what fashion would best become the said orator, whether the martingal fashion, wherein is a spunge-hole with a drawbridge, for the more easy caguing; or the fashion of the mariners, for the greater solace and comfort of his kidneys; or that of the Switzers,

45

which keeps warm the belly-tabret; or round breeches with straight cannions, having in the seat a piece like a cod's tail; all which considered, for fear of over-heating his reins, he caused to be given him seven ells of white cloth for the linings. The wood was carried by the porters, the masters of arts carried the sausages and the dishes (*dish*), and Master Janotus himself would carry the cloth. One of the said masters (called Jousse Bandouille) shewed him that it was not seemly nor decent for one of his degree and quality to do so, and that therefore he should deliver it to one of them. "Ha," said Janotus, "blockhead, blockhead, thou dost not conclude *in modo & figura;* for lo, to this end serve the *Suppositions & Parva Logicalia. Pannus pro quo supponit?" Confusè,"* said Baudouille, *"& distributivè."* "I do not ask thee," said Janotus, "blockhead, *quomodo supponit,* but *pro quo?* It is blockhead, *pro tibiis meis,* and therefore I will carry it, *Egomet, sicut suppositum portat appositum";* so did he carry it away very close, as Patelin did his cloth. The best was, that when this cougher, in a full assembly held at the Mathurins, had with great confidence demanded his breeches and sausages, and that they were flatly denied him, because he had them of Gargantua, according to the informations thereupon taken; he shewed them that this was gratis, and out of pure liberality, by which they were not in any sort quit of their promises. Notwithstanding this, it was answered him, that he should be content with reason, without expectation of any other *bribe* (*boon*) there. "Reason?" said Janotus, "we use none of that here; unlucky traitors, you are not worth the hanging; the earth beareth not more arrant villains than you are; I know it well enough; halt not before cripples; I have practised wickedness with you: By God's rattle I will inform the king of the enormous abuses that are forged here, and carried under hand by you, and let me be a leper if he do not burn you alive like bougres, traitors, heretics, and seducers, enemies to God and virtue."

Upon these words they framed articles against him; he on the other side cited them to appear. In sum, the process was retained by the court, and there it is yet depending. Hereupon the magisters made a vow, never to rub off the dirt from either shoes or clothes; and Master Janotus, with his adherents, vowed never to blow their noses, until judgment was given by a definitive sentence.

By reason of those vows, both parties continue dirty and snotty to this day; for the court hath not yet fully looked into all the proceedings; so that the judgment is not like to be declared till *latter*

46

Lammas; that is to say, never. So you find that they do more than Nature, and contrary to their own articles. The *Articles of Paris* maintain, that to God alone belongs infinity; and Nature produceth nothing that is immortal, for she putteth an end and period to all things by her engendered, according to the saying, *Omnia orta cadunt. &c.* But these *thick-mist swallowers* make the suits in law, depending upon them, both infinite and immortal; in doing whereof, they have given occasion to, and verified the saying of Chilo the Lacedæmonian, consecrated at Delphos: That misery goes along with law-suits, and suitors are miserable; for sooner shall they attain to the end of their lives, than to the final decision of their pretended rights.

CHAPTER XXI

THE STUDY OF GARGANTUA, ACCORDING TO THE DISCIPLINE OF HIS SCHOOLMASTERS THE SOPHISTERS

THE first day being thus spent, and the bells put up again in their own place, the citizens of Paris, in acknowledgment of this courtesy, offered to maintain and feed his mare as long as he pleased, which Gargantua took in good part, and they sent her to graze in the forest of Biere. I think she is not there now. This done, he with all his heart submitted his study to the discretion of Ponocrates; who first of all appointed that he should do as he was accustomed to the end it might be understood by what means, in so long time, his old masters had made him such a sot and puppy. He disposed therefore of his time in such fashion, that ordinarily he did awake betwixt eight or nine o'clock, whether it was day or night (for so had his ancient governors ordained), alleging that which David saith; *Vanum est vobis ante lucem surgere.* Then did he tumble and toss, wag his legs, and wallow in the bed some time, the better to stir up and rouse his vital spirits, and apparelled himself according to the season; but willingly he would wear a great long gown of thick frieze, furred with fox skins. Afterwards he combed his head with a comb *de al-main,* which is the four fingers and the thumb, for his preceptors had said that to comb himself otherways, to wash and make himself neat, was to lose time in this world. Then he dunged, pissed, spued, belched, cracked, yawned, spitted, coughed, hawked, sneezed, and snotted himself like an archdeacon: and, to fortify against the fog and bad air, went to breakfast, having some good fried tripes, fair rashers on the coals, good gammons of bacon, store of good minced meat, and a great deal of sippet-brewis, made up of the fat of the beef-pot, laid upon bread, cheese, and chopped parsley strewed together.

Ponocrates shewed him, that he ought not to eat so soon after rising out of his bed, unless he had performed some exercise before-hand. Gargantua answered, "What! have I not sufficiently well exercised myself? I have wallowed and rolled myself six or seven turns in my bed, before I rose; is not that enough? Pope Alexander did so, by the advice of a *Jew* his physician, and lived till his dying day in despite of his enemies. My first masters have used me to it, saying, that to eat breakfast made a good memory; and therefore they drank first. I am very well after it, and dine but the better. And Master Tubal (who was the first licentiate at Paris) told me, that it was not enough to run apace, but to set forth betimes. So the total welfare of our humidity doth not depend upon drinking, switter-swatter like ducks, but in being at it early in the morning; *Unde versus,*

"Lever matin n'est point bonheur,
Boire matin est le meilleur."

To rise betimes is good for nothing.
To drink betimes is meat and cloathing.

After a good breakfast he went to church, and they carried to him in a great basket a huge breviary, weighing, what in grease, clasps, parchment, and cover, little more or less than eleven hundred and six pounds: There he heard six and twenty or thirty masses: This while, to the same place came his mattin-mumbler, muffled up about the chin, round as a hoop, and his breath pretty well antidoted with the vine-tree sirrup: with him he mumbled all his *kiriels,* which he so curiously thumbed and fingered, that there fell not so much as one bead of them to the ground. As he went from the church, they brought him, upon a dray drawn with oxen, a confused heap of *patinotres* of Saint Claude, every one of the bigness of a hat-block; and sauntering along through the cloisters, galleries, or garden, he riddled over more of them than sixteen hermits would have done. Then did he study some paultry half hour with his eyes fixed upon his book; but (as the comedy has it) *his mind was in the kitchen.*

48

Pissing then a whole potfull, he sat down at table; and because he was naturally phlegmatic, he began his meal with some dozens of gammons, dried neats' tongues, botargos, sausages, and such other forerunners of wine; in the meanwhile, four of his folks did cast into his mouth, one after another continually, mustard by the whole shovels full. Immediately after that, he drank a horrible draught of white wine for the comfort of his kidneys. When that was done, he ate according to the season, meat agreeable to his appetite; and then left off eating when his belly was like to crack for fulness. As for his drinking, he had in that neither end nor rule; for he was wont to say that the limits and bounds of drinking were, that a man might drink till the cork of his shoes swells up half a foot high.

CHAPTER XXII

THE GAMES OF GARGANTUA

THEN with a starched phiz mumbling over some scraps of a scurvy grace, he washed his hands in fresh wine, picked his teeth with the foot of a hog, and talked merrily with the people; then the carpet being spread, they brought plenty of cards, many dice, with great store and abundance of checkers and chess-boards.

There he played,

At flusse.	At the last couple in hell.
At primero.	At the hock.
At the beast.	At the surly.
At the rifle.	At the lanskenet.
At trump.	At the cuckow.
At the prick and spare not.	At puff or let him speak that
At the hundred.	hath it.
At the peenie.	At take nothing and throw out.
At the unfortunate woman.	At the marriage.
At the fib.	At the frolic, or jackdaw.
At the pass ten.	At the opinion.
At one and thirty.	At who doth the one doth the
At post and pair, or even and	other.
sequence.	At the sequences.
At three hundred.	At the ivory bundles.
At the unlucky man.	At the tarots.

49

At losing load him.
At he's gulled and *esto*.
At the torture.
At the handruff.
At the click.
At honours.
At love.
At the chess.
At Reynard the fox.
At the squares.
At the cowes.
At the lottery.
At the chance or mumchance.
At three dice or maniest bleaks.
At the tables.
At nivinivinack.
At the lurch.
At doublets or queen's game.
At the failie.
At the *French* tictac.
At the long tables or ferkeering.
At felldown.
At tods body.
At needs must.
At the dames or draughts.
At bob and mow.
At *primus secundus*.
At mark-knife.
At the keys.
At span-counter.
At even and odd.
At cross or pile.
At ball and huckle-bone.
At ivory balls.
At the billiards.
At bob and hit.
At the owl.
At the charming of the hare.
At pull yet a little.
At trudge-pig.

At the magatapies.
At the horn.
At the flower over shrovetide ox.
At the madge-owlet.
At pinch without laughing.
At prickle me tickle me.
At the unshoeing of the ass.
At the cocksess.
At hari hohi.
At I set me down.
At earle beardie.
At the old mode.
At draw the spit.
At put out.
At gossip lend me your sack.
At ramcod ball.
At thrust out the harlot.
At marfeil figs.
At nicknamrie.
At stick and hole.
At boke or him, or flaying the fox.
At the branching it.
At trill madam, or grapple my lady.
At the cat selling.
At blow the coal.
At the re-wedding.
At the quick and dead judge.
At unoven the iron.
At the false clown.
At the flints or at the nine stones.
At to the cruch hulchback.
At the sanct is found.
At hinch, pinch, and laugh not.
At the leek.
At bumdockdousse.
At the loosegig.
At the hoop.
At the sow.

At belly to belly.
At the dales or straths.
At the twigs.
At the quoits.
At I'm for that.
At tilt at Weekie.
At nine pins.
At the cock *quintin.*
At tip and hurle.
At the flat bowls.
At the veere and tourn.
At rogue and ruffian.
At bumbatch touch.
At the mysterious trough.
At the short bowls.
At the dapple gray.
At cock and crank it.
At break pot.
At my desire.
At twirly whirlytril.
At the rush bundles.
At the short staff.
At the whirling gigge.
At hide and seek, or are you all
  hid.
At the picket.
At the blank.
At the care sin.
At the pilferers.
At prison bars.
At have at the nuts.
At cherry pit.
At rub and rice.
At whip top.
At the casting top.
At the hobgobling.
At the O wonderful.
At sollile smutchy.
At the fast and loose.
At sutch-breech.

At the broom-beesom.
At St. Cosme I come to adore
  thee.
At the lusty brown boy.
At I take you napping.
At fair and softly passeth Lent.
At the forked oak.
At truss.
At the wolf's tail.
At bum to buss or nose in breech.
At *Goerdy* give me my lance.
At swagay, waggy, or shoggy-
  shou.
At stook and rook, shear and
  threave.
At the birch.
At the musse.
At the dilly dilly darling.
At ox moudy.
At purpose in purpose.
At blind-man buff.
At the fallen bridges.
At bridle *nick.*
At the white at buts.
At thwack swinge him.
At apple, pear, plum.
At mumgi.
At the toad.
At cricket.
At the pounding stick.
At nine less.
At jack and the box.
At the queens.
At the trades.
At heads and points.
At the vine-tree hug.
At black be thy fall.
At ho the distaff.
At Joane Tomson.
At the boulting cloth.

At the oats seed.
At greedy glutton.
At the moorish dance.
At Feeby.
At the whole frisk and gambole.
At battabum, or riding of the wild mare.
At Hind the plowman.
At the good mawkin.
At the dead beast.
At climb the ladder Billy.
At the dying hog.
At the salt doup.
At the pretty pigeon.
At barley break.
At the bavine.
At the bush leap.
At crossing.
At the hardit arsepursy.
At the harrowers' nest.
At forward hey.
At the fig.
At mustard peel.
At gunshot crack.
At the Gome.
At the relapse.
At jog breech or prickle him forward.
At knock-pate.
At the Cornish chough.
At the crane dance.
At slash and cut.
At bobbing, or the flirt on the nose.
At the larks.
At filipping.

After he had thus well played, shuffled, clogged, and thrown away his time, it was thought fit to drink a little, and that was every man eleven bumpers; and afterwards make much of himself, and stretch upon a fair bench, or a good large bed, and there sleep for two or three hours together, without thinking or speaking any hurt: After he was awakened, he would shake his ears a little, and then they brought him fresh wine, and he drank better than ever. Ponocrates shewed him, that it was an ill diet to drink after sleeping. "It is." answered Gargantua, "the very life of the Patriarchs and holy Fathers. For naturally I sleep: Salt and sleep to me is so many gammons."

Then began he to study a little, and out came the *patenotres;* which the more formally to despatch, he got upon an old mule, which had served nine kings; and so mumbling with his mouth, nodding and doddling his head, would go and see a coney ferreted or caught in a grinne. At his return he went into the kitchen, to know what roast meat was on the spit, and supped very well, upon my conscience; and commonly did invite some of his neighbors that were good drinkers, with whom, carousing merrily, they told stories of all sorts, from the old to the new. Among others, he had for domestics the Lord of Fouille, of Grouville, of Griviot, and of Marigny. After supper, were

52

brought into the room, the fair wooden gospels, and the books of the four kings; that is to say, the tables and cards, with a deal of *cockalls, mumblety-pegs,* and *wheels* of fortune; or else they went to see the wenches thereabouts with their wakes, their junketings, and little collations; then to sleep without control till eight o'clock the next morning.

CHAPTER XXIII

HOW GARGANTUA WAS INSTRUCTED BY PONOCRATES, AND IN SUCH SORT DISCIPLINATED, THAT HE LOST NOT ONE HOUR OF THE DAY

WHEN Ponocrates knew Gargantua's vicious manner of living, he resolved to bring him up in another guise way; but for a while bore with him, considering *that Nature cannot endure a sudden change without great violence.* Therefore, to begin his work the better he requested a learned physician of that time, called Master Theodore, seriously to perpend, if it were possible, how to bring Gargantua unto a better course; the said physician purged him canonically with Anticyrian hellebore, by which medicine he cleansed all that foulness and perverse habit of his brain. By this means, also, Ponocrates made him forget all that he had learned under his ancient preceptors, as Timotheus did to his scholars who had been instructed under other musicians: to do this the better they brought him into the company of learned men, which stirred in him an emulation and desire to whet his wit and improve his parts, and to bend his study another way; so as that the world might have a value for him. And afterwards he put himself into such a road, that he lost not any one hour in the day, but employed all his time in learning and honest knowledge. Gargantua awaked about four o'clock in the morning. Whilst they were in rubbing of him, there was read unto him some chapter of the Holy Scripture aloud and clearly, with a pronunciation fit for the matter; and hereunto was appointed a young page, born in Basché, named Anagnostes. According to the purpose and argument of that lesson, he oftentimes gave himself to worship, adore, pray, and send up his supplications to that good God, whose word did shew his majesty and marvellous judgment. Then went he unto the secret places to make excretion of his natural digestions; there his master repeated what had been read, expounding unto him the most obscure and difficult points. In returning, they considered the face of the sky, if it were such as they had observed it the night before, and into what signs the sun was entering, as also the moon for that day. This done he was apparelled, combed, curled, trimmed, and perfumed, during which time they repeated to him the lessons of the day before; he himself said them by heart, and upon them would ground some practical cases concerning the estate of man, which he would prosecute sometimes two or three hours, but ordinarily they ceased as soon as he was fully cloathed. Then for three good hours he had a lecture read unto him: this done, they went forth, still conferring on the substance of the lecture, either unto a field near the University, called the Brack, or unto the meadows, where they played at the ball, tennis, and at the pelitrigone, most gallantly exercising their bodies, as before they had done their minds: all their play was but in liberty, for they left off when they pleased, and that was commonly when they did sweat over all their body, or were otherwise weary. Then were they very well wiped and rubbed, shifted their shirts, and walking soberly, went to see if dinner was ready. Whilst they stayed for that, they did clearly and eloquently pronounce some sentences that they had retained of the lecture. In the meantime Master Appetite came, and then very orderly sat they down at table. At the beginning of the meal, there was read some pleasant history of the warlike actions of former times, until he had taken a glass of wine. Then (if they thought good) they continued reading, or began to discourse merrily together; speaking first of the virtue, propriety, efficacy, and nature of all that was served in at the table: of bread, of wine, of water, of salt, of fleshes, fishes, fruits, herbs, roots, and of their dressing; by means whereof he learned in a little time, all the passages competent for this, that were to be found in Pliny, Athenæus, Dioscorides, Julius Pollux, Galen, Porphyry, Oppian, Polybius, Heliodorus, Aristotle, Elian, and others. Whilst they talked of these things many times, to be more certain they caused the very books to be brought to the table. And so well and perfectly did he in his memory retain the things above said, that in those days there was not a physician that knew half so much as he did. Afterwards they conferred of the lessons read in the morning, and ending their repast with some conserve or marmalade of quinces, he picked his teeth with mastic tooth-pickers; washed his hands and eyes with fair fresh water, and gave thanks unto God in some neat hymn, made in the praise of the divine bounty and munificence. This done they brought in cards, not to play, but to learn a thousand pretty tricks and new inventions, which were all grounded upon arithmetic. By this means he fell in love with that numerical science, and every day after dinner and supper he passed his time in it as pleasantly as he was wont to do at cards and dice; so that at last he understood so well both the theory and practical part thereof, that Tunstal, the Englishman, who had written very largely to that purpose, confessed that verily, in comparison of him, he understood no more High Dutch.

And not only in that, but in the other mathematical sciences, as geometry, astronomy, and music. For, in waiting on the concoction, and attending the digestion of his food, they made a thousand pretty instruments and geometrical figures, and did in some measure practise the astronomical canons.

After this they recreated themselves with singing musically, in four or five parts, or upon a set scheme or ground at random, as it best pleased them; in matter of musical instruments he learned to play upon the lute, the virginals, the harp, the all-man flute with nine holes, the viol, and the sackbut. This hour thus spent, and digestion finished, he did purge his body of natural excrements; then betook himself to his principal study for three hours together or more, as well to repeat his morning lectures, as to proceed in the book he had in hand, as also to write handsomely, to draw and form the antique and Roman letters. This being done they went abroad, and with them a young gentleman of Tourain, named the Esquire Gymnast, who taught him the art of riding. Changing then his cloaths, he rode a Naples courser, a Dutch roussin, a Spanish gennet, a barded, or trapped steed, then a light fleet horse, unto whom he gave a hundred carieres, made him go the high saults, bounding in the air, free the ditch with a skip, leap over a stile or pale, turn short in a ring both to the right and left hand. There he broke not his lance; for it is the greatest foolery in the world to say I have broken ten lances at tilt, or in fight; a carpenter can do even as much; but it is a glorious and praiseworthy action, with one lance to break and overthrow ten enemies: therefore with a sharp, stiff, strong, and well-steeled lance would he usually force up a door, pierce a harness, beat down a tree, carry away the ring, lift up a cuirassier saddle, with the mail coat and gauntlet; all this he did in complete armour from head to foot. As for the prancing flourishes, and smacking poppisms, for the better cherishing of the horse commonly used in riding, none did them better than he. The great vaulter of Ferrara was but an ape compared to him. He was singularly skilful in leaping nimbly from one horse to another, without putting foot to ground, and these horses were called *desultories;* he could likewise, from either side, with a lance in his hand, leap on horseback without stirrups, and rule the horse at his pleasure, without a bridle, for such things are useful in military engagements. Another day he exercised the battle-ax, which he so dexterously wielded both in the nimble, strong, and smooth management of that weapon, and that in all the feats practiseable by it, that he passed knight of arms in the field, and at all essays.

Then tossed he the pike, play with the two-handed sword, with the back-sword, with the Spanish tuck, the dagger, poniard, armed or unarmed, with a buckler, with a cloak, with a target.

Then would he hunt the hart, the roe-buck, the bear, the fallow deer, the wild boar, the hare, the pheasant, the partridge, and the bustard. He played at the balloon, and made it bound in the air, both with fist and foot.

He wrestled, ran, jumped, not at three steps and a leap, nor at the hare's leap, nor yet at the *almanes;* "for," said Gymnast, "these jumps are for the wars altogether unprofitable, and of no use"; but at one leap he would skip over a ditch, spring over a hedge, mount six paces upon a wall, ramp and grapple after this fashion up against a window, of the full height of a lance. He did swim in deep waters on his belly, on his back, sideways, with all his body, with his feet only, with one hand in the air, wherein he held a book, crossing thus the breadth of the River Seine without wetting it, and dragged along his cloak with his teeth, as did Julius Cæsar; then, with the help of one hand he entered forcibly into a boat, from whence he cast himself again headlong into the water, sounded the depths, hollowed the rocks, and plunged into the pits and gulphs. Then turned he the boat about, governed it, led it swiftly or slowly with the stream and against the stream, stopped it in its course, guided it with one hand, and with the other laid hard about him with a huge great oar, hoisted the sail, hied up along the mast by the shrowds, ran upon the edge of the decks, set the compass in order, tackled the bow-lines, and steered the helm. Coming out of the water, he ran furiously up against a hill, and with the same alacrity and swiftness ran down again; he climbed up trees like a cat, and leaped from one to the other like a squirrel; he did pull down the great boughs and branches like another Milo; then with two sharp, well steeled daggers, and two tried bodkins, would he run up by the wall to the very top of a house, like a rat;

then suddenly came down from the top to the bottom, with such an even composition of members, that by the fall he would catch no harm.

He did cast the dart, throw the bar, put the stone, practise the javelin, the boar-spear, or partisan, and the halbert; he broke the strongest bows in drawing, bended against his breast the greatest cross-bows of steel, took his aim by the eye with the hand-gun, and shot well, traversed, and planted the cannon, shot at butmarks, at the papgay from below upwards, from above downwards, then before him, sideways, and behind him, like the Parthians.

They tied a cable rope to the top of a high tower, by one end whereof hanging near the ground he wrought himself with his hands to the very top: then upon the same track came down so sturdily and firm, that they could not, on a plain meadow, have run with more assurance. They set up a great pole, fixed upon two trees, there would he hang by his hands, and with them alone, his feet touching at nothing, would go back and fore along the aforesaid rope, with so great swiftness that hardly could one overtake him with running; and then, to exercise his breast and lungs, he would shout like all the devils in hell: I heard him once call Eudemon, from St. Victor's gate to Monmertre; Stentor had never such a voice at the siege of Troy.

Then, for the strengthening of his nerves or sinews, they made him two great sows of lead, each of them weighing eight thousand and seven hundred kintals, which they called *alteres;* those he took up from the ground, in each hand one, then lifted them up over his head, and held them without stirring, three quarters of an hour or more, which was an inimitable force.

He fought at barriers with the stoutest and most vigorous champions; and when it came to the cope, he stood so sturdily on his feet that he abandoned himself to the strongest, in case they could remove him from his place, as Milo was wont to do of old; in whose imitation likewise he held a pomegranate in his hand, to give it unto him that could take it from him. The time being thus bestowed, and himself rubbed, cleansed, wiped, and refreshed with other cloaths, he returned fair and softly, and passing through certain meadows, or other grassy places, beheld the trees and plants, comparing them with what is written of them in the books of the ancients, such as Theophrast, Dioscorides, Marinus, Pliny, Nicander, Macer, and Galen, and carried home to the house great handfuls of them, whereof a young page, called Rhizotomos, had charge; together with little mattocks, pickaxes, grubbing hooks, cabbies, pruning knives, and other instruments requisite for gardening. Being come to their lodging whilst supper was making ready, they repeated certain passages of that which had been read, and then sat down at table. Here remark, that his dinner was sober and thrifty, for he did then eat only to prevent the gnawings of his stomach, but his supper was copious and large, for he took then as much as was fit to maintain and nourish him; which, indeed, is the true diet prescribed by the art of good and sound physic; although a rabble of logger-headed physicians, nuzzeled in the brabbling shop of Sophisters, counsel the contrary. During that repast, was continued the lesson read at dinner, as long as they thought good; the rest was spent in good discourse, learned and profitable. After they had given thanks, he set himself to sing vocally, and play upon harmonious instruments, or otherwise passed his time at some pretty sports, made with cards or dice, or in practising the feats of legerdemain, with cups and balls. There they stayed some nights in frolicking thus, and making themselves merry till it was time to go to bed; and, on other nights they would go make visits unto learned men, or to such as had been travellers in strange and remote countries. When it was full night, before they retired themselves, they went unto the most open place of the house, to see the face of the sky, and there beheld the comets, if any were, as likewise the figures, situations, aspects, opposition, and conjunctions, of both fixed stars, and planets.

Then with his master did he briefly recapitulate, after the manner of the Pythagoreans, that which he had read, seen, learned, done, and understood, in the whole course of that day.

Then prayed they unto God the Creator, in falling down before him, and strengthening their faith towards him, and glorifying him for his boundless bounty; and giving thanks to him for the time that was past, they recommended themselves to his divine clemency for the future, which being done they went to bed, and betook themselves to their repose.

CHAPTER XXIV

HOW GARGANTUA SPENT HIS TIME IN RAINY WEATHER

IF it happened that the weather was anything cloudy, foul, and rainy, all the forenoon was employed as before specified, according to custom, with this difference only, that they had a good clear fire lighted, to correct the distempers of the air; but, after dinner, instead of their wonted exercitations, they did abide within, and by way of *Apotherapie,* did recreate themselves in bottling of hay, in cleaving and sawing of wood, and in threshing sheaves of corn at the barn. Then they studied the art of painting or carving, or brought into use the antique (ancient) play of *Tables,* as Leonicus has written of it; and as our good friend Lascaris playeth at it. In playing, they examined the passages of ancient authors, wherein the said play is mentioned, or any metaphor drawn from it. They went likewise to see the drawing of metals, or the casting of great ordnance; how the lapidaries did work, as also the goldsmiths, and cutters of precious stones: nor did they omit to visit the alchymists, money-coiners, upholsterers, weavers, velvet-workers, watch-makers, looking-glass framers, printers, organists, dyers, and other such kind of artificers, and everywhere giving them somewhat to drink, did learn and consider the industry and invention of the trade.

They went also to hear the public lectures, the solemn commencements, the repetitions, the acclamations, the pleadings of the lawyers, and sermons of evangelical preachers.

He went through the halls and places appointed for fencing, and there played against the masters themselves at all weapons, and shewed them by experience, that he knew as much in it as (yea more than) they: and, instead of simpling, they visited the shops of druggists, herbalists, and apothecaries, and diligently considered the fruits, roots, leaves, gums, seeds, the grease and ointments of some foreign parts, as also how they did adulterate them (*i.e.,* all the said drugs). He went to see the jugglers, tumblers, mountebanks, and quack-salvers; and considered their cunning, their shifts, their summersaults, and smooth tongue, especially of those of Chauny in Picardy, who are naturally great praters, and will banter and lye as fast as a dog can trot.

Being returned home, they did eat at supper more soberly than at other times; and meats more *desiccative and extenuating;* to the end, *that the intemperate moisture of the air, communicated to the body by a necessary confinity, might by this means be corrected;* and that they might not receive any prejudice for want of their ordinary bodily exercise.

Thus was Gargantua governed, and kept on in this course of education from day to day profiting, as you understand such a young man of his age and good sense, so kept to his exercise, may well do; which, although at the beginning seemed difficult, became a little after so sweet, so easy, and so delightful, that it seemed rather the recreation of a king, than the study of a scholar. Nevertheless, Ponocrates, to divert him from this vehement intension of the spirits, thought fit, once in a month, upon some fair and clear day, to go out in the city betimes in the morning, either towards Gentilly or Boulogne, or to Montrouge, or Charentonbridge, or to Vanves, or St. Clou, and there spend all the day long in making the greatest cheer that could be devised, sporting, making merry, drinking healths, playing, singing, dancing, tumbling in some fair meadow, unnestling of sparrows, taking of quails, and fishing for frogs and crabs.

But, although that day was passed without books or lecture, yet was it not spent without profit; for, in the said meadows they usually repeated certain pleasant verses of Virgil's Agriculture, of Hesiod, and of Politian's Husbandry, would set abroach some witty Latin Epigrams, then immediately turned them into roundelays and songs in the French language. In their feasting, they would sometimes separate the water from the wine that was therewith mixed, as Cato teacheth *de re rustica,* and Pliny, with an ivy cup, would wash the wine in a bason full of water, then take it out again with a funnel as pure as ever. They made the water go from one glass to another, and contrived a thousand little *automatory* engines, that is to say, moving of themselves.

CHAPTER XXV

HOW THERE WAS GREAT STRIFE AND DEBATE RAISED BETWIXT THE CAKE-BAKERS OF LERNÉ, AND THOSE OF GARGANTUA'S COUNTRY, WHEREUPON WERE WAGED GREAT WARS

AT that time, which was the season of vintage, in the beginning of harvest, when the country shepherds were set to keep the vines, and hinder the starlings from eating up the grapes; as some cake bakers of Lerné happened to pass along the broad highway, driving unto the city ten or twelve horses loaded with cakes, the said shepherds courteously intreated them to give them some for their money, as the price then ruled in the market. For here it is to be remarked, that it is a celestial food to eat for breakfast hot fresh cakes with grapes, especially the frail clusters, the great red grapes, muscadine, the verjuice grape, and the luskard, for those that are costive in their belly; because it will make them gush out, and squirt the length of a hunter's staff, like the very tap of a barrel; and oftentimes *thinking* to let a squib, they did all-to-besquatter and conshite themselves, whereupon they are commonly called the *vintage thinkers*.

The cake-bakers were in nothing inclinable to their request; but which was worse, did injure them most outrageously, calling them prating gablers, lickorous gluttons, freckled bittors, mangy rascals, shite-a-bed scoundrels, drunken roysters, sly knaves, drowsy loiterers, slapsauce fellows, slabberdegullion druggels, lubbardly louts, cousening foxes, ruffian rogues, paltry customers, sycophant varlets, drawlatch hoydons, flouting milk-sops, jeering companions, staring clowns, forlorn snakes, ninny lobcocks, scurvy sneaksbies, fondling fips, base loons, saucy coxcombs, idle lusks, scoffing braggards, noddy meacocks, blockish grutnols, doddipol joltheads, jobbernol goosecaps, foolish loggerheads, slutch calf-lollies, grout-head gnatsnappers, lob-dotterels, gaping changelings, codshead loobies, woodcock slangams, ninny-hammer flycatchers, noddipeak simpletons, turgy gut, shitten shepherds, and other such defamatory epithets, saying further, that it was not for them to eat of these dainty cakes, but might very well content themselves with the coarse unraunged bread, or to eat of the great brown household loaf. To which provoking words, one amongst them called Forgier (an honest fellow of his person, and a notable springall) made answer very calmly thus: "How long is it since you have got horns, that you are become so proud? Indeed, formerly, you were wont to give us some freely, and will you not now let us have some for our money? This is not the part of good neighbours, neither do we serve you thus when you come hither to buy our good corn, whereof you make your cakes and buns. Besides that, we should have given you to the bargain some of our grapes, but, *by his zounds,* you may chance to repent it, and possibly have need of us another time, when we shall use you after the like manner, and therefore remember it."

Then Marquet, a prime man in the confraternity of the cake-bakers, said unto him, "Yea, Sir, thou art pretty well crest-risen this morning, thou didst eat yesternight too much millet and bolymong; come hither, sirrah, come hither, I will give thee some cakes." Whereupon Forgier, dreading no harm, in all simplicity went towards him, and drew a sixpence out of his leather satchel, thinking that Marquet would have sold him some of his cakes; but instead of cakes, he gave

him with his whip such a rude lash overthwart his legs, that the
marks remained; then would have fled away, but Forgier cried out
as loud as he could, "O! Murder, murder, help, help, help, help"; and
in the meantime threw a great cudgel after him, which he carried
under his arm, wherewith he hit him in the coronal joint of his head,
upon the crotophic artery of the right side thereof, so forcibly, that
Marquet fell down from his mare, more like a dead than a living
man.

Meanwhile, the farmers and country swains that were watching
their walnuts near to that place, came running with their great poles
and long staves, and laid such load on these cake-bakers, as if they
had been to thresh upon green rye. The other shepherds and shepherdesses, hearing the lamentable shout of Forgier, came with their
slings and slackies following them, and throwing great stones at
them, as thick as hail. At last, these overtook them, and took from
them about four or five dozen of their cakes: Nevertheless, they paid
for them the ordinary price, and gave them over and above one hundred eggs, and three baskets full of mulberries. Then did the cake-
bakers help to get Marquet mounted upon his mare again, who was
most shrewdly wounded; and forthwith they returned to Lerné,
changing the resolution they had to go to Pareille, threatening very
sharp and boisterously the cowherds, shepherds, and farmers of Sevilé
and Sinays. This done, the shepherds and shepherdesses made merry
with these cakes and fine grapes, and sported themselves together at
the sound of the pretty small pipe, scoffing and laughing at those vain-
glorious cake-bakers who had that day met with mischief for want
of crossing themselves with a good hand in the morning. Nor did
they forget to apply to Forgier's leg some fair great, red, and medicinal
grapes, and so handsomely dressed it and bound it up, that it was
quickly cured.

CHAPTER XXVI

HOW THE INHABITANTS OF LERNÉ, BY THE COMMANDMENT
OF PICROCHOLE, THEIR KING, ASSAULTED THE SHEPHERDS
OF GARGANTUA, UNEXPECTEDLY AND ON A SUDDEN

THE cake-bakers being returned to Lerné, went presently, before
they either did eat or drink, to the Capitol, and there, before

their king, called Picrochole, the third of that name, made their complaint, shewing their paniers broken, their caps all crumpled, their coats torn, their cakes taken away; but above all, Marquet most enormously wounded, saying, that all that mischief was done by the shepherds and herdsmen of Grangousier, near the broad highway beyond Sevilé.

Picrochole incontinent grew angry and furious; and, without asking any farther, what, how, why or wherefore, commanded the Ban and Arrier Ban to be sounded throughout all his country, that all his vassals of what condition soever, should upon pain of the halter, come in the best arms they could unto the great place before the castle, at the hour of noon; and, better to expedite his design, he caused the drum to beat about the town. Whilst his dinner was making ready, he went himself to see his artillery mounted upon the carriages, to display his colours, and set up the great royal standard, and loaded wains with store of ammunition both for the field and for the belly, arms and victuals. At dinner he dispatched his commissions, and by his express edict my lord Shagrag was appointed to command the van guard, wherein were numbered sixteen thousand and fourteen harquebusiers, together with thirty thousand eleven volunteers. The great Touquedillon, master of the horse, had the charge of the ordnance, wherein were reckoned nine hundred and fourteen of brass, in cannons, double-cannons, basilisks, serpentines, culverins, bombards, falcons, passevolans, spiroles, and other sort of great guns. The rear-guard was committed to the duke of Scrapegood. In the main battle was the king and the princes of his kingdom. Thus being hastily equipped, before they would set forward, they sent three hundred light horsemen under the conduct of captain Swillwind, to discover the country, clear the avenues, and see whether there was any ambush laid for them. But after they had made diligent search, they found all the land round about in peace and quiet, without any meeting or convention at all; which Picrochole understanding, commanded that every one should march speedily under his colours. Then in all disorder, without keeping either rank or file, they took the fields, one amongst another, wasting, spoiling, destroying, and making havoc of all wherever they went, not sparing poor nor rich, privileged nor unprivileged places, church or laity; drove away oxen and cows, bulls, calves, heifers, wethers, ewes, lambs, goats, kids, hens, capons, chickens, geese, ganders, goslings, hogs, swine, pigs, and the like. Beating down the walnuts, plucking the grapes, tearing the hedges,

63

shaking the fruit-trees, and committing such incomparable abuses, that the like abomination was never heard of. Nevertheless, they met with none to resist them; for every one submitted to their mercy: beseeching them, that they might be dealt with courteously; in regard that they had always carried themselves as became good and loving neighbours; and that they had never been guilty of any wrong or outrage done upon them, to be thus suddenly surprised, troubled, and disquieted, and that, if they would not desist, God would punish them very shortly. To which expostulations and remonstrances no other answer was made, but, that they would learn them to eat cakes.

CHAPTER XXVII

HOW A MONK OF SEVILÉ SAVED THE CLOSE OF THE ABBEY FROM BEING RAVAGED BY THE ENEMY

SO much they did, and so far they went pillaging and stealing, that at last they came to Sevilé, where they robbed both men and women, and took all they could catch: Nothing was either too hot or too heavy for them. Although the plague was there in the most part of all the houses, they nevertheless entered everywhere; then plundered and carried away all that was within, and yet, for all this, not one of them took any hurt, which is a most wonderful case. For the curates, vicars, preachers, physicians, chirurgeons, and apothecaries, who went to visit, to dress, to cure, to heal, to preach unto, and admonish those that were sick, were all dead of the infection; and these devilish robbers and murderers caught never any harm at all. Whence comes this to pass (my masters), I beseech you think upon it?

The town being thus pillaged, they went unto the abbey with a horrible noise and tumult, but they found it shut and made fast against them; whereupon, the body of the army marched forward towards a ford, called Sue (Gue) de Vede, except seven companies of foot, and two hundred lanciers, who, staying there, broke down the walls of the close to waste, spoil and make havoc of all the vines and vintage within that place. The monks (poor devils) knew not in that extremity, to which of all their sancts they should vow themselves; nevertheless, at all adventures they rang the bells *ad capitulum capitulantes.* There it was decreed, that they should make a fair procession, stuffed with good lectures, prayers, and litanies, *contra hostium insidias,* and jolly responses *pro pace.*

64

There was then in the abbey, a claustral monk, called Friar John de Entoumeures, young, gallant, frisk, lusty, nimble, quick, active, bold, adventurous, resolute, tall, lean, wide-mouthed, long-nosed, a rare mumbler of mattins, unbridler of masses, and runner over of vigils: and to conclude summarily, in a word, a right monk, if ever there were any, since the monking world monked a monkery. For the rest a clerk, even to the teeth, in matter of breviary. This monk, hearing the noise that the enemy made within the inclosure of the vineyard, went out to see what they were doing, and perceiving that they were cutting and gathering the grapes, whereon was grounded the foundation of all their next year's wine, returned unto the choir of the church where the other monks were, all amazed and astonished like so many bell-melters, whom, when he heard sing, *im, nim, pe, ne, ne, ne, ne, nede, tum ne, num, num, ini, i, mi, co, o, no, o, o, neno ne, no, no, no, rum, nenum, num:* "This is," said he, "*bien chié chanté,* well shit, well sung. By the virtue of God; why do you not sing paniers farewell, vintage is done. The devil snatch me if they be not already within the middle of our close and cut so well both vines and grapes, that by Cods Body, there will not be found for these four years to come so much as a gleaning in it. By the belly of Sanct James, what shall we (poor devils) drink the while? Lord God! *da mihi potum.*" Then said the prior of the convent, "What should this drunken fellow do here, let him be carried to prison for troubling the divine service?" "Nay," said the monk, "the wine service? let us behave ourselves so that it be not troubled; for you yourself, my lord prior, love to drink of the best, and so doth every honest man. Never yet did a man of worth dislike good wine; it is a monastical apophthegm: But these responses that you chaunt here, by G——, are not in season. Wherefore is it, that our devotions were instituted to be short in the time of harvest and vintage, and long in the advent and all the winter?

"The late friar Messepelosse, of good memory, a true zealous man (or the devil take me) of our religion, told me, and I remember it well, how the reason was, that in this season we might press and make the wine, and in the winter whiff it up. Hark you, my masters, you that love the wine, Cods Body, follow me, for Sanct Anthony burn me as freely as a faggot, if they taste one drop of the liquor, that will not now come and fight in defence of the vine. Hog's belly, the goods of the church! Ha, no, no: What the devil would have Sanct Thomas

65

of England died for them; If I die, shall not I be a Sanct likewise? Yet will not I die for all this, but send others a packing."

As he spake this, he threw off his great monk's habit, and laid hold upon the staff of the cross, which was made of the heart of a sorb-apple-tree, it being of the length of a lance, round, of a full gripe, and a little powdered with *flower de luces,* almost all defaced and worn out. Thus went he out in a fair long-skirted jacket, putting his frock scarfways, athwart his breast, and with his staff of the cross laid on so lustily upon his enemies, who without any order, or ensign, or trumpet, or drum, were busied in gathering the grapes of the vineyard; for the cornets, guidons, and ensign-bearers had lain down their standards, banners, and colours by the wall-sides: The drummers had knocked out the heads of their drums on one end, to fill them with grapes: The trumpeters were loaded with great bundles of bunches, and huge knots of clusters: In sum, every one of them was out of array, and all in disorder. He hurried therefore upon them so rudely, without crying *gare,* or beware, that he overthrew them like hogs, tumbled them over like swine, striking athwart and alongst, and by one means or other laid so about him, after the old fashion of fencing, that to some he beat out their brains, to others he crushed their arms, battered their legs, and bethwacked their sides till their ribs cracked with it; to others again, he unjointed the spondyles of the neck, disfigured their chaps, gashed their faces, made their cheeks hang flapping over their chin, and so swinged and belamed them, that they fell down before him like hay before a mower: to some others he spoiled the frame of their kidnies, marred their backs, broke their thigh bones, pushed in their noses, poached out their eyes, cleft their mandibules, tore their jaws, dashed their teeth into their throat, shook asunder their *omoplates,* or shoulder-blade, *sphacelated* their shins, mortified their shanks, inflamed their ancles, heaved off of the hinges theis ishies, their *sciatica* or hip-gout, dislocated the joints of their knees, squattered into pieces the boughs or pestles of their thighs, and so thumped, mauled, and belaboured them everywhere, that never was corn so thick and threefold threshed upon by ploughmen's flails, as were the pitifully disjointed members of their mangled bodies, under the merciless baton of the cross.

If any offered to hide himself amongst the thickest of the vines, he laid him squat as a flounder, bruised the ridge of his back, and dashed his reins like a dog. If any thought by his flight to escape, he made his head to fly in pieces by the *lambdoidal commissure.* If anyone did scramble up into a tree, thinking there to be safe, he rent up his perinee, and impaled him in at the fundament. If any one of his old acquaintance happened to cry out, "Ha, Friar John, my friend; Friar John, quarter, quarter, I yield myself to you; to you I render myself." "So thou shalt," said he, "*per* force, and thy soul to all the devils in hell"; then suddenly gave him *dronos*. If any was so rash and full of temerity as to resist him to his face, then was it he did shew the strength of his muscles; for without more ado he did transpierce him, by running him at the breast through the *mediatestine* and the heart. Others again he so quashed and be-bumped, that with a sound bounce under the hollow of their short ribs, he overturned their stomachs, so that they died immediately. To some, with a smart souse on the *epigaster,* he would make their midriff swag; then redoubling the blow, gave them such a home push on the navel, that he made their puddings gush out. To others, through their ballocks he pierced their bumgut, and left not bowel, tripe, nor entrail in their body, that had not felt the impetuosity, fierceness, and fury of his violence. Believe, that it was the most horrible spectacle that ever one saw: Some cried unto Sanct Barbe, others to St. George; "O, the holy Lady Nytouch," said one, "the good sanctess"; "O, *our lady of succours,*" said another, "help, help!" Others cried, "Our lady of Cunaut, of Loretta, of *good tidings,* on the other side of the water St. Mary-over": Some vowed a pilgrimage to St. James, and others to the *holy handkerchiefs* at Chamberry, which three months after that burnt so well in the fire, that they could not get one thread of it saved: others sent up their vows to St. Cadouin, others to St. John d'Angelie, and to St. Eutropius of Xantes: Others again invoked St. Mesmes of Chinon, St. Martin of Candes, St. Cloud of Sinays, the holy relics of Laurezay, with a thousand other jolly little sancts and santrels. Some died without speaking, others spoke without dying; some died in speaking, others spoke in dying. Others shouted aloud, *"Confession, confession, confiteor, miserere, in manus."* So great was the cry of the wounded, that the prior of the abbey with all his monks came forth; who, when they saw these poor wretches so slain amongst the vines, and wounded to death, confessed some of them. But whilst the priests were busy in confessing them, the little monkies ran all to the place where Friar John was, and asked him wherein he would be pleased to require their assistance.

To which he answered, that they should cut the throats of those he had thrown down upon the ground. They, presently leaving their outer habits and cowls upon the rails, began to throttle and make an end of those whom he had already crushed. Can you tell with what instruments they did it? With fair *gullicks,* which are little hulched-backed demi-knives, wherewith the little boys in our country cut ripe walnuts in two.

In the meantime, Friar John with his formidable baton (staff) of the cross, got to the breach which the enemies had made, and there stood to snatch up those that endeavoured to escape. Some of the monkitos carried the standards, banners, ensigns, guidons, and colours into their cells and chambers, to make garters of them, but when those that had been shriven would have gone out at the gap of the said breach, the sturdy monk quashed and felled them down with blows, saying, "These men have had confession and are penitent souls, they have got their absolution, and gained the pardons: they go into Paradise as straight as a sickle, or as the way is to Faye (*like Crooked-lane at Eastcheap*)."

Thus by his prowess and valour were discomfited all those of the army that entered into the close of the abbey, unto the number of thirteen thousand six hundred twenty and two, besides the women and little children, which is always to be understod. Never did Maugis the hermit bear himself more valiantly with his *pilgrim's staff* against the Saracens, of whom it is written in the Acts of the four sons of Haymon, than did this *monk* against *his enemies with the staff of the cross.*

CHAPTER XXVIII

HOW PICROCHOLE STORMED AND TOOK BY ASSAULT THE ROCK CLERMOND, AND OF GRANGOUSIER'S UNWILLINGNESS AND AVERSION FROM THE UNDERTAKING

WHILST the monk did thus skirmish, as we have said, against those which were entered within the close, Picrochole in great haste passed the ford Vede with all his soldiery, and set upon the rock Clermond, where there was made him no resistance at all: And because it was already night, he resolved to quarter himself and his army in that town, and to refresh himself of his pugnative choler. In the morning, he stormed and took the bulwarks and castle, which afterwards he fortified with rampiers, and furnished with all ammunition requisite, intending to make his retreat there, if he should happen to be otherwise worsted; for it was a strong place both by art and nature, in regard of the situation of it. But let us leave them there, and return to our good Gargantua, who is at Paris, very assiduous and earnest at the study of good letters, and athletical exercitations; and to the good old man Grangousier his father, who, after supper, warmeth his ballocks by a good, clear, great fire, and, whilst his chestnuts are a roasting, is very serious in drawing scratches on the hearth with a stick burned at one end, wherewith they did stir up the fire, telling to his wife and the rest of the family, pleasant old stories and tales of former times.

Whilst he was thus employed, one of the shepherds which did keep the vines (named Pillot), came towards him, and to the full related the enormous abuses which were committed, and the excessive spoil that was made by Picrochole, king of Lerné, upon his lands and territories, and how he had pillaged, wasted, and ravaged all the country, except the enclosure at Sevilé, which Friar John *des Entoumeures,* to his great honour, had preserved; and that at the same present time, the said king was in the rock Clermond; and there with great industry and circumspection, was strengthening himself and his whole army. *"Halas, halas, alas,"* said Grangousier, "what is this, good people? Do I dream, or is it true that they tell me? Picrochole, my ancient friend of old time, of my own kindred and alliance, comes he to invade me? What moves him? What provokes him? What sets him on? What drives him to it? Who hath given him this counsel? *Ho, ho, ho, ho, ho,* my God, my Saviour, help me, inspire me, and advise me what I shall do. I protest, I swear before thee, so be thou favourable to me, if ever I did him or his subjects any damage or displeasure, or committed any the least robbery in his country; but, on the contrary, I have succoured and supplied him with men, money, friendship and counsel upon any occasion, wherein I could be steadable for his good; that he hath therefore at this nick of time so outraged and wronged me; it cannot be but by the malevolent and wicked spirit. Good God, thou knowest my courage, for nothing can be hidden from thee. If perhaps he be grown mad, and that thou hast sent him hither to me for the better recovery and re-establishment of his brain, grant me power and wisdom to bring him to the yoke of thy holy will by good discipline. *Ho, ho, ho, ho,* my good people, my friends, and my faithful servants, must I hinder you from helping me? Alas! my old age required henceforward nothing else but

69

rest, and all the days of my life I have laboured for nothing so much as peace: But now I must (I see it well) load with arms my poor, weary, and feebled shoulders, and take in my trembling hand the lance and horseman's mace, to succour and protect my honest subjects. Reason will have it so; for by their labour am I maintained, and with their sweat am I nourished, I, my children, and my family. This notwithstanding I will not undertake war, until I have first tried all the ways and means of peace; that I resolve upon."

Then assembled he his counsel, and proposed the matter, as it was indeed, whereupon it was concluded that they should send some discreet man unto Picrochole, to know wherefore he had thus suddenly broken the peace, and invaded those lands unto which he had no right nor title. Furthermore, that they should send for Gargantua, and those under his command, for the preservation of the country, and defence thereof, now at need. All this pleased Grangousier very well, and he commanded that so it should be done. Presently, therefore, he sent Basque, his lackey, to fetch Gargantua with all diligence, and wrote to him as followeth.

CHAPTER XXIX

THE TENOR OF THE LETTER WHICH GRANGOUSIER WROTE TO HIS SON GARGANTUA

THE fervency of thy studies did require, that I should not in a long time recall thee from that philosophical rest thou now enjoyest, if the confidence reposed in our friends and ancient confederates had not at this present disappointed the assurances of my old age. But seeing such is my fatal destiny, that I should be now disquieted by those in whom I trusted most, I am forced to call thee back to defend the people and goods, which, by the right of nature, belong unto thee. For even as arms are weak abroad if there be not counsel at home; so is that study vain, and counsel unprofitable, which, in a due and convenient time, is not by virtue executed and put in effect. My intention is not to provoke, but appease; not to assault, but to defend; not to conquer, but to preserve my faithful subjects and hereditary dominions; into which Picrochole is entered in a hostile manner, without any ground or cause, and from day to day pursueth his furious enterprise with great height of insolence, that is intolerable to freeborn spirits.

"I have endeavoured to moderate his tyrannical choler, offering him all that which I thought might give him satisfaction; and oftentimes have I sent lovingly unto him, to understand wherein, by whom, and how he found himself to be wronged: but of him could I obtain no other answer, but a mere defiance; and that in my lands he did pretend only to the right of a civil correspondency and good behaviour. Whereby I knew that the eternal God hath given him over to the disposure of his own free will and sensual appetite, which cannot choose but be wicked, if by divine grace it be not continually guided: and, to contain him within his duty, and bring him to know himself, hath sent him hither to me by a grievous token. Therefore, my beloved son, as soon as thou canst, upon sight of these letters, repair hither with all diligence, to succour, not me so much (which, nevertheless, by natural piety thou oughtest to do) as thine own people, which by reason thou oughtest to save and preserve. The exploit shall be done with as little effusion of blood as may be; and, if possible, by means more expedient, by policy and stratagems of war, we will save all the souls, and send them home merry unto their own houses. My dearest son, the peace of Jesus Christ our Redeemer be with thee. Salute from me Ponocrates, Gymnastes, and Eudemon.

"The 20th of
September. Thy father,
"GRANGOUSIER."

CHAPTER XXX

HOW ULRICH GALLET WAS SENT UNTO PICROCHOLE

THE letter being dictated, signed, and sealed, Grangousier ordained, that Ulrich Gallet (master of the requests), a very wise and discreet man, of whose prudence and sound judgment he had made trial in several difficult and debateful matters, to go unto Picrochole, to shew what had been resolved amongst them. At the same hour departed the good man Gallet, and, having passed the Ford, asked the miller, in what condition Picrochole was? who answered, That *his soldiers had left neither cock nor hen;* that they were retired and shut up into the rock Clermond, and that he would not advise him to go any further, for fear of the scouts, because they were enormously furious; which he easily believed, and therefore lodged that night with the miller.

The next morning he went with a trumpeter to the gate of the castle, and required of the guards he might be admitted to speak to the king, of somewhat that concerned him. These words being told unto the king, he would by no means consent that they should open the gate; but, getting upon the top of the bulwark, said unto the ambassador, "What is the news? What have you to say?" Then the ambassador began to speak as followeth:

CHAPTER XXXI

THE SPEECH MADE BY GALLET TO PICROCHOLE

THERE cannot arise amongst men a juster cause of grief, than when they receive hurt and damage, where they may justly expect for favour and good will; and not without cause (though without reason) have many, after they had fallen into such a calamitous accident, esteemed this indignity less supportable than the loss of their own lives; in such sort, that if they could not by force of arms, or otherwise, correct it, they have deprived themselves of this light.

"It is, therefore, no wonder if King Grangousier, my master, be full of high displeasure, and much disquieted in mind upon thy outrageous and hostile coming; but truly it would be a marvel, if he were not sensible of, and moved with, the incomparable abuses and injuries perpetrated by thee and thine upon those of his country, towards whom there hath been no example of inhumanity omitted; which in itself is to him so grievous for the cordial affection wherewith he hath always cherished his subjects, that more it cannot be to any mortal man; yet in this (above human apprehension) is it to him the more grievous, that these wrongs and sad offences have been committed by thee and thine, who, time out of mind, from all antiquity, thou and thy predecessors, have been in a continual league and amity with him, and all his ancestors, which, even until this time, you have, as sacred, together inviolably preserved, kept, and maintained so well, that not he and his only, but the very barbarous nations, the Poictevins, Bretons, Manceaux, and those that dwell beyond the isles of the Canaries, and that of Isabella, have thought it as easy to pull down the firmament, and to set up depths above the clouds, as to make a breach in your alliance; and have been so afraid of it in their enterprise, that they have never dared to provoke, incense, or endamage the one for fear of the other. Nay, which is more, this sacred league hath so filled the world, that there are few nations at this day inhabiting throughout all the continent and isles of the ocean, who have not ambitiously aspired to be received into it, upon your own covenants and conditions, holding your joint confederacy in as high esteem as their own territories and dominions; in such sort, that, from the memory of man, there hath not been either prince or league so wild and proud, that durst have offered to invade, I say, not your countries, but not so much as those of your confederates. And if by rash and heady counsel they have attempted any new design against them, as soon as they heard the name and title of your alliance, they have suddenly desisted from their enterprises. What rage and madness, therefore, doth now incite thee, all old alliance infringed, all amity trod under foot, and all right violated, thus in a hostile manner to invade his country, without having been by him or his in any thing prejudiced, wronged or provoked? Where is faith? Where is law? Where is reason? Where is humanity? Where is the fear of God? Dost thou think that these atrocious abuses are hidden from the eternal spirits, and the Supreme God, who is the just rewarder of all our undertakings? If thou so think, thou deceivest thyself; for all things shall come to pass, as in his incomprehensible judgment he hath appointed.

"Is it thy fatal destiny, or influence of the stars, that would put an end to thy so long enjoyed ease and rest? For all things have their end and period, so as that, when they are come to the superlative point of their greatest height, they are in a trice tumbled down again, as not being able to abide long in that state. This is the conclusion and end of those who cannot, by reason and temperance, moderate their fortunes and prosperities. But, if it be predestinated that thy happiness and ease must now come to an end, must it needs be by wronging my king? Him, by whom thou wert established? If thy house must come to ruin, should it, therefore, in its fall, crush the heels of him that set it up? The matter is so unreasonable, and so dissonant from common sense, that hardly can it be conceived by human understanding, and altogether incredible unto strangers, till, by the certain and undoubted effects thereof, it be made apparent, that nothing is either sacred or holy to those, who, having emancipated themselves from God and reason, do merely follow the perverse affections of their own depraved nature.

"If any wrong had been done by us to thy subjects and dominions; if we have favoured thy ill-willers; if we had not assisted thee in thy need; if thy name and reputation had been wounded by us; or (to speak more truly) if the calumniating spirit, tempting to induce thee to evil, had, by false illusions and deceitful fantasies, put into thy conceit the impression of a thought, that we had done unto thee anything unworthy of our ancient correspondence and friendship, thou oughtest first to have enquired out the truth, and afterwards by a seasonable warning to admonish us thereof; and we should have so satisfied thee, according to thine own heart's desire, that thou shouldest have had occasion to be contented. But (O, Eternal God), what is thy enterprise? Wouldest thou, like a perfidious tyrant, thus spoil and lay waste my master's kingdom? Hast thou found him so silly and blockish, that he would not; or so destitute of men and money, of counsel, and skill in military discipline, that he cannot withstand thy unjust invasion? March hence presently, and to-morrow, some time of the day, retreat unto thine own country, without doing any kind of violence or disorderly act by the way; and pay withal a thousand besans of gold, for reparations of damages thou hast done in his country: half thou shalt pay to-morow, and the other half at the ides of May next coming, leaving with us in the meantime, for hostages, the Dukes of Turnebank, Lowbuttock, and Smalltrash; together with the Prince of Itches [Scrubbado], and Viscount of Snatchbit."

CHAPTER XXXII

HOW GRANGOUSIER, TO BUY PEACE, CAUSED THE CAKES TO BE RESTORED

WITH that the good man Gallet held his peace: but Picrochole to all his discourse answered nothing, but *"Come and fetch them, come and fetch them; they have ballocks fair and soft; they will knead some cakes for you."* Then returned he to Grangousier, whom he found upon his knees, bare-headed, crouching in a little corner of his cabinet, and humbly praying unto God, that he would vouchsafe to assuage the choler of Picrochole, and bring him to the rule of reason without proceeding by force.—When the good man came back, he asked him, "Ha, my friend, my friend, what news do you bring me?" "There is neither hope nor remedy," said Gallet; "the man is quite out of his wits, and forsaken of God."—"Yea, but," said Grangousier, "my friend, what cause doth he pretend for his outrages?" "He did not shew me any cause at all," said Gallet, "only

74

that, in a great anger, he spoke some words of *cakes*. I cannot tell if they have done any wrong to his *cake-bakers*." "I will know," said Grangousier, "the matter thoroughly, before I resolve any more upon what is to be done." Then sent he to learn concerning that business, and found, by true information, that some of his men had taken violently some *cakes* from Picrochole's people, and that Marquet had his head broken: that, nevertheless, all was well paid, and that the said Marquet had first hurt Forgier with a stroke of his whip athwart the legs, and it seemed good to his whole counsel, that he should defend himself with all his might. "Notwithstanding all this," said Grangousier, "seeing the question is but about a few cakes, I will labour to content him; for I am very unwilling to wage war against him." He enquired then what quantity of cakes they had taken away, and, understanding that it was but some four or five dozen, he commanded five cart-loads of them to be baked that same night, and that there should be one full of cakes made with fine butter, fine yolks of eggs, fine saffron, and fine spice, to be bestowed upon Marquet, unto whom likewise he directed to be given seven hundred thousand and three Philips, for reparation of his losses, and for satisfaction of the chirurgeon that had dressed his wound; and furthermore settled upon him and his, for ever in freehold, the apple-orchard called La Pomardiere; for the conveyance and passing of all which, was sent Gallet, who, by the way, as they went, made them gather near the willow trees great store of boughs, canes, and reeds, wherewith all the carriers were enjoined to garnish and deck their carts, and each of them to carry one in his hand, as himself likewise did, thereby to give all men to understand, that they demanded but peace, and that they came to buy it.

Being come to the gate, they required to speak with Picrochole, from Grangousier. Picrochole would not so much as let them in, nor go to speak with them, but sent them word that he was busy, and that they should deliver their mind to Captain Touquedillon, who was then planting a piece of ordnance upon the wall. Then said the good man unto him, "My Lord, to ease you of all this labour, and to take away all excuses why you may not return unto our former alliance, we do here presently restore unto you the cakes upon which the quarrel arose.—Five dozen did our people take away; they were well paid for: we love peace so well that we restore unto you five cart-loads, of which this cart shall be for Marquet, who doth most complain. Besides, to content him entirely, here are seven hundred thousand and three Philips, which I deliver to him; and for the losses he may pretend to have sustained, I resign for ever the farm of the Pomardiere, to be possessed in fee simple by him and his for ever, without the payment of any duty, or acknowledgment of homage, fealty, fine, or service whatsoever; and here is the deed of conveyance; and for God's sake let us live henceforward in peace; and go you home merrily into your own country from this place, unto which you have no right at all, as yourselves must needs confess, and let us be good friends as before." Touquedillon related all this to Picrochole, and more and more exasperated his courage, saying to him: "These clowns are afraid to some purpose. By cocks, Grangousier conshites himself for fear; the poor *drinker* he is not skilled in warfare, nor hath he any stomach for it; he knows better how to empty the flaggons—that is his art. I am of opinion that it is fit we send back the carts and the money; and for the rest, that very speedily we fortify ourselves here, then prosecute our fortune. But what, do they think they have to do with a Ninniewhoop, to feed you thus with cakes? You may see what it is, the good usage and great familiarity which you have had with them heretofore, hath made you contemptible in their eyes; *ungenton purget purgentom rustius unget.*"

"Sa, sa, sa," said Picrochole, "by St. James, you have given a true character of them." "One thing I will advise you," said Touquedillon; "we are here but badly victualled, and very slenderly provided with stores for the mouth: if Grangousier should come to besiege us, I would go presently and pluck out of all your soldiers' heads and mine own all the teeth, except three to each of us, and with them alone we should make an end of our provision but too soon."

"We shall have," said Picrochole, "but too much sustenance and feeding stuff. Came we hither to eat or to fight?" "To fight indeed," said Toquedillon; "yet *from the paunch comes the dance, and where famine rules force is exiled.*" "Leave off your prating," said Picrochole, "and forthwith seize upon what they have brought." Then took he the money and cakes, oxen and carts, and sent away the messengers, without speaking a word, only that they would come no more so near, for a reason that would be told them the morrow after. Thus, without doing anything, returned they to Grangousier, and related the whole matter unto him, subjoining that there was *no hope left to draw them to peace, but by sharp and fierce wars.*

CHAPTER XXXIII

HOW SOME MINISTERS OF PICROCHOLE, BY HAIR-BRAINED
COUNSEL, PUT HIM IN EXTREME DANGER

THE carts being unloaded, and the money and cakes secured, there came before Picrochole the Duke of Smalltrash, the Earl Swashbuckler, and Captain Durtaille, who said unto him, "Sir, this day we make you the happiest, the most warlike and chivalrous prince that ever was since the death of Alexander of Macedonia." "Be covered, be covered," said Picrochole. "Cry you mercy," said they, "we do but our duty. The matter is thus—you shall leave some captain here to have the charge of this garrison, with a party competent for keeping of the place, which, besides its natural strength, is made stronger by the rampiers and fortresses of your devising. Your army you are to divide into two parts, as you know very well how to do; one part thereof shall fall upon Grangousier and his forces; by it shall he be easily, at the very first shock, routed, and then shall you get money by heaps; for the *clown* had store of ready coin. *Clown* we call him, because a noble and generous prince had never a penny, and that to hoard up treasure is the part of a clown. The other part of the army, in the meantime, shall draw towards Onys, Xaintonge, Angoumois, and Gascony; then march to Perigourt, Medos, and Elanes, taking, wherever you come, without resistance, towns, castles, and forts. Afterwards to Bayonne, St. John de Luz, to Fuentarabia, where you shall seize upon all the ships, and coasting along Gallicia and Portugal, shall pillage all the maritime places, even unto Lisbon, where you shall be supplied with all necessaries befitting a conqueror. By Copsodi, Spain will yield, for they are but a race of loobies. Then are you to pass the Straits of Gibraltar, where you shall erect two pillars more stately than those of Hercules, to the perpetual memory of your name; and the narrow entrance there shall be called the Picrochonical sea.

"Having past the Picrochonical sea, behold, Barbarossa yields himself your slave." "I will," said Picrochole, "give him *fair quarter.*" "Yea," said they, "so that he be content to be christened. And you shall conquer the kingdoms of Tunés, of Hippos Argier [Algiers], Bomine, Corode, yea, all Barbary.—Furthermore, you shall take into your hands Majorca, Minorca, Sardinia, Corsica, with the other islands of the Ligustick and Balcarian seas [Balearian]. Going along on the left hand, you shall subdue all Gallia Narbonensis, Provence, the Allobrogians, Genoa, Florence, Lucca, and then *God by Rome, our poor Monsieur the pope dies now for fear.*" "By my faith," said Picrochole, "I will not then *kiss his pantoffle.*"

"Italy being thus taken, behold Naples, Calabria, Aputia [Apulia] and Sicily, all ransacked, and Malta too. I wish those jovial quondam knights of Rhodes would but come to resist you, that we might see their urine." "I would," said Picrochole, "very willingly go to Loretta." "No, no," said they, "that shall be at our return. From hence we will sail eastwards, and take Candia, Cyprus, Rhodes, and the Cyclade Island, and set upon the Morea. It is ours by St. Trenian, the Lord preserve Jerusalem; for the great Soldan is not comparable to you in power." "I will then," said he, "cause Solomon's Temple to be built." "No," said they, "not yet; have a little patience; stay awhile; be never too sudden in your enterprises.

"Can you tell what Octavian Augustus said, *Festina lentè*. It is requisite that you first have the Lesser Asia, Carra, Lycia, Pamphylia, Cilicia, Lydia, Phrygia, Mysia, Bithynia, Cara, Zia, Satalia, Samagaria, Castamena, Luga, Sanasta, even unto Euphrates." "Shall we see," said Picrochole, "Babylon and Mount Sinai?" "There is no need," said they, "at this time. Have we not hurried up and down, travelled and toiled enough, in having transfretted and past over the Hircanian Sea, marched along the two Armenias and the three Arabias?" "By my faith," said he," "we have played the fools, and are undone. Ha, poor souls!" "What's the matter?" said they. "What shall we have," said he, "to drink in these desarts? for Julian Augustus, with his whole army, died there for thirst, as they say." "We have already," said they, "given order for that. In the Syriac sea, you have nine thousand and fourteen great ships laden with the best wines in the world; they arrived at Port-Joppa; there you shall find two and twenty thousand camels, and sixteen hundred elephants, which you shall find at one hunting about Sigelmes, when you enter into Lybia: and, besides this, you will have all the Mecca caravan. Will not they furnish you sufficiently with wine?" "Yes; but," said he, "we shall not drink it fresh." 'That," said they, "is for a little fish; but a mighty man, a pretender, one that aspires to the monarchy of the world, cannot always have his ease. God be thanked that you and your men are come safe and sound unto the banks of the River Tigris."

"But," said he, "what doth that part of our army, in the meantime, which overthrows that worthy swill-pot Grangousier?" "They are not idle," said they; "we shall meet with them by-and-by. They shall have won you Brittany, Normandy, Flanders, Hainault, Brabant, Artois, Holland, Zealand; they have past the Rhine, over the bellies of the Switzers and Lanskennets, and a party of them hath subdued Luxemburg, Lorrain, Champaign, and Savoy, even to Lyons, in which place they have met with your forces returning from the naval conquests of the Mediterranean Sea; and have rallied again in Bohemia, after they had plundered and sacked Suevia, Wittemberg, Bavaria, Austria, Moravia, and Styria.—Then they set fiercely together upon Lubeck, Norway, Swedeland, Rie, Denmark, Guitland, Greenland, the Sterlins, even unto the Frozen Sea. This done, they conquered the Isles of Orkney, and subdued Scotland, England, and Ireland. From thence sailing through the Sandy Sea, and by the Sarmates, they have vanquished and overcome Prussia, Poland, Lithuania, Russia, Wallachia, Transylvania, Hungaria, Bulgaria, Turquieland, and are now at Constantinople." "Come," said Picrochole, "let us go join them quickly; for I will be emperor of Trebezonde also. Shall we not kill all these dog Turks and Mahometans?" "What a devil should we do else?" said they; *and you shall give their goods and lands to such as shall have served you honestly.* "Reason," said he, "will have it so; that is but just. I give unto you Carmania, Suria, and all Palestine." "Ah, sir," said they, *It is your goodness*: grammercy God grant you may always prosper." There was present at the time an old gentleman well experienced in the wars—a stern soldier, and who had been in many great hazards, named Echephron, who hearing this discourse, said: "I do heartily doubt that all this enterprise will be like the tale of the *pitcher full of milk,* wherewith a shoemaker made himself rich in conceit; but, when the pitcher was broken, he had not whereupon to dine. What do you pretend by these large conquests? What shall be the end of so many labours and crosses?" "Thus it shall be," said Picrochole, "that when we return we shall sit down, rest, and be merry." "But," said Echephron, "if by chance you should never come back, for the voyage is long and dangerous, were it not better for us to take our rest now, than unnecessarily to expose ourselves to so many dangers?" "O," said Swashbuckler, "by G—, here is a good dotard; come, let us go hide ourselves in the corner of a chimney, and there spend the whole time of our life amongst ladies, in threading of pearls, or spinning like Sardanapalus. *'He that nothing ventures hath neither horse nor mule,'* said Solomon." " *'He who adventureth too much,'* said Echephron;

"'*loseth both horse and mule*,' as Malchon answered." "Enough," said Picrochole, "go forward; I fear nothing, but that these devilish legions of Grangousier, whilst we are in Mesopotamia, will come on our backs and charge upon our rear; what remedy then?" "A very good one," said Durtaille; "send a pretty round commission to the Muscovites, and they will bring instantly into the field for you four hundred and fifty thousand choice fighting men. O, that you would but make me your lieutenant-general, how I should truss up the rogues with discipline! I fret, I charge, I strike, I take, I kill, I slay, I play the devil." "On, on," said Picrochole, "he that loves me, follow me."

CHAPTER XXXIV

HOW GARGANTUA LEFT THE CITY OF PARIS, TO SUCCOUR HIS COUNTRY, AND HOW GYMNAST ENCOUNTERED WITH THE ENEMY

IN this same very hour, Gargantua, who was gone out of Paris, as soon as he had read his father's letters, coming upon his great mare, had already passed the Nunnery-bridge. Ponocrates, Gymnast, and Eudemon, to go follow him, took post-horses; the rest of his train came after him by even journies, bringing with them all his books and philosophical instruments. As soon as he had alighted at Parillé, he was informed by a farmer of Gouget, how Picrochole had fortified himself within the rock Clermond, and had sent Captain Tripet with a great army to set upon the wood of Vede and Vaugaudry; and that they had already plundered the whole country, not leaving cock nor hen, even as far as to the wine-press of Billard; and that it was a strange thing, and hardly to be credited, what ravage they had committed over all the land; which so affrighted Gargantua, that he knew not what to say, nor what to do. But Ponocrates counselled him to go unto the lord of Vauguyon, who, at all times had been their friend and confederate; and that by him they should be better advised in their business; which they did incontinently, and found him very willing to assist them; and he was of opinion, that they should send some one of his company to scout along and discover the country; to learn in what condition and posture the enemy was, that they might take counsel, and proceed according to the present occasion. Gymnast offered himself to go; whereupon it was con-

cluded, that for his safety, and the better expedition, he should have
with him some one that knew the ways, avenues, turnings, windings,
and rivers thereabout. Then away went he and Prelingot, gentleman
of Vauguyon's horse, who scouted and espied on all quarters without
any fear. In the meantime Gargantua took a little refreshment, ate
somewhat himself, the like did those that were with him, and caused
to give his mare a *picotine* of oats, that is, threescore and fourteen
quarters and three bushels. Gymnast and his companion rode so
long, that at last they met with the enemy's forces, all scattered and
out of order, plundering, stealing, robbing, and pillaging, all they could
lay their hands on; and, as far off as they could perceive him, they
ran thronging upon the back of one another in all haste towards
him, to unload him of his money, and untruss his portmantles. Then
cried he out unto them, "My masters, *I am a poor devil,* I desire you
to spare me, I have yet one crown left; come, we must drink it, for it
is *aurum potabile,* and this horse here shall be sold to pay *my welcome;* afterwards take me for one of your own, for never yet was
there any man that knew better how to take, lard, roast, and dress,
yea, by G—, to tear asunder and devour a hen, than I that am here;
and for my beverage, I drink to all good fellows." With that he
unscrued his leathern bottle, and, without putting in his nose, drank
very handsomely; the rogues looked upon him, and opening their
throats a foot wide, and putting out their tongues like greyhounds,
in hopes to drink after him; but Captain Tripet, in the very nick,
came running to him to see who it was. To him Gymnast offered his
bottle, saying, "Hold, Captain, drink boldly and spare not. I have
been thy taster; it is wine of *La Fay Monjau.*" "What," says Tripet,
"this fellow gibes and flouts us; who art thou?" said Tripet. "I am,"
said Gymnast, "*A poor devil*" (*pauvre diable*). "Ha," said Tripet,
"seeing thou art a poor devil, it is reason that thou shouldst be permitted to go whithersoever thou wilt, for all *poor devils* pass everywhere without toll or tax; but it is not the custom of *poor devils* to
be so well mounted, therefore, sir *devil,* come down, and let me have
your horse, and if he do not carry me well, you, master devil, must
do it; for I love a life that such a devil as you should carry me away."

CHAPTER XXXV

WHEN they heard these words, some amongst them began to be afraid, and blessed themselves with both hands, thinking, indeed, that he had been a devil disguised; insomuch, that one of them, named Good John, captain of the trained bands, took his psalter out of his codpiece, and cried out aloud, *"Hagios ho Theos.* If thou be of God, speak; if thou be of the other spirit, avoid hence, and get thee going." Yet he went not away; which words being heard by all the soldiers that were there, divers of them being a little inwardly terrified, departed from the place. All this did Gymnast very well remark and consider, and therefore making as if he would have alighted from off his horse, as he was poising himself on the mounting side, he most nimbly, with his short sword by his thigh, shifting his feet in the stirrup, performed the stirrup-leather feat, whereby, after the inclining of his body downwards, he forthwith launched himself aloft in the air, and placed both his feet together on the saddle, standing upright, with his back turned towards the horse's head; "Now," said he, "my case goes backward." Then suddenly, in the very same posture wherein he was, he fetched a gambol upon one foot, and, turning to the left hand, failed not to carry his body perfectly round, just into his former stance [position] without missing one jot. "Ha," said Tripet, "I will not do that at this time," and not without cause. "Well," said Gymnast, "I have failed, I will undo this leap"; then, with a marvellous strength and agility, turning towards the right hand, he fetched another frisking gambol as before; which done, he set his right-hand thumb upon the hind bow of the saddle, raised him up, and sprung in the air, poising and upholding his whole body upon the muscle and nerve of the said thumb, and so turned and whirled himself about three times. At the fourth, reversing his body, and overturning it upside down, and foreside back, without touching anything, he brought himself betwixt the horse's two ears, springing with all his body into the air, upon the thumb of his left hand, and in that posture, turning like a windmill, did most acticely do that trick which is called the *miller's pass*. After this, clapping his right hand flat upon the midle of the saddle, he gave himself such a jerking swing, that he thereby seated himself upon the crupper, after the manner of gentlewomen.

This done, he easily passed his right leg over the saddle and placed himself like one that rides in *croup*. "But," said he, "it were better for me to get into the saddle"; then putting the thumbs of both hands upon the crupper before him, and thereupon leaning himself, as upon the only supporters of his body, he incontinently turned heels over head in the air, and straight found himself betwixt the bow of the saddle, in a good seat. Then, with a *summersault*, springing into the air again, he fell to stand with both his feet close together upon the saddle, and there made above an hundred frisks, turns, and demi-pommads, with his arms held out across, and in so doing, cried out aloud, "I rage, I rage, devils, I am stark mad; devils, I am mad; hold me, devils, hold me; hold, devils, hold, hold!"

Whilst he was thus vaulting, the rogues in great astonishment, said to one another, "By cock's death, he is a goblin or a devil thus disguised; *ab hoste maligno libera nos, domine*," and ran away as in a total rout, looking now and then behind them like a dog that has stolen a pudding.

Then Gymnast, spying his advantage, alighted from his horse, drew his sword, and laid on great blows upon the thickest and highest-crested amongst them, and overthrew them in great heaps, hurt, wounded, and bruised, being resisted by nobody, they thinking he had been a *starved devil,* as well in regard of his wonderful feats in vaulting, which they had seen, as for the talk Tripet had with him, calling him *poor devil*. Only Tripet would have traitorously cleft his head with his fauchion; but he was well armed, and felt nothing of the blow, but the weight of the stroke; whereupon, turning suddenly about, he gave Tripet a home thrust, and, upon the back of that, whilst, he was about to ward his head from a slash, he ran him in at the breast with a hit, which at once cut his stomach, the colon, and the half of his liver, wherewith he fell to the ground; and, in falling, gushed forth above four pottles of pottage, and his soul mingled with the pottage.

This done, Gymnast withdrew himself, very wisely considering that a case of great adventure and hazard should not be pursued unto its utmost period, and that it becomes all cavaliers modestly to use their good fortune, without troubling or stretching it too far. Wherefore, getting to horse, he gave him the spur, taking the right way unto Vauguyon, and Prelingot with him.

83

CHAPTER XXXVI

HOW GARGANTUA DEMOLISHED THE CASTLE AT THE FORD
OF VEDE, AND HOW THEY PASSED THE FORD

AS soon as he came thither, he related the estate and condition wherein they found the enemy, and the stratagem which he alone had used against all their multitude; affirming that they were but rascally rogues, plunderers, thieves, and robbers, ignorant of all military discipline; and that they might boldly set forward unto the field, it being an easy matter to fell and strike them down like beasts. Then Gargantua mounted his great mare, accompanied, as we have said before, and finding in his way a high and great tree (which commonly was called St. Martin's tree, because heretofore St. Martin planted a pilgrim's staff there; which grew to that height and greatness), said "That is that which I lacked; this tree shall serve me both for a staff and lance." With that he pulled it up easily, plucked off the boughs, and trimmed it at his pleasure. In the meantime his mare pissed to ease her belly but it was in such abundance, that it did overflow the country seven leagues, and all the flood ran glib away towards the ford of Vede, wherewith the water was so swollen, that all the forces the enemy had there, were with great horror drowned, except some who had taken the way on the left hand towards the hills. Gargantua, being come to the wood of Vede, was informed by Eudemon, that there was some remainder of the enemy within the castle; which to know, Gargantua cried out as loud as he was able, "Are you there, or are you not there? if you be there, be there no more; and if you be not there, I have no more to say." But a ruffian gunner, at the portcullis, let fly a cannon-ball at him, and hit him with that shot most furiously on the right temple of his head, yet did him no more hurt than if he had but cast a grape-stone at him. "What is this?" said Gargantua, "do you throw at us grape-stones here? The vintage shall cost you dear," thinking indeed that the bullet had been the stone of a grape.

Those who were within the castle being till then busy at the pillage, when they heard this noise, ran to the towers and fortresses, from whence they shot at him above nine thousand and five and twenty falcon-shot and harbuscades, aiming all at his head; and so thick did they shoot at him that he cried out, "Ponocrates, my friend, these flies are like to put out mine eyes; give me a branch of those willow-trees to drive them away," thinking that the bullets and stones shot out of the great ordnance had been but dun-flies. Ponocrates looked and saw there were no other flies, but great shot which they had shot from the castle. Then was it that he rushed with his great tree against the castle, and with mighty blows overthrew both towers and fortresses, and laid all level with the ground, by which means all that were within were slain and broken in pieces.

Going from thence, they came to the bridge at the *mill,* where they found all the *ford* covered with dead bodies, so thick, that they had choaked up the *mill,* and stopped the current of its water; and these were those that were destroyed in the urinal deluge of the mare. There they were at a stand, consulting how they might pass without hindrance by these dead carcasses. But Gymnast said, "If the devils have passed there, I will pass well enough." "The devils have passed there," said Eudemon, "to carry away the damned souls." "By St. Rhenian," said Ponocrates, "then by necessary consequence he shall pass there." "Yes, yes," said Gymnastes, "or I shall stick in the way." Then, setting spurs to his horse, he passed through freely, his horse not fearing, nor being any ways affrighted at the sight of the dead bodies; for he had accustomed him, according to the doctrine of Ælian, not to fear armour, nor the carcasses of dead men; and that not by killing men, as Diomedes did the Thracians, or as Ulysses did in throwing the corpse of his enemies at his horse's feet, as Homer saith; but by putting a *Jack-a-lent* amongst his hay, and making him go over it ordinarily when he gave him his oats.

The other three followed him very close, except Eudemon only, whose horse's far fore-foot sunk up to the knee in the paunch of a great fat chuff, who lay there upon his back drowned, and could not get it out. There was he pestered, until Gargantua, with the end of his staff, thrust down the rest of the villain's tripes into the water, whilst the horse pulled out his foot; and, which is a wonderful thing in hippiatry, the said horse was thoroughly cured of a ringbone which he had in that foot, by the touch of the burst guts of that great looby.

CHAPTER XXXVII

HAVING got over the river of Vede, they came very shortly after to Grangousier's castle, who waited for them with great longing. At their coming there was such hugging and embracing, never was seen a more joyful company; for *supplementum, supplementi chronicorum* saith, that Gargamelle died there with joy. For my part, truly I cannot tell, neither do I care very much for her, nor for anybody else. The truth was, that Gargantua, in shifting his clothes and combing his head with a comb nine hundred feet long, and the teeth all tusks of elephants, whole and entire, he made fall at every rake above seven balls that stuck in his hair, at the razing the castle at the wood of Vede; which his father Grangousier seeing, thought they had been lice, and said unto him, "What, my dear son, hast thou brought us thus far some short-winged hawks of the college of Montague? I did not mean that thou shouldest reside there." Then answereed Ponocrates, "My sovereign lord, think not that I have placed him in that lowsy college, which they call Montague; I had rather have put him amongst the grave diggers of Sanct Innocent, so enormous is the cruelty and villany that I have known there: for the galley-slaves are far better used amongst the Moors and Tartars, the murderers in the criminal dungeons, yea, the very dogs in your house, than are poor wretched students in the aforesaid college. And were I king of Paris, the devil take me if I would not set it on fire, and burn both principal and regents, for suffering this inhumanity to be exercised before their eyes." Then, taking up one of these bullets, he said, "These are cannon-shot, which your son Gargantua hath lately received by the treachery of your enemies, as he was passing before the wood of Vede.

"But they have been so rewarded, that they are all destroyed in the ruin of the castle, as were the Philistines by the policy of Sampson, and those whom the tower of Silohim slew, as it is written, Luke 13. My opinion is, that we pursue them whilst the luck is on our side, for Occasion hath all her hair on her forehead; when she is past you may not recal her; she is bald in the hind part of her head, and never returneth again." "Truly," said Grangousier, "it shall not be at this time, for I will make you a feast this night, and bid you welcome."

This said, they made ready supper, and, of extraordinary, besides

86

his daily fare, were roasted sixteen oxen, three heifers, two and thirty calves, threescore and three fat kids, fourscore and fifteen wethers, three hundred barrow pigs souced in sweet wine, eleven score partridges, seven hundred snipes and woodcocks, four hundred Loudon and Cornwal capons, six thousand pullets, and as many pigeons, six hundred crammed hens, fourteen hundred leverets, three hundred and three buzzards, and one thousand and seven hundred cockerels. For venison, they could not so suddenly come by it, only eleven wild boars, which the Abbot of Turpenay sent, and eighteen fallow deer, which the Lord of Grammont bestowed; together with seven score pheasants, which were sent by the Lord of Essars, and some dozens of quests, cushots, ringdoves, and woodculvers; river-fowl, teals and awteals, bitterns, courtes, plovers, Francolins, briganders, tyrasons, young lapwings, tame ducks, shovelers, woodlanders, herons, moorhens, criels, storks, canepetiers, oranges, flamans which are phænicopters, terrigoles, turkies, arbens, coots, solingeese, curlews, termagants, and water-wagtails, with a great deal of cream, curds, and fresh cheese and store of soup, pottages, and *brewis,* with variety. Without doubt there was meat enough, and it was handsomely dressed by Snapsauce, Hotch-pot, and Braverjuice, Grangousier's cooks. Jenken, Trudge-a-pace, and Clean-glass, were very careful to fill them drink.

CHAPTER XXXVIII

HOW GARGANTUA DID EAT UP SIX PILGRIMS IN A SALLAD

THE story requireth, that we relate what happened unto six pilgrims, who came from Sebastian near to Nantes; and who for shelter that night, being afraid of the enemy, had hid themselves in the garden upon the chicheling pease, among the cabbages and lettices. Gargantua, finding himself somewhat dry, asked whether they could get any lettice to make him a sallad; and hearing that there were the greatest and fairest in the country (for they were as great as plum-trees, or as walnut-trees) he would go thither himself, and brought thence in his hand what he thought good, and withal carried away the six pilgrims, who were in so great fear, they did not dare to speak nor cough.

Washing them, therefore, first at the fountain, the pilgrims said one to another softly, *"What shall we do? we are almost drowned here amongst these lettices, shall we speak? but if we speak he will kill us for spies."* As they were thus deliberating what to do, Gargantua put them with the lettices into a platter of the house as large as the huge tun of the Cistertians, which done, with oil, vinegar, and salt, he eat them up, to refresh himself a little before supper, and had already swallowed up five of the pilgrims, the sixth being in the platter, totally hid under a lettice, except his staff that appeared and nothing else; which Grangousier seeing, said to Gargantua, "I think that is the horn of a shell snail, do not eat it." "Why not?" said Gargantua; "they are good all this month," which he no sooner said, but drawing up the staff, and therewith taking up the pilgrim, he eat him very well, then drank a terrible draught of excellent white-wine, and expected supper to be brought up.

The pilgrims, thus devoured, made shift to save themselves as well as they could, by withdrawing their bodies out of the reach of the grinders of his teeth, but could not escape from thinking they had been put in the lowest dungeon of a prison. And when Gargantua whiffed the great draught, they thought to have been drowned in his mouth, and the flood of wine had almost carried them away in the gulph of his stomach. Nevertheless, skipping with their staves, as St. Michael's palmers used to do, they sheltered themselves from the danger of that inundation, under the banks of his teeth. But one of them by chance, groping or sounding the country with his staff to try whether they were in safety or no, struck hard against the cleft of a hollow tooth, and hit the *mandibulary* sinew or nerve of the jaw, which put Gargantua to very great pain, so that he began to cry for the rage that he felt. To ease himself therefore of his smarting ach, he called for his tooth-picker, and, rubbing towards a young walnut-tree, unnestled you my gentlemen pilgrims.

For he caught one by the legs, another by the scrip, another by the pocket, another by the scarf, another by the band of the breeches, and the poor fellow that had hurt him with the staff, him he hooked to him by the codpiece, which snatch nevertheless did him a great deal of good, for it broke upon him a pocky botch he had in the groin, which grievously tormented him ever since they were past Ancenis. The pilgrims, thus dislodged, ran athwart the plain a pretty fast pace, and the pain ceased, even just at the time when by Eudemon he was called to supper, for all was ready. "I will go then," said he, "and piss away my misfortune," which he did do in such a copious measure, that, the urine taking away the feet from the pilgrims, they

88

were carried along with the stream unto the bank of a tuft of trees: upon which, as soon as they had taken footing, and that for their self-preservation they had run a little out of the road, they on a sudden fell all six, except Fourniller, into a trap that had been made to take wolves by a train; out of which they escaped nevertheless by the industry of the said Fourniller, who broke all the snares and ropes. Being gone from thence, they lay all the rest of that night in a lodge near unto Coudry, where they were comforted in their miseries, by the gracious words of one of their company, called Sweertogo, who shewed them that this adventure had been foretold by the prophet David in the Psalms. *"Quum exurgerent homines in nos, fortè vivos deglutissent nos;* when we were eaten in the sallad, with salt, oil and vinegar. *Quum irasceretur furor eorum in nos, forsitan aqua absorbuisset nos;* when he drank the great draught. *Torrentem pertransivit anima nostra;* when the stream of his water carried us to the thicket. *Forsitan pertransisset anima nostra aquam intolerabilem;* that is, the water of his urine, the flood whereof, cutting our way, took our feet from us. *Benedictus dominus qui non dedit nos in captionem dentibus eorum: anima nostra sicut passer erepta est de laqueo venantiam;* when we fell in the trap. *Laqueus contritus est,* by Fourniller. *Et nos liberati sumus. Adjutorium nostrum, &c."*

CHAPTER XXXIX

HOW THE MONK WAS FEASTED BY GARGANTUA, AND OF THE JOVIAL DISCOURSE THEY HAD AT SUPPER

WHEN Gargantua was set down at table, and all of them had somewhat stayed their stomachs, Grangousier began to relate the source and cause of the war raised between him and Picrochole, and came to tell how Friar John of *des Entoumeures,* the Funnels, had triumphed at the defence of the close of the abbey, and extolled him for his valour above Camillus, Scipio, Pompey, Cæsar, and Themistocles. Then Gargantua desired that he might be presently sent for, to the end that with him they might consult of what was to be done; whereupon, by a joint consent, the *master d'hotel* went for him, and brought him along merrily, with his staff of the cross upon Grangousier's mule. When he was come, a thousand huggings, a thousand embracements, a thousand good days were given. "Ha,

89

Friar John, my friend, Friar John, my brave cousin Friar John, from the devil, let me clip thee about the neck; let me have thee in my arms; I must gripe thee (my cod) till thy back crack"; and, Friar John, the gladdest man in the world, never was man made welcomer, never was any more courteously and graciously received than Friar John. "Come, come," said Gargantua, "a stool here close by me at this end." "With all my heart," said the monk, "seeing you will have it so." "Some water, page, fill, my boy, fill, it is to refresh my liver." "Give me some, *child*, to gargle my throat withal. *Depositâ cappâ*," said Gymnast, "let us pull off this frock." "Ho, by G—, gentlemen," said the monk, "there is a chapter in *Statutis Ordinis,* which opposeth my laying it down." "Pish," said Gymnast, "a fig for your chapter. This frock breaks both your shoulders; put it off." "My friend," said the monk, "let me alone with it, for by G— I'll drink the better that it is on, it makes all my body jocund: if I should lay it aside, the waggish pages would cut to themselves garters out of it, as I was once served at Coulaines; and, which is worse, I should lose my appetite, but if in this habit I sit down at table, I will drink by G— both to thee and thy horse, and so courage, frolic, God save the company, I have already supped, yet I will eat never a whit the less for that, for I have a paved stomach, as hollow as St. Benet's boots, always open like a lawyer's pouch. Of all fishes but the tench, take the wing of a partridge, or the thigh of a nun: doth not he die like a good fellow that dies with a stiff *cazzo?* Our prior loves exceedingly the white of a capon." "In that," said Gymnast, "he doth not resemble the foxes; for of the capons, hens, and pullets which they carry away, they never eat the white." "Why?" said the monk. "Because," said Gymnast, "they have no cooks to dress them, and, if they be not competently made ready, they remain red and not white, the redness of meats being a token that they have not enough of the fire, except the shrimps, lobsters, crabs, and crayfishes, which are cardinalized with boiling." "God's fish," said the monk, "the porter of our abbey then hath not his head well-boiled, for his eyes are as red as a mazer made of an alder-tree. The thigh of this leveret is good for those that have the gout. Some *natural* philosophy; *ha, ha,* what is the reason that the *thighs* of a gentlewoman are always fresh and cool?" "This problem," said Gargantua, "is neither in Aristotle, in Alexander Aphrodiseus, nor in Plutarch." "There are *three causes,*" said the monk, "by which *that place* is naturally refreshed. *Primò,* because the water runs all along it. *Secundò,* because it is a shady place, obscure and dark, upon which the sun never shines. And thirdly, because it is continually blown upon, and aired by a reverberation from the *back-door,* by the fan of the *smock,* and *flipflat* of the cod-piece. And lusty my lads, some bousing liquor, page; so *crack, crack, crack,* O, what a good God have we, that gives us this excellent juice; I call him to witness, if I had been in the time of Jesus Christ, I would have kept him from being taken by the Jews in the Garden of Olivet; and the devil fail me, if I should have failed to cut off the hams of these gentlemen *apostles* who ran away so basely after they had so well supped, and left their good master in the lurch. I hate that man worse than poison that offers to run away, when he should fight and lay stoutly about him. O, that I were but king of France for fourscore or an hundred years! by G— I should whip like curtailed dogs these *run-aways* of Pavia. A plague take them, why, did they not chuse rather to die there than to leave their good prince in that pinch and necessity? Is it not better and more honourable to perish in fighting valiantly, than to live in disgrace by cowardly running away? We are like to eat no great store of goslings this year, therefore, friend, reach me some of that roasted pig there.

"Diavolo, is there no more must? No more sweet wine! *Germinavit radix jesse.* I renounce my life, I die for thirst. This wine is none of the worst; what wine drank you at Paris? I give myself to the devil, if I did not once keep open house at Paris for all comers six months together. Do you know Friar Claude of the High Kilderkins? O, the good fellow that he is! But what fly hath stung him of late, he is become so hard a student? For my part I study not at all. In our abbey we never study, for fear of the mumps. Our late abbot was wont to say, that it is a monstrous thing to see a learned monk: by G— master my friend, *magis, magnos, clericos, non sunt, magis magnos sapientes.* You never saw so many hares as there are this year. I could not anywhere come by a gos-hawk, nor tassel of falcon; my lord Beloniere promised me a *lanner* (hawk), but he wrote to me not long ago, that he was become pursy. The partridges will so multiply henceforth, that they will go near to eat up our ears; I take no delight in the stalking-horse, for I catch such cold, that I am like to founder myself at that sport; if I do not run, toil, travel and trot about, I am not well at ease. True it is, that in leaping over hedges and bushes my frock leaves always some of its wool behind it; I have recovered a dainty grey-hound; I give him to the devil if he suffer a hare to escape him. A groom was leading him to my lord Hunt-little, and I robbed him of him; did I ill?" "No, Friar John," said Gymnast, "no, by all the devils that are, no." "So," said the monk, "do I attest these same devils so long as they last; Virtue G— what could that gouty limpard have done with so fine a dog? By the body of G— he is better pleased, when one presents him with a good yoke of oxen." "How now," said Ponocrates, "you swear, Friar John." "It is only," said the monk, "but to grace and adorn my speech; they are colours of a Ciceronian rhetoric."

CHAPTER XL

WHY MONKS ARE THE OUTCASTS OF THE WORLD, AND WHEREFORE SOME HAVE BIGGER NOSES THAN OTHERS

BY the faith of a Christian," said Eudemon, "I am highly transported, when I consider what an honest fellow this *monk* is, for he makes us all merry. How is it then that they exclude the *monks* from all good companies; calling them feast-troublers, as the bees drive away the drones from their hives? *Ignavum fucos, pecus,* said Maro, *à præsepibus arcent."* "Hereunto," answered Gargantua, "there is nothing so true, as that the frock and cowle draw to them the opprobries, injuries, and maledictions of the world, just as the wind called Cecias attracts the clouds; the peremptory reason is because they eat the turd of the world, that is to say, they feed upon the sins of the people: and as a noisome thing, they are cast into the privies; that is, the convents and abbies, separated from civil conversation, as the privies and retreats of a house are; but if you conceive how an *ape* in a family is always mocked, and provokingly incensed, you shall easily apprehend how *monks* are shunned of all men, both young and old: the ape keeps not the house as a dog doth: he draws not in the plough as the ox: he yields neither milk nor wool as the sheep: he carrieth no burthen as a horse doth: That which he doth is only to conskit, spoil and defile all, which is the cause wherefore he hath of all men mocks, frumperies, and bastinadoes.

"After the same manner a *monk* (I mean those little, idle, lazy *monks*) doth not labour and work as do the peasant and artificer, doth not ward and defend the country as doth the soldier, cureth not the sick and diseased as the physician doth, doth neither preach nor teach as do the evangelical doctors and schoolmasters, doth not import commodities and things necessary for the commonwealth as the merchant doth; therefore is it, that by and of all men they are hooted at, hated and abhorred." "Yea, but," said Grangousier, "they pray to God for us." "Nothing less," answered Gargantua: "true it is, with a tingle tangle, jangling of bells, they trouble and disquiet all their neighbours about them." "Right," said the monk, " *a mass, a matine, a vesper well rung is half said.*" "They mumble out great store of legends and psalms, by them not at all understood, they say many *patenotres,* interlarded with *ave maries,* without thinking upon, or apprehending the meaning of what it is they say, which truly I call *mocking of God, and not prayers.* But so help them God, as they pray for us, and not for being afraid to lose their victuals, their manchets, and good fat pottage. All true Christians, of all estates and conditions, in all places and at all times, send up their prayers to God, and the spirit prayeth and intercedeth for them, and God is gracious to them. Now such a one is our good Friar John, therefore every man desireth to have him in his company, he is no bigot, he is not for division; he is an honest heart, plain, resolute, good fellow; he travels, he labours, he defends the oppressed, comforts the afflicted, helps the needy, and keeps the close of the abbey." "Nay," said the monk, "I do a great deal more than that; for whilst we are dispatching our matines and anniversaries, in the choir, I make withal some cross-bow-strings, polish glass bottles and boults; I twist lines, and weave pursenets, wherein to catch conies. I am never idle; but *hola,* fill, fill, some drink, some drink, here, bring the fruit; these chestnuts are of the wood of Estrox, and, with good new wine, will make you a composer of bum-sonnets. You are not yet well liquored; by G— I drink at all fords like a promoter's (proctor's) horse." "Friar John," said Gymnast, "take away the snot that hangs at your nose." "Ha, ha," said the monk, "am not I in danger of drowning, seeing I am in water even to the nose?" "No, no, *quare? quia,* though it comes out thence abundantly, yet there never goes in any; for it is well antidoted with syrup of the vine."

"O, my friend, he, that hath winter boots made of such leather, may boldly fish for oysters, for they will never take water." "What is the cause," said Gargantua, "that Friar John hath such a goodly nose?" "Because," said Grangousier, "that God would have it so, who frameth us in such form, and for such end, as is most agreeable to his divine will, even as a potter fashioneth his vessels." "Because," said Ponocrates, "he came with the first to the fair of noses, and therefore made choice of the fairest and the greatest." "Pish," said the monk, "that is not the reason of it, but according to the true monastical philosophy, it is because my nurse had soft teats, by virtue whereof, whilst she gave me suck, my nose did sink in, as in so much butter. The hard breasts of nurses make children short nosed. But hey dey, *ad forman nasi cognoscitur ad te levavi.* I am for no sweet stuff with my tipple, boy: *Item,* rather some toasts."

CHAPTER XLI

HOW THE MONK MADE GARGANTUA SLEEP, AND OF HIS HOURS AND BREVIARIES

SUPPER being ended, they consulted of the business in hand, and concluded, that about midnight they should fall unawares upon the enemy, to know what manner of watch and ward they kept; and in the meanwhile take a little rest, the better to refresh themselves. But Gargantua could not sleep by *any means, on which side soever he turned himself.* Whereupon the monk said to him, "I never sleep soundly but when I am at *sermon* or *prayers.* Let us therefore begin, you and I, the seven penitential psalms, to try whether you shall not quickly fall asleep." The conceit pleased Gargantua very well, and beginning the first of these psalms, as soon as they came to *beati quorum,* they fell asleep both the one and the other. But the monk for his being formerly accustomed to the hour of claustral matines, failed not to wake a little before midnight, and being up himself, awaked all the rest, in singing aloud, and with a full, clear voice, the song,

> "Awake, O Reinian, awake,
> Awake, O Reinian, ho:
> Get up for a pot and a cake;
> With a diddle dum, diddle dum, do."

When they were all rouzed and up, he said, "My masters, it is a usual saying, *that we begin matines with coughing, and supper with drinking;* let us now (in doing clean contrarily) begin our matins with drinking, and, at night, before supper, we will cough as hard as we can." "What!" said Gargantua, "to drink so soon after sleep, this is not to live by the rule of physicians; for you ought first to scour and cleanse your stomach of all its superfluities." "O, rot your physicians," said the monk, "a hundred devils leap into my body, if there be not *more old drunkards than old physicians*. I have made this paction and covenant with my appetite that it always lieth down and goeth to bed with me, for of that I take very good care, and then it also riseth with me the next morning. Tend your cures as much as you will, I will get me to my *tiring*." "What tiring do you mean?" said Gargantua. "My breviary," said the monk, "for just as the falconers, before they feed their hawks do make them tire at a hen's leg, to purge their brains of phlegm, and sharpen them to a good appetite; so, by taking this jolly little breviary in the morning, I scour all my lungs, and find myself ready to drink."

"After what manner," said Gargantua, "do you say these *belly heures* of yours?" "After the manner of Whipfield," said the monk, "by three psalms and three lessons, or nothing all, he that will. I never tie myself to hours, *les heures* are made for the man, and not the man for *les heures;* therefore is it that I make my prayers in fashion of stirrup-leathers; I shorten or lengthen them when I think good. *Brevis oratio penetrat cœlos, & longa potatio evacuat scyphos."* "Where is that written?" "By my faith," said Ponocrates, "I cannot tell, my pillicock, but thou art worth gold." "Like you, sir," said the monk. "But *venite, apotemus."* Then made they ready rashers on the coals in abundance, and good fat brewis with sippets, and the monk drank at pleasure. Some kept him company, and did as he did; others let it alone. Afterwards, every man began to arm and equip himself for battle, and they armed the monk against his will, for he desired no other armour for back and breast, but his frock, nor any other weapon in his hand, but the staff of the cross; yet at their pleasure was he armed *cap-a-pee,* and mounted upon one of the best horses in the kingdom, with a good slashing sabre by his side; together with him were Gargantua, Ponocrates, Gymnast, Eudemon, and five and twenty more of the most resolute and adventurous of Grangousier's house, all armed at proof, with their lances in their hands, mounted like St. George, and every one of them having a harquebuse behind him.

95

CHAPTER XLII

HOW THE MONK ENCOURAGED HIS FELLOW CHAMPIONS, AND HOW HE HANGED UPON A TREE

THUS went out those valiant champions on their adventure in full resolution, to know what enterprise they should undertake, and what to be aware of in the day of the great and horrible battle. And the monk encouraged them saying: "My children, do not fear nor doubt, I will conduct you safely. God and St. Benedict be with us. If I had strength answerable to my courage, by 'sdeath I would plume them for you like ducks. I fear nothing but the great ordnance; yet I know a prayer, which the sub-sexton of our abbey taught me, that will preserve a man from the violence of guns and all manner of fire-engines; *but it will do me no good, because I do not believe it.* However, my staff of the cross will beat the devil. *Parbleu,* whoever is a duck amongst you, I give myself to the devil, if I do not make a monk of him in my stead, and hamper (swaddle) him within my frock, which is a cure for cowardice.

"Did you never hear of my lord Meurles his greyhound which was not worth a straw in the fields! he put a frock about his neck; by the body of G— there was neither hare nor fox that could escape him; and which is more, he lined all the bitches in the country, though before that he was feeble-reined, and *ex frigidis & maleficiates.*"

The monk uttering these words in choler as he passed under a walnut-tree, in his way towards the causey, he broached the vizor of his helmet on the stump of a great branch of the tree; nevertheless, he set his spurs so fiercely to the horse, who was full of mettle, and quick on the spur, that he bounded forwards, and the monk, going about to ungrapple his vizor, let go his hold of the bridle, and so hanged by his hand upon the bough, whilst his horse stole away from under him. By this means was the monk left hanging on the walnut-tree, and crying for help: "Murder! murder!" and swearing also that he was betrayed. Eudemon perceived him first, and calling Gargantua, said: "Sir, come and see Absalom hanging." Gargantua being come, considered the countenance of the monk, and in what posture he hanged; wherefore he said to Eudemon, "You were mistaken in comparing him to Absalom, for Absalom hung by his hair, but this shaveling monk hangeth by the ears." "Help me," said the monk, "in the devil's name; is this a time for you to flout? You seem to me the *decretalist* preachers, who say, 'that whosoever shall see his neighbour in danger of death, ought, upon pain of trisulk excommunication, rather to admonish him to make confession and put his conscience in the state of grace, than to help him.' And therefore, when I shall see them fallen into a river, and ready to be drowned instead of lending them my hand and pulling them out, I shall make them a fine long sermon, *de contemptu mundi, & fuga seculi,* and when they are stark dead, then go to fish for them." "Be quiet," said Gymnast, "and stir not, my minion; I am now coming to unhang thee, for thou art a pretty little gentle *Monachus: Monachus in claustro non valet ova duo; sed quando est extra bene valet triginta.* I have seen above five hundred hanged, but I never saw any hang with so good a grace; truly, if I had so good a one, I would willingly hang thus all my life-time." "What!" said the monk; "have you almost done preaching? Help me, in the name of God, seeing you will not in the name of the other spirit; or by the habit which I wear, you shall repent it. *Tempore & loco prœlibatis."*

Then Gymnast alighted from his horse, and climbing up the walnut-tree, lifted up the monk with one hand, by the gushets of his armour under the armpits, and with the other undid his vizor from the stump of the broken branch; which done, he let him fall to the ground and himself after. As soon as the monk was down he put off all his armour, and threw away one piece after another about the field, and taking to him again his staff of the cross, remounted up his horse, which Eudemon had caught in his running away. Then went they on merrily, riding on the highway.

CHAPTER XLIII

HOW THE SCOUTS AND FORE-PARTY OF PICROCHOLE WERE MET WITH BY GARGANTUA, AND HOW THE MONK SLEW CAPTAIN DRAWFORTH, AND THEN WAS TAKEN PRISONER BY HIS ENEMIES

PICROCHOLE, at the relation of those who had escaped out of the broil and defeat wherein Tripet was untriped, grew very angry that the devils should have so run upon his men, and held all that night a council of war, at which Rashcalf and Touchefaucet concluded his power to be such, that he was able to defeat all the devils of hell, if they should come to justle with his forces.

97

This Picrochole did not fully believe, though he doubted not much of it. Therefore sent he under the command and conduct of the Count Drawforth, for discovering of the country, the number of sixteen hundred horsemen, all well mounted upon light horses for skirmish, and thoroughly besprinkled with holy water; and every one for their cognizance had a star in his scarf to serve at all adventures, in case they should happen to encounter with devils; that by the virtue, as well of that Gregorian water, as of the stars, they might make the devils disappear and vanish.

In this equipage they made an excursion upon the country, until they came near to Vauguyon, and to the hospital, but could never find anybody to speak unto; whereupon they returned a little back, and by chance, in a shepherd's cottage near to Coudray, they found five pilgrims; these they carried away bound and manacled as if they had been spies, for all the exclamations, adjurations, and requests that they could make. Being come down from thence towards Sevilé, they were heard by Gargantua, who said then unto those that were with him, "Comrades and fellow-soldiers, we have here met with an encounter, and they are ten times in number more than we: shall we charge them or no?" "What a devil," said the monk, "shall we do else? Do you esteem men by their number, rather than by their valour and prowess?" With this he cried out, "Charge! devils, charge!" Which when the enemies heard, they thought certainly that they had been very devils, and therefore, even then began all of them to run away as hard as they could drive, Drawforth only excepted, who immediately settled his lance on its rest, and therewith hit the monk with all his force on the very middle of his breast; but coming against his horrific frock, the point of the iron, being with the blow either broke off or blunted, it was in matter of execution, as if you had struck against an anvil with a little wax-candle. Then did the monk, with his staff of the cross, give him such a sturdy thump and whirret betwixt his neck and shoulders, upon the acromion bone, that he made him lose both sense and motion, and fall down stone dead at his horse's feet. And seeing the *star* (stole) which he wore on his scarf, he said unto Gargantua: "These men are but priests, which is but the beginning of a monk. By St. John I am a perfect monk, I will kill them like flies. Then ran he after them at a swift and full gallop, till he overtook the rear, and felled them down like rye, striking athwart and alongst, and every way. Gymnast presently asked

98

Gargantua if they should pursue them. To whom Gargantua answered, "By no means; for, according to right military discipline, *you must never drive your enemy unto despair.* For that such a streight doth multiply his force, and increase his courage, which was before broken and cast down. Neither is there any better help for men that are out of heart, toiled, and spent, than to *hope for no favour at all.* How many victories have been taken out of the hands of the victors by the vanquished, when they would not rest satisfied with reason, but attempt to put all to the sword, and totally to destroy all their enemies, without leaving so much as one to carry home the news of the defeat of his fellows. Open therefore unto your enemies all the gates and ways, and make to them a bridge of silver rather than fail, that you may be rid of them." "Yea, but," said Gymnast, "they have the monk." "Have they the monk?" said Gargantua; "upon mine honour then it will prove to their cost. But to prevent all dangers let us not yet retreat, but halt here quietly, for I think I do already understand the policy of our enemies; they are truly more directed by chance and mere fortune than by good advice and counsel." In the meanwhile, whilst these made a stop under the walnut-trees, the monk pursued on the chase, charging all he overtook and giving quarter to none, until he met with a trooper, who carried behind him one of the poor pilgrims, and there would have rifled him. The pilgrim, in hope of relief at the sight of the monk, cried out, "Ha, my lord prior, my good friend, my lord prior, save me! I beseech you, save me!" Which words being heard by those that rode in the van, they instantly faced about, and seeing there was nobody but the monk that made this great havock and slaughter among them, they lodged (loaded) him with blows as thick as they used to do an ass with wood. But of all this he felt nothing, especially when they struck upon his frock, his skin was so hard. Then they committed him to two of the marshal's men to keep, and looking about, saw nobody coming against them, whereupon they thought that Gargantua and his party were fled. Then was it that they rode as hard as they could towards the walnut-trees to meet with them, and left the monk there all alone, with his two foresaid men to guard him. Gargantua heard the noise and neighing of the horses, and said to his men, "Comrades, I hear the track and beating of the enemies' horse-feet, and withal perceive that some of them come in a troop and full body against us; let us rally and close here, then set forward in order; and by this means we shall be able to receive their charge, to their loss and our honour."

CHAPTER XLIV

HOW THE MONK RID HIMSELF OF HIS KEEPERS, AND HOW
PICROCHOLE'S FORLORN HOPE WAS DEFEATED

THE monk, seeing them break off thus without order, conjectured that they were to set upon Gargantua and those that were with him, and was wonderfully grieved that he could not succour them. Then considered he the countenance of the two keepers in whose custody he was, who would have willingly run after the troops to get some booty and plunder, and were always looking towards the valley unto which they were going. Farther, he *syllogised,* saying, "These men are but badly skilled in matters of war, for they have not required my *parole;* neither have they taken my sword from me." Suddenly hereupon he drew his long sword, wherewith he gave the keeper which held him on the right side, such a sound slash, that he cut clean through the jugulary veins, and the sphagitid arteries of the neck with the gargareon, even unto the two adenes, and redoubling the blow, he opened the spinal marrow between the second and the third vertebræ; there fell down that keeper stark dead to the ground. Then the monk, reining his horse to the left, ran upon the other, who seeing his fellow dead, and the monk to have the advantage of him, cried with a loud voice, "Ah, my lord prior, quarter; I yield, my lord prior, quarter, quarter; my good friend, my lord prior." And the monk cried likewise, "My lord posterior, my friend, my lord posterior, you shall have it upon your *posteriorums.*" "Ha," said the keeper, "my lord prior, my dear lord prior, I pray God make you an abbot." "By the habit," said the monk, "which I wear, I will here make you a cardinal. What do you use to pay ransoms to religious men; you shall have now *a red hat* of my giving." And the fellow cried, "Ha, my lord prior, my lord prior, my lord abbot that shall be, my lord cardinal, my lord *All. Ha, ha, hes;* no, my lord prior, my good little lord prior, I yield, render, and deliver myself up to you." "And I deliver thee," said the monk, "to all the devils in hell"; then at one stroke he struck off his head; cutting his *scalp* upon the *temple*-bones and lifting up the two bones, *brigmatis,* together with the *sagittal commissure,* as also a great part of the *coronal* bone; by which terrible blow likewise he cut the two *meninges,* and made a deep wound in the two posterior *ventricles* of the brain; so that the *cranium* remained hanging upon his shoulders by the skin of the *pericranium* behind, in form of *a doctor's bonnet,* black without and red within. Thus fell he down also to the ground stark dead.

And presently the monk gave his horse the spur, and kept the way that the enemy held, who had met with Gargantua and his companions in the broad highway, and were so diminished of their number, for the enormous slaughter that Gargantua had made with his great tree amongst them, as also Gymnast, Ponocrates, Eudemon, and the rest, that they began to retreat disorderly, and in great haste, as men altogether affrighted, and troubled in both sense and understanding; and as if they had seen the very proper *species* and form of death before their eyes. Or rather, as when you see an ass with a *brizze* under his tail, or fly that stings him, run hither and thither, without keeping any path or way, throwing down his load to the ground, breaking his bridle and reins, and taking no breath nor rest, and no man can tell what ails him, for they see not anything touch him. So fled these people destitute of wit, without having any cause of flying, only pursued by a *panic* terror, which in their minds they had conceived. The monk perceiving that their whole intent was to betake themselves to their heels, alighted from his horse, and got upon a big large rock, which was in the way, and with his great *brackmard sword,* laid such load upon those runaways, and with main strength fetching a compass with his arm, without feigning or sparing, slew and overthrew so many, that his sword broke in two pieces. Then thought he within himself, that he had slain and killed sufficiently; and that the rest should escape to carry news. Therefore he took up a battle-axe of those that lay there dead, and got upon the rock again, passing his time to see the enemy thus flying, and to tumble himself amongst the dead bodies, only that he suffered none to carry pike, sword, lance, nor gun with him, and those who carried the *pilgrims* bound, he made to alight, and gave their horses unto the said *pilgrims,* keeping them there with him under the hedge, and also Touchefaucet, who was then his prisoner.

CHAPTER XLV

THIS skirmish being ended, Gargantua retreated with his men, excepting the monk, and about the dawning of the day they came unto Grangousier, who in his bed was praying unto God for their safety and victory: and seeing them all safe and sound, he embraced them lovingly, and asked what was become of the monk? Gargantua answered him, "That without doubt the enemies had the monk." "Then have they mischief and ill-luck," said Grangousier, which was very true. Therefore it is a common proverb to this day, *To give a man the monk.* Then commanded he a good breakfast to be provided for their refreshment. When all was ready they called Gargantua, but he was so aggrieved that the monk was not to be heard of, that he would neither eat nor drink. In the meanwhile the monk comes, and from the gate of the outer court cries out aloud, "Fresh wine, fresh wine, Gymnast, my friend." Gymnast went out and saw that it was Friar John, who brought along with him five pilgrims, and Touchefaucet, prisoners. Whereupon Gargantua likewise went forth to meet him, and all of them made him the best welcome that possibly they could, and brought him before Grangousier, who asked him of all his adventures. The monk told him all, both how he was taken, how he rid himself of his keepers, and of the slaughter he had made by the way, and how he had rescued the pilgrims, and brought along with him Capt. Touchefaucet. Then did they altogether fall to banqueting most merrily. In the meantime Grangousier asked the pilgrims what countrymen they were, whence they came, and whither they went? Sweertogo, in the name of the rest, answered, "My Sovereign Lord. I am of St. Genou, in Berry, this man is of Paluau, this other is of Anzay, this of Argy, and this man of Villebrenin. We came from St. Sebastian, near Nantes, and are now returning, as we best may, by easy journeys." "Yea, but," said Grangousier, "what went you to do at St. Sebastian?" "We went," said Sweertogo, "to offer unto that saint our vows, against the plague." "Ah, poor men," said Grangousier, "do you think that the plague comes from St. Sebastian?" "Yes, truly," answered Sweertogo, "our preachers tell us so, indeed." "But is it so," said Grangousier, "do the false prophets teach you such abuses? Do they thus blaspheme the sancts and holy men of God, as to make them like unto the devils, who do nothing but hurt unto mankind? as Homer writeth that the plague was sent into the camp of the Greeks by Apollo; and as the poets feign a great rabble of vejoves and mischievous gods. So did a certain old hypocrite preach, at Sinay, that St. Anthony sent the fire into men's legs; that St. Eutropius made men hydropick; St. Gildas, fools; and that St. Genou made them goutish. But I punished him so exemplarily, though he called me heretic for it, that since that time no such hypocritical rogue durst set his foot within my territories. And truly I wonder that your king should suffer them, in their sermons, to publish such scandalous doctrine in his dominions. For they deserve to be chastised with greater severity than those who, by magical art, or any other device, have brought the pestilence into a country. The pest killeth but the bodies, but such abominable impostors empoison our very souls." As he spake these words, in came the monk very resolute, and asked them, "Whence are you, you poor wretches?" "Of St. Genou," said they. "And how," said the monk, "doth the Abbot Galligut, that true toper; and the monks, what cheer make they? Morbleau, they will have a fling at your wives, whilst you are upon your gadding pilgrimage." *"Hin, hen,"* said Sweertogo, "I am not afraid of mine; for he that shall see her by day, will never break his neck to come to her in the night-time." "Yea, marry," said the monk, "now you have hit it; let her be as ugly as ever was Proserpina, she will not keep her arse dry, if there dwell any monks near her. For *a good carpenter will make use of any kind of timber.* Let me be peppered with the pox if you find not all your wives with child at your return; for the very shadow of an abbey steeple is prolific."

"It is," said Gargantua, "like the water of Nilus, in Egypt, if you believe Strabo and Pliny, lib. 7, cap. 3. What virtue will there be then in their bullets of concupiscense, their habits, and their bodies?"

"Then," said Grangousier, "go your ways, poor men, in the name of God the Creator, to whom I pray to guide you perpetually; and henceforward, be not so ready to undertake these idle and unprofitable journeys. Look to your families, labour every man in his vocation, instruct your children, and live as the good apostle St. Paul directeth you. In doing whereof God, his angels, and saints, will guard and protect you, and no evil or plague at any time shall befal you."

Then Gargantua led them into the hall to take their refection; but

103

the pilgrims did nothing but sigh, and said to Gargantua, "O, how happy is that land which hath such a man for their Lord! We have been more edified and instructed by the talk which he hath had with us, than by all the sermons that ever were preached in our town." "This is," said Gargantua, "that which Plato saith, lib. v. De Republ. That those commonwealths are happy, whose rulers philosophise, and whose philosophers rule." Then caused he their wallets to be filled with victuals, and their bottles with wine, and gave unto each of them a horse to ease them upon the way, together with some pence to live upon.

CHAPTER XLVI

HOW GRANGOUSIER DID VERY KINDLY ENTERTAIN TOUCHEFAUCET HIS PRISONER

TOUCHEFAUCET was presented unto Grangousier, and by him examined upon the enterprise and attempt of Picrochole, what it was he could pretend to, by this tumultuary invasion; whereunto he answered, that his end and purpose was to conquer all the country, if he could, for the injury done to his *cake bakers*. "It is too great an undertaking," said Grangousier, "and, as the proverb is '*He that gripes too much, holds fast but little.*' The time is not *now* so to conquer kingdoms, to the loss of our nearest christian brother. This imitation of the ancient Herculeses, Alexanders, Hannibals, Scipios, Cæsars, and other such heroes, is quite contrary to the profession of the gospel of Christ, by the which we are commanded to preserve, keep, rule, and govern every man his own country and lands, and not in a hostile manner to invade others; and that which heretofore the Saracens and Barbarians called *prowess*, we do now call *robbery* and *wickedness*. It would have been more commendable in him to have contained himself within the bounds of his own territories, royally governing them, than to insult and domineer in mine, pillaging and plundering everywhere, for, *by ruling his own with discretion, he might have increased his greatness; but by robbing me, he cannot escape destruction.* Go your ways in the name of God; do what is righteous; shew your king what is amiss, and never counsel him with regard unto your own particular profit; for with the public will also be swallowed up the private. As for your ransom, I do freely remit it to you, and will that your arms and horse be restored to you; so should good neighbours do, and ancient friends, seeing this our difference is not properly *war*. As Plato, lib. 5 De Repub. would not have it called *war,* but *sedition,* not when the Greeks took up arms against one another; and therefore, when such combustions should arise, his advice was to behave themselves with all discretion and modesty. Although you call it *war* it is but superficial; it entereth not in the inmost cabinets of our hearts; for neither of us hath been wronged in his honour, nor is there any question about us in the main; but only how to redress, by the by, some pretty faults committed by our men; I mean both yours and ours; which, although you knew, you ought to let pass; for these quarrelsome persons deserve rather to be contemned than mentioned, especially seeing I offered them satisfaction according to the wrong.

"God shall be the just judge of our variances, whom I beseech, by death, rather to take me out of this life, and to permit my goods to perish and be destroyed before mine eyes, than that by me, or mine, he should in any sort be wronged (offended)." These words uttered, he called the monk, and before them all spoke thus unto him: "Friar John, my good friend, is it you that took prisoner the Captain Touchefaucet here present?" "Sir," said the monk, "seeing himself is here, and that he is of the years of discretion, I had rather you should know it by his confession than by any words of mine." Then said Touchefaucet: "My sovereign lord, it is he, indeed, that took me; and I do, therefore, most freely yield myself his prisoner." "Have you put him to any ransom?" said Grangousier to the monk. "No," said the monk, "of that I take no care." "How much would you have for having taken him?" "Nothing, nothing," said the monk; "I am not swayed by that, nor do I regard it." Then Grangousier commanded, that, in presence of Touchefaucet, should be delivered to the monk, for taking him, the sum of threescore and two thousand saluts, which was done, whilst they made a collation to the said Touchefaucet; of whom Grangousier asked if he would stay with him, or chuse rather to return to his king. Touchefaucet answered, that he was content to take whatever course he would advise him to. Then said Grangousier, "Return unto your king; and God be with you."

Then he gave him an excellent sword, a *Vienna* blade, with a golden scabbard, wrought with vine-branch like flourishes, of fine goldsmith's work, and a collar of gold, weighing seven hundred and two thousand marks, garnished with precious stones of the finest sorts, esteemed at a hundred and sixty thousand ducats, and ten thousand crowns more as an honourable present.

After this Touchefaucet got to his horse, and Gargantua, for his safety, allowed him the guard of thirty men-at-arms and sixscore archers to attend him, under the conduct of Gymnast, to bring him even unto the gate of the rock Clermond, if there were need. As soon as he was gone, the monk restored unto Grangousier the threescore and two thousand saluts which he had received, saying, "Sir, it is not as yet the time for you to give such gifts. Stay till this war be at an end, for none can tell what accidents may occur, and war begun without good provision of money beforehand, is but as a blast that will quickly pass away. *Coin is the sinews of war.*" "Well, then," said Grangousier, "at the end I will content you by some honest recompence, as also all those who shall do me good service."

CHAPTER XLVII

HOW GRANGOUSIER SENT FOR HIS LEGIONS, AND HOW TOUCHE-
FAUCET SLEW RASHCALF, AND WAS AFTERWARDS EXECUTED
BY THE COMMAND OF PICROCHOLE

ABOUT this same time those of Besse, of the *old market,* of St. James Bourg, of the Draggage, of Parillé, of the Rivers, of the Rocks St. Pol, of the Vaubreton, of Pautillé, of the Brahemont, of Clainbridge, of Cravant, of Grandmont, of the town at the Badger-holes, of Huymes, of Segré, of Husse, of St. Livant, of Panzoust, of Celdraux, of Vernon, of Coulaines, of Chose, of Varenes, of Bourgueil, of the Bouchard Claud, of the Croulay, of Narsie, of Cande, of Monsoreau, and other bordering places, sent ambassadors unto Grangousier to tell him that they were advised of the great wrongs which Picrochole had done him; and in regard of their ancient confederacy offered him what assistance they could afford, both in men, money, victuals, ammunition, and other necessaries for war. The money which, by the joint agreement of them all, was sent unto him, amounted to six score and fourteen millions two crowns and a half of pure gold.

The forces wherewith they did assist him did consist of fifteen thousand cuirassiers, two and thirty thousand light horsemen, fourscore and nine thousand dragoons, and a hundred and forty thousand volunteer adventurers. These had with them eleven thousand and two hundred cannons, double cannons, *basilisks.* Of pioneers they had seven and forty thousand, all victualled and paid for six months and four days of advance; which offer Gargantua did not altogether refuse nor wholly accept of, but giving them hearty thanks, said that he would compound and order the war by such a device, that there should not be found great need to put so many honest men to trouble in the managing of it; and therefore was content at that time to give order only for bringing along the legions, which he maintained at his ordinary garrison towns of the Deernier (Deviniere), Chavignie, of Granot (Gravot) and of Quinquenais, amounting to the number of two thousand cuirassiers, threescore and six thousand foot-soldiers, and six and twenty thousand dragoons, attended by two hundred pieces of great ordnance, two and twenty thousand pioneers, and six thousand light horsemen, all drawn up in troops, so well befitted and accommodated with their commissaries, sutlers, farriers, harness-makers, and other such like necessary members in a military camp, so fully instructed in the art of warfare, so perfectly knowing and following their colours, so ready to hear and obey their captains, so nimble to run, so strong at their charging, so prudent in their adventures, and every day (way) so well disciplined, that they seemed rather to be a concert of organ-pipes, or mutual concord of the wheels of a clock, than an infantry and cavalry, or army of soldiers.

Touchefaucet, immediately after his return, presented himself before Picrochole, and related unto him at large all that he had done and seen, and at last endeavoured to persuade him with strong and forcible arguments, to capitulate, and make an agreement with Grangousier, whom he found to be the honestest man in the world; saying further, that it was neither right nor reason thus to trouble his neighbours, of whom they never received anything but good; and, in regard of the main point, that they should never be able to go through stitch with that war, but to their great damage and mischief; for the forces of Picrochole were not so considerable, but that Grangousier could easily overthrow them.

He had not well done speaking when Rashcalf said out loud: "Unhappy is that prince which is by such men served, who are so easily corrupted as I know Touchefaucet is; for I see his courage so changed, that he had willingly joined with our enemies to fight against us, and betray us, if they would have received him; but, as virtue is of all, both friends and foes, praised and esteemed, so is wickedness soon known and suspected; and, although it happen the enemies do make use thereof for their profit, yet have they always the *wicked and the traitors in abomination.*"

Touchefaucet, being at these words very impatient, drew out his sword, and therewith ran Rashcalf through the body, a little under the nipple of his left side, whereof he died presently, and, pulling back his sword out of his body, said boldly, *"So let him perish that shall a faithful servant blame."* Picrochole incontinently grew furious, and seeing Touchefaucet's new sword, and his scabbard so richly diapered with flourishes of most excellent workmanship, said, "Did they give thee this weapon so feloniously therewith to kill before my face my so good friend Rashcalf?" Then immediately commanded he his guard to hew him in pieces, which was instantly done, and that so cruelly that the chamber was all dyed with blood. Afterwards he appointed the corpse of Rashcalf to be honourably buried, and that of Touchefaucet to be cast over the wall into the ditch.

The news of these excessive violences was quickly spread through the army; whereupon many began to murmur against Picrochole, in so far that Pinchpenny said to him, "My sovereign lord, I know not what the issue of this enterprise will be: I see your men much dejected, and not well resolved in their minds, by considering that we are here very ill provided of victuals, and that our number is already much diminished by three or four sallies. Furthermore, great supplies and recruits come daily in to your enemies; but we so moulder away, that if we be once besieged, I do not see how we can escape a total destruction." *"Tush, pish,"* said Picrochole; "you are like the Melun eels, you cry before they come to you. *Let them come, let them come if they dare."*

CHAPTER XLVIII

HOW GARGANTUA SET UPON PICROCHOLE, WITHIN THE ROCK
CLERMOND, AND UTTERLY DEFEATED THE ARMY OF THE
SAID PICROCHOLE

GARGANTUA had the charge of the whole army, and his father, Grangousier, staid in his castle, who, encouraging them with good words, promised great rewards unto those that should do any notable service. As soon as they had gained the Ford of Vede, boats and bridges being speedily made, they past over in a trice; then, considering the situation of the town, which was on a high and advantageous place, Gargantua thought fit to call his council, and pass that night in deliberation upon what was to be done. But Gymnast said unto him, "My sovereign Lord, such is the nature and complexion of the French, that *they are worth nothing but at the first push.*—Then are they more fierce than devils; but if they be wearied with delays, they prove more faint than women. My opinion is, therefore, that now, presently, after your men have taken breath, and some small refection, you give order for a resolute assault." The advice was found very good, and, for effectuating thereof, he brought forth his army into the plain field, and placed the reserves on the skirt or rising of a little hill. The monk took along with him six companies of foot, and two hundred horsemen well armed, and with great diligence crossed the marsh, and valiantly got up to the top of the green hillock, even to the highway which leads to Loudun. Whilst the assault was thus begun, Picrochole's men could not tell well which was best, to issue out and receive the assailants, or keep within the town, and not stir: himself, in the meantime, without deliberation, sallied forth, in a rage, with the cavalry of his guard, who were forthwith received, and royally entertained with great cannon-shot, that fell upon them like hail from the high grounds, on which the artillery was planted; whereupon the Gargantuists betook themselves unto the vallies, to give the ordnance leave to play and range with the larger scope.

Those of the town defended themselves as well as they could, but their shot past over, without doing any hurt at all. Some of Picrochole's men, that had escaped our artillery, set most fiercely upon our soldiers, but prevailed little; for they were all let in betwixt the files, and there knocked down to the ground; which their fellow-soldiers seeing, they would have retreated, but the monk having seized upon the pass by the which they were to return, they ran away and fled in all the disorder and confusion that could be imagined.

Some would have pursued after them and followed the chase; but the monk withheld them, apprehending that, in their pursuit, the pursuers might lose their ranks, and so give occasion to the besieged to sally out of town upon them. Then staying there some space, and none coming against him, he sent the Duke Phrontist to advise Gargantua to advance towards the hill upon the left hand, to hinder Picrochole's retreat at that gate; which Gargantua did with all expedition, and sent thither four brigades, under the conduct of Sebast, which had no sooner reached the top of the hill, but they met Picrochole in the teeth, and those that were with him scattered.

Then charged they upon them stoutly, yet were they much in-damaged by those that were upon the walls, who galled them with all manner of shot, both from the great ordance, small guns, and bows; which Gargantua perceiving, he went with a strong party to their relief, and with his artillery began to thunder so terribly upon that canton of the wall, and so long, that all the strength within the town, to maintain and fill up the breach, was drawn thither. The monk seeing that quarter which he kept besieged, void of men and competent guards, and in a manner altogether naked and abandoned, did most magnanimously, on a sudden, lead up his men towards the fort, and never left till he had got up upon it, knowing *that such as come to the reserve, in a conflict,* bring with them always more fear and terror, than those that deal about them with their hands in the fight.

Nevertheless, he gave no *alarm* till all his soldiers had got within the wall, except the two hundred horsemen, whom he left without to secure his entry. Then did he give a most terrible shout, so did all those who were with him, and immediately thereafter, without re-sistance, putting to the edge of the sword the guard that was at that gate, they opened it to the horsemen, with whom most furiously they altogether ran towards the *east-gate,* where all the hurly-burly was, and coming close upon them in the rear, overthrew all their forces.

The besieged, seeing that the Gargantuists had won the town upon them, and that they were like to be secure in no corner of it, sub-mitted themselves to the mercy of the monk, and asked for quarter, which the monk very nobly granted them, yet made them lay down their arms. Then, shutting them up within churches, gave orders to seize upon all the *staves* of the *crosses,* and placed men at the doors to keep them from coming forth. Then opening the *east-gate,* he is-sued out to succour and assist Gargantua. But Picrochole, thinking it had been some relief coming to him from the town, adventured more forwardly than before, and was upon the giving of a most desperate home charge, when Gargantua cried out, "Ha, Friar John, my friend Friar John, you are come in a good hour": which unexpected accident so affrighted Picrochole and his men, that giving all for lost, they be-took themselves to their heels, and fled on all hands. Gargantua chased them till they came near to Vaugaudry, killing and slaying all the way, and then sounded the retreat.

CHAPTER XLIX

PICROCHOLE, thus in despair, fled towards the Bouchard island, and, in the way to Rivere, his horse stumbled, and fell down, whereat he was on a sudden so incensed, that he, with his sword, without more ado, killed him in his choler. Then, not finding any other whereon to remount, he was about to have taken an ass at the mill that was thereby; but the miller's men did so baste his bones, and so soundly bethwacked him, that they made him both black and blue with strokes; then, stripping him of all his cloaths, gave him a scurvy old canvas jacket, wherewith to cover his nakedness. Thus went along this poor choleric wretch, who, passing the water at Porthuaux, and relating his misadventurous disaster, was foretold by an old Lourpidon hag, that his kingdom should be restored to him at the coming of the cocklicranes. What is become of him since, we cannot certainly tell; yet was I told that he is now a porter at Lyons, as testy and choleric as ever, and always, with great lamentation, enquiring of all strangers of the coming of the cocklicranes, expecting assuredly (according to the old woman's prophecy) that at their coming he shall be re-established in his kingdom. The first thing Gargantua did, after his return into the town, was to call the muster-roll of his men, which when he had done, he found that there were very few either killed or wounded, only some few foot of Captain Tolmere's company, and Ponocrates, who was shot with a musket-ball, through the doublet. Then he caused them all, and in their several posts and divisions, to take a little refreshment, which was very plenteously provided for them, in the best drink and victuals that could be had for money; and gave order to the treasurers and commissaries of the army, to pay for and defray that repast, and that there should be no outrage at all, nor abuse committed in the town, seeing it was his own. And furthermore commanded that, immediately after the soldiers had done with eating and drinking, they should be drawn up on the Piazza before the castle, there to receive six months' pay: all which was done. After this, by his direction, were brought before him, in the said place, all those that remained of Picrochole's party; unto whom, in the presence of the princes, nobles, and officers of his court and army, he spoke as followeth.

III

CHAPTER L

OUR forefathers and ancestors, in all times, have been of this nature and disposition, that, upon the winning of a battle, they have chosen rather, for a sign and memorial of their triumphs and victories, to erect trophies and monuments in the *hearts* of the vanquished by *clemency,* than by *architecture,* in the *lands* which they had conquered. For they hold in greater estimation the lively remembrance of men purchased by liberality, than the dumb inscription of *arches, pillars,* and *pyramids,* subject to the injury of storms and tempests, and to the envy of every one. You may very well call to mind the courtesy which by them was used towards the Bretons, in the battle of St. Aubin of Cormier, and at the demolishing of Partenay. You have heard, and hearing admire, their gentle comportment towards those at the barriers of Spaniola, when they had plundered, wasted, and ransacked the maritime borders of Olone and Talmondois. All this hemisphere of the world was filled with the praises and congratulations which yourselves and your fathers made when Alpharbal King of Canarre, not satisfied with his own fortunes, did most furiously invade the Land of Onyx, and with cruel pyracies molest all the Armorick Islands, and confine regions of Britany. Yet was he, in a set fight, justly taken and vanquished by my father, *whom God preserve and protect.* But what? Whereas other kings and emperors, yea, those who entitle themselves *Catholics,* would have dealt roughly with him, kept him a close prisoner, and put him to an extreme high ransom: He entreated him very courteously, lodged him kindly with himself in his own palace, and, out of his incredible mildness and gentle disposition, sent him back with a safe conduct, loaden with gifts, loaden with favours, loaden with all offices of friendship. What fell out upon it? Being returned into his country, he called a *parliament,* where all the princes and states of his kingdom being assembled, he shewed them the humanity which he had found in us, and therefore wished them to take such course, by way of compensation therein, as that the whole world might be edified by the example, as well of their honest graciousness to us, as of our gracious honesty towards them. The result hereof was, that it was voted and decreed by an unanimous consent, that they should offer up entirely their lands, dominions, and kingdoms, to be disposed of by us according to our pleasure.

"Alpharbal, in his own person, presently returned with nine thousand and thirty-eight great ships of burden, bringing with him the treasures, not only of his house and royal lineage, but almost of all the country beside. For he imbarking himself to set sail with a *west-north-east* wind, every one, in heaps, did cast into the ship gold, silver, rings, jewels, spices, drugs, and aromatical perfumes, parrots, pelicans, monkies, civit-cats, black-spotted weasels, porcupines, &c. He was accounted *no good mother's son* that did not cast in all the rare and precious things he had.

"Being safely arrived, he came to my said father, and would have kissed his feet: that action was found too submissively low, and therefore was not permitted, but in exchange he was most cordially embraced: he offered his presents—they were not received, because they were too excessive: he yielded himself voluntarily a servant and vassal, and was content his whole posterity should be liable to the same bondage: this was not accepted of, because it seemed not equitable. He surrendered, by virtue of the decree of his great *parliamentary council,* his whole countries and kingdoms to him, offering the deed and conveyance, signed, sealed, and ratified by all those that were concerned in it. This was altogether refused, and the parchments cast into the fire. In the end, this free good will and simple meaning of the Canarrines wrought such tenderness in my father's heart, that he could not abstain from shedding tears, and wept most profusely; then, by choice words, very congruously adapted, strove, in what he could, to diminish the estimation of the good offices which he had done them, saying, that any courtesy he had conferred upon them was not worth a rush, and what favour soever he had shewed them, he was bound to do it. But so much the more did Alpharbal augment the repeat thereof: What was the issue? Whereas for his ransom, in the greatest extremity of rigour and most tyrannical dealing, could not have been exacted above *twenty times a hundred thousand crowns,* and his eldest sons detained as hostages, till that sum had been paid, they made themselves perpetual tributaries, and obliged to give us every year two millions of gold, at four and twenty carats fine: The first year we received the whole sum of two millions; the second year, of their own accord, they paid freely to us three and twenty hundred thousand crowns; the third year, six and twenty hundred thousand; the fourth year, three millions; and do so increase it always out of their own good will, that we shall be constrained to forbid them to bring us any more. This is the nature of gratitude and true thankfulness: for time, which gnaws and diminisheth all things else, augments and increaseth benefits; because a noble action of liberality done to a man of reason, doth grow continually by his generous thinking of it, and remembering it.

"But, unwilling, therefore, any way to degenerate from the hereditary mildness and clemency of my parents, I do now forgive you, set you at liberty, and every way make you as frank and free as ever you were before. Moreover, at your going out of the gate, you shall have every one of you three months' pay, to bring you home unto your houses and families, and shall have a safe convoy of six hundred cuirassiers, and eight thousand foot, under the conduct of Alexander, esquire of my body, that the clubmen of the country may not do you any injury. God be with you. I am sorry from my heart that Picrochole is not here; for I would have given him to understand, that this war was undertaken against my will, and without any hope to increase either goods or renown; but seeing he is lost, and that no man can tell where, nor how he went away, *it is my will,* that this kingdom remain entire to his son, who, because he is too young (he not being yet full five years old), shall be brought up and instructed by the ancient princes and learned men of the kingdom. And because a realm thus desolate may easily come to ruin, if the covetousness and avarice of those who, by their places, are obliged to administer justice in it, be not curbed and restrained, I ordain, and will have it so, that Ponocrates be overseer and superintendent above all his governors, with whatever power and authority is requisite thereto, and that he be continually with the child, until he find him able and capable to rule and govern by himself.

"Now I must tell you, that you are to understand how a too feeble and dissolute facility in pardoning evil-doers giveth them occasion to commit wickedness afterward more readily; upon this pernicious confidence of receiving favour, I consider that Moses, the meekest man that was in his time upon the earth, did severely punish the mutinous and seditious people of Israel. I consider likewise, that Julius Cæsar, who was so gracious an emperor, that Cicero said of him 'that his fortune had nothing more excellent than that he could, and his virtue nothing better than that he would always save and pardon every man': He, notwithstanding all this did in certain places most rigorously punish the authors of rebellion. After the example of these good men, it is my will and pleasure that you deliver unto me before you depart hence, first, that fine fellow Marquet, who was the prime origin and groundwork of this war, by his vain presumption and over-weening. Secondly his fellow cake-bakers, who were neglective in checking and reprehending his idle hair-brained humour in the instant time. And lastly, all the counsellors, captains, officers and domestics of Picrochole, who had been incendiaries or fomenters of the war, by provoking, praising, or counselling him to come out of his limits thus to trouble us."

CHAPTER LI

HOW THE VICTORIOUS GARGANTUISTS WERE RECOM-PENSED AFTER THE BATTLE

WHEN Gargantua had finished his speech, the seditious men, whom he had required, were delivered up unto him, except Swashbuckler, Durtaille, and Smalltrash, who ran away six hours before the battle; one of them as far as to the neck of Laniel at one course, another to the valley of Vire, and the third even unto Logroine, without looking back, or taking breath by the way; and two of the cake-bakers, who were slain in the fight. Gargantua did them no other hurt but that he appointed them to pull at the presses of his printing-house, which he had newly set up. Then those who died there he caused to be honourably buried in Blacksoille valley, and Burn-hag-field, and gave order, that the wounded should be dressed and had care of, in his great hospital or osocome. After this, considering the great prejudice done to the town and its inhabitants, he reimbursed their charges, and repaired all the losses, that, by their confession upon oath, could appear they had sustained. And for their better defence, and security in times coming, against all sudden up-roars and invasions, commanded a strong citadel to be built there with a competent garrison to maintain it. At his departure, he did very graciously thank all the soldiers of the brigades, that had been at this overthrow, and sent them back to their winter quarters in their several stations and garrisons: the *Decumane legion* only excepted, whom in the field on that day he saw do some great exploit, and their captains also, whom he brought along with himself unto Grangousier.

At the sight and coming of them, the good man was so joyful, that it is not possible fully to describe it. He made them a feast, the most magnificent, plentiful, and delicious that ever was seen since the time of the king Assuerus. At the taking up of the table, he distributed amongst them his whole cupboard of plate, which weighed eight hundred thousand and fourteen besants of gold, in great antique vessels, huge pots, large basons, big tasses, cups, goblets, candlesticks, comfit-boxes, and other such plate, all of pure massy gold, besides the precious stones, enamelling, and workmanship, which by all men's estimation was more worth than the matter of the gold. Then unto every one of them out of his efforts caused he to be given the sum of twelve hundred thousand crowns ready money. And further, he gave to each of them for ever and in perpetuity (unless he should happen to decease without heirs), such castles and neighbouring lands of his, as were most commodious for them. To Ponocrates he gave the rock Clermond; to Gymnast, the Coudray; to Eudemon, Monpensier; Rivau, to Tolmere; to Ithibolle, Monsaureau; to Acamas, Cande; Varenes, to Chironacte; Gravot, to Sebast; Quinquenais, to Alexander; Legre, to Sophrone; and so of his other places.

CHAPTER LII

HOW GARGANTUA CAUSED TO BE BUILT FOR THE MONK THE ABBEY OF THELEME

THERE was left only the monk to provide for, whom Gargantua would have made abbot of Sevilé, but he refused it. He would have given him the abbey of Bourgueil, or of Sanct Florent, which was better, or both if it pleased him. But the monk gave him a very peremptory answer, that he would never take upon him the charge nor government of monks. "For how shall I be able," said he, "to rule over others, that have not power and command over myself? If you think I have done you, or may hereafter do you any acceptable service, give me leave to found an abbey after my own mind and fancy." The notion pleased Gargantua very well, who thereupon offered him all the country of Theleme by the river of Loire, till within two leagues of the great forest of Porthuaut. The monk then requested Gargantua to institute his religious order *contrary* to all others. "First then," said Gargantua, "you must not build a wall about your convent, for all other abbeys are strongly walled and mured about."

"See," said the monk, "and without cause, where there is *mur* before and *mur* behind, there is store of *murmur,* envy, and mutual conspiracy."

Moreover, seeing there are certain convents in the world, whereof the custom is, if any woman come (I mean chaste and honest women) they immediately sweep the ground which they have trod upon. Therefore was it ordained, that if any man or woman, entered into religious orders, should by chance come within this new abbey, all the *rooms* should be thoroughly *washed* and cleansed, through which they had passed. And because in all other monasteries and nunneries all is compassed, limited, and regulated by *hours,* it was decreed, that in this new structure there should be neither clock nor dial, but that, according to the opportunities and incident occasions, all *their hours* should be disposed of. "For," said Gargantua, "the greatest loss of time that I know, is, to count the *hours.* What good comes of it? Nor can there be any *greater dotage* in the world, than for one to guide and direct his courses by the sound of a bell, and not by his own judgment and discretion."

Item, because at that time they put no *women* into nunneries, but such as were either purblind, blinkards, lame, crooked, ill-favoured, mis-shapen, fools, senseless, spoiled, or corrupt; nor encloistered *any men,* but those that were *either sickly,* subject to defluxions, ill-bred louts, simple sots, or peevish trouble-houses. "But to the purpose," said the monk: "a woman that is neither fair nor good, to what use serves she?" "To make a *nun* of," said Gargantua. "Yea," said the monk, "and to make shirts and smocks." Therefore was it ordained, that *into this religious* order should be admitted *no women* that were not fair, well featured, and of a sweet disposition; nor *men that* were not comely, personable, and well-conditioned.

Item, because in the convents of women, men come not but underhand, privily, and by stealth; it was therefore enacted, that in this house there shall be no women in case there be not men, nor men in case there be not women.

Item, because both men and women that are received into religious orders, after the expiring of their *novitiat,* or probation year, were constrained and forced perpetually to stay there all the days of their life; it was therefore ordered, that all whatever men or women, admitted within this abbey, should have full leave to depart with peace and contentment, whensoever it should seem good to them so to do.

117

Item, for that the religious men and women did ordinarily make three vows, to wit, those of *chastity, poverty,* and *obedience;* it was therefore constituted and appointed, that in this convent they might be honourably *married,* that they might be *rich,* and live at *liberty.* In regard of the legitimate time of the persons to be initiated, and years under and above which they were not capable of reception, the women were to be admitted from *ten till fifteen,* and the men from *twelve to eighteen.*

CHAPTER LIII

HOW THE ABBEY OF THE THELEMITES WAS BUILT
AND ENDOWED

FOR the fabric and furniture of the abbey Gargantua caused to be delivered out, in ready money, seven and twenty hundred thousand eight hundred and one, and thirty of those golden rams of Berrie, which have a sheep stamped on the one side, and a flowered cross on the other. And for every year, until the whole work were compleated, he allotted threescore and nine thousand crowns of the *sun,* and as many of the *seven stars,* to be charged all upon the receipt of the *custom.* For the foundation and maintenance thereof for ever, he settled a perpetual fee-farm-rent of three and twenty hundred, threescore and nine thousand, five hundred and fourteen *rose-nobles,* exempt from all homage, fealty, service, or burden whatsoever, and payable every year *at the gate of the abbey;* and of this, by letters patent, passed a very good grant. The architecture was in a figure *hexagonal,* and in such a fashion that in every one of the six corners there was built a great round tower of threescore feet in diameter; and were all of a like form and bigness. Upon the north side ran along the river of Loire, on the bank whereof was situated the tower called Arctic. Going towards the east, there was another, called Calaer; the next following Anatole; the next Mesembrine; the next Hesperia, and the last Criere. Every tower was distant from the other the space of three hundred and twelve paces. The whole edifice was everywhere six stories high, reckoning the cellars underground for one. The second was arched after the fashion of a basket-handle. The rest were cieled with pure wainscoat, flourished with Flanders fret-work, in the form of the foot of a lamp; and covered above with fine slates, with an indorsement of lead, carrying the antique figures of little puppets, and animals of all sorts, notably well suited to one another, and gilt, together with the gutters, which jetting without the walls, from betwixt the cross bars in a diagonal figure, painted with gold and azure, reached to the very ground, where they ended into great conduit pipes, which carried all away unto the river from under the house.

This same building was a hundred times more sumptuous and magnificent than ever was Bonnivet, Chambourg, or Chantilly. For there were in it nine thousand, three hundred, and two and thirty chambers; every one whereof had a withdrawing room, a handsome closet, a wardrobe, an oratory, and neat passage, leading into a great and spacious hall. Between every tower, in the midst of the said body of building, there was a pair of winding stairs, whereof the steps were part of porphyry, part of *Numidian* stone, and part of *serpentine* marble; each of those steps being two and twenty feet in length, and three fingers thick, and the just number of twelve betwixt every rest or landing-place. In every resting-place were two fair antique arches, where the light came in; and by those they went into a cabinet (closet), made even with, and of the breadth of the said winding, and the reascending above the roofs of the house ending *conically* in a pavilion. By that *vize,* or winding, they entered on every side into a great hall, and from the halls into the chambers. From the Arctic tower unto the Criere, were the fair great libraries in Greek, Latin, Hebrew, French, Italian, and Spanish, respectively distributed in their several cantons, according to the diversity of these languages. In the midst there was a wonderful winding stair, the entry whereof was without the house, in a vault or arch, six fathoms broad. It was made in such symmetry and largeness that six men-at-arms, with their lances in their rests, might together in a breast ride all up to the very top of all the palace. From the tower Anatole to the Mesembrine were spacious galleries, all coloured over and painted with the ancient prowesses, histories, and descriptions of the world. In the midst thereof was likewise such another ascent and gate, as we said there was on the river side. Upon that gate was written, in great antique letters, that which followeth.

CHAPTER LIV

THE INSCRIPTION SET UPON THE GREAT GATE OF THELEME

HERE enter not, religious boobies, sots,
   Impostors, sniveling hypocrites, bigots:
Dark-brain distorted owls, worse than the Huns
Or Ostrogots; fore-runners of baboons:
Curs'd snakes, dissembling varlets, seeming sancts,
Slipshop caffards, beggars pretending wants;
Fomentors of divisions and debates,
Elsewhere, not here, make sale of your deceits.
      Your filthy trumperies,
       Stuff'd with pernicious lies.
        (Not worth a bubble)
        Would only trouble
      Our earthly Paradise.
      Your filthy trumperies.

"Here enter not attorneys, barraters,
Nor bridle-champion-law practitioners:
Clerks, commissaries, scribes, nor pharisees,
Wilful disturbers of the people's ease,
Judges, destroyers, with an unjust breath,
That, like dogs, worry honest men to death.
We want not your *demurrers*, nor your *pleas;*
So at the gibbet go and seek your fees.
We are not for attendance or delays;
But would with ease and quiet pass our days.
      Law-suits, debates, and wrangling
      Hence are exil'd, and jangling.
        Here we are very
        Frolic and merry,
      And free from all intangling
      Law-suits, debates, and wrangling.

"Here enter not base pinching usurers,
Pelf-lickers, everlasting gatherers;
Gold-graspers, coin-gripers, gulpers of mists,
With harpy-griping claws, who, tho' your chests

Vast sums of money should to you afford,
Would nevertheless be adding to the hoard:
And yet not be content; ye cluntch-fist dastards,
Insatiable friends, and Pluto's bastards;
Greedy devourers, chichy, sneak-bill rogues;
Hell-mastiff's gnaw your bones, you rav'nous dogs.
    You beastly looking fellows,
    Reason doth plainly tell us,
      That we should not
      To you allot
    Room here, but at the gallows;
    You beastly looking fellows.

"Here enter not, unsociable wight,
Humoursome churl, by day, nor yet by night.
No grumbling awf, none of the sharping trade,
No huff-cap squire, or brother of the blade.
A Tartar bred, or in Alsatia wars,
The ruffian comes not hither with his bears.
Elsewhere for shelter scour, ye bully-rocks.
And rogues, that rot with infamy and pox.
    Grace, honour, praise, delight,
    Here sojourn day and night,
      Sound bodies, lin'd
      With a good mind,
    Do here pursue with might
    Grace, honour, praise, delight.

"Here enter you, and welcome from our hearts,
All noble sparks, endow'd with gallant parts.
This is the glorious place which nobly shall
Afford sufficient to content you all;
Were you a thousand, here you shall not want
For anything; for what you ask, we grant.
The brave, the witty, here we entertain,
And, in a word, all worthy gentlemen,
    Men of heroic breasts
    Shall taste here of the feasts,
      Both privily
      And civilly

All you are welcome guests,
Men of heroic breasts.

"Here enter you, pure, honest, faithful, true,
Expounders of the *Scriptures,* old and new;
Whose glosses do not the plain truth disguise,
And with false light distract or blind our eyes.
Here shall we find a safe and warm retreat,
When Error beats about and spreads her net.
Strange doctrines here must neither reap nor sow,
But Faith and Charity together grow.
In short, confounded be their first device,
Who are the holy *Scriptures'* enemies.
  Here in the *holy word*
  Trust all, with one accord;
   It will some help afford:
   Tho' you be knight or lord,
  You may find shield and sword,
  Here in the *holy word*.

"Here enter ladies all, of high degree,
Of goodly shape, of humour gay and free;
Of lovely looks, of sprightly flesh and blood:
Here take, here chuse, here settle your abode.
The gent, the brisk, the fair, whoever comes,
With eyes that sparkle, or whose beauty blooms.
This *bower* is fashion'd by a gentle knight,
Ladies, for you, and innocent delight.
  This is design'd a place
  For every charming grace;
   The witty and the fair
   Hither may all repair;
  For every lovely face
  This is design'd a place."

CHAPTER LV

WHAT MANNER OF DWELLING THE THELEMITES HAD

IN the middle of the lower court there was a stately fountain of fair
alabaster; upon the top thereof stood the three Graces, with their
cornucopias, and did jett out the water at their breasts, mouth, ears,
eyes, and other open passages of the body. The inside of the build-
ings in this lower court, stood upon great pillars of *cassydony* stone,
and *porphyry* marble, made archways, after a goodly antique fashion:
within those were spacious galleries, long and large, adorned with
curious pictures, the horns of bucks and unicorns; with rhinoceroses,
water-horses, called *hippopotames;* the teeth and tusks of elephants,
and other things well worth the holding (beholding). The lodging
of the ladies took up all from the tower Arctic unto the gate Mesembrine. The men possessed the rest. Before the said lodging of the
ladies, that they might have their recreation between the two first
towers, on the outside were placed the *tilt-yard,* the *theatre* and *nat-
atory,* with most admirable baths in three stages, situated above one
another, well furnished with all necessary accommodations and store
of *myrtle-water.* By the river side was a fine pleasure-garden, and in
the midst of that a *labyrinth.* Between the two other towers were
the courts for *tennis* and the *baloon.* Towards the tower Criere stood
the *orchard,* full of all fruit-trees, set and ranged in a *quincuncial*
order. At the end of that was the great *park,* abounding with all
sorts of venison. Betwixt the third couple of towers were the *butts*
and marks for shooting with a snap-work gun, an ordinary bow for
common archery, or with a cross-bow. The office-houses were without the tower Hesperia, of one story high. The stables were beyond
the offices, and before them stood the falconry, managed by ostridge-
keepers and falconers, very expert in the air (art). And it was yearly
supplied and furnished by the Candians, Venetians, and Sarmates
with all sorts of most excellent hawks, eagles, gerfalcons, gosse-hawks,
sacres, laniers, falcons, spar-hawks, marlins, and all other kinds of
them; so gentle and perfectly well manned, that flying of themselves
sometimes from the castle, for their own disport, they would not fail
to catch whatever they encountered. The *venery,* where the beagles
and hounds were kept, was a little farther off drawing towards the
park.

All the halls, chambers, and closets, or cabinets, were richly hung with tapestry, and hangings of divers sorts, according to the variety of the seasons of the year. All the pavements and floors were covered with green cloth; the beds were all embroidered. In every back chamber or withdrawing-room, there was a looking-glass of pure crystal, set in a frame of fine gold, garnished all about with pearls, and was of such greatness, that it would represent to the full the whole lineaments and proportion of the person that stood before it. At the going out of the halls, which belong to the ladies' lodgings, were the perfumers and trimmers, through whose hands the gallants passed when they were to visit the ladies. Those sweet artificers did every morning furnish the ladies' chambers with the spirit of roses, orange-flower water and angelica; and to each of them gave a little precious casket, vapouring forth the most odoriferous exhalations of the choicest aromatical scents.

CHAPTER LVI

HOW THE MEN AND WOMEN OF THE RELIGIOUS ORDER
OF THELEME WERE APPARELLED

THE ladies at the foundation of this order were apparelled after their own pleasure and liking; but since that, of their *own accord* and free-will, they have reformed themselves; their accoutrements were in manner as followeth. They wore stockings of scarlet crimson, or ingrained purple die, which reached just three inches above the knee, having a list beautified with exquisite embroideries, and rare incisions of the cutter's art; their garters were of the colour of their bracelets, and circled the knee a little, both over and under: their shoes, pumps, and slippers, were either of red, violet, or crimson velvet, pinked and jagged like lobsters' wadles.

Next to their smock they put on the pretty kirtle or vasquin of pure silk camblet; above that went the taffety or tabby vardingale, of white, red, tawny, grey, or of any other colour: Above this taffety petticoat they had another of cloth, of tissue or brocade, embroidered with fine gold, and interlaced with needle-work, or as they thought good, and according to the temperature and disposition of the weather, had their upper coats of satin, damask, or velvet, and those either orange, tawny, green, ash-coloured, blue, yellow, bright red, crimson, or white, and so forth; or had them of cloth of gold, cloth of silver, or some other choice stuff, enriched with purple, or embroidered according to the dignity of the festival days and times wherein they wore them.

Their gowns, being still correspondent to the season, were either of cloth of gold, frizzled with a silver-raised work; of red satin, covered with gold purple; of tabby or taffety, white, blue, black, tawny, &c., of silk serge, silk camblet, velvet, cloth of silver, silver tissue, cloth of gold, gold wire, figured velvet, or figured satin, tinselled and overcast with golden threads, in divers variously purfled draughts.

In *summer*, some days, instead of gowns, they wore light handsome mantles, made either of the stuff of the aforesaid attire, or like Moresco rugs, of violet velvet frizzled, with a raised work of gold upon silver purl; or with a knotted cord work of gold embroidery, everywhere garnished with little Indian pearls. They always carried a fair *pannache* or plume of feathers of the colour of their muff, bravely adorned and tricked out with glistering spangles of gold. In the *winter* time they had their taffety gowns, of all colours, as above-named: And those lined with the rich furrings of hind-wolves or speckled lynxes, black-spotted weasels, martlet-skins of Calabria, sables and other costly furs of inestimable value. Their beads, rings, bracelets, collars, carcanets, and neck chains, were all of precious stones, such as carbuncles, rubies, baleus, diamonds, sapphires, emeralds, turquoises, garnets, agates, berilles, and excellent margarites. Their head-dressing also varied with the season of the year, according to which they decked themselves. In *winter* it was of the French fashion; in the *spring* of the Spanish; in *summer* of the fashion of Tuscany, except only upon the holidays and Sundays, at which time they were accoutred in the French mode, because they accounted it more honourable, and better befitting the garb of a *matronal pudicity*.

The men were apparelled after their fashion. Their stockings were of tamine or of cloth serge, of white, black, scarlet, or some other ingrained colour. Their breeches were of velvet, of the same colour with their stockings, or very near, embroidered and cut according to their fancy. Their doublet was of cloth of gold, of cloth of silver, of velvet, satin, damask, taffeties, &c. of the same colours, cut, embroidered and suitably trimmed up in perfection. The points were of silk of the same colours; the tags were of gold well enamelled. Their coats and jerkins were of cloth of gold, cloth of silver, gold tissue, or velvet embroidered, as they thought fit. Their gowns were every whit as costly as those of the ladies. Their girdles were of silk, of the colour of their doublets. Every one had a gallant sword by his side, the hilt and handle whereof were gilt, and the scabbard of velvet of the colour of his breeches, with a chape of gold, and pure goldsmiths' work. The dagger was of the same. Their caps or bonnets were of black velvet, adorned with jewels and buttons of gold; upon that they wore a white plume, most prettily and minion-like parted by so many rows of gold spangles, at the end whereof hung dangling in a more sparkling resplendency, fair rubies, emeralds, diamonds, &c., but there was such a sympathy betwixt the gallants and the ladies, that every day they were apparelled in the same livery. And that they might not miss, there were certain gentlemen appointed to tell the youths every morning, what vestments the ladies would on that day wear; for all was done according to the pleasure of the ladies. In these so handsome cloaths and habiliments so rich, think not that either one or the other of either sex did waste any time at all; for the masters of the wardrobes had all their raiments and apparels so ready for every morning and the chamber ladies were so well skilled, that in a trice they would be dressed, and completely in their clothes from head to foot. And to have those accoutrements with the more conveniency, there was about the wood of Theleme a row of houses of the extent of half a league, very neat and cleanly, wherein dwelt the goldsmiths, lapidaries, jewellers, embroiderers, taylors, gold-drawers, velvet-weavers, tapestry-makers, and upholsterers, who wrought there every one in his own trade, and all for the aforesaid jolly friars and nuns of the new stamp. They were furnished with matter and stuff from the hands of the Lord Nausiclete, who every year brought them seven ships from the Perlas and Cannibal islands, laden with ingots of gold, with raw silk, with pearls, and precious stones. And if any *unions* (*pearls*) began to grow old, and lose somewhat of their natural whiteness and lustre, those by their art did renew, by tendering them to eat to some pretty cocks, as they use to give casting unto hawks.

CHAPTER LVII

HOW THE THELEMITES WERE GOVERNED, AND OF THEIR MANNER OF LIVING

ALL their life was spent not in laws, statutes, or rules, but according to their own free will and pleasure. They rose out of their

126

beds when they thought good; they did eat, drink, labour, sleep, when they had a mind to it, and were disposed for it. None did awake them, none did offer to constrain them to eat, drink, nor do any other thing; for so had Gargantua established it. In all their rule and strictest tie of their order, there was but this one clause to be observed:

DO WHAT THOU WILT

Because men that are free, well-born, well-bred, and conversant in honest companies, have naturally an *instinct* and spur that prompteth them unto virtuous actions, and withdraws them from vice, which is called *honour*. Those same men, when by base subjection and constraint they are brought under and kept down, turn aside from that noble disposition, by which they formerly were inclined to *virtue,* to shake off that bond of servitude, wherein they are so tyrannously inslaved for it is agreeable to the nature of man to long after things forbidden, and to desire what is denied us. By this liberty they entered into a very laudable emulation, to do all of them what they saw did please one. If any of the gallants or ladies should say, *"Let us drink,"* they would all drink. If any one of them said, *"Let us play,"* they all played. If one said, *"Let us go a walking into the fields,"* they went all. If it were to go a hawking, or a hunting, the ladies mounted upon dainty well-paced nags, seated in a stately palfrey saddle, carried on their lovely fists *miniardly begloved* every one of them, either a sparhawk, or a laneret, or a marlin, and the young gallants carried the other kind of hawks. So nobly were they taught, that there was neither he nor she amongst them, but could read, write, sing, play upon several musical instruments, speak five or six several languages, and compose in them all very quaintly, both in verse and prose. Never were seen so valiant *knights,* so noble and worthy, so dexterous and skilful both on foot and horseback, more brisk and lively, more nimble and quick, or better handling all manner of weapons, than were there. Never were seen *ladies* so proper and handsome, so miniard and dainty, less froward, or more ready with their hand, and with their needle, in every honest and free action belonging to that sex, than were there. For this reason, when the time came that any *man* of the said *abbey,* either at the request of his parents, or for some other cause, had a mind to go out of it, he carried along with him one of the *ladies,* namely, her, whom he had before that chosen for his *mistress,* and they were married together. And if they had formerly in Theleme lived in good devotion and amity,

127

they did continue therein, and increase it to a greater height in their state of matrimony; and did entertain that mutual love till the very last day of their life, in no less vigour and fervency than at the very day of their wedding. Here must I not forget to set down unto you a riddle which was found under the ground, as they were laying the foundation of the *abbey,* engraven on a copperplate, and it was thus as followeth.

CHAPTER LVIII

A PROPHETICAL RIDDLE

POOR mortals who wait for a happy day,
   Cheer up your hearts, and hear what I shall say,
If it be lawful firmly to believe,
That the *cœlestial body* can us give
Wisdom to judge of things that are not yet,
Or if from Heaven such wisdom we may get,
As may with confidence make us discourse
Of years to come, their destiny and course;
I to my hearer give to understand,
That this next *winter,* tho' it be at hand,
Yea, and before, there shall appear a *race*
Of *men,* who, loath to sit still in one place,
Shall boldly go before all people's eyes
Suborning men of divers qualities,
To draw them unto covenants and sides,
In such a manner, that whate'er betides,
They'll move you, if you give them ear (no doubt)
With both your *friends* and kindred to fall out.

   They make a *vassal* to withstand his lord,
And *children* their own *parents;* in a word,
All *reverences* shall then be banished,
No true respect to others shall be had.
   They'll say, that every *man* should have his turn,
Both in his going forth and his return;
And hereupon there shall arise such woes,
Such jarrings, and confused *to's* and *fro's;*
That never were in history such coyles,

Set down as yet, such tumults and garboyles;
Then shall you many *gallant men* see by
Valour stirr'd up, and youthful fervency;
Who, trusting too much in their hopeful time,
Live but a while, and perish in their *prime;*
Neither shall any, who this course shall run,
Leave off the *race* which he hath once begun;
Till they the Heavens with *noise* by their contention
Have fill'd, and with their *steps* the earth's dimension.
Then those shall have no less *authority,*
That have no *faith,* than those that will not lie;
For then shall all be govern'd by a rude,
Base, ignorant, and foolish *multitude;*
The veriest *lowt* of all shall be their *judge,*
O, horrible and dangerous *deluge!*
Deluge I call it, and that for good reason,
For this shall be omitted in no season;
Nor shall the earth of this foul stir be free,
Till suddenly you in great store shall see,
The waters issue out, with whose *streams* the
Most moderate of all shall *moisten'd* be;
And justly too, because they did not spare
The *flocks* of beasts that *innocentest* are;
But did their *sinews;* and their bowels take,
Not to the gods a *sacrifice* to make;
But usually to serve themselves for sport,
And now consider, I do you exhort.
  In such *commotions* so continual,
What rest can take the *globe terrestrial?*
  Most happy then are they, that can it hold,
And use it carefully as precious gold,
By keeping it in *gaol,* whence it shall have
No help but him, who being to it gave;
And to increase his mournful accident
The *sun,* before it set in th' *occident,*
Shall cease to dart upon it any light
More than in an *eclipse,* or in the night:
So that at once its favour shall be gone,
And *liberty* with it be left alone:
And yet, before it come to ruin thus,

129

Its *quaking* shall be as impetuous
As Ætna's was, when Titan's sons lay under,
And yield, when *lost,* a fearful sound like thunder.
Inarimé did not more *quickly move,*
When Typheus did the vast huge hills remove;
And for despite, into the sea them threw.
   Thus shall it then be *lost* by ways not few,
And *changed* suddenly, when those, that have it,
To *other men* that after come shall leave it.
Then shall it be high time to cease from this
So long, so great, so tedious *exercise;*
For the *great waters* now foretold by me,
Will make each think where his retreat shall be;
And yet before that they be clean dispersed,
You may behold in the air, were nought was erst,
The *burning-heat* of a great flame to rise,
Lick up the water, and the enterprise.
   It resteth after these things to declare,
That those shall sit content, who *chosen* are;
With all good things, and with cœlestial *manne*
And richly recompensed every *man;*
The other at the last all *stripp'd* shall be,
That after this great work all men may see,
How each shall have his *due,* this is their *lot,*
O, he is worthy praise that shrinketh not.

No sooner was this ænigmatical monument read over, but Gargantua, fetching a deep sigh, said unto those that stood by, "It is not now only (I perceive) that people called to the faith of the gospel, and convinced with the certainty of evangelical truths, are persecuted; but happy is that man that shall not be scandalized, but shall always continue to the end in aiming at that mark, which God by his dear Son hath set before us, without being distracted or diverted by his carnal affections and depraved nature."

The monk then said, "What do you think in your conscience is meant and signified by this riddle?" "What?" said Gargantua, "the progress and carrying on of the divine truth." "By St. Goderan," said the monk, "that is not my exposition; it is the style of the prophet Merlin; make upon it as many grave allegories and glosses as you will, and dote upon it, you and the rest of the world as long as you please; for my part, I can conceive no other meaning in it, but a description of a set at *tennis* in dark and obscure terms.

"The suborners of men are the makers of matches, which are commonly *friends*. After the two *chases* are made, he that has the upper end of the *tennis-court* goeth out, and the other cometh in. They believe the first that saith, the *ball* was over or under the *line*. The *waters* are the heats that the players take till they sweat again. The cords of the rackets are made of the guts of sheep or goats. The globe terrestrial is the *tennis-ball*. After playing, when the game is done they refresh themselves before a clear fire, and change their shirts; then very willingly they make all good cheer, but most merrily those that have gained; and so farewell."

THE TRANSLATOR TO THE READER

ELSEWHERE, I taught physicians doubtful skill,
 Like other doctors, how to cure or kill:
Here is my *nostrum,* that can ne'er miscarry;
For all I here prescribe is to be merry.
One *dram* of mirth will sooner mend thy crasis,
Than twenty bitter draughts, with scurvy faces.
Let chemist or the Galenist prevail;
Yet sure a course of mirth is worth 'em all.
No drug, nor hellebore, no rhubarb safe;
O still, the only physic is to laugh:
To which, if this small book cannot provoke thee,
Let pills, let bolus, quack, or Radcliff choke thee.

THE AUTHOR'S PROLOGUE

TO

THE SECOND BOOK

MOST illustrious and thrice valorous champions, gentlemen, and others, who willingly apply your minds to the high flights and harmless sallies of wit. You have, not long ago, seen, read, and understood the great and inestimable chronicles of the huge giant Gargantua; and like true *men of faith,* have firmly believed all that is contained in them, and have very often past your time amongst honourable ladies and gentlewomen, telling them fair long stories, when you are out of all other talk, for which you are worthy of great praise and sempiternal memory. And I do heartily wish, that every man would lay aside his own business, meddle no more with his profession nor trade, and throw all affairs concerning himself behind his back, to attend this wholly, without distracting or troubling his mind with anything else, until he have learned all without book; that if, by chance, the art of printing should cease, or in case that, in time to come, all books should perish, every man might truly teach them to his children, and deliver them over to his successors and survivors, from hand to hand as a religious *cabala:* for there is in it more profit than a rabble of great pocky logger-heads are able to discern, who surely understand far less in these little merriments, than Raclet did in the institutes.

I have known great and mightly lords, and those not a few, who going a deer-hunting, or a hawking after wild ducks, when the chace had not encountered with the blinks, that were cast in her way to retard her course, or that the hawk did but plain and smoothly fly, without moving her wings, perceiving the prey, by force of flight, to have gained bounds of her, have been much chafed and vexed, as you understand well enough; but the comfort unto which they had refuge, and that they might not take cold, was to relate the inestimable deeds of the said Gargantua. There are others in the world, these are no flimflam stories, who being much troubled with the tooth-ach, after they had spent their goods upon physicians, without receiving at all any ease of their pain, have found no more ready remedy, than to put the said *chronicles* betwixt two pieces of linen cloth, made very hot, and so apply them to the place that smarteth, *synapising* them with a little powder of *projection,* otherwise called *doribus.*

133

But what shall I say of those poor men that are plagued with the pox and the gout? O, how often have we seen them, even immediately after they were anointed and thoroughly greased, till their faces did glister like the key-hole of a powdering-tub, their teeth dance like the jacks of a pair of little organs or virginals, when they are played upon, and that they foamed from their very throats like a boar, which the mongrel mastiff-hounds have driven in, and overthrown amongst the toils: what did they then? All their consolation was to have some page of the said jolly book read unto them. And we have seen those who have given themselves to an *hundred puncheons of old devils,* in case that they did not feel a manifest ease and assuagement of pain, at the hearing the said book read, even when they were kept in a purgatory of torment: no more nor less than women in travail used to find their sorrow abated, when the life of St. Margarite is read unto them. Is this nothing? Find me a book in any language, in any faculty or science whatsoever, that hath such virtues, properties, and prerogatives, and I will be content to pay you a chopine of tripes. No, no, my masters, it is peerless, incomparable, and not to be matched; and this am I resolved for ever to maintain, even unto the fire exclusive. And those that will pertinaciously hold the contrary opinion, let them be accounted abusers, predestinators, impostors, and seducers of the people. It is very true, that there are found in some noble and famous books, certain occult and hidden properties, in the number of which are reckoned, Whippot, Orlando Furioso, Robert the Devil, Fierabras, William without Fear, Huon of Bourdeaux, Monteville, and Matabrune: but they are not comparable to that which we speak of; and the world hath well known, by infallible eyperience, the great emolument and utility which it hath received by this *Gargantuine Chronicle;* for the printers have sold more of them in two months' time, than there will be bought of bibles in nine years.

I therefore, your humble slave, being very willing to increase your solace and recreations yet a little more, do offer you, for a present, another book of the same stamp, only that it is a little more reasonable and worthy of credit than the other was; for think not unless you wilfully will err against your knowledge, that I speak of it as the Jews do of the law. I was not born under such a planet, neither did it ever befal me to lie, or affirm a thing for true that was not: I speak of it like a jolly *onocrotarie,* I should say *crotenotary* of the martyrized lovers, and *croquenotaire* of love: *quod vidimus, testamur.* It is of the horrible and dreadful feats and prowesses of Pantagruel, whose menial servant I have been ever since I was a page till this hour, that by his leave I am permitted to visit my cow-country, and to know if any of my kindred there be alive.

And therefore, to make an end of this prologue, even as I give myself fairly to an hundred thousand panniers full of devils, body and soul, tripes and guts, in case that I lie so much as one single word in this whole history: just so St. Anthony's fire burn you, Mawmet's disease whirl you, the squinzy choke you, botches, crinckums sink you plumb down to Pegtrantums, plagues of Sodom and Gomorrah cram your pocky arse with sorrow. Fire, brimstone, and pits bottomless swallow you all alive, in case you do not firmly believe all that I shall relate unto you in this present chronicle.

THE SECOND BOOK

OF

RABELAIS'S WORKS

TREATING OF THE HEROIC DEEDS AND SAYINGS OF

THE

GOOD PANTAGRUEL

CHAPTER I

OF THE ORIGINAL AND ANTIQUITY OF THE GREAT PANTAGRUEL

IT will not be an idle or unprofitable thing, seeing we are at leisure, to put you in mind of the fountain and original source, whence is derived unto us the good Pantagruel: for I see that all good historiographers have thus handled their *chronicles,* not only the Arabians, Barbarians, and Latins, but also the gentle Greeks, who were eternal drinkers. You must therefore remark, that at the beginning of the world, I speak of a long time, it is above forty quarantains of nights, according to the supputation of the ancient Druids, a little after that Abel was killed by his brother Cain, the earth embrued with the blood of the just, was one year so exceedingly fertile in those fruits which it usually produceth to us, and especially in *medlars,* that, ever since, throughout all ages, it hath been called the year of the great *medlars,* for three of them did fill a bushel. In that year the *calends* were found by the Grecian almanacks. There was that year nothing of the month of March in the time of Lent, and the middle of August was in May. In the month of October, as I take it, or at least September, that I may not err, for I will carefully take heed of that, was the week so famous in the annals, which they call *the week of the three Thursdays;* for it had three of them, by means of the irregular *bissextile,* occasioned by the sun's having tripped and stumbled a little towards the left hand, like a debtor afraid of serjeants; and the moon varied from her course above five fathom; and there was manifestly

136

seen the motion of *trepidation* in the firmament called *aplanes:* so that the middle *pleiade,* leaving her fellows, declined toward the *equinoctial;* and the star named *Spica* left the constellation of the *Virgin,* withdrawing itself towards the *Balance:* which are cases very terrible, and matters so hard and difficult, that astrologians cannot set their teeth in them; and indeed their teeth had been pretty long if they could have reached thither.

However, account you it for a truth, that everybody did then most heartily eat of these *medlars,* for they were fair to the eye, and in taste delicious. But even as Noah, that holy man, to whom we are so much beholden, bound, and obliged, for that he planted to us the vine, from whence we have that nectarian, delicious, precious, heavenly, joyful, and deific liquor, which they call the *piot,* or *tiplage,* was deceived in the drinking of it, for he was ignorant of the great virtue and power thereof; so likewise the men and women of that time did delight much in the eating of that fair great fruit; but divers and very different accidents did ensue thereupon: for there fell upon them all in their bodies a most terrible *swelling,* but not upon all in the same place; for some were *swollen* in the belly, and their belly strouted out big like a great tun; of whom it is written, *ventrem omnipotentem;* who were all very honest men, and merry blades: and of this race came St. Fatgulch and Shrovetuesday. Others did *swell* at the shoulders, who in that place were so crump and nobby, that they were therefore called *montifers,* which is as much as to say *hill-carriers,* of whom you see some yet in the world, of divers sexes and degrees: of this race came Æsop, some of whose excellent words and deeds you have in writing. Some other *puffes* did *swell* in length by the *member,* which they call the *labourer of nature,* in such sort, that it grew marvellous long, plump, jolly, lusty, stirring, and crest-risen in the antique fashion; so that they made use of it as of a girdle, winding it five or six times about their waste; but if it happened the aforesaid *member* to be in good case, spooming with a full sail, bunt fair before the wind, then to have seen those strouting champions, you would have taken them for men that had their lances settled on their rest, to run at the ring, or tilting *quintain.* Of these the race is utterly lost, and quite extinct, as the women say; for they do lament continually, that there are none extant now of those *long, plump, &c.,* you know the rest of the song. Others did grow in matter of ballocks so enormously, that three of them would fill a sack: from them are descended the ballocks of Lorrain, which never dwell in cod-pieces, but fall down to the bottom of the breeches. Others grew in the hams, and to see them, you would have said they had been cranes, or flamans, or else men walking upon stilts; the little schoolboys called these *iambicks*. In others, their nose did grow so, that it seemed to be the beak of a *limbeck*, in every part thereof most variously diapered with the twinkling sparkles of crimson blisters budding forth, and purpled with pimples, all enamelled with thick-set wheals of a sanguine colour, bordered with *gules;* and such have you seen the prebend Panzoul, and Woodenfoot, the physician of Angiers: of which race there were few that liked the *ptisane,* but all of them were perfect lovers of the pure *septembral juice.* Naso and Ovid had their extraction from thence, and all those of whom it is written, *Ne reminiscaris.* Others grew in *ears,* which they had so big, that out of one would have been stuff enough to make a doublet, a pair of breeches, and a jacket, whilst with the other they might have covered themselves as with a Spanish cloak: and they say, that in Bourbonois this race remaineth yet; and from thence they are called the *ears of Bourbon.* Others grew in length of body, and of those came the giants, and of them Pantagruel.

And the first was Chalbroth,
who begat Sarabroth,
who begat Faribroth,
who begat Hurtali, that was a brave eater of pottage, and reigned in
   the time of the flood;
who begat Nembroth,
who begat Atlas, that with his shoulders kept the sky from falling;
who begat Goliah,
who begat Erix, that invented the *hocus pocus* plays of legerdemain;
who begat Titius,
who begat Eryon,
who begat Polyphemus,
who begat Cacus,
who begat Etion, the first man that ever had the pox, for not
   drinking fresh in summer, as Bartachin witnesseth;
who begat Enceladus,
who begat Ceus,
who begat Tiphæus,
who begat Alæus,
who begat Othus,

who begat Ægeon,

who begat Briareus, that had an hundred hands;

who begat Porphyrio,

who begat Adamastor,

who begat Antæus,

who begat Agatho,

who begat Porus, against whom fought Alexander the Great;

who begat Aranthas,

who begat Gabbara, that was the first inventor of drinking of
   healths;

who begat Goliah of Secondille,

who begat Offot, that was terribly well-nosed for drinking at the
   barrel head;

who begat Artachæus,

who begat Oromedon,

who begat Gemmagog, the first inventor of Poulan shoes, which are
   open on the foot, and tied over the instep with a latchet;

who begat Sisyphus,

who begat the Titans, of whom Hercules was born;

who begat Enay, the most skilful man that ever was, in matter of
   taking the little worms out of the hands;

who begat Fierabras, that was vanquished by Oliver peer of
   France, and Rowland's Camerade;

who begat Morgan, the first in the world that played at dice with
   spectacles;

who begat Fracassus, of whom Merlin Coccaius hath written, and
   of him was born Ferragus;

who begat Hapmouche, the first that ever invented the drying of
   neat's-tongues in the chimney; for before that people salted them
   as they do now gammons of bacon;

who begat Bolivorax,

who begat Longis,

who begat Gayoffo, whose cods were of poplar, and his pendulum
   of the servise, or sorb-apple-tree;

who begat Maschefain,

who begat Bruslefer,

who begat Angoulevent,

who begat Galehault, the inventor of flaggons;

who begat Mirelangant,

who begat Gallaffre,

who begat Salourdin,
who begat Roboast,
who begat Sortibrant of Conimbres,
who begat Brusbant of Mommiere,
who begat Bruyer, that was overcome by Ogier the Dane, peer of
 France;
who begat Mabrun,
who begat Foutasnon,
who begat Haquelebac,
who begat Vitdegrain,
who begat Grangousier,
who begat Gargantua,
who begat the noble Pantagruel, my master.

I know that, reading this passage, you will make a doubt within yourselves, and that grounded upon very good reason, which is this, How is it possible that this relation can be true, seeing at the time of the flood all the world was destroyed, except Noah, and seven persons more with him in the ark, into whose number Hurtali is not admitted? Doubtless the demand is well made, and seemingly just; but the answer shall satisfy you, or my wit is not rightly caulked: and because I was not at that time to tell you anything of my own fancy, I will bring unto you the authority of the Masorites, good honest fellows, true ballockeering blades, and exact Hebraical bag-pipers, who affirm, that verily the said Hurtali was not within the ark of Noah, neither could he get in, for he was too big, but he sat astride upon it, with one leg on the one side, and another on the other, as little children used to do upon their wooden horses; or as the great bull of Berne, which was killed at Marinian, did ride for his hackney the great murdering-piece, a pretty beast, of a fair and pleasant amble, without all question.

In that posture he, after God, saved the said ark from danger; for with his legs he gave it the balance that was needful, and with his foot turned it whither he pleased, as a ship answereth her rudder. Those that were within sent him up victuals in abundance, by a chimney, as people very thankfully acknowledging the good that he did them: and sometimes they did talk together, as Icaromenippus did to Jupiter, according to the report of Lucian. Have you understood all this well? Drink then one good draught without water; for if you believe it not: *"No, truly do I not,"* quoth she.

CHAPTER II

GARGANTUA, at the age of four hundred fourscore forty and four years, begat his son Pantagruel, upon his wife named Badebec, daughter to the king of the Amaurots in Utopia, who died in child-birth; for he was so wonderfully great and lumpish, that he could not possibly come forth into the light of the world, without thus suffocating his mother. But that we may fully understand the cause and reason of the name of Pantagruel, which, at his baptism, was given him, you are to remark, that in that year there was so great a drought over all the country of Afric, that there past thirty and six months, three weeks, four days, thirteen hours, and a little more, without rain, but with a heat so vehement that the whole earth was parched and withered by it; neither was it more scorched and dried up with heat in the days of Elijah, than it was at that time; for there was not a tree to be seen that had either leaf or bloom upon it: the grass was without verdure or greenness, the rivers were drained, the fountains dried up, the poor fishes abandoned and forsaken by their proper element, wandering and crying upon the ground most horribly; the birds did fall down from the air, for want of moisture and dew wherewith to refresh them: the wolves, foxes, harts, wild-boars, fallow-deer, hares, conies, weesils, brocks, badgers, and other such beasts were found dead in the fields, with their mouths open. In respect of men, there was the pity, you should have seen them lay out their tongues like greyhounds that had run six hours; many did throw themselves into the wells; others entered within a cow's belly to be in the shade; those Homer calls Alibants: all the country was at a stand, and nothing could be done; it was a most lamentable case, to have seen the labour of mortals in defending themselves from the vehemency of this horrific drought; for they had work enough to do to save the holy water in the churches from being wasted: but there was such order taken by the counsel of my lords the cardinals, and of our holy father, that none did dare to take above one lick; yet when any one came into the church you should have seen above twenty poor thirsty fellows hang upon him that was the distributor of the water, and that with a wide open throat, gaping for some little drop, like the rich glutton in St. Luke, that might fall by, lest anything should be lost. O how happy was he that year who had a cool cellar under ground, well plenished with fresh wine!

The philosopher reports in moving the question, *wherefore is it that the sea-water is salt?* that at the time when Phœbus gave the government of his resplendent chariot to his son Phæton, the said Phæton, unskilful in the art, and not knowing how to keep the *ecliptic* line betwixt the two *tropics* of the *latitude* of the sun's course, strayed out of his way, and came so near the earth, that he dried up all the countries that were under it, burning a great part of the heaven, which the *philosophers* call *Via lactea,* and the huff-snuffs, St. James's way; although the most lofty and high-crested poets affirm that to be the place where Juno's milk fell when she gave suck to Hercules.

The earth at that time was so excessively heated, that it fell into an enormous sweat, yea, such an one that made it sweat out the sea, which is therefore *salt,* because all *sweat* is *salt;* and this you cannot but confess to be true, if you will taste of your own, or of those that have the pox, when they are put into a *sweating;* it is all one to me. Just such another case fell out this same year; for on a certain Friday, when the whole people were bent upon their devotions, and had made goodly *processions,* with store of *litanies,* and fair *preachings,* and beseechings of God Almighty to look down with his eye of mercy upon their miserable and disconsolate condition, there was even then visibly seen issue out of the ground great drops of water, such as fall from a man in a top *sweat;* and the poor hoydons began to rejoice, as if it had been a thing very profitable unto them; for some said, that there was not one drop of moisture in the air, whence they might have any rain, and that the earth did supply the default of that. Other learned men said, that it was a shower of the *antipodes,* as Seneca saith in his fourth book *Quæstionum Naturalium,* speaking of the source and spring of Nilus; but they were deceived; for the procession being ended, when every one went about to gather of this dew, and to drink of it with full bowls, they found it was nothing but *pickle,* and the very *brine* of salt, more brackish in taste than the saltest water of the sea: and because in that very day Pantagruel was born, his father gave him that name; for *Panta* in Greek is as much as to say *all,* and *Gruel* in the Hagarene language doth signify *thirsty;* inferring hereby, that *at his birth the whole world was a-dry and thirsty;* as likewise' foreseeing that he would be some day supreme lord and sovereign of the thirsty companions, which was shewn to him at that very same hour, by a more evident sign; for when his mother Badebec was in the bringing of him forth, and that the midwives did wait to receive him, there came first out of her belly threescore and eight *sellers* of *salt,* every one of them leading in a halter a *mule,* heavy loaded with *salt;* after whom issued forth nine *dromedaries,* with great loads of gammons of bacon, and dried neat's-tongues on their backs; then followed seven *camels* loaded with links and chitterlings, hog's pudding, and sausages; after them came out twenty-five great *wains* full of leeks, garlic, onions, and chibals. At the sight hereof the midwives were much amazed; yet some of them said, *"Lo, here is good provision, and indeed we need it, for we drink but lazily, as if our tongues walked on crutches: truly this is a good sign, there is nothing here but what is fit for us, these are the spurs of wine that set it going."* As they were tattling thus together, after their own manner of chat, behold! out comes Pantagruel, all hairy like a bear; whereupon one of them, inspired with a prophetical spirit, said, *"This will be a terrible fellow; he is born with all his hair, he is undoubtedly to do wonderful things; and, if he live, he will be of age."*

CHAPTER III

OF THE GRIEF WHEREWITH GARGANTUA WAS MOVED AT THE DECEASE OF HIS WIFE BADEBEC

WHEN Pantagruel was born, there was none more astonished and perplexed than was his father Gargantua: for, on the one side seeing his wife Badebec dead, and on the other side his son Pantagruel born, so fair and so goodly, *he knew not what to say, nor what to do;* and the doubt, that troubled his brain, was to know whether he should *cry* for the death of his wife, or *laugh* for the joy of his son: he was on either side choked with sophistical arguments; for he framed them very well in *modo & figura,* but he could not resolve them, remaining pestered and entangled by this means, like a mouse catched in a trap, or a kite snared in a gin. "Shall I weep?" said he: "yes. For why? my so good wife is dead, who was the most *this,* the most *that,* that ever was in the world: never shall I see her, never shall I recover such another; it is unto me an inestimable loss! O my good God, what had I done, that thou shouldest thus punish me? Why didst thou not take me away before her, seeing for me to live, without her, is but to languish? Ah! Badebec, Badebec, my minion, my dear heart, my pigsney, my duck, my honey, my *little coney* (yet it hath in circumference full six acres, three rods, five poles, four yards, two feet, one inch and a half of good woodland measure), my tender Peggy, my cod-piece-darling, my bob and hit, my slip-shoe-lovy, never shall I see thee! Ah! poor Pantagruel, thou hast lost thy good mother, thy sweet nurse, thy well-beloved lady! O false death, how injurious and delightful hast thou been to me! how malicious and outrageous have I found thee, in taking her from me, my well-beloved wife, who should, of right, have been immortal!"

With these words he did cry like a cow; but on a sudden fell a laughing like a calf, when Pantagruel came into his mind. "Ha! my little son," said he, "my childilolly, fedlifondy, dandlichucky, my ballocky, my pretty rogue: O how jolly thou art, and how much I am bound to my gracious God, that hath been pleased to bestow on me a son so fair, so spriteful, so lively, so smiling, so pleasant, and so gentle. *Ho, ho, ho, ho,* how glad I am! let us drink, *ho,* and put away melancholy: bring of the best: rinse the glasses; lay the cloth; drive out these dogs; blow this fire; light candles; shut that door there; cut this bread in sippets for brewis; send away these poor folks; give them what they ask; hold my gown; I will strip myself into my doublet, *en cuerpo,* to make the gossips merry, and keep them company."

As he spoke this, he heard the litanies and the momentos of the priests that carried his wife to be buried! which dashed all his merriment again, and he was suddenly ravished another away, saying "Lord God, must I again *contrist* myself? This grieves me; I am no longer young; I grow old; the weather is dangerous; I am sick; I faint away. By the faith of a gentleman, it were better to *cry* less, and *drink* more.

"My wife is dead, well, by G—(*da jurandi*) I shall not raise her again by my crying: she is well; she is in paradise at least, if she be no higher: she prayeth to God for us; she is happy; she is above the sense of our miseries, nor can our calamities reach her. What though she be dead, must not we also die? The same debt, which she hath paid, hangs over our heads; nature will require it of us, and we must all of us, some day, taste of the same sauce: let her pass then, and the Lord preserve the survivors, for I must now cast about how to get another wife. But I will tell you what you shall do," said he to the midwives "(where be they? good folks, I cannot see you), go to my wife's interment, and I will the while *rock* my son; for I find

144

myself strangely altered, and in danger of falling sick; but drink one good draught first; you will be the better for it, believe me, upon my honour." They, at his request, went to her burial and funeral obsequies: in the meanwhile, poor Gargantua staying at home, and willing to have somewhat in remembrance of her to be engraven upon her tomb, made this epitaph, in the manner as followeth:

> "Dead is the noble Badebec,
> Who had a face like a rebec;
>   A Spanish body, and a belly
> Of Swisserland; she died, I tell ye,
> In child-birth; pray to God that her
> He pardon wherein she did err.
> Here lies her body, which did live
> Free from all vice, as I believe;
>   And did decease at my bed-side,
>   The year and day in which she died."

CHAPTER IV

OF THE INFANCY OF PANTAGRUEL

I FIND, by the ancient historiographers and poets, that divers have been born in this world after very strange manners, which would be too long to repeat; read therefore the seventh book of Pliny, if you have so much leisure: yet have you never heard of any so wonderful as that Pantagruel; for it is a very difficult matter to believe how, in the little time he was in his mother's belly, he grew both in body and strength. That which Hercules did was nothing, when in his cradle he slew two serpents; for those serpents were but little and weak: but Pantagruel, being yet in his cradle, did far more admirable things, and more to be amazed at. I pass by here the relation of how at every one of his meals he supped up the milk of four thousand six hundred cows; and how to make him a skillet to boil his milk in, there were set a-work all the braziers of Saumure in Anjou, of Villedieu in Normandy, and of Bramont in Lorrain: and they served in this whitepot-meat to him in a huge great bell, which is yet to be seen in the city of Bourges in Berry, near the palace; but his teeth were already so well grown, and so strengthened in vigour, that of the said bell he bit off a great morsel, as very plainly doth appear till this hour.

One day in the morning, when they would have made him suck one of his cows—for he never had any other nurse, as the history tells us—he got one of his arms loose from the swaddling bands, wherewith he was kept fast in the cradle, laid hold on the said cow under the left fore-arm, and grasping her to him, ate up her udder, and half her paunch, with the liver and the kidnies, and had devoured all up, if she had not cried out most horribly, as if the wolves had held her by the legs; at which noise company came in, and took away the said cow from Pantagruel: yet could they not so well do it, but that the quarter whereby he caught her was left in his hand, of which quarter he gulped up the flesh in a trice, even with as much ease as you would eat a sausage; and that so greedily, with desire of more, that when they would have taken away the bone from him, he swallowed it down whole, as a cormorant would do a little fish, and afterwards began fumblingly to say, *"Good, good, good!"* for he could not yet speak plain; giving them to understand thereby that he had found it very good, and that he did lack but so much more: which when they saw that attended him, they bound him with great cable-ropes, like those that are made at Tain for the carriage of salt to Lyons, or such as those are whereby the great French ship rides at anchor in the road of Newhaven in Normandy. But on a certain time a great bear, which his father had bred, got loose, came towards him, began to lick his face, for his nurses had not thoroughly wiped his chaps: at which unexpected approach, being on a sudden offended, he as lightly rid himself of those great cables as Sampson did of the hauser ropes wherewith the Philistines had tied him, and, by your leave, takes up monsieur the bear, and tears him to pieces like a pullet, which served him for a gorge full, or good warm bit for that meal.

Whereupon Gargantua, fearing lest the child should hurt himself, caused four great chains of iron to be made to bind him, and so many strong wooden arches unto his cradle, most firmly stocked and mortised in huge frames: of those chains you have one at Rochel, which they draw up at night betwixt the two great towers of the haven; another is at Lyons; a third at Angiers; and the fourth was carried away by the devils, to bind Lucifer, who broke his chains at that time by reason of a cholic that did extraordinarily torment him, taken with eating a serjeant's soul fricasseed for his breakfast; and therefore you may believe that which Nicolas de Lyre saith upon that place of the psalter, where it is written, "Et Og regem Basan"; that

146

the said Og, being yet little, was so strong and robustious, that they were fain to bind him with chains of iron in his cradle. Thus continued Pantagruel for awhile very calm and quiet, for he was not able so easily to break those chains, especially having no room in the cradle to give a swing with his arms. But see what happened; once upon a great holiday, that his father Gargantua made a sumptuous banquet to all the princes of his court: I am apt to believe that the menial officers of the house were so imbusied in waiting each on his proper service at the feast, that nobody took care of poor Pantagruel, who was left *a reculorum,* behindhand all alone and as forsaken. What did he? Hark what he did, good people: he strove and essayed to break the chains of the cradle with his arms, but could not, for they were too strong for him; then did he keep with his feet such a stamping stir, and so long, that at last he beat out the lower end of his cradle, which notwithstanding was made of a great beam five foot in square; and as soon as he had gotten out his feet, he slid down as well as he could, till he had got his soles to the ground; and then, with a mighty force, he rose up, carrying his cradle upon his back, bound to him like a tortoise that crawls up against a wall; and to have seen him, you would have thought it had been a great carrick of five hundred tun upon one end. In this manner he entered into the great hall, where they were banquetting, and that very boldly, which did much affright the company: yet because his arms were tied in, he could not reach anything to eat, but, with great pain, stooped now and then a little, to take, with the whole flat of his tongue, some lick, good bit, or morsel.

Which when his father saw, he knew well enough that they had left him without giving him anything to eat, and therefore commanded that he should be loosed from the said chains, by the counsel of the princes and lords there present: besides that, also the physicians of Gargantua said, that if they did thus keep him in the cradle, he would be all his lifetime subject to the stone. When he was unchained, they made him to sit down, where, after he had fed very well, he took his cradle, and broke it into more than five hundred thousand pieces, with one blow of his fist that he struck in the midst of it, swearing that he would never come into it again.

147

CHAPTER V

THUS grew Pantagruel from day to day, and, to every one's eye,
waxed more and more in all his dimensions, which made his
father to rejoice by a natural affection; therefore caused he to be made
for him, whilst he was yet little, a pretty cross-bow, wherewith to
shoot at small birds, which now they call the great cross-bow at Chan-
telle. Then he sent him to school to learn, and to spend his youth
in virtue: in the prosecution of which design he came first to Poitiers,
where, as he studied and profited very much, he saw that the scholars
were oftentimes idle, and knew not how to bestow their time, which
moved him to take such compassion on them, that one day he took
from a long ledge of rocks (called there Passelourdin) a hugh great
stone, of about twelve fathom square and fourteen handfuls thick,
and with great ease set it upon four pillars, in the midst of a field,
to no other end, but that the said scholars, when they had nothing else
to do, might pass their time in getting up on that stone, and feast it
with store of gammons, pasties, and flaggons, and carve their names
upon it with a knife! in token of which deed, till this hour, the stone is
called the *lifted stone:* and in remembrance hereof, there is none entered into the register and matricular book of the said university of
Poitiers, till he have first drunk in the caballine fountain of Crous-
telles, passed at Passelourdin, and got up upon the *lifted stone.*

Afterwards reading the delectable chronicles of his ancestors, he
found that Jeffrey of Lusinian, called *Jeffrey with the great tooth,*
grandfather to the cousin-in-law of the eldest sister of the aunt of the
son-in-law of the uncle of the good daughter of his step-mother, was
interred at Maillezais; therefore he took a *play-day* to pay his respects
to him in a visit; and going from Poitiers with some of his companions, they passed by Legugé, visiting the noble Abbot Ardillon:
then by Lusinian, by Sansay, by Celles, by Colonges, by Fontenay le
Comte, saluting the learned Tiraqueau, and from thence arrived at
Maillezais, where he went to see the sepulchre of the said *Jeffrey with
the great tooth;* which made him somewhat afraid, looking upon the
portraiture, representing a man in an extreme fury, drawing his great
malchus faulchion half-way out of his scabbard. When the reason
hereof was demanded, the canons of the said place told him, that there

was no other cause of it, but that *pictoribus atque poetis,* &c., that is to say, that painters and poets have liberty to paint and devise what they list after their own fancy: but he was not satisfied with their answer, and said, "He is not thus painted without a cause; and I suspect that at his death there was some wrong done him, whereof he requireth his kindred to take revenge: I will inquire further into it, and then do what shall be reasonable." Then he returned not to Poitiers, but would take a view of the other universities of France: therefore going to Rochel, he took shipping, and arrived at Bourdeaux, where he found no great diversion, only now and then he would see some mariners and lightermen a wrestling on the key, or strand, by the river-side. From thence he came to Thoulouse, where he learned to *dance* very well, and to play with the *two-handed sword,* as the fashion of the scholars of the said university is. But he staid not long there, when he saw that they stuck not to burn their regents alive, like red-herrings, saying, "Now, God forbid that I should die this death, for I am by nature sufficiently dry already, without being *heated* any further."

He went then to Montpellier, where he met with the good wives of Mirevaux, and good jovial company withal, and thought to have set himself to the study of *physic;* but he considered that that calling was too troublesome and melancholy, and that *physicians* did smell of *glisters* like old devils; therefore he resolved he would study the laws; but seeing that there were but three scalled, an one bald-pated legist in that place, he departed from thence, and in his way made the bridge of Guard, and the amphitheatre of Nemes, in less than three hours, which nevertheless seems to be more than mortal man could do. After that he came to Avignon, where he was not above three days before he fell in love; for the women there take great delight in playing at the close buttock-game, because it is papal ground; which his tutor Epistemon perceiving, he drew him out of that place, and brought him to Valence in the Dauphiny, where he saw no great matter of recreation, only that the lubbards of the town did beat the scholars; which so incensed him with anger that when, upon a certain very fair Sunday, the people being at their public dancing in the streets, and one of the *scholars* offering to put himself into the ring, the bumkins would not let him; whereupon Pantagruel taking the scholar's part, so belaboured them with blows, and laid such load upon them, that he drove them all before him, even to the brink of the river Rhosne, and would have there drowned them, but that they did squat into the ground like moles, and there lay close a full half league under the river. The hole is to be seen there yet.

After that, he departed from thence, and in three strides and a leap came to Angiers, where he found himself very well, and would have continued there some space, but that the plague drove them away. So from thence he came to Bourges, where he studied a good long time, and profited very much in the faculty of the laws; and would sometimes say that *law books* were like a wonderful rich cloth of gold, edged with sirreverence; for in the world are no goodlier books to be seen, more ornate, nor more eloquent than the texts of the pandects; but the *bordering* of them, that is to say, the *gloss* of Accursius, is so vile, mean, and scandalous, that it is nothing but dirt and excrement.

Going from Bourges he came to Orleans, where he found store of sparkish *scholars* that made him great entertainment at his coming, and with whom he learned to play at *tennis* so well, that he was a master at that game: for the students there are excellent at it. And sometimes they carried him unto Cupid's gardens, there to recreate his person at the poussevant, or in and in. As for breaking his head with over-much study, he had an especial care not to do it in any case, for *fear of spoiling his eyes;* which he the rather observed, for that one of the *regents* there had often in his *lectures maintained, that nothing could be so hurtful to the sight as to have sore eyes.* So one day, when a scholar of his acquaintance (who had of learning not much more than his brethren, though, instead of that, he could *dance* very well, and play at *tennis*) was made a licentiate in law, he blazoned the licentiates of that university in this manner:

> "In his hand is always a racket,
> Or his tennis-ball in a placket:
> In a dance he neatly can trip it;
> And for law, it is all in his tippet."

CHAPTER VI

HOW PANTAGRUEL MET WITH A LIMOSIN, WHO AFFECTED TO SPEAK IN LEARNED PHRASE

UPON a certain day, I know not when, Pantagruel walking, after supper, with some of his fellow-students, without that gate of the city through which we enter on the road to Paris, encountered with a young handsome spruce scholar, that was coming upon the very same way; and, after they had saluted one another, asked him thus: "My friend, from whence comest thou now?" The scholar answered him, "From the *alme, inclyte* and celebrate academy, which is *vocitated Lutetia.*" "What is the meaning of this?" said Pantagruel to one of his men. "It is," answered he, "from Paris." "Thou comest from Paris, then," said Pantagruel; "and how do you spend your time there, you, my masters, the students of Paris?" The *scholar* answered, "We *transfretate* the *sequan* at the *ditucal* and *crepuscul;* we *deambulate* by the *compites* and *quadrives* of the urb; we *despumate* the *latial verbocination;* and like *verisimilarie amorabons,* we *captat* the benevolence of the *omnijugal, omniform,* and *omnigenal fœminine sex;* upon certain *diecules* we *invisat* the *lupanares,* and in a *venerian extase incultate* our *veretres,* into the *penitissime recesses* of the *pudends* of these *amicabilissim meretricules:* then do we *cauponisate* in the *meritory taberns* of the *pineapple,* the *castle,* the *magdalene,* and the *mule,* goodly *vervecine spatules performinated* with *petrosile:* and if by fortune there be rarity, or penury of *pecune* in our *marsupies;* and that they be exhausted of *ferruginean* metal for the shot, we *dimit* our *codices,* and *oppignerat* our vestiments, whilst we *prestolate* the coming of the *tabellaries* from the *penates,* and *patriotic lares.*" To which Pantagruel answered, "What devilish language is this? By the Lord, I think thou art some kind of heretic." "My Lord, no," said the scholar; "for *libentissimally,* as soon as it *illucesceth* any minutle slice of the day, I *demigrate* into one of these so well *architected* minsters, and there *irrorating* myself with fair *lustral* water, I mumble off little parcels of some *missick precation* of our *sacrificals;* and *submurmurating* my *horary precules,* I *elevate* and *absterg* my *anime* from its nocturnal *inquinations.* I *revere* the *olympicols;* I *latrially venere* the supernal *astripotent;* I *dilige* and *redame* my *proxims;* I observe the *decalogical precepts;* and, according to the *facultatule* of my *vires,* I do not *discede* from them one breadth of an *unguicule:* nevertheless it is *veriform,* that because *Mammona* doth not *supergurgitate* anything in my *locules,* that I am somewhat *rare* and *lent* to *supererrogate* the *elemosynes* to those *egents* that *ostially queritate* their *stipe.*"

"Prut, tut," said Pantagruel, "what doth this fool mean to say? I think he is upon the forging of some *diabolical* tongue, and that, incanter-like, he would *charm* us." To whom one of his men said, "Without doubt, sir, this fellow would counterfeit the language of the

Parisians; but he doth only flay the Latin, imagining, by so doing, that he doth mightily pindarize it in most eloquent terms, and strongly conceiteth himself to be therefore a great orator in the French, because he disdaineth the common manner of speaking." To which Pantagruel said, "Is it true?" The scholar answered, "My worshipful lord, my *genie* is not *apt nate* to that which this *flagitious nebulon* saith, to *excoriate* the *cuticle* of our *vernacular Gallick;* but *viceversally* I *gnave opere,* and by *veles* and *rames enite* to *locupletate* it with the *Latinicome* redundance." "By G—," said Pantagruel, "I will teach you to speak: but first come hither, and tell me whence thou art?" To this the scholar answered: "The *primeval origin* of my *aves* and *ataves* was *indigenary* of the *Lemovick* regions, where *requiesceth* the *corpor* of the *hagiotat* St. Martial." "I understand thee very well," said Pantagruel; "when all comes to all, thou art a Limosin, and thou wilt here, by thy affected speech, counterfeit the Parisians. Well now, come hither; I must shew thee a new trick, and handsomely give thee one fling." With this he took him by the throat, saying to him, "Thou flayest the Latin; by St. John, I will make thee flay the fox, for I will now flay thee alive." Then began the poor Limosin to cry: "Haw, gwid maaster! haw, Laord, my halp, and St. Marshaw! haw, I am worried: haw, my thropple, the bean of my cragg is bruk: haw, for Guaad's seck, lawt me lean, mawster; waw, waw, waw." "Now," said Pantagruel, "thou speakest naturally"; and so let him go: for the poor Limosin had totally bewrayed and thoroughly conshit his breeches, which were not deep and large, but made *à queüe de merlus.* "Then," said Pantagruel, "St. Alipantin, what civette? Foh, fah; to the devil with this turnip-eater. How he stinks!" And so let him depart. But this hug of Pantagruel's was such a terror to him all the days of his life, and he had such a thirst upon him, that he would often cry out that Pantagruel held him by the throat. And after some few years he died a Rowland death; a work of divine vengeance, shewing us that which saith the philosopher, and Aulus Gellius, *that it becometh us to speak according to the common language;* and that we should, as said Octavian Augustus, shun all strange words, with as much care as pilots of ships avoid the rocks in the sea.

CHAPTER VII

AFTER that Pantagruel had studied very well at Orleans, he resolved to see the great university of Paris: but before his departure he was informed that there was a huge big bell at St. Anian, in the said town of Orleans, under the ground, which had been there above two hundred and fourteen years: for it was so great, that they could not, by any device, get it so much as above the ground, although they used all the means that are found in Vitruvius de architectura, Alburtus de re ædificatoria, Euclid, Theon, Archimedes, and Hero de ingeniis; for all that was to no purpose. Wherefore, condescending heartily to the humble request of the citizens and inhabitants of the said town, he determined to remove it to the tower that was erected for it. With that he came to the place where it was, and lifted it out of the ground with his little finger, as easily as you would have done a hawk's bell: but before he would carry it to the aforesaid tower, he would needs make some music with it about the town, and ring it along all the streets, as he carried it in his hand; wherewith all the people were very glad: but there happened one great inconveniency; for with carrying it so, and ringing it about the streets, all the good Orleans wine *turned* instantly, and was spoiled: which nobody there did perceive till the night following; for every man found himself so a-dry with drinking these *flat* wines, that they did nothing but spit, and that as white as Maltha cotton, saying: "We have got the Pantagruel, and our very *throats are salted.*"

This done, he came to Paris with his retinue, and at his entry every one came out to see him (as you know well enough, that the people of Paris are sots by nature, by *b flat,* and *b sharp*) and beheld him with great astonishment, mixed with no less fear, that he would carry away the palace into some other country *à remotis,* as his father formerly had done the great bells at our *lady's* church, to tie about his *mare's* neck. Now after he had staid there a pretty space, and studied very well in all the seven liberal arts, he said it was a good town to live in, but not to die in, because the grave-digging rogues of St. Innocent used, in frosty nights, to warm their bums with dead man's bones. In his abode there, he went to see the library of St. Victor, very magnificent, especially in some books which

were there, of which followeth the catalogue.
Et primó,

> The two-horse tumbrel of salvation.
> The cod-piece of the law.
> The slippers or pantofles of the decretals.

The pomegranate of vice.
The clew-bottom of theology.
The duster, or foxtail-flap of preachers, composed by Turlupin.
The churning ballock of the valiant.
The henbane of the bishops.
Marmotretus de baboonis & apis, cum commento Dorbellis.
Decretum universitatis Parisiensis super gorgiositate muliercularum ad placitum.
The apparition of sancte Geltrude to a nun of Poissie, being in travel, at the bringing forth of a child.
Ars honestè fartandi (petandi) in societate, per M. Ortuinum.
The mustard pot of penance.
The gamashes, aliàs the boots of patience.
Formicarium artium.
De brodiorum usu, & honestate chopinandi, per Sylvestrem Prioratem Jacobinum.
The cuckold in court.
The frail of the scriveners.
The marriage-packet.
The crucible of contemplation.
The flimflams of the law.
The goad of wine.
The spur of cheese.
Decrotatorium scholarium.
Tartaretus de modo cacandi.
The bravades of Rome.
Bricot de differentiis souparum.
The tail-piece cushion, or close-breech of discipline.
The cobbled shoe of humility.
The trevet of good thoughts.
The kettle of magnanimity.
The cavilling intanglements of confessors.
The curates rap o'er the knuckles.
Reverendi patris fratris Lubini provincialis Bavardiæ, de coquendis lardonibus, libri tres.

Pasquilli doctoris marmorei, de capreolis cum chardoneta comedendis tempore papali ad ecclesia interdicto.

The invention of the holy cross, personated by six wilie clerks.

The spectacles of pilgrims bound for Rome.

Majoris, de modo faciendi boudinos puddings.

The bag-pipe of the prelates.

Beda de optimitate triparum.

The complaint of the barristers upon the reformation of comfits or sweetmeats.

The furred cat of the solicitors and attornies.

Of pease and bacon, cum commento.

The small vales, or drinking money of the indulgences.

Præclarissimi juris utriusque doctoris magistri Pilloti Raquedenari de bobelinandis glossæ Accursianæ baguenaudis repetitio enucidiluculidissima.

Stratagemata francharchieri de Baniolet.

Franctopinus or Churlbumpkinus de re militari, cum figuris Tevoti.

De usu et utilitate escorchandi—*i.e.,* flayandi equos et equas, authore magistro nostro de Quebecu.

The sauciness of country stewards.

M. N. Rostocostojambedanesse, de mustarda post prandium servienda, libri quatuordecim apostillati, per M. Vaurillonis.

The couillage or ballock-money of proctors.

Jabolenus de cosmographia purgatorii.

Quæstio subtilissima, utrum chimæra in vacuo bombinans posset comedere secundas intentiones; & fuit debatuta per decem hebdomadas in consilio Constantiensi.

The bridle-champer of the advocates.

Barbouillamenta Scoti.

The rasping and hard scraping of the cardinals.

De calcaribus removendis decades undecim, per M. Albericum de Rosata.

Ejusdem de castrametandis criminibus, libri tres.

The entrance of Antony de Leive into the territories of Brasil, or of the Greeks.

Marforii bacalarii cubantis Roma, de pelendis mascarendisque cardinalium mulis.

The said author's apology against those who alledge, that the pope's mule doth eat but at his hours.

Prognosticatio quæ incipit, Silvii Triquebille, balata, per M. N. Songecrusion.

Boudarini episcopi de emulgentiarum profectibus enneades novem, cum privilegio papali ad triennium & postea non.

The shitabrenna of the maids.

The bald arse of the widows.

The cowl or capouch of the monks.

The brimborions of the cælestine friars.

The passage-toll of beggarliness.

The teeth-chatter or gum-didder of lubberly lusks.

The paring-shovel of the theologues.

The drenching-horn of the masters of arts.

The scullions of Olkam the uninitiated clerk.

Magistri N. Fripesaucetis de grabellationibus horarum canonicarum, libri quadraginta.

Cullebutatorium confratriarum, incerto authore.

The rasher of cormorants, or greedy gluttons.

The rammishness of the Spaniards, supercoquelicanticked by friar Inigo.

The muttering of pitiful wretches.

Poltronismus rerum Italicarum, authore magistro Burnegad.

R. Lullius de batisfolagiis principum.

Calibistratorium caffardiæ, authore M. Jacobo Hocstraten hereti-cometrâ.

Codtickler de magistro nostrandorum magistro nostratorúmque beu-vetis, librî octo galantissimi.

The crackarades of bullists, copists, scriveners, clerks, abbreviators, notaries and reporters, lately compiled by Regis.

A perpetual almanack for those that have the gout and the pox.

Manera sweepandi fornacellos, per mag. Eccium.

The shable, or scimetar of merchants.

The pleasures of the monachal life.

The hodge-podge of hypocrites.

The history of the hobgoblins.

The ragamuffianism of the pensionary maimed soldiers.

The gulling fibs of commissaries.

The litter of treasurers.

The juglingatorium of sophisters.

Antipericatametanaparbeugedamphicribrationesmendicantium.

The periwinkle of ballad-makers.

The push-forward of the alchymists.

The niddy-noddy of the satchel-loaded seekers, by friar Bind-fastatis.

The shackles of religion.

The racket of swaggerers.

The leaning stock of old age.

The muzzle of nobility.

The ape's paternoster.

The crickets and hawks-bells of devotion.

The pot of the ember weeks.

The mortar of the politic life.

The flap of the hermits.

The riding-hood of the penitentiaries.

The trictrac of the knocking friars.

Blockheadodus de vita & honestate bragardochiorum.

Lyrippii sorbonici moralisationes, per M. Lupoldum.

The carrier horse bells of travellers.

The bibbings of the tippling bishops.

Tarrabalationes doctorum Coloniensium adversus Reuchlin.

The cymbals of ladies.

The dungers' martingale.

Whirling-friskorum Chasemarkerorum, per fratrem Crackwood-loguetis.

The clouted patches of a stout heart.

The mummery of the robin-good-fellows.

Gerson de auferibilitate papæ ab ecclesia.

The catalogue of nominated and graduated persons.

Jo. Dytebrodij de terribilitate excommunicationis, libellus acephalos.

Ingeniositas invocandi diabolo & diabolas, per M. Guingolphum.

The gallimaufry of the perpetually begging friars.

The morris-dance of the heretics.

The whinings of Cajetan.

Muddisnout doctoris cherubici de origine roughfootedarum & wry-neckedorum ritibus, libri septem.

Sixty-nine fat breviaries, or breviars.

The night-mare of the five orders of beggars.

The skinnery of the new start-ups, extracted out of the fallow butt, incornifistibulated upon in the Summa Angelica.

The raver in cases of conscience.

The fat belly of the presidents.

The baffling flowter of the abbots.

Sutoris adversus quendam qui vocaverat eum fripponatorem, & quod
fripponatores non sunt damnati ab ecclesia.
Cacatorium medicorum.
The chimney-sweeper of astrology.
Campi clysteriorum per C.
The bumsquibcracker of apothecaries.
The kiss-breech of chirurgery.
Justinianus de white-leperotis tollendis.
Antidotarium animæ.
Merlinus Coccaius de patria diabolorum.

Of which library some books are already printed, and the rest are
now in the press, in this noble city of Tubingen.

CHAPTER VIII

HOW PANTAGRUEL, BEING AT PARIS, RECEIVED LETTERS FROM HIS FATHER GARGANTUA, AND THE COPY OF THEM

PANTAGRUEL studied very hard, as you may well conceive, and
profited accordingly: for he had an excellent understanding, and
notable wit, together with a capacity. in point of memory, equal to
the measure of twelve oil-budgets, or butts of olives. And as he was
there abiding, one day, he received a letter from his father, in manner
as followeth:

"MOST DEAR SON,
"Amongst the gifts, graces, and prerogatives, with which the sovereign psalmator God Almighty hath endowed and adorned human
nature from the beginning, that seems to me most singular and excellent, by which we may in a mortal estate attain to a kind of immortality, and in the course of this transitory life perpetuate our name
and seed, which is done by a progeny issued from us in the lawful
bonds of matrimony; whereby, that, in some measure, is restored unto
us, which was taken from us by the sin of our first parents; to whom
it was said, that because they had not obeyed the commandment of
God their creator, they should die, and by death should be brought
to nought that so stately frame and psalmature, wherein the man at
first had been created. But by this means of seminal propagation,
there continueth in the children what was lost in the parents, and in
158

the grandchildren, that which perished in their fathers, and so successively until the day of the last judgment, when Jesus Christ shall have rendered up to God the Father his kingdom in a peaceable condition, out of all danger and contamination of sin: for then shall cease all generations and corruptions, and the elements leave off their continual transmutations; seeing the so much desired peace shall be attained unto and enjoyed, and that all things shall be brought to their end and period. And therefore, not without just and reasonable cause, do I give thanks to God my saviour and preserver, for that he hath enabled me to see my bald old age reflourish in thy youth: for when at his good pleasure, who rules and governs all things, my soul shall leave this mortal habitation, I shall not account myself wholly to die, but to pass from one place unto another: considering that in and by thee, I continue in my visible image living in the world, visiting and conversing with people of honour, and other my good friends, as I was wont to do. Which conversation of mine, although it was not without sin (because we are all of us trespassers, and therefore do continually beseech his divine majesty to blot our transgressions out of his memory), yet was it, by the help and grace of God, without all manner of reproach before men. Wherefore if those qualities of the mind but shine in thee, wherewith I am endowed, as in thee remaineth the perfect image of my body, thou wilt be esteemed by all men to be the perfect guardian and treasure of the immortality of our name: but if otherwise, I shall truly take but small pleasure to see it, considering that the lesser part of me, which is the body, would abide in thee; and the best, to wit, that which is the soul, and by which our name continues blessed amongst men, would be degenerate and bastardized. This I do not speak out of any distrust that I have of thy virtue, which I have heretofore already tried, but to encourage thee yet more earnestly to proceed from good to better. And that, which I now write unto thee, is not so much that thou should'st live in this virtuous course, as that thou should'st rejoice in so living, and, having lived, cheer up thyself with the like resolution in time to come. To the prosecution and accomplishment of which enterprise and generous undertaking, thou may'st easily remember how that I have spared nothing, but have so helped thee, as if I had had no other treasure in this world, but to see thee once in my life completely well-bred and accomplished, as well in virtue, honesty, and valour, as in all liberal knowledge and civility: and so to leave thee after my death, as a mirror, representing the person of me thy father; and if not so excellent, and such indeed as I do wish thee, yet such in desire.

"But although my deceased father, of happy memory, Grangousier, had bent his best endeavours to make me profit in all perfection and political knowledge, and that my labour and study was fully corre-spondent to, yea, went beyond his desire; nevertheless, as thou may'st well understand, the time was not so proper and fit for learning as it is at present, neither had I plenty of such good masters as thou hast had: for that time was darksome, obscured with clouds of ignor-ance, and savouring a little of the infelicity and calamity of the Goths, who had, wherever they set footing, destroyed all good literature, which in my age hath by the divine goodness been restored unto its former light and dignity, and that with such amendment and increase of knowledge, that now hardly should I be admitted unto the first form of the little grammar school-boys: I say, I, who in my youthful days was (and that justly) reputed the most learned of that age. Which I do not speak in vain-boasting, although I might lawfully do it in writing unto thee, by the authority of Marcus Tullius, in his book of old age, and the sentence of Plutarch, in the book, entitled, How a man may praise himself without envy: but to give thee an emulous encouragement to strive yet farther.

"Now it is that the minds of men are qualified with all manner of discipline, and the old sciences revived, which for many ages were extinct: now it is, that the learned languages are to their pristine purity restored—viz., Greek (without which a man may be ashamed to account himself a scholar), Hebrew, Arabic, Chaldean, and Latin. Printing likewise is now in use, so elegant, and so correct, that better cannot be imagined, although it was found out in my time but by divine inspiration; as by a diabolical suggestion, on the other side, was the invention of ordnance. All the world is full of knowing men, of most learned school-masters, and vast libraries; and it appears to me as a truth, that neither in Plato's time, nor Cicero's, nor Papinian's, there was ever such conveniency for studying, as we see at this day there is. Nor must any adventure henceforward to come in public, or represent himself in company, that hath not been pretty well pol-ished in the shop of Minerva. I see robbers, hangmen, free-booters, tapsters, ostlers, and such like, of the very rubbish of the people, more learned now, than the doctors and preachers were in my time.

"What shall I say? The very women and children have aspired to this praise and celestial manna of good learning: yet so it is that at the age I am now of, I have been constrained to learn the Greek tongue, which I contemned not like Cato, but had not the leisure in my younger years to attend the study of it. And I take much delight in the reading of Plutarch's morals, the pleasant dialogues of Plato, the monuments of Pausanias, and the antiquities of Athenæus, whilst I wait the hour wherein God my creator shall call me, and command me to depart from this earth and transitory pilgrimage. Wherefore, my son, I admonish thee to employ thy youth to profit as well as thou canst, both in thy studies and in virtue. Thou art at Paris, where the laudable examples of many brave men may stir up thy mind to many gallant actions; and hast likewise for thy tutor the learned Epistemon, who by his lively and vocal documents may instruct thee in the arts and sciences.

"I intend, and will have it so, that thou learn the languages perfectly. First of all, the Greek, as Quintilian will have it: secondly, the Latin; and then the Hebrew, for the holy Scripture-sake. And then the Chaldee and Arabic likewise. And that thou frame thy style in Greek, in imitation of Plato; and for the Latin, after Cicero. Let there be no history which thou shalt not have ready in thy memory; and to help thee therein, the books of cosmography will be very conducible. Of the liberal arts of geometry, arithmetic, and music, I gave thee some taste when thou wert yet little, and not above five or six years old; proceed further in them, and learn the remainder if thou canst. As for astronomy, study all the rules thereof: let pass nevertheless the divining and judicial astrology and the art of Lullius, as being nothing else but plain cheats and vanities. As for the civil law, of that I would have thee to know the texts by heart, and then to confer them with philosophy.

"Now in matter of the knowledge of the works of nature, I would have thee to study that exactly; so that there be no sea, river, or fountain, of which thou dost not know the fishes; all the fowls of the air; all the several kinds of shrubs and trees, whether in forest or orchard: all sorts of herbs and flowers that grow upon the ground; all the various metals that are hid within the bowels of the earth; together with all the diversity of precious stones that are to be seen in the orient and south parts of the world: let nothing of all these be hidden from thee. Then fail not most carefully to peruse the books of the Greek, Arabian and Latin physicians; not despising the talmudists and cabalists; and by frequent anatomies get thee the perfect knowledge of the microcosm, which is man. And at some hours of the day apply thy mind to the study of the holy Scriptures: first in Greek, the New Testament with the Epistles of the Apostles; and then the Old Testament in Hebrew. In brief, let me see thee an abyss and bottomless-pit of knowledge: for from henceforward, as thou growest great and becomest a man, thou must part from this tranquillity and rest of study; thou must learn chivalry, warfare, and the exercise of the field, the better thereby to defend my house and our friends, and to succour and protect them at all their needs against the invasion and assaults of evil-doers.

"Furthermore, I will that very shortly thou try how much thou hast profited, which thou canst not better do than by maintaining publicly theses and conclusions in all arts, against all persons whatsoever, and by haunting the company of learned men, both at Paris and otherwhere. But because, as the wise man Soloman saith, wisdom entereth not into a malicious mind, and that science without conscience is but the ruin of the soul; it behoveth thee to serve, to love, to fear God, and on him to cast all thy thoughts and all thy hope, and, by faith formed in charity, to cleave unto him, so that thou mayest never be separated from him by thy sins. Suspect the abuses of the world: set not thy heart upon vanity, for this life is transitory, but the word of the Lord endureth for ever. Be serviceable to all thy neighbours, and love them as thyself: reverence thy præceptors; shun the conversation of those whom thou desirest not to resemble, and receive not in vain the graces which God hath bestowed upon thee. And when thou shall see that thou hast attained to all the knowledge that is to be acquired in that part, return unto me, that I may see thee, and give thee my blessing before I die. My son, the peace and grace of our Lord be with thee. Amen.

"From Utopia, the 17th day
 of the month of March.

"Thy father, GARGANTUA."

These letters being received and read, Pantagruel plucked up his heart, took a fresh courage to him, and was inflamed with a desire to profit in his studies more than ever; so that if you had seen him, how he took pains, and how he advanced in learning, you would have said that the vivacity of his spirit, amidst the books, was like a great fire amongst dry wood; so active it was, vigorous, and indefatigable.

CHAPTER IX

HOW PANTAGRUEL FOUND PANURGE, WHOM HE LOVED
ALL HIS LIFE-TIME

ONE day as Pantagruel was taking a walk without the city, towards St. Anthony's abbey, discoursing and philosophating with his own servants, and some other scholars, he met wth a young man of a very comely stature, and surpassing handsome in all the lineaments of his body, but in several parts thereof most pitifully wounded; in such bad equipage in matter of his apparel, which was but tatters and rags, and every way so far out of order, that he seemed to have been fighting with mastiff-dogs, from whose fury he had made an escape; or, to say better, he looked, in the condition wherein he then was, like an apple-gatherer of the country of Perche.

As far off as Pantagruel saw him, he said to those that stood by, "Do you see that man there, who is coming hither upon the road from Charenton-bridge? By my faith, he is only poor in fortune; for I may assure you, that by his physiognomy it appeareth that nature hath extracted him from some rich and noble race, and that too much curiosity hath thrown him upon adventures, which possibly have reduced him to this indigence, want, and penury." Now as he was just among them, Pantagruel said unto him, "Let me entreat you, friend, to stop here a little, and answer me to that which I shall ask you, and I am confident you will not think your time ill bestowed; for I have an extreme desire (according to my ability) to give you some supply in this distress wherein I see you are; because I do very much commiserate your case, which truly moves me to great pity: therefore, my friend, tell me who you are? whence you come? whither you go? what you desire? and what your name is?" The companion answered him in the German tongue thus:

"*Iunker, gott geb euch gluck und heil zuvor. Lieber yunker, ich las euch wissen das daihr mich von fragt, ist ein arm und erbamlich ding, und wer viel darvon zu sagen, welches euch verdrussig zu horen und mir zu erzelen, wer, wiewol die poeten und oratorn vortzeiten haben gesagt in ihren spruchen und sentenzen das die gedecktnus des ellendz und armuts vorlangst erlitten ist ein grosse lust.*" "My friend," said Pantagruel, "I have no skill in that gibberish of yours; therefore, if you would have us to understand you, speak to us in some other language." Then did the drole answer him thus:

163

"Albarildim gotfano dechmin brin alabo dordio falbroth ringuam albaras. Nin porthzadikin almucatin milko prin alelmin en thoth dalheben ensouim: kuthim al dum alkatin nim broth dechoth porth min michais im endoth, pruch dalmaisulum hol moth danfrihim lupaldas im voldemoth. Nin hur diavosth munarbotim dalgousch pulfrapin duch in scoth pruch galeth dal Chinon, minfoulchrich al conin butathen doth dal prin." "Do you understand none of this?" said Pantagruel to the company. "I believe," said Epistemon, "that this is the language of the antipodes, and such a hard one, that the devil himself knows not what to make of it." Then said Pantagruel, "Gossip, I know not if the walls do comprehend the meaning of your words; but none of us here doth so much as understand one syllable of them." Then said my blade again:

"Signor mio, voi vedete per essempio che la cornemusa non suona mai, se non ha il ventre pieno: cosi io parimente non vi saprei contare le mie fortune, se prima il tribulato ventre non ha la solita refectione. Alquale è adviso che le mani e li denti abbiano perso il loro ordine naturale e del tutto annichilati." To which Epistemon answered, "As much of the one as of the other, and nothing of either." Then said Panurge:

"My lord, if the generosity of your mind be suitable to your body, you would naturally have pity of me. For nature made us equal: but fortune has exalted some, and other some has depressed. Nevertheless, though virtue is despised, and worthy men depressed; yet, till the end, none can be pronounced happy." "Yet less do I understand of this," said Pantagruel. Then said Panurge:

"Jona andie gaussa goussey etan beharda er remedio beharde de versela ysser landa. Anbat es otoy y es nausu ey nessassut gourray propposian ordine den. Non yssena bayte facheria egabe gen herassy badea sadassu noura assia: aran hondavan gaulde cydassu nydassuna: estou oussye ecvinau soury hin er darstura eguy harm: Genicoa plasar vadu." "Are you there," said Eudemon, "Genicoa?" To this, said Carpalim, "St. Trinian's rammer unstitch your bum, for I had almost understood it." Then answered Panurge:

"Prug frest frinst sorgdmand strochdi dyhds pag breleland Gravot chavygni pomardiere rusth pkalldracg Deviniere pres Nays; couille Kalmuch monach drupp del meupplist rincque drind dodelp up drent loch mine stzincq jald de vins ders cordelis bur jocst stzanpenards." "Do you speak christian," said Epistemon, "or the gypsey language?" "Nay, it is lantern language," said another.

Then said Panurge:

"Heere, ik en spreck anders gheen taele dankersten taele; my dunkt nogtans, al en seg ik u niet een wordt, mynen noot verklaert genoegh wat ik begeere: geeft my uyt bermhertigheyt yets waar van ik gevoet magh syn." To which answered Pantagruel, "As much of that." Then said Panurge:

"Sennor, de tanto hablar yo Soy cansado, porque supplico à vuestra excellencia que mire a los precettos evangelicos, para que ellos muevan vuestra excellencia a lo que es de consciencia, y si ellos no bastaren: para mover vuestra reverlencia a piedad supplico que mire a la piedad natural, laqual yo creo que le movera, como es de razon: y con esso, no digo mas." "Truly, my friend," said Pantagruel, "I doubt not but you can speak divers languages; but tell us that which you would have us to do for you in some tongue, which you conceive we may understand." Then said the companion:

"Myn herr, eendog ieg met ingen tunge talede lygesom boern, oeg uskellig creatuer: mine claedebon och mit legioms magerhed udviser alligevel klarlig huad ting mig best behof gioris, som er sandelig mad ock dricke: huorfor forbarme dig ofvermig, oc befal at gisve mig noget, af huilket jeg kand styre min giocendis mage, ligerviis som mand Cerbero en suppe forsetter: saa skalt du lefve lœnge oc lyksalig." "I think, really," said Eusthenes, "that the Goths spoke thus of old: and that, if it pleased God, we should all of us speak so with our tails." Then again said Panurge:

"Adon, sealom lechai im ischar harob hal hebdeca bimeherath thithén li kikar lehem: chanchat ub laah al Adonai cho nen ral." To which answered Epistemon, "At this time have I understood him very well; for it is the Hebrew tongue most rhetorically pronounced." Then again said the merry fellow:

"Despota tinyn panagathe, diati si mi ouk artodotis? Horas gar limo analiscomenon eme athlion, ke en to metaxi me ouk eleis oudamos, zetis de par emou ha ou chre. Ke homos philologi pantes homologousi tote logous te ke remata peritta hyparchin opote pragma afto pasi delon esti. Entha gar anankei monon logi isin, hina pragmata [hon peri amphisbetoumen] me prosphoros epiphinete." "What!" said Carpalim, Pantagruel's footman, "it is Greek, I have understood him: and how? hast thou dwelt any while in Greece?" Then said the drole again:

"Agonou dont oussys vous desdaignez algarou: nou den faron zamist vous mariston ulbrou, fousquez voubrol tam bredaguez maupreton

165

*den goulhoust, daguez daguez non croupys fost bardonnoffist nou-
grou: agou paston tol nalprissys hourtou los echatonous, prou
dhouguys, brol pany gou den bascrou noudous caguons goufren goul
oustarouppassou?"* "Methinks I understand him," said Pantagruel;
"for either it is the language of my country of Utopia, or sounds very
like it." And as he was about to have begun some argument, the companion said:

"*Jam toties vos per sacra, perque deos deasque omnes obtestatus
sum, ut si qua vos pietas permovet, egestatem meam solaremini, nec
hilum proficio clamans & ejulans: sinite, quæso, sinite, viri impii,
quo me fata vocant abire: nec ultrà vanis vestris interpellationibus
obtundatis, memores veteris illius adagii, quo venter famelicus auriculis
carere dicitur.*" "Well, my friend," said Pantagruel, "but cannot
you speak French?" "That I can do, sir, very well," said the companion, "God be thanked: it is my natural language and mother-
tongue; for I was born and bred in my younger years in the garden
of France, to wit, Touraine." Then said Pantagruel, "Tell us what
is your name, and from whence you are come; for by my faith, I
have already stamped in my mind such a deep impression of love
towards you, that, if you will condescend unto my will, you shall
not depart out of my company, and you and I shall make up another
couple of friends, such as Æneas and Achates were." "Sir," said the
companion, "my true and proper christian name is Panurge; and I am
just come out of Turky, to which country I was carried away prisoner
at that time, when they went to Metelin with a mischief: and willingly
would I relate unto you my fortunes, which are more wonderful
than those of Ulysses were; but seeing that it pleaseth you to retain
me with you, I most heartily accept of the offer, protesting never to
leave you, should you go to all the devils in hell. We shall have
therefore more leisure at another time, and a fitter opportunity wherein to report them: for at this present I am in a very urgent necessity
to feed; my teeth are sharp, my belly empty, my throat dry, and my
stomach fierce and craving; all is ready, if you will but set me to
work: it will be as good as a balsam for sore eyes. to see me gulch
and raven it; for God's sake give order for it." Then Pantagruel
commanded that they should carry him home, and provide him good
store of victuals; which being done, he eat very well that evening,
and, capon-like, went early to bed, then slept until dinner-time the
next day; so that he made but three steps and one leap from the bed
to the board.

CHAPTER X

HOW PANTAGRUEL EQUITABLY DECIDED A CAUSE WHICH WAS WONDERFULLY
INTRICATE AND OBSCURE: WHEREBY HE WAS REPUTED TO HAVE A
MOST ADMIRABLE JUDGMENT

PANTAGRUEL, very well remembering his father's letter and
admonitions, would one day make trial of his knowledge. Thereupon, in all the *carrefours* (cross-ways) streets and corners of the
city he set up conclusions to the number of nine thousand seven hundred sixty and four, in all manner of learning, touching in them the
hardest doubts that are in any science. And first of all in the Fodder-
street he held dispute against all the regents, professors of arts, and
orators, and did so gallantly, that he overthrew them, and set them
all upon their tails. He went afterwards to the Sorbonne, where he
maintained arguments against all the theologians, for the space of six
weeks, from four o'clock in the morning until six in the evening;
except an interval of two hours to refresh themselves, and take their
repast. And at this were present the greatest part of the lords of the
court, the masters of request, presidents, counsellors, those of the
accompts, secretaries, advocates and others: as also the sheriffs of the
said town, with the physicians and professors of the canon-law.
Amongst which it is to be remarked, that the greatest part were resty
and head-strong, and in their opinions obstinate: but he took such
course with them, that, for all their ergoes and fallacies, he put their
backs to the wall, gravelled them in the deepest questions, and made
it visibly appear to the world, that, compared to him, they were but
monkies and a knot of muffled calves. Whereupon everybody began to keep a bustling noise, and talk of his so marvellous knowledge,
through all degrees of persons in both sexes, even to the very lan-
dresses, brokers, roast-meat-sellers, pen-knife-makers and others; who,
when he past along in the street, would say, "This is he!" In which
he took delight, as Demosthenes the prince of Greek orators did, when
a mumping old hag, pointing at him with her fingers, said, "This is
the man."

Now at this same very time there was a suit in law, depending
in court between two great lords; of which one was called my lord
Kissbreech, plaintiff, of one side; and the other my lord Suckfist, defendant, of the other: whose controversy was so high and difficult
in law, that the court of parliament could make nothing of it. And

therefore, by the commandment of the king, there were assembled ·
four of the greatest and most learned of all the parliaments of France
together with the great council, and all the principal regents of the
universities, not only of France, but of England also and Italy; such
as Jason, Philippus-Decius, Petrus de Petronibus, and a rabble of
other old Rabanists; who being thus met together, after they had
thereupon consulted for the space of six and forty weeks, finding that
they could not fasten their teeth in it, nor with such clearness understand the case, as that they might in any manner of way be able to
right it, or take up the difference betwixt the two aforesaid parties,
it did so grievously vex them, that they most villainously conshit themselves for shame. In this great extremity, one amongst them, named
du Douhet, the learnedest of all, and more expert and prudent than
any of the rest, whilst one day they were thus at their wit's-end, all-
to-be-dunced and philogrobolized in their brains, said unto them:
"We have been here, my masters, a good long space, without doing
anything else than trifle away both time and money, and can find
neither brim nor bottom in this matter: for the more we study about
it, the less we understand therein, which is a great shame and disgrace
to us, and a heavy burthen to our consciences; yea, such, that in my
opinion we should not rid ourselves of it without dishonour, unless
we take some other course; for we do nothing but dote in our consultations.

"See therefore what I have thought upon: you have heard much
talking of that worthy personage named master Pantagruel, who hath
been found to be learned above capacity of this present age, by the
proofs he gave in those great disputations, which he held publicly
against all men. My opinion is, that we send for him, to confer with
him about this business: for never any man will compass the bringing
of it to an end, if he do it not."

Hereunto all the counsellors and doctors willingly agreed, and according to that their result, having instantly sent for him, they entreated him to be pleased to canvas the process and sift it thoroughly;
that, after a deep search and narrow examination of all the points
thereof, he might forthwith make the report unto them, such as he
shall think good in true and legal knowledge. To this effect they
delivered into his hands the bags wherein were the writs and pancarts
concerning that suit, which, for bulk and weight, were almost enough
to lade four great stoned asses. But Pantagruel said unto them, "Are
the two lords, between whom this debate and process is, yet living?"

It was answered him, "Yes." "To what a devil then," said he, "serve so many paltry heaps, and bundles of papers and copies which you give me? Is it no better to hear their controversy from their own mouths, whilst they are face to face before us, than to read these vile fopperies, which are nothing but chicaneries, deceits, diabolical cozenages of Cepola, pernicious sleights, and subversions of equity? For I am sure that you, and all those through whose hands this process hath passed, have by your devices added what you could to in *pro & contra;* in such sort, that, although their difference perhaps was clear and easy enough to determine at first, you have perplexed and puzzled the cause, by the frivolous, sottish, unreasonable, and foolish reasons and opinions of Accursius, Baldus, Bartolus de Castro, de Imola, Hippolytus, Panormitanus, Bertachin, Alexander, Curtius, and those other old mastiffs, who never understood the least law of the pandects: they being but mere blockheads and great tithe-calves, ignorant of all that which was needful for the understanding of the laws. For (as it is most certain) they had not the knowledge either of the Greek or Latin tongue, but only of the Gothic and Barbarian. The laws nevertheless were first taken from the Greeks, according to the testimony of Ulpian, l. poster. de origine juris; which we likewise may perceive, by that all the laws are full of Greek words and sentences. And then we find that they are reduced into a Latin style, the most elegant and ornate that whole language is able to afford, without excepting that of any that ever wrote therein; nay, not of Sallust, Varro, Cicero, Seneca, Titus Livius, nor Quintilian. How then could these old dotards be able to understand aright the text of the laws, who never in their time had looked upon a good Latin book, as doth evidently enough appear by the rudeness of their style; which is fitter for a chimney-sweeper, a cook, or a scullion, than for a jurisconsult and doctor in the laws?

"Furthermore, seeing the laws are excerpted out of the middle of moral and natural philosophy, how should these fools have understood it, that have, by G——, studied less in philosophy than my mule? In respect of human learning, and the knowledge of antiquities and histories, they were truly laden with those faculties as a toad is with feathers; and yet of all this the laws are so full, that without it they cannot be understood; as I intend more fully to shew unto you in a peculiar treatise, which on that purpose I am about to publish. Therefore if you will that I meddle in this process; first, cause all these papers to be burnt; secondly, make the two gentlemen come

169

personally before me! and afterwards, when I shall have heard them, I will tell you my opinion freely, without any fiction or dissimulation whatsoever."

Some amongst them did contradict this motion; as you know that in all companies there are more fools than wise men, and that the greater part always surmounts the better; as saith Titus Livius, in speaking of the Carthaginians. But the aforesaid du Douhet held the contrary opinion, maintaining that Pantagruel had said well, and what was right, in affirming that these records, bills of inquest, replies, rejoinders, exceptions, depositions, and other such diableries of truth-entangling writs, were but engines wherewith to overthrow justice, and unnecessarily to prolong such suits as did depend before them; and that therefore the devil would carry them all away to hell, if they did not take another course, and proceeded not in times coming according to the prescripts of evangelical and philosophical equity. In fine, all the papers were burnt, and the two gentlemen summoned and personally convented; at whose appearance before the court, Pantagruel said unto them, "Are you they that have this great difference betwixt you?" "Yes, my lord," said they. "Which of you," said Pantagruel, "is the plaintiff?" "It is I," said my lord Kissbreech. "Go too then, my friend," said he, "and relate your matter unto me from point to point, according to the real truth; or else (by cock's body) if I find you to lie so much as in one word, I will make you shorter by the head, and take it from off your shoulders; to shew others, by your example, that in justice and judgment men ought to speak nothing but the truth: therefore take heed you do not add nor impair anything in the narration of your case. Begin."

CHAPTER XI

HOW THE LORDS OF KISSBREECH AND SUCKFIST DID PLEAD
BEFORE PANTAGRUEL, WITHOUT ADVOCATES

THEN began Kissbreech in manner as followeth: "My lord, it is true that a good woman of my house carried eggs to the market to sell." "Be covered, Kissbreech," said Pantagruel. "Thanks to you, my lord," said the lord Kissbreech: "but to the purpose. There passed, betwixt the two tropics, the sum of threepence towards the zenith, and a halfpenny; forasmuch as the Riphæan mountains had been that year oppressed with a great sterility of counterfeit gudgeons, and shews without substance, by means of the babbling tattle and fond fibs, seditiously raised between the gibble-gabblers and Accursian gibberish-mongers, for the rebellion of the Swissers, who assembled themselves to the full number of the bumbees and myrmidons, to go a handsel-getting on the first day of the new year, at that very time when they give brewis to the oxen, and deliver the key of the coals to the country-girls, for serving in of the oats to the dogs. All the night long they did nothing else (keeping their hands still upon the pot) but dispatch bulls a-foot, and bulls a-horseback, to stop the boats: for the tailors and salesmen would have made of the stolen shreads a goodly sagbut to cover the face of the ocean, which then was great with child of a potful of cabbage, according to the opinion of the hay-bundle-makers: but the physicians said, that by the urine they could discern no manifest sign of the bustard's pace, nor how to eat double-tongued mattocks with mustard, unless the lords and gentlemen of the court should be pleased to give by b. mol. express command to the pox, not to run about any longer, in gleaning up of copper-smiths and tinkers: for the jobbernowls had already a pretty good beginning in their dance of the Bretish jig, called the estrindore, to a perfect diapason, with one foot in the fire, and their heads in the middle, as good man Ragot was wont to say.

"Ha, my masters, God moderates all things, and disposeth of them at His pleasure; so that against unlucky fortune a carter broke his frisking whip, which was all the wind-instrument he had: this was done at his return from the little paultry town, even then when master Antitus of Cresseplots was licentiated, and had past his degrees in all dullery and blockishness, according to this sentence of the canonists, *Beati dunces, quoniam ipsi stumblaverunt.* But that which makes lent to be so high, by St. Fiacre of Bry, is for nothing else but that the pentecost never comes but to my cost: yet on afore there, ho: a little rain stills a great wind; and we must think so, seeing that the sergeant hath propounded the matter so far above my reach, that the clerks and secondaries could not with the benefit thereof lick their fingers feathered with ganders, so orbicularly, as they were wont in other things to do. And we do manifestly see, that every one acknowledgeth himself to be in the error, wherewith another hath been charged, reserving only those cases whereby we are obliged to take an ocular inspection in a prospective glass of these things, towards the place in the chimney, where hangeth the sign of the wine of forty girths which have been always accounted very necessary for the number of twenty panels and pack-saddles of the bankrupt protectionaries of five years' respite. Howsoever, at least he, that would not let fly the fowl before the cheesecakes, ought in law to have discovered his reason why not; for the memory is often lost with a wayward shooing. Well, God keep Theobald Mitain from all danger." Then said Pantagruel, "Hold there: ho my friend, soft and fair; speak at leisure, and soberly, without putting yourself in choler: I understand the case, go on." "Now then, my lord, "said Kissbreech, "the foresaid good woman, saying her gaudez and audinos, could not cover herself with a treacherous back-blow ascending by the wounds and passions of the privileges of the university; unless by the virtue of a warming-pan she had angelically fomented every part of her body, in covering them with a hedge of garden beds: then giving in a swift unavoidable thrust very near to the place where they sell the old rags, whereof the painters of Flanders make great use, when they are about neatly to clap on shoes on grashoppers, locusts, cigals, and such like fly-fowls; so strange to us, that I am wonderfully astonished why the world doth not lay, seeing it is so good to hatch."

Here the lord of Suckfist would have interrupted him, and spoken somewhat: whereupon Pantagruel said unto him, "Hush! by St. Anthony's belly, doth it become thee to speak without command? I sweat, here, and crack my brain to understand the proceeding of your mutual difference, and yet thou comest to trouble and disquiet me. Peace, in the devil's name, peace; thou shalt be permitted to speak thy belly-full when this man hath done, and no sooner. Go on," said he to Kissbreech, "speak calmly, and do not overheat yourself with too much haste."

"I perceiving then," said Kissbreech, "that the pragmatic sanction did make no mention of it, and that the holy pope to every one gave liberty to fart at his own ease, provided the blankets had no streaks: wherein the liars were to be crossed with a ruffian-like crew, and the rainbow, being newly sharpened at Milan to bring forth larks, gave his full consent, that the good woman should tread down the heel of the hip-gut pangs, by virtue of a solemn protestation put in by the little testiculated or codsted fishes; which, to tell the truth, were at that time very necessary for understanding the syntax and construction of old boots. Therefore John Calfe, her cousin-gervais once removed, with a log from the woodstack, very seriously advised her not to put herself into the hazard of quagswagging in the lee, to be scowred with buck of linen cloths, till first she had kindled the paper. This counsel she laid hold on, because he desired her to take nothing, and throw out, for *non de ponte vadit, qui cum sapientia cadit*. Matters thus standing, seeing the members of that committee did not fully agree amongst themselves in casting up the number of the Almany whistles, whereof were framed those spectacles for princes, which have been lately printed at Antwerp, I must needs think that it makes a bad return of the writ, and that the adverse party is not to be believed, *in sacer verbo dotis*. For that having a great desire to obey the pleasure of the king, I armed myself from toe to top with belly-furniture, of the soles of good venison-pasties, to go see how my grape-gatherers and vintagers had pinked and cut full of small holes their high-coped caps, to lecher it the better, and play at in and in. And indeed the time was very dangerous in coming from the fair, in so far that many trained bowmen were cast at the muster, and quite rejected, although the chimney-tops were high enough, according to the proportion of the windgalls, and the malaunders lamibaudichon. And by this means there was that year great abundance, throughout all the country of Artois, of tawny buzzing beetles, to the no small profit of the gentlemen-great-stick-faggot-carriers, when they did eat without disdaining the cocklicranes, till their belly was like to crack with it again. As for my part, such is my christian charity towards my neighbours, that I could wish from my heart every one had as good a voice: it would make us play the better at the tennis and the baloon. And truly, my lord, to express the real truth without dissimulation, I cannot but say, that those pretty subtle devices, which are found out in the etymologizing of patins, would descend more easily into the river of Seine, to serve for ever at the miller's bridge; as it was heretofore decreed by the king of the Canarians, which is to be seen in the registry and records within the clerk's office of this house.

"And therefore, my lord, I do most humbly require that by your lordship there may be said and declared upon the case what is reasonable, with costs, damages, and interest." Then said Pantagruel, "My friend, is this all you have to say?" Kissbreech answered, "Yes, my lord; for I have told all the tu-autem, and have not varied at all, upon mine honour, in so much as one single word." "You then," said Pantagruel, "my lord of Suckfist, say what you will, and be brief, without omitting nevertheless anything that may serve to the purpose."

CHAPTER XII

THEN began the lord Suckfist in manner as followeth: "My lord, and you my masters, if the iniquity of men were as easily seen in categorical judgment, as we can discern flies in a milk-pot, the world's four oxen had not been so eaten up with rats, nor had so many ears upon the earth been nibbled away so scurvily. For although all that my adversary hath spoken be of down, insomuch as concerns the letter and history of the factum; yet nevertheless the subtilties, the fineness, the little sly intanglements are hid under the rose-pot.

"Should I endure, that when I am eating my pottage, equal with the best, and that without thinking or speaking any manner of ill, they rudely come to vex, trouble, and perplex my brains ringing in my ears that old jingle.

'He that will in his pottage drink,
When he is dead, shall not see one wink.'

And, good lady! how many great captains have we seen in the day of battle, when in open field the sacrament was distributed in luncheons of the sanctified bread of the confraternity, the more honestly to nod their heads, play on the lute, crack with their tails, and make pretty little platform leaps? But now the world is unshackled from the corners of the packs of Leicester, one flies out lewdly and becomes debauched; another likewise, five, four and two, and that at such random, that if the court take not some course therein, it will make as bad a season in matter of gleaning this year, as ever it made, or it will make goblets. If any poor creature goes to the stoves to illuminate his muzzle a cowturd, or to buy winter boots, and that the serjeants passing by, or those of the watch happen to receive the decoction of a clyster, or the fecal matter of a close stool, upon their rustling-wrangling-clutter-keeping masterships; should any because of that make bold to clip the shillings and testers, and fry the wooden dishes? Sometimes when we think one thing, God does another; and when the sun is set, all beasts are in the shade. Let me never be believed again, if I do not gallantly prove it by several people that have seen the light of the day.

"In the year thirty and six, buying a Dutch curtail, which was a middle-sized horse, both high and short, of a wool good enough, and

174

dyed in grain, as the goldsmiths assured me, although the notary put an &c. in it: I told really that I was not a clerk of so much learning as to snatch at the moon with my teeth; but as for the butter-firkin, where Vulcanian's deeds and evidences were sealed, the rumour was, and that report, thereof went current, the salt-beef will make one find the way to the wine without a candle, though it were hid in the bottom of a collier's sack, and that with his drawers on he were mounted on a barbed horse furnished with a fronstal, and such arms, thighs, and leg-pieces as are requisite for the well frying and broiling of a swaggering sauciness. Here is a sheep's-head, and it is well they make a proverb of this, that it is good to see black cows in burnt wood, when one attains to the enjoyment of his love. I had a consultation upon this point with my masters the clerks, who for resolution concluded in frisesomorum, that there is nothing like to mowing in the summer, and sweeping clean away in water, well garnished with paper, ink, pens, and penknives of Lyons upon the river of Rhosne; dolopym dolop of, tarabin tarabas, tut prut pish: for incontinently after that armour begins to smell of garlic, the rust will go near to eat the liver, not of him that wears it; and then do they nothing else but withstand others courses, and wryneckedly set up their bristles against one another, in lightly passing over their afternoon's sleep: and this is that which maketh salt so dear. My lords, believe not, when the said good woman had, with birdlime, caught the shovelar fowl, the better before a serjeant's witness, to deliver the younger son's portion to him, that the sheep's pluck, or hog's haslet, did dodge and shrink back in the userer's purses, or that there could be anything better to preserve one from the cannibals, than to take a rope of onions, knit with three hundred turnips, and a little of a calf's chaldern of the best allay that the alchymists have: and that they lute and calcine these pantofflés, muf in muf out, mouflin mouflard, with the fine sauce of the juice of the rabble-rout, whilst they hide themselves in some pretty moldwarphole, saving always the bacon. Now if the dice will not favour you with any other throw but ambesace, and the chance of three at the great end, mark well the ace; then take me your dame, settle her in a corner of the bed, and whisk me her up drille trille, there, there: then a hearty draught of the best depiscando grenovillibus, in despite of the frogs; whose fair coarse bebuskined stockings shall be set apart for the little mued goslings which, fattened in a coop, take delight to sport themselves at the wag-

175

tail game, waiting for the beating of the metal, and heating of the wax, by the slavering drivellers of consolation.

"Very true it is, that the four oxen which are in debate, and whereof mention was made, were somewhat short in memory: nevertheless, to understand the game aright, they feared neither the cormorant nor mallard of Savoy, which put the good people of my country in great hope, that their children sometime should become very skilful in algorism: therefore is it, that by a law rubrick and special sentence thereof that we cannot fail to take the wolf, if we make our hedges higher than the windmill, whereof somewhat was spoken by the plaintiff. But the great devil did envy it, and put the High-dutch far behind, who played the devils in swilling down and tippling at the good liquor: trink meen-heer, trink, trink. By two of my table-men, in the corner-point I have gained the lurch; for it is not probable, nor is there any appearance of truth in this saying, At Paris, upon a little bridge, the hen is proportionable: and were they as copped and high-crested as marish whoops, if veritably they did not sacrifice the printers pumpet-balls at Moreb, with a new edge set upon them by text letters, or those of a swift-writing hand, it is all one to me; so that the headband of the book breed not moths or worms in it. And put the case, that the coupling together of the buck-hounds, the little puppies should have waxed proud before the notary could have given an account of the serving of his writ by the cabalistic art, it will necessarily follow (under correction of the better judgment of the court) that six acres of meadow-ground of the greatest breadth will make three buts of fine ink, without paying ready money. Considering that at the funeral of king Charles, we might have had the fathom in open market for deuce-ace: this I may affirm with a safe conscience, upon my oath of wool.

"And I see ordinarily in all good bagpipes, that when they go to the counterfeiting of the chirping of small birds, by swinging a broom three times about a chimney, and putting his name upon record; they do nothing but bend a cross-bow backward, and wind a horn, if perhaps it be too hot; and that by making it fast to a rope he was to draw, immediately after the sight of the letters, the cows were restored to him. Such another sentence after the homeliest manner was pronounced in the seventeenth year, because of the bad government of Louzefougarouse; whereunto it may please the court to have regard. I desire to be rightly understood; for truly I say not, but that in all equity, and with an upright conscience, those may very

176

well be dispossessed, who drink holy-water, as one would do a weaver's shuttle; whereof suppositories are made to those that will not resign, but on the terms of ell and tell, and giving of one thing for another. Tunc, my lords, *quid juris pro minoribus?* For the common custom of the Salic law is such, that the first incendiary or firebrand of sedition, that flays the cow, and wipes his nose in a full concert of music, without blowing in the cobler's stitches, should in the time of the nightmare sublimate the penury of his member by moss gathered when people are like to founder themselves at the mass at midnight, to give the estrapade to these white wines of Anjou, that do gambetta, neck to neck, after the fashion of Britanny. Concluding, as before, with costs, damages, and interests."

After that the lord of Suckfist had ended, Pantagruel said to the lord of Kissbreech, "My friend, have you a mind to make any reply to what is said?" "No, my lord," answered Kissbreech; "for I have spoke all I intended, and nothing but the truth: therefore put an end for God's sake to our difference: for we are here at great charge."

CHAPTER XIII

HOW PANTAGRUEL GAVE JUDGMENT UPON THE DIFFERENCE OF THE TWO LORDS

THEN Pantagruel, rising up, assembled all the presidents, counsellors, and doctors that were there, and said unto them; "Come now, my masters, you have heard, *vivæ vocis oraculo,* the controversy that is in question, what do you think of it?" They answered him, "We have indeed heard it; but have not understood (the devil) so much as one circumstance of the case: and therefore we beseech you *unâ voce,* and in courtesy request you, that you would give sentence as you think good; and *ex nunc prout ex tunc,* we are satisfied with it, and do ratify it with our full consents." "Well, my masters," said Pantagruel, "seeing you are so pleased, I will do it: but I do not truly find the case so difficult as you make it. Your paragraph Caton, the law frater, the law gallus, the law quinque pedum, the law vinum, the law si dominus, the law mater, the law mulier bona, the law si quis, the law Pomponius, the law fundi, the law emtor, the law prætor, the law venditor, and a great many others, are far more intricate in my opinion." After he had spoke this, he walked a turn or two about the hall, plodding very profoundly as one may think: for he did groan like an ass, whilst they girt him too hard, with the intensiveness of considering how he was bound in conscience to do right to both parties, without varying or accepting of persons. Then he returned, sat down, and began to pronounce sentence as followeth:

"Having seen, heard, calculated, and well considered of the difference between the lords of Kissbreech and Suckfist; the court saith unto them, that in regard of the sudden shivering of the flickermouse, bravely declining from the estival solstice, to attempt by private means the surprisal of toyish trifles in those who are a little unwell for having taken a draught too much, through the lewd demeanour and vexation of the beetles, that inhabit the diarodal climate of an hypocritical ape on horseback, bending a cross-bow backwards. The plaintiff truly had just cause to calset [caulk], and stop the chinks of the gallion, which the good woman blew up with wind, having one foot shod and the other bare, reimbursing and restoring to him, low and stiff in his conscience, as many bladder nuts and wild pistaches as there is of hair in eighteen cows, with as much for the embroiderer, and so much for that. He is likewise declared innocent of the case privileged from the knapdardies, into the danger whereof it was thought he had incurred; because he could not jocundly and with fulness of freedom untruss and dung, by the decision of a pair of gloves perfumed with the scent of bum-gunshot, at the walnut-tree taper, as is usual in his country of Mirobalais. Slacking therefore the top-sail, and letting go the boulin with the brazen bullets, wherewith the mariners did by way of protestation bake in paste meat great store of pulse interquilted with the dormouse, whose hawks bells were made with a puntinaria, after the manner of Hungary or Flanders lace, and which his brother-in-law carried in a pannier, lying near to three chevrons or bordered gueules, whilst he was clean out of heart, drooping and crest-fallen by the too narrow sifting, canvassing, and curious examining of the matter, in the angulary dog-hole of nasty scoundrels, from whence we shoot at the vermiformal popingay, with the flap made of a fox-tail.

"But in that he chargeth the defendant that he was a botcher, a cheese-eater, and trimmer of man's flesh embalmed; which in the arsiversy swagfal tumble was not found true, as by the defendant was very well discussed.

"The court therefore doth condemn and amerce him in three porringers of curds, well cemented and closed together, shining like pearls, and cod-pieced after the fashion of the country, to be paid unto the said defendant about the middle of August in May: but on the other part, the defendant shall be bound to furnish him with hay and stubble, for stopping the caltrops of his throat, troubled and impulregafixed, with gabardines garbled shuffingly, and friends as before, without costs and for cause."

Which sentence being pronounced, the two parties departed both contented with the decree; which was a thing almost incredible: for it never came to pass since the great rain, nor shall the like occur in thirteen jubilees hereafter, that two parties, contradictorily contending in judgment, be equally satisfied and well pleased with the definitive sentence. As for the counsellors, and other doctors in the law that were there present, they were all so ravished with admiration at the more than human wisdom of Pantagruel, which they did most clearly perceive to be in him, by his so accurate decision of this so difficult and thorny cause, that their spirits, with the extremity of the rapture, being elevated above the pitch of actuating the organs of the body, they fell into a trance and sudden ecstasy, wherein they stayed for the space of three long hours; and had been so as yet, in that condition, had not some good people fetched store of vinegar and rose-water to bring them again unto their former sense and understanding. For the which God be praised everywhere: and so be it.

CHAPTER XIV

HOW PANURGE RELATED THE MANNER HOW HE ESCAPED OUT OF THE HANDS OF THE TURKS

THE great wit and judgment of Pantagruel was immediately after this made known to all the world, by setting forth his praises in print, and putting upon record this late wonderful proof he had given thereof amongst the rolls of the crown, and registers of the palace; in such sort, that everybody began to say that Solomon, who by a probable guess only, without any further certainty, caused the child to be delivered to his own mother, shewed never in his time such a masterpiece of wisdom, as the good Pantagruel had done: happy are we therefore that have him in our country. And indeed they would have made him thereupon master of the requests, and president in the court; but he refused all, very graciously thanking them for their offer; "for," said he, "there is too much slavery in these offices, and very hardly can they be saved that do exercise them, considering the great corruption that is amongst men; which makes me believe, if the empty seats of angels be not filled with other kind of people than those, we shall not have the final judgment these seven thousand sixty and seven jubilees yet to come: and so Cusanus will be deceived in his conjecture. Remember that I have told you of it, and given you fair advertisement in time and place convenient. But if you have any hogsheads of good wine, I willingly will accept of a present of that." Which they very heartily did do, in sending him of the best that was in the city; and he drank reasonably well. But poor Panurge bibbed and bowsed of it most villainously: for he was as dry as a red-herring, as lean as a rake, and like a poor lank slender cat, walked gingerly as if he had trod upon eggs; so that by some one being admonished, in the midst of his draught of a large deep bowl, full of excellent claret, with these words: "Fair and softly, gossip, you suck up as if you were mad"; "I give thee to the devil," said he; "thou hast not found here thy tippling sippers of Paris, that drink no more than the chaffinch, and never take in their beak full of liquor, till they be bobbed on the tails after the manner of the sparrows. O companion, if I could mount up as well as I can get down, I had been long ere this above the sphere of the moon with Empedocles. But I cannot tell what a devil this means. This wine is so good and delicious, that the more I drink thereof, the more I am athirst. I believe the shadow of my master Pantagruel maketh men a-thirsty, as the moon makes the catarrhs and defluxions." At which word the company began to laugh; which Pantagruel perceiving, said: "Panurge, what is that which moves you to laugh so?" "Sir," said he, "I was telling them that those devilish Turks are very unhappy, in that they never drink one drop of wine; and that though there were no other harm in all Mahomet's alcoran, yet for this one base point of abstinence from wine, which therein is commanded, I would not submit myself unto their law." "But now tell me," said Pantagruel, "how you escaped out of their hands." "By G—, sir," said Panurge, "I will not lie to you in one word.

"The rascally Turks had broached me upon a spit, all larded like a rabbit: for I was so dry and meagre, that otherwise of my flesh they would have made but very bad meat: and in this manner began to roast me alive. As they were thus roasting me, I recommended myself unto the divine grace, having in my mind the good St. Lawrence, and always hoped in God that he would deliver me out of this torment; which came to pass, and that very strangely; for as I did commit myself with all my heart to God, crying, 'Lord God, help me! Lord God, save me! Lord God, take me out of this pain and hellish torture, wherein these traitorous dogs detain me for my sincerity in the maintenance of thy law!' the turnspit fell asleep by the divine will, or else by the virtue of some good Mercury, who cunningly brought Argus into a sleep for all his hundred eyes. When I saw that he did no longer turn me in roasting, I looked upon him, and perceived that he was fast asleep: then took I up in my teeth a firebrand, by the end where it was not burnt, and cast it into the lap of my roaster; and another did I throw as well as I could under a field bed, that was placed near to the chimney, wherein was the straw-bed of my master turnspit. Presently the fire took hold in the straw, and from the straw to the bed, and from the bed to the loft, which was planked and cieled with fir, after the fashion of the foot of a lamp. But the best was that the fire, which I had cast into the lap of my paltry roaster, burnt all his groin, and was beginning to seize upon his cullions, when he became sensible of the danger: for his smelling was not so bad, but that he felt it sooner than he could have seen daylight. Then suddenly getting up, and in great amazement running to the window, he cried out to the streets as high as he could, 'Dal-baroth! dal-baroth! dal-baroth!' which is as much to say, fire! fire! fire! Incontinently turning about, he came straight towards me, to throw me quite into the fire; and, to that effect, had already cut the ropes wherewith my hands were tied, and was doing the cords from off my feet, when the master of the house hearing him cry fire, and smelling the smoke from the very street where he was walking with some other bashaws and mustaphas, ran with all the speed he had to save what he could, and to carry away his jewels; yet such was his rage, before he could well resolve how to go about it, that he caught the broach whereon I was spitted, and therewith killed my roaster stark dead, of which wound he died there for want of regimen, or otherwise: for he ran him in with the spit a little above the navel, towards the right flank, till he pierced the third lappet of his liver, and the blow slanting upwards from the diaphragm, through which it had made penetration, the spit pass'd athwart the pericardium, and came out above at his shoulders, betwixt the spondyls and the left homoplat.

"True it is, for I will not lie, that in drawing the spit out of my body, I fell to the ground near unto the andirons, and so by the fall took some hurt; which indeed had been greater, but that the lardons, or little slices of bacon wherewith I was stuck, kept off the blow. My bashaw then seeing the case to be desperate, his house burnt without remission, and all his goods lost, gave himself over unto all the devils in hell, calling upon some of them by their names, Grilgoth, Astarot, Rappalus, and Gribouillis, nine several times; which when I saw, I had above five pennyworth if fear, dreading that the devils would come even then to carry away this fool, and seeing me so near him would perhaps snatch me up too. I am ready, thought I, half roasted, and my lardons will be the cause of my mischief; for these devils are very lickorous of lardons, according to the authority which you have of the philosopher Jamblicus and Murmault, in the apology of Bossutis, adulterated *pro magistros nostros:* but for my better security I made the sign of the cross; crying, *'Hagios, athanatos ho theos!'* and none came. At which, my rogue bashaw, being very much aggrieved, would in transpiercing his heart with my spit have killed himself; and to that purpose had set it against his breast, but it could not enter, because it was not sharp enough. Whereupon I, perceiving that he was not like to work upon his body the effect which he intended, although he did not spare all the force he had to thrust it forward, came up to him, and said, 'Master Bugrino, thou dost here but trifle away thy time, for thou wilt never kill thyself thus as thou dost. Well, thou may'st hurt or bruise somewhat within thee, so as to make thee languish all thy life time most pitifully amongst the hands of the chirurgeons: but if thou wilt be counselled by me, I will kill thee clear outright, so that thou shalt not so much as feel it; and trust me, for I have killed a great many others, who never have complained afterwards.' 'Ha, my friend,' said he, 'I prythee do so, and for thy pains I will give thee my codpiece: take, here it is, there are six hundred seraphs in it, and some fine diamonds, and most excellent rubies.'" "And where are they?" said Epistemon. "By St. John!" said Panurge, "they are a good way hence, if they always keep going: but where is the last year's snow? This was the greatest care that Villon the Parisian poet took." "Make an end," said Pantagruel, "that we may know how thou didst dress thy bashaw." "By the faith of an honest man," said Panurge, "I do not lie in one word; I swaddled him in a scurvy swathel-binding, which I found lying there half-burnt, and with my cords tied him royster-like both hand and foot, in such sort that he was not able to wince; then past my spit through

182

his throat, and hanged him thereon, fastening the end thereof at two great hooks, or cramp-irons, upon which they did hang their halberds; and then, kindling a fire under him, did flame you up my milourt, as they use to dry herrings in a chimney: with this, taking his budget, and a little javelin that was upon the foresaid hooks, I ran away a fair gallop-rake, and God he knows how I did smell my shoulder of mutton.

"When I was come down into the street, I found everybody come to put out the fire with store of water, and seeing me so half-roasted, they did naturally pity my case, and threw all their water upon me, which by a most joyful refreshing of me, did me very much good. Then did they present me with some victuals; but I could not eat much, because they gave me nothing to drink but water, after their fashion. Other hurt they did me none; only one little villainous Turkey knob-breasted rogue came to snatch away some of my lardons; but I gave him such a sturdy thump, and sound rap on the fingers, with all the weight of my javelin, that he came no more the second time. Shortly after this, there came towards me a pretty young Corinthian wench, who brought me a box full of conserves, of round Myrabolan plums, called emblicks, and looked upon my poor Roger with an eye of great compassion, as it was flea-bitten and pinked with the sparkles of the fire from whence it came; for it reached no further in length, believe me, than my knees. But note, that this roasting cured me entirely of a sciatica, whereunto I had been subject above seven years before, upon that side which my roaster, by falling asleep, suffered to be burnt.

"Now whilst they were thus busy about me, the fire triumphed; never ask, how? for it took hold on above two thousand houses; which one of them espying, cried out, saying, 'By Mahoom's belly all the city is on fire, and we do nevertheless stand gazing here, without offering to bring any relief.' Upon this, every one ran to save his own. For my part, I took my way towards the gate. When I was got upon the knap of a little hillock, not far off, I turned me about as did Lot's wife, and looking back, saw all the city burning in a fair fire: whereat I was so glad, that I had almost beshit myself for joy; but God punished me well for it." "How?" said Pantagruel. "Thus," said Panurge; "for when with pleasure I beheld this jolly fire, jesting with myself, and saying, 'Ha poor fleas, ha poor mice, you will have a bad winter of it this year; the fire is in your reeks, it is in your bed-straw'; out came more than six, yea more than thirteen hundred and eleven dogs, great and small, all together out of the town, flying away from the fire. At the first approach they ran all upon me, being carried on by the scent of my leacherous half-roasted flesh, and had even then devoured me in a trice, if my good angel had not then inspired me with the instruction of a remedy, very sovereign against the pain of the teeth." "And wherefore," said Pantagruel, "wert thou afraid of the pain of the teeth? wert thou not cured of thy rheums?" "By Palm-Sunday," said Panurge, "is there any greater pain of the teeth than when the dogs have you by the legs? But on a sudden, as my good angel directed me, I thought upon my lardons, and threw them into the midst of the field amongst them: then did the dogs run, and fight with one another at fair teeth, which should have the lardons; by this means they left me, and I left them also bustling with, and haring one another. Thus did I escape frolic and lively, grammercy roast-meat and cookery."

CHAPTER XV

HOW PANURGE SHEWED A VERY NEW WAY TO BUILD
THE WALLS OF PARIS

PANTAGRUEL, one day to refresh himself of his study, went a walking towards St. Marcel's suburbs, to see the extravagancy of the Gobeline building, and to taste of their spiced bread. Panurge was with him, having always a flagon under his gown, and a good slice of a gammon of bacon; for without this he never went, saying, "That it was his life-guard! other sword carried he none." And when Pantagruel would have given him one, he answered that he needed none, for that it would but heat his milt. "Yea, but," said Epistemon, "if thou should'st be set upon, how would'st thou defend thyself?" "With great brodkin blows," answered he, "provided thrusts were forbidden." At their return, Panurge considered the walls of the city of Paris, and in derision said to Pantagruel, "See what fair walls are here! O how strong they are, and well fitted to keep geese in a coop to fatten them! By my beard, they are very sorry walls for such a city as this is; for a cow with one fart would go near to overthrow above six fathoms of them." "O my friend," said Pantagruel, "dost thou know what Agesilaus said, when he was asked, why the great city of Lacedemon was not enclosed with walls? Shewing them the inhabitants and citizens, so strong, so well armed,

184

and so expert in military discipline; 'Lo here,' said he, 'the walls of the city': signifying thereby, that there is no wall but of bones, and that towns and cities cannot have a surer wall, nor better fortification, than the prowess and virtue of the citizens and inhabitants. So is this city so strong, by the great number of warlike people that are in it, that they care not for making any other walls.

"Besides, whosoever would go about to wall it, as Strasburgh, Orleans, or Ferrara, would find it almost impossible, the cost and charges would be so excessive." "Yea, but," said Panurge, "it is good nevertheless to have an outside of stone, when we are invaded by our enemies, were it but to ask, who is below there? As for the enormous expense, which you say would be needful for undertaking the great work of walling this city about, if the gentlemen of the town will be pleased to give me a good round cup of wine, I will shew them a pretty strange, and new way how they may build them cheap enough." "How?" said Pantagruel. "Do not speak of it then," said Panurge, "and I will tell it you. I see that the what d'ye call-ums of the women of this country are cheaper than stones; of them should the walls be built, ranging them in good symmetry by the rules of architecture, and placing the largest in the first ranks, then sloping downwards ridge-ways, like the back of an ass; the middle-sized ones must be ranked next, and last of all the least and smallest. This done, there must be a fine little interlacing of them, like points of diamonds, as is to be seen in the great tower of Bourges, with a like number of the lusty catsoes that dwell in the claustral codpieces. What devil were able to overthrow such walls? There is no metal like it to resist blows, in so far that if culverin-shot should come to graze upon it, you would incontinently see distil from thence the blessed fruit of the great pox, as small as rain. Beware in the name of the devils, and hold off. Furthermore, no thunderbolt or lightning would fall upon it: for why? They are all either blessed or consecrated. I see but one inconveniency in it." "Ho, ho, ha, ha, ha," said Pantagruel, "and what is that?" "It is that the flies would be so lickorish of them, to a wonder, and would quickly gather there together; and there leave their ordure and excretions; and so all the work would be spoiled. But see how that might be remedied: they must be wiped and made rid of the flies with fair fox tails, or good great ass-pizzles of Provence. And to this purpose I will tell you, as we go to supper, a brave example set down by *frater Lubinus, libro de compotationibus mendicantium.*

185

"In the time that the beasts did speak, which is not yet three days ago, a poor lion walking through the forest of Bieure, and saying his own little private devotions, past under a tree where there was a roguish collier gotten up to cut down wood: who seeing the lion, cast his hatchet at him, and wounded him enormously in one of his legs: whereupon the lion halting, so long toiled and turmoiled himself in roaming up and down the forest to find help, till at last he met with a carpenter, who willingly looked upon his wound, cleansed it as well as he could, and filled it with moss; telling him that he must wipe his wound well, that the flies might not do their excrements in it, whilst he should go search for some millefoil, commonly called the carpenter's herb. The lion, being thus healed, walking along in the forest; at what time, a sempiternous old hag was picking up, and gathering some sticks in the said forest; who, seeing the lion coming towards her, for fear fell down backwards, in such sort, that the wind blew up her gown, coats, and smock even as far as above her shoulders. Which the lion perceiving, for pity ran to see whether she had taken any hurt by the fall; and thereupon considering her what d'you call it, said, 'O poor woman, who hath thus wounded thee?' Which words when he had spoken, he espied a fox, whom he called to come to him, saying, 'Gossip Renard, hau, hither, hither, and for cause.'

"When the fox was come, he said unto him, 'My gossip and friend, they have hurt this good woman between the legs most villainously, and there is a manifest solution of continuity: see how great a wound it is, even from the tail up to the navel, in measure four, nay full five handfulls and a half! This is the blow of an hatchet; I doubt me it is an old wound; and therefore, that the flies may not get into it, wipe it lustily, well and hard, I prithee, both within and without: thou hast a good tail and long: wipe, my friend, wipe, I beseech thee, and in the meanwhile I will go get some moss to put into it. For thus ought we to succour and help one another. Wipe it hard, thus, my friend, wipe it well; for this wound must be often wiped, otherwise the party cannot be at ease. Go to, wipe well, my little gossip, wipe: God hath furnished thee with a tail: thou hast a long one, and of a bigness proportionable; wipe hard and be not weary. A good wiper, who, in wiping continually, wipeth with his wipard, by wasps shall never be wounded. Wipe, my pretty minion, wipe, my little bully, I will not stay long.' Then went he to get store of moss; and, when he was a little way off, he cried out, in speaking to the fox, thus,

'Wipe well still, gossip, wipe, and let it never grieve thee to wipe well, my little gossip: I will put thee into service to be wiper to don Pedro de Castille; wipe, only wipe, and no more.' The poor fox wiped as hard as he could, here and there, within and without: but the false old trot did so fizzle and foist, that she stunk like a hundred devils. Which put the poor fox to a great deal of ill ease! for he knew not to what side to turn himself, to escape the unsavoury perfume of this old woman's postern blasts. And whilst to that effect he was shifting hither and thither, without knowing how to shun the annoyance of those unwholesome gusts, he saw that behind there was yet another hole, not so great as that which he did wipe, out of which came this filthy and infectious air. The lion at last returned, bringing with him of moss more than eighteen packs would hold, and began to put into the wound, with a staff which he had provided for that purpose; and had already put in full sixteen packs and a half, at which he was amazed. 'What a devil!' said he, 'this wound is very deep, it would hold above two cart-loads of moss.' The fox, perceiving this, said unto the lion, 'O gossip lion, my friend, I pray thee do not put in all thy moss there, keep some of it: for there is yet here another little hole, that stinks like five hundred devils. I am almost choked with the smell thereof, it is so pestiferous and impoisoning.'

"In this manner," said Panurge, "must these walls be kept from the flies and wages allowed to some for wiping of them.' Then said Pantagruel, "How dost thou know that the privy parts of women are at such a cheap rate? for in this city there are many virtuous, honest, and chaste women, besides the maids." *"Et ubi prenus?"* said Panurge. "I will give you my opinion of it, and that upon certain and assured knowledge. I do not brag that I have bumbasted four hundred and seventeen, since I came into this city, though it be but nine days ago. But this very morning I met with a good fellow, who in a wallet, such as Æsop's was, carried two little girls of two or three years old at the most, one before, and the other behind. He demanded alms of me: but I made him answer, that I had more cods than pence. Afterwards I asked him, 'Good man, these two girls are they maids?' 'Brother,' said he, 'I have carried them thus two years, and in regard of her that is before, whom I see continually, in my opinion she is a virgin; nevertheless I will not put my finger in the fire for it: as for her that is behind, doubtless I can say nothing.' " "Indeed," said Pantagruel, "thou art a merry companion, I will have thee to be apparelled in my livery"; and therefore caused him to be

187

cloathed most gallantly, according to the fashion that then was: only that Panurge would have the codpiece of his breeches three foot long, and in shape square, not round; which was done, and was well worth the seeing. Oftentimes he was wont to say, that the world had not yet known the emolument and utility that is in wearing great codpieces; but time would one day teach it them, as all things had been invented in time.

"God keep from hurt," said he, "the good fellow whose great codpiece hath saved his life. God keep from hurt him, whose great codpiece hath been worth to him, in one day, one hundred threescore thousand and nine crowns. God keep from hurt him, who by his great codpiece hath saved a whole city from dying by famine. And by G—, I will make a book of the commodity of great codpieces, when I shall have more leisure." And indeed he composed a fair great book with figures; but it is not printed as yet, that I know of.

CHAPTER XVI

OF THE QUALITIES AND CONDITIONS OF PANURGE

PANURGE was of a middle stature, not too high nor two low, and had somewhat an aquiline nose, made like the handle of a razor. He was at that time five and thirty years old, or thereabouts, fine to gild like a leaden dagger: for he was a very gallant man of his person, only that he was a little lewd, and naturally subject to a kind of disease, which at that time they called lack of money; a malady of nonpariel: yet notwithstanding he had threescore and three tricks to help himself at his need; of which the most honourable and most ordinary was by the way of filching: for he was a quarrelsome fellow, a sharper, drinker, royster, scowerer, and a very dissolute and debauched fellow, if there were any in Paris; otherwise, and in all matters else, the best man in the world. And he was still contriving some plot, and devising mischief against the serjeants and the watch.

At one time he assembled three or four especial good hacksters and roaring boys; made them in the evening drink like templars; afterwards led them till they came above St. Genevieve, or about the college of Navarre; and at the hour that the watch was coming up that way, which he knew by putting his sword upon the pavement, and his ear by it (and when he heard his sword shake, it was an infallible sign that the watch was near) at that instant he and his companions took a tumbrel or dung-cart, and gave it the brangle, hurling it with all their force down the hill, and so overthrow all the poor watchmen like pigs, and then ran away upon the other side; for, in less than two days, he knew all the streets, lanes, and turnings in Paris, as well as his Deus det.

At another time he laid in some fair place, where the said watch was to pass, a train of gunpowder, and, at the very instant that they went along, set afire to it, and then made himself sport to see what good grace they had in running away, thinking that St. Anthony's fire had caught them by the legs. As for the poor masters of arts and theologues, he did persecute them above all others. When he met with any of them upon the street, he would never fail to put some trick or other upon them; sometimes putting a fried turd in their graduate hoods; at other times pinning on little fox-tails, or hares-ears, behind them, or some such other roguish prank. One day that the theologians were appointed all to meet in the Sorbonne, be made a barbonnesa tart, made of store of garlic, galbanum, assa fœtida, castoreum, dogs' turds very warm: which he steeped, tempered, and liquified in the corrupt matter of pocky biles and pestiferous blotches; and, very early in the morning, therewith anointed all the lattices and grates of the Sorbonne in such sort, that the devil could not have endured it. Which made all these good people there to give up their gorges, and vomit what was upon their stomachs before all the world, as if they had flayed the fox. And ten or twelve of them died of the plague; fourteen became lepers, eighteen grew lousy, and above seven and twenty had the pox; but he did not care a button for it. He commonly carried a whip under his gown, wherewith he whipped, without remission, the pages, whom he found carrying wine to their masters, to make them mend their pace. In his coat he had above six and twenty little fobs and pockets always full, one with some lead-water, and a little knife as sharp as a glover's needle, wherewith he used to cut purses: another with some kind of bitter stuff, which he threw into the eyes of those he met: another with clotburs, penned with little geese or capons feathers, which he cast upon the gowns and caps of honest people; and often made them fair horns, which they wore about all the city, sometimes all their life. Very often also upon the women's hoods would he stick, in the hind-part, somewhat made in the shape of a man's member. In another he had a great many little horns full

189

of fleas and lice, which he borrowed from the beggars of St. Innocent, and cast them with small canes or quills to write with, into the necks of the daintiest gentlewomen that he could find, yea, even in the church: for he never seated himself above in the choir, but always sat in the body of the church amongst the women, both at mass, at vespers, and at sermon. In another he used to have good store of hooks and buckles, wherewithal he would couple men and women together, that sat in company close to one another; but especially those that wore gowns of crimson taffaties; that when they were about to go away, they might rend all their gowns. In another, he had a squib furnished with tinder, matches, stones to strike fire, and all other tackling necessary for it. In another, two or three burning glasses, wherewith he made both men and women sometimes mad, and in the church put them quite out of countenance; for he said that there was but an antistrophe between a woman, *folle a la messe,* and *molle a la fesse.*

In another he had a good deal of needles and thread, wherewith he did a thousand little devilish pranks. One time, at the entry of the palace unto the great hall, where a Cordelier was to say mass to the counsellors, he did help to apparel him, and put on his vestments; but in the accoutring of him, he sewed on his alb, surplice, or stole, to his gown and shirt, and then withdrew himself, when the said lords of the court, or counsellors, came to hear the said mass: but when it came to the *Ite, missa est,* that the poor frater would have laid by his stole, or surplice, he plucked off withall both his frock and shirt, which were well sewed together, and thereby stripping himself up to the shoulders, shewed his what d'ye call-um to all the world; which was no small one, as you may imagine: and the friar still kept haling, but so much the more did he discover himself, and lay open his backparts; till one of the lords of the court said, "How now, what is the matter? Will this good father make us here an offering of his tail to kiss it? Nay, St. Anthony's fire kiss it for us." From thenceforth was made an ordinance, that the poor fathers should never disrobe themselves any more before the world, but in their vestry-room, especially in the presence of women, lest it should tempt them to the sin of longing, and disordinate desire. The people then asked, why it was the friars had so long and large genitories? The said Panurge resolved the problem very neatly, saying, "That which makes asses to have such great ears is, that their dams did put no biggins on their heads, as d'Alliaco mentioneth in his suppositions. By the like reason, that which makes the generation-tools of those fair fraters so long, is, for that they wear no bottomed breeches, and therefore their jolly member, having no impediment, hangeth dangling at liberty, as far as it can reach, with a wiggle-waggle down to their knees, as women carry their patinotre beads. And the cause, wherefore they have it so correspondently great, is, that in this constant wig-wagging the humours of the body descend into the said member; for, according to the legists, agitation and continual motion is cause of attraction."

Item, He had another pocket full of itching powder, called stone-allum; whereof he would cast some into the backs of those women, whom he judged to be most beautiful and stately; which did so ticklishly gall them, that some would strip themselves in open view of the world, and others dance like a cock upon hot embers, or a drum-stick on a taber: others again ran about the streets, and he would run after them: to such as were in the stripping-vein, he would very civilly come to offer his attendance, and cover them with his cloak, like a courteous and very gracious man.

Item, In another he had a little leather-bottle full of old oil; wherewith, when he saw any man or woman in a rich new handsome suit, he would grease, smutch, and spoil all the best parts of it, under colour and pretence of touching them, saying, "This is good cloth, this is good satin, good taffaties: madam, God give you all that your noble heart desireth: you have a new suit, pretty sir; and you a new gown, sweet mistress; God give you joy of it, and maintain you in all prosperity." And with this would lay his hand upon their shoulders; at which touch such a villainous spot was left behind, so enormously engraven to perpetuity in the very soul, body, and reputation, that the devil himself could never have taken it away. Then upon his departing, he would say, "Madam, take heed you do not fall, for there is a filthy great hole before you."

Another he had all full of euphorbium, very finely pulverized: in that powder did he lay a fair handkerchief curiously wrought, which he had stolen from a pretty semstress of the palace, in taking away a louse from off her bosom, which he had put there himself. And when he came into the company of some good ladies, he would trifle them into a discourse of some fine workmanship of bone-lace; then immediately put his hand into their bosom, asking them, "And this work, is it of Flanders, or of Hainault?" And then drew out his handkerchief, and said, "Hold, hold, look what work here is: it is of Foutiman, or of Fontarabia": and shaking it hard at their nose, made them sneeze for four hours without ceasing. In the meanwhile he would fart like a horse, and the women would laugh, and say, "How now, do you fart, Panurge?" "No, no, madam," said he, "I do but tune my tail to the plain song of the music, which you make with your nose." In another he had a picklock, a pelican, a crampiron, a crook, and some other iron tools, wherewith there was no door nor coffer which he would not pick open. He had another full of little cups, wherewith he played very artificially; for he had his fingers made to his hand, like those of Minerva or Arachne, and had heretofore cried treacle. And when he changed a teston, cardecu, or any other piece of money, the changer had been more subtle than a fox, if Panurge had not at every time made five or six sols vanish away visibly, openly, and manifestly, without making any hurt or lesion, where of the changer should have felt nothing but the wind.

CHAPTER XVII

HOW PANURGE GAINED THE PARDONS, AND MARRIED THE OLD WOMEN: AND OF THE SUIT IN LAW WHICH HE HAD IN PARIS

ONE day I found Panurge very much out of countenance, melancholic and silent, which made me suspect that he had no money; whereupon I said unto him, "Panurge, you are sick, as I do very well perceive by your physiognomy; and I know the disease, you have a flux in your purse: but take no care, I have yet seven-pence half-penny, that never saw father nor mother, which shall not be wanting no more than the pox in your necessity." Whereunto he answered me, "Well, well, for money, one day I shall have but too much; for I have a philosopher's stone, which attracts money out of men's purses, as the loadstone doth iron. But will you go with me to gain the pardons?" said he. "By my faith," said I, "I am no great pardon-taker in this world; if I shall be any such in the other, I cannot tell. Yet let us go in God's name, it is but one farthing more or less." "But," said he, "lend me then a farthing upon interest?" "No, no," said I, "I will give it you freely, and from my heart." *"Grates vobis dominos,"* said he.

So we went along, beginning at St. Gervase, and I got the pardons at the first box only; for in those matters very little contenteth me. Then did I say my small suffrages, and the prayers of St. Brigid. But he gained them at all the boxes, and always gave money to every one of the pardoners. From thence we went to our Lady's church, to St. John's, to St. Anthony's, and so to the other churches, where there was a bank of pardons. For my part, I gained no more of them. But he at all the boxes kissed the relics, and gave at every one. To be brief, when we were returned, he brought me to drink at the castle tavern, and there shewed me ten or twelve of his little bags full of money; at which I blessed myself, and made the sign of the cross, saying, "Where have you recovered so much money in so little time?" Unto which he answered me, that he had taken it out of the basons of the pardons. "For in giving them the first farthing," said he, "I put it in with such sleight of hand, and so dexterously, that it appeared to be a three-pence, thus with one hand I took three-pence, nine-pence, or six-pence at the least, and with the other as much, and so through all the churches where we have been."

"Yea, but," said I, "you damn yourself like a snake, and are withal a thief and sacrilegious person." "True," said he, "in your opinion, but I am not of that mind: for the pardoners do give me it, when they say unto me, in presenting the relics to kiss, *Centuplum accipies;* that is, that for one penny I should take a hundred. For *accipies,* is spoken according to the manner of the Hebrews, who use the future tense instead of the imperative: as you have in the law, *Diliges Dominum;* that is, *dilige:* even so when the pardon-bearer says to me, *Centuplum accipies;* his meaning is *Centuplum accipe:* and so doth Rabbi Kimi and Rabbi Eben Ezra expound it, and all the Masorets, & ibi Bartholus. Moreover, pope Sixtus gave me fifteen hundred franks of yearly pension upon his ecclesiastical revenues and treasure, for having cured him of a cankerous botch, which did so torment him, that he thought to have been a cripple by it all his life. Thus do I pay myself at my own hand (for otherwise I get nothing) upon the said ecclesiastical treasure.

"Ho, my friend!" said he, "if thou didst know how well I feathered my nest, by the pope's bull of the croisade, thou would'st wonder exceedingly. It was worth to me above six thousand florins." "And what a devil is become of them?" said I; "for of that money thou hast not one half-penny." "They returned from whence they came," said he; "they did no more but change their master.

"But I employed at least three thousand of them in marrying (not young virgins, for they find but too many husbands) but great old sempiternous trots, which had not so much as one tooth in their heads. And that out of the consideration I had, that these good old women had very well spent the time of their youth in playing at the close-buttock game to all comers, serving the foremost first, till no man would have any more dealing with them. And by G— I will have their skin-coat shaken once yet before they die. By this means, to one I gave a hundred florins, to another six score, to another three hundred, according as they were infamous, detestable, and abominable. For by how much the more horrible and execrable they were, so much the more must I needs have given them. Otherwise the devil would not have jumm'd them. Presently I went to some great and fat woodporters, or such like, and did myself make the match: but before I did shew him the old hags, I made a fair muster to him of the crowns, saying, 'Good fellow, see what I will give thee, if thou wilt but condescend to dufle, dinfredaille, or leacher it one good bout.' They began the poor rogues to gape like old mules, and I caused to be provided for them a banquet, with drink of the best, and store of spiceries, to put the old women in rut and heat of lust. To be short, they occupied all like good souls; only to those that were horribly ugly and ill-favoured, I caused their heads to be put within a bag to hide their face.

"Besides, all this, I have lost a great deal in suits of law." "And what law-suits could'st thou have?" said I. "Thou hast neither house nor lands." "My friend," said he, "the gentlewomen of this city had found out, by the instigation of the devil of hell, a manner of high-mounted gorgets, and neckerchiefs for women, which did so closely cover their bosoms, that men could no more put their hands under; for they had put the slit behind, and those neckcloths were wholly shut before; whereat the poor sad contemplative lovers were much discontented. Upon a fair Tuesday, I presented a petition to the court, making myself a party against the said gentlewomen, and shewing the great interest that I pretended therein; protesting that, by the same reason, I would cause the codpiece of my breeches to be sewed behind, if the court would not take order for it. In sum, the gentlewomen put in their defences, shewed the grounds they went upon, and constituted their attorney for the prosecuting of the cause: but I pursued them so vigorously, that by a sentence of the court it was decreed those high neckcloths should be no longer worn, if they were not a little cleft and open before; but it cost me a good sum of money.

I had another very filthy and beastly process against master Fohfoh and his deputies, that they should no more read privily by night the pipe, puncheon, nor quart of sentences; but in fair full-day, and that in the Sorbonne, in the face of the Arrian sophisters; where I was ordained to pay the charges, by reason of some clause mistaken in the relation of the sergeant. Another time I framed a complaint to the court, against the mules of the presidents, counsellors and others, tending to this purpose: That when, in the lower court of the palace, they left them to champ on their bridles, some bibs might be made for them, that with their driveling they might not spoil the pavement, to the end that the pages of the palace might play upon it at dice, or cox body, at their own ease, without spoiling their breeches at the knees. And for this I had a fair decree: but it cost me dear. Now reckon up what expence I was at in little banquets, which from day to day I made to the pages of the palace." "And to what end?" said I. "My friend," said he, "thou hast no pastime at all in this world. I have more than the king; and if thou wilt join thyself with me, we will do the devil together."

"No, no," said I: "by St. Adauras that will I not; for thou wilt be hanged one time or another." "And thou," said he, "wilt be interred some time or other. Now which is most honourable, the air or the earth? *Ho, grosse pecore!* (dull beast).

"Whilst the pages are at their banqueting, I keep their mules, and to some one I cut the stirrup-leather of the mounting side, till it hang but by a thin strap or thread, that when the great puff-guts of the counsellor, or some other, has taken his swing to get up, he may fall flat on his side like a porker, and so furnish the spectators with more than a hundred franks' worth of laughter. But I laugh yet further, to think how at his home-coming the master-page is to be whipped like green rie, which makes me not repent what I have bestowed in feasting them." In brief, he had (as I said before) threescore and three ways to acquire money: but he had two hundred and fourteen to spend it, besides his drinking.

CHAPTER XVIII

IN that same time a certain learned man, named Thaumast, hearing
the fame and renown of Pantagruel's incomparable knowledge,
came out of his own country of England, with an intent only to see
him, to try thereby, and prove whether his knowledge in effect was
so great as it was reported to be. In this resolution, being arrived at
Paris, he went forthwith unto the house of Pantagruel, who was
lodged in the palace of St. Denys, and was then walking in the garden with Panurge, philosophizing after the fashion of the Peripatetics. At his first entrance he startled, and was almost out of his wits
for fear, seeing him so great and so tall: then did he salute him courteously, as the manner is, and said unto him, "'Very true it is,' saith
Plato, the prince of philosophers, 'that if the image of knowledge and
wisdom were corporeal, and visible to the eyes of mortals, it would
stir up all the world to admire her.' Which we may the rather believe, since the very bare report thereof, scattered in the air, if it happen to be received into the ears of men, who, for being studious, and
lovers of virtuous things, are called philosophers, doth not suffer them
to sleep nor rest in quiet, but so pricketh them up and sets them on
fire, to run unto the place where the person is, in whom the said
knowledge is said to have built her temple, and uttered her oracles.
As it was manifestly shewn unto us in the queen of Sheba, who came
from the utmost borders of the east and Persian sea, to behold the
order of Solomon's house, and hear his wisdom. In Anacharsis,
who came out of Scythia, even unto Athens, to see Solon. In Pythagoras, who travelled far to visit the memphitical vaticinators. In
Plato, who went a great way off to see the magicians of Egypt, and
Architas of Tarentum. In Apollonius Tyaneus, who went as far as
unto mount Caucasus, passed along the Scythians, the Massagetes,
the Indians, and sailed over the great river Phison, even to the Brach-
mans to see Hiarchas: as likewise unto Babylon, Chaldea, Media, As-
syria, Parthia, Syria, Phœnicia, Arabia, Palestina, and Alexandria,
even unto Æthiopia, to see the Gymnosophists. The like example
have we of Titus Livius, who, to see and hear divers studious persons,
came to Rome, from the confines of France and Spain. I dare not
reckon myself in the number of those so excellent persons; but well

would be called studious, and a lover, not only of learning, but of learned men also. And indeed, having heard the report of your so inestimable knowledge, I have left my country, my friends, my kindred, and my house, and am come thus far, valuing as nothing the length of the way, the tediousness of the sea, nor strangeness of the land, and that only to see you, and to confer with you about some passages in philosophy, of geomancy, and of the cabilistic art; whereof I am doubtful, and cannot satisfy my mind; which if you can resolve, I yield myself unto you for a slave, henceforward, together with all my posterity: for other gift have I none, that I can esteem a recompence sufficient for so great favour. I will reduce them into writing, and to-morrow publish them to all the learned men in the city, that we may dispute publicly before them.

"But see in what manner I mean that we shall dispute. I will not argue *pro & contra,* as do the sottish sophisters of this town, and other places. Likewise I will yet not dispute after the manner of the academics, by declamation. Nor yet by numbers, as Pythagoras was wont to do, and as Picus de la Mirandula did of late at Rome. But I will dispute by signs only, without speaking: for the matters are so abstruse, hard, and arduous, that words, proceeding from the mouth of man, will never be sufficient for unfolding of them to my liking. May it therefore please your magnificence to be there, it shall be at the great hall of Navarre, at seven o'clock in the morning." When he had spoke these words, Pantagruel very honourably said unto him, "Sir, of the graces that God hath bestowed upon me, I would not deny to communicate unto any man to my power: for whatever comes from him is good, and his pleasure is, that it should be increased when we come amongst men worthy and fit to receive this celestial manna of honest literature. In which number, because that in this time (as I do already very plainly perceive) thou holdest the first rank, I give thee notice that at all hours thou shalt find me ready to condescend to every one of thy requests, according to my poor ability: although I ought rather to learn of thee, than thou of me. But as thou hast protested, we will confer of thy doubts together, and will seek out the resolution, even unto the bottom of that undrainable well, where Heraclitus says the truth lies hidden. And I do highly commend the manner of arguing which thou hast proposed, to wit, by signs without speaking: for by this means thou and I shall understand one another well enough, and yet shall be free from that clapping of hands, which these blockish sophisters make, when any of the

197

arguers hath gotten the better of the argument. Now to-morrow I will not fail to meet thee at the place and hour thou hast appointed: but let me entreat thee, that there be not any strife or uproar between us, and that we seek not the honour and applause of men, but the truth only." To which Thaumast answered, "The Lord God maintain you in his favour and grace; and, instead of my thankfulness to you, pour down his blessings upon you, for that your highness and magnificent greatness hath not disdained to descend to the grant of the request of my poor baseness: so farewell till to-morrow." "Farewell," said Pantagruel. Gentlemen, you that read this present discourse, think not that ever men were more elevated and transported in their thoughts, than all this night were both Thaumast and Pantagruel: for Thaumast said to the keeper of the inn of Cluny, where he was lodged, that in all his life he had never known himself so dry as he was that night: "I think," said he, "that Pantagruel held me by the throat: give order, I pray you, that we may have some drink, and see that some fresh water be brought unto us to gargle my palate."

On the other side, Pantagruel stretched his wits as high as he could, entering into very deep and serious meditations, and did nothing all that night but plod upon, and turn over the book of Beda, de numeris & signis; Plotius's book, de Inenarrabilibus; the book of Proclus, de Magia; the book of Artemidorus, περι ὀνειροκριτικῶν; of Anaxagoras, περι σημείων; Dinarius, περι ἀφάτων; the books of Philistion; Hipponax, περι ἀνεκφωνητῶν; and a rabble of others so long, that Panurge said unto him:

"My lord, leave all these thoughts and go to bed: for I perceive your spirits to be so troubled by a too intensive bending of them, that you may easily fall into some quotidian fever with this so excessive thinking and plodding: but having first drank twenty-five or thirty good draughts, retire yourself and sleep your fill; for in the morning I will argue against, and answer your Monsieur the Englishman; and if I drive him not *ad metam non loqui*, then call me knave." "Yea, but," said Pantagruel, "my friend Panurge, he is marvellously learned; how wilt thou be able to answer him?" "Very well," answered Panurge; "I pray you talk no more of it, but let me alone. Is any man so learned as the devils are?" "No, indeed," said Pantagruel, "without God's especial grace." "Yet for all that," said Panurge, "I have many a time and often argued against them, gravelled and blanked them in disputation, and laid them so squat upon their tails, that I have made them look like monkies: therefore be assured, that to-mor-

198

row I will make this vain-glorious Englishman to skite vinegar before all the world." So Panurge spent the night with tippling amongst the pages, and played away all the points of his breeches at *primus & secundus,* and at peckpoint. Yet when the appointed time was come he failed not to conduct his master Pantagruel to the place, unto which, believe me, there was neither great nor small in Paris but came; thinking with themselves that this devilish Pantagruel, who had overthrown and vanquished in dispute all those doting and freshwater sophisters, would now get full payment, and be tickled to some purpose; for this Englishman is another devil of a disputant; we shall see who will be conqueror.

Thus, all being assembled, Thaumast stayed for them; and then, when Pantagruel and Panurge came into the hall, all the schoolboys, professors of art, senior-sophisters, and bachelors, began to clap their hands, as their scurvy custom is: but Pantagruel cried out with a loud voice, as if it had been the sound of a double cannon, saying, "Peace with a devil to you, peace: by G— you rogues, if you trouble me here, I will cut off the heads of every one of you." At which words they remained all daunted and astonished, like so many ducks, and durst not so much as cough, although they had swallowed fifteen pounds of feathers: withal they grew so dry with this only voice, that they laid out their tongues a full half foot beyond their mouths, as if Pantagruel had salted all their throats. Then began Panurge to speak, saying to the Englishman, "Sir, are you come hither to dispute contentiously in those prepositions you have set down, or otherwise but to learn and know the truth?" To which answered Thaumast, "Sir, no other thing brought me hither, but the great desire I had to learn, and to know that of which I have doubted all my life long, and have neither found book nor man able to content me in the resolution of those doubts which I have proposed.

"And as for disputing contentiously, I will not do it, for it is too base a thing, and therefore leave it to these sottish sophisters, who in their disputes, do not search for the truth, but for contradiction only and debate."

Then said Panurge, "If I, who am but a mean and inconsiderable disciple of my master, my lord Pantagruel, content and satisfy you in all and everything, it were a thing below my said master, wherewith to trouble him: therefore it is fitter that he be chairman, and sit as judge and moderator of our discourse and purpose, and give you satisfaction in many things, wherein, perhaps, I shall be wanting to

199

your expectation." "Truly," said Thaumast, "it is very well said: begin then." Now you must note that Panurge had set at the end of his long codpiece a pretty tuft of red silk, as also of white, green, and blue, and within it, had put a fair orange.

CHAPTER XIX

HOW PANURGE PUTS TO A NON-PLUS THE ENGLISHMAN
THAT ARGUED BY SIGNS

EVERYBODY then taking heed, and harkening with great silence, the Englishman lifted up on high into the air his two hands severally, clinching in all the tops of his fingers together, after the manner they call, in Chinonnois, the hen's arse, and struck the one hand on the other by the nails four several times; then he, opening them, struck the one with the flat of the other, till it yielded a clashing noise, and that only once: again, in joining them as before, he struck twice, and afterwards four times in opening them: then did he lay them joined, and extended the one towards the other, as if he had been devoutly to send up his prayers unto God. Panurge suddenly lifted up in the air his right hand, and put the thumb thereof into the nostril of the same side, holding his four fingers straight out, and closed orderly in a parallel line to the point of his nose, shutting the left eye wholly, and making the other wink with a profound depression of the eye-brows and eye-lids. Then lifted he up his left hand, with hard wringing and stretching forth his four fingers, and elevating his thumb, which he held in a line directly correspondent to the situation of his right hand, with the distance of a cubit and a half between them. This done, in the same form he abased towards the ground both the one and the other hand. Lastly, he held them in the midst, as aiming right at the Englishman's nose. "And if Mercury——," said the Englishman. There Panurge interrupted him, and said, "You have spoken, mask."

Then made the Englishman this sign: His left hand all open he lifted up into the air, then instantly shut into his fist the four fingers thereof, and his thumb extended at length he placed upon the gristle of his nose. Presently after, he lifted up his right hand all open and abased, and bent it downwards, putting the thumb thereof in the very place where the little finger of the left hand did close in the fist, and the four right hand fingers he softly moved in the air. Then contrarily he did with the right hand what he had done with the left and with the left what he had done with the right.

Panurge, being not a whit amazed at this, drew out into the air his trismegist codpiece with the left hand, and with his right drew forth a truncheon of a white ox rib, and two pieces of wood of a like form, one of black ebony, and the other of incarnation brasil, and put them betwixt the fingers of that hand in good symmetry: then knocking them together, made such a noise as the lepers of Britany use to do with their clappering clickets, yet better resounding and far more harmonious, and with his tongue contracted in his mouth, did very merrily warble it, always looking fixedly upon the Englishman. The divines, physicians, and chirurgeons that were there, thought that by this sign he would have inferred that the Englishman was a leper. The counsellors, lawyers, and decretalists conceived, that by doing this, he would have concluded some kind of human felicity to consist in leprosy, as the Lord maintained heretofore.

The Englishman for all this was nothing daunted, but holding up his two hands in the air, kept them in such form, that he closed the three master fingers in his fist; and passing his thumbs through his indical and middle fingers, his auricular fingers remained extended and stretched out, and so presented he them to Panurge: then joined he them so, that the right thumb touched the left, and the left little finger touched the right. Hereat Panurge, without speaking one word, lifted up his hands and made this sign.

He put the nail of the fore finger of his left hand to the nail of the thumb of the same, making in the middle of the distance as it were a buckle; and of his right hand shut up all the fingers into his fist, except the fore finger, which he often thrust in and out thro' the said two others of the left hand: then stretched he out the fore finger and middle finger, or medical of his right hand, holding them asunder as much as he could, and thrusting them towards Thaumast. Then did he put the thumb of his left hand upon the corner of his left eye, stretching out all his hand like the wing of a bird, or the fin of a fish, and moving it very daintily this way and that way. He did as much with his right hand upon the corner of his right eye. Thaumast began then to wax somewhat pale, and to tremble, and made him this sign.

With the middle finger of his right hand he struck against the muscle of the palm or pulp, which is under the thumb; then put he the fore finger of the right hand in the like buckle of the left; but he put it under and not over, as Panurge did. Then Panurge knocked one hand against another, and blowed in his palm, and put again the fore finger of his right hand into the aperture or mouth of the left, pulling it often in and out: then held he out his chin, most intensively looking upon Thaumast. The people there, which understood nothing in the other signs, knew very well that therein he demanded, without speaking a word to Thaumast, What do you mean by that? In effect, Thaumast then began to sweat great drops, and seemed, to all the spectators, a man strangely ravished in high contemplation. Then he bethought himself, and put all the nails of his left hand against those of his right, opening his fingers as if they had been semicircles; and with this sign, lifted up his hands as high as he could; whereupon Panurge presently put the thumb of his right hand under his jaws, and the little finger thereof in the mouth of the left hand; and, in this posture, made his teeth to sound very melodiously, the upper against the lower. With this, Thaumast with great toil and vexation of spirit rose up; but in rising let a great baker's fart, for the bran came after; and pissing withal very strong vinegar, stunk like all the devils in hell. The company began to stop their noses; for he had conskitted himself with mere anguish and perplexity; then lifted he up his right hand, clinching it in such sort, that he brought the ends of all his fingers to meet together; and his left hand he laid flat upon his breast. Whereat Panurge drew out his long cod-piece with his tuft, and stretched it forth a cubit and a half, holding it in the air with his right hand, and with his left took out his orange, and casting it up into the air seven times, at the eighth he hid it in the fist of his right hand, holding it steadily up on high; and then began to shake his fair cod-piece shewing it to Thaumast.

After that, Thaumast began to puff up his two cheeks like a player on a bagpipe, and blew as if he had been to puff up a pig's bladder. Whereupon Panurge put one finger of his left hand in his nockandrow, and with his mouth sucked in the air, in such a manner as when one eats oysters in the shell, or when we sup our broth; this done, he opened his mouth somewhat, and struck his right hand flat upon it, making therewith a great and a deep sound, as if it came from the superficies of the diaphragma through the trachean artery: and this he did for sixteen times. But Thaumast did always keep blowing like a goose. Then Panurge put the fore finger of his right hand into his mouth, pressing it very hard to the muscles thereof:

202

then he drew it out, and withal made a great noise, as when little boys shoot pellets out of the pot cannons, made of the hollow sticks of the branch of an elder tree; and he did it nine times.

Then Thaumast cried out, "Ha, my masters, a great secret." With this he put in his hand up to the elbow; then drew out a dagger that he had, holding it by the point downwards. Whereat Panurge took his long codpiece, and shook it as hard as he could against his thighs: then put his two hands entwined in manner of a comb upon his head, laying out his tongue as far as he was able; and turning his eyes in his head, like a goat that is ready to die. "Ha, I understand," said Thaumast, "but what?" making such a sign, that he put the haft of his dagger against his breast, and upon the point thereof the flat of his hand, turning in a little the ends of his fingers. Whereat Panurge held down his head on the left side, and put his middle finger into his right ear, holding up his thumb bolt upright: then he crossed his two arms upon his breast, and coughed five times, and, at the fifth time, he struck his right foot against the ground: then he lifted up his left arm, and closing all his fingers into his fist, held his thumb against his forehead, striking with his right hand six times against his breast. But Thaumast, as not content therewith, put the thumb of his left hand upon the top of his nose, shutting the rest of his said hand. Whereupon Panurge set his two master fingers upon each side of his mouth, drawing it as much as he was able, and widening it so, that he shewed all his teeth: and with his two thumbs plucked down his two eye-lids very low, making therewith a very-ill-favoured countenance as it seemed to the company.

CHAPTER XX

HOW THAUMAST RELATETH THE VIRTUES AND KNOWLEDGE OF PANURGE

THEN Thaumast rose up, and putting off his cap, did very kindly thank the said Panurge, and with loud voice said unto all the people that were there, "My lords, gentlemen, and others, at this time may I to some good purpose speak that evangelical word, *Et ecce plus quàm Salomon hic.* You have here in your presence an incomparable treasure, that is, my lord Pantagruel, whose great renown hath brought me hither, out of the very heart of England, to confer with him about the insoluble problems, both in magic, alchemy, the cabala, geomancy, astrology, and philosophy, which I had in my mind. But at present I am angry even with fame itself, which I think was envious to him, for that it did not declare the thousandth part of the worth that indeed is in him. You have seen how his disciple only hath satisfied me, and hath told me more than I asked of him: besides, he hath opened unto me and resolved other inestimable doubts, wherein I can assure you he hath to me discovered the very true well, fountain, and abyss of the encyclopedia of learning; yea, in such sort, that I did not think I should ever have found a man that could have made his skill appear, in so much as the first elements of word or half word. But in fine I will reduce into writing that which we have said and concluded, that the world may not take them to be fooleries, and will hereafter cause them to be printed, that every one may learn as I have done. Judge then what the master had been able to say, seeing the disciple hath done so valiantly; for, *non est discipulus super magistrum.* Howsoever, God be praised, and I do very humbly thank you for the honour that you have done us at this act: God reward you for it eternally." The like thanks gave Pantagruel to all the company; and, going from thence, he carried Thaumast to dinner with him: and believe that they drank as much as their skins could hold; or, as the phrase is, with unbottoned bellies; (for in that age they made fast their bellies with buttons, as we do now the collars of our doublets) even till they neither knew where they were, nor whence they came. Blessed lady, how they did carouse it, and pluck, as we say, at the kid's leather; and flaggons to trot, and they to toot, Draw, give (page) some wine; here, reach hither, fill with a devil. So! There was not one but did drink five and twenty or thirty pipes: can you tell how? Even *sicut terra sine aqua;* for the weather was hot; and besides that, they were very dry. In matter of the exposition of the propositions set down by Thaumast, and the signification of the signs which they used in their disputation, I would have set them down for you according to their own relation; but I have been told that Thaumast made a great book of it, imprinted at London, wherein he hath set down all, without omitting anything, and therefore at this time I do pass by it.

CHAPTER XXI

HOW PANURGE WAS IN LOVE WITH A LADY OF PARIS

PANURGE began to be in great reputation in the city of Paris, by means of this disputation, wherein he prevailed against the Englishman, and from thenceforth made his cod-piece to be very useful to him; to which effect he had it pinked with pretty little embroideries, after the Romanese fashion: and the world did praise him publicly, in so far that there was a song made of him, which little children did use to sing when they went to fetch mustard. He was withal made welcome in all companies of ladies and gentlewomen; so that at last he became presumptuous, and went about to bring to his lure one of the greatest ladies in the city; and indeed, leaving a rabble of long prologues and protestations, which ordinarily these dolent contemplative lent-lovers make, who never meddle with the flesh; one day said he unto her, "Madam, it would be a very great benefit to the common-wealth, delightful to you, honourable to your progeny, and necessary for me, that I cover you for the propagating of my race; and believe it, for experience will teach it you." The lady at this word thrust him back above a hundred leagues, saying, "You mischievous fool, is it for you to talk thus unto me? Whom do you think you have in hand? Begone! never come in my sight again; for, if it were not for one thing, I would have your legs and arms cut off."

"Well," said he, "that were all one to me, to want both legs and arms, provided you and I had but one merry bout together at the brangle buttock-game: for here within is (in shewing her his long codpiece) master John Thursday, who will play you such an antique, that you shall feel the sweetness thereof even to the very marrow of your bones: he is a gallant, and doth so well know how to find out all the corners, creeks, and ingrained inmates in your carnal trap, that after him there needs no broom, he'll sweep so well before, and leave nothing to his followers to work upon." Whereunto the lady answered, "Go, villain! go! if you speak to me one such word more, I will cry out, and have you knocked down with blows." "Ha," said he, "you are not so bad as you say; no, or else I am deceived in your physiognomy: for sooner shall the earth mount up into the heavens, and the highest heavens descend into the abyss of hell, and all the course of nature be quite perverted, than that, in so great

205

beauty and neatness as in you is, there should be one drop of gall or malice. They say, indeed, that hardly shall a man ever see a fair woman that is not also stubborn: yet that is spoke only of those vulgar beauties; but yours is so excellent, so singular, and so heavenly, that I believe nature hath given it you as a paragon and masterpiece of her art, to make us know what she can do, when she will employ all her skill, and all her power. There is nothing in you but honey, but sugar, but a sweet and celestial manna. To you it was to whom Paris ought to have adjudged the golden apple, not to Venus, no, nor to Juno, nor to Minerva: for never was there so much magnificence in Juno, so much wisdom in Minerva, nor so much comeliness in Venus, as there is in you.

"O heavenly Gods and Goddesses! how happy shall that man be to whom you will grant the favour to embrace her, to kiss her, and to rub his bacon with hers! By G— that shall be I, I know it well; for she loves me already her belly-full, I am sure of it; and so was I predestinated to it by the fairies. And therefore that we lose no time, put on, thrust out your gammons." Then he would have embraced her; but she made as if she would put out her head at the window, to call her neighbours for help. Then Panurge on a sudden ran out, and in his running away said, "Madam, stay here till I come again; I will go call them myself, do not you take so much pains." Thus went he away, not much caring for the repulse he had got, nor made he any whit the worse cheer for it. The next day he came to the church, at the time that she went to mass: at the door he gave her some of the holy-water, bowing himself very low before her: afterwards, he kneeled down by her very familiarly, and said unto her, "Madam, know that I am so amorous of you, that I can neither piss nor dung for love: I do not know (lady) what you mean, but if I should take any hurt by it, how much would you be to blame?"

"Go," said she, "go, I do not care; let me alone to say my prayers." "Ay, but," said he, "equivocate upon a *Beaumont le viconte.*" "I cannot," said she. "It is," said he, "a *beau con le vit monte:* and upon this pray to God to give you that which your noble heart desireth; and I pray you give me these patenotres." "Take them," said she, "and trouble me no longer." This done, she would have taken off her patenotres, which were made of a kind of yellow stone, called cestrin, and adorned with great spots of gold: but Panurge nimbly drew out one of his knives, wherewith he cut them off very handsomely; and whilst he was going away to carry them to the brokers, he said to her,

206

"Will you have my knife?" "No, no," said she. "But," said he, "to the point; I am at your commandment, body and goods, tripes and bowels."

In the meantime the lady was not well content with the want of her patenotres; for they were one of her implements to keep her countenance by in the church: then thought with herself, "This bold flouting royster is some giddy, fantastical, light-headed fool of a strange country; I shall never recover my patenotres again. What will my husband say? He will, no doubt, be angry with me; but I will tell him that a thief hath cut them off from my hands in the church; which he will easily believe, seeing the end of the ribbon left at my girdle." After dinner Panurge went to see her, carrying in his sleeve a great purse full of palace-crowns, called counters, and began to say unto her, "Which of us two loveth other best, you me, or I you?" Whereunto she answered, "As for me, I do not hate you; for, as God commands, I love all the world." "But to the point," said he, "are not you in love with me?" "I have," said she, "told you so many times already, that you should talk so no more to me; and, if you speak of it again, I will teach you that I am not one to be talked unto dishonestly: get you hence packing, and deliver me my patenotres, that my husband may not ask me for them."

"How now, madam," said he, "your patenotres? Nay, by mine oath I will not do so, but I will give you others: had you rather have them of gold well enamelled in great round knobs, or after the manner of love-knots, or otherwise all massive, like great ingots? or if you had rather have them of ebony, of jacinth, or of grained gold, with the marks of fine turquoises, or of fair topazes, marked with fine sapphires, or of baleu rubies, with great marks of diamonds of eight and twenty squares. No, no, all this is too little. I know a fair bracelet of fine emeralds, marked with spotted ambergris, and at the buckle a Persian pearl as big as an orange; it will cost not above five and twenty thousand ducats: I will make you a present of it; for I have ready coin enough": and withal he made a noise with his counters as if they had been French crowns.

"Will you have a piece of velvet, either of the violet colour, or of crimson died in grain; or a piece of broached or crimson satin? Will you have chains, gold, tablets, rings? You need no more but say yes; so far as fifty thousand ducats may reach, it is but as nothing to me." By the virtue of which words he made the water come in her mouth. But she said unto him, "No, I thank you; I will have nothing of you." "By G—" said he, "but I will have somewhat of you; yet shall it be that which shall cost you nothing, neither shall you have a jot the less, when you have given it: hold" (shewing his long codpiece), "this is Master John Goodfellow, that asks for lodging"; and with that would have embraced her; but she began to cry out, yet not very loud. Then Panurge put off his counterfeit garb, changed his false visage, and said unto her, "You will not then otherwise let me do a little? A turd for you; you do not deserve so much good, nor so much honour; but by G— I will make the dogs ride you." And with this he ran away as fast as he could, for fear of blows, whereof he was naturally fearful.

CHAPTER XXII

HOW PANURGE SERVED THE PARISIAN LADY A TRICK THAT PLEASED HER NOT VERY WELL

NOW you must note that the next day was the great festival of Corpus Christi, called the sacre, wherein all women put on their best apparel; and on that day the said lady was cloathed in a rich gown of crimson satin, under which she wore a very costly white velvet petticoat.

Now on the vigil, Panurge searched so long of one side and another, that he found a hot or salt bitch, which, when he had tried her her with his girdle, he led her to his chamber, and fed her very well all that day and night; in the morning thereafter he killed her, and took that part of her which the Greek geomancers know, and cut it into several pieces as small as he could: then carrying it away as close as might be, he went to the place where the lady was to come along to follow the procession, as the custom is upon the said holyday. And when she came in, Panurge sprinkled some holy water on her, saluting her very courteously. Then, a little while after she same bench, and gave her this roundelay in writing, in manner as had said her petty devotions, he sat down close by her upon the followeth:—

"A ROUNDELAY
"Lady for once, because my case
I told you, am I out of grace?
That you should so severely call
208

Me to be gone for good-and-all,
Who never had deserved your frown
By word, deed, letter, or lampoon.
You might deny me what I sought,
And not have call'd me all to nought
Because I would have had a bout,
                    Lady for once.

"It hurts you not that I complain
Of my intolerable pain;
Of bloody wound, and deadly dart,
Wherewith your beauty thrills my heart:
And since from thence my torment came,
O grant some little of that same,
                    Lady for once."

As she was opening this paper to see what it was, Panurge very promptly and lightly scattered the drug that he had upon her in divers places, especially in the pleats of her sleeves, and of her gown: then said he unto her, "Madam, the poor lovers are not always at ease. As for me, I hope that those heavy nights, those pains and troubles which I suffer for love of you, shall be a deduction to me of so much pain in purgatory: yet at the least pray to God to give me patience in my misery." Panurge had no sooner spoke this, but all the dogs that were in the church came running to this lady with the smell of the drugs that he had strewed upon her, both small and great, big and little, all came, laying out their member; smelling to her, and pissing everywhere upon her: it was the greatest villany in the world.

Panurge made some offers of driving them away; then took his leave of her, and withdrew himself into a chapel or oratory of the said church, to see the sport; for these villanous dogs did compiss all her habiliments, and left none of her attire unbesprinkled with their staling; insomuch that a tall greyhound pissed upon her head; others in her sleeves; others on her crupper-piece; and the little ones pissed upon her pattins; so that all the women that were round about her, had much ado to save her. Whereat Panurge very hartily laughing, he said to one of the lords of the city, "I believe that same lady is hot, or else that some greyhound hath covered her lately." And when he saw that all the dogs were flocking about her, yarring at the retardment of their access to her, and every way keeping such a coil with her, as they are wont to do about a proud or salt bitch; he forth-with departed from thence, and went to call Pantagruel; not forget-ting in his way along the street through which he went, where he found any dogs, to give them a bang with his foot, saying, "Will you not go with your fellows to the wedding? Away hence! avant! avant! with a devil avant!" And being come home, he said to Pantag-ruel, "Master, I pray you come and see all the dogs of the country, how they are assembled about a lady, the fairest in the city, and would duffle and line her." Whereunto Pantagruel willingly conde-scended, and saw the mystery, which he found very pretty and strange. But the best was at the procession, in which were seen above six hundred thousand and fourteen dogs about her, which did very much trouble and molest her! and whithersoever she passed, those dogs that came afresh, tracing her footsteps, followed her at the heels, and pissed in the way, where her gown had touched. All the world stood gazing at this spectacle, considering the action of those dogs, who leaping up, got about her neck, and spoiled all her gorgeous accoutre-ments; for the which she could find no remedy, but to retire unto her house, which was a palace. Thither she went, and the dogs after her: she ran to hide herself, but the chambermaids could not abstain from laughing. When she was entered into the house, and had shut the door upon herself, all the dogs came running, of half a league round, and did so well bepiss the gate of her house, that there they made a stream with their urine wherein a duck might very well have swum; and it is the same current that now runs at St. Victor, in which Gobelin dyeth scarlet by the specifical virtue of these piss-dogs, as our master Doribus did heretofore preach publicly. So may God help you, a mill would have ground corn with it; yet not so much as those of Basacle at Toulouse.

CHAPTER XXIII

HOW PANTAGRUEL DEPARTED FROM PARIS, HEARING THE NEWS THAT THE DIPSODES HAD INVADED THE LAND OF THE AMAUROTS: AND THE CAUSE WHEREFORE THE LEAGUES ARE SO SHORT IN FRANCE

A LITTLE while after Pantagruel heard news that his father Gar-gantua had been translated into the land of the fairies by Morgue, as heretofore were Oger and Arthur: and that, the report of his translation being spread abroad, the Dipsodes had issued out beyond their borders, with inroads, had wasted a great part of Utopia, and at that very time had besieged the great city of the Amaurots. Whereupon departing from Paris, without bidding any man farewell, for the business required diligence, he came to Rouen.

Now Pantagruel, in his journey, seeing that the leagues of that little territory about Paris, called France, were very short in regard of those of other countries, demanded the cause and reason of it from Panurge; who told him a story which Marotus du Lac, monachus, set down in the acts of the kings of Canarre; saying that, "In old times countries were not distinguished into leagues, miles, furlongs, nor parasanges, until that king Pharamond divided them, which was done in manner as followeth:—The said king chose at Paris a hundred fair, gallant, lusty, brisk young men, all resolute and bold adventurers in Cupid's duels, together with a hundred comely, pretty, handsome, lovely, and well-complexioned wenches of Picardy; all which he caused to be well entertained and highly fed for the space of eight days: then, having called for them, he delivered to every one of the young men his wench, with store of money to defray their charges, and this injunction besides, to go unto divers places here and there. And wheresoever they should biscot and thrum their wenches, that they, setting a stone there, it should be accounted for a league. Thus went away those brave fellows and sprightly blades most merrily, and because they were fresh, and had been at rest, they were jumming and tumbling almost at every field's end; and this is the cause why the leagues about Paris are so short. But when they had gone a great way, and were now as weary as poor devils, all the oil in their lamps being almost spent, they did not chink and duffle so often, but contented themselves (I mean for the men's part) with one scurvy paultry bout in a day. And this is that which makes the leagues in Britany, Delanes, Germany, and other more remote countries, so long. Other men give other reasons for it; but this seems to me of all other the best." To which Pantagruel willingly adhered. Parting from Rouen, they arrived at Honfleur, and there took shipping, Pantagruel, Panurge, Epistemon, Eusthenes, and Carpalim.

In which place, waiting for a favourable wind, and caulking their ship, he received from a lady of Paris (that had formerly been kept by him a long time) a letter, directed on the outside thus.

"To the best beloved of the fair,
And the least loyal of the brave;

"P.N.T.G.R.L."

CHAPTER XXIV

WHEN Pantagruel had read the superscription, he was much amazed, and therefore demanded of the said messenger the name of her that had sent it. Then opened he the letter, and found nothing written in it nor otherwise inclosed, but only a gold ring, with a square table diamond. Wondering at this, he called Panurge to him, and shewed him the case; whereupon Panurge told him, that the leaf of paper was written upon, but with such cunning and artifice that no man could see the writing at first sight. Therefore, to find it out, he set it by the fire, to see if it was made with sal ammoniac, soaked in water. Then put he it into the water, to see if the letter was written with the juice of tithymalle. After that, he held it up against the candle, to see if it was written with the juice of white onions.

Then he rubbed one part of it with oil of nuts, to see if it were not written with the lee of a fig-tree; and another part of it with the milk of a woman giving suck to her eldest daughter, to see if it was written with the blood of red toads, or green earth-frogs. Afterwards he rubbed one corner with the ashes of a swallow's nest, to see if it were not written with the dew that is found within the herb alcakengy, called the winter-cherry. He rubbed after that one end with ear-wax, to see if it were not written with the gall of a raven. Then did he dip it into vinegar, to try if it was not written with the juice of the garden spurge. After that he greased it with the fat of a bat or flitter-mouse, to see if it was not written with the sperm of a whale, which some call ambergris. Then put it very fairly into a bason full of fresh water, and forthwith took it out, to see whether it were written with stone-allum. But after all experiments, when he perceived that he could find out nothing, he called the messenger, and asked him, "Good fellow, the lady that sent thee hither, did she not give thee a staff to bring with thee?" thinking that it had been according to the conceit whereof Aulus Gellius maketh mention: and the messenger answered him, "No, sir." Then Panurge would have caused his head to be shaven, to see whether the lady had written upon his bald pate, with the hard lee whereof soap is made, that which she meant: but perceiving that his hair was very long, he forbore, considering that it could not have grown to so great a length in so short a time.

Then he said to Pantagruel, "Master, by the virtue of G— I cannot tell what to do nor say in it. For to know whether there be anything written upon this or no, I have made use of a good part of that which master Francisco di Nianto, the Tuscan, sets down, who hath written the manner of reading letters that do not appear: that which Zoroastes published, *peri grammaton acriton:* and Calphurnius Bassus, *de litteris illegibilibus.* But I can see nothing, nor do I believe that there is anything else in it than the ring. Let us therefore look upon it." Which when they had done, they found this in Hebrew written within, *Lama sabachthani:* whereupon they called Epistemon and asked him what that meant? To which he answered, "That they were Hebrew words, signifying, wherefore hast thou forsaken me?" Upon that Panurge suddenly replied, "I know the mystery. Do you see this diamond? It is a false one. This then is the exposition of that which the lady means, *Diamant faux;* that is, false lover, why hast thou forsaken me?" Which interpretation Pantagruel presently understood; and withal remembering, that at his departure he had not bid the lady farewel, he was very sorry, and would fain have returned to Paris to make his peace with her. But Epistemon put him in mind of Æneas's departure from Dido, and the saying of Heraclitus of Tarentum, that the ship being at anchor, when need requireth, we must cut the cable rather than lose time about untying of it. And that he should lay aside all other thoughts to succour the city of his nativity, which was then in danger. And indeed within an hour after that, the wind arose at the north-north-west; wherewith they hoisted sail, and put out, even into the main sea; so that within few days, passing by Porto Sancto, and by the Madeiras, they went ashore in the Canary islands; parting from thence, they passed by Capo-bianco, by Senega, by Capo-verde, by Gambra, by Sagres, by Melli, by the Cap di buona Speranza, and set ashore again in the kingdom of Melinda; parting from thence, they sailed away with a tramontan or northerly wind, passing by Meden, by Uti, by Uden, by Gelasim, by the isles of the Fairies, and along the kingdom of Achory, till at last they arrived at the port of Utopia, distant from the city of the Amaurots three leagues and somewhat more.

When they were ashore, and pretty well refreshed, Pantagruel said, "Gentlemen, the city is not far from hence; therefore were it not amiss, before we set forward, to advise well what is to be done, that we be not like the Athenians, who never took counsel until after the fact: are you resolved to live and die with me?" "Yes, sir," said they all, "and be as confident of us, as of your own fingers." "Well," said he, "there is but one thing that keeps my mind in great doubt and suspense, which is this; that I know not in what order, nor of what number the enemy is, that layeth siege to the city: for if I were certain of that, I should go forward and set on with the better assurance. Let us therefore consult together, and bethink ourselves by what means we may come to this intelligence." Whereunto they all said, "Let us go thither and see, and stay you here for us: for this very day, without further respite, do we make account to bring you a certain report thereof."

"Myself," said Panurge, "will undertake to enter into their camp within the very midst of their guards, unespied by their watch, and merrily feast and lecher it at their cost, without being known of any, to see the artillery and the tents of all the captains, and thrust myself in with a grave and magnific carriage, amongst all their troops and companies, without being discovered; the devil would not be able to pick me out with all his circumventions; for I am of the race of Zopyrus."

"And I," said Epistemon, "know all the plots and stratagems of the valiant captains and warlike champions of former ages, together with all the tricks and subtilties of the art of war. I will go; and though I be detected and revealed, I will escape, by making them believe of you whatever I please; for I am of the race of Sinon."

"I," said Eusthenes, "will enter and set upon them in their trenches, in spite of their sentries, and all their guards: for I will tread upon their bellies, and break their legs and arms, yea though they were every whit as strong as the devil himself; for I am of the race of Hercules."

"And I," said Carpalim, "will get in there, if the birds can enter: for I am so nimble of body, and light withal, that I shall have leaped over their trenches, and ran clean through all their camp, before that they perceive me: neither do I fear shot, nor arrow, nor horse, how swift soever, were he the Pegasus of Perseus, or Pacelot; being assured that I shall be able to make a safe and sound escape before them all without any hurt. I will undertake to walk upon the ears of corn, or grass in the meadows, without making either of them do so much as bow under me; for I am of the race of Camilla the Amazon.

CHAPTER XXV

AS he was speaking this, they perceived six hundred and three-score light horsemen, gallantly mounted, who came to discover what ship and company it was that was newly arrived in the harbour, and came in full gallop to take them if they had been able. Then said Pantagruel, "My lads, retire yourselves into the ship; here are some of our enemies coming apace, but I will kill them here before you like beasts, although they were ten times so many: in the mean-time withdraw yourselves, and take your sport at it." Then answered Panurge, "No, sir, there is no reason that you should do so; but on the contrary, retire you into the ship, both you and the rest; for I alone will here discomfit them: but we must not linger, come, set forward." Whereunto the others said, "It is well advised; sir, with-draw yourself, and we will help Panurge here, so shall you know what we are able to do." Then said Pantagruel, "Well, I am content; but if that you be too weak, I will not fail to come to your assistance."

With this, Panurge took two great cables of the ship, and tied them to the capstan which was on the deck towards the hatches, and fas-tened them in the ground, making a long circuit, the one further off, the other within that. Then said he to Epistemon, "Go aboard the ship, and, when I will give you a call, turn about the capstan upon the orlop diligently, drawing unto you the two cable-ropes": and said to Eusthenes and to Carpalim, "My bullies, stay you here, and of-fer yourselves freely to your enemies; do as they bid you, and make as if you would yield unto them: but take heed you come not within the compass of the ropes; be sure to keep yourselves free of them." And presently he went aboard the ship, and took a bundle of straw and a barrel of gunpowder, strewed it round about the compass of the cords, and stood by with a brand of fire, or match, lighted in his hand. Presently came the horsemen with great fury, and the foremost ran almost home to the ship; and by reason of the slipperiness of the bank they fell, they and their horses, to the number of four and forty: which the rest seeing, came on, thinking that resistance had been made them at their arrival. But Panurge said unto them, "My masters, I believe that you have hurt yourselves: I pray you pardon us, for it is

215

not our fault, but the slipperiness of the sea water that is always flow-ing: we submit ourselves to your good pleasure." So said likewise his two other fellows, and Epistemon, that was upon the deck. In the meantime, Panurge withdrew himself, and seeing that they were all within the compass of the cables, and that his two companions were retired, making room for all those horses which came in a crowd, thronging upon the neck of one another to see the ship and such as were in it, cried out on a sudden to Epistemon, "Draw, draw." Then began Epistemon to wind about the capstan, by doing whereof, the two cables so entangled and impestered the legs of the horses, that they were all of them thrown down to the ground easily, together with their riders. But they, seeing that, drew their swords, and would have cut them. Whereupon Panurge set fire to the train, and there burnt them up all like damned souls, both men and horses, not one escaping save one alone; who being mounted on a fleet Turkey courser, by mere speed in flight, got himself out of the circle of the ropes. But when Carpalim perceived him, he ran after him with such nimbleness and celerity, that he overtook him in less than a hundred paces: then leaping close behind him upon the crupper of his horse, clasped him in his arms, and brought him back to the ship.

This exploit being ended, Pantagruel was very jovial, and won-drously commended the ingenuity of these gentlemen, whom he called his fellow soldiers, and made them refresh themselves, and feed well and merrily upon the sea-shore, and drink heartily with their bellies upon the ground, and their prisoner with them, whom they admitted to that familiarity; only that the poor devil was not well assured but that Pantagruel would have eat him up whole: which, considering the wideness of his mouth, and capacity of his throat, was no great matter for him to have done; for he could have done it as easily as you would eat a small comfit, he shewing no more in his throat than would a grain of millet seed in the mouth of an ass.

CHAPTER XXVI

HOW PANTAGRUEL AND HIS COMPANY WERE WEARY OF EATING SALT MEATS; AND HOW CARPALIM WENT A HUNTING TO HAVE SOME VENISON

THUS as they talked and chatted together, Carpalim said, "And by the belly of St. Quenet, shall we never eat any venison? This salt meat makes me horribly dry. I will go fetch you a quarter of one of those horses which we have burnt, it is well roasted already." As he was rising up to go about it, he perceived under the side of a wood a fair great roe-buck, which was come out of his fort, as I conceive, at the sight of Panurge's fire. Him did he pursue and run after with so much vigour and swiftness, as if it had been a bolt out of a cross-bow, and caught him in a moment; and, whilst he was in his course, he with his hands took in the air four great bastards, seven bitterns, six and twenty grey partridges, two and thirty red-legged ones, sixteen pheasants, nine woodcocks, nineteen herons, two and thirty coushots and ring-doves; and with his feet killed ten or twelve hares and rabbits, which were then at relief, and pretty big withal; eighteen rayles in a knot together, with fifteen young wild boars, two little bevers, and three great foxes. So, striking the kid with his falchion athwart the head, he killed him, and bearing him on his back, he in his return took up his hares, rayles, and young wild boars, and as far off as he could be heard, cried out, and said, "Panurge, my friend, vinegar, vinegar." Then the good Pantagruel, thinking he had fainted, commanded them to provide some vinegar. But Panurge knew well that there was some good prey in hands, and forthwith shewed unto noble Pantagruel how he was bearing upon his back a fair roe-buck, and all his girdle bordered with hares. Then immediately did Epistemon make, in the name of the nine muses, nine antique wooden spits. Eusthenes did help to flay, and Panurge placed two great cuirassier saddles in such sort that they served for andirons; and making their prisoner to be their cook, they roasted their venison by the fire where the horsemen were burnt. And making great cheer with a good deal of vinegar, the devil a one of them did forbear from his victuals: it was a triumphant and incomparable spectacle, to see how they ravened and devoured. Then said Pantagruel, "Would to God every one of you had two pair of sacring bells hanging at your chin, and that I had at mine the great clocks of Rennes, of Poitiers, of Tours, and of Cambray, to see what a peal they would ring with the wagging of our chaps."

"But," said Panurge, "it were better we thought a little upon our business, and by what means we might get the upper hand of our enemies." "That is well remembered," said Pantagruel: therefore spoke he thus to the prisoner: "My friend, tell us here the truth, and do not lie to us at all, if thou wouldest not be flayed alive, for it is I that eat the little children: relate unto us, at full, the order, the number, and the strength of the army." To which the prisoner answered, "Sir, know for a truth, that in the army there are three hundred giants, all armed with armour of proof, and wonderful great; nevertheless, not fully so great as you, except one that is their head, named Loupgarou, who is armed from head to foot with cyclopical anvils. Furthermore, one hundred threescore and three thousand foot, all armed with the skins of hobgoblings, strong and valiant men; eleven thousand four hundred cuirassiers; three thousand six hundred double cannons, and harquebusiers without number; fourscore and fourteen thousand pioneers: one hundred and fifty thousand whores, fair like goddesses ('That is for me," said Panurge), whereof some are Amazons, some Lionnoises, others Parisiennes, Taurangelles, Angevines, Poictevines, Normands, and High Dutch: there are of them of all countries and all languages."

"Yea, but," said Pantagruel, "is the king there?" "Yes, sir," said the prisoner, "he is there in person, and we call him Anarchus, king of the Dipsodes; which is as much as to say, thirsty people; for you never saw men more thirsty, or more willing to drink: and his tent is guarded by the giants." "It is enough," said Pantagruel, "come, brave boys, are you resolved to go with me?" To which Panurge answered, "God confound him that leaves you. I have already bethought myself how I will kill them all like pigs, and so that the devil one leg of them shall escape. But I am somewhat troubled about one thing." "And what is that?" said Pantagruel. "It is," said Panurge, "how I shall be able to set forward to the justling and bragmardising of all the whores that be there this afternoon, in such sort, that there escape not one unbumped by me, breasted and jummed after the ordinary fashion of men and women." "Ha, ha, ha, ha, ha," said Pantagruel.

And Carpalim said, "The devil take these sink-holes, if by G— I do not bumbaste some one of them."

"And I," said Eusthenes, "what d'ye make of me, who, since we came from Rouen, have never been wound up, at least that my needle could mount above to ten or eleven o'clock? It is now stiff and strong, like a hundred devils." "Truly," said Panurge, "thou shalt have of the fattest, and of those that are the most plump, and in the best case."

"How now," said Epistemon, "every one shall ride, and I must lead the ass? The devil take him that will do so. We will make use of the right of war. *Qui potest capere, capiat.*" "No, no," said Panurge, "but tie thine ass to a crook, and ride as the world doth." And the good Pantagruel laughed at all this, and said unto them, "You reckon without your host. I am much afraid, that before it be night I shall see you in such taking, that you will have no great stomach to ride, but are more like to be rode upon, with sound blows of pike and lance."

"Enough of that," said Epistemon: "I will not fail to bring them to you, either to roast or boil, to fry or put in paste. They are not so many in number as were in the army of Xerxes: for he had thirty hundred thousand fighting men, if you will believe Herodotus and Trogus Pompeius; and yet Themistocles with a few men overthrew them all. For God's sake take you no care for that." "Cobsminnie, Cobsminnie," said Panurge, "my codpiece alone shall suffice to overthrow all the men; and St. Sweephole, that dwells within, shall lay all the women squat on their backs." "Up then, my lads," said Pantagruel, "and let us march along."

CHAPTER XXVII

HOW PANTAGRUEL SET UP ONE TROPHY IN MEMORIAL OF THEIR VALOUR, AND PANURGE ANOTHER IN REMEMBRANCE OF THE HARES. HOW PANTAGRUEL LIKEWISE WITH HIS FARTS BEGAT LITTLE MEN, AND WITH HIS FISGS [FIZZLES] LITTLE WOMEN: AND HOW PANURGE BROKE A GREAT STAFF OVER TWO GLASSES

BEFORE we depart hence," said Pantagruel, "in remembrance of the exploit that you have now performed, I will in this place erect a fair trophy." Then every man amongst them, with great joy, and fine little country songs, set up a huge big post, whereunto they hanged a great cuirassier saddle, the fronstal of a barbed horse, bridle-bosses, pulley-pieces for the knees, stirrup-leathers, spurs, stirrups, a coat of mail, a corslet tempered with steel, a battle-axe, a strong, short, and sharp horseman's sword; a gantlet, a horseman's mace, gusset-armour for the arm-pits, leg-harness, and a gorget, with all other furniture needful for a triumphant arch, or trophy. And then Pantagruel, for an eternal memorial, wrote this victorial ditton as followeth:

> "Here four bold champions had a rubbers
> With sixty and six hundred lubbers;
> Destroyed 'em all; yet when they fought 'em,

219

Had not their arms, but wits about 'em:
So play'd the scoundrels such a trick,
Old Scipio never knew the like.
Learn hence, kings, dukes, all great and little,
'Tis wit, not strength, that wins the battle.
              For victory,
              As all agree,
              Hangs on the beck
                  Of pow'rs above,
                  Who surely move,
              The proud to check.
The strong are baffled without question,
  Or doubt of any that's a christian:
And he ('tis only he) can have it,
Who has the grace and faith to crave it."

Whilst Pantagruel was writing these foresaid verses, Panurge halved, and fixed upon a great stake, the horns of the roebuck, together with the skin, and the right fore foot thereof; the ears of three leverets, the chine of a coney, the jaws of a hare, the wings of two bustards, the feet of four questdoves, a bottle full of vinegar, a horn wherein to put salt, a wooden spit, a larding stick, a scurvy kettle full of holes, a dripping-pan, a skillet to make sauce in, an earthen salt-cellar, and a goblet of Beauvois. Then, in imitation of Pantagruel's verses and trophy, wrote that which followeth:

"Here four brave topers sitting on their bums,
  With flagons, nobler noise than drums,
Carous'd it, bous'd it, toss'd the liquor,
Each seem'd a Bacchus-priest, or vicar:
Hares, conies, bustards, pigs were brought 'em,
With jugs and pipkins strew'd about 'em;
For trophy-spoils to each good fellow,
  That is hereafter to be mellow.
              In every creed,
              'Tis on all hands agreed,
          And plainly confest;
              When the weather is hot,
              That we stick to the pot,
          And drink o' the best.

220

First note, that in your bill of fare,
Sauce be provided for the rare.
But vinegar the most extol;
'Tis of an hare the very soul."

Then said Pantagruel, "Come, my lads, let us be gone, we have staid here too long about our victual; for very seldom doth it fall out, that the greatest eaters do the most martial exploits. There is no shadow like that of flying colours, no smoke like that of horses, no clattering like that of armour." At this Epistemon began to smile, and said, "There is no shadow like that of the kitchen, no smoke like that of pasties, and no clattering like that of goblets." Unto which answered Panurge, "There is no shadow like that of curtains, no smoke like that of women's breasts, and no clattering like that of ballocks." Then, forthwith rising up, he gave a fart, a leap, and a whistle, and most joyfully cried aloud, "Ever live, Pantagruel." When Pantagruel saw that, he would have done as much, but, with the fart that he let, the earth trembled nine leagues about: wherewith, and with the corrupted air, he begot above three and fifty thousand little men, ill-favoured dwarfs; and with one fisg [fizzle] that he let, he made as many little women, crouching down, as you shall see in divers places, which never grow but like cows' tails, downwards, or like the Limosin rad-ishes, round. "How now," said Panurge, "are your farts so fertile? By G—, here be brave farted men and fisgued women; let them be married together, they will beget fine hornets and dorflies." So did Pantagruel, and called them pigmies. Those he sent to live in an is-land thereby, where, since that time, they are increased mightily; but the cranes make war with them continually, against which they do most courageously defend themselves; for these little ends of men and dandiprats (whom in Scotland they call whip-handles, and knots of a tar-barrel) are commonly very testy and choleric. The physical rea-son whereof is, because their heart is near their turd.

At this same time, Panurge took two drinking glasses that were there, both of one bigness, and filled them up with water to the brim, and set one of them upon one stool, and the other upon another, plac-ing them above five feet from one another: then he took the staff of a javelin, about five feet and a half long, and put it upon the two glasses, so that the two ends of the staff did come just to the brims of the glasses. This done, he took a great stake, and said to Pantagruel, and to the rest, "My masters, behold how easily we shall have the victory

221

over our enemies: for just as I shall break this staff here upon these glasses, without either breaking or crasing of them; nay, which is more, without spilling one drop of the water that is within them; even so shall we break the heads of our Dipsodes, without receiving any of us any wound or loss in our person or goods. But that you may not think there is any witchcraft in this, hold," said he to Eusthenes, "strike upon the midst as hard as thou canst with this log." Eusthenes did so, and the staff was broken in two pieces, and not one drop of the water fell out of the glasses. Then said he, "I know a great many such other tricks, let us now therefore march boldly."

CHAPTER XXVIII

HOW PANTAGRUEL GOT THE VICTORY VERY STRANGELY OVER THE DIPSODES, AND THE GIANTS

AFTER all this talk Pantagruel took the prisoner to him, and sent him away, saying, "Go thou unto thy king in his camp, and tell him tidings of what thou hast seen, and let him resolve to feast me to-morrow about noon; for as soon as my gallies shall come, which will be to-morrow at farthest, I will prove unto him, by eighteen hundred thousand fighting men, and seven thousand giants, all of them greater than I am, that he hath done foolishly, and against reason, thus to invade my country": wherein Pantagruel feigned that he had an army at sea. But the prisoner answered, that he would yield himself to be his slave; and that he was content never to return to his own people, but rather with Pantagruel to fight against them; and for God's sake besought him, that he might be permitted so to do. Whereunto Pantagruel would not give consent, but commanded him to depart thence speedily, and be gone, as he had told him: and to that effect gave him a box full of euphorbium, together with some grains of the black chameleon thistle, steeped in aqua vitæ, and made up into the condiment of a wet sucket; commanding him to carry it to his king, and to say unto him, that if he were able to eat one ounce of that without drinking after it, he might be able to resist him, without any fear or apprehension of danger.

The prisoner then besought him, with joined hands, that in the hour of battle he would have compassion upon him. Whereat Pantagruel said unto him, "After that thou hast delivered all unto the king, put thy whole confidence in God, and he will not forsake thee: because, although for my part I be mighty, as thou mayest see, and have an infinite number of men in arms, I do nevertheless trust neither in my force nor in my industry; but all my confidence is in God my protector, who doth never forsake those that in him do put their trust and confidence." This done, the prisoner requested him that he would be contented wth some reasonable composition for his ransom. To which Pantagruel answered, that his end was not to rob nor ransom men, but to enrich them, and reduce them to total liberty. "Go thy way," said he, "in the peace of the living God, and never follow evil company, lest some mischief befal thee." The prisoner being gone, Pantagruel said to his men, "Gentlemen, I have made this prisoner believe that we have an army at sea, as also that we will not assault them till to-morrow at noon, to the end that they, doubting of the great arrival of our men, may spend this night in providing, and strengthening themselves; but in the meantime my intention is, that we charge them about the hour of the first sleep."

Let us leave Pantagruel here with his apostles, and speak of king Anarchus and his army. When the prisoner was come, he went unto the king, and told him there was a great giant come, called Pantagruel, who had overthrown, and made to be cruelly roasted, all the six hundred and fifty-nine horsemen, and he alone escaped to bring the news. Besides that, he was charged by the said giant to tell him, that the next day about noon he must make a dinner ready for him; for at that hour he was resolved to set upon him. Then did he give him that box wherein were those confitures: but, as soon as he had swallowed down one spoonful of them, he was taken with such a heat in the throat, together with an ulceration in the flap of the top of the wind-pipe, that his tongue peeled with it in such sort, that for all they could do unto him, he found no ease at all, but by drinking only without cessation: for as soon as ever he took the goblet from his head, his tongue was on fire; and therefore they did nothing but still pour wine into his throat with a funnel. Which when his captains, bashaws, and guard of his body did see, they tasted of the same drugs, to try whether on them they would have the same operation or no: but it so befel them as it had done their king; and they plied the flaggon so well, that the noise ran throughout all the camp, how the prisoner was returned; that the next day they were to have an assault; that the king and his captains did already prepare themselves for it, together with his guards, and that with carousing lustily, and quaffing as hard as they could. Every man therefore in the army began to tipple, ply the pot, swill and guzzle, till in fine they fell asleep like pigs, all out of order throughout the whole camp.

Let us now return to the good Pantagruel, and relate how he carried himself in this business. Departing from the place of the trophies, he took the mast of their ship in his hand, like a pilgrim's staff, and put within the top of it two hundred and thirty-seven puncheons of white-wine of Anjou, the rest was of Rouen; and tied up to his girdle the barque all full of salt, as easily as the Lanskennets carry their little panniers; and so set onward on his way with his fellow-soldiers. When he was come near to the enemy's camp, Panurge said unto him, "Sir, if you would do well, let down this white-wine of Anjou from the scuttle of the mast of the ship, that we may all drink thereof, like Bretons."

Hereunto Pantagruel very willingly consented; and they drank so neat, that there was not so much as one poor drop left of two hundred and thirty-seven puncheons, except one leathern bottle of Tours, which Panurge filled for himself (for he called that his vade mecum) and some scurvy lees of wine in the bottom, which served him instead of vinegar. After they had whittled and curried the can pretty handsomely, Panurge gave Pantagruel to eat some devilish drugs, compounded of lithotripton, nephrocatarticon, the marmalade of quinces, with cantharides, and other diureticks. This done, Pantagruel said to Carpalim, "Go into the city, scrambling like a cat up against a wall, as you can well do, and tell them that now presently they come out, and charge their enemies as rudely as they can; and having said so, come down, taking a lighted torch with you, wherewith you shall set on fire all the tents and pavilions in the camp; then cry as loud as you are able with your great voice, and then come away from thence." "Yea, but," said Carpalim, "were it not good to nail all their ordnance?" "No, no," said Pantagruel, "only blow up all their powder." Carpalim, obeying him, departed suddenly, and did as he was appointed by Pantagruel; and all the combatants came forth that were in the city: and, when he had set fire to the tents and pavilions, he passed so lightly through them, and so highly and perfoundly did they snore and sleep, that they never perceived him. He came to the place where their artillery was, and set their munition on fire: but here was the danger, the fire was so sudden, that poor Carpalim had almost been burnt; and had it not been for his wonderful agility, he had been scorched like a roasting pig: but he departed away so speedily, that a bolt or arrow out of a cross-bow could not have a swifter motion.

When he was clear of their trenches, he shouted aloud, and cried out so dreadfully, and with such amazement to the hearers, that it seemed all the devils of hell had been let loose. At which noise the enemies awaked, but can you tell how? Even no less astonished than are the monks at the ringing of the first peal to matins, which in Lusonnois is called rub-ballock.

In the meantime Pantagruel began to sow the salt that he had in his barque, and, because they slept with an open gaping mouth, he filled all their throats with it, so that those poor wretches were by it made to cough like foxes, crying, "Ha, Pantagruel, how thou addest greater heat to the firebrand that is in us." Suddenly Pantagruel had will to piss, by means of the drugs which Panurge had given him, and pissed amidst the camp so well and so copiously, that he drowned them all, and there was a particular deluge ten leagues round about; though history saith, if his father's great mare had been there, and pissed likewise, it would undoubtedly have been a more enormous deluge than that of Deucalion: for she did never piss but she made a river, greater than is either the Rhosne or the Danube. Those that were come out of the city, seeing this, said, "They are all cruelly slain, see how the blood runs along": but they were deceived in thinking Pantagruel's urine had been the blood of their enemies; for they could not see but by the light of the fire of the pavilions, and some small light of the moon.

The enemies, after they were awaked, seeing on one side the fire in the camp, and on the other the inundation of the urinal deluge, could not tell what to say, nor what to think. Some said, that it was the end of the world, and the final judgment which ought to be by fire. Others again thought, that the sea-gods, Neptune, Proteus, Triton, and the rest of them, did persecute them; for that indeed they found it to be like sea-water and salt.

O who were able now condignly to relate how Pantagruel did demean himself against the three hundred giants! O my muse, my Calliope, my Thalia, inspire me at this time, restore unto me my spirits, for this is the logical bridge of asses: here is the pitfall, here is the difficulty, to have ability enough to express the horrible battle that was fought. Ah, would to God that I had a bottle of the best wine that ever those drank who shall read this so veridical history!

CHAPTER XXIX

HOW PANTAGRUEL DISCOMFITED THE THREE HUNDRED GIANTS ARMED WITH FREESTONE, AND LOUPGAROU THEIR CAPTAIN

THE giants, seeing all their camp drowned, carried away their king Anarchus upon their backs, as well as they could, out of the fort; as Æneas did his father Anchises, in the time of the conflagration of Troy. When Panurge perceived them, he said to Pantagruel, "Sir, yonder are the giants coming forth against you; lay on them with your mast gallantly, like an old fencer; for now is the time that you must shew yourself a brave and an honest man: and for our part, we will not fail you; I myself will kill ye a good many gallantly enough: for why, David killed Goliah very easily; and then, this great letcher Eusthenes, who is stronger than four oxen, will nor spare himself. Be of good courage, therefore, and valiant; charge amongst them with point and edge, and by all manner of means." "Well," said Pantagruel, "of courage I have more than for fifty franks: but let us be wise; for Hercules never undertook against two." "That is well cacked, well scummered," said Panurge: "do you compare yourself with Hercules? You have by G—, more strength in your teeth, and more scent in your bum, than ever Hercules had in all his body and soul. So much is a man worth as he esteems himself." Whilst they spake those words, behold Loupgarou was come with all his giants, who seeing Pantagruel in a manner alone, was carried away with temerity and presumption, for hopes that he had to kill the good man: whereupon he said to his companions the giants, "You wenchers of the Low-country, by Mahoon, if any of you undertake to fight against these men here, I will put you cruelly to death: It is my will that you let me fight single; in the meantime you shall have good sport to look upon us." Then all the other giants retired with their king to the place where the flaggons stood, and Panurge and his comrades with them, who counterfeited those that have had the pox; for he writhed about his mouth, shrunk up his fingers, and with a harsh voice said unto them, "I forsake —od, fellow soldiers, if I would have it to be believed, that we make any war at all: give us somewhat to eat with you, whilst our masters fight against one another." To this the king and giants jointly condescended, and accordingly made them to banquet with them.

In the meantime Panurge told them the fables of Turpin, the examples of St. Nicholas, and the tale of a tub. Loupgarou then set forward towards Pantagruel, with a mace all of steel, and that of the best sort, weighing nine thousand seven hundred kintals, and two quarterons; at the end whereof were thirteen pointed diamonds, the least whereof was as big as the greatest bell of our lady's church at Paris; there might want perhaps the thickness of a nail, or at most (that I may not lie) of the back of those knives which they call cutlugs; but for a little off or on, more or less, it is no matter: and it was enchanted in such sort, that it could never break, but contrarily all that it did touch did break immediately. Thus then as he approached with great fierceness and pride of heart, Pantagruel, casting up his eyes to heaven, recommended himself to God with all his soul, making such a vow as followeth:

"O thou Lord God, who hast always been my protector and my saviour, thou seest the distress wherein I am at this time: nothing brings me hither but a natural zeal, which thou hast permitted unto mortals, to keep and defend themselves, their wives and children, country and family, in case thy own proper cause were not in question, which is the faith; for in such a business thou wilt have no co-adjutors, only a catholic confession and service of thy word, and hast forbidden us all arming and defence: for thou art the Almighty, who in thine own cause, and where thine own business is taken to heart, canst defend it far beyond all that we can conceive; thou who hast thousand thousands of hundreds of millions of legions of angels, the least of which is able to kill all mortal men, and turn about the heavens and earth at his pleasure, as heretofore it very plainly appeared in the army of Sennacherib. If it may please thee therefore at this time to assist me, as my whole trust and confidence is in thee alone, I vow unto thee, that in all countries whatsoever, wherein I shall have any power or authority, whether in this Utopia, or elsewhere, I will cause thy holy gospel to be purely, simply, and entirely preached; so that the abuses of a rabble of hypocrites and false prophets, who by human constitutions and depraved inventions have impoisoned all the world, shall be quite exterminated from about me." This vow was no sooner made, but there was heard a voice from heaven, saying, *"Hoc fac, & vinces"*; that is to say, "Do this, and thou shall overcome."

Then Pantagruel, seeing that Loupgarou with his mouth wide open was drawing near to him, went against him boldly, and cried out, as loud as he was able, "Thou diest, villain, thou diest!" purposing by his horrible cry to make him afraid, according to the discipline of the Lacedemonians. Withal, he immediately cast at him, out of his barque, which he wore at his girdle, eighteen cags and four bushels of salt, wherewith he filled both his mouth, throat, nose, and eyes. At this Loupgarou was so highly incensed, that most fiercely setting upon him, he thought even then with a blow of his mace to have beat out his brains: but Pantagruel was very nimble, and had always a quick foot and a quick eye, and therefore with his left foot did he step back one pace; yet not so nimbly, but that the blow, falling upon the barque, broke it in four thousand fourscore and six pieces, and threw all the rest of the salt about the ground. Pantagruel, seeing that, most gallantly displayed the vigour of his arms, and, according to the art of the ax, gave him with the great end of his mast a home thrust a little above the breast; then bringing along the blow to the left side with a slash, struck him between the neck and shoulders: after that, advancing his right foot, he gave him a push upon the couillons, with the upper end of his said mast; wherewith breaking the scuttle on the top thereof, he split three or four puncheons of wine that were left therein.

Upon that, Loupgarou thought that he had pierced his bladder, and that the wine that came forth had been urine. Pantagruel, being not content with this, would have doubled it by a side-blow, but Loupgarou lifting up his mace, advanced one step upon him, and with all his force would have dashed it upon Pantagruel; wherein (to speak the truth) he so sprightfully carried himself, that, if God had not succoured the good Pantagruel, he had been cloven from the top of his head to the bottom of his milt; but the blow glanced to the right side by the brisk nimbleness of Pantagruel, and his mace sunk into the ground above threescore and thirteen feet, through a huge rock, out of which the fire did issue greater than nine thousand and six tuns. Pantagruel seeing him busy about plucking out his mace, which struck in the ground between the rocks, ran upon him, and would have clean cut off his head, if by mischance his mast had not touched a little against the stock of Loupgarou's mace, which was enchanted, as we have said before. By this means his mast broke off about three handfuls above his hands; whereat he stood amazed like a bell-founder, and cried out, "Ah, Panurge, where art thou?" Panurge, seeing that, said to the king and the giants, "By G— they will hurt one another if they be not parted." But the giants were as merry as if they had been at a wedding. Then Carpalim would have risen from thence to help his master, but one of the giants said to him, "By Golfarin the nephew of Mahom, if thou stir hence I will put thee in the bottom of my breeches instead of a suppository, which cannot chuse but do me good; for in my belly I am very costive, and cannot well cagar without gnashing my teeth, and making many filthy faces."

Then Pantagruel, thus destitute of a staff, took up the end of his mast, striking athwart and alongst upon the giant; but he did him no more hurt than you would do with a filip upon a smith's anvil. In the meantime Loupgarou was drawing his mace out of the ground, and, having already plucked it out, was ready therewith to have struck Pantagruel, who, being very quick in turning, avoided all his blows in taking only the defensive part in hand; until on a sudden he saw that Loupgarou did threaten him with these words, saying, "Now, villain! will not I fail to chop thee as small as minced meat, and keep thee henceforth from ever making any more poor men athurst." Then, without any more ado, Pantagruel struck him such a blow with his foot against the belly, that he made him fall backwards, his heels over his head, and dragged him thus along at flay-buttock above a flight-shot. Then Loupgarou cried out, bleeding at the throat, "Mahom! Mahom! Mahom!" At which noise all the giants arose to succour him: but Panurge said unto them, "Gentlemen, do not go; if you will believe me: for our master is mad, and strikes athwart and alongst, he cares not where; he will do you a mischief." But the giants made no account of it, seeing that Pantagruel had never a staff.

And when Pantagruel saw those giants approach very near unto him, he took Loupgarou by the two feet, and lifted up his body like a pike in the air, wherewith, it being harnessed with anvils, he laid such heavy load amongst those giants, armed with freestone, that, striking them down as a mason doth little knobs of stones, there was not one of them that stood before him, whom he threw not flat to the ground; and, by the breaking of this stony armour, there was made such a horrible rumble, as put me in mind of the fall of the butter-tower of St. Stephen's at Bourges, when it melted before the sun. Panurge, with Carpalim, and Eusthenes, did cut in the meantime the throats of those that were struck down, in such sort, that there escaped not one. Pantagruel to any man's sight was like a mower, who with his scithe, which was Loupgarou, cut down the meadow grass, to wit, the giants. But with this fencing of Pantagruel's, Loupgarou lost his head, which happened when Pantagruel struck down one whose name was Riflandouille, who was armed cap-a-pie with grison-stones, one chip whereof splintering abroad cut off Epistemon's neck clean and fair. For otherwise the most part of them were but lightly armed, with a kind of sandy brittle-stone, and the rest with slates. At last when he saw that they were all dead, he threw the body of Loupgarou as hard as he could against the city, where, falling like a frog upon his belly, in the great piazza, he with the fall killed a singed he-cat, a wet she-cat, a farting duck, and a bridled goose.

CHAPTER XXX

HOW EPISTEMON, WHO HAD HIS HEAD CUT OFF, WAS FINELY HEALED BY PANURGE; AND OF THE NEWS WHICH HE BROUGHT FROM THE DEVILS, AND DAMNED PEOPLE IN HELL

THIS gigantal victory being ended, Pantagruel withdrew himself to the place of the flaggons, and called for Panurge and the rest, who came unto him safe and sound, except Eusthenes (whom one of the giants had scratched a little in the face, whilst he was about the cutting of his throat) and Epistemon, who appeared not at all. Whereat Pantagruel was so aggrieved, that he would have killed himself. But Panurge said unto him, "Nay, sir, stay awhile, and we will search for him among the dead and find out the truth of all." Thus as they went seeking after him, they found him stark dead, with his head between his arms all bloody. Then Eusthenes cried out, "Ah, cruel death! hast thou taken from me the perfectest amongst men?" At which words Pantagruel rose up with the greatest grief that ever any man did see, and said to Panurge, "Ha, my friend! the prophecy of your two glasses, and the Javelin staff, was a great deal too deceitful." But Panurge answered, "My dear bullies all, weep not one drop more; he being yet all hot, I will make him as sound as ever he was." In saying this, he took the head, and held it warm fore-against his cod-piece, that the wind might not enter into it. Eusthenes and Carpalim carried the body to the place where they had banqueted, not out of any hope that ever he would recover, but that Pantagruel might see it.

Nevertheless Panurge gave them very good comfort, saying, "If I do not heal him, I will be content to lose my head, which is a fool's wager; leave off therefore crying, and help me." Then cleansed he his neck very well with pure white-wine, and, after that, took his head, and into it synapised some powder of diamerdis, which he always carried about him in one of his bags. Afterwards he anointed it with I know not what ointment, and set it on very just, vein against vein, sinew against sinew, and spondyle against spondyle that he might not be wry-necked, for such people he mortally hated. This done, he gave it round about some fifteen or sixteen stitches with a needle, that it might not fall off again; then on all sides, and everywhere, he put a little ointment on it, which he called resuscitative.

Suddenly Epistemon began to breathe, then opened his eyes, yawned, sneezed, and afterwards let a great houshold fart. Whereupon Panurge said, "Now certainly he is healed"; and therefore gave him to drink a large full glass of strong white-wine with a sugared toast. In this fashion was Epistemon finely healed, only that he was somewhat hoarse for above three weeks together, and had a dry cough, of which he could not be rid, but by the force of continual drinking. And now he began to speak, and said that he had seen the devil, had spoken with Lucifer familiarly, and had been very merry in hell, and in the Elysian fields; affirming very seriously before them all, that the devils were boon companions and merry fellows: but, in respect of the damned, he said he was very sorry that Panurge had so soon called him back into this world again: "For," said he, "I took wonderful delight to see them." "How so?" said Pantagruel. "Because they do not use them there," said Epistemon, "so badly, as you think they do. Their estate and condition of living is but only changed after a very strange manner. For I saw Alexander the Great there mending old stockings, whereby he got but a very poor living.

Xerxes was a crier of mustard.

Romulus, a salter and patcher of pattens.

Numa, a nail-smith.

Tarquin, a porter.

Piso, a clownish swain.

Sylla, a ferry-man.

Cyrus, a cowherd.

Themistocles, a glass-maker.

Epaminondas, a maker of looking-glasses.

Brutus and Cassius, surveyors of land.

Demosthenes, a vine-dresser.

Cicero, a fire kindler.
Fabius, a threader of patenotres.
Artaxerxes, a rope-maker.
Æneas, a miller.
Achilles, a scald-pated maker of hay-bundles.
Agamemnon, a lick-box.
Ulysses, a hay-mower.
Nestor, a forester.
Darius, a gold-finder.
Ancus Martius, a ship-trimmer.
Camillus, a foot-post.
Marcellus, a sheller of beans.
Drusus, a taker of money at the doors of play-houses.
Scipio Africanus, a crier of lee in a wooden slipper.
Asdrubal, a lanthorn-maker.
Hannibal, a kettle-maker and seller of egg-shells.
Priamus, a seller of old clouts.
Lancelot of the lake, a flayer of dead horses.

All the knights of the round table were poor labouring slaves, employed to row over the rivers of Cocytus, Phlegeton, Styx, Acheron, and Lethe, when messieurs the devils had a mind to recreate themselves upon the water; as on the like occasion are hired the boat-men at Lions, the gondeliers of Venice [and the oars at London]; but with this difference, that these poor knights have only for their fare a bob or flirt on the nose, and in the evening a morsel of coarse mouldy bread.

Trajan was a fisher of frogs.
Antoninus, a lacquey.
Commodus, a bag-piper.
Pertinax, a peeler of walnuts.
Lucullus, a maker of rattles and hawks' bells.
Justinian, a pedlar.
Hector, a snap sauce scullion.
Paris, a poor beggar.
Cambyses, a mule-driver.
Nero, a base blind fiddler.

Fierabas was his serving man, who did him a thousand mischievous tricks, and would make him eat of the brown bread, and drink of the turned wine, when himself did both eat and drink of the best.

Julius Cæsar and Pompey were boat-wrights and tighters of ships.

232

Valentine and Orson did serve in the stoves of hell, and were sweat-rubbers in hot-houses.

Giglan and Govian were poor swineherds.

Jeffrey with the great tooth was a tinder maker, and seller of matches.

Godfrey de Bullion, a hood-maker.

Jason was a bracelet-maker.

Don Pietro de Castille, a carrier of indulgences.

Morgan, a beer-brewer.

Huon of Bourdeaux, a hooper of barrels.

Pyrrhus, a kitchen scullion.

Antiochus, a chimney-sweeper.

Octavian, a scraper of parchment.

Nerva, a mariner.

Pope Julius was a crier of pudding-pies; but he left off wearing there his great buggerly beard.

John of Paris was a greaser of boots.

Arthur of Britain, an ungreaser of caps.

Perce-forest, a carrier of faggots.

Pope Boniface VIII. a scummer of pots.

Pope Nicholas III. a maker of paper.

Pope Alexander, a rat-catcher.

Pope Sixtus, an anointer of those that have the pox."

"What," said Pantagruel, "have they the pox there too?" "Surely," said Epistemon, "I never saw so many; there are there, I think, above a hundred millions. For be assured, that those who have not had the pox in this world, must have it in the other."

"Cotsbody," said Panurge, "then am I free; for I have been as far as the hole of Gibraltar reached unto the utmost bounds of Hercules, and gathered of the ripest."

"Ogier the Dane was a furbisher of armour.

The king Tigranes, a mender of thatched houses.

Galien restored, a taker of moldwarps.

The four sons of Aymon were all tooth-drawers.

Pope Calixtus was the barber of a woman's sine quo non.

Pope Urban, a bacon-picker.

Melusina was a kitchen drudge wench.

Mettabrune, a laundress.

Cleopatra, a crier of onions.

Helen, a broker for chamber-maids.

233

Semiramis, the beggars lice-killer.
Dido sold mushrooms.
Penthesilea sold cresses.
Lucretia was an ale-house-keeper.
Hortensia, a spinstress.
Livia, a grater of verdigrise.

"After this manner those that had been great lords and ladies here, got but a poor scurvy wretched livelihood below. And, on the contrary, the philosophers and others, who in this world had been altogether indigent and wanting, were great lords there in their turn. I saw Diogenes there strut it out most pompously, and in great magnificence, with a rich purple gown on him, and a gold scepter in his right-hand. And which is more, he would now and then make Alexander the great mad, so enormously would he abuse him, when he had not well patched his breeches [stockings]; for he used to pay his skin with sound bastinadoes. I saw Epictetus there most gallantly apparelled, after the French fashion, sitting under a pleasant arbour, with store of handsome gentlewomen, frolicing, drinking, dancing and making good cheer, with abundance of crowns of the sun. Above the lattice were written these verses for his device.

" 'Sauter, dancer, faire les tours,
    Et boire vin blanc, & vermeil;
Et ne faire rien tous les jours,
    Que compter escuts au soleil.'

To dance, to skip, and to play,
    The best white and claret to swill,
And nothing to do all the day,
    But rolling in money at will.

"When he saw me, he invited me to drink with him very courteously; and I being willing to be entreated, we tippled and chopined together most theologically. In the meantime came Cyrus to beg one farthing of him for the honour of Mercury, therewith to buy a few onions for his supper. 'No, no,' said Epictetus, 'I do not use in my alms-giving to bestow farthings; hold, thou varlet, there is a crown for thee, be an honest man.' Cyrus was exceeding glad to have met with such a booty. But the other poor rogues, the kings that are there below, as Alexander, Darius, and others, stole it away from him by night. I saw Patelin, the treasurer of Rhadamanthus, who, in cheapening the pudding-pies that pope Julius cried, asked him, how much a dozen? 'Three blanks,' said the pope. 'Nay,' said Patelin, 'three blows with a cudgel; lay them down here, you rascal, and go fetch more.' The poor pope went away weeping; who, when he came to his master the pie-maker, told him, that they had taken away his pudding-pies. Whereupon, his master gave him such a sound lash with an eel-skin, that his own skin would have been worth nothing to make bag-pipe-bags of. I saw master John le Maire there, personate the pope in such fashion, that he made all the poor kings and popes of this world kiss his feet; and, taking great state upon him, gave them his benediction, saying, 'Get the pardons, rogues, get the pardons, they are good and cheap: I absolve you of bread and pottage, and dispense with you to be never good for anything.' Then, calling Caillet and Triboulet, to them he spoke these words: 'My lords the cardinals, dispatch their bulls, to wit, to each of them a blow with a cudgel upon the reins.' Which accordingly was forthwith performed.

"I heard master Francis Villon ask Xerxes, how much the mess of mustard? 'A farthing,' said Xerxes. To which the said Villon answered, 'The pox take thee for a villain; as much of square-ear'd wheat is not worth half that price, and now thou offerest to enhance the price of victuals.' With this he pissed in his pot, as the mustard-makers of Paris use to do. I saw the franc archer de Baignolet, who was one of the inquisition against heretics. When he saw Pierce-forest making water against a wall, on which was painted the fire of St. Anthony, he declared him a heretic, and would have caused him to be burnt alive, had it not been for Morgant, who for his proficiat and other small fees, gave him nine tuns of beer."

"Well," said Pantagruel, "reserve all these stories for another time; only tell us how the usurers are there handled." "I saw them," said Epistemon, "all very busily employed in seeking of rusty pins and old nails in the kennels of the streets, as you see poor wretched rogues do in this world: but the quintal, or hundred-weight of this old iron-ware, is there valued but at the price of a cantle of bread; and yet they have but a very bad dispatch and riddance in the sale of it. Thus the poor misers are sometimes three whole weeks without eating one morsel or crumb of bread, and yet work both day and night looking for the fair to come: nevertheless, of all this labour, toil, and misery, they reckon nothing; so cursedly active they are in the prosecution

235

of that their base calling in hopes, at the end of the year, to earn some scurvy penny by it."

"Come," said Pantagruel, "let us now make ourselves merry one bout, and drink, my lads, I beseech you; for it is very good drinking all this month." Then did they uncase their flaggons by heaps and dozens, and with their leaguer-provision made excellent good cheer. But the poor king Anarchus could not all this while settle himself towards any fit of mirth: whereupon Panurge said, "Of what trade shall we make my lord the king here, that he may be skilful in the art, when he goes thither to sojourn amongst the devils of hell?" "Indeed," said Pantagruel, "that was well advised of thee, do with him what thou wilt: I give him to thee." "Grammercy," said Panurge, "the present is not to be refused, and I love it from you."

CHAPTER XXXI

HOW PANTAGRUEL ENTERED INTO THE CITY OF THE AMAUROTS, AND HOW PANURGE MARRIED KING ANARCHUS TO AN OLD LANTERN-CARRYING HAG, AND MADE HIM A CRIER OF GREEN-SAUCE

AFTER this wonderful victory, Pantagruel sent Carpalim unto the city of the Amaurots, to declare and signify unto them how the king Anarchus was taken prisoner, and all the enemies of the city overthrown: which news, when they heard, all the inhabitants of the city came forth to meet him in good order, and with a great triumphant pomp conducting him with a heavenly joy into the city, where innumerable bonfires were kindled everywhere, and fair round tables furnished with store of good victuals set out in the middle of the streets. This was a renewing of the golden age; so good was the cheer which then they made.

But Pantagruel, having assembled the whole senate and common-council-men of the town said, "My masters, we must now strike the iron whilst it is hot; it is therefore my will that, before we frolic it any longer, we advise how to assault and take the whole kingdom of the Dipsodes. To which effect, let those that will go with me provide themselves against to-morrow after drinking; for then I will begin to march. Not that I need any more men than I have to help me to conquer it; for I could make it as sure that way as if I had it already: but I see this city is so full of inhabitants, that they scarce can turn in the streets; I will therefore carry them as a colony into Dipsody, and will give them all that country, which is fair, wealthy, fruitful, and pleasant above all other countries in the world, as many of you can tell who have been there heretofore. Every one of you therefore that will go along, let him provide himself as I have said." This counsel and resolution being published in the city, the next morning there assembled in the piazza, before the palace, to the number of eighteen hundred fifty six thousand and eleven, besides women and little children. Thus began they to march straight into Dipsody, in such good order as did the people of Israel when they departed out of Egypt, to pass over the Red Sea.

But before we proceed any further, I will tell you how Panurge handled his prisoner the king Anarchus. For having remembered that which Epistemon had related, how the kings and rich men in this world were used in the Elysian fields, and how they got their living there by base and ignoble trades; he therefore one day apparelled his king in a pretty little canvas doublet, all jagged and pinked like the tippet of a light horseman's cap, together with a pair of large mariner's breeches, and stockings without shoes ("For," said he, "they would but spoil his sight"), and a light peach-coloured bonnet, with a great capon's feather in it. I lie, for I think he had two; and a very handsome girdle, de pers & vert; saying, that such a livery did become him well, for that he had always been perverse. And in this plight, bringing him before Pantagruel, said unto him, "Do you know this royster?" "No, indeed," said Pantagruel. "It is," said Panurge, "my lords the king of the clouted hose. I intend to make him an honest man. These devils of kings here are but as so many calves; they know nothing, and are good for nothing but to do a thousand mischiefs to their poor subjects, and to trouble all the world with war for their unjust and detestable pleasure. I will put him to a trade, and make him a crier of green-sauce. Go to, begin and cry; Do you lack any green-sauce?" And the poor devil fell to crying. "That is too low," said Panurge; then took him by the ear, saying, "Sing higher in ge, sol, re, ut. So, so, poor wretch; thou hast a good throat: thou could'st never have been so happy, hadst thou continued longer king."

And Pantagruel made himself merry with all this. For I dare boldly say, that he was the best little gaffer that was to be seen between this and the end of a staff. Thus was Anarchus made a good crier of green-sauce. Two days thereafter, Panurge married him with

237

an old lantern-carrying hag; and he himself made the wedding, with fine sheeps-heads, brave haslets with mustard, gallant salligots with garlic, of which he sent five horse-loads unto Pantagruel, which he eat up all, he found them so appetizing. And, for their drink, they had a kind of small well-water'd wine, and some fine sorb-apple cyder. And, to make them dance, he hired a blind man, that made music to them with a wind-broach.

After dinner he led them to the palace, and shewed them to Pantagruel, and said, pointing to the married woman, "You need not fear that she will crack" [fart]. "Why?" said Pantagruel. "Because," said Panurge, "she is well slit and broke up already." "What do you mean by that?" said Pantagruel. "Did you never see," said Panurge, "that the chestnuts which are roasted in the fire, if they be whole, they crack as if they were mad; and, to keep them from cracking, they make an incision in them, and slit them: so this new bride is in her lower parts well slit before, and therefore will not crack behind."

Pantagruel gave them a little lodge near the lower-street, and a mortar of stone wherein to bray and pound their sauce. And in this manner did they do their little business, he being as pretty a crier of green-sauce as ever was seen in the country of Utopia. But I have been told since that his wife doth beat him like plaster, and the poor sot dares not defend himself, he is so simple.

CHAPTER XXXII

HOW PANTAGRUEL WITH HIS TONGUE COVERED A WHOLE ARMY, AND WHAT THE AUTHOR SAW IN HIS MOUTH

THUS as Pantagruel with all his army had entered into the country of the Dipsodes, every one was glad of it, and incontinently rendered themselves unto him, bringing him out of their own good wills the keys of all the cities where he went, the Almirods only excepted; who, being resolved to hold out against him, made answer to his heralds, that they would not yield but upon very honourable and good conditions.

"What!" said Pantagruel, "do they ask any better terms than the hand at the pot, and the glass in their fist? Come, let us go sack them, and put them all to the sword." Then did they put themselves in good order, as being fully determined to give an assault. But by the way, passing through a large field, they were overtaken by a great

238

shower of rain, whereat they began to shiver and tremble, to crowd, press, and thrust close to one another. When Pantagruel saw that, he made their captains tell them that it was nothing, and that he saw well above the clouds, that it would be nothing but a little dew; but howsoever, that they should put themselves in order, and he would cover them. Then did they put themselves in a close order, and stood as near to each other as they could; and Pantagruel drew out his tongue only half way, and covered them all, as a hen doth her chickens.

In the meantime I, who relate to you these so veritable stories, hid myself under a burdock-leaf, which was not much less in largeness than the arch of the bridge of Montrible; but when I saw them thus covered, I went towards them, to shelter myself likewise, which I could not do; for that (as the saying is) at the yard's end there is no cloth left. Then, as well as I could, I got upon it, and went forwards full two leagues upon his tongue; and so long marched, that at last I came into his mouth. But, O gods and goddesses, what did I see there! Jupiter confound me with his trisulk lightning if I lie. I walked there as they do in Sophie at Constantinople, and saw there great rocks, like the mountains in Denmark; I believe that those were his teeth: I saw also fair meadows, large forests, great and strong cities, not a jot less than Lyons or Poictiers. The first man I met with there was a good honest fellow planting colworts; whereat being very much amazed, I asked him, "My friend, what art thou doing here?" "I am planting colworts," said he. "But how, and wherewith?" said I. "Ha, sir," said he, "every one cannot have his baws as heavy as a mortar; neither can we be all rich. Thus do I get my poor living, and carry them to the market to sell in the city, which is here behind." "Jesus!" said I, "is there here a new world?" "Sure," said he, "it is never a jot new: but it is commonly reported, that without this there is an earth, whereof the inhabitants enjoy the light of a sun and moon; and that it is full of, and replenished with, very good commodities; but yet, this is more ancient than that." "Yea, but," said I, "my friend, what is the name of that city whither thou carriest thy colworts to sell?" "It is called Alpharage," said he, "and all the indwellers are Christians, very honest men, and will make you good cheer." To be brief, I resolved to go thither. Now, in my way, I met with a fellow that was lying in wait to catch pigeons, of whom I asked, "My friend, from whence come these pigeons?" "Sir," said he, "they come from the other world." Then I thought, that when Pantagruel yawned the pigeons went into his mouth in whole flocks, thinking that it had been a pigeon house.

Then I went into the city, which I found fair, very strong, and seated in a good air; but, at my entry, the guard demanded of me my pass or ticket; whereat I was much astonished, and asked them, "My masters, is there any danger of the plague here?" "O Lord," said they, "they die hard by here so fast, that the cart runs about the streets." "Good God!" said I," "and where?" Whereunto they answered, that it was in Larinx and Phærinx; which are two great cities, such as Rouen and Nantz, rich, and of great trading; and the cause of the plague was, by a stinking and infectious exhalation which lately vapoured out of the abismes, whereof there have died above two and twenty hundred and threescore thousand and sixteen persons within this sevennight. Then I considered, calculated, and found that it was a rank and unsavoury breathing, which came out of Pantagruel's stomach when he did eat so much garlic, as we have aforesaid.

Parting from thence, I passed amongst the rocks, which were his teeth, and never left walking till I got upon one of them; and there I found the pleasantest places in the world, great large tennis-courts, fair galleries, sweet meadows, store of vines, and an infinite number of banqueting summer out-houses in the fields, after the Italian fashion, full of pleasure and delight; where I staid full four months, and never made better cheer in my life than at that time. After that, I went down by the hinder teeth to come to the chaps; but in the way I was robbed by thieves in a great forest, that is in the territory towards the ears. Then (after a little further travelling) I fell upon a pretty village (truly I have forgot the name of it) where I was yet merrier than ever, and got some certain money to live by. Can you tell how? by sleeping; for there they hire men by the day to sleep, and they get by it sixpence a day; but they that can snore hard, get at least nine-pence. How I had been robbed in the valley I informed the senators, who told me, that in very truth the people of that side were bad livers, and naturally thievish; whereby I perceived well, that as we have with us the countries Cisalpine and Transalpine, so have they there the countries Cidentine and Tradentine, that is, behither and beyond the teeth; but it is far better living on this side, and the air is purer. There I began to think, that it is very true which is commonly said, that the one half of the world knoweth not how the other half liveth. Seeing none before myself had ever written of that country, wherein are above five and twenty kingdoms inhabited, besides deserts, and a great arm of the sea, I have composed a great book, intituled, "The History of the Gorgians," because they dwell in the gorge of my master Pantagruel.

At last I was willing to return, and, passing by his beard, I cast myself upon his shoulders, and from thence slid down to the ground, and fell before him. As soon as I was perceived by him, he asked me, "Whence comest thou, Alcofribas?" I answered him, "Out of your mouth, my lord." "And how long hast thou been there?" said he. "Since the time," said I, "that you went against the Almirods." "That is about six months ago," said he. "And wherewith didst thou live? What didst thou drink?" I answered, "My lord, of the same that you did, and of the daintiest morsels that passed through your throat I took toll." "Yea, but," said he, "where didst thou shite?" "In your throat, my lord," said I. "Ha, ha, thou art a merry fellow," said he. "We have, with the help of God, conquered all the land of the Dipsodes; I will give thee the Chastelleiny of Salmigondin." "Grammercy, my lord," said I, "you gratify me beyond all that I have deserved of you."

CHAPTER XXXIII

HOW PANTAGRUEL BECAME SICK, AND THE MANNER HOW HE WAS RECOVERED

A WHILE after this the good Pantagruel fell sick, and had such an illness in his stomach, that he could neither eat nor drink; and because one mischief seldom comes alone, he had got also the hot piss, which tormented him more than you would believe. His physicians, nevertheless, helped him very well, and with store of lenitives and diuretic drugs, made him piss away his pain. His urine was so hot, that since that time it is not yet cold, and you have of it in divers places of France, according to the course that it took, and they are called the hot baths; as at Coderets; at Limous; at Dast; at Ballervie; at Nerie; at Bourbonensy, and elsewhere. In Italy, at Mongros; at Appone; at Sancto Petro de Padua; at St. Helen; at Casa Nuova; at St. Bartolomee in the county of Bologna; at the Loretta; and a thousand other places.

And I wonder much at a rabble of foolish philosophers and phy-

sicians, who spend their time in disputing, whence the heat of the
said waters cometh, whether it be by reason of borax, or sulphur, or
allum, or saltpetre, that is within the mine: for they do nothing but
dote, and better were it for them to rub their arse against a thistle,
than to waste away their time thus in disputing of that whereof they
know not the original; for the resolution is easy, neither need we to inquire any further, than that the said baths came by a hot piss of the
good Pantagruel.

Now to tell you after what manner he was cured of his principal
disease, I let pass how for a minorative he took four hundred pound
weight of colophoniac scammony; sixscore and eighteen cart-loads of
cassia; eleven thousand and nine hundred pounds weight of rhubarb;
besides other confused jumblings of sundry drugs. You must understand, that, by the advice of the physicians, it was ordered, that what
did offend his stomach should be taken away; and therefore they
made seventeen great balls of copper, each whereof was bigger than
that which is to be seen on the top of St. Peter's needle at Rome, and
in such sort, that they did open in the midst, and shut with a spring.
Into one of them entered one of his men, carrying a lantern and a
torch lighted, and so Pantagruel swallowed him down like a little
pill: into seven others went seven country fellows, having every one
of them a shovel on his neck: into nine others entered nine wood-
carriers, having each of them a basket hung at his neck: and so were
they swallowed down like pills. When they were in his stomach,
every one undid his spring, and came out of their cabins; the first
whereof was he that carried the lantern: and so they fell more than
half a league into a most horrible gulph, more stinking and infectious
than ever was Mephitis, or the marishes of Camerina, or the abominably unsavoury lake of Sorbona, whereof Strabo maketh mention. And
had it not been that they had very well antidoted their stomach, heart,
and wine-pot, which is called the noddle, they had been altogether
suffocated and choked with these detestable vapours. O what a perfume! O what an evaporation, wherewith to bewray the masks or
mufflers of young mangy queans! After that, with groping and
smelling, they came near to the fecal matter, and the corrupted humours. Finally, they found a montjoy or heap of ordure and filth: then
fell the pioneers to work to dig it up, and the rest with their shovels
filled the baskets; and, when all was cleansed, every one retired himself into his ball.

This done, Pantagruel, enforcing himself to a vomit, very easily brought them out, and they made no more show in his mouth than a fart in yours; but when they came merrily out of their pills, I thought upon the Grecians coming out of the Trojan horse. By this means was he healed, and brought unto his former state and convalescence. And of these brazen pills you have one at Orleans, upon the steeple of the holy cross church.

CHAPTER XXXIV

THE CONCLUSION OF THIS PRESENT BOOK, AND THE EXCUSE OF THE AUTHOR

NOW, my masters, you have heard a beginning of the horrific history of my lord and master Pantagruel. Here will I make an end of the first book. My head aches a little, and I perceive that the registers of my brain are somewhat jumbled and disordered with the septembral juice. You shall have the rest of the history at Frankfort mart next coming, and there shall you see how Panurge was married, and made a cuckold within a month after his wedding: how Pantagruel found out the philosopher's stone, the manner how he found it, and the way how to use it: how he past over the Caspian mountains, and how he sailed through the Atlantic sea, defeated the cannibals, and conquered the isles of Perles; how he married the daughter of the king of India, called Prestham; how he fought against the devil, and burnt up five chambers of hell; ransacked the great black chamber, threw Proserpine into the fire, broke four teeth of Lucifer, and the horn that was in his arse. How he visited the regions of the moon, to know whether indeed the moon were not entire and whole; or if the women had three quarters of it in their heads; and a thousand other little merriments, all veritable. These are brave things truly. Good night, gentlemen. *Perdonate mi,* and think not so much upon my faults, that you forget your own. If you say to me, "Master, it would seem that you were not very wise in writing to us these flim-flam stories, and pleasant fooleries"; I answer you, that you are not much wiser, to spend your time in reading them. Nevertheless, if you read them to make yourselves merry, as in manner of pastime I wrote them, you and I both are far more worthy of pardon than a great rabble of squint-minded fellows, counterfeit saints, demure lookers, hypocrites, zealots, tough friars, buskin-monks, and other such sects of men, who disguise themselves like maskers, to deceive the world: for whilst they give the common people to understand that they are busied about nothing but contemplation and devotion in fastings, and maceration of their sensuality, and that only to sustain and aliment the small frailty of their humanity, it is so far otherwise, that, on the contrary, God knows what cheer they make *Et Curios simulant, sed Bacchanalia vivunt.* You may read it in great letters in the colouring of their red snouts, and gulching bellies, as big as a tun, unless it be when they perfume themselves with sulphur. As for their study, it is wholly taken up in reading of Pantagruelin books: not so much to pass the time merrily, as to hurt some one or other mischievously, to wit, in articling, sole-articling, wryneckifying, buttock-stirring, ballocking, and diabliculating, that is, calumniating: wherein they are like unto the poor rogues of a village, they are busy in stirring up and scraping in the ordure and filth of little children, in the season of cherries and guinds, and that only to find the kernels, that they may sell them to the druggists, to make thereof pomander oil. Fly from these men, abhor and hate them as much as I do, and upon my faith you will find yourselves the better for it. And if you desire to be good Pantagruelists, that is to say, to live in peace, joy, health, making yourselves always merry, never trust those men that always peep out at one hole.

FRANCIS   RABELAIS

TO THE SOUL OF

THE DECEASED QUEEN OF NAVARRE

ABSTRACTED soul, ravished with ecstasies,
    Gone back, and now familiar in the skies:
Thy former host, thy body, leaving quite,
Which to obey thee always took delight,
Obsequious, ready: now from motion free,
Senseless, and, as it were, in apathy.
Deign now to issue forth, for a short space,
From that divine, eternal, heavenly place,
To see the third part, in this earthly cell,
Of the brave acts of good Pantagruel.

THE AUTHOR'S PROLOGUE

TO

THE THIRD BOOK

GOOD people, most illustrious drinkers, and you thrice precious gouty gentlemen; did you ever see Diogenes the cynic philosopher? If you have seen him, you then had your eyes in your head, or I am very much out of my understanding and logical sense. It is a gallant thing to see the clearness of (wine, gold) the sun. I'll be judged by the blind-born, so renowned in the sacred scriptures; who having at his choice to ask whatever he would from Him who is Almighty, and whose word in an instant is effectually performed, asked nothing else but that he might see. Item, you are not young, which is a competent quality for you to philosophize (*de vino*) upon wine (not in *vano*), rather than upon matters physical, and henceforwards to be of the Bacchick council: to the end that opening, *i.e.* your jaws to guttle and guzzle, there you may opine, *i.e.* give your opinion, faithfully of the substance, colour, excellent odour, eminency, propriety, faculty, virtue, and effectual dignity of the said blessed and desired liquor.

If you have not seen him (as I am easily induced to believe that you have not) at least you have heard some talk of him. For through the air, and the whole extent of this hemisphere of the heavens, hath his report and fame, even until this present time, remained very memorable and renowned. Then all of you are derived from the Phrygian blood (if I be not deceived). And if you have not so many crowns as Midas had, yet have you something (I know not what) of him. which the Persians of old esteemed more of in all their otacusts, and which was more desired by the Emperor Antoninus; and gave occasion thereafter to the Basilisco at Rohan to be sirnamed goodly ears. If you have not heard of him, I will presently tell you a story to make your wine relish. Drink then; and so to the purpose. Hearken now, whilst I give you notice (to the end that you may not, like infidels, be by your simplicity abused) that in his time he was a rare philosopher, and the cheerfullest of a thousand. If he had some imperfection, so have you, so have we; for there is nothing (but God) that is perfect. Yet so it was, that by Alexander the Great, although he had Aristotle for his instructor and domestic, was he held in such estimation, that he wished, if he had not been Alexander, to have been Diogenes the Sinopian.

When Philip King of Macedon enterprised the siege and ruin of Corinth, the Corinthians, having received certain intelligence, by their spies, that he with a numerous army in battle array was coming against them, were all of them, not without cause, most terribly afraid; and therefore were not neglective of their duty, in doing their best endeavours to put themselves in a fit posture to resist his hostile approach, and defend their own city.

Some from the fields brought into the fortified places their moveables, cattle, corn, wine, fruit, victuals, and other necessary provisions.

Others did fortify and rampire their walls, set up little fortresses, bastions, squared ravelins, digged trenches, cleansed countermines, fenced themselves with gabions, contrived platforms, emptied casemates, barricadoed the false brayes, erected the cavalliers, repaired the conterscarpes, plaistered the courtines, lengthened ravelins, stopped parapets, mortaised barbacans, new pointed the portcullices with fine steel or good iron, fastened the herses and cataracts, placed their centries, and doubled their patrouille.

Every one did watch and ward, and not one was exempted from carrying the basket.

Some polished corselets, varnished backs and breasts, cleaned the head-pieces, mailcoats, brigandins, salads, helmets, murrions, jacks, gushets, gorgets, hoguines, brassars and cuissars, corselets, haubergeons, shields, bucklers, targets, greves, gantlets, and spurs.

Other made ready bows, slings, and crossbows, pellets, catapults, migraines, or fireballs, firebrands, balists, scorpions, and other such warlike engines, repugnatory, and destructive to the helepolides.

They sharpened and prepared spears, staves, pikes, brown bills, halberts, long hooks, lances, zagages, quarterstaves, eelspears, partisans, troutstaves, clubs, battle-axes, maces, darts, dartlets, glaves, javelins, javelots, and truncheons.

They set edges upon scymetars, cutlasses, badelairs, backswords, tucks, rapiers, bayonets, arrow-heads, dags, daggers, mandousians, poignards, whynyards, knives, skenes, sables, chipping knives, and raillons.

Every man exercised his weapon; every man scowered off the rust

247

from his natural hanger: nor was there a woman amongst them (though never so reserved or old) who made not her harness to be well furbished; as you know the Corinthian women of old were reputed very courageous combatants.

Diogenes, seeing them all so warm at work, and himself not employed by the magistrates in any business whatsoever, he did very seriously (for many days together without speaking one word) consider and contemplate the countenances of his fellow-citizens.

Then on a sudden, as if he had been roused up and inspired by a martial spirit, he girded his cloak, scarf-ways, about his left arm, tucked up his sleeves to the elbow, trussed himself like a clown gathering apples, and giving to one of his old acquaintance his wallet, books, and opistographs, away went he out of town towards a little hill or promontory of Corinth called Craneum: and there on the strand, a pretty level place, did he roll his jolly tub, which served him for an house to shelter him from the injuries of the weather; there, I say, in a great vehemency of spirit, did he turn it, veer it, wheel it, whirl it, frisk it, jumble it, shuffle it, huddle it, tumble it, hurry it, joult it, justle it, overthrow it, evert it, invert it, subvert it, overturn it, beat it, thwack it, bump it, batter it, knock it, thrust it, push it, jerk it, shock it, shake it, toss it, throw it, overthrow it up-side down, topsy-turvy, arsiversy, tread it, trample it, stamp it, tap it, ting it, ring it, tingle it, towl it, sound it, resound it, stop it, shut it, unbung it, close it, unstopple it. And then again, in a mighty bustle, he bandied it, slubbered it, hacked it, whittled it, wayed it, darted it, hurled it, staggered it, reeled it, swinged it, brangled it, tottered it, lifted it, heaved it, transformed it, transfigured it, transposed it, transplaced it, reared it, raised it, hoised it, washed it, dighted it, cleansed it, rinced it, nailed it, settled it, fastened it, shackled, fettered it, levelled it, blocked it, tugged it, tewed it, carried it, bedashed it, bewrayed it, parched it, mounted it, broached it, nicked it, notched it, bespattered it, decked it, adorned it, trimmed it, garnished it, gaged it, furnished it, bored it, pierced it, trapped it, rumbled it, slid it down the hill, and precipitated it from the very height of the Craneum; then from the foot to the top, like another Sisyphus with his stone, bore it up again, and every way so banged it and belaboured it, that it was ten thousand to one he had not struck the bottom of it out.

Which when one of his friends had seen, and asked him why he did so toil his body, perplex his spirit, and torment his tub? The philosopher's answer was, "That not being employed in any other office by the republic, he thought it expedient to thunder and storm it so tempestuously upon his tub, that amongst a people so fervently busy, and earnest at work, he alone might not seem a loitering slug and lazy fellow." To the same purpose may I say of myself.

> Tho' I be rid from fear,
> I am not void of care.

For perceiving no account to be made of me towards the discharge of a trust of any great concernment, and considering that through all the parts of this most noble kingdom of France, both on this and on the other side of the mountains, every one is most diligently exercised and busied; some in the fortifying of their own native country, for its defence; others, in the repulsing of their enemies by an offensive war; and all this with a policy so excellent, and such admirable order, so manifestly profitable for the future, whereby France shall have its frontiers most magnificently enlarged, and the French be assured of a long and well-grounded peace, that very little withholds me from the opinion of good Heraclitus, which affirmeth war to be the parent of all good things; and therefore do I believe that war is in Latin called *bellum,* not by antiphrasis, as some patchers of old rusty Latin would have us to think, because in war there is little beauty to be seen; but absolutely and simply, for that in war *bellum* in Latin appears all that is so good and graceful, *bon* and *bel* in French, and that by the wars is purged out all manner of wickedness and deformity. For proof whereof, the wise and pacific Solomon could no better represent the unspeakable perfection of the divine wisdom, than by comparing it to the due disposure and ranking of an army in battle array, well provided and ordered.

Therefore, by reason of my weakness and inability, being reputed by my compatriots unfit for the offensive part of warfare; and on the other side, being no way employed in matter of the defensive, although it had been but to carry burthens, fill ditches, or break clods, each whereof had been to me indifferent; I held it not a little disgraceful to be only an idle spectator of so many valorous, eloquent, and warlike persons, who in the view and sight of all Europe act this notable interlude or tragi-comedy, and not exert myself, and contribute thereto this nothing, my all; which remained for me to do. For in my opinion, little honour is due to such as are mere lookers-on, liberal of their eyes, and of their strength parsimonious; who conceal their crowns and hide their silver; scratching their head with one finger like grumbling puppies; gaping at the flies like tithe calves; clapping down their ears like Arcadian asses at the melody of musicians, who with their very countenances in the depth of silence express their consent to the prosopopeia.

Having made this choice and election, it seemed to me that my exercise therein would be neither unprofitable nor troublesome to any, whilst I should thus set a-going my Diogenical tub, which is all that is left me safe from the shipwreck of my former misfortunes.

At this dingle-dangle wagging of my tub, what would you have me to do? By the virgin that tucks up her sleeve, I know not as yet. Stay a little, till I suck up a draught of this bottle; it is my true and only Helicon; it is my Cabaline fountain; it is my sole enthusiasm. Drinking thus I meditate, discourse, resolve, and conclude. After that the epilogue is made, I laugh, I write, I compose, and drink again. Ennius drinking wrote, and writing drank. Æschylus (if Plutarch, in his symposiacs, merit any faith) drank composing, and drinking composed. Homer never wrote fasting, and Cato never wrote till after he had drank. These passages I have brought before you, to the end you may not say that I live without the example of men well praised, and better prized. It is good and fresh enough, even as if you would say it is entering upon the second degree. God, the good God sabaoth, that is to say of armies, be praised for it eternally. If you after the same manner would take one great draught, or two little ones, whilst you have your gown about you, I truly find no kind of inconveniency in it, provided you send up to God for all some small scantling of thanks.

Since then my luck or destiny is such as you have heard (for it is not for everybody to go to Corinth), I am fully resolved to be so little idle and unprofitable, that I will set myself to serve the one and the other sort of people. Amongst the diggers, pioneers, and rampire-builders, I will do as did Neptune and Apollo at Troy under Laomedon, or as did Renault of Montauban, in his latter days: I will serve the masons; I'll set on the pot to boil for the bricklayers; and when the jay-work's over, by the sound of my small pipe I'll measure the muzzle of the musing dotards.

For the use of the warriors I am about to broach off a new barrel to give them a taste (which by two former books of mine, if by the deceitfulness and falsehood of printers they had not been jumbled, marred, and spoiled, you would have very well relished), and draw unto them of the growth of our own trippery pastimes, a gallant third part of a gallon, and consequently a jolly cheerful quart of Pantagruelic sentences, which you may lawfully call, if you please, Diogenical; and shall have me, seeing I cannot be their fellow-soldier, for their faithful butler, refreshing and cheering, according to my little power, their return from the alarms of the enemy; as also for an indefatigable extoller of their martial exploits and glorious achievements. I shall not fail therein, *par lapathium (acutum) de Dieu,* if Mars fail not in Lent; which the cunning lecher, I warrant you, will not be such a fool as to do.

I remember nevertheless to have read, that Ptolemy, the son of Lagus, one day, amongst the many spoils and booties which by his victories he had acquired, presenting to the Egyptians, in the open view of the people, a Bactrian camel all black, and a party-coloured slave, in such sort, as that the one half of his body was black, and the other white, not in partition of breadth by the diaphragma, as was that woman consecrated to the Indian Venus, whom the Tyanean philosopher did see between the river Hydaspes and mount Caucasus, but in a perpendicular dimension of altitude, which were things never before that seen in Egypt; he expected by the show of these novelties to win the love of the people. But what happened thereupon? At the production of the camel they were all affrighted, and offended at the sight of the party-coloured man. Some scoffed at him as a detestable monster, brought forth by the error of nature. In a word, of the hope which he had to please these Egyptians, and by such means to increase the affection which they naturally bore him he was altogether frustrate and disappointed; understanding fully, by their deportments, that they took more pleasure and delight in things that were proper, handsome and perfect, than in misshapen, monstrous, and ridiculous creatures. After which time he had both the slave and the camel in such dislike, that it was not long before, either through negligence, or for want of ordinary sustenance, they both tipt over the perch.

This example makes me fluctuate between hope and fear, my heart misgiving me that for the contentment which I am at, I shall but reap what will be most distasteful to me, my treasure become coals, my cake dough, and for my Venus, I shall have but some deformed puppy dog; instead of serving them, I shall but vex them, and offend them whom I purpose to exhilarate; resembling in this dubious adventure Euclio's cock, so renowned by Plautus in his pot, and by Ausonius in his griphon, and by divers others; which cock, for having by his scraping discovered a treasure, had his neck twisted round. Put

251

the case I get no anger by it; yet formerly such things fell out, and the like may occur again; but, by Hercules, it will not. So I perceive in them all one and the same specifical form, and the like individual proprieties, which our ancestors called Pantagruelism; by virtue whereof they will bear with anything that floweth from a good, free, and loyal heart. I have seen them ordinarily take goodwill in part of payment, and remain satisfied therewith, when one was not able to do better. Having dispatched this point, I return to my barrel.

Up my lads, to this wine, spare it not; drink, boys, and trowl it off at full bowls. If you do not think it good, let it alone. I am not like those officious and importunate sots, who by force, outrage, and violence costrain an easy good-natured fellow to quaff, carouse, and spend whole days and nights in drinking. All honest tiplers, all honest gouty men, all such as are a-dry, coming to this little barrel of mine, need not drink thereof, if it please them not: but if they have a mind to it, and that the wine proves agreeable to the tastes of their worshipful worships, let them drink frankly, freely, and boldly, without paying anything, and welcome. This is my decree, my statute and ordinance; and let none fear there shall be any want of wine, as at the marriage of Cana in Galilee: for how much soever you shall draw forth at the faucet, so much shall I tun in at the bung. Thus shall the barrel remain inexhaustible; it hath a lively spring and perpetual current. Such was the beverage contained within the cup of Tantalus, which was figuratively represented amongst the Brachman sages. Such was, in Iberia, the mountain of salt, so highly written of by Cato. Such was the branch of gold consecrated to the subterranean goddess, which Virgil treats of so sublimely. It is a true *cornucopia* of merriment and raillery. If at any time it seem to you to be emptied to the very lees, yet shall it not for all that be drawn wholly dry: good hope remains there at the bottom, as in Pandora's box: and not despair, as in the leaky tub of the Daniads. Mark well what I have said, and what manner of people they be whom I do invite: for to the end that none be deceived, I (in imitation of Lucilius, who did protest that he wrote only to his own Tarentines and Consentines) have not pierced this vessel for any else, but you honest men, who are drinkers of the first edition, and gouty blades of the highest degree. The great dorophages, bribe-mongers, have on their hands occupation enough, and sacks enough on the hooks for their venison. There may they follow their prey; here is no garbage for them. You pettifoggers, garblers of syllables and masters of chicanery, speak not to me I beseech you, in the name of, and for the reverence you bear to the four hips that engendered you, and to the quickening peg which at that time conjoined them. As for the Levitical hypocrites, much less; although they were all of them unsound in body, pockified, scurfy, furnished with unquenchable thirst, and insatiable eating; because indeed they are not of good, but of evil, and of that evil from which we daily pray to God to deliver us. And albeit we see them sometimes counterfeit devotion, yet never did old ape make pretty moppet. Hence, mastiffs, dogs in a doublet, get you behind; aloof villains, out of my sun-shine; curs, to the devil. Do you come hither, wagging your tails, pant at my wine, and then bepiss my barrel? Look here is the cudgel, which Diogenes, in his last will, ordained to be set by him after his death, for beating away, crushing the reins, and breaking the backs of these bustuary hobgoblins, and cerberian hell-hounds. Pack you hence therefore, you hypocrites: to your sheep, dogs; get you gone, you dissemblers, to the devil. Hay! what, are you there yet? I renounce my part of Papimanie, if I snap you, grr, grrr, grrrrr. Avant! avant! Will you not be gone? May you never shit till you be soundly lashed with stirrup leather; never piss but by the strappado; nor be otherways warmed, than by the bastinado.

THE THIRD BOOK

OF

RABELAIS'S WORKS

CHAPTER I

HOW PANTAGRUEL TRANSPORTED A COLONY OF UTOPIANS
INTO DIPSODIE

PANTAGRUEL, having wholly subdued the land of Dipsodie, transported there unto a colony of Utopians, to the number of 9876543210 men, besides the women and little children, artificers of all trades, and professors of all liberal sciences; to refresh, cultivate, and improve that country, which otherwise was ill inhabited, and in the greatest part thereof but a mere desert and wilderness. And he did transport them not so much for the excessive multitude of men and women, which were, in Utopia, multiplied like grasshoppers upon the face of the land. You understand well enough, nor is it needful further to explain it to you, that the Utopian men had so rank and fruitful genitories, and that the Utopian women carried matrixes so ample, so glutinous, so tenaciously retentive, and so architectonically cellulated, that, at the end of every ninth month, seven children at the least, what male what female, were brought forth by every married woman; an imitation of the people of Israel in Egypt, if de Lyra be to be trusted. Nor yet was this transplantation made so much for the fertility of the soil, the wholesomeness of the air, or commodity of the country of Dipsodie, as to retain that rebellious people within the bounds of their duty and obedience, by this new draught of his ancient and most faithful subjects, who, from all time out of mind, never knew, acknowledged, owned, or served any other sovereign lord but him; and who likewise, from the very instant of their birth, as soon as they were entered into this world, had, with the milk of their mothers and nurses, sucked in the sweetness, humanity and mildness of his government; to which they were always so nourished, seasoned and habituated, that

255

there was nothing surer, than they would sooner abandon their lives than swerve from this singular and primitive obedience naturally due to their prince, whithersoever they should be dispersed or removed.

And not only should they, and their children successively descending from their blood, be such, but would also keep and maintain in this same fealty and obsequious observance, all the nations lately annexed to his empire; which so truly came to pass that therein he was not disappointed of his intent. For if the Utopians were before their transplantation thither dutiful and faithful subjects, the Dipsodes, after some few days conversing with them, were every whit as loyal, if not more so, than they; and that by virtue of I know not what natural fervency, incident to all human creatures at the beginning of any labour wherein they take delight: solemnly attesting the heavens and supreme intelligencies of their being only sorry that no sooner unto their knowledge had arrived the great renown of the good Pantagruel.

Remark therefore here, honest drinkers, that the manner of preserving and retaining countries newly conquered in obedience, is not as hath been the erroneous opinion of some tyrannical spirits, to their detriment and dishonour, to pillage, plunder, force, spoil, trouble, oppress, vex, disquiet, ruin and destroy the people, ruling, governing and keeping them in awe with rods of iron; and, in a word, eating and devouring them, after the fashion that Homer calls an unjust and wicked king, Δημόβορον, that is to say, a devourer of his people.

I will not bring you to this purpose the testimony of ancient writers; it shall suffice to put you in mind of what your fathers have seen thereof, and yourselves too, if you be not very babes. New-born, they must be given suck to, rocked in a cradle, and dandled. Trees newly planted must be supported, underpropped, strengthened and defended against all tempests, mischiefs, injuries, and calamities. And one lately saved from a long and dangerous sickness and now upon his recovery, must be forborn, spared and cherished, in such sort, that they may harbour in their own breasts this opinion, that there is not in the world a king or a prince, who does not desire fewer enemies, and more friends.

Thus Osiris, the great king of the Egyptians, conquered almost the whole earth, not so much by force of arms, as by easing the people of their troubles; teaching them how to live well, and honestly, giving them good laws, and using them with all possible affability, courtesy, gentleness and liberality: therefore was he by all men deservedly entitled the great king Euergetes, that is to say, benefactor, which style he obtained by virtue of the command of Jupiter to one Pamyla.

And indeed, Hesiod, in his hierarchy, places the good demons (call them angels if you will, or geniuses) as intercessors and mediators betwixt the gods and men, they being of a degree inferior to the gods, but superior to men; and for that through their hands the riches and benefits we get from heaven are dealt to us; and that they are continually doing us good, and still protecting us from evil. He saith, that they exercise the offices of kings, because to do always good, and never ill, is an act most singularly royal.

Just such another was the emperor of the universe, Alexander the Macedonian. After this manner was Hercules, sovereign possessor of the whole continent, relieving men from monsters or monstrous oppressions, exactions, and tyrannies; governing them with discretion, maintaining them in equity and justice, instructing them with seasonable policies and wholesome laws, convenient for and suitable to the soil, climate, and disposition of the country; supplying what was wanting, abating what was superfluous, and pardoning all that was past, with a sempiternal forgetfulness of all preceding offences; as was the amnesty of the Athenians, when, by the prowess, valour and industry of Thrasybulus, the tyrants were exterminated; afterwards at Rome by Cicero set forth, and renewed under the Emperor Aurelian. These are the philtres, allurements, jynges, inveiglements, baits, and enticements of love, by the means whereof that may be peaceably retained, which was painfully acquired. Nor can a conqueror reign more happily, whether he be a monarch, emperor, king, prince, or philosopher, than by making his justice to second his valour. His valour shews itself in victory and conquest; his justice will appear in the good will and affection of the people, when he maketh laws, publisheth ordinances, establisheth religion, and doth what is right to every one, as the noble poet Virgil writes of Octavian Augustus:

> "*Victorque volentes*
> *Per populos dat jura.*"

Therefore is it that Homer, in his Iliads, calleth a good prince and great king κοσμήτορα λαῶν, that is, the ornament of the people.

Such was the consideration of Numa Pompilius, the second king of the Romans, a just politician and wise philosopher, when he ordained that to god Terminus, on the day of his festival called Terminales, nothing should be sacrificed that had died; teaching us thereby that the bounds, limits, and frontiers of kingdoms should be guarded and preserved in peace, amity, and meekness, without polluting our hands with blood and robbery. Who doth otherwise, shall not only lose what he hath gained, but also be loaded with this scandal and reproach, that he is an unjust and wicked purchaser, and his acquests perish with him: *juxta illud, malè parta, malè dilabuntur.* And although during his whole lifetime he should have peaceable possession thereof, yet, if what hath been so acquired moulder away in the hands of his heirs, the same opproby, scandal and imputation will be charged upon the defunct, and his memory remain accursed for his unjust and unwarrantable acquest: *juxta illud: de malè quæsitis, vix gaudet tertius hæres.*

Remark likewise, gentlemen, you gouty feoffees, in this main point worthy of your observation, how by these means Pantagruel of one angel made two; which was a contingency opposite to the counsel of Charlemaine, who made two devils of one, when he transplanted the Saxons into Flanders, and the Flemings into Saxony. For not being able to keep in such subjection, the Saxons, whose dominions he had joined to the empire, but that ever and anon they would break forth into open rebellion, if he should casually be drawn into Spain, or other remote kingdoms; he caused them to be brought into his own country of Flanders, the inhabitants whereof did naturally obey him; and transplanted the Haynaulters and Flemings, his ancient loving subjects, into Saxony, not mistrusting their loyalty, although they were transplanted into a strange land. But it happened that the Saxons persisted in their rebellion and primitive obstinacy: and the Flemings, dwelling in Saxony, did imbibe the stubborn manners and conditions of the Saxons.

CHAPTER II

HOW PANURGE WAS MADE LAIRD OF SALMYGONDIN IN DIPSODIE, AND DID WASTE HIS REVENUE BEFORE IT CAME IN

WHILST Pantagruel was giving order for the government of all Dipsodie, he assigned to Panurge the lairdship of Salmygondin, which was yearly worth 6789106789 ryals of certain rent, besides the uncertain revenue of the locusts and periwinkles, amounting one year with another to the value of 2435768, or 2435769 French crowns of Berry. Sometimes it did amount to 1234554321 seraphs, when it was a good year, and that locusts and periwinkles were in request; but that was not every year.

Now his worship, the new laird, husbanded this his estate so providently well and prudently, that in less than fourteen days he wasted and dilapidated all the certain and uncertain revenue of his lairdship for three whole years: yet did not he properly dilapidate it as you might say, in founding of monasteries, building of churches, erecting of colleges, and setting up of hospitals, or casting his bacon flitches to the dogs; but spent it in a thousand little banquets and jolly collations, keeping open house for all comers and goers; yea, to all good fellows, young girls and pretty wenches; felling timber, burning the great logs for the sale of the ashes, borrowing money before hand, buying dear, selling cheap, and eating his corn, as it were, whilst it was but grass.

Pantagruel, being advertised of this his lavishness, was in good sooth no way offended at the matter, angry nor sorry: for I once told you, and again tell it you, that he was the best little great good man that ever girded a sword to his side: he took all things in good part, and interpreted every action to the best sense: he never vexed nor disquieted himself with the least pretence of dislike to anything, because he knew that he must have most grossly abandoned the divine mansion of reason, if he had permitted his mind to be never so little grieved, afflicted, or altered on any occasion whatsoever. For all the goods that the heaven covereth, and that the earth containeth, in all their dimensions of height, depth, breadth, and length, are not of so much worth, as that we should for them disturb or disorder our affections, trouble or perplex our senses or spirits.

He only drew Panurge aside, and then making to him a sweet remonstrance and mild admonition, very gently represented before him, in strong arguments, "That if he should continue in such an unthrifty course of living, and not become a better husband, it would prove altogether impossible for him, or at least hugely difficult, at any time to make him rich." "Rich!" answered Panurge; "have you fixed your thoughts there? Have you undertaken the task to enrich me in this world? Set your mind to live merrily in the name of God and good folks; let no other cark nor care be harboured within the sacrosanctified domicile of your celestial brain. May the calmness and tranquillity thereof be never incommodated with, or over-shadowed by, any frowning clouds of sullen imaginations and displeasing annoyance. For if you live joyful, merry, jocund, and glad, I cannot be

259

but rich enough. Everybody cries up thrift, thrift, and good husbandry: but many speak of Robin Hood that never shot in his bow; and talk of that virtue of husbandry, who know not what belongs to it. It is by me that they must be advised. From me therefore take this advertisement and information; that what is imputed to me for a vice, hath been done in imitation of the university and parliament of Paris; places in which is to be found the true spring and source of the lively idea of pantheology, and all manner of justice. Let him be counted an heretic that doubteth thereof, and doth not firmly believe it. Yet they in one day eat up their bishop, or the revenue of the bishoprick (is it not all one?) for a whole year; yea, sometimes for two. This is done on the day he makes his entry, and is installed: nor is there any place for an excuse; for he cannot avoid it, unless he would be hooted at and stoned for his parsimony.

"Ill-husbandry hath been also esteemed an act flowing from the four cardinal virtues. 1. Of prudence, in borrowing money beforehand: for none knows what may fall out. Who is able to tell if the world shall last yet three years? But although it should continue longer, is there any man so foolish as to have the confidence to promise himself three years?

<blockquote>
" 'What fool so confident to say,
That he shall live one other day?'
</blockquote>

"2. Of commutative justice, in buying dear, I say upon trust, and selling good cheap, that is, for ready money. What says Cato in his book of husbandry to this purpose? 'The father of a family,' says he, 'must be a perpetual seller': by which means it is impossible but that at last he shall become rich, if he have of vendible ware enough still ready for sale. Of distributive justice it doth partake, in giving entertainment to good (remark good) and gentle fellows, whom fortune had shipwrecked, like Ulysses, upon the rock of a hungry stomach without provision of sustenance; and likewise to the good and young wenches (remark the good and young): for according to the sentence of Hippocrates, youth is impatient of hunger, chiefly if it be vigorous, lively, frolic, brisk, stirring, and bouncing; which wanton lasses willingly and heartily devote themselves to the pleasure of honest men; and are so far both Platonic and Ciceronian, that they do acknowledge their being born into this world, not to be for themselves alone, but that in their proper persons their acquaintance may claim one share, and their friends another.

260

"3. The virtue of fortitude appears therein, by the cutting down and overthrowing of the great trees, like a second Milo; making havoc of dark forests, which did serve only to furnish dens, caves, and shelter to wolves, wild boars, and foxes; and afford receptacles, withdrawing-corners, and refuges to robbers, thieves and murderers; lurking holes and skulking places for cut-throat assassinators; secret obscure shops for coiners of false money, and safe retreats for heretics; laying woods even and level with the plain champaign fields and pleasant heathy ground; at the sound of the hautboys and bag-pipes playing reeks with the high and stately timber, and preparing seats and benches for the eve of the dreadful day of judgment.

"4. I gave thereby proof of my temperance, in eating my corn whilst it was but grass, like an hermit feeding upon sallads and roots; that so affranchising myself from the yoke of sensual appetites, to the utter disclaiming of their sovereignty, I might the better reserve somewhat in store for the relief of the lame, blind, crippled, maimed, needy poor, and wanting wretches.

"In taking this course I save the expence of the weed-grubbers, who gain moncy; of the reapers in harvest-time, who drink lustily, and without water; of gleaners, who will expect their cakes and bannocks; of threshers, who leave no garlic, scallions, leeks, nor onions in our gardens, by the authority of Thestilis in Virgil; and of the millers, who are generally thieves; and of the bakers, who are little better. Is this small saving or frugality? Besides the mischief and damage of the field mice, the decay of barns, and the destruction usually made by mites and weevils.

"Of corn in the blade, you may make good green sauce, of a light concoction, and easy digestion, which recreates the brain, and exhilarates the animal spirits, rejoiceth the sight, openeth the appetite, delighteth the taste, comforteth the heart, tickleth the tongue, cheereth the countenance; striking a fresh and lively colour, strengthening the muscles; tempers the blood, disburthens the midriff, refresheth the liver, disobstructs the spleen, easeth the kidneys, suppleth the reins, quickens the joints of the back, cleanseth the urine-conduits, dilates the spermatic vessels, shortens the cremasters, purgeth the bladder, puffeth up the genitals, correcteth the prepuce, hardens the nut and rectifies that member. It will make you have a current belly to trot, fart, dung, piss, sneeze, cough, spit, belch, spew, yawn, snuff, blow, breathe, snort, sweat, and set agog your robin, with a thousand other rare advantages." "I understand you very well," says Pantagruel;

261

"you would thereby infer, that those of a mean spirit and shallow capacity, have not the skill to spend much in a short time: you are not the first in whose conceit that heresy hath entered: Nero maintained it, and above all mortals admired most his uncle Caius Caligula, for having, in a few days, by a most wonderfully pregnant invention, totally spent all of the goods and patrimony which Tiberius had left him.

"But instead of observing the sumptuary supper-curbing laws of the Romans—viz., the *lex orchia,* the *fannia,* the *didia,* the *licinia,* the *cornelia,* the *lepidiana,* the *antia;* and of the Corinthians, by the which they were inhibited, under pain of great punishment, not to spend more in one year than their annual revenue did amount to: you have offered up the oblation of *protervia,* which was with the Romans such a sacrifice as the paschal lamb was amongst the Jews, wherein all that was eatable was to be eaten, and the remainder to be thrown into the fire, without reserving anything for the next day. I may very justly say of you, as Cato did of Albidius, who after that he had, by a most extravagant expence, wasted all the means and possessions he had to one only house, he fairly set it on fire, that he might the better say, *Consummatum est.* Even just as, since his time, St. Thomas Aquinas did when he had eaten up the whole lamprey. But let that pass."

CHAPTER III

HOW PANURGE PRAISETH THE DEBTORS AND BORROWERS

BUT," quoth Pantagruel, "when will you be out of debt?" "At the ensuing term of the Greek calends," answered Panurge, "when all the world shall be content, and that it be your fate to become your own heir. The Lord forbid that I should be out of debt, as if, indeed, I could be trusted. Who leaves not some leaven over night, will hardly have paste the next morning.

"Be still indebted to somebody or other, that there may be somebody always to pray for you; that the giver of all good things may grant unto you a blessed, long, and prosperous life: fearing if fortune should deal crossly with you, that it might be his chance to come short of being paid by you; he will always speak good of you in every company, ever and anon purchase new creditors unto you; to the end that through their means you may make a shift by borrowing from Peter to pay Paul, and with other folks' earth fill up his ditch. When of old in the region of the Gauls, by the institution of the Druids, the servants, slaves and bond-men were burnt quick at the funerals and obsequies of their lords and masters; had not they fear enough, think you, that their lords and masters should die? For, per force, they were to die with them for company. Did not they incessantly send up their supplications to their great God Mercury, as likewise unto Dis the father of wealth, to lengthen out their days, and preserve them long in health? Were not they very careful to entertain them well, punctually to look unto them, and to attend them faithfully and circumspectly? For by those means were they to live together at least until the hour of death. Believe me, your creditors with a more fervent devotion will beseech Almighty God to prolong your life, they being of nothing more afraid than that you should die: for that they are more concerned for the sleeve than the arm, and love the penny better than their own lives; as it evidently appeareth by the usurers of Landerousse, who not long since hanged themselves, because the price of the corn and wines was fallen, by the return of a gracious season." To this Pantagruel answering nothing, Panurge went on in his discourse, saying, "Truly, and in good sooth, sir, when I ponder my destiny aright, and think well upon it, you put me shrewdly to my plunges, and have me at a bay in twitting me with the reproach of my debts and creditors: and yet did I, in this only respect and consideration of being a debtor, esteem myself worshipful, reverend and formidable. For, against the opinion of most philosophers, that of nothing ariseth nothing; yet without having bottomed on so much as that which is called the first matter, did I out of nothing become such a maker and creator, that I have created,—what? A gay number of fair and jolly creditors. Nay, creditors, I will maintain it, even to the very fire itself exclusively, are fair and goodly creatures. Who lendeth nothing is an ugly and wicked creature, and an accursed imp of the infernal old Nick. And there is made,—what? Debts: a thing most precious and dainty, of great use and antiquity. Debts, I say, surmounting the number of syllables which may result from the combinations of all the consonants with each of the vowels, heretofore projected, reckoned and calculated by the noble Xenocrates. To judge of the perfection of debtors by the numerosity of their creditors, is the readiest way for entering into the mysteries of practical arithmetic.

"You can hardly imagine how glad I am, when every morning I perceive myself environed and surrounded with brigades of creditors;

humble, fawning and full of their reverences: and whilst I remark, that as I look more favourably upon, and give a more cheerful countenance to one than another, the fellow thereupon buildeth a conceit that he shall be the first dispatched, and the foremost in the date of payment; and he valueth my smiles at the rate of ready money. It seemeth unto me, that I then act and personate the god of the passion of Saumure, accompanied with his angels and cherubims.

"These are my flatterers, my soothers, my clawbacks, my smoothers, my parasites, my saluters, my givers of good morrows, and perpetual orators; which makes me verily think, that the supremest height of heroic virtue, described by Hesiod, consisteth in being a debtor, wherein I held the first degree in my commencement. Which dignity, though all human creatures seem to aim at, and aspire thereto, few nevertheless, because of the difficulties in the way, and incumbrances of hard passages, are able to reach it; as is easily perceivable by the ardent desire and vehement longing harboured in the breast of every one, to be still creating more debts, and new creditors.

"Yet doth it not lie in the power of every one to be a debtor. To acquire creditors is not at the disposure of each man's arbitrament. You nevertheless would deprive me of this sublime felicity. You ask me when I will be out of debt.

"Well, to go yet farther on, and possibly worse in your conceit, may sanct Bablin, the good sanct, snatch me, if I have not all my lifetime held debt to be as an union or conjunction of the heavens with the earth, and the whole cement whereby the race of mankind is kept together; yea, of such virtue and efficacy, that, I say, the whole progeny of Adam would very suddenly perish without it. Therefore, perhaps, I do not think amiss, when I repute it to be the great soul of the universe, which according to the opinion of the academics, vivifieth all manner of things. In confirmation whereof, that you may the better believe it to be so, represent unto yourself, without any prejudice of spirit, in a clear and serene fancy, the idea and form of some other world than this; take, if you please, and lay hold on the thirtieth of those which the philosopher Metrodorus did enumerate, wherein it is to be supposed there is no debtor or creditor, that is to say, a world without debts. There amongst the planets will be no regular course. All will be in disorder. Jupiter reckoning himself to be nothing indebted unto Saturn, will go near to detrude him out of his sphere, and with the Homeric chain will be like to hang up all the intelligences, gods, heavens, demons, heroes, devils, earth and sea, together

264

with the other elements. Saturn, no doubt, combining with Mars, will reduce the world into a chaos of confusion.

"Mercury then would be no more subjected to the other planets; he would scorn to be any longer their Camillus, as he was of old termed in the Hetrurian tongue: for it is to be imagined that he is no way a debtor to them. Venus will be no more venerable, because she shall have lent nothing. The moon will remain bloody and obscure: for to what end should the sun impart unto her any of his light? He owed her nothing. Nor yet will the sun shine upon the earth, nor the stars send down any good influence; because the terrestrial globe hath desisted from sending up their wonted nourishment by vapours and exhalations, wherewith Heraclitus said, the stoics proved, Cicero maintained they were cherished and alimented. There would likewise be in such a world no manner of symbolization, alternation, nor transmutation amongst the elements; for the one will not esteem itself obliged to the other, as having borrowed nothing at all from it. Earth then will not become water; water will not be changed into air; of air will be made no fire, and fire will afford no heat unto the earth; the earth will produce nothing but monsters, Titans, giants; no rain will descend upon it, nor light shine thereon; no wind will blow there, nor will there be in it any summer or autumn. Lucifer will break loose, and issuing forth of the depth of hell, accompanied with his furies, fiends, and horned devils, will go about to unnestle and drive out of heaven all the gods, as well of the greater as of the lesser nations. Such a world, without lending, will be no better than a dog-kennel, a place of contention and wrangling, more unruly and irregular than that of the rector of Paris; of a devil of an hurly-burly, and more disordered confusion, than that of the plagues of Doüay. Men will not then salute one another; it will be but lost labour to expect aid or succour from any, or to cry, 'Fire, water, murder'; for none will put to their helping hand. Why? He lent no money; there is nothing due to him. Nobody is concerned in his burning, in his shipwreck, in his ruin. or in his death; and that because he hitherto had lent nothing, and would never thereafter have lent anything. In short, faith, hope and charity would be quite banished from such a world; for men are born to relieve and assist one another: and in their stead would succeed and be introduced defiance, disdain, and rancour, with the most execrable troop of all evils, all imprecations and all miseries. Whereupon you will think, and that not amiss, that Pandora had there spilt her unlucky bottle. Men unto men will be wolves, hob-

thrushers and goblins (as were Lycaon, Bellerophon, Nebuchodono-
sor); plunderers, highway-robbers, cut-throats, rapperees, murderers,
poisoners, assassinators, lewd, wicked, malevolent, pernicious haters,
set against everybody, like to Ismael, Metabus, or Timon the Athenian, who for that cause was named Misanthropos; in such sort, that
it would prove much more easy in nature to have fish entertained in
the air, and bullocks fed in the bottom of the ocean, than to support
or tolerate a rascally rabble of people that will not lend. These fellows, I vow, do I hate with a perfect hatred; and if, conformable to the
pattern of this grievous, peevish and perverse world, which lendeth
nothing, you figure and liken the little world, which is man, you will
find in him a terrible jostling coyle and clutter. The head will not
lend the sight of his eyes to guide the feet and hands; the legs will
refuse to bear up the body; the hands will leave off working any more
for the rest of the members; the heart will be weary of its continual
motion for the beating of the pulse, and will no longer lend his assistance; the lungs will withdraw the use of their bellows; the liver will
desist from conveying any more blood through the veins, for the good
of the whole; the bladder will not be indebted to the kidneys so that
the urine thereby will be totally stopped. The brains, in the interim,
considering this unnatural course, will fall into a raving dotage, and
withhold all feeling from the sinews, and motion from the muscles.
Briefly, in such a world without order and array, owing nothing, lending nothing, and borrowing nothing, you would see a more dangerous
conspiration than that which Æsop exposed in his apologue. Such a
world will perish undoubtedly; and not only perish, but perish very
quickly. Were it Æsculapius himself, his body would immediately
rot, and the chafing soul, full of indignation, take its flight to all the
devils of hell after my money.

CHAPTER IV

PANURGE CONTINUETH HIS DISCOURSE IN PRAISE OF
BORROWERS AND LENDERS

ON the contrary, be pleased to represent unto your fancy another
world, wherein every one lendeth, and every one oweth, all are
debtors, and all creditors. O how great will that harmony be, which
shall thereby result from the regular motions of the heavens! Me-

thinks I hear it every whit as well as ever Plato did. What sympathy will there be amongst the elements! O how delectable then unto nature will be her own works and productions! Whilst Ceres appeareth loaden with corn, Bacchus with wines, Flora with flowers, Pomona with fruits, and Juno fair in a clear air, wholesome and pleasant. I lose myself in this high contemplation.

"Then will among the race of mankind peace, love, benevolence, fidelity, tranquillity, rest, banquets, feastings, joy, gladness, gold, silver, small money, chains, rings, with other ware, and chaffer of that nature be found to trot from hand to hand; no suits at law, no wars, no strife, debate, nor wrangling: none will be there an usurer, none will be there a pinch-penny, a scrape-good wretch, or churlish hardhearted refuser. Good God! Will not this be the golden age in the reign of Saturn? The true idea of the Olympic regions, wherein, all other virtues ceasing, charity alone ruleth, governeth, domineereth and triumpheth? All will be fair and goodly people there, all just and virtuous.

"O happy world! O people of that world most happy! Yea, thrice and four times blessed is that people; I think in very deed that I am amongst them, and swear to you, by my good forsooth, that if this glorious aforesaid world had a pope, abounding with cardinals, that so he might have the association of a sacred college, in the space of very few years you should be sure to see the sancts much thicker in the roll, more numerous, wonderworking and mirific, more services, more vows, more staff-bearers, more wax-candles than are all those in the nine bishoprics of Brittany, St. Yves only excepted. Consider, sir, I pray you, how the noble Patelin, having a mind to deify, and extol even to the third heavens, the father of William Josseaume, said no more but this: 'And he did lend his goods to those who were desirous of them.'

"O the fine saying! Now let our microcosm be fancied conformable to this model in all its members; lending, borrowing and owing, that is to say, according to its own nature: for nature hath not to any other end created man, but to borrow and lend: no greater is the harmony amongst the heavenly spheres, than that which shall be found in its well-ordered policy. The intention of the founder of this microcosm is, to have a soul therein to be entertained, which is lodged there, as a guest with its host, that it may live there for a while. Life consisteth in blood; blood is the seat of the soul: therefore the chiefest work of the microcosm, is, to be making blood continually.

"At this forge are exercised all the members of the body: none is exempted from labour; each operates a-part and doth its proper office. And such is their hierarchy, that perpetually the one borrows from the other, the one lends the other, and the one is the other's debtor. The stuff and matter convenient, which nature giveth to be turned into blood, is bread and wine. All kind of nourishing victuals is understood to be comprehended in these two, and from hence in the Langue Goth is called the coampanage. To find out this meat and drink, to prepare and boil it, the hands are put to work, the feet do walk and bear up the whole bulk of the corporal mass; the eyes guide and conduct all; the appetite, in the orifice of the stomach, by means of a little sourish black humour, called melancholy, which is transmitted thereto from the milt, giveth warning to shut in the food. The tongue doth make the first essay, and tastes it; the teeth do chew it, and the stomach doth receive, digest and chilify it; the meseraic veins suck out of it what is good and fit, leaving behind the excrements, which are, through special conduits for that purpose, voided by an expulsive faculty: thereafter it is carried to the liver, where it being changed again, it, by the virtue of that new transmutation, becomes blood. What joy, conjecture you, will then be found amongst those officers, when they see this rivulet of gold, which is their sole restorative? No greater is the joy of alchymists, when, after long travel, toil and expence, they see in their furnaces the transmutation. Then is it that every member doth prepare itself, and strive anew to purify and to refine this treasure. The kidneys, through the emulgent veins, draw that aquosity from thence which you call urine, and there send it away through the ureters to be slipt downwards; where, in a lower receptacle, and proper for it, to wit, the bladder, it is kept, and stayeth there until an opportunity to void it out in his due time. The spleen draweth from the blood its terrestrial part—viz, the grounds, lees, or thick substance settled in the bottom thereof, which you term melancholy. The bottle of the gall substracts from thence all the superfluous choler; whence it is brought to another shop or workhouse to be yet better purified and fined, that is the heart, which, by its agitation of diastolic and systolic motions, so neatly subtilizeth and inflames it, that in the right-side ventricle it is brought to perfection, and through the veins is sent to all the members: each parcel of the body draws it then unto itself, and after its own fashion is cherished and alimented by it: feet, hands, thighs, arms, eyes, ears, back, breast, yea, all; and then it is that who before were lenders, now become

268

debtors. The heart doth in its left-side ventricle so thinnify the blood, that it thereby obtains the name of spiritual; which being sent through the arteries to all the members of the body, serveth to warm, and winnow, or fan the other blood which runneth through the veins. The lights never cease with its lappets and bellows to cool and refresh it; in acknowledgment of which good the heart, through the arterial vein, imparts unto it the choicest of its blood. At last it is made so fine and subtle within the rete mirabile, that thereafter those animal spirits are framed and composed of it; by means whereof the imagination, discourse, judgment, resolution, deliberation, ratiocination and memory have their rise, actings, and operations.

"Cops body, I sink, I drown, I perish, I wander astray, and quite fly out of myself, when I enter into the consideration of the profound abyss of this world, thus lending, thus owing. Believe me, it is a divine thing to lend; to owe, an heroic virtue. Yet is not this all: this little world thus lending, owing, and borrowing, is so good and charitable, that no sooner is the above-specified alimentation finished, but that it forthwith projecteth, and hath already forecast, how it shall lend to those who are not as yet born, and by that loan endeavour, what it may, to eternize itself, and multiply in images like the pattern, that is, children. To this end every member doth, of the choicest and most precious of its nourishment, pare and cut off a portion: then instantly dispatcheth it downwards to that place, where nature hath prepared for it very fit vessels and receptacles, through which descending to the genitories by long ambages, circuits and flexuosities, it receiveth a competent form, and rooms apt enough both in the man and woman for the future conservation and perpetuating of human kind. All this is done by loans and debts of the one unto the other; and hence have we this word, the debt of marriage. Nature doth reckon pain to the refuser, with a most grievous vexation to his members, and an outragous fury amidst his senses. But on the other part, to the lender, a set reward, accompanied with pleasure, joy, solace, mirth and merry glee."

CHAPTER V

I UNDERSTAND you very well," quoth Pantagruel, "and take you
to be very good at topics, and thoroughly affectioned to your own
cause: but preach it up, and patrocinate it; prattle on it, and defend it
as much as you will, even from hence to the next Whitsuntide, if you
please so to do; yet in the end will you be astonished to find how you
shall have gained no ground at all upon me, nor persuaded me by
your fair speeches and smooth talk to enter ever so little into the
thraldom of debt. 'You shall owe to none,' saith the holy apostle,
'anything save love, friendship, and a mutual benevolence.'

"You serve me here, I confess, with fine graphides and diatyposes,
descriptions and figures, which truly please me very well: but let me
tell you, if you will represent unto your fancy an impudent blustering
bully, and an importunate borrower, entering afresh and newly into
a town already advertised of his manners, you shall find that at
his ingress the citizens will be more hideously affrighted and
amazed, and in a greater terror and fear, dread and trembling, than
if the pest itself should step into it, in the very same garb and accoutrement wherein the Tyanæan philosopher found it within the city
of Ephesus. And I am fully confirmed in the opinion, that the Persians erred not when they said, 'That the second vice was to lie,' the
first being that of owing money. For in very truth, debts and lying
are ordinarily joined together. I will nevertheless not from hence infer, that none must owe anything, or lend anything. For who so rich
can be, that sometimes he may not owe? or who can be so poor, that
sometimes he may not lend?

"Let the occasion notwithstanding in that case, as Plato very wisely
saith, and ordaineth in his laws, be such, that none be permitted to
draw any water out of his neighbour's well, until first, they by continual digging and delving into their own proper ground, shall have
hit upon a kind of potter's earth, which is called ceramite, and there
had found no source or drop of water: for that sort of earth, by reason of its substance, which is fat, strong, firm and close, so retaineth its
humidity, that it doth not easily evaporate it by any outward excur-
sions or evaporation.

"In good sooth, it is a great shame to chuse rather to be still borrowing in all places from every one, than to work and win. Then only in my judgment should one lend, when the diligent, toiling and industrious person is no longer able by his labour to make any purchase unto himself; or otherwise, when by mischance he hath suddenly fallen into an unexpected loss of his goods.

"Howsoever let us leave this discourse, and from henceforwards do not hang upon creditors, nor tie yourself to them. I make account for the time past to rid you freely of them, and from their bondage to deliver you."

"The least I should in this point," quoth Panurge, "is to thank you, though it be the most I can do: and if gratitude and thanksgiving be to be estimated and prized by the affection of the benefactor, that is to be done infinitely and sempiternally: for the love which you bear me of your own accord and free grace, without any merit of mine, goeth far beyond the reach of any price or value; it transcends all weight, all number, all measure, it is endless and everlasting: therefore should I offer to commensurate and adjust it, either to the size and proportion of your own noble and gracious deeds, or yet to the contentment and delight of the obliged receivers, I would come off but very faintly and flaggingly. You have verily done me a great deal of good and multiplied your favours on me more frequently than was fitting to one of my condition. You have been more bountiful towards me than I have deserved, and your courtesies have by far surpassed the extent of my merits; I must needs confess it. But it is not as you suppose, in the proposed matter: for there it is not where I itch, it is not there where it fretteth, hurts or vexeth me; for henceforth being quit and out of debt, what countenance shall I be able to keep? You may imagine that it will become me very ill, for the first month; because I have never hitherto been brought up or accustomed to it, I am very much afraid of it. Furthermore, there shall not one hereafter, native of the country of Salmigondy, but he shall level the shot towards my nose: all the back-cracking fellows of the world, in discharging of their postern petarades, use commonly to say *Voila pour les quittes:* that is, for the quit. My life will be of very short continuance, I do foresee it. I recommend to you the making of my epitaph; for I perceive I shall die confected in the very stench of farts. If at any time to come, by way of restorative to such good women as shall happen to be troubled with the grievous pain of the wind-cholic, the ordinary medicaments prove nothing effectual, the mummy of all my befarted body will straight be as a present remedy appointed by the physicians; whereof they taking any small modicum, it will incontinently for their case afford them a rattle of bumshot, like a sal of muskets.

"Therefore would I beseech you to leave me some few centuries of debts; as king Louis the eleventh, exempting from suits in law the reverend Miles d'Illiers, bishop of Chartres, was by the said bishop most earnestly solicited to leave him some few for the exercise of his mind. I had rather give them all my revenue of the periwinkles, to-gether with the other incomes of the locusts, albeit I should not there-by have any parcel abated from off the principal sums which I owe." "Let us waive this matter," quoth Pantagruel, "I have told it you over again."

CHAPTER VI

WHY NEW MARRIED MEN WERE PRIVILEGED FROM GOING TO THE WARS

BUT, in the interim," asked Panurge, "by what law was it con-stituted, ordained and established, that such as should plant a new vineyard, those that should build a new house, and the new married men, should be exempted and discharged from the duty of warfare for the first year?" "By the law," answered Pantagruel, "of Moses." "Why," replied Panurge, "the lately married? As for the vine-plant-ers, I am now too old to reflect on them; my condition, at this present, induceth me to remain satisfied with the care of vintage, finishing and turning the grapes into wine: nor are those pretty new build-ers of dead stones written or pricked down in my book of life; it is all with live stones that I set up and erect the fabrics of my architec-ture, to wit, men." "It was, according to my opinion," quoth Pantag-ruel, "to the end, first, That the fresh married folks should for the first year reap a full and complete fruition of their pleasures in their mutual exercise of the act of love, in such sort, that in waiting more at leisure on the production of posterity and propagating of their prog-eny, they might the better increase their race, and make provision of new heirs: that if in the years thereafter men should, upon their un-dergoing of some military adventure, happen to be killed, their names and coats of arms might continue with their children in the same families: and next, that the wives thereby coming to know whether they were barren or fruitful (for one year's trial, in regard of the maturity of age, wherein, of old, they married, was held sufficient for the discovery) they might pitch the more suitably, in case of their first husband's decease, upon a second match. The fertile women to be wedded to those who desire to multiply their issue; and the sterile ones to such other mates, as misregarding the storing of their lineage, chose them only for their virtues, learning, genteel behaviour, domestic consolation, management of the house, and matrimonial conveniences and comforts, and such like." "The preachers of Varennes," saith Panurge, "detest and abhor the second marriages, as altogether foolish and dishonest."

"Foolish and dishonest," quoth Pantagruel: "a plague take such preachers!" "Yea, but," quoth Panurge, "the like mischief also befel the friar Charmer, who, in a full auditory, making a sermon at Parcilly, and therein abominating the reiteration of marriage, and the entering again in the bonds of a nuptial tie, did swear, and heartily give himself to the swiftest devil in hell, if he had not rather choose, and would much more willingly undertake the unmaidening or depucelating of a hundred virgins, than the simple drudgery of one widow. Truly I find your reason in that point right good, and strongly grounded.

"But what would you think, if the cause why this the exemption or immunity was granted had no other foundation, but that, during the whole space of the said first year, they so lustily bobbed it with their female consorts, as both reason and equity require they should do, that they had drained and evacuated their spermatic vessels; and were become thereby altogether feeble, weak, emasculated, drooping, and flaggingly pithless; yea, in such sort, that they in the day of battle, like ducks which plunge over head and ears, would sooner hide themselves behind the baggage, than, in the company of valiant fighters and daring military combatants, appear where stern Bellona deals her blows, and moves a bustling noise of thwacks and thumps. Nor is it to be thought that under the standard of Mars they will so much as once strike a fair stroke, because their most considerable knocks have been already jirked and whirreted within the curtains of his sweetheart Venus.

"In confirmation whereof, amongst other relics and monuments of antiquity, we now as yet often see, that in all great houses, after the expiring of some few days, these young married blades are readily sent away to visit their uncles, that in the absence of their wives, reposing themselves a little, they may recover their decayed strength by the recruit of a fresh supply, the more vigorous to return again, and

273

face about to renew the duelling shock and conflict of an amorous dalliance: albeit, for the greater part, they have neither uncle nor aunt to go to.

"Just so did the king Crackart, after the battle of the cornets, not cashier us, speaking properly, I mean me and the quail-piper, but for our refreshment remanded us to our houses; and he is as yet seeking after his own. My grandfather's godmother was wont to say to me, when I was a boy,

> " 'Patenosters et oraisons
> Sont pour ceux-là qui les retiennent.
> Un fiffre en fenaisons
> Est plus fort que deux qui en viennent.'

> " 'Not orisons nor paternotres
> Shall ever disorder my brain.
> One cadet, to the field as he flutters,
> Is worth two when they end the campaign.'

"That which prompteth me to that opinion is, that the vine-planters did seldom eat of the grapes, or drink of the wine of their labour, till the first year was wholly elapsed; during all which time also the builders did hardly inhabit their new structured dwelling places, for fear of dying suffocated through want of respiration; as Galen hath most learnedly remarked, in the second book of the difficulty of breathing. Under favour, sir, I have not asked this question without cause causing, and reason truly very ratiocinant. Be not offended, I pray you."

CHAPTER VII

HOW PANURGE HAD A FLEA IN HIS EAR, AND FOREBORE TO WEAR ANY LONGER HIS MAGNIFICENT COD-PIECE

PANURGE, the day thereafter, caused pierce his right ear, after the Jewish fashion, and thereto clasped a little gold ring, of a fearny-like kind of workmanship, in the beazil or collet whereof was set and inchased a flea; and to the end you may be rid of all doubts, you are to know that the flea was black. O what a brave thing it is, in every case and circumstance of a matter, to be thoroughly well informed! The sum of the expence hereof being cast up, brought in, and laid down upon his council-board carpet, was found to amount to no more quarterly than the charge of the nuptials of an Hyrcanian tigress; even as you would say 609000 maravedis. At these vast costs and excessive disbursements, as soon as he perceived himself to be out of debt, he fretted much; and afterwards, as tyrants and lawyers use to do, he nourished and fed her with the sweat and blood of his subjects and clients.

He then took four French ells of a coarse brown russet cloth, and therein apparelling himself, as with a long, plain-seamed, and single-stitched gown, left off the wearing of his breeches, and tied a pair of spectacles to his cap. In this equipage did he present himself before Pantagruel; to whom this disguise appeared the more strange, that he did not, as before, see that goodly, fair and stately codpiece, which was the sole anchor of hope, wherein he was wonted to rely, and the last refuge he had amidst all the waves and boisterous billows, which a stormy cloud in a cross fortune would raise up against him. Honest Pantagruel, not understanding the mystery, asked him, by way of interrogatory, what he did intend to personate in that new-fangled prosopopeia? "I have," answered Panurge, "a flea in mine ear, and have a mind to marry." "In a good time!" quoth Pantagruel; "you have told me joyful tidings; yet would not I hold a red hot iron in my hand for all the gladness of them. But it is not the fashion of lovers to be accoutred in such daggling vestments, so as to have their shirts flagging down over their knees, without breeches, and with a long robe of a dark brown mingled hue, which is a colour never used in talarian garments amongst any persons of honour, quality or virtue. If some heretical persons, and schismatical sectaries, have at any time formerly been so arrayed and cloathed (though many have imputed such a kind of dress to cosenage, cheat, imposture, and an affectation of tyranny upon credulous minds of the rude multitude), I will nevertheless not blame them for it, nor in that point judge rashly or sinistrously of them; every one overflowing aboundeth in his own sense and fancy: yea, in things of a foreign consideration, altogether extrinsical and indifferent, which in and of themselves are neither commendable nor bad, because they proceed not from the interior of the thoughts and heart, which is the shop of all good and evil: of goodness, if it be upright, and that its affections be regulated by the pure and clean spirit of righteousness; and on the other side, of wickedness, if its inclinations, straying beyond the bounds of equity, be cor-

rupted and depraved by the malice and suggestions of the devil. It is
only the novelty and new-fangledness thereof which I dislike, together
with the contempt of common custom, and the fashion which is in
use."

"The colour," answered Panurge, "is convenient, for it is conform
to that of my council-board carpet: therefore will I henceforth hold me
with it, and more narrowly and circumspectly, than ever hitherto I
have done, look to my affairs and business. Seeing I am once out of
debt, you never yet saw man more unpleasing than I will be, if God
help me not. Lo here be my spectacles. To see me afar off, you
would readily say, that it were friar John Burgess. I believe certainly,
that in the next ensuing year, I shall once more preach the croisade,
bounce buckram. Do you see this grey rug? Doubt not but there
lurketh under it some hid property and occult virtue, known to very
few in the world. I did not take it on before this morning: and
nevertheless, am already in a rage of lust, mad after a wife, and
vehemently hot upon untying the cod-piece-point: I itch, I tingle, I
wriggle, and long exceedingly to be married; that, without the danger
of cudgel-blows, I may labour my female cops-mate with the hard
push of a bull-horned devil. O the provident and thrifty husband that
I then will be! After my death, with all honour and respect due to
my frugality, will they burn the sacred bulk of my body, of purpose
to preserve the ashes thereof, in memory of the choicest pattern that
ever was, of a perfectly wary, and complete householder. Cops-body,
this is not the carpet whereon my treasurer shall be allowed to play
false in his accompts with me, by setting down an X for a V, or an
L for an S: for in that case, should I make a hail of fisti-cuffs to fly
into his face. Look upon me, sir, both before and behind: it is made
after the manner of a toge, which was the ancient fashion of the Romans in time of peace. I took the mode, shape, and form thereof in
Trajan's column at Rome, as also in the triumphant arch of Septimus
Severus. I am tired of the wars, weary of wearing buff-coats, cassocks,
and hoquetons. My shoulders are pitifully worn, and bruised with the
carrying of harness; let armour cease, and the long robe bear sway: at
least it must be so for the whole space of the succeeding year, if
I be married, as yesterday by the Mosaic law you evidenced. In what
concerneth the breeches, my great aunt Laurence did long ago tell
me, that the breeches were only ordained for the use of the cod-piece,
and to no other end; which I, upon a no less forcible consequence,
give credit to every whit as well, as to the saying of the fine fellow

Galen, who, in his ninth book of the use and employment of our members, alledgeth, that the head was made for the eyes: for nature might have placed our heads in our knees or elbows; but having before-hand determined that the eyes should serve to discover things from afar, she, for the better enabling them to execute their designed office, fixed them in the head (as on the top of a long pole) in the most eminent part of all the body: no otherwise than we see the phares, or high towers erected in the mouths of havens, that navigators may the further off perceive with ease the light of the nightly fires and lanterns. And because I would gladly, for some short while (a year at least) take a little rest and breathing-time from the toilsome labour of the military profession; that is to say, be married; I have desisted from wearing any more a cod-piece, and consequently have laid aside my breeches: for the cod-piece is the principal and most essential piece of armour that a warrior doth carry; and therefore do I maintain even to the fire (exclusively, understand you me) that no Turks can properly be said to be armed men, in regard that cod-pieces are by their law forbidden to be worn."

CHAPTER VIII

WHY THE COD-PIECE IS HELD TO BE THE CHIEF (OR RATHER FIRST) PIECE OF ARMOUR AMONGST WARRIORS

WILL you maintain," quoth Pantagruel, "that the cod-piece is the first piece of a military harness? It is a new kind of doctrine, and very paradoxical: for we say, at the spurs begins the arming of a man." "Sir, I maintain it," answered Panurge, "and not wrongfully do I maintain it. Behold how nature having a fervent desire after its production of plants, trees, shrubs, herbs, sponges, and plant-animals, to eternize, and continue them unto all succession of ages (in their several kinds or sorts at least, although the individual perish) unruinable, and in an everlasting being, hath most curiously armed and fenced their buds, sprouts, shoots and seeds, wherein the above-mentioned perpetuity consisteth, by strengthening, covering, guarding, and fortifying them with an admirable industry, with husks, cases, scarfs and swads, hulls, cods, stones, films, cartels, shells, ears, rinds, barks, skins, ridges, and prickles, which serve them instead of strong, fair, and natural cod-pieces: as is manifestly apparent in pease, beans, fasels, pomegranates, peaches, cottons, gourds, pumpions, melons, corn, lemons, almonds, walnuts, filberts, and chestnuts; as likewise in all plants, slips, or sets whatsoever, wherein it is plainly and evidently seen, that the sperm and semina is more closely veiled, overshadowed, corroborated, and thoroughly harnessed than any other part, portion, or parcel of the whole.

"Nature, nevertheless, did not after that manner provide for the sempiternizing of the human race: but on the contrary created man naked, tender and frail, without either offensive or defensive arms; and that in the estate of innocence, in the first age of all, which was the golden season: not as a plant, but living creature, born for peace, not war, and brought forth into the world with an unquestionable right and title to the plenary fruition and enjoyment of all fruits and vegetables; as also to a certain calm and gentle rule and dominion over all kinds of beasts, fowls, fishes, reptiles, and insects. Yet afterwards it happening in the time of the iron age, under the reign of Jupiter, when the multiplication of mischievous actions, wickedness and malice began to take root and footing within the then perverted hearts of men, that the earth began to bring forth nettles, thistles, thorns, briars, and such other stubborn and rebellious vegetables to the nature of man; nor scarce was there any animal, which by a fatal disposition did not then revolt from him, and tacitly conspire, and covenant with one another to serve him no longer, nor, as far as they had ability to resist, to do him any manner of obedience; but rather, to the uttermost of their power, to annoy him with all the hurt and harm they could. The man then, that he might maintain his primitive right and prerogative, and continue his sway and dominion over all, both vegetable and sensitive creatures; and knowing of a truth, that he could not be so well accommodated as he ought, without the servitude and subjection of several animals, bethought himself, that of necessity he must needs put on arms, and make provision of harness against wars and violence." "By the holy saint Babingoose," cried out Pantagruel, "you are become, since the last rain, a great lifrelofre,—philosopher I should say." "Take notice, sir," quoth Panurge, "when dame nature had prompted him to his own arming, what part of the body it was, where, by her inspiration, he clapped on the first harness: it was forsooth by the double pluck of my little dog the ballock, and good senor don Priapus stabo stando; which done, he was content, and sought no more. This is certified by the testimony of the great Hebrew captain and philosopher Moses, who affirmeth, that he fenced that member with a brave and gallant cod-piece, most exquisitely framed, and by right curious devices of a notably pregnant invention, made up and composed of fig-tree leaves; which by reason of their solid stiffness, incisory notches, curled, frisling, sleeked smoothness, large ampleness, together with their colour, smell, virtue, and faculty, were exceeding proper, and fit for the covering and arming of the sachels of generation, the hideously big Lorrain cullions being from thence only excepted; which swaggering down to the lowermost bottom of the breeches, cannot abide (for being quite out of all order and method) the stately fashion of the high and lofty cod-piece; as is manifest by the noble Valentin Viardiere, whom I found at Nancy, on the first day of May (the more flauntingly to gallantize it afterwards) rubbing his ballocks, spread out upon a table after the manner of a Spanish cloak. Wherefore it is, that none should henceforth say, who would not speak improperly, when any country-bumkin hyeth to the wars, Have a care, my royster, of the wine pot, that is the skull, but, Have a care, my royster, of the milk pot, that is, the testicles. By the whole rabble of the horned fiends of hell, the head being cut off, that single person only thereby dieth: but if the ballocks be marred, the whole race of human kind would forthwith perish, and be lost for ever.

"This was the motive which incited the goodly writer Galen, lib. 1, de spermate, to aver with boldness, that it were better (that is to say, a less evil) to have no heart at all, than to be quite destitute of genitories: for in them is laid up, conserved, and put in store, as in a secessive repository, and sacred warehouse, the semina, and original source of the whole offspring of mankind. Therefore would I be apt to believe, for less than a hundred franks, that those are the very same stones, by means whereof Deucalion and Pyrrha restored the human race, in peopling with men and women the world, which, a little before that, had been drowned in the overflowing waves of a poetical deluge. This stirred up the valiant Justinian, l. 1, 4, de cagotis tollendis, to collocate his summum bonum, in braguibus, & braguetis. For this, and other causes, the lord Humphry de Merville, following his king to a certain warlike expedition, whilst he was in trying upon his own person a new suit of armour (for of his old rusty harness he could make no more use, by reason that some few years since, the skin of his belly was a great way removed from his kidneys) his lady thereupon, in the profound musing of a contemplative spirit, very maturely considering that he had but small care of the staff of love, and packet of marriage, seeing he did no otherwise arm that part of the body, than with links of mail, advised him **to** shield, fence, and gabionate it with a big tilting helmet, which she had lying in her closet, to her otherways utterly unprofitable. On this lady was penned these subsequent verses, which are extant in the third book of the Shitbrana of paultry wenches.

> " 'When Yoland saw her spouse, equipt for fight,
> And, save the cod-piece, all in armour dight,
> My dear, she cry'd, why, pray, of all the rest
> Is that expos'd, you know I love the best:
> Was she to blame for an ill-manag'd fear,
> Or rather pious, conscionable care?
> Wise lady, she! in hurly-burly fight,
> Can any tell where random blows may light?' '

"Leave off then, sir, from being astonished, and wonder no more at this new manner of decking and trimming up myself as you now see me."

CHAPTER IX

HOW PANURGE ASKETH COUNSEL OF PANTAGRUEL WHETHER HE SHOULD MARRY, YEA, OR NO

TO this Pantagruel replying nothing, Panurge prosecuted the discourse he had already broached; and therewithal fetching, as from the bottom of his heart, a very deep sigh, said, "My lord and master, you have heard the design I am upon, which is to marry, if by some disastrous mischance, all the holes in the world be not shut up, stopped, closed, and bushed. I humbly beseech you, for the affection which of a long time you have borne me, to give me your best advice therein." "Then," answered Pantagruel, "seeing you have so decreed and taken deliberation thereon, and that the matter is fully determined, what need is there of any further talk thereof, but forthwith to put into execution what you have resolved." "Yea, but," quoth Panurge, "I would be loth to act anything therein without counsel had thereto." "It is my judgment also," quoth Pantagruel, "and I advise you to it." "Nevertheless," quoth Panurge, "if you think that it were much better for me to remain a bachelor, as I am, than to run headlong upon new hair-brained undertakings of conjugal adventure, I would rather choose not to marry." "Not marry then," said Pantagruel. "Yea, but," quoth Panurge, "would you have me so solitarily drag out the whole course of my life, without the comfort of a matrimonial consort? You know it is written *Væ soli;* and a single person is never seen to reap the joy and solace that is found among those that are wedlockt." "Wedlock it then, in the name of God," quoth Pantagruel. "But if," quoth Panurge, "my wife should make me a cuckold; as it is not unknown unto you, how this hath been a very plentiful year in the production of that kind of cattle; I should fly off the hinges, and grow impatient, beyond all measure and mean. I love cuckolds indeed at my heart; for they seem unto me to be of a right honest conversation, and I, truly, do very willingly frequent their company: but should I die for it, I would not be one of their number: that is a point for me of a too sore prickling point, and too hard a knot." "Not marry then," quoth Pantagruel: "for without all controversy, this sentence of Seneca is infallibly true, 'what thou to others shalt have done, others will do the like to thee.'" "Do you," quoth Panurge, "aver that without all exception?" "Without all exception," quoth Pantagruel. "Ho, ho," says Panurge, "by the wrath of a devil, his meaning is, either in this world, or in the other, which is to come. Yet seeing I can no more do without a wife, than a blind man without his staff, for the funnel must be in agitation, without which manner of occupation I cannot live; were it not a great deal better for me to apply and associate myself to some one honest, lovely, and virtuous woman, than (as I do) by a new change of females every day, run a hazard of being bastinadoed, or (which is worse) of the great pox, if not of both together? for never had I enjoyment yet of an honest woman, be it spoken by leave and favour of the husbands." "Husband then be, in God's name," quoth Pantagruel. "But if," quoth Panurge, "it were the will of God, and that my destiny did unluckily lead me to marry an honest woman who would beat me, I should be stored with more than two third parts of the patience of Job, if I were not stark mad by it, and quite distracted with such rugged dealings: for it hath been told me, that those exceeding honest women have ordinarily very perverse headpieces; therefore is it that their family lacketh not for good vinegar. Yet in that case should it go worse with me, if I did not then in such sort bang her back and breast, so thumpingly bethwack her giblets, to wit, her arms, legs, head, lights, liver, and milt, with her other en-

281

trails, and mangle, jag, and slash her coats, so after the cross-billet fashion, that the greatest devil of hell should wait at the gate for the reception of her damned soul. I could make a shift for this year to waive such molestation and disquiet, and be content to lay aside that trouble, and engage not in it." "Engage not in it then," answered Pantagruel. "Yea, but," quoth Panurge, "considering the condition wherein I now am, out of debt and unmarried: mark what I say, free from all debt, in an ill hour! for were I deeply on the score, my creditors would be chary of my sweet paternity: but being quit, and not married, nobody will be so regardful of me, or carry towards me a love like that which is said to be in a conjugal affection. And if by some mishap I should fall sick, I should be looked to very waywardly. The wise man saith, where there is no woman (I mean the mother of a family, and wife in the union of a lawful wedlock) the crazy and diseased are in danger of being ill used, and of having much brabling and strife about them; as by clear experience hath been made apparent in the persons of popes, legates, cardinals, bishops, abbots, priors, priests, and monks: but there, assure yourself, you shall not bind me." "Bind thee then, in the name of God," answered Pantagruel. "But if," quoth Panurge, "being ill at ease, and possibly through that distemper, made unable to discharge the matrimonial duty that is incumbent to an active husband; my wife, impatient of that drooping sickness, and faint fits of a pining languishment, should abandon and prostitute herself to the embraces of another man; and not only then not help and assist me in my extremity and need, but withal flout at, and make sport of that my grievous distress and calamity; or peradventure (which is worse) embezzle my good, and steal from me, as I have seen it often-times befal unto the lot of many other men; it were enough to undo me utterly, to fill brimful the cup of my misfortune, and make me play the madpate reeks of a bedlamite, or wild bear." "Bear without marrying then," quoth Pantagruel. "Yea, but," said Panurge, "I shall never by any other means come to have lawful sons and daughters, in whom I may harbour some hope of perpetuating my name and arms, and to whom also I may leave and bequeath my inheritances and purchased goods (of which latter sort you need not doubt, but that, in some one or other of these mornings, I will make a fair and goodly show) that so I may cheer up and make merry, when otherwise I should be plunged into a peevish mood of pensive sullenness; as I do perceive daily by the carriage of your gracious father towards you; as all honest folks use to do at their own homes and private dwelling-houses. For being free from debt, and yet not married, if casually I should fret and be angry, although the cause of my grief and displeasure were never so just, I am afraid, instead of consolation, that I should meet with nothing else but scuffs, frumps, gibes, and mocks at my misadventure." "Venture then, in the name of God," quoth Pantagruel: "and thus have I given you my advice."

CHAPTER X

HOW PANTAGRUEL REPRESENTETH UNTO PANURGE THE DIFFICULTY
OF GIVING ADVICE IN THE MATTER OF MARRIAGE; AND TO
THAT PURPOSE MENTIONETH SOMEWHAT OF THE HOMERIC
AND VIRGILIAN LOTTERIES

YOUR counsel," quoth Panurge, "under your correction and favour, seemeth unto me not unlike to the song of gammer yea-by-nay; it is full of sarcasms, mockeries, bitter taunts, nipping bobs, derisive quips, biting jerks, and contradictory iterations, the one part destroying the other. I know not," added Panurge, "which of all your answers to lay hold on." "Good reason why," quoth Pantagruel: "for your proposals are so full of ifs and buts, that I can ground nothing on them, nor pitch upon any solid and positive determination satisfactory to what is demanded by them. Are not you assured within yourself of what you have a mind to? The chief and main point of the whole matter lieth there: all the rest is merely casual, and totally dependeth upon the fatal disposition of the heavens. We see some so happy in the fortune of this nuptial encounter, that their family shineth, as it were, with the radiant effulgency of an idea, model, or representation of the joys of Paradise; and perceive others again to be so unluckily matched in the conjugal yoke, that those very basest of devils, which tempt the hermits that inhabit the deserts of Thebais and Montserrat, are not more miserable than they. It is therefore expedient, seeing you are resolved for once to make a trial of the state of marriage, that, with shut eyes, bowing your head, and kissing the ground, you put the business to a venture, and give it a fair hazard, in recommending the success of the residue to the disposure of Almighty God. It lieth not in my power to give you any other manner of assurance, or otherways to certify you of what shall ensue on this your undertaking. Nevertheless, if you think fit, this you may do: bring hither Virgil's

283

poems, that, after having opened the book, and with our nails severed the leaves thereof three several times, we may, according to the number agreed upon betwixt ourselves, explore the future hap of your intended marriage: for frequently, by an Homeric lottery, have many hit upon their destinies; as is testified in the person of Socrates, who, whilst he was in prison, hearing the recitation of this verse of Homer, said of Achilles, in the ninth of the Iliads:

"'We, the third day, to fertile Pthia come.'

Thereby foresaw that on the third subsequent day he was to die; of the truth whereof he assured Æschines (as Plato in Critone; Cicero, in primo de divinatione; Diogenes, Laërtius, and others, have to the full recorded in their works). The like is also witnessed by Opilius Macrinus, to whom, being desirous to know if he should be the Roman Emperor, befel, by chance of lot, this sentence in the eighth of the Iliads:

"'Dotard, new warriors urge thee to be gone:
Thy life decays, and old age weighs thee down.'

"[In fact, he being then somewhat ancient, had hardly enjoyed the sovereignty of the empire for the space of fourteen months, when by Heliogabulus, then both young and strong, he was dispossessed thereof, thrust out of all and killed.] Brutus also doth bear witness of another experiment of this nature, who willing, through this exploratory way by lot, to learn what the event and issue should be of the Pharsalian battle, wherein he perished, he casually encountered on this verse, said of Patroclus in the sixteenth of the Iliads:

"'Fate, and Latona's son have shot me dead.'

"And accordingly Apollo was the field-word in the dreadful day of that fight. Divers notable things of old have likewise been foretold and known by casting of Virgilian lots; yea, in matters of no less importance than the obtaining of the Roman empire; as it happened to Alexander Severus, who trying his fortune at the said kind of lottery, did hit upon this verse, written in the sixth of the Æneids:

"'Know, Roman, that thy business is to reign,' &c.

"He, within very few years thereafter, was effectually and in good earnest created and installed Roman emperor. A resembling story thereto is related of Adrian, who being hugely perplexed within himself, out of a longing humour, to know in what account he was with the emperor Trajan, and how large the measure of that affection was, which he did bear unto him, had recourse, after the manner above specified, to the Maronian lottery, which by haphazard tendered him these lines out of the sixth of the Æneids:

> " 'But who is he conspicuous from afar,
> With olive boughs that doth his offerings bear?
> By the white hair, and beard I know him plain,
> The Roman king.'

Shortly thereafter was he adopted by Trajan, and succeeded to him in the empire. Moreover to the lot of the praise-worthy emperor Claudius befel this line of Virgil, written in the sixth of his Æneids:

> " 'Whilst the third summer saw him reign a king
> In Latium.'

"And in effect he did not reign above two years. To the said Claudius also, enquiring concerning his brother Quintilius, whom he proposed as a colleague with himself in the empire, happened the response following in the sixth of the Æneids:

> " '——Whom fate let us see,
> And would no longer suffer him to be.'

And so it fell out; for he was killed on the seventeenth day after he had attained unto the management of the imperial charge. The very same lot also with the like misluck, did betide the emperor Gordian the younger. To Claudius Albinus, being very solicitous to understand somewhat of his future adventures, did occur this saying, which is written in the sixth of the Æneids:

> " 'The Romans boiling with tumultuous rage,
> This warrior shall the dangerous storm assuage:
> With victories he the Carthaginian mauls,
> And with strong hand shall crush the rebel Gauls.'

"Likewise when the emperor Claudius, Aurelian's predecessor, did, with great eagerness, research after the fate to come of his posterity, his hap was to alight on this verse in the first of the Æneids:

"'No bounds are to be set, no limits here.'

Which was fulfilled by the goodly genealogical row of his race who succeeded him.

"When Mr. Peter Amy did in like manner explore and make trial, if he should escape the ambush of the Hobgoblins, who lay in wait all to bemaul him, he fell upon this verse in the third of the Æneids:

"'Oh flee the bloodly land, the wicked shore!'

Which counsel he obeying, got forthwith out of their hands, safe and sound, and avoided all their ambuscades.

"Were it not to shun prolixity, I could enumerate a thousand such like adventures, which, conformable to the dictate and verdict of the verse, have by that manner of lot-casting-encounter befallen to the curious researchers of them. Do not you nevertheless imagine, lest you should be deluded, that I would upon this kind of fortune-flinging-proof infer an uncontrollable and not to be gainsaid infallibility of truth."

CHAPTER XI

HOW PANTAGRUEL SHEWETH THE TRIAL OF ONE'S FORTUNE
BY THE THROWING OF DICE TO BE UNLAWFUL

IT would be sooner done," quoth Panurge, "and more expeditely, if we should try the matter at the chance of three fair dice." Quoth Pantagruel, "That sort of lottery is deceitful, abusive, illicitous, and exceeding scandalous; never trust in it: the accursed book of the re-creation of dice was a great while ago excogitated in Achaia near Bourre, by that ancient enemy to mankind, the infernal calumniator, who, before the statue or massive image of the Bouraic Hercules, did of old, and doth in several places of the world as yet, make many simple souls to err and fall into his snares. You know how my father Gargantua hath forbidden it over all his kingdoms and dominions;

how he hath caused to burn the moulds and draughts thereof, and altogether suppressed, abolished, driven forth and cast it out of the land, as a most dangerous plague and infection to any well-polished state or commonwealth. What I have told you of dice, I say the same of the play at cockall. It is a lottery of the like guile and deceitfulness; and therefore do not, for convincing of me, alledge in opposition to this my opinion, or bring in the example of the fortunate cast of Tiberius, within the fountain of Appona, at the oracle of Gerion. These are the baited hooks, by which the devil attracts and draweth unto him the foolish souls of silly people into eternal perdition.

"Nevertheless, to satisfy your humour in some measure, I am content you throw three dice upon this table, that, according to the number of the blots which shall happen to be cast up, we may hit upon a verse of that page, which in the setting open of the book you shall have pitched upon.

"Have you any dice in your pockets?" "A whole bag full"; answered Panurge. "That is provision against the devil, as is expounded by Merlin Coccajus, lib, ii: *De patria diabolorum*. The devil would be sure to take me napping, and very much at unawares, if he should find me without dice." With this the three dice being taken out, produced and thrown, they fell so pat upon the lower points, that the cast was five, six and five. "These are," quoth Panurge, "sixteen in all. Let us take the sixteenth line of the page; the number pleaseth me very well; I hope we shall have a prosperous and happy chance. May I be thrown amidst all the devils of hell, even as a great bowl cast athwart at a set of nine-pins, or a cannon-ball shot among a battalion of foot, in case so many times I do not boult my future wife the first night of our marriage." "Of that, forsooth, I make no doubt at all," quoth Pantagruel: "you needed not to have rapped forth such a horrid imprecation, the sooner to procure credit for the performance of so small a business, seeing possibly the first bout will be amiss, and that you know is usually at tennis called fifteen. At the next justling turn you may amend that fault, and so complete your reckoning of sixteen." "Is it so," quoth Panurge, "that you understand the matter? and must my words be thus interpreted? Nay, believe me, never yet was any solecism committed by that valiant champion, who often hath for me in Bellydale stood centry at the hypogastrian crany. Did you ever hitherto find me in the confraternity of the faulty? Never, I trow; never, nor ever shall, for ever and a day. I do the feat like a goodly friar, or father confessor, without default: and therein am I willing to be judged by the players." He had no sooner spoke these words, than the works of Virgil were brought in: but before the book was laid open, Panurge said to Pantagruel, "My heart, like the furch of a hart in rut, doth beat within my breast. Be pleased to feel and grope my pulse a little on this artery of my left arm: at its frequent rise and fall you would say that they swinge and belabour me after the manner of a probationer posed, and put to a peremptory trial, in the examination of his sufficiency for the discharge of the learned duty of a graduate in some eminent degree in the college of the Sorbonists.

"But would you not hold it expedient, before we proceed any farther, that we should invocate Hercules and the Tenetian goddesses, who in the chamber of lots are said to rule, sit in judgment, and bear a presidental sway?" "Neither him nor them," answered Pantagruel; "only set your nails at work, and with them open the leaves of the book."

CHAPTER XII

HOW PANTAGRUEL DOTH EXPLORE BY THE VIRGILIAN LOTTERY WHAT FORTUNE PANURGE SHALL HAVE IN HIS MARRIAGE

THEN at the opening of the book, in the sixteenth row of the lines of the disclosed page, did Panurge encounter upon this following verse:

"Nec deus hunc mensa, dea nec dignata cubili est."

"The god him from his table banished,
Nor would the goddess have him in her bed."

"This response," quoth Pantagruel, "maketh not very much for your benefit or advantage: for it plainly signifies and denoteth, that your wife will be a strumpet, and yourself by consequence a cuckold. The goddess, whom you shall not find propitious nor favourable unto you, is Minerva, a most redoubtable and dreadful virgin, powerful and fulminating goddess, an enemy to cuckolds and effeminate young-sters, to cuckold-makers, adulterers and adulteresses. The god is Ju-piter, a terrible and thunder-making god from heaven: and withal, it is to be remarked, that conform to the doctrine of the ancient He-trurians, the manubes (for so they did call the darting hurls, or slinging casts of the Vulcanian thunderbolts) did only appertain to her, and to Jupiter her father capital. This was verified in the conflagration of the ships of Ajax Oileus. Nor doth this fulminating power belong to any other of the Olympic gods: men therefore stand not in such fear of them. Moreover, I will tell you, and you may take it as extracted out of the profoundest mysteries of mythology, that when the giants had enterprized the waging of a war against the powers of the celestial orbs, the gods at first did laugh at those attempts, and scorned such despicable enemies, who were, in their conceit, not strong enough to cope in feats of warfare with their pages: but when they saw, by the gigantic labour, the high hill Pelion set on lofty Ossa, and that the mount Olympus was made shake, in order to be erected on the top of both; then did they all stand aghast.

"Then was it that Jupiter held a parliament, or general convention, wherein it was unanimously resolved upon, and concluded, by all the gods, that they should worthily and valiantly stand to their defence. And because they had often seen battles lost by the cumbersome lets and disturbing incumbrances of women, confusedly huddled in amongst armies, it was at that time decreed and enacted, that they should expel and drive out of heaven into Egypt, and the confines of Nile, that whole crew of goddesses, disguised in the shapes of weasels, polecats, bats, shrew-mice, ferrets, fulmarts, and other such like odd transformations: only Minerva was reserved, to participate with Jupiter in the horrific fulminating power; as being the goddess both of war and learning, of arts and arms, of council and dispatch; a goddess armed from her birth, a goddess dreaded in heaven, in the air, by sea and land." "By the belly of Saint Buff," quoth Panurge, "should I be Vulcan, whom the poet blazons? Nay, I am neither a cripple, coiner of false money, nor smith, as he was.

"My wife possibly will be as comely and as handsome as ever was his Venus, but not a whore like her, nor I a cuckold like him.

"The crook-legged slovenly slave made himself to be declared a cuckold, by a definitive sentence and judgment, in the open view of all the gods: for this cause ought you to interpret the aforementioned verse quite contrary to what you have said. This lot importeth, that my wife will be honest, virtuous, chaste, loyal, and faithful; not armed, surly, wayward, cross, giddy, humorous, heady, hare-brained, or extracted out of brains, as was the goddess Pallas: nor shall this fair jolly Jupiter be my corrival; he shall never dip his bread in my broth, though we should sit together at one table.

"Consider his exploits and gallant actions; he was the most manifest ruffian, wencher, and whoremonger, and infamous cuckold-maker that ever breathed: he did always lecher it like a boar; and no wonder, for he was fostered by a sow in the isle of Candia, if Agathocles, the Babylonian be not a liar, and more rammishly lascivious than a he-goat; whence it is that he is said by others, to have been suckled and fed with the milk of the goat Amalthæa. By the virtue of Acheron, he stitcht and bulled, in one day, the third part of the world, beasts, and people, floods and mountains; that was Europa.

"For this grand subagitatory achievement, the Ammonians caused draw, delineate, and paint him in the figure and shape of a ram, ramming, and horned ram. But I know well enough how to shield and preserve myself from that horned champion: he will not, trust me, have to deal, in my person, with a sottish, dunsical Amphytrion; nor with a silly witless Argus, for all his hundred spectacles; nor yet with the cowardly Acrisius; the simple goosecap Lycus of Thebes; the doating blockhead Agenor; the phlegmatic Asopus; rough-footed Lycaon: the luskish misshapen Corytus of Tuscany; nor with the large backed and strong reigned Atlas: let him alter, change, transform, and metamorphose himself into a hundred various shapes and figures; into a swan, a bull, a satyr, a shower of gold, or into a cuckoo, as he did when he unmaidened his sister Juno; into an eagle, ram, or dove, as when he was enamoured of the virgin Phthia, who then dwelt in the Ægean territory; into fire, a serpent; yea, even into a flea, into Epicurean and Democratical atoms, or more magistronostrally, into those sly intentions of the mind, which in the schools are called second notions: I'll catch him in the neck, and take him napping.

"And would you know what I would do unto him? Even that which Saturn did to his father Cœlum. Seneca foretold it of me, and Lactantius hath confirmed it; what the goddess Rhea did to Athys: I would make him two stone lighter, rid him of his Cyprian cymbals, and cut so close and neatly by the breech, that there should not remain thereof so much as one small hair; so cleanly would I shave him, and disable him for ever from being pope; for *testiculos non habet.*" "Hold there," said Pantagruel; "hoc, soft and fair, my lad, enough of that: cast up, turn over the leaves, and try your fortune for the second time." Then did he fall up on this ensuing verse.

"Membra quatit, gelidusque coït formidine sanguis."

"His joints and members quake, he becomes pale,
And sudden fear doth his cold blood conjeal."

"This importeth," quoth Pantagruel, "that she will soundly bang your back and belly." "Clean and quite contrary," answered Panurge: "it is of me that he prognosticates, in saying that I will beat her like a tiger, if she vex me. Sir Martin Wagstaff will perform that office, and in default of a cudgel, the devil gulp me if I should not eat her up quick; as Candaules the Lydian king did his wife, whom he ravened and devoured."

"You are very stout," says Pantagruel, "and courageous: Hercules himself durst hardly adventure to scuffle with you in this your raging fury: nor is it strange; for *a jan* is worth two; and two in fight against Hercules are too strong." "Am I *a jan?*" quoth Panurge. "No, no," answered Pantagruel; "my mind was only running upon lurch and trick track." Thereafter did he hit, at the third opening of the book, upon this verse:

"Fœmineo prœdœ & spoliorum ardebat amore."

"After the spoil and pillage, as in fire,
He burnt with a strong feminine desire."

"This portendeth," quoth Pantagruel, "that she will steal your goods, and rob you. Hence this, according to these three drawn lots, will be your future destiny, I clearly see; you will be a cuckold, you will be beaten, and you will be robbed." "Nay, it is quite otherwise," quoth Panurge; "for it is certain that this verse presageth, that she will love me with perfect liking: nor did the satire-writing poet lie in proof hereof, when he affirmed, that a woman burning with extreme affection, takes sometimes pleasure to steal from her sweetheart. And what, I pray you? A glove, a point, or some such trifling toy of no importance, to make him keep a gentle kind of stirring in the research and quest thereof. In like manner these small scolding debates, and petty brabling contentions, which frequently we see spring up, and for a certain space boil very hot betwixt a couple of high-spirited lovers, are nothing else but recreative diversions for their refreshment, spurs to, and incentives of a more fervent amity than ever. As for example: we do sometimes see cutlers with hammers mawl their finest whetstones, therewith to sharpen their iron tools the better.

"And therefore do I think, that these three lots make much for my advantage; which if not, I from their sentence totally appeal." "There is no appealing," quoth Pantagruel, "from the decrees of fate or destiny, of lot or chance: as is recorded by our ancient lawyers: witness Baldus, lib. ult. cap. de leg. The reason hereof is, fortune doth not acknowledge a superior, to whom an appeal may be made from her, or any of her substitutes. And in this case the pupil cannot be restored to his right in full, as openly by the said author is alleged in L. dit. prætor § ult. ff. de minor."

CHAPTER XIII

HOW PANTAGRUEL ADVISETH PANURGE TO TRY THE FUTURE GOOD OR BAD LUCK OF HIS MARRIAGE BY DREAMS

NOW seeing we cannot agree together in the manner of expounding or interpreting the sense of the Virgilian lots, let us bend our course another way, and try a new sort of divination." "Of what kind?" asked Panurge. "Of a good, ancient and authentic fashion," answered Pantagruel; "it is by dreams: for in dreaming, such circumstances and conditions being thereto adhibited, as are clearly enough described by Hippocrates, in lib. Περὶ τῶν ἐνυπνίων, by Plato, Plotin, Iamblicus, Synesius, Aristotle, Xenophon, Galen, Plutarch, Artemidorus, Daldianus, Herophilus and others, the soul doth oftentimes foresee what is to come.

"How true this is, you may conceive by a very vulgar and familiar example: as when you see that at such a time as sucking babes, well nourished, fed and fostered with good milk, sleep soundly and profoundly, the nurses in the interim get leave to sport themselves, and are licentiated to recreate their fancies at what range to them shall seem most fitting and expedient; their presence, sedulity and attendance on the cradle being, during all that space, held unnecessary.

"Even just so, when our body is at rest, that the concoction is everywhere accomplished, and that, till it awake, it lacks for nothing, our soul delighteth to disport itself, and is well pleased in that frolic to take a review of its native country, which is the heavens; where it receiveth a most notable participation of its first beginning, with an imbuement from its divine source; and in contemplation of that infinite and intellectual sphere, whereof the centre is everywhere, and the circumference in no place of the universal world, to wit, God (according to the doctrine of Hermes Trismegistus) to whom no new thing happeneth, whom nothing that is past escapeth, and unto whom all things are alike present; remarketh not only what is preterit, and gone in the inferior course and agitation of sublunary matters, but withal taketh notice what is to come; then bringeth a relation of those future events unto the body, by the outward senses and exterior organs, it is divulged abroad unto the hearing of others. Whereupon the owner of that soul deserveth to be termed a vaticinator, or prophet.

"Nevertheless, the truth is, that the soul is seldom able to report those things in such sincerity as it hath seen them, by reason of the imperfection and frailty of the corporeal senses, which obstruct the effectuating of that office: even as the moon doth not communicate unto this earth of ours, that light which she receiveth from the sun with so much splendour, heat, vigour, purity and liveliness as it was given her. Hence it is requisite for the better reading, explaining and unfolding of these somniatory vaticinations, and predictions of that nature, that a dexterous, learned, skilful, wise, industrious, expert, rational and peremptory expounder or interpreter be pitched upon, such a one as by the Greeks is called *onirocritic,* or *oniropolist.*

"For this cause Heraclitus was wont to say, that nothing is by dreams revealed to us, that nothing is by dreams concealed from us, and that only we thereby have a mystical signification and secret evidence of things to come, either for our own prosperous or unlucky fortune, or for the favourable or disastrous success of another. The sacred scriptures testify no less, and profane histories assure us of it; in both which are exposed to our view a thousand several kinds of strange adventures, which have fallen pat according to the nature of the dream, and that as well to the party dreamer as to others. The Atlantic people, and those that inhabit the land of Thasos (one of the Cyclades) are of this grand commodity deprived: for in their countries none yet ever dreamed. Of this sort were Cleon of Daulia, Thrasymedes, and in our days the learned Frenchman Villanovanus, neither of all which knew what dreaming was.

"Fail not therefore to-morrow, when the jolly and fair Aurora with her rosy fingers draweth aside the curtains of the night, to drive away the sable shades of darkness, to bend your spirits wholly to the task of sleeping sound, and thereto apply yourself. In the meanwhile you must denude your mind of every human passion or affection, such as are love and hatred, fear and hope: for as of old the great vaticinator, most famous and renowned prophet Proteus, was not able in his disguise, or transformation into fire, water, a tiger, a dragon, and other such like uncouth shapes and visors, to presage anything that was to come, till he was restored to his own first natural and kindly form; just so doth man: for at his kind reception of the art of divination, and faculty of prognosticating future things, that part in him which is most divine (to wit, the νοῦς, or *mens*) must be calm, peaceable, untroubled, quiet, still, husht, and not imbusied or distracted with foreign, soul disturbing perturbations." "I am content," quoth Panurge. "But I pray you, sir, must I this evening, ere I go to bed, eat much or little? I do not ask this without cause; for if I sup not well, large, round, and amply, my sleeping is not worth a turnip; all the night long I then but doze and rave, and in my slumbering fits talk idle nonsense; my thoughts being in a dull brown study, and as deep in their dumps as is my belly hollow."

"Not to sup," answered Pantagruel, "were best for you, considering the state of your complexion, and healthy constitution of your body. A certain very ancient prophet, named Amphiaraus, wished such as had a mind by dreams to be imbued with any oracles, for four and twenty hours to taste no victuals, and to abstain from wine three days together, yet shall not you be put to such a sharp, hard, rigorous and extreme sparing diet.

"I am truly right apt to believe, that a man whose stomach is replete with various cheer, and in a manner surfeited with drinking, is hardly able to conceive aright of spiritual things: yet am not I of the opinion of those, who, after long and pertinacious fastings, think by such means to enter more profoundly into the speculation of celestial mysteries. You may very well remember how my father Gargantua, whom here for honour sake I name, hath often told us, that the writings of abstinent, abstemious, and long fasting hermits, were every whit as saltless, dry, jejune and insipid, as were their bodies when they did compose them. It is a most difficult thing for the spirits to be in good plight, serene and lively, when there is nothing in the body but a kind of voidness and inanity: seeing the philosophers with the physicians jointly affirm, that the spirits, which are styled animal, spring from, and have their constant practice in, and through the arterial blood, refined and purified to the life within the admirable net, which wonderfully framed lieth under the ventricles and tunnels of the brain. He gave us also the example of the philosopher, who, when he thought most seriously to have withdrawn himself unto a solitary privacy, far from the rustling clutterments of the tumultuous and confused world, the better to improve his theory, to contrive, comment and ratiocinate, was, notwithstanding his uttermost endeavours to free himself

294

from all untoward noises, surrounded and environed about so with the barking of curs, howling of wolves, neighing of horses, bleating of sheep, barring of elephants, hissing of serpents, braying of asses, chirping of grasshoppers, cooing of turtles, prating of parrots, tatling of jackdaws, grunting of swine, girning of boars, yelping of foxes, mewing of cats, cheeping of mice, squeaking of weasels, croaking of frogs, crowing of cocks, kekling of hens, calling of partridges, chanting of swans, chattering of jays, pieping of chickens, singing of larks, cackling of geese, chattering of swallows, clucking of moorfowls, cucking of cuckows, bumbling of bees, rammage of hawks, chirming of linnets, croaking of ravens, screeching of owls, whicking of pigs, gushing of hogs, curring of pigeons, grumbling of cushet doves, howling of panthers, curkling of quails, chirping of sparrows, crackling of crows, nuzzing of camels, wheening of whelps, buzzing of dromedaries, mumbling of rabbits, cricking of ferrets, humming of wasps, mioling of tigers, bruzzing of bears, sussing of kittnings, clamoring of scarfes, whimpering of fulmarts, boing of buffalos, warbling of nightingales, quavering of meavises, drintling of turkies, conniating of storks, frantling of peacocks, clattering of magpies, murmuring of stock-doves, crouting of cormorants, cigling of locusts, charming of beagles, guarring of puppies, snarling of messens, rantling of rats, guerieting of apes, snuttering of monkies, pioling of pelicans, quacking of ducks, yelling of wolves, roaring of lions, that he was much more troubled than if he had been in the middle of the crowd at the fair of Fontenay or Niort.

"Just so is it with those who are tormented with the grievous pangs of hunger; the stomach begins to gnaw and bark as it were, the eyes to look dim, and the veins, by greedily sucking some refection to themselves from the proper substance of all the members of a fleshy consistence, violently pull down and draw back that vagrant roaming spirit, careless and neglecting of his nurse and natural host, which is the body. As when a hawk upon the fist, willing to take her flight by soaring aloft into the open spacious air, is on a sudden drawn back by a leash tied to her feet.

"To this purpose also did he allege unto us the authority of Homer, the father of all philosophy, who said, that the Grecians did not put an end to their mournful mood for the death of Patroclus, the most intimate friend of Achilles, till hunger in a rage declared herself, and their bellies protested to furnish no more tears unto their grief. For from bodies emptied and macerated by long fasting, there could not be such supply of moisture and brackish drops, as might be proper on that occasion.

"Mediocrity at all times is commendable; nor in this case are you to abandon it. You may take a little supper, but thereat must you not eat of a hare, nor of any other flesh. You are likewise to abstain from beans; from the preak (by some called the polyp); as also from cole-worts, cabbage, and all other such like windy victuals, which may endanger the troubling of your brains, and the dimning or casting a kind of mist over your animal spirits. For as a looking-glass cannot exhibit the semblance or representation of the object set before it, and exposed to have its image to the life expressed, if that the polished sleekedness thereof be darkened by gross breathings, dampish vapours, and foggy, thick, infectious exhalations: even so the fancy cannot well receive the impression of the likeness of those things, which divination doth afford by dreams, if any way the body be annoyed or troubled with the fumish steam of meat, which it had taken in a while before; because betwixt these two there still hath been a mutual sympathy and fellow-feeling, of an indissolubly-knit affection. You shall eat good eusebian and bergamot-pears, one apple of the short-shank pepin-kind, a parcel of the little plums of Tours, and some few cherries of the growth of my orchard. Nor shall you need to fear, that thereupon will ensue doubtful dreams, fallacious, uncertain, and not to be trusted to, as by some peripatetic philosophers hath been related; for that, say they, men do more copiously in the season of harvest feed on fruitages, than at any other time. The same is mystically taught us by the ancient prophets and poets, who alledge, that all vain and deceitful dreams lie hid and in covert, under the leaves which are spread on the ground; by reason that the leaves fall from the trees in the autumnal quarter; for the natural fervour, which abounding in ripe, fresh, recent fruits, cometh, by the quickness of its ebullition, to be with ease evaporated into the animal parts of the dreaming person (the experiment is obvious in most) is a pretty while before it be expired, dissolved and evanished. As for your drink, you are to have it of the pure, fair water of my fountain."

"The condition," quoth Panurge, "is somewhat hard; nevertheless, cost what price it will, or whatsoever come of it, I heartily condescend thereto; protesting, that I will to-morrow break my fast betimes, after my somniatory exercitations. Furthermore, I recommend myself to Homer's two gates, to Morpheus, to Iselon, to Phantasus, and unto Phobetor. If they in this my great need succour me, and grant me that assistance which is fitting, I will, in honour of them all, erect a jolly, genteel altar, composed of the softest down. If I were now Laconia, in the temple of Juno, betwixt Oetile and Thalamis, she suddenly would disintangle my perplexity, resolve me of my doubts, and cheer me up with fair and jovial dreams in a deep sleep." Then did he say thus unto Pantagruel: "Sir, were it not expedient for my purpose, to put a branch or two of curious laurel betwixt the quilt and bolster of my bed, under the pillow on which my head must lean?" "There is no need at all of that," quoth Pantagruel; "for besides that it is a thing very superstitious, the cheat thereof hath been at large discovered unto us, in the writings of Serapion, Ascalonites, Antiphon, Philochorus, Artemon, and Fulgentius Planciades. I could say as much to you of the left shoulder of a crocodile, as also of a chameleon, without prejudice be it spoken to the credit which is due to the opinion of old Democritus; and likewise of the stone of the Bactrians, called Eumetrides, and of the Hammonian horn: for so by the Æthiopians is termed a certain precious stone, coloured like gold, and in the fashion, shape, form, and proportion of a ram's horn, as the horn of Jupiter Hammon is reported to have been: they over and above assuredly affirming, that the dreams of those who carry it about them are no less veritable and infallible, than the truth of the divine oracles. Nor is this much unlike to what Homer and Virgil wrote of those two gates of sleep, to which you have been pleased to recommend the management of what you have in hand. The one is of ivory, which letteth in confused, doubtful, and uncertain dreams: for through ivory, how small and slender soever it be, we can see nothing; the density, opacity, and close compactedness of its material parts hindering the penetration of the visual rays, and the reception of the species of such things as are visible. The other is of horn, at which an entry is made to sure and certain dreams: even as through horn, by reason of the diaphanous splendour, and bright transparency thereof, the species of all objects of the sight distinctly pass, and so without confusion appear, that they are clearly seen." "Your meaning is, and you would thereby infer," quoth friar John, "that the dreams of all horned cuckolds (of which number Panurge, by the help of God, and his future wife, is without controversy to be one) are always true and infallible."

CHAPTER XIV

A T seven o'clock of the next following morning, Panurge did not fail to present himself before Pantagruel, in whose chamber were at that time Epistemon, friar John of the Funnels, Ponocrates, Eudemon, Carpalim, and others: to whom, at the entry of Panurge, Pantagruel said, "Lo here cometh our dreamer." "That word," quoth Epistemon, "in ancient times cost very much, and was dearly sold to the children of Jacob." Then said Panurge, "I have been plunged into my dumps so deeply, as if I had been lodged with gaffer Noddy-cap: dreamed indeed I have, and that right lustily; but I could take along with me no more thereof, that I did truly understand, save only that I in my vision had a pretty, fair, young, gallant, handsome woman, who no less lovingly and kindly treated and entertained me, hugged, cherished, cockered, dandled, and made much of me, as if I had been another neat dillidarling minion, like Adonis. Never was man more glad than I was then: my joy at that time was incomparable: she flattered me, tickled me, stroaked me, groped me, frizzled me, curled me, kissed me, embraced me, laid her hands about my neck, and now and then made, jestingly, pretty little horns above my forehead. I told her, in the like disport, as I did play the fool with her, that she should rather place and fix them in a little below mine eyes, that I might see the better what I should stick at with them: for being so situated, Momus then would find no fault therewith, as he did once with the position of the horns of bulls. The wanton, toying girl, notwithstanding any remonstrance of mine to the contrary, did always drive and thrust them further in: yet thereby (which to me seemed wonderful) she did not do me any hurt at all. A little after, though I know not how, I thought I was transformed into a tabor or drum, and she into a chough, or madgehowlet.

"My sleeping there being interrupted, I awaked in a start, angry, displeased, perplexed, chafing, and very wroth. There have you a large platterful of dreams; make thereupon a good cheer, and if you please, spare not to interpret them according to the understanding which you may have in them. Come, Carpalim, let us to breakfast."

"To my sense and meaning," quoth Pantagruel, "if I have skill or knowledge in the art of divination by dreams, your wife will not really, and to the outward appearance of the world, plant, or set horns, and stick them fast in your forehead, after a visible manner, as satyrs use to wear and carry them; but she will be so far from preserving herself loyal in the discharge and observance of a conjugal duty, that on the contrary she will violate her plighted faith, break her marriage-oath, infringe all matrimonial ties, prostitute her body to the dalliance of other men, and so make you a cuckold. This point is clearly and manifestly explained and expounded by Artemidorus, just as I have related it. Nor will there be any metamorphosis, or transmutation made of you into a drum or tabor; but you will surely be as soundly beaten, as e'er was tabor at a merry wedding: nor yet will she be changed into a chough, or madgehowlet; but will steal from you, chiefly in the night, as is the nature of that thievish bird. Hereby may you perceive your dreams to be in every jot conform and agreeable to the Virgilian lots: a cuckold you will be, beaten and robbed." Then cried out friar John, with a loud voice: "He tells the truth upon my conscience: thou wilt be a cuckold, an honest one, I warrant thee, O the brave horns that will be borne by thee! ha, ha, ha, our good master de Cornibus, God save thee, and shield thee; wilt thou be pleased to preach but two words of a sermon to us, and I will go through the parish church to gather up alms for the poor."

"You are," quoth Panurge, "very far mistaken in your interpretation; for the matter is quite contrary to your sense thereof. My dream presageth, that I shall, by marriage, be stored with plenty of all manner of goods; the hornifying of me shewing, that I shall possess a cornucopia, that amalthæan horn, which is called the horn of abundance, whereof the fruition did still portend the wealth of the enjoyer. You possibly will say, that they are rather like to be satyrs' horns; for you of these did make some mention: Amen, Amen. *Fiat, fiatur, ad differentiam papæ.* Thus shall I have my touch-her-home still ready; my staff of love, sempiternally in a good case, will, satyr-like, be never toiled out; a thing which all men wish for, and send up their prayers to that purpose; but such a thing as nevertheless is granted but to few. Hence doth it follow, by a consequence as clear as the sunbeams, that I shall never be in the danger of being made a cuckold: for the defect hereof is, *causa sine qua non;* yea, the sole cause (as many think) of making husbands cuckolds. What makes poor scoundrel rogues to beg, I pray you? Is it not because they have not enough at home, wherewith to fill their bellies, and their poaks? What is it makes the wolves to leave the woods? is it not the want of fresh meat? What maketh women whores? you understand me well enough. And herein I submit my opinion to the judgment of learned lawyers, presidents, counsellors, advocates, procurers, attorneys, and other glossers and commentators on the venerable rubric, *de frigidis & maleficiatis*. You are in truth, sir, as it seems to (excuse my boldness if I have erred or transgressed) in a most palpable and absurd error, to attribute my horns to cuckoldry: Diana wears them on her head, after the manner of a crescent: is she a cucquean for that? how the devil can she be cuckolded, who never yet was married? Speak somewhat more correctly, I beseech you, lest she, being offended, furnish you with a pair of horns, shapen by the pattern of those which she made for Actæon. The goodly Bacchus also carries horns; Pan, Jupiter Hammon, with a great many others: are they all cuckolds? If Jove be a cuckold Juno is a whore: this follows by the figure metalepsis: as to call a child, in the presence of his father and mother, a bastard, or whore's son, is, tacitly and underboard, no less than if one had said openly, the father is a cuckold, and his wife a punk. Let our discourse come nearer to the purpose: the horns that my wife did make me are horns of abundance, planted and grafted in my head for the increase and shooting up of all good things: this will I affirm for truth, upon my word, and pawn my faith and credit both upon it. As for the rest, I will be no less joyful, frolic, glad, cheerful, merry, jolly, and gamesome than a well-bended tabor in the hands of a good drummer, at a nuptial feast, still making a noise, still rolling, still buzzing and cracking. Believe me, Sir, in that consisteth none of my least good fortunes. And my wife will be jocund, feat, compt, neat, quaint, dainty, trim, tricked up, brisk, smirk and smug, even as a pretty little Cornish chough: who will not believe this, let hell or the gallows be the burden of his Christmas carol."

"I remark," quoth Pantagruel, "the last point or particle which you did speak of, and having seriously conferred it with the first, find that at the beginning you were delighted with the sweetness of your dream; but in the end and final closure of it, you startlingly awaked, and, on a sudden, were forthwith vexed in choler, and annoyed." "Yea," quoth Panurge; "the reason of that was, because I had fasted too long." "Flatter not yourself," quoth Pantagruel; "all will go to ruin: know for a certain truth, that every sleep that endeth with a starting, and leaves the person irksome, grieved, and fretting, doth either signify a present evil, or otherways presageth and portendeth a future imminent mishap. To signify an evil, that is to say, to shew some sickness hardly curable, a kind of pestilentious or malignant bile, botch or sore, lying and lurking, hid, occult, and latent within the very centre of the body, which many times doth by the means of sleep (whose nature is to reinforce and strengthen the faculty and virtue of concoction) begin, according to the theorems of physic, to declare itself, and moves to the outward superficies. At this sad stirring is the sleeper's rest and ease disturbed and broken, whereof the first feeling and stinging smart admonisheth, that he must patiently endure great pain and trouble, and thereunto provide some remedy: as when we say, proverbially, to increase hornets, to move a stinking puddle, and to awake a sleeping lion; instead of these more usual expressions, and of a more familiar and plain meaning, to provoke angry persons, to make a thing the worse by meddling with it, and to irritate a testy choleric man when he is at quiet. On the other part, to presage or foretell an evil, especially in what concerneth the exploits of the soul, in matter of somnial divinations, is as much as to say, that it giveth us to understand, that some dismal fortune or mischance is destinated and prepared for us, which shortly will not fail to come to pass. A clear and evident example hereof is to be found in the dream and dreadful awaking of Hecuba; as likewise in that of Eurydice, the wife of Orpheus; neither of which was no sooner finished, saith Ennius, but that incontinently thereafter they awaked in a start, and were affrighted horribly: thereupon these accidents ensued; Hecuba had her husband Priamus, together with her children, slain before her eyes, and saw then the destruction of her country; and Eurydice died speedily thereafter, in a most miserable manner. Æneas, dreaming that he spoke to Hector a little after his decease, did on a sudden in a great start awake, and was afraid: now hereupon did follow this event; Troy that same night was spoiled, sacked and burnt. At another time the same Æneas, dreaming that he saw his familiar geniuses and penates, in a ghastly fright and astonishment awaked; of which terror and amazement the issue was, that the very next day subsequent, by a most horrible tempest on the sea, he was like to have perished, and been cast away. Moreover, Turnus being prompted, instigated, and stirred up, by the fantastic vision of an infernal fury, to enter into a bloody war against Æneas, awaked in a start, much troubled and disquieted in spirit; in sequel whereof, after many notable and famous routs, defeats and discomfitures in open field, he came at last to be killed in a single combat, by the said Æneas. A thousand other instances I could afford, if it were needful of this matter. Whilst I relate these stories of Æneas, remark the saying of Fabius

Pictor, who faithfully averred, that nothing had at any time befallen unto, was done, or enterprized by him, whereof he previously had not notice, and before-hand foreseen it to the full, by sure predictions, altogether founded on the oracles of somnial divination. To this there is no want of pregnant reasons, no more than of examples: for if repose and rest in sleeping be a special gift and favour of the gods, as is maintained by the philosophers, and by the poet attested in these lines:

> "'Then sleep, that heavenly gift, came to refresh,
> Of human labourers, the wearied flesh.'

Such a gift of benefit can never finish or terminate in wrath and indignation, without portending some unlucky fate, and most disastrous fortune to ensue: otherways it were a molestation, and not an ease; a scourge, and not a gift, at least proceeding from the gods above, but from the infernal devils our enemies, according to the common vulgar saying: εχθρῶν ἄδωρα δῶρα.

"Suppose the lord, father, or master of a family, sitting at a very sumptuous dinner, furnished with all manner of good cheer, and having at his entry to the table his appetite sharp set upon his victuals, whereof there was great plenty, should be seen rise in a start, and on a sudden fling out of his chair, abandoning his meat, frighted, appalled, and in a horrid terror; who should not know the cause hereof would wonder, and be astonished exceedingly: But what? he heard his male servants cry, 'Fire, fire, fire, fire,' his serving maids and women yell, 'Stop thief, stop thief": and all his children shout as loud as ever they could, 'Murder, murder, murder.' Then was it not high time for him to leave his banqueting, for application of a remedy in haste, and to give speedy order for succouring of his distressed houshold? Truly, I remember, that the Cabalists and Massorets, interpreters of the sacred scriptures, in treating how with verity one may judge of angelical apparitions (because oftentimes the angel of Satan is disguised and transfigured into an angel of light) said, that the difference of these two mainly did consist in this: the favourable and comforting angel useth in his appearing unto man at first to terrify and hugely affright him; but in the end he bringeth consolation, leaveth the person who hath seen him, joyful, well pleased, fully content, and satisfied: on the other side, the angel of perdition, that wicked, devilish, and malignant spirit, at his appearance unto any person, in the beginning cheereth up the heart of his beholder; but at last forsakes him, and leaves him troubled, angry, and perplexed."

CHAPTER XV

THE Lord save those who see, and do not hear," quoth Panurge.
"I see you well enough, but know not what it is that you have
said: the hunger-starved belly wanteth ears: for lack of victuals, before
God, I roar, bray, yell and fume as in a furious madness. I have performed too hard a task to-day, an extraordinary work indeed: he shall
be craftier, and do far greater wonders than ever did Mr. Mush, who
shall be able any more this year to bring me on the stage of preparation
for a dreaming verdict. Fie! not to sup at all, that is the devil. Pox
take that fashion. Come friar John, let us go break our fast: for if I
hit on such a round refection in the morning, as will serve thoroughly
to fill the mill-hopper and hogshide of my stomach, and furnish it
with meat and drink sufficient; then at a pinch, as in the case of some
extreme necessity which presseth, I could make a shift that day to forbear dining. But not to sup; a plague rot that base custom, which is
an error offensive to nature. That lady made the day for exercise, to
travel, work, wait on and labour in each his negotiation and employment; and that we may with the more fervency and ardour prosecute
our business, she sets before us a clear burning candle, to wit, the sun's
resplendency; and at night, when she begins to take the light from
us, she thereby tacitly implies no less, than if she would have spoken
thus unto us: My lads and lasses, all of you are good and honest folks,
you have wrought well to-day, toiled and turmoiled enough; the night
approacheth, therefore cast off these moiling cares of yours, desist
from all your swinging painful labours, and set your minds how to refresh your bodies in the renewing of their vigour with good bread,
choice wine, and store of wholesome meats: then may you take some
sport and recreation, and after that lie down and rest yourselves, that
you may strongly, nimbly, lustily, and with the more alacrity to-morrow attend on your affairs as formerly.

"Falconers, in like manner, when they have fed their hawks, will
not suffer them to fly on a full gorge, but let them on a perch abide
a little, that they may rouse, bait, tour and soar the better. That
good pope, who was the first instituter of fasting, understood this
well enough; for he ordained that our fast should reach but to the
hour of noon; all the remainder of that day was at our disposure,

freely to eat and feed at any time thereof. In ancient times there were but few that dined, as you would say, some church-men, monks, and canons: for they have little other occupation: each day is a festival unto them who diligently heed the claustral proverb, *de missa ad mensam.* They do not use to linger and defer their sitting down and placing of themselves at table, only so long as they have a mind in waiting for the coming of the abbot: so they fell to without ceremony, terms or conditions; and everybody supped, unless it were some vain, conceited, dreaming dotard. Hence was a supper called *cœna,* which sheweth that it is common to all sorts of people. Thou knowest it well, friar John. Come let us go, my dear friend, in the name of all the devils of the infernal regions, let us go: the gnawings of my stomach, in this rage of hunger, are so tearing, that they make it bark like a mastiff. Let us throw some bread and beef into his throat to pacify him, as once the Sibyl did to Cerberus. Thou likest best monastical brewess, the prime, the flower of the pot. I am for the solid, principal verb that comes after: the good brown loaf, always accompanied with a round slice of the nine-lecture-pounded labourer." "I know thy meaning," answered friar John; "this metaphor is extracted out of the Claustral kettle: the labourer is the ox, that hath wrought and done the labour; after the fashion of nine lectures, that is to say, most exquisitely well and thoroughly boiled. These holy religious fathers, by a certain cabalistic institution of the ancients, not written, but carefully by tradition conveyed from hand to hand, rising betimes to go to morning prayers, were wont to flourish that their matutinal devotion with some certain notable preambles before their entry into the church—viz., They dunged in the dungeries, pissed in the pisseries, spit in the spitteries, melodiously coughed in the cougheries, and doted in their doteries, that to the divine service they might not bring anything that was unclean and foul.

"These things thus done, they very zealously made their repair to the holy chapel (for so was, in their canting language, termed the convent kitchen): where they, with no small earnestness, had care that the beef pot should be put on the crook, for the breakfast of the religious brothers of our Lord and Saviour; and the fire they would kindle under the pot themselves. Now the matins, consisting of nine lessons, were so incumbent on them, that they must have risen the sooner for the more expedite dispatching of them all. The earlier that they rose, the sharper was their appetite, and the barkings of their stomachs, and the gnawing increased in the like proportion; and consequently made these godly men thrice more a-hungered and a-thirst, than when their matins were hemmed over only with three lessons.

"The more betimes they rose, by the said cabal, the sooner was the beef pot put on; the longer that the beef was on the fire, the better it was boiled; the more it boiled, it was the tenderer; the tenderer that it was, the less it troubled the teeth, delighted more the palate, less charged the stomach, and nourished our good religious men the more substantially: which is the only end and prime intention of the first founders, as appears by this, that they eat not to live, but live to eat, and in this world have nothing but their life. Let us go, Panurge."

"Now have I understood thee," quoth Panurge, "my plushcod friar, my caballine and claustral ballock. I freely quit the costs, interest and charges, seeing you have so egregiously commented upon the most especial chapter of the culinary and monastic cabal. Come along my Carpalim, and you friar John, my inseparable friend. Good morrow to you all, my good lords; I have dreamed enough to drink. Let us go." Panurge had no sooner done speaking, than Epistemon, with a loud voice said these words: "It is a very ordinary and common thing amongst men to conceive, foresee, know, and presage the misfortune, bad luck, or disaster of another; but to have the understanding, providence, knowledge, and prediction of a man's own mishap, is very scarce and rare to be found anywhere. This is exceeding judiciously and prudently deciphered by Æsop in his apologues, who there affirmeth, that every man in the world carrieth about his neck a wallet, in the fore-bag whereof are contained the faults and mischances of others, always exposed to his view and knowledge; and in the other scrip thereof, which hangs behind, are kept the bearer's proper transgressions and inauspicious adventures, at no time seen by him, nor thought upon, unless he be a person that hath a favourable aspect from the heavens."

CHAPTER XVI

HOW PANTAGRUEL ADVISED PANURGE TO CONSULT WITH THE SYBIL OF PANZOUST

A LITTLE while thereafter, Pantagruel sent for Panurge, and said to him: "The affection which I bear you being now inveterate, and settled in my mind by a long continuance of time, prompteth me to the serious consideration of your welfare and profit; in order whereto remark what I have thought thereon: it hath been told me that at Panzoust, near Crouly, dwelleth a very famous sybil, who is endowed with the skill of foretelling all things to come. Take Epistemon in your company, repair towards her, and hear what she will say unto you." "She is possibly," quoth Epistemon, "some Canidia, Sagana, or Pythonissa, either whereof with us is vulgarly called a witch: I being the more easily induced to give credit to the truth of this character of her, that the place of her abode is vilely stained with the abominable repute of abounding more with sorcerers and witches than ever did the plains of Thessaly. I should not, to my thinking, go thither willingly; for that it seems to me a thing unwarrantable, and altogether forbidden in the law of Moses." "We are not Jews," quoth Pantagruel; "nor is it a matter judically confessed by her, nor authentically proved by others that she is a witch. Let us for the present suspend our judgment, and defer, till after you return from thence, the sifting and garbeling of those niceties. How know we but that she may be an eleventh sybil, or a second Cassandra? But although she were neither, and she did not merit the name or title of any of these renowned prophetesses, what hazard, in the name of God, do you run, by offering to talk and confer with her of the instant perplexity and perturbation of your thoughts? seeing especially (and which is most of all) she is, in the estimation of those that are acquainted with her, held to know more, and to be of a deeper reach of understanding, than is either customary to the country wherein she liveth, or to the sex whereof she is. What hindrance, hurt, or harm doth the laudable desire of knowledge bring to any man, were it from a sot, a pot, a fool, a stool, a winter-mittain, a truckle for a pully, the lid of a goldsmith's crucible, an oil-bottle, or old slipper? You may remember to have read, or heard at least, that Alexander the Great, immediately after his having obtained a glorious victory over the king Darius at Abela, refused, in the presence of the splendid and illustrious courtiers that were about him, to give audience to a certan poor despicable fellow, who, through the solicitations and mediation of some of his royal attendants, was admitted humbly to beg that grace and favour of him: but sore did he repent, although in vain, a thousand and ten thousand times thereafter, the surly state which he then took upon him to the denial of so just a suit, the grant whereof would have been worth unto him the value of a brace of potent cities. He was indeed victorious in Persia, but withal so far distant from Macedonia, his hereditary kingdom, that the joy of the one did not expel the grief, which through occasion of the other he had inwardly conceived: for not being able with all his power to find or invent a convenient mean and expedient, how to get or come by the certainty of any news from thence; both by reason of the huge remoteness of the places from one to another; as also, because of the impeditive interposition of many great rivers, the interjacent obstacles of divers wild deserts, and obstructive interjection of sundry almost inaccessible mountains: whilst he was in this sad quandary and solicitous pensiveness, which, you may suppose, could not be of a small vexation to him; considering that it was a matter of no great difficulty to run over his whole native soil, possess his country, seize on his kingdom, install a new king on the throne, and plant thereon foreign colonies, long before he could come to have any advertisement of it: for obviating the jeopardy of so dreadful inconveniency, and putting a fit remedy thereto, a certain Sydonian merchant of a low stature, but high fancy, very poor in shew, and to outward appearance of little or no account, having presented himself before him, went about to affirm and declare, that he had excogitated and hit upon a ready mean and way, by the which those of his territories at home should come to the certain notice of his Indian victories, and himself be perfectly informed of the state and condition of Egypt and Macedonia, within less than five days. Whereupon the said Alexander, plunged into a sullen animadvertency of mind, through his rash opinion of the improbability of performing a so strange and impossible-like undertaking, dismissed the merchant without giving ear to what he had to say, and vilified him. What could it have cost him to hearken unto what the honest man had invented and contrived for his good; what detriment, annoyance, damage or loss could he have undergone to listen to the discovery of that secret, which the good man would have most willingly revealed unto him? Nature, I am persuaded, did not without a cause frame our ears open, putting thereto no gate at all, nor shutting them up with any manner of inclosures, as she hath done unto the tongue, the eyes, and other such out-jetting parts of the body. The cause, as I imagine, is, to the end, that every day and every night, and that continually, we may be ready to hear, and by a perpetual hearing apt to learn: for of all the senses, it is the fittest for the reception of the knowledge of arts, sciences and disciplines; and it may be, that man was an angel (that is to say, a messenger sent from God) as Raphael was to Toby. Too suddenly did he contemn, despise and misregard him; but too long thereafter, by an untimely and too late repentance, did he do penance for it." "You say very well," answered Epistemon; "yet shall you never for all that induce me to believe, that it can tend any way to the advantage or commodity of a man, to take advice and counsel of a woman, namely, of such a woman, and a woman of such a country." "Truly I have found," quoth Panurge, "a great deal of good in the counsel of women, chiefly in that of the old wives amongst them; who for every time I consult with them, I readily get a stool or two extraordinary, to the great solace of my bumb-gut passage. They are as sloth hounds in the infallibility of their scent, and in their saying no less sententious than the rubrics of the law. Therefore, in my conceit, it is not an improper kind of speech to call them sage or wise women. In confirmation of which opinion of mine, the customary style of my language alloweth them the denomination of presage women. The epithet of sage is due unto them, because they are surpassing dextrous in the knowledge of most things. And I give them the title of presage, for that they divinely foresee, and certainly foretell future contingencies and events of things to come. Sometimes I call them maunettes, but monettes, from their wholesome monitions like the Roman Juno. Whether it be so, ask Pythagoras, Socrates, Empedocles, and our master Ortuinus. I furthermore praise and commend above the skies the ancient memorable institution of the pristine Germans, who ordained the responses and documents of old women to be highly extolled, most cordially reverenced, prized at a rate in nothing inferior to the weight, test and standard of the sanctuary: and as they were respectfully prudent in receiving of these sound advices, so by honouring and following them did they prove no less fortunate in the happy success of all their endeavours. Witness the old wife Aurinia, and the good mother Vellede, in the days of Vespasian. You need not any way doubt, but that feminine old age is always fructifying in qualities sublime; I would have said sybilline. Let us go, by the help; let us go by the virtue of God, let us go. Farewell, friar John; I recommend the care of my cod-piece to you." "Well," quoth Epistemon, "I will follow you, with this protestation nevertheless, that if I happen to get a sure information, or otherways find that she doth use any kind of charm or enchantment in her responses, it may not be imputed to me for a blame to leave you at the gate of her house, without accompanying you any further in."

308

CHAPTER XVII

HOW PANURGE SPOKE TO THE SYBIL OF PANZOUST

THEIR voyage was six days' journeying. On the seventh was
shewn unto them the house of the vaticinatress, standing on the
knape or top of a hill, under a large and spacious walnut-tree. Without great difficulty they entered into that straw-thatched cottage, scurvily built, naughtily moveabled, and all besmoaked. "It matters not,"
quoth Epistemon: "Heraclitus, the grand Scotist, and tenebrous darksome philosopher, was nothing astonished at his introit in such a
coarse and paultry habitation; for he did usually shew forth unto his
sectators and disciples, that the gods made as cheerfully their residence
in these mean homely mansions, as in sumptuous, magnific palaces,
replenished with all manner of delight, pomp, and pleasure. [I
withal do really believe, that the dwelling place of the so famous
and renowned Hecate was just such another petty cell as this is, when
she made a feast therein to the valiant Theseus.] And that of no better structure was the cott or cabin of Ayreus, or Oenopion, wherein
Jupiter, Neptune, and Mercury were not ashamed, all three together,
to harbour and sojourn a whole night, and there to take a full and
hearty repast: for the payment of the shot they thankfully pissed
Orion."

They found the old woman sitting in a corner of her chimney.
Upon which, says Epistemon, "She is indeed a true sybil, and the
lively portrait of one represented by the τῇ καμινοῖ of Homer. The
old hag was in a pitiful bad plight and condition, in matter of the outward state and complexion of her body, the ragged and tattered equipage of her person, in the point of accoutrements, and beggarly poor
provision of fare for her diet and entertainment: for she was ill apparelled, worse nourished, toothless, blear-eyed, crook-shouldered,
snotty, her nose still dropping, and herself still drooping, faint, and
pithless; whilst in this wofully wretched case she was making ready,
for her dinner, porridge of wrinkled green colworts, with a sword of
yellow bacon, mixed with a twice before cooked sort of waterish, unsavoury poor broth, extracted out of bare and hollow bones. Epistemon said, "By the cross of a groat, we are to blame, nor shall we get
from her any response at all; for we have not brought along with us
the branch of gold." "I have," quoth Panurge, "provided pretty well
for that; for here I have it within my bag, in the substance of a

309

gold ring, accompanied with some fair pieces of small money."
No sooner were these words spoken, when Panurge coming towards her, after the ceremonial performance of a profound and humble
salutation, presented her with six neats'-tongues dried in the smoke, a
great butter-pot full of fresh cheese, a boracho furnished with good
beverage, and a ram's cod stored with single pence newly coined. At
last he, with a low bow, put on her medical finger a pretty handsome
golden ring, whereinto was right artificially inchased a precious toad-
stone of Beausse. This done, in a few words, and very succinctly did
he set open, and expose unto her, the motive reason of his coming;
most civilly and courteously entreated her, that she might be pleased
to vouchsafe to give him an ample and plenary intelligence concerning the future good luck of his intended marriage.

The old trot for a while remained silent, pensive, and grinning like
a dog: then, after she had set her withered breech upon the bottom
of a bushel, she took into her hands three old spindles, which when
she had turned and whirled betwixt her fingers very diversly, and
after several fashions, she pried narrowly into, by the trial of their
points: the sharpest whereof she retained in her hand, and threw
the other two under a stone trough. After this she took a pair of
yarn windles or reels, which she nine times unintermittedly veered
and frisked about; then at the ninth revolution, or turn, without
touching them any more, maturely perpending the manner of their
motion, she very demurely waited on their repose and cessation from
any further stirring. In sequel whereof she pulled off one of her
wooden pattens, put her apron over her head, as a priest use to do
his amice, when he is going to sing mass, and with a kind of antic,
gaudy, party-coloured string, knit it under her neck. Being thus covered and muffled, she whiffed off a lusty good draught out of the boracho, took three several pence forth of the ramcod fob, put them into as
many walnut shells, which she set down upon the bottom of a feather
pot; and then, after she had given them three whisks of a broom-
besom athwart the chimney, casting into the fire half a bevin of long
heather, or furz, together with a branch of dry laurel, she observed,
with a very hush and coy silence, in what form they did burn, and
saw, that although they were in a flame, they made no kind of noise,
or crackling din. Hereupon she gave a most hideous horribly dreadful shout, muttering betwixt her teeth some few barbarous words,
of a strange termination.

This so terrified Panurge, that he forthwith said to Epistemon, "The devil mince me into a gallymaufry, if I do not tremble for fear. I do not think but that I am now enchanted; for she uttereth not her voice in the terms of any christian language. O look, I pray you, how she seemeth unto me to be by three full spans higher than she was, when she began to hood herself with her apron. What meaneth this restless wagging of her slouchy chaps? What can be the signification of the uneven shrugging of her hulchy shoulders? To what end doth she quaver with her lips, like a monkey in the dismembering of a lobster? My ears through horror glow; ah! how they tingle. I think I hear the shrieking of Proserpina; the devils are breaking loose to be all here. O the foul, ugly and deformed beast! Let us run away! By the hook of God, I am like to die for fear! I do not love the devils; they vex me, and are unpleasant fellows. Now let us fly, and betake us to our heels. Farwell, gammer; thanks and grammercy for your goods. I will not marry; no, believe me, I will not; I fairly quit my interest therein, and totally abandon and renounce it, from this time forward, even as much as at present." With this, as he endeavoured to make an escape out of the room, the old crone did anticipate his flight, and make him stop. The way how she prevented him was this: whilst in her hand she held the spindle, she hurried out to a back-yard, close by her lodge, where, after she had peeled off the bark of an old sycamore, three several times, she very summarily, upon eight leaves which dropt from thence, wrote with the spindle-point some curt and briefly couched verses, which she threw into the air; then said unto them, "Search after them if you will: find them if you can; the fatal destinies of your marriage are written in them."

No sooner had she done thus speaking, when she did withdraw herself unto her lurking hole, where, on the upper seat of the porch, she tucked up her gown, her coats and smock, as high as her armpits, and gave them a full inspection of the nockandroe: which being perceived by Panurge, he said to Epistemon, "God's bodkins, I see the sybil's hole, where many have perished: let's fly this hole." She suddenly then bolted the gate behind her, and was never since seen any more. They jointly ran in haste after the fallen and dispersed leaves, and gathered them up at last; though not without great labour and toil, for the wind had scattered them amongst the thorn bushes of the valley. When they had ranged them each after other in their due places, they found out their sentence, as it is metrified in this octastic.

"Thy fame upheld,

Even so, so:
And she with child
Of thee: no.
Thy good end
Suck she shall,
And flay thee, friend,
But not all."

CHAPTER XVIII

HOW PANTAGRUEL AND PANURGE DID DIVERSLY EXPOUND
THE VERSES OF THE SYBIL OF PANZOUST

THE leaves being thus collected, and orderly disposed, Epistemon
and Panurge returned to Pantagruel's court, partly well pleased,
and other part discontented: glad for their being come back, and vexed
for the trouble they had sustained by the way, which they found to be
craggy, rugged, stony, rough, and ill-adjusted. They made an ample
and full relation of their voyage unto Pantagruel; as likewise of
the estate and condition of the sybil. Then having presented to him
the leaves of the sycamore, they shew him the short and twattle verses
that were written in them. Pantagruel, having read and considered
the whole sum and substance of the matter, fetched from his heart a
deep and heavy sigh, then said to Panurge: "You are now, forsooth,
in a good taking, and have brought your hogs to a fine market: the
prophecy of the sybil doth explain, and lay out before us, the very
same predictions which have been denoted, foretold, and presaged to
us by the decree of the Virgilian lots, and the verdict of your own
proper dreams; to wit, that you shall be very much disgraced, shamed,
and discredited by your wife: for that she will make you a cuckold
in prostituting herself to others, being big with child by another than
you; will steal from you a great deal of your goods, and will beat
you, scratch and bruise you, even to plucking the skin in part from
off you; will leave the print of her blows in some member of your
body." "You understand as much," answered Panurge, "in the veritable interpretation, and expounding of recent prophecies, as a sow
in the matter of spicery. Be not offended, sir, I beseech you, that I
speak thus boldly; for I find myself a little in choler, and that not
without cause, seeing it is the contrary that is true: take heed and give

312

attentive ear unto my words. The old wife said, that as the bean is not seen till first it be unhusked, and that its swad or hull be shelled, and peeled from off it: so it is that my virtue and transcendent worth will never come, by the mouth of fame, to be blazed abroad proportionable to the height, extent, and measure of the excellency thereof, until previously I get a wife, and make the full half of a married couple. How many times have I heard you say, that the function of a magistrate, or office of dignity, discovereth the merits, parts, and endowments of the person so advanced and promoted, and what is in him; that is to say, we are then best able to judge aright of the deservings of a man, when he is called to the management of affairs: for when before he lived in a private condition, we could have no more certain knowledge of him, than of a bean within its husk. And thus stands the first article explained: otherwise could you imagine, that the good fame, repute, and estimation of an honest man, should depend upon the tail of a whore?

"Now to the meaning of the second article. My wife will be with child (here lies the prime felicity of marriage) but not of me. Copsbody, that I do believe indeed: it will be of a pretty little infant: O how heartily I shall love it! I do already dote upon it; for it will be my dainty feedle-darling, my gentel dilli-minion. From thenceforth, no vexation, care, or grief, shall take such deep impression in my heart, how hugely great or vehement soever it otherways appear; but that it shall evanish forthwith, at the sight of that my future babe, and at the hearing of the chat and prating of its childish gibberish: and blessed be the old wife. By my truly I have a mind to settle some good revenue or pension upon her, out of the readiest increase of the lands of my Salmygondinois; not an inconstant and uncertain rentseek, like that of witless, giddy-headed bachelors, but sure and fixed of the nature of the well-payed incomes of regenting doctors.

"If this interpretation doth not please you, think you my wife will bear me in her womb? conceive with me? be of me delivered as women use in childbed to bring forth their young ones; so as that it may be said, Panurge is a second Bacchus; he hath been twice born; he is re-born, as was Proteus, one time of Thetis, and, secondly, of the mother of the philosopher Apollonius: as were the two Palici near the flood Simæthos, in Sicily. His wife was big of child with him. In him is renewed and begun again the palintocy of the Megarians, and the palingenesie of Democritus. Fie upon such errors! to hear stuff of that nature rends mine ears.

"The words of the third article are: she will suck me at my best end. Why not? that pleaseth me right well. You know the thing, I need not tell you, that it is my intercrural pudding with one end. I swear and promise, that in what I can, I will preserve it sappy, full of juice, and as well victualled for her use as may be: she shall not suck me, I believe, in vain, nor be destitute of her allowance; there shall her justum, both in peck and lippy, be furnished to the full eternally. You expound this passage allegorically, and interpret it to theft and larceny. I love the exposition, and the allegory pleaseth me; but not according to the sense whereto you stretch it. It may be that the sincerity of the affection, which you bear me, moveth you to harbour in your breast those refractory thoughts concerning me, with a suspicion of my adversity to come. We have this saying from the learned, that a marvellously fearful thing is love, and that true love is never without fear. But, sir, according to my judgment, you do understand both of and by yourself, that here stealth signifieth nothing else, no more than in a thousand other places of Greek and Latin, old and modern writings, but the sweet fruits of amorous dalliance, which Venus liketh best when reaped in secret, and culled by fervent lovers filchingly."

"Why, so? I prithee tell." "Because when the feat of the loosecoat skirmish happeneth to be done underhand and privily, between two doors, athwart the steps of a pair of stairs, lurkingly, and in covert, behind a suit of hangings, or close hid and trussed upon an unbound faggot, it is more pleasing to the Cyprian goddess (and to me also, I speak this without prejudice to any better, or more sound opinion) than to perform that culbusting art, after the Cynic manner, in the view of the clear sun-shine; or in a rich tent, under a precious stately canopy, within a glorious and sublime pavilion; or yet on a soft couch, betwixt rich curtains of cloth of gold, without affrightment, at long intermediate respites, enjoying of pleasures and delights a belly-full, all at great ease, with a huge fly-flap fan of crimson satin, and a bunch of feathers of some East-India ostrich, serving to give chase unto the flies all around about: whilst, in the interim, the female picks her teeth with a stiffstraw, picked even then from out of the bottom of the bed she lies on.

"If you be not content with this my exposition, are you of the mind that my wife will suck and sup me up, as people use to gulp and swallow oysters out of the shell? or as the Cilician women, according to the testimony of Dioscorides, were wont to do the grain of Alkermes?

Assuredly that is an error. Who seizeth on it, doth neither gulch up, nor swill down: but takes away what hath been packed up, catcheth, snatcheth, and plies the play of hey-pass, repass.

"The fourth article doth imply that my wife will flay me, but not at all. O the fine word! You interpret this to beating strokes and blows. Speak wisely: will you eat a pudding? Sir, I beseech you to raise up your spirits above the low-sized pitch of earthly thoughts, unto that height of sublime contemplation, which reacheth to the apprehension of the mysteries and wonders of dame nature. And here be pleased to condemn yourself, by a renouncing of those errors which you have committed very grossly, and somewhat perversely, in expounding the prophetic sayings of the holy sybil. Yet put the case (albeit I yield not to it) that, by the instigation of the devil, my wife should go about to wrong me, make me a cuckold downwards to the very breech, disgrace me otherways, steal my goods from me; yea, and lay violently her hands upon me: she nevertheless should fail of her attempts, and not attain to the proposed end of her unreasonable undertakings. The reason which induceth me hereto, is grounded totally on this last point, which is extracted from the profoundest privacies of a monastic pantheology. The good friar Arthur Wagtail told me once, upon a Monday morning, as we were (if I have not forgot) eating a bushel of trotter-pies; and I remember well it rained hard: God give him the good to-morrow. The women at the beginning of the world, or a little after, conspired to flay the men quick, because they found the spirit of mankind inclined to domineer it and bear rule over them upon the face of the whole earth. In pursuit of this their resolution, they promised, swore, and covenanted amongst themselves by the pure faith they owe to the nocturnal sanct Rogero. But O the vain enterprises of women! O the great fragility of that sex feminine! They did begin to flay the man, or peel him (as says Catullus) at that member, which of all the body they loved best; to wit, the nervous and cavernous cane; and that above five thousand years ago: yet have they not of that small part alone flayed any more till this hour but the head. In mere despite whereof the Jews snip off that parcel of the skin in circumcision, chusing rather to be called clip-yards, and rascals, than to be flayed by women, as are other nations. My wife, according to this female covenant, will flay it to me, if it be not so already. I heartily grant my consent thereto, but will not give her leave to flay it all: nay, truly will I not, my noble king."

"Yea, but," quoth Epistemon, "you say nothing of her most dreadful cries and exclamations, when she and we both saw the laurel-bough burn without yielding any noise or crackling. You know it is a very dismal omen, and inauspicious sign, unlucky indice, and token formidable, bad, disastrous, and most unhappy; as is certified by Propertius, Tibullus, the quick philosopher Porphyrius, Eustathius on the Iliads of Homer, and by many others."

"Verily, verily," quoth Panurge, "brave are the allegations which you bring me, and testimonies of two-foot calves. These men were fools, as they were poets; and dotards, as they were philosophers; full of folly, as they were of philosophy."

CHAPTER XIX

HOW PANTAGRUEL PRAISETH THE COUNSEL OF DUMB MEN

PANTAGRUEL, when this discourse was ended, held for a pretty while his peace, seeming to be exceeding sad and pensive; then said to Panurge, "The malignant spirit misleads, beguileth and seduceth you: I have read that in times past the surest and most veritable oracles were not those which either were delivered in writing, or uttered by word of mouth in speaking: for many times, in their interpretation, right, witty, learned, and ingenious men have been deceived through amphibologies, equivoques and obscurity of words, no less than by the brevity of their sentences. For which cause Apollo, the God of vaticination, was surnamed Λοξίας. Those which were represented then by signs and outward gestures, were accounted the truest and the most infallible. Such was the opinion of Heraclitus: and Jupiter did himself in this manner give forth in Ammon frequently predictions: nor was he single in this practice; for Apollo did the like amongst the Assyrians. His prophesying thus unto those people, moved them to paint him with a large long beard, and clothes beseeming an old settled person, of a most sedate, staid, and grave behaviour; not naked, young, and beardless, as he was portrayed most usually amongst the Grecians. Let us make trial of this kind of fatidicency; and go you to take advice of some dumb person without any speaking." "I am content," quoth Panurge. "But," says Pantagreul, "it were requisite that the dumb you consult with be such as have been deaf from the hour of their nativity, and consequently dumb: for none can be so lively, natural, and kindly dumb, as he who never heard."

"How is it," quoth Panurge, "that you conceive this matter? If you apprehend it so, that never any spoke, who had not before heard the speech of others, I will from that antecedent bring you to infer very logically a most absurd and paradoxical conclusion. But let it pass; I will not insist on it. You do not then believe what Herodotus wrote of two children, who at the special command and appointment of Psammeticus, king of Egypt, having been kept in a petty country cottage, where they were nourished and entertained in a perpetual silence, did at last, after a certain long space of time, pronounce this word, bee, which in the Phrygian language signifieth bread." "Nothing less," quoth Pantagruel, "do I believe, than that it is a mere abusing of our understandings, to give credit to the words of those, who say that there is any such thing as a natural language. All speeches have had their primary origin from the arbitrary institutions, accords and agreements of nations, in their respective condescendments to what should be noted and betokened by them. An articulate voice (according to the dialecticians) had naturally no signification at all; for that the sense and meaning thereof did totally depend upon the good will and pleasure of the first deviser and imposer of it. I do not tell you this without a cause: for Bartholus, l. v. de verb. oblig. very seriously reporteth, that even in his time there was in Eugubia, one named sir Nello de Gabrielis, who although he by a sad mischance became altogether deaf, understood nevertheless everyone that talked in the Italian dialect, howsoever he expressed himself: and that only by looking on his external gestures, and casting an attentive eye upon the divers motions of his lips and chaps. I have read, I remember also, in a very literate and eloquent author, that Tyridates king of Armenia, in the days of Nero, made a voyage to Rome, where he was received with great honour and solemnity, and with all manner of pomp and magnificence: yea, to the end there might be a sempiternal amity and correspondence preserved betwixt him and the Roman senate, there was no remarkable thing in the whole city, which was not shown unto him. At his departure, the emperor bestowed upon him many ample donations of an inestimable value: and besides, the more entirely to testify his affection towards him, heartily entreated him to be pleased to make choice of any whatsoever thing in Rome was most agreeable to his fancy; with a promise juramentally confirmed, that he should not be refused of his demand. Thereupon,

317

after a suitable return of thanks for so gracious an offer, he required a certain jack-pudding, whom he had seen to act his part most egregiously upon the stage, and whose meaning (albeit he knew not what it was he had spoken) he understood perfectly enough by the signs and gesticulations which he has made. And for this suit of his, in that he asked nothing else, he gave this reason; that in several wide and spacious dominions, which were reduced under the sway and authority of his sovereign government, there were sundry countries and nations much differing from one another in language, with whom, whether he was to speak unto them, or give any answer to their requests, he was always necessitated to make use of divers sorts of truchmen and interpreters: now with this man alone, sufficient for supplying all their places, will that great inconveniency hereafter be totally removed; seeing he is such a fine gesticulator, and in the practice of chirology an artist so complete, expert and dextrous, that with his very fingers he doth speak. Howsoever, you are to pitch upon such a dumb one as is deaf by nature, and from his birth; to the end that his gestures and signs may be the more naturally and truly prophetic, and not counterfeit by the intermixture of some adulterate lustre and affectation. Yet whether this dumb person shall be of the male or female sex is in your option, lieth at your discretion, and altogether dependeth on your election."

"I would more willingly," quoth Panurge, "consult with and be advised by a dumb woman, were it not that I am afraid of two things. The first is, that the greater part of women, whatever it be that they see, do always represent unto their fancies, think and imagine, that it hath some relation to the sugred entering of the goodly ithyphallos, and graffing in the cleft of the overturned tree, the quick-set imp of the pin of copulation. Whatever signs, shews, or gestures we shall make, or whatever our behaviour, carriage, or demeanour shall happen to be in their view and presence, they will interpret the whole in reference to the act of androgynation, and the culbatizing exercise; by which means we shall be abusively disappointed of our designs, in regard that she will take all our signs for nothing else but tokens and representations of our desire to entice her unto the lists of a Cyprian combat, or catsenconny skirmish. Do you remember what happened at Rome two hundred and threescore years after the foundation thereof? A young Roman gentleman encountering by chance, at the foot of mount Celion, with a beautiful Latin lady, named Verona, who from her very cradle upwards had always been both deaf and dumb, very civilly asked her (not without a chironomatic italianising of his demand, with various jectigation of his fingers, and other gesticulations, as yet customary amongst the speakers of that country) what senators in her descent from the top of the hill she had met with going up thither. For you are to conceive, that he knowing no more of her deafness than dumbness, was ignorant of both. She, in the meantime, who neither heard nor understood so much as one word of what he had said, straight imagined, by all that she could apprehend in the lovely gesture of his manual signs, that what he then required of her was, what herself had a great mind to, even that which a young man doth naturally desire of a woman. Then was it, that by signs (which in all occurrences of venereal love are incomparably more attractive, valid and efficacious than words) she beckoned to him to come along with her to her house; which when he had done, she drew him aside to a privy room, and then made a most lively alluring sign unto him, to shew that the game did please her. Whereupon, without any more advertisement, or so much as uttering of one word on either side, they fell to, and bringuardised it lustily.

"The other cause of my being averse from consulting with dumb women, is, that to our signs they would make no answer at all, but suddenly fall backwards in a divaricating posture, to intimate thereby unto us the reality of their consent to the supposed motion of our tacit demands. Or if they should chance to make any counter-signs responsory to our propositions, they would prove so foolish, impertinent, and ridiculous, that by them ourselves should easily judge their thoughts to have no excursion beyond the duffling academy. You know very well how at Brignoles, when the religious nun, sister Fatbum, was made big with child by the young Stiffly-stand-to't, her pregnancy came to be known, and she cited by the abbess, and, in a full convention of the convent, accused of incest. Her excuse was, that she did not consent thereto, but that it was done by the violence and impetuous force of the friar Stiffly-stand-to't. Hereto the abbess very austerely replying, 'Thou naughty wicked girl, why didst thou not cry, a rape? then should all of us have run to thy succour.' Her answer was, that the rape was committed in the dorter, where she durst not cry, because it was a place of sempiternal silence. 'But,' quoth the abbess, 'thou naughty wench, why didst not thou then make some sign to those that were in the next chamber beside thee?' To this she answered, that with her buttocks she made a sign unto them, as vigorously as she could; yet never one of them did so much

319

as offer to come to her help and assistance. 'But,' quoth the abbess, 'thou scurvy baggage, why didst thou not tell it immediately after the perpetration of the fact, that so we might orderly, regularly, and canonically have accused him? I would have done so, had the case been mine, for the clearer manifestation of mine innocency.' 'I truly, madam, would have done the like with all my heart and soul,' quoth sister Fatbum; 'but that fearing I should remain in sin, and in the hazard of eternal damnation, if prevented by a sudden death, I did confess myself to the father friar before he went out of the room; who, for my penance, enjoined me not to tell it, or reveal the matter unto any. It were a most enormous and horrid offence, detestable before God and the angels, to reveal a confession: such an abominable wickedness would have possibly brought down fire from heaven, wherewith to have burnt the whole nunnery, and sent us all headlong to the bottomless pit, to bear company with Corah, Dathan, and Abiram.'" "You will not," quoth Pantagruel, "with all your jesting, make me laugh: I know that all monks, friars, and nuns had rather violate and infringe the highest of the commandments of God, than break the least of their provincial statutes.

"Take you therefore Goatsnose, a man very fit for your present purpose: for he is, and hath been, both dumb and deaf from the very remotest infancy of his childhood."

CHAPTER XX

HOW GOATSNOSE BY SIGNS MAKETH ANSWER TO PANURGE

GOATSNOSE being sent for, came the day thereafter to Pantagruel's court; at his arrival to which Panurge gave him a fat calf, the half of a hog, two puncheons of wine, one load of corn, and thirty franks of small money: then having brought him before Pantagruel, in presence of the gentlemen of the bed-chamber, he made this sign unto him. He yawned a long time, and in yawning made, without his mouth, with the thumb of his right hand, the figure of the Greek letter Tau, by frequent reiterations. Afterwards he lifted up his eyes to heavenwards; then turned them in his head, like a she-goat in the painful fit of an abortive birth, in doing whereof he did cough and sign exceeding heavily: this done, after that he had made demonstration of the want of his codpiece, he from under his shirt took his placket-racket in a full gripe, making it therewithal clack very melodiously betwixt his thighs: then no sooner had he with his body stooped a little forwards, and bowed his left knee, but that immediately thereupon, holding both his arms on his breast, in a loose faintlike posture, the one over the other, he paused awhile. Goatsnose looked wistly upon him, and having heedfully enough viewed him all over, he lifted up into the air his left hand, the whole fingers whereof he retained fist-ways, closed together, except the thumb of his forefinger, whose nails he softly joined and coupled to one another. "I understand," quoth Pantagruel, "what he meaneth by that sign: it denotes marriage, and withal the number thirty, according to the profession of the Pythagorians. You will be married." "Thanks to you," quoth Panurge, in turning himself towards Goatsnose, "my little sewer, pretty master's-mate, dainty baily, curious serjeant-marshal, and jolly catchpole-leader." Then did he lift higher up than before his said left hand, stretching out all the five fingers thereof, and severing them as wide from one another as he possibly could get done. "Here," says Pantagruel, "doth he more amply and fully insinuate unto us, by that token which he sheweth forth of the quinary number, that you shall be married; yea, that you shall not only be affianced, betrothed, wedded, and married, but that you shall farthermore cohabit, and live jollily and merrily with your wife: for Pythagoras called five the nuptial number, which, together with marriage, signifieth the consummation of matrimony, because it is composed of a ternary, the first of the odd, and binary, the first of the even numbers, as of a male and female knit and united together. In very deed it was the fashion of old, in the city of Rome, at marriage festivals to light five wax tapers; nor was it permitted to kindle any more at the magnific nuptials of the most potent and wealthy; nor yet any fewer at the penurious weddings of the poorest and most abject of the world. Moreover, in times past, the heathen, or paynims, implored the assistance of five deities, or of one deity helpful, at least, in five several good offices to those that were to be married: of this sort were the nuptial Jove; Juno, president of the feast; the fair Venus; Pitho, the goddess of eloquence and persuasion; and Diana, whose aid and succour was required to the labour of child-bearing." Then shouted Panurge, "O the gentle Goatsnose! I will give him a farm near Cinais, and a wind-mill hard by Mirebalais." Hereupon the dumb fellow sneezeth with an impetuous vehemency, and huge concussion of the spirits of the whole body, withdrawing himself in so doing with a jerking turn towards the left hand. "By the body of a fox new slain," quoth Pantagruel, "what is that? This maketh nothing for your advantage; for he betokeneth thereby that your marriage will be inauspicious and unfortunate. This sneezing (according to the doctrine of Terpsion) is the Socratic dæmon: which if done towards the right side, it imports and portendeth, that boldly, and with all assurance, one may go whither he will, and do what he listeth, according to what deliberation he shall be pleased to have thereupon taken: his entries in the beginning, progress in his proceedings, and success in the events and issues will be all lucky, good, and happy. The quite contrary thereto is thereby implied and presaged, if it be done towards the left." "You," quoth Panurge, "do take always the matter at the worst, and continually, like another Davus, cast in new disturbances and obstructions. I believe nothing of the matter; nor ever yet did I know this old paltry Terpsion worthy of citation, but in points only of cousenage and imposture." "Nevertheless," quoth Pantagruel, "Cicero hath written I know not what to the same purpose, in his second book of divinations."

Panurge then turning himself towards Goatsnose, made this sign unto him. He inverted his eye-lids upwards, wrenched his jaws from the right to the left side, and drew forth his tongue half out of his mouth: this done, he posited his left hand wholly open (the mid-finger only excepted, which was perpendicularly placed upon the palm thereof) and set it just in the room where his codpiece had been. Then did he keep his right hand altogether shut up in a fist, save only the thumb, which he straight turned backwards directly under the right arm-pit, and settled it afterwards on that most eminent part of the buttocks which the Arabs call the al-katim. Suddenly thereafter he made this interchange; he held his right hand after the manner of the left, and posited it on the place wherein his codpiece sometime was, and retaining his left hand in the form and fashion of the right, he placed it upon his al-katim. This altering of hands did he reiterate nine several times; at the last whereof, he reseated his eye-lids in their own first natural position. Then doing the like also with his jaws and tongue, he did cast a squinting look upon Goatsnose, diddering and shivering his chaps, as apes use to do, and rabbits, whilst almost starved with hunger, they are eating oats in the sheaf.

Then was it that Goatsnose, lifting up into the air his right hand wholly open and displayed, put the thumb thereof, even close to its first articulation, between the two third joints of the middle and ring fingers, pressing about the said thumb thereof very hard with them both, and whilst the remanent joints were contracted and shrunk in towards the wrist, he stretched forth, with as much straightness as he could, the fore and little fingers. That hand, thus framed and disposed of, he laid and posited upon Panurge's navel, moving withal continually the aforesaid thumb, and bearing up, supporting, or under-propping that hand upon the above specified, and fore and little fingers, as upon two legs. Thereafter did he make in this posture his hand by little and little, and by degrees and pauses, successively to mount from athwart the belly to the stomach, from whence he made it to ascend to the breast, even upwards to Panurge's neck, still gaining ground, till having reached his chin, he had put within the concave of his mouth his aforementioned thumb: then fiercely brandishing the whole hand, which he made to rub and grate against his nose, he heaved it further up, and made the fashion, as if with the thumb thereof he would have put out his eyes. With this Panurge grew a little angry, and went about to withdraw, and rid himself from this ruggedly untoward dumb devil. But Goatsnose, in the meantime, prosecuting the intended purpose of his prognosticatory response, touched very rudely with the above-mentioned shaking thumb, now his eyes, then his forehead, and after that, the borders and corners of his cap. At last Panurge cried out, saying, "Before God, master fool, if you do not let me alone, or that you will presume to vex me any more, you shall receive from the best hand I have a mask, wherewith to cover your rascally scoundrel face, you paltry shitten varlet." Then said friar John, "He is deaf, and doth not understand what thou sayest unto him. Bulliballock, make sign to him of a hail of fisticuffs upon the muzzle."

"What the devil," quoth Panurge, "means this busy restless fellow? What is it that this polypragmonetic ardelion to all the fiends of hell doth aim at? He hath almost thrust out mine eyes, as if he had been to poach them in a skillet with butter and eggs. By God, *da jurandi,* I will feast you with flirts and raps, on the snout interlarded with a double row of bobs and finger-filipings." Then did he leave him, in giving him by way of salvo a volley of farts for his farewel. Goatsnose, perceiving Panurge thus to slip away from him, got before him, and by mere strength enforcing him to stand, made this sign unto him. He let fall his right arm towards his knee on the same side as low as he could, and raising all the fingers of that hand into a close fist, past his dexter thumb betwixt the foremost and midfingers thereto belonging. Then scrubbing and swinging a little with his left hand alongst, and upon the uppermost in the very bow of the elbow of the said dexter arm, the whole cubit thereof, by leisure fair and softly, at these thumpatory warnings, did raise and elevate itself even to the elbow, and above it: on a sudden did he then let it fall down as low as before: and after that, at certain intervals and such spaces of time, raising and abasing it, he made a shew thereof to Panurge. This so incensed Panurge, that he forthwith lifted his hand to have strucken the dumb royster, and given him a sound whirret on the ear, but that the respect and reverence which he carried to the presence of Pantagruel restrained his choler, and kept his fury within bounds and limits. Then said Pantagruel, "If the bare signs now vex and trouble you, how much more grievously will you be perplexed and disquieted with the real things, which by them are represented and signified? All truths agree, and are consonant with one another. This dumb fellow prophesieth and foretelleth that you will be married, cuckolded, beaten and robbed." "As for the marriage," quoth Panurge, "I yield thereto, and acknowledge the verity of that point of his prediction: as for the rest, I utterly abjure and deny it: and believe, sir, I beseech you, if it may please you so to do, that in the matter of wives and horses, never any man was predestinated to a better fortune than I."

CHAPTER XXI

HOW PANURGE CONSULTETH WITH AN OLD FRENCH POET, NAMED RAMINAGROBIS

I NEVER thought," said Pantagruel, "to have encountered with any man so headstrong in his apprehensions, or in his opinions so wilful, as I have found you to be, and see you are. Nevertheless, the better to clear and extricate your doubts, let us try all courses, and leave no stone unturned, nor wind unsailed by. Take good heed to what I am to say unto you. The swans, which are fowls consecrated to Apollo, never chant but in the hour of their approaching death, especially in the Meander flood, which is a river that runneth along some of the territories of Phrygia. This I say, because Ælianus and Alexander Myndius write, that they had seen several swans in other places die, but never heard any of them sing or chant before their death. However, it passeth for current that the imminent death of

324

a swan is presaged by his foregoing song, and that no swan dieth until previously he hath sung.

"After the same manner poets, who are under the protection of Apollo, when they are drawing near their latter end, do ordinarily become prophets, and by the inspiration of that god sing sweetly, in vaticinating things which are to come. It hath been likewise told me frequently, that old decrepit men, upon the brinks of Charon's banks, do usher their decease with a disclosure, all at ease (to those that are desirous of such informations) of the determinate and assured truth of future accidents and contingencies. I remember also that Aristophanes, in a certain comedy of his, calleth old folks sybils; Ἴσϑ᾽ ὁ γέρων Σιϐυλλιᾶς. For as when being upon a pier by the shore, we see afar off mariners, sea-faring men, and other travellers alongst the curled waves of azure Thetis within their ships, we then consider them in silence only, and seldom proceed any further than to wish them a happy and prosperous arrival: but when they do approach near to the haven, and come to wet their keels within their harbour, then both with words and gestures we salute them, and heartily congratulate their access safe to the port wherein we are ourselves: just so the angels, heroes, and good demons (according to the doctrine of the Platonics) when they see mortals drawing near unto the harbour of the grave, as the most sure and calmest port of any, full of repose, ease, rest, tranquillity; free from the troubles and solicitudes of this tumultuous and tempestuous world; then is it that they with alacrity hail and salute them, cherish and comfort them, and speaking to them lovingly, begin even then to bless them with illuminations, and to communicate unto them the abstrusest mysteries of divination. I will not offer here to confound your memory; by quoting antique examples of Isaac, of Jacob, of Patroclus towards Hector, of Hector towards Achilles, of Polymnestor towards Agamemnon, of Hecuba, of the Rhodian celebrated by Possidonius, of Calanus the Indian towards Alexander the Great, of Orodes towards Mezentius, and of many others; it shall suffice for the present, that I commemorate unto you the learned and valiant knight and cavalier William of Bellay, late lord of Langey, who died on the hill of Tarara, the tenth of January, in the climacteric year of his age, and of our supputation 1543, according to the Roman account. The last three or four hours of his life he did employ in the serious utterance of a very pithy discourse, whilst with a clear judgment, and spirit void of all trouble, he did foretel several important things, whereof a great deal is come to pass, and the rest we wait for. Howbeit, his prophecies did at that time seem unto us somewhat strange, absurd, and unlikely; because there did not then appear any sign of efficacy enough to engage our faith to the belief of what he did prognosticate.

"We have here, near to the town of Villomere, a man that is both old and a poet, to wit, Raminagrobis, who to his second wife espoused my Lady Broadsow, on whom he begot the fair Basoche. It hath been told me, he is a dying, and so near his latter end, that he is almost upon the very last moment, point, and article thereof: repair thither as fast as you can, and be ready to give an attentive ear to what he shall chant unto you: it may be, that you shall obtain from him what you desire, and that Apollo will be pleased, by his means, to clear your scruples." "I am content," quoth Panurge; "let us both go thither, Epistemon, and that instantly in all haste, lest otherways his death prevent our coming. Wilt thou come along with us, friar John?" "Yes, that I will," quoth friar John, "right heartily to do thee a courtesy, my billy-ballocks; for I love thee with the best of my milt and liver." Thereupon, incontinently, without any farther lingering or delay, they all three went, and quickly thereafter (for they made good speed) arriving at the poetical habitation, they found the jolly old man, albeit in the agony of his departure from this world, looking cheerfully, with an open countenance, splendid aspect, and behaviour full of alacrity. After that Panurge had very civilly saluted him, he in a free gift did present him with a gold ring, which he even then put upon the medical finger of his left hand, in the collet or bezle whereof was inchased an oriental sapphire, very fair and large. Then, in imitation of Socrates, did he make an oblation unto him of a fair white cock; which was no sooner set upon the tester of his bed, than that with a high-raised head and crest, lustily shaking his feather-coat, he crowed stentoriphonically loud. This done, Panurge very courteously required of him, that he would vouchsafe to favour him with the grant and report of his sense and judgment, touching the future destiny of his intended marriage. For answer hereto, when the honest man had forthwith commanded pen, paper, and ink to be brought unto him, and that he was at the same call conveniently served with all the three, he wrote these following verses.

> "Take, or not take her,
>   Off, or on:
>   Handy-dandy is your lot.

326

When her name you write, you blot.
'Tis undone, when all is done,
Ended e'er it was begun:
Hardly gallop if you trot;
Set not forward when you run,
Nor be single, tho' alone.
Take, or not take her.

"Before you eat, begin to fast;
For what shall be was never past.
Say, unsay, gainsay, save your breath:
Then wish at once her life and death.
Take, or not take her."

These lines he gave out of his own hands unto them, saying unto them, "Go, my lads, in peace; the great God of the highest heavens be your guardian and preserver; and do not offer any more to trouble or disquiet me with this or any other business whatsoever. I have this same very day (which is the last both of May and me) with a great deal of labour, toil, and difficulty, chased out of my house a rabble of filthy, unclean, and plaguily pestilentious rake-hells, black-beasts, dusk, dun, white, ash-coloured, speckled, and foul vermin of other hues, whose obtrusive importunity would not permit me to die at my own ease: for by fraudulent and deceitful pricklings, ravenous, harpy-like graspings, waspish stingings, and such-like unwelcome approaches, forged in the shop of I know not what kind of insatiabilities; they went about to withdraw, and call me out of those sweet thoughts, wherein I was already beginning to repose myself, and acquiesce in the contemplation and vision, yea, almost in the very touch and taste of the happiness and felicity which the good God hath prepared for his faithful saints and elect in the other life, and state of immortality. Turn out of their courses, and eschew them; step forth of their ways, and do not resemble them; meanwhile, let me be no more troubled by you, but leave me now in silence, I beseech you."

CHAPTER XXII

HOW PANURGE PATROCINATES AND DEFENDETH THE ORDER
OF THE BEGGING FRIARS

PANURGE, at his issuing forth of Raminagrobis's chamber, said, as if he had been horribly affrighted, "By the virtue of God, I believe he is a heretic; the devil take me if I do not; he doth so villainously rail at the mendicant friars, and jacobins: who are the two hemispheres of the Christian world; by whose gyronomonic circumbilivaginations, as by two celivagous filopendulums, all the autonomatic metagrobolism of the Romish church, when tottering and emblustricated with the gibble-gabble gibberish of this odious error and heresy, is homocentrically poised. But what harm, in the devil's name, have those poor devils the capuchins and minims done unto him? Are not those beggarly devils sufficiently wretched already? Who can imagine that these poor snakes, the very extracts of ichthiophagy, are not thoroughly enough besmoaked and besmeared with misery, distress, and calamity? Dost thou think, friar John, by thy faith, that he is in the state of salvation? He goeth, before God, as surely damned to thirty thousand baskets full of devils, as a pruning-bill to the lopping of a vine-branch.

"To revile with opprobrious speeches the good and couragious props and pillars of the church, is that to be called a poetical fury? I cannot rest satisfied with him; he sinneth grossly, and blasphemeth against the true religion. I am very much offended at his scandalizing words, and contumelious obloquy." "I do not care a straw," quoth friar John, "for what he hath said: for although everybody should twit and jerk them, it were but a just retaliation, seeing all persons are served by them with the like sauce: therefore do I pretend no interest therein. Let us see nevertheless what he hath written." Panurge very attentively read the paper, which the old man had penned, then said to his fellow-travellers, "The poor drinker doteth: howsoever, I excuse him; for that I believe he is now drawing near to the end and final closure of his life: let us go make his epitaph.

"By the answer which he hath given us, I am not, I protest, one jot wiser than I was. Hearken here, Epistemon, my little bully, dost not thou hold him to be very resolute in his responsory verdicts? He is a witty, quick, and subtle sophister. I will lay an even wager, that he is a miscreant apostate. By the belly of a stalled ox, how careful he is not to be mistaken in his words! He answereth but by disjunctives, there-fore can it not be true which he saith; for the verity of such like prop-ositions is inherent only in one of its two members. O the cozening prattler that he is! I wonder if St. Iago of Bressure be one of these cogging shirks." "Such was of old," quoth Epistemon, "the custom of the grand vaticinator and prophet Tiresias, who used always (by way of a preface) to say openly and plainly, at the beginning of his divin-ations and predictions, that what he was to tell would either come to pass, or not: and such is truly the style of all prudently presaging prog-nosticators." "He was nevertheless," quoth Panurge, "so unfortu-nately misadventurous in the lot of his own destiny, that Juno thrust out both his eyes."

"Yes," answered Epistemon, "and that merely out of a spight and spleen, for having pronounced his award more veritably than she, upon the question which was merrily proposed by Jupiter." "But," quoth Panurge, "what arch-devil is it that hath possest this master Ramina-grobis, that so unreasonably, and without any occasion, he should have so snappishly and bitterly inveighed against these poor honest fathers, jacobins, minors, and minims? It vexeth me grievously, I assure you; nor am I able to conceal my indignation: his soul goeth infallibly to thirty thousand panniers full of devils."

"I understand you not," quoth Epistemon, "and it disliketh me very much, that you should so absurdly and perversely interpret that of the friar mendicants, which by the harmless poet was spoken of black beasts, dun, and other sorts of other coloured animals. He is not, in my opinion, guilty of such a sophistical and fantastic allegory, as by that phrase of his to have meaned the begging brothers: he in downright terms speaketh absolutely and properly of fleas, punies, handworms, flies, gnats, and other such like scurvy vermin, whereof some are black, some dun, some ash-coloured, some tawny, and some brown and dusky, all noisome, molesting, tyrannous, cumbersome, and unpleasing creatures, not only to sick and diseased folks, but to those also who are of a sound, vigorous, and healthy temperament and constitution. It is not unlike that he may have the ascarids, and the lumbrics, and worms within the entrails of his body. Possibly doth he suffer (as is frequent and usual amongst the Ægyptians, to-gether with all those who inhabit the Erythræan confines, and dwell along the shores and coasts of the Red Sea) some sour prickings, and smart stingings in his arms and legs of those little speckled dragons, which the Arabians call meden. You are to blame for offering to

329

expound his words otherways and wrong the ingenious poet, and outrageously abuse and miscal the said fraters, by an imputation of baseness undeservedly laid to their charge. We still should, in such like discourses of fatiloquent soothsayers, interpret all things to the best."
"Will you teach me," quoth Panurge, "how to discern flies among milk, or shew your father the way how to beget children? He is, by the virtue of God, an arrant heretic, a resolute formal heretic; I say, a rooted, riveted, combustible heretic, one as fit to burn as the little wooden clock at Rochel. His soul goeth to thirty thousand carts full of devils. Would you know whither? Cocks-body, my friend, straight under Proserpina's close-stool, to the very middle of the self-same infernal pan, within which she by an excrementitious evacuation voided the fecal stuff of her stinking clysters, and that just upon the left side of the great cauldron of three fathom height, hard by the claws and talons of Lucifer, in the very darkest part of the passage which leadeth towards the black chamber of Demigorgon. Oh the villain!"

CHAPTER XXIII

HOW PANURGE MAKETH THE MOTION OF A RETURN TO RAMINAGROBIS

LET us return," quoth Panurge, not ceasing, "to the uttermost of our abilities, to ply him with wholesome admonitions, for the furtherance of his salvation. Let us go back for God's sake, let us go in the name of God: it will be a very meritorious work, and of great charity in us, to deal so in the matter, and provide so well for him, that albeit he come to lose both body and life, he may at least escape the risk and danger of the eternal damnation of his soul. We will by our holy peruasions bring him to a sense and feeling of his escapes, induce him to acknowledge his faults, move him to a cordial repentance of his errors, and stir up in him such a sincere contrition of heart for his offences, as will prompt him with all earnestness to cry mercy, and to beg pardon at the hands of the good fathers, as well of the absent, as of such as are present: whereupon we will take instrument formally and authentically extended, to the end he be not, after his decease, declared an heretic, and condemned, as were the hobgoblins of the provost's wife of Orleans, to the undergoing of such punishments, pains and tortures, as are due to, and inflicted on

330

those that inhabit the horrid cells of the infernal regions: and withal incline, instigate, and persuade him to bequeath, and leave in legacy (by way of an amends and satisfaction for the outrage and injury done) to those good religious fathers, throughout all the convents, cloisters, and monasteries of this province, many pittances, a great deal of mass-singing, store of obits, and that sempiternally, on the anniversary day of his decease, every one of them all be furnished with a quintuple allowance: and that the great boracho, replenished with the best liquor, trudge apace along the tables, as well of the young duckling monkitoes, lay-brothers, and lowermost degree of the abbey-lubbards, as of the learned priests, and reverend clerks. The very meanest of the novices, and mitiants unto the order, being equally admitted to the benefit of those funerary and obsequial festivals with the aged rectors, and professed fathers. This is the surest ordinary means, whereby from God he may obtain forgiveness.

"Ho, ho, I am quite mistaken, I digress from the purpose, and fly out of my discourse, as if my spirits were a wool-gathering. The devil take me if I go thither. Virtue God! the chamber is already full of devils. O what a swinging, thwacking noise is now amongst them! O the terrible coil that they keep. Hearken; do you not hear the rustling thumping bustle of their strokes and blows, as they scuffle with one another, like true devils indeed, who shall gulp up Raminagrobis's soul, and be the first bringer of it, whilst it is hot, to monsieur Lucifer? Beware, and get you hence: for my part, I will not go thither; the devil roast me if I go. Who knows but that these hungry mad devils may, in the haste of their rage and fury of their impatience, take a *quid* for a *quo,* and instead of Raminagrobis snatch up poor Panurge frank and free? Though formerly, when I was deep in debt, they always failed. Get you hence: I will not go thither. Before God, the very bare apprehension thereof is like to kill me. To be in the place where there are greedy, famished, and hunger-starved devils; amongst factious devils; amidst trading and trafficking devils: O the Lord preserve me! Get you hence: I dare pawn my credit on it, that no jacobin, cordelier, carmelite, capucin, theatin, or minim, will bestow any personal presence at his interment. The wiser they, because he hath ordained nothing for them in his latter will and testament.

"The devil take me, if I go thither: if he be damned, to his own loss and hindrance be it. What the deuce moved him to be so snappish, and depravedly bent against the good fathers of the true reli-

331

gion? Why did he cast them off, reject them, and drive them quite out of his chamber, even in that very nick of time when he stood in greatest need of the aid, suffrage, and assistance of their devout prayers, and holy admonitions? Why did not he by testament leave them, at least, some jolly lumps and cantles of substantial meat, a parcel of cheek-puffing victuals, and a little bellytimber, and provision for the guts of those poor folks, who have nothing but their life in this world.

"Let him go thither, who will; the devil take me, if I go; for if I should, the devil would not fail to snatch me up. Cancro: ho, the pox! Get you hence, friar John. Art thou content that thirty thousand wainload of devils should get away with thee at this same very instant? If thou be, at my request, do these three things. First, give me thy purse; for, besides that thy money is marked with crosses, and the cross is an enemy to charms, and the same may befal to thee, which not long ago happened to John Dodin, collector of the excise of Coudray, at the fort of Vede, when the soldiers broke the planks: this moneyed fellow meeting at the very brink of the bank of the ford, with friar Adam Crank-cod, a Franciscan observantin of Mirebeau, promised him a new frock, provided that, in the transporting of him over the water, he would bear him upon his neck and shoulders, after the manner of carrying dead goats: for he was a lusty, strong-limbed, sturdy rogue.

"The condition being agreed upon, friar Crank-cod trusseth himself up to his very ballocks, and layeth upon his back, like a fair little saint Christopher, the load of the said supplicant Dodin, and so carried him gaily and with a good will; as Æneas bore his father Anchises through the conflagration of Troy, singing in the meanwhile a pretty Ave maris-stella. When they were in the deepest place of all the ford, a little above the master-wheel of the water-mill, he asked if he had any coin about him. 'Yes,' quoth Dodin, 'a whole bag full'; and that he needed not to mistrust his ability in the performance of the promise which he had made unto him concerning a new frock. 'How?' quoth friar Crank-cod, 'thou knowest well enough, that by the express rules, canons and injunctions of our order, we are forbidden to carry about us any kind of money: thou art truly unhappy, for having made me in this point to commit a heinous trespass. Why didst thou not leave thy purse with the miller? Without fail thou shalt presently receive thy reward for it; and if ever hereafter I may but lay hold upon thee within the limits of our chancel at Mirebeau, thou shalt have the miserere even to the vitulos.'

332

With this suddenly discharging himself of his burthen, he throws me down your Dodin headlong.

"Take example by this Dodin, my dear friend friar John, to the end that the devils may the better carry thee away at thine own ease. Give me thy purse. Carry no manner of cross upon thee. Therein lieth an evident and manifestly apparent danger: for if you have any silver coined with a cross upon it, they will cast thee down head-long upon some rocks; as the eagles use to do with the tortoises for the breaking of their shells, as the bald pate of the poet Æschylus can sufficiently bear witness. Such a fall would hurt thee very sore, my sweet bully, and I should be sorry for it. Or otherways, they will let thee fall, and tumble thee down into the high swollen waves of some capacious sea, I know not where; but I warrant thee far enough hence, as Icarus fell; which from thy name would afterwards get the denomination of the Funnelian sea.

"Secondly, Be out of debt; for the devils carry a great liking to those that are out of debt. I have sore felt the experience thereof in mine own particular: for now the lecherous varlets are always woo-ing me, courting me, and making much of me, which they never did when I was all to pieces. The soul of one in debt is insipid, dry, and no meat for the devil.

"Thirdly, With thy cowl and thy domino de grobis, return to Raminagrobis; and in case, being thus qualified, thirty thousand boats full of devils forthwith come not to carry thee quite away, I shall be content to be at the charge of paying for the pinte and faggot. Now if for the more security thou wouldst have some associate to bear thee company, let not me be the comrade thou searchest for: think not to get a fellow traveller of me; nay, do not, I advise thee for the best. Get you hence; I will not go thither; the devil take me if I go." "Notwithstanding all the fright that you are in," quoth friar John, "I would not care so much as might possibly be expected I should, if I once had but my sword in my hand." "Thou hast verily hit the nail on the head," quoth Panurge, "and speakest like a learned doctor, subtle, and well skilled in the art of devilry.

"At the time when I was a student in the university of Toulouse, that same reverend father in the devil, Picatrix, rector of the diabol-ical faculty, was wont to tell us, that the devils did naturally fear the bright glancing of swords, as much as the splendour and light of the sun. In confirmation of the verity whereof he related this story: That Hercules, at his descent into hell to all the devils of those regions, did not by half so much terrify them with his club and lion's skin, as afterwards Æneas did with his clear shining armour upon him, and his sword in his hand well furbished and unrusted, by the aid, and counsel and assistance of the Sybilla Cumana. That perhaps was the reason why the senior John James Trivolse, whilst he was dying at Chartres, called for his cutlass, and died with a drawn sword in his hand, laying about him alongst and athwart around the bed, and everywhere within his reach, like a stout, doughty, valorous and knight-like cavalier. By which resolute manner of fence he scared away and put to flight all the devils that were then lying in wait for his soul at the passage of his death. When the massorets and cabalists are asked, Why it is that none of all the devils do at any time enter into the terrestrial paradise? their answer hath been, is, and will be still, That there is a cherubim standing at the gate thereof, with a flame-like glistering sword in his hand. Although, to speak in the true diabolical sense or phrase of Toledo, I must needs confess and acknowledge, that veritably the devils cannot be killed, or die by the stroke of a sword: I do nevertheless avow and maintain, according to the doctrine of the said diabology, that they may suffer a solution of continuity, and (as if with thy sabre thou shouldst cut athwart the flame of a burning fire, or the gross opacous exhalations of a thick and obscure smoak,) cry out, like very devils, at their sense and feeling of this dissolution, which in real deed I must aver and affirm is devilish painful, smarting and dolorous.

"When thou seest the impetuous shock of two armies, and vehement violence of the push in the horrid encounter with one another; dost thou think, Ballockasso, that so horrible a noise as is heard there, proceedeth from the voice and shouts of men? The dashing and jolting of harness? The clattering and clashing of armies? The hacking and slashing of battle-axes? The justling and crashing of pikes? The bustling and breaking of lances? The clamour and shrieks of the wounded? The sound and din of drums? The clangour and shrillness of trumpets? The neighing and rushing in of horses? With the fearful claps and thundering of all sorts of guns, from the double cannon to the pocket pistol inclusively? I cannot, goodly, deny, but that in these various things which I have rehearsed, there may be somewhat occasionative of the huge yell and tintamarre, of the two engaged bodies.

"But the most fearful and tumultuous coil and stir, the terriblest and most boisterous garboil and hurry, the chiefest rustling black

334

santus of all, and most principal hurly burly, springeth from the grievously plangorous howling and lowing of devils, who pell-mell, in a hand-over-head confusion, waiting for the poor souls of the maimed and hurt soldiery, receive unawares some strokes with swords, and so by those means suffering a solution of, and division in, the continuity of their aërial and invisible substances: as if some lackey, snatching at the lardslices stuck in a piece of roast-meat on the spit, should get from Mr. Greasyfist a good rap on the knuckles with a cudgel, they cry out and shout like devils. Even as Mars did, when he was hurt by Diomedes at the siege of Troy, who (as Homer testifieth of him) did then raise his voice more horrifically loud, and sonoriferously high, than ten thousand men together would have been able to do. What maketh all this for our present purpose? I have been speaking here of well-furbished armour and bright shining swords. But so is it not, friar John, with thy weapon: for by a long discontinuance of work, cessation from labour, desisting from making it officiate, and putting it into that practice wherein it had been formerly accustomed; and in a word, for want of occupation, it is, upon my faith, become more rusty than the key-hole of an old powdering-tub. Therefore it is expedient that you do one of these two things; either furbish your weapon bravely, and as it ought to be, or otherwise have a care that in the rusty case it is in, you do not presume to return to the house of Raminagrobis. For my part, I vow I will not go thither, the devil take me if I go."

CHAPTER XXIV

HOW PANURGE CONSULTETH WITH EPISTEMON

HAVING left the town of Villaumere, as they were upon their return towards Pantagruel, Panurge, in addressing his discourse to Epistemon, spoke thus: "My most ancient friend and gossip, thou seest the perplexity of my thoughts, and knowest many remedies for the removal thereof; art thou not able to help and succour me?" Epistemon thereupon taking the speech in hand, represented unto Panurge, how the open voice and common fame of the whole country did run upon no other discourse, but the derision and mockery of his new disguise: wherefore his counsel unto him was, that he would in the first place be pleased to make use of a little Hellebore, for the

335

purging of his brain of that peccant humour, which, through that extravagant and fantastic mummery of his, had furnished the people with a too just occasion of flouting and gibing, jeering and scoffing him; and that next he would resume his ordinary fashion of accoutrement, and go apparelled as he was wont to do. "I am," quoth Panurge, "my dear gossip Epistemon, of a mind and resolution to marry; but am afraid of being a cuckold, and to be unfortunate in my wedlock: for this cause have I made a vow to young St. Francis (who at Plessis les Tours is much reverenced of all women, earnestly cried unto by them, and with great devotion; for he was the first founder of the confraternity of good men, whom they naturally covet, affect and long for), I say, I have vowed to him to wear spectacles in my cap, and to carry no codpiece in my breeches, until the present inquietude and perturbation of my spirits be fully settled."

"Truly," quoth Epistemon, "that is a pretty jolly vow, of thirteen to a dozen: it is a shame to you, and I wonder much at it, that you do not return unto yourself, and recal your senses from this their wild swerving and straying abroad, to that rest and stillness which becomes a virtuous man. This whimsical conceit of yours, brings me to the remembrance of a solemn promise, made by the shag-haired Argives, who having in their controversy against the Lacedemonians for the territory of Thyræa lost the battle, which they hoped should have decided it for their advantage, vowed to carry never any hair on their heads, till they had recovered the loss of both their honour and lands: as likewise to the memory of the vow of a pleasant Spaniard, called Michael Doris, who vowed to carry in his hat a piece of the skin of his leg, til he should be revenged of him who had struck it off. Yet do not I know which of these two deserveth most to wear a green and yellow hood, with a hare's ears tied to it, either the aforesaid vain-glorious champion, or that Enguerrant, who having forgot the art and manner of writing histories, set down by the Samosatian philosopher, maketh a most tediously long narrative and relation thereof. For at the first reading of such a profuse discourse, one would think it had been broached for the introducing of a story of great importance and moment, concerning the waging of some formidable war, or the notable change and mutation of potent states and kingdoms; but in conclusion, the world laughed at the capricious champion, at the Englishman who had affronted him, as also at their scribbler Enguerrant, more drivelling at the mouth than a mustardpot. The jest and scorn thereof is not unlike to that of the mountain of Horace, which by the poet was made to cry out and lament most enormously, as a woman in the pangs and labour of child-birth; at which deplorable and exorbitant cries and lamentations the whole neighbourhood being assembled, in expectation to see some marvellous monstrous production, could at last perceive no other but a paltry ridiculous mouse."

"Your mousing," quoth Panurge, "will not make me leave my musing why folks should be so frumpishly disposed; seeing I am certainly persuaded that some flout, who merit to be flouted at: yet as my vow imports, so will I do. It is now a long time since, by Jupiter, we did swear faith and amity to one another: give me your advice, Billy, and tell me your opinion freely, should I marry or no?"

"Truly," quoth Epistemon, "the cause is hazardous, and the danger so eminently apparent, that I find myself too weak and insufficient to give you a punctual and peremptory resolution therein; and if ever it was true, that the judgment is difficult (in matters of the medicinal art, as was said by Hippocrates of Lango) it is certainly so in this case. True it is that in my brain there are some rolling fancies, by means whereof somewhat may be pitched upon of a seeming efficacy to the disentangling your mind of those dubious apprehensions, wherewith it is perplexed; but they do not thoroughly satisfy me. Some of the platonic sect affirm, that whosoever is able to see his proper genius, may know his own destiny. I understand not their doctrine; nor do I think that you adhere to them: there is a palpable abuse. I have seen the experience of it in a very curious gentleman of the country of Estangourre. This is the first point. There is yet another, not much better. If there were any authority now in the oracles of Apollo in Lebadia, Delphos, Delos, Cyrrha, Patara, Tegyres, Preneste, Lycia, Colophon; of Bacchus in Dodona; of Mercury in Phares, near Patras; of Apis, in Egypt; of Serapis in Canopie; of Faunus in Menalia, and Albunes near Tivoli; of Tiresias in Orchomente; of Mopsus in Cilicia; of Orpheus in Lesbos; and of Trophonius in Leucadia: I would in that case advise you, and possibly not, to go thither for their judgment concerning the design and enterprise you have in hand. But you know that they are all of them become as dumb as so many fishes since the advent of that Saviour King, whose coming to this world hath made all oracles and prophecies to cease; as the approach of the sun's radiant beams expelleth goblins, bugbears, hobthrushes, broams, screech-owl-mates, night-walking spirits, and tenbrions. These now are gone: but although they were as yet in con-

337

tinuance, and in the same power, rule and request that formerly they were; yet would not I counsel you to be too credulous in putting any trust in their responses: too many folks have been deceived thereby. It stands furthermore upon record, how Agrippina did charge the fair Lollia with the crime of having interrogated the oracle of Apollo Clarius, to understand if she could be at any time married to the emperor Claudius: for which cause she was first banished, and thereafter put to a shameful and ignominious death."

"But," said Panurge, "let us do better. The Ogygian islands are not far distant from the haven of Sammalo: let us, after that we shall have spoken to our king, make a voyage thither. In one of those four isles, to wit, that which hath its primest aspect towards the sun-setting, it is reported (and I have read in good antique and authentic authors) that there reside many sooth-sayers, fortune-tellers, vaticinators, prophets, and diviners of things to come; that Saturn inhabiteth that place, bound with fair chains of gold, and within the concavity of a golden rock, being nourished with divine ambrosia and nectar, which are daily in great store and abundance transmitted to him from the heavens, by I do not well know what kind of fowls (it may be that they are the same ravens, which in the deserts are said to have fed St. Paul, the first hermit), he very clearly foretelleth unto every one, who is desirous to be certified of the condition of his lot, what his destiny will be, and what future chance the fates have ordained for him: for the parcæ or weard sisters do not twist, spin, or draw out a thread; nor yet doth Jupiter perpend, project, or deliberate anything, which the good old celestial father knoweth not the full, even whilst he is asleep. This will be a very summary abbreviation of our labour, if we but hearken unto him a little upon the serious debate and canvassing of this my perplexity." "That is," answered Epistemon, "a gullery too evident, a plain abuse, and a fib too fabulous. I will not go, not I, I will not go."

CHAPTER XXV

HOW PANURGE CONSULTETH WITH HER TRIPPA

NEVERTHELESS," quoth Epistemon, continuing his discourse, "I will tell you what you may do, if you will be ruled by me, before we return to our king. Hard by here, in the brown-wheat island (Bouchart) dwelleth Her Trippa. You know how, by the arts of astrology, geomancy, chiromancy, and others of a like stuff and nature, he fortelleth all things to come: let us talk a little, and confer with him about your business." "Of that," answered Panurge, "I know nothing. But of this much concerning him I am assured, that one day, and that not long since, whilst he was prating to the great king of celestial, sublime, and transcendent things, the lacqueys and footboys of the court, upon the upper steps of stairs between two doors, jumbled one after another, as often as they listed, his wife; who is a passable, fair, and pretty snug hussey. Thus he, who seemed very clearly to see all heavenly and terrestrial things without spectacles, who discoursed boldly of adventures past, with great confidence opened up present cases and accidents, and stoutly professed the presaging of all future events and contingencies, was not able, with all the skill and cunning that he had, to perceive the bumbasting of his wife, whom he reputed to be very chaste; and hath not, till this hour, got notice of anything to the contrary. Yet let us go to him, seeing you will have it so: for surely we can never learn too much."

They, on the very next ensuing day, went to Her Trippa's lodging. Panurge, by way of donative, presented him with a long gown lined all through with wolves-skins, with a short sword mounted with a gilded hilt, and covered with a velvet scabbard, and with fifty good single angels: then, in a familiar and friendly way, did he ask of him his opinion touching the affair. At the very first Her Trippa, looking on him very wistly in the face, said unto him; "Thou hast the metoposcopy and physiognomy of a cuckold; I say, of a notorious and infamous cuckold." With this, casting an eye on Panurge's right hand in all the parts thereof, he said; "This rugged draught which I see here, just over the mount of Jove, was never yet but in the hand of a cuckold." Afterwards he, with a white lead pencil, swiftly and hastily drew a certain number of diverse kinds of points, which by rules of geomancy he coupled and joined together; then said, "Truth itself is not truer, than that it is certain thou wilt be a cuckold, a little after thy marriage." That being done, he asked of Panurge the horoscope of his nativity: which was no sooner by Panurge tendered unto him, than that, erecting a figure, he very promptly and speedily formed and fashioned a complete fabric of the houses of heaven, in all their parts; whereof when he had considered the situation and the aspects in their triplicities, he fetched a deep sigh, and said: "I have clearly enough already discovered unto you the fate of your cuckoldry, which is unavoidable; you cannot escape it; and here have I got a new and further assurance thereof: so that I may now hardly pronounce, and affirm without any scruple or hesitation at all, that thou wilt be a cuckold; that furthermore, thou wilt be beaten by thine own wife, and that she will purloin, filch, steal of thy goods from thee: for I find the seventh house, in all its aspects, of a malignant influence, and every one of the planets threatening thee with disgrace, according as they stand seated towards one another, in relation to the horned signs of Aries, Taurus, Capricorn, and others: in the fourth house I find Jupiter in a decadence, as also in a tertagonal aspect to Saturn, associated with Mercury. Thou wilt be soundly peppered, my good honest fellow, I warrant thee." "Shall I so?" answered Panurge: "a plague rot thee, thou old fool, and doating sot, how graceless and unpleasant thou art.

"When all cuckolds shall be at a general rendezvous, thou shalt be their standard-bearer. But whence comes this ciron-worm betwixt these two fingers?" This Panurge said, holding towards Her Trippa his two fore-fingers open after the manner of two horns, and shutting into his palm, his thumb, with the other fingers. Then in turning to Epistemon, he said, "Lo, here the true Olus of Martial, who addicted and devoted himself wholly to the observing the miseries, crosses, and calamities of others; whilst his own wife, in the interim, did keep an open bawdyhouse.

"This varlet is poorer than ever Irus was, and yet he is proud, vaunting, arrogant, self-conceited, over-weening, and more insupportable than seventeen devils: in one word, a very πτωχαλάζων: which term of old was applied to the like beggarly strutting cox-combs.

"Come, let us leave this madpash bedlam, this hare-brained fop, and give him leave to rave and doze his belly-full, with his private and intimately acquainted devils; who, if they were not the very worst of all the infernal fiends, would never have deigned to serve such a knavish, barking cur as this is. He hath not learnt the first precept of philosophy, which is, 'Know thyself': for whilst he braggeth and boasteth, that he can discern the least mote in the eye of another, he is not able to see the huge block that puts out the sight of both his eyes. This is such another Polypragmon, as is by Plutarch described: he is of the nature of the Lamian witches, who in foreign places, in the houses of strangers, in public, and amongst the common people, had a sharper and more piercing inspection into their affairs than any lynx; but at home, in their own proper dwelling mansions, were

340

blinder than molewarps, and saw nothing at all: for their custom was at their return from abroad, when they were by themselves in private, to take their eyes out of their head, from whence they were as easily removable as a pair of spectacles from their nose, and to lay them up into a wooden slipper, which for that purpose did hang behind the door of their lodging."

Panurge had no sooner done speaking, when Her Trippa took into his hand a tamarisk branch. "In this," quoth Epistemon, "he doth very well, right, and like an artist; for Nicander calleth it the divinatory tree." "Have you a mind," quoth Her Trippa, "to have the truth of the matter yet more fully and amply disclosed unto you by pyromancy, by aeromancy, (whereof Aristophanes in his Clouds maketh great estimation) by hydromancy, by lecanomancy, of old in prime request amongst the Assyrians, and thoroughly tried by Hermolaus Barbarus? Come hither, and I will shew thee, in this platter-full of fair fountain-water, thy future wife, lechering, and secroupiersing (buttocking it) with two swaggering ruffians, one after another." "Yea, but have a special care," quoth Panurge, "when thou comest to put thy nose within my arse, that thou forget not to pull off thy spectacles." Her Trippa going on in his discourse, said: "By catoptromancy, likewise held in such account by the emperor Didius Julianus, that by means thereof he ever and anon foresaw all that which at any time did happen or befal unto him. Thou shalt not need to put on thy spectacles: for in a mirror thou wilt see her as clearly and manifestly nebrundiated, and billibodring it, as if I should shew it in the fountain of the temple of Minerva near Patras. By coscinomancy, most religiously observed of old, amidst the ceremonies of the ancient Romans. Let us have a sieve and shears, and thou shalt see devils. By alphitomancy, cried up by Theocritus in his pharmaceutria. By alentomancy, mixing the flour of wheat with oatmeal. By astragalomancy, whereof I have the plots and models all at hand ready for the purpose. By tyromancy, whereof we make some proof in a great Brehemont cheese, which I here keep by me. By giromancy, if thou shouldst turn round circles, thou mightest assure thyself from me, that they would fall always on the wrong side. By sternomancy, which maketh nothing for thy advantage for thou hast an ill-proportioned stomach. By libanomancy, for the which we shall need but a little frankincense. By gastromancy, which kind of ventral fatiloquency was for a long time together used in Ferrara, by lady Giacoma Rodogina, the engastrimythian prophetess. By cephalomancy, often practised amongst the High Germans, in their boiling of an ass's head upon burning coals. By ceromancy, where, by the means of wax dissolved into water, thou shalt see the figure, portrait, and lively representation of thy future wife, and of her fredin fredaliatory belly-thumping blades. By capnomancy: O the gallantest and most excellent of all secrets! By axionomancy: we want only a hatchet and a jet-stone to be laid together upon a quick fire of hot embers. O how bravely Homer was versed in the practice hereof towards Penelope's suiters! By onymancy; for that we have oil and wax. By tephromancy; thou wilt see the ashes, thus aloft dispersed, exhibiting thy wife in a fine posture. By botonomancy; for the nonce I have some few leaves in reserve. By sicomancy: O divine art in fig-tree leaves! By icthyomancy, in ancient times so celebrated, and put in use by Tireias and Polydamus, with the like certainty of event as was tried of old at the Dina-ditch, within that grove consecrated to Apollo, which is in the territory of the Lycians. By choiromancy; let us have a great many hogs, and thou shalt have the bladder of one of them. By cheromancy, as the bean is found in the cake at the epiphany vigil. By anthropomancy, practised by the Roman emperor Heliogabalus; it is somewhat irksome, but thou wilt endure it well enough, seeing thou art destinated to be a cuckold. By a sybilline stichomancy. By onomatomancy. How do they call thee?" "Chaw-turd," quoth Panurge. "Or else by alectryomancy. If I should here with a compass draw a round, and in looking upon thee, and considering thy lot, divide the circumference thereof into four and twenty equal parts, then form a several letter of the alphabet upon every one of them; and lastly, posit a barley corn or two upon each of these so-disposed letters; I durst promise, upon my faith and honesty, that if a young virgin cock be permitted to range alongst and athwart them, he should only eat the grains which are set and placed upon these letters, A. c.u.c.k. o.l.d. t.h.o.u. s.h.a.l.t. b.e. And that as fatidically, as under the emperor Valens, most perplexedly desirous to know the name of him, who should be his successor to the empire, the cock vaticinating and alectryomantic, ate up only the grains that were posited on the letters Θ. E. O. Δ. T.h.e.o.d. Or, for the more certainty, will you have a trial of your fortune by the art of aruspiciny? By augury? or by extispicine?" "By turdispicine," quoth Panurge. "Or yet by the mystery of necromancy? I will, if you please, suddenly set up again, and revive some one lately deceased: as Apollonius of Tyana did to Achilles, and the Pythoness in the presence of Saul; which body so raised up and requickened, will tell us the sum of all you shall require of him; no more nor less than at the invocation of Erictho, a certain defunct person foretold to Pompey the whole progress and issue of the fatal battle fought in the Pharsalian fields. Or, if you be afraid of the dead, as commonly all cuckolds are, I will make use of the faculty of sciomancy." "Go, get thee gone," quoth Panurge, "thou frantic ass, to the devil, and be buggered, filthy bardachio that thou art, by some Albanian for a steeple-crowned hat. Why the devil didst not thou counsel me as well to hold an emerald, or the stone of a hyena under my tongue? Or to furnish and provide myself with tongues of whoops, and hearts of green frogs? Or to eat of the liver and milt of some dragon? To the end that by those means I might, at the chanting and chirping of swans and other fowls, understand the substance of my future lot and destiny, as did of old the Arabians in the country of Mesopotamia? Fifteen brace of devils seize upon the body and soul of this horned renegado, miscreant cuckold, the enchanter, witch, and sorcerer of antichrist; away to all the devils of hell.

"Let us return towards our king: I am sure he will not be well pleased with us, if he once come to get notice that we have been in the kennel of this muffled devil. I repent my being come hither. I would willingly dispense with a hundred nobles, and fourteen yeomans, on condition that he, who not long since did blow in the bottom of my breeches, should instantly with his squirting spittle inluminate his mustaches. O Lord God! how the villain hath besmoaked me with vexation and anger, with charms and witchcraft, and with a terrible coil and stir of infernal and tartarian devils! The devil take him! Say amen; and let us go drink. I shall not have any appetite for my victuals (how good cheer soever I make) these two days to come; hardly these four."

CHAPTER XXVI

HOW PANURGE CONSULTETH WITH FRIAR JOHN OF THE FUNNELS

PANURGE was indeed very much troubled in mind, and disquieted at the words of Her Trippa, and therefore as he passed by the little village of Huymes, after he had made his address to friar

John, in pecking at, rubbing and scratching his own left ear, he said unto him; "Keep me a little jovial and merry, my dear and sweet bully: for I find my brains altogether metagrabolized and confounded, and my spirits in a most dunsical puzzle at the bitter talk of this devilish, hellish, damned fool. Hearken, my dainty cod,

Mellow c.	Furious c.	Poudred beef c.
Lead-coloured c.	Packed c.	Positive c.
Knurled c.	Hooded c.	Spared c.
Suborned c.	Varnished c.	Bold c.
Desired c.	Renowned c.	Lascivious c.
Stuffed c.	Matted c.	Gluttonous c.
Speckled c.	Genetive c.	Resolute c.
Finley mettled c.	Gigantal c.	Cabbage-like c.
Arabian-like c.	Oval c.	Courteous c.
Trussed-up-grey-	Claustral c.	Fertil c.
hound-like c.	Viril c.	Whizzing c.
Mounted c.	Stayed c.	Neat c.
Sleeked c.	Massive c.	Common c.
Diapred c.	Manual c.	Brisk c.
Sotted c.	Absolute c.	Quick c.
Master c.	Well-set c.	Barelike c.
Seeded c.	Gemel c.	Partitional c.
Lusty c.	Turkish c.	Patronymic c.
Jupped c.	Burning c.	Cockney c.
Milked c.	Thwacking c.	Auromercuriated c.
Calfeted c.	Urgent c.	Robust c.
Raised c.	Handsome c.	Appetizing c.
Odd c.	Prompt c.	Succourable c.
Steeled c.	Fortunate c.	Redoubtable c.
Stale c.	Boxwood c.	Affable c.
Orange-tawny c.	Latten c.	Memorable c.
Embroidered c.	Unbridled c.	Palpable c.
Glazed c.	Hooked c.	Barbable c.
Interlarded c.	Researched c.	Tragical c.
Burger-like c.	Encompassed c.	Transpontine c.
Impoudred c.	Strouting out c.	Digestive c.
Ebonized c.	Jolly c.	Active c.
Brasiliated c.	Lively c.	Vital c.
Organized c.	Gerundive c.	Magistral c.
Passable c.	Franked c.	Monachal c.
Trunkified c.	Polished c.	Subtil c.

344

Hammering c.
Clashing c.
Tingling c.
Usual c.
Exquisite c.
Trim c.
Succulent c.
Factious c.
Clammy c.
Fat c.
High-prized c.
Requisite c.
Laycod c.
Hand-filling c.
Insuperable c.
Agreeable c.
Formidable c.
Profitable c.
Notable c.
Musculous c.
Subsidiary c.
Satyrick c.
Repercussive c.
Convulsive c.
Restorative c.
Masculinating c.
Incarnative c.
Sigillative c.
Sallying c.
Plump c.
Thundering c.
Lechering c.
Fulminating c.
Sparkling c.
Ramming c.
Lusty c.
Household c.
Pretty c.
Astrolabian c.
Algebraical c.
Venust c.

Aromatizing c.
Trixy c.
Paillard c.
Gaillard c.
Broaching c.
Addle c.
Syndicated c.
Boulting c.
Snorting c.
Pilfering c.
Shaking c.
Bobbing c.
Chiveted c.
Fumbling c.
Topsiturvying c.
Raging c.
Piled up c.
Filled up c.
Manly c.
Idle c.
Membrous c.
Strong c.
Twin c.
Belabouring c.
Gentil c.
Stirring c.
Confident c.
Nimble c.
Roundheaded c.
Figging c.
Helpful c.
Spruce c.
Plucking c.
Ramage c.
Fine c.
Fierce c.
Brawny c.
Compt c.
Repaired c.
Soft c.
Wild c.

Renewed c.
Quaint c.
Starting c.
Fleshy c.
Auxiliary c.
New vamped c.
Improved c.
Malling c.
Sounding c.
Batled c.
Burly c.
Seditious c.
Wardian c.
Protective c.
Twinkling c.
Able c.
Algoristical c.
Odoriferous c.
Pranked c.
Jocund c.
Routing c.
Purloining c.
Frolic c.
Wagging c.
Ruffling c.
Jumbling c.
Rumbling c.
Thumping c.
Bumping c.
Cringeling c.
Berumpling c.
Jogging c.
Nobbing c.
Touzing c.
Tumbling c.
Fambling c.
Overturning c.
Shooting c.
Culeting c.
Jagged c.
Pinked c.

Arsiversing c.	Affected c.	Superlative c.
Polished c.	Grapled c.	Clashing c.
Slashed c.	Stuffed c.	Wagging c.
Hamed c.	Well-fed c.	Scriplike c.
Leisurely c.	Flourished c.	Encremastered c.
Cut c.	Fallow c.	Bouncing c.
Smooth c.	Sudden c.	Levelling c.
Depending c.	Grasp-full c.	Fly-flap c.
Independent c.	Swillpow c.	Perinæ-tegminal c.
Lingring c.	Crushing c.	Squat-coughing c.
Rapping c.	Creaking c.	Short-hung c.
Reverend c.	Dilting c.	Hypogastrian c.
Nodding c.	Ready c.	Witness bearing c.
Disseminating c.	Vigorous c.	Testigerous c.
Affecting c.	Scoulking c.	Instrumental c.

"My harcabuzing cod, and buttock-stirring ballock, friar John, my friend; I do carry a singular respect unto thee, and honour thee with all my heart; thy counsel I hold for a choice and delicate morsel: therefore have I reserved it for the last bit. Give me thy advice freely, I beseech thee; should I marry, or no?" Friar John, very merrily, and with a sprightly cheerfulness, made this answer to him: "Marry in the devil's name; why not? What the devil else should'st thou do, but marry? Take thee a wife, and furbish her harness to some tune: swinge her skin-coat, as if thou wert beating on stock-fish; and let the repercussion of thy clapper, from her resounding metal, make a noise, as if a double peal of chiming-bells were hung at the cremasters of thy ballocks. As I say, marry, so do I understand, that thou should'st fall to work as speedily as may be: yea, my meaning is, that thou oughtest to be so quick and forward therein, as on this same very day, before sun-set, to cause proclaim thy banns of matrimony, and make provision of bedsteads. By the blood of a hog's-pudding, till when should'st thou delay the acting of a husband's part? Dost thou not know, and is it not daily told unto thee, that the end of the world approacheth? We are nearer by three poles, and half a fathom, than we were two days ago. The antichrist is already born, at least is so reported by many. The truth is, that hitherto the effects of his wrath have not reached farther than to the scratching of his nurse and governesses; his nails are not sharp enough as yet, nor have his claws attained to their full growth: he is little.

346

Crescat; nos qui vivimus, multiplicemur.

It is written so, and it is holy stuff, I warrant you: the truth whereof is like to last as long as a sack of corn may be had for a penny, and a puncheon of pure wine for three-pence. Would'st thou be content to be found with thy genitories full in the day of judgment? *Dum venerit judicare."* "Thou hast," quoth Panurge, "a right, clear, and neat spirit, friar John, my metropolitan cod; thou speak'st in very deed pertinently, and to purpose: that belike was the reason which moved Leander of Abydos, in Asia, whilst he was swimming through the Hellespontic sea, to make a visit to his sweetheart, Hero, of Sestus, in Europe, to pray unto Neptune, and all the other marine gods, thus:

"Now, whilst I go, have pity on me,
And at my back returning drown me.

"He was loath, it seems, to die with his cods overgorged. He was to be commended. Therefore do I promise, that from henceforth no malefactor shall by justice be executed within my jurisdiction of Salmigondinois, who shall not for a day or two at least before, be permitted to culbut, and foraminate, onocrotalwise, that there remain not in all his vessels, to write a Greek Y. Such a precious thing should not be foolishly cast away. He will perhaps therewith beget a male, and so depart the more contentedly out of this life, that he shall have left behind him one for one."

CHAPTER XXVII

HOW FRIAR JOHN MERRILY AND SPORTINGLY COUNSELLETH PANURGE

BY saint Rigomé," quoth friar John, "I do advise thee to nothing, my dear friend Panurge, which I would not do myself, were I in thy place. Only have a special care, and take good heed thou solder well together the joints of the double-backed, and two-bellied beast, and fortify thy nerves so strongly, that there be no discontinuance in the knocks of the venerean thwacking: else thou art lost, poor soul: for if there pass long intervals betwixt the priapising feats, and that thou make an intermission of too long a time, that will befal thee, which betides the nurses, if they desist from giving suck to children; they lose their milk: and if continually thou do not hold thy aspersory tool in exercise, and keep thy metal going, thy lacticinian nectar will be gone, and it will serve thee only as a pipe to piss out at, and thy cods for a wallet of lesser value than a beggar's scrip. This is certain truth, I tell thee, friend, and doubt not of it: for myself have seen the sad experiment thereof in many, who cannot now do what they would, because before they did not want what they might have done. *Ex desuetudine amittuntur privilegia:* non-usage oftentimes destroys one's right, say the learned doctors of the law. Therefore, my Billy, entertain as well as possibly thou canst, that hypogastrian, lower sort of troglodytic people, that their chief pleasure may be placed in the case of sempiternal labouring. Give order that henceforth they live not like idle gentlemen, idly upon their rents and revenues; but that they may work for their livelihood, by breaking ground within the Paphian trenches." "Nay, truly," answered Panurge, "friar John, my left ballock, I will believe thee; for thou dealest plain with me, and fallest downright square upon the business, without going about the bush with frivolous circumstances, and unnecessary reservations. Thou, with the splendour of a piercing wit, hast dissipated all the louring clouds of anxious apprehensions and suspicions which did intimidate and terrify me: therefore the heavens be pleased to grant to thee, at all she conflicts, a stiff-standing fortune. Well then, as thou hast said, so will I do: I will, in good faith, marry: in that point there shall be no failing, I promise thee; and I shall have always by me pretty girls cloathed with the name of my wife's waiting-maids, that lying under thy wings, thou mayest be night-protector of their sister-hood when thou comest to see me."

"Let this serve for the first part of the sermon. Hearken," quoth friar John, "to the oracle of the bells of Varenes: What say they?" "I hear and understand them," quoth Panurge: "their sound is, by my thirst, more uprightly fatidical, than that of Jove's great kettles in Dodona. Hearken! 'Take thee a wife, take thee a wife, and marry, marry: for if thou marry, thou shalt find good therein; here in a wife thou shalt find good; so marry, marry.' I will assure thee, that I will be married; all the elements invite and prompt me to it: let this word be to thee a brazen wall, by diffidence not to be broken through. As for the second part of this our doctrine: thou seemest in some measure to mistrust the readiness of my paternity, in the practising of my placket-racket within the aphrodisian tennis-court at all times

348

fitting, as if the stiff god of gardens were not favourable to me. I pray thee, favour me so much as to believe, that I still have him at a beck, attending always my commandments, docile, obedient, vigorous, and active in all things, and everywhere, and never stubborn or refractory to my will or pleasure.

"I need no more but let go the reins, and slacken the leash, which is the belly-point, and when the game is shewn unto him, say, 'Hey, Jack, to thy booty!' he will not fail even then to flesh himself upon his prey, and tuzzle it to some purpose. Hereby you may perceive, although my future wife were as unsatiable and guttonous in her voluptuousness, and the delights of venery, as ever was the empress Messalina, or yet the marchioness of Oincester in England; yet I desire thee to give credit to it, that I lack not for what is requisite to overlay the stomach of her lust, but have wherewith aboundingly to please her.

"I am not ignorant that Solomon said, who indeed of that matter speaketh clerk-like and learnedly, as also how Aristotle after him declared for a truth, that the lechery of a woman is ravenous and unsatisfiable: nevertheless, let such as are my friends, who read those passages, receive from me for a most real verity, that I for such a Gill, have a fit Jack; and that, if women's things cannot be satiated, I have an instrument indefatigable; an implement as copious in the giving, as can in craving be their vade mecums. Do not here produce ancient examples of the paragons of paillardise, and offer to match with my testiculatory ability, the priapæan prowess of the fabulous fornicators, Hercules, Proculus Cæsar, Mahomet, who in his koran doth vaunt that in his cods he had the vigour of threescore bully-ruffians: but let no zealous Christian trust the rogue; the filthy ribald rascal is a liar. Nor shalt thou need to urge authorities, or bring forth the instance of the Indian prince, of whom Theophrastus, Pliny, and Athenæus testify, that, with the help of a certain herb, he was able, and had given frequent experiments thereof, to toss his sinewy piece of generation, in the act of carnal concupiscence, above threescore and ten times in the space of four and twenty hours. Of that I believe nothing; the number is supposititious, and too prodigally foisted in: give no faith unto it, I beseech thee; but prithee trust me in this, and thy credulity therein shall not be wronged; for it is true, and probatum est, that my pioneer of nature, the sacred ithyphallion champion, is of all stiff-intruding blades the primest: come hither, my ballockette, and hearken. Didst thou ever see the monk of Castre's cowl? When

349

in any house it was laid down, whether openly in the view of all, or covertly out of the sight of any, such was the ineffable virtue thereof, for exciting and stirring up the people of both sexes unto lechery, that the whole inhabitants and indwellers, not only of that, but likewise of all the circumjacent places thereto, within three leagues around it, did suddenly enter into rut, both beasts and folks, men and women, even to the dogs and hogs, rats and cats.

"I swear to thee, that many times heretofore I have perceived, and found in my codpiece a certain kind of energy, or efficacious virtue, much more irregular, and of a greater anomaly, than what I have related: I will not speak to thee either of house or cottage, nor of church or market, but only tell thee, that once, at the representation of the passion, which was acted at St. Maxent's, I had no sooner entered within the pit of the theatre, but that forthwith, by the virtue and occult property of it, on a sudden all that were there, both players and spectators, did fall into such an exorbitant temptation of lust, that there was not angel, man, devil, nor deviless, upon the place, who would not then have bricollitched it with all their heart and soul.

"The prompter forsook his copy; he who played St. Michael's part, came down to rights; the devils issued out of hell, and carried along with them most of the pretty little girls that were there: yea, Lucifer got out of his fetters: in a word, seeing the huge disorder, I disparked myself forth of that inclosed place, in imitation of Cato the censor, who perceiving, by reason of his presence, the floralian festivals out of order, withdrew himself."

CHAPTER XXVIII

HOW FRIAR JOHN COMFORTETH PANURGE IN THE DOUBTFUL MATTER OF CUCKOLDRY

I UNDERSTAND thee well enough," said friar John; "but *time makes all things plain.* The most durable marble or porphyry is subject to old age and decay. Though, for the present, thou possibly be not weary of the exercise, yet is it like I shall hear thee confess, a few years hence, that thy cods hang dangling downwards for want of a better truss. I see thee waxing a little hoar-headed already: thy beard, by the distinction of grey, white, tawny, and black, hath, to my thinking, the resemblance of a map of the terrestrial globe, or geographical chart. Look attentively upon, and take inspection of what I shall shew unto thee. Behold there Asia; here are Tigris and Euphrates: lo there Afric; here is the mountain of the moon: yonder thou mayest perceive the fenny marshes of Nilus; on this side lieth Europe. Dost thou not see the Abbey of Thelema? This little tuft, which is altogether white, is the Hyperborean Hills. By the thirst of my throple, friend, when snow is on the mountains (I mean the head and the chin), there is not then any considerable heat to be expected in the valleys and low-countries of the codpiece." "By the kibes of thy heels," quoth Panurge, "thou dost not understand the topics. When the snow is on the tops of the hills, lightning, thunder, tempest, whirlwinds, storms, hurricanes, and all the devils of hell, rage in the valleys. Wouldst thou see the experience thereof, go to the territory of the Swissers, and earnestly perpend with thyself there the situation of the Lake of Wunderberlich, about four leagues distant from Berne, on the Sion side of the land. Thou twittest me with my grey hairs, yet considerest not how I am of the nature of leeks, which, with a white head, carry a green, fresh, straight, and vigorous tail.

"The truth is, nevertheless (why should I deny it?), that I now and then discern in myself some indicative signs of old age. Tell this, I prithee, to nobody, but let it be kept very close and secret betwixt us two; for I find the wine much sweeter now, more savoury to my taste, and unto my palate of a better relish, than formerly I was wont to do; and withal, besides mine accustomed manner, I have a more dreadful apprehension, than I ever heretofore have had, of lighting on bad wine. Note and observe, that this doth argue and portend I know not what of the west and occident of my time, and signifieth that the south and meridian of mine age is past. But what then, my gentle companion? That doth but betoken that I shall hereafter drink so much the more. That is not, the devil hale it, the thing that I fear; not is it there where my shoe pinches. The thing, that I doubt most, and have greatest reason to dread and suspect, is, that, through some long absence of our King Pantagruel (to whom I must needs bear company, should he go to all the devils of Barathum), my future wife will make me a cuckold. This is, in truth, the long and the short of it; for I am, by all those whom I have spoke to, menaced and threatened with a horned fortune; and all of them affirm it is the lot to which from heaven I am predestinated." "Every one," answered friar John, "that would be a cuckold, is not one. If it be thy fate to be hereafter of the number of that horned cattle, then may I conclude with an *ergo*, thy wife will be beautiful, and *ergo* thou wilt be kindly used by her: likewise with this *ergo* thou shalt be blessed with the fruition of many friends and well-willers; and finally with this other *ergo* thou shalt be saved and have a place in Paradise. These are monachal topics and maxims of the cloister: thou mayst take more liberty to sin: thou shalt be more at ease than ever: there will be never the less left for thee. Nothing diminished, but the goods shall increase notably; and, if so be it was pre-ordinated for thee, wouldst thou be so impious as not to acquiesce in thy destiny? Speak, thou jaded cod,

Faded c.	Broken-reined c.	Mitified c.
Mouldy c.	Defective c.	Goat-ridden c.
Musty c.	Crest-fallen c.	Weakened c.
Paultry c.	Felled c.	Ass-ridden c.
Senseless c.	Fleeted c.	Puff-pasted c.
Foundered c.	Cloyed c.	St. Antonified c.
Distempered c.	Squeezed c.	Untriped c.
Bewrayed c.	Resty c.	Blasted c.
Inveigled c.	Pounded c.	Cut-off c.
Dangling c.	Loose c.	Beveraged c.
Stupid c.	Coldish c.	Scarified c.
Seedless c.	Pickled c.	Dashed c.
Soaked c.	Churned c.	Slashed c.
Louting c.	Filiped c.	Infeebled c.
Discouraged c.	Singlefied c.	Whore-hunting c.
Surfeited c.	Begrimed c.	Deteriorated c.
Peevish c.	Wrinkled c.	Chill c.
Translated c.	Fainted c.	Scrupulous c.
Forlorn c.	Extenuated c.	Crazed c.
Unsavoury c.	Grim c.	Tasteless c.
Worm-eaten c.	Wasted c.	Hacked c.
Over-toiled c.	Inflamed c.	Flaggy c.
Miserable c.	Unhinged c.	Scrubby c.
Steeped c.	Scurfy c.	Drained c.
Kneaded with cold water c.	Straddling c.	Haled c.
Appealant c.	Putrified c.	Lolling c.
Swagging c.	Maimed c.	Drenched c.
Withered c.	Over-lechered c.	Burst c.
	Druggely c.	Stirred up c.

352

Mitred c.
Pedlingly furnished c.
Rusty c.
Exhausted c.
Perplexed c.
Unhelved c.
Fizzled c.
Leprous c.
Bruised c.
Spadonic c.
Boughty c.
Mealy c.
Wrangling c.
Gangreened c.
Crustrissen c.
Ragged c.
Quelled c.
Braggadochio c.
Beggarly c.
Trepanned c.
Bedusked c.
Emasculated c.
Corked c.
Transparent c.
Vile c.
Antedated c.
Chopped c.
Pinked c.
Cup-glassified c.
Fruitless c.
Riven c.
Pursy c.
Fusty c.
Jadish c.
Fistulous c.
Languishing c.
Maleficiated c.
Hectic c.
Worn-out c.
Ill-favoured c.

Duncified c.
Macerated c.
Paralytic c.
Degraded c.
Benumbed c.
Bat-like c.
Fart-shotten c.
Sun-burnt c.
Pacified c.
Blunted c.
Rankling-tasted c.
Rooted-out c.
Costive c.
Hailed-on c.
Cuffed c.
Buffeted c.
Whirreted c.
Robbed c.
Neglected c.
Lame c.
Confused c.
Unsavoury c.
Overthrown c.
Boulted c.
Trod-under c.
Desolate c.
Declining c.
Stinking c.
Sorrowful c.
Murthered c.
Matachin-like c.
Besotted c.
Customerless c.
Minced c.
Exulcerated c.
Patched c.
Stupefied c.
Annihilated c.
Spent c.
Foiled c.

Aguish c.
Disfigured c.
Disabled c.
Forceless c.
Censured c.
Cut c.
Rifled c.
Undone c.
Corrected c.
Slit c.
Skittish c.
Spungy c
Botched c.
Dejected c.
Jagged c.
Pining c.
Deformed c.
Mischieved c
Cobbled c
Imbased c.
Ransacked c.
Despised c.
Mangey c.
Abased c.
Supine c.
Mended c.
Dismayed c.
Harsh c.
Beaten c.
Barred c.
Abandoned c.
Confounded c.
Loutish c.
Borne-down c
Sparred c.
Abashed c.
Unreasonable c.
Oppressed c.
Grated c.
Falling-away c.

Small-cut c.
Disordered c.
Latticed c.
Ruined c.
Exasperated c.
Rejected c.
Belamed c.
Febricitant c.
Perused c
Emasculated c.
Roughly-handled c.
Examined c.
Cracked c.
Wayward c.
Hagled c.
Gleaning c.
Ill-favoured c.
Pulled c.
Drooping c.
Faint c.
Parched c.
Paultry c.
Cankered c.
Void c.
Vexed c.
Bestunk c.
Crooked c.
Brabling c.
Rotten c.
Anxious c.
Clouted c.
Tired c.
Proud c.
Fractured c.
Melancholy c.
Coxcombly c.
Base c.
Bleaked c.
Detested c
Turned-over c.

Harried c.
Flawed c.
Froward c.
Ugly c.
Drawn c.
Riven c.
Distasteful c.
Hanging c.
Broken c.
Limber c.
Effeminate c.
Kindled c.
Evacuated c.
Grieved c.
Carking c.
Disorderly c.
Empty c.
Bisquoted c.
Desisted c.
Confounded c.
Hooked c.
Devourous c.
Wearied c.
Sad c.
Vain-glorious c.
Poor c.
Brown c.
Shrunken c.
Abhorred c.
Troubled c.
Scornful c.
Dishonest c.
Reproved c.
Cocketed c.
Diaphanous c.
Unworthy c.
Checked c.
Mangled c.
Filthy c.
Shred c.

Chawned c.
Short-winded c.
Branchless c.
Chapped c.
Failing c.
Deficient c.
Lean c.
Consumed c.
Used c.
Puzzled c.
Allayed c.
Spoiled c.
Clagged c.
Palsy-strucken c.
Amazed c.
Bedunced c.
Extirpated c.
Banged c.
Stripped c.
Hoary c.
Winnowed c.
Decayed c.
Disastrous c.
Unhandsome c.
Stummed c.
Barren c.
Wretched c.
Feeble c.
Cast-down c.
Stopped c.
Kept-under c.
Stubborn c.
Ground c.
Retchless c.
Weather-beaten c.
Flayed c.
Bald c.
Tossed c.
Flapping c.
Cleft c.

Meagre c.
Dumpified c.
Suppressed c.
Hagged c.
Jawped c.
Havocked c.
Astonished c.
Dulled c.
Slow c.
Plucked-up c.
Constipated c.
Blown c.
Blockified c.
Pommelled c.
All-to-bemauled c.
Fallen-away c.
Unlucky c.
Sterile c.
Beshitten c.
Appeased c.
Caitif c.
Woful c.
Unseemly c.
Heavy c.
Weak c.
Prostrated c.
Uncomely c.
Naughty c.
Laid flat c.
Suffocated c.
Held-down c.
Barked c.
Hairless c
Flamping c.
Hooded c.

Wormy c.
Besisted c.
Faulty c.
Bemealed c.
Mortified c.
Scurvy c.
Bescabbed c.
Torn-out c.
Subdued c.
Sneaking c.
Bare c.
Swart c.
Smutched c.
Raised-up c.
Chopped c.
Flirted c.
Blained c.
Blotted c.
Sunk-in c.
Ghastly c.
Unpointed c.
Beblistered c.
Wizened c.
Beggar-plated c.
Douf c.
Clarty c.
Lumpish c.
Abject c.
Side c.
Choked-up c.
Backward c.
Prolix c.
Spotted c.
Crumpled c.
Frumpled c.

State c.
Corrupted c.
Beflowered c.
Amated c.
Blackish c.
Underlaid c.
Lothing c.
Ill-filled c.
Bobbed c.
Matted c.
Tawny c.
Whealed c.
Besmeared c.
Hollow c.
Pantless c.
Guizened c.
Demiss c.
Refractory c.
Rensy c.
Frowning c.
Limping c.
Ravelled c.
Rammish c.
Gaunt c.
Beskimmered c.
Scraggy c.
Lank c.
Swashring c.
Moyling c.
Swinking c.
Harried c.
Tugged c.
Towed c.
Misused c.
Adamitical c.

"Balockatso to the devil, my dear friend Panurge, seeing it is so decreed by the gods, wouldst thou invert the course of the planets, and make them retrograde? Wouldst thou disorder all the celestial

355

spheres, blame the intelligences, blunt the spindles, join the wherves, slander the spinning-quills, reproach the bobbins, revile the clew-bottoms, and finally ravel and untwist all the threads of both the warp and the weft of the weird-sister Parcæ? What, a pox to thy bones, dost thou mean, stony cod? Thou wouldst, if thou couldst, a great deal worse than the giants of old intended to have done. Come hither, Billicullion; whether wouldst thou be jealous without cause, or be a cuckold and know nothing of it?" "Neither the one nor the other," quoth Panurge, "would I choose to be: but, if I get an inkling of the matter, I will provide well enough, or there shall not be one stick of wood, within five hundred leagues about me, whereof to make a cudgel. In good faith, friar John, I speak now seriously unto thee; I think it will be my best not to marry: hearken to what the bells do tell me, now that we are nearer to them: *Do not marry; marry not, not, not, not, not; marry, marry, not, not, not, not, not: if thou marry, thou wilt miscarry, carry, carry; thou'lt repent it, resent it, sent it: if thou marry, thou a cuckold, a cou-cou-cuckoe, cou-cou, cuckold thou shalt be.* By the worthy wrath of God, I begin to be angry; this Campanilian oracle fretteth me to the guts; a March hare was never in such a chafe as I am. O how I am vexed! You monks and friars of the cowl-pated and hood-polled fraternity, have you no remedy nor salve against this malady of grafting horns in heads? Hath nature so abandoned human kind, and of her help left us so destitute, that married men cannot know how to sail through the seas of this mortal life, and be safe from the whirlpools, quicksands, rocks, and banks, that lie along the coast of Cornwall?"

"I will," said friar John, "shew thee a way, and teach thee an expedient, by means whereof thy wife shall never make thee a cuckold without thy knowledge and thine own consent." "Do me the favour, I pray thee," quoth Panurge, "my pretty soft downy cod; now tell it, Billy, I beseech thee." "Take," quoth friar John, "Hans Carvel's ring upon thy finger, who was the king of Melinda's chief jeweller: besides that this Hans Carvel had the reputation of being very skilful and expert in the lapidary's profession, he was a studious, learned, and ingenious man, a scientific person, full of knowledge, a great philosopher, of a sound judgment, of a prime wit, good sense, clear-spirited, an honest creature, courteous, charitable, giver of alms, and of a jovial humour, a boon companion, and a merry blade, if ever there was any in the world: he was somewhat gorbellied, had a little shake in his head, and in effect unwieldly of his body: in his old age

356

he took to wife the bailiff of Concordat's daughter, a young, fair, jolly, gallant, spruce, frisky, brisk, neat, feat, smirk, smug, compt, quaint, gay, fine, trixy, trim, decent, proper, graceful, handsome, beautiful, comely, and kind a little too much to her neighbours and acquaintance.

"Hereupon it fell out, after the expiring of a scantling of weeks, that Master Carvel became as jealous as a tiger, and entered into a very profound suspicion that his new-married gixy did keep a buttock-stirring with others; to prevent which inconvenience, he did tell her many tragical stories of the total ruin of several kingdoms by adultery; did read unto her the legend of chaste wives; then made some lectures to her in the praise of the choice virtue of pudicity, and did present her with a book in commendation of conjugal fidelity, wherein the wickedness of all licentious women was odiously detested; and withal he gave her a chain enriched with pure oriental sapphires. Notwithstanding all this, he found her always more and more inclined to the reception of her neighbour Copes-mates, that day by day his jealousy increased; in sequel whereof, one night as he was lying by her, whilst in his sleep, the rambling fancies of the lecherous deportments of his wife did take up the cellules of his brain; he dreamt that he encountered with the devil, to whom he had discovered to the full the buzzing of his head, and suspicion that his wife did tread her shoe awry: the devil, he thought, in his perplexity, did, for his comfort, give him a ring, and therewithal did kindly put it on his middle-finger, saying, 'Hans Carvel, I give thee this ring: whilst thou carriest it upon that finger, thy wife shall never carnally be known by any other than thyself, without thy special knowledge and consent.' 'Grammercy,' quoth Hans Carvel, 'my lord devil, I renounce Mahomet if ever it shall come off my finger.' The devil vanished, as is his custom, and then Hans Carvel, full of joy, awaking, found that his middle-finger was as far as it could reach within the what-do-you-call-it of his wife. I did forget to tell thee, how his wife, as soon as she had felt the finger there, said, in recoiling her buttocks, 'Off, yes, nay, tut, pish, tush, aye, Lord, that is not the thing which should be put up in that place.' With this, Hans Carvel thought that some pilfering fellow was about to take the ring from him.

"Is not this an infallible and sovereign preservation? Therefore, if thou wilt believe me, in imitation of this example, never fail to have continually the ring of thy wife's commodity upon thy finger."
—When that was said, their discourse and their way ended.

CHAPTER XXIX

HOW PANTAGRUEL CONVOCATED TOGETHER A THEOLOGIAN,
PHYSICIAN, LAWYER, AND PHILOSOPHER, FOR EXTRICATING
PANURGE OUT OF THE PERPLEXITY WHEREIN HE WAS

NO sooner were they come into the royal palace than they, to the
full, made report unto Pantagruel of the success of their expedition, and shewed him the response of Raminagrobis. When Pantagruel had read it over and over again, the oftener he perused it, being the better pleased therewith, he said, in addressing his speech to Panurge, "I have not as yet seen any answer framed to your demand which affordeth me more contentment; for, in this his succinct copy of verses, he summarily and briefly, yet fully enough, expresseth how he would have us to understand, that every one, in the project and enterprise of marriage, ought to be his own carver, sole arbitrator of his proper thoughts, and from himself alone take counsel in the main and peremptory closure of what his determination should be, in either his assent to, or dissent from it. Such always hath been my opinion to you; and, when at first you spoke thereof to me, I truly told you this same very thing: but tacitly you scorned my advice, and would not harbour it within your mind. I know for certain, and therefore may I with the greater confidence utter my conception of it, that philauty, or self-love, is that which blinds your judgment and deceiveth you.

"Let us do otherwise, and that is this: whatever we are, or have, consisteth in three things; the soul, the body, and the goods: now, for the preservation of these three, there are three sorts of learned men ordained, each respectively to have care of that one which is recommended to his charge. Theologues are appointed for the soul, physicians for the welfare of the body, and lawyers for the safety of our goods: hence it is that it is my resolution to have, on Sunday next, with me at dinner, a divine, a physician, and a lawyer; that, with those three assembled thus together, we may, in every point and particle, confer at large of your perplexity." "By St. Picot," answered Panurge, "we never shall do any good that way: I see it already, and you see yourself, how the world is vilely abused, as when with a fox-tail one claps another's breech to cajole him. We give our souls, to keep, to the theologues, who for the greater part are heretics: our bodies we commit to the physicians, who never themselves take any physic: and then we entrust our goods to law-yers, who never go to law against one another." "You speak like a courtier," quoth Pantagruel: "but the first point of your assertion is to be denied; for we daily see how good theologues make it their chief business, their whole and sole employment, by their deeds, their words and writings, to extirpate errors and heresies out of the hearts of men, and in their stead profoundly plant the true and lively faith. The second point you spoke of I commend; for, whereas the professors of the art of medicine give so good order to the *prophy-lactic* or *conservative* part of their faculty in what concerneth their proper healths, they stand in no need of making use of the other branch, which is the *curative,* or *therapeutic,* by medicaments. As for the third, I grant it to be true; for learned advocates and coun-sellors at law are so much taken up with the affairs of others in their consultations, pleadings, and such like patrocinations of those who are their clients, that they have no leisure to attend any controversies of their own. Therefore, on the next ensuing Sunday, let the divine be our godly father Hippothadeus, the physician our honest master Rondibilis, and the legist our good friend Bridlegoose: nor will it be (to my thinking) amiss, that we enter into the pythagoric Te-trade, and choose, for an assistant to the three aforenamed doctors, our ancient faithful acquaintance the philosopher Trouillogan; es-pecially seeing a perfect philosopher, such as is Trouillogan, is able positively to resolve all whatsoever doubts you can propose. Car-palim, have you a care to have them here all four on Sunday next at dinner, without fail."

"I believe," quoth Epistemon, "that throughout the whole country, in all the corners thereof, you could not have pitched upon such other four: which I speak not so much in regard of the most ex-cellent qualifications and accomplishments wherewith all of them are endowed for the respective discharge and management of each his own vocation and calling (wherein, without all doubt or controversy, they are the paragons of the land, and surpass all others), besides that Rondibilis is married now, who before was not: Hippothadeus was not before, nor is yet: Bridlegoose was married once, but is not now: and Trouillogan is married now, who was wedded to another wife before. Sir, if it may stand with your good liking, I will ease Carpalim of some parcel of his labour, and invite Bridlegoose myself, with whom I of a long time have had a very intimate familiarity, and unto whom I am to speak on the behalf of a pretty, hopeful youth, who now studieth at Toulouse, under the most learned, virtuous Dr. Boissonet." "Do what you deem most expedient," quoth Pantagruel, "and tell me, if my recommendation can in anything be serviceable for the promoting of the good of that youth, or otherways tend to the bettering of the dignity and office of the worthy Boissonet, whom I do so love and respect, for one of the ablest and most sufficient in his way, that anywhere are extant." "Sir, I will use therein my best endeavours, and heartily bestir myself about it."

CHAPTER XXX

HOW THE THEOLOGUE, HIPPOTHADEUS, GIVETH COUNSEL TO PANURGE IN THE MATTER AND BUSINESS OF HIS NUPTIAL ENTERPRIZE

THE dinner on the subsequent Sunday, was no sooner made ready, than the afore-named invited guests gave thereto their appearance, all of them, Bridlegoose only excepted, who was the deputy-governor of the Fonsbeton. At the ushering in of the second service, Panurge, making a low reverence, spake thus: "Gentlemen, the question I am to propound unto you shall be uttered in very few words; *Should I marry or not?* If my doubt herein be not resolved by you, I shall hold it altogether insolvable, as are the *Insolubilia de Aliaco;* for all of you are elected, chosen, and culled out, from amongst others, every one in his own condition and quality, like so many picked peas on a carpet."

The father Hippothadeus, in obedience to the bidding of Pantagruel, and with much courtesy to the company, answered exceeding modestly, after this manner: "My friend, you are pleased to ask counsel of us; but first you must consult with yourself. Do you find any trouble or disquiet in your body, by the importunate stings and pricklings of the flesh?" "That I do," quoth Panurge, "in a hugely strong and almost irresistible measure: be not offended, I beseech you, good father, at the freedom of my expression." "No, truly, friend, not I," quoth Hippothadeus; "there is no reason why I should be displeased therewith: but in this carnal strife and debate of yours, have you obtained from God the gift and *special grace* of continency?" "In good faith, not," quoth Panurge. "My counsel to you in that case, my friend, is, that you marry," quoth Hippothadeus;

"for you should rather choose to marry once than to burn still in fires of concupiscence." Then Panurge, with a jovial heart and a loud voice, cried out, "That is spoke gallantly, without circumbilivaginating about and about, and never hitting it in its centred point. Grammercy, my good father: in truth, I am resolved now to marry, and without fail I shall do it quickly. I invite you to my wedding: by the body of a hen we shall make good cheer, and be as merry as crickets: you shall wear the bridegroom's colours; and, if we eat a goose, my wife shall not roast it for me. I shall intreat you to lead up the first dance of the bridesmaids, if it may please you to do me so much favour and honour. There resteth yet a small difficulty, a little scruple, yea, even less than nothing, whereof I humbly crave your resolution: shall I be a cuckold, father, yea or no?" "By no means," answered Hippothadeus, "will you be cuckolded, if it please God." "O the Lord help us now," quoth Panurge; "whither are we driven, good folks? To the *conditionals,* which, according to the rules and precepts of the dialectic faculty, admit of all contradictions and impossibilities. *If my Transalpine mule had wings, my Transalpine mule would fly.* If it please God, I shall not be a cuckold; but I shall be a cuckold, if it please him. Good God! if this were a condition which I knew how to prevent, my hopes should be as high as ever, nor would I despair: but you here send me to God's privy-council, to the closet of his *little* pleasures. You, my French countrymen, which is the way you take to go thither?

"My honest father, I believe it will be your best not to come to my wedding: the clutter and dingle-dangle noise of marriage guests will disturb you, and break the serious fancies of your brain. You love repose, with solitude and silence: I really believe you won't come: And then you dance but indifferently, and would be out of countenance at the first entry. I will send you some good things to your chamber, together with the *bride's favour,* and there you may drink our health, if it may stand with your good liking." "My friend," quoth Hippothadeus, "take my words in the sense wherein I mean them, and do not misinterpret me. When I tell you, *if it please God,* do I to you any wrong therein? is it an ill expression? is it a blaspheming clause or reserve, anyways scandalous unto the world? Do not we thereby honour the Lord God Almighty, creator, protector, and conserver of all things? Is not that a mean whereby we do acknowledge him to be the sole giver of all whatsoever is good? Do not we in that manifest our faith, that we believe all

361

things to depend upon his infinite and incomprehensible bounty; and that without him nothing can be produced, nor after its production be of any value, force, or power, without the concurring aid and favour of his assisting grace? Is it not a canonical and authentic exception, worthy to be premised to all our undertakings? Is it not expedient that what we propose unto ourselves be still referred to what shall be disposed of by the sacred will of God, unto which all things must acquiesce, in the heavens as well as on the earth? Is not that verily a sanctifying of his holy name? My friend, you shall not be a cuckold, if it please God; nor shall we need to despair of the knowledge of his goodwill and pleasure herein, as if it were such an abstruse and mysteriously-hidden secret that for the clear understanding thereof it were necessary to consult with those of his celestial privy-council, or expressly make a voyage into the *empyrean* chamber, where order is given for the effectuating of his most holy pleasures. The great God hath done us this good, that he hath declared and revealed them to us openly and plainly, and described them in the Holy Bible. There will you find that you shall never be a cuckold, that is to say, your wife shall never be a strumpet, if you make choice of one of a commendable extraction, descended of honest parents, and instructed in all piety and virtue; such a one as hath not at any time haunted or frequented the company or conversation of those that are of corrupt or depraved manners; one loving and fearing God, who taketh a singular delight in drawing near to him by faith and the cordial observing of his sacred commandments; and, finally, one who, standing in awe of the divine majesty of the most high, will be loth to offend him and lose the favourable kindness of his grace, through any defect of faith, or transgression against the ordinances of his holy law, wherein adultery is most rigorously forbidden, and a close adherence to her husband alone most strictly and severely enjoined; yea, in such sort, that she is to cherish, serve, and love him, above anything next to God, that meriteth to be beloved. In the interim, for the better schooling of her in these instructions, and that the wholesome doctrine of a matrimonial duty may take the deeper root in her mind, you must needs carry yourself so on your part, and your behaviour is to be such, that you are to go before her in a good example, by entertaining her unfeignedly with a conjugal amity, by continually approving yourself, in all your words and actions, a faithful and discreet husband, and by living not only at home and privately with your own household and family, but in the face also of all men and open view of the world, devoutly, virtuously, and chastely, as you would have her on her side to deport and demean herself towards you, as becomes a godly, loyal, and respectful wife, who maketh conscience to keep inviolable the tie of the matrimonial oath: For, as that *looking-glass* is not the best which is most decked with gold and precious stones, but that which representeth to the eye the liveliest shapes of objects set before it; even so that wife should not be most esteemed who richest is, and of the noblest race, but she who, fearing God, conforms herself nearest unto the humour of her husband. Consider how the moon doth not borrow her light from Jupiter, Mars, Mercury, or any other of the planets; nor yet from any of those splendid stars which are set in the spangled firmament; but from her husband only, the bright sun, which she receiveth from him, more or less, according to the manner of his *aspect* and variously bestowed eradiations. Just so should you be a pattern to your wife, in virtue, goodly zeal, and true devotion; that, by your radiance in darting on her the *aspect* of an exemplary goodness, she, in your imitation, may outshine the luminaries of all other women. To this effect you daily must implore God's grace to the protection of you both." "You would have me then," quoth Panurge, twisting the whiskers of his beard on either side, with his thumb and forefinger of his left hand, "to espouse and take to wife the prudent frugal woman described by Solomon: without all doubt she is dead, and truly, to my best remembrance, I never saw her; the Lord forgive me! nevertheless I thank you, father: eat this slice of marchpane; it will help your digestion; then shall you be presented with a cup of claret hypocras, which is right healthful and stomached. Let us proceed."

CHAPTER XXXI

HOW THE PHYSICIAN RONDIBILIS COUNSELLETH PANURGE

PANURGE, continuing his discourse, said, "The first word which was spoken by him who gelded the lubbardly quaffing monks of Saussiniac, after that he had unstoned friar Caulderiel, was this, *'To the rest.'* In like manner I say, *to the rest.* Therefore I beseech you, my good master Rondibilis, should *I marry or not?*" "By the ambling of my mule," quoth Rondibilis, "I know not what answer to make to this problem of yours. You say that you feel in you the *pricking strings* of sensuality, by which you are stirred up to venery. I find, in our faculty of *medicine* (and we have founded our opinion therein upon the deliberate resolution and final decision of the ancient Platonics), that *carnal concupiscence* is cooled and quelled five several ways.

"First, by the means of *wine,* I shall easily believe that," quoth friar John; "for, when I am well whittled with the juice of the grape, I care for nothing else, so I may sleep." "When I say," quoth Rondibilis, "that *wine* abateth lust, my meaning is, *wine* immoderately taken; for, by intemperance proceeding from the excessive drinking of strong liquor, there is brought upon the body of such a swill-down bouser a chillness in the blood, a slackening in the sinews, a dissipation of the generative seed, a numbness and hebetation of the senses, with a perversive wryness and convulsion of the muscles; all which are great lets and impediments to the act of generation. Hence it is that Bacchus, the god of bibbers, tipplers, and drunkards, is most commonly painted beardless, and clad in a woman's habit, as a person altogether effeminate, or like a libbed eunuch. *Wine,* nevertheless, taken moderately, worketh quite contrary effects, as is implied by the old proverb, which saith, that Venus takes cold when not accompanied with Ceres and Bacchus. This opinion is of great antiquity, as appeareth by the testimony of Diodorus the Sicilian, and confirmed by Pausanias, and universally held amongst the Lampsacians, that Don Priapus was the son of Bacchus and Venus.

"Secondly, the fervency of lust is abated by certain drugs, plants, herbs, and roots, which make the taker cold, maleficiated, unfit for, and unable to perform the act of generation; as hath been often experimented in the water-lily, Heraclea, Agnus-castus, willow-twigs, hemp-stalks, wood-bind, honeysuckle, tamarisk, chaste-tree, mandrake, bennet, kecbugloss, the skin of hippopotamus, and many other such, which by convenient doses, proportioned to the peccant humour and constitution of the patient, being duly and seasonably received within the body, what by their elementary virtues on the one side, and peculiar properties on the other, do either benumb, mortify, and beclumpse with cold, the prolific semence; or scatter and disperse the spirits, which ought to have gone along with and conducted the sperm to the places destinated and appointed for its reception; or, lastly, shut up, stop, and obstruct, the ways, passages, and conduits, through which the seed should have been expelled, evacuated, and ejected. We have nevertheless of those ingredients which, being of a contrary operation, heat and blood, bend the nerves, unite the spirits, quicken the senses, strengthen the muscles, and thereby rouse up, provoke, excite, and enable a man to the vigorous accomplishment of the feat of amorous dalliance." "I have no need of those," quoth Panurge, "God be thanked, and you, my good master. Howsoever, I pray you take no exception or offence at these my words; for what I have said was not out of any ill-will I did bear to you, the Lord knows."

"Thirdly, the ardour of lechery is very much subdued and mated (checked) by frequent *labour* and continual toiling; for, by painful exercises and laborious working, so great a dissolution is brought upon the whole body, that the blood, which runneth along the channels of the veins thereof for the nourishment and alimentation of each of its members, hath neither time, leisure, nor power, to afford the seminal resudation, or superfluity of the third concoction, which nature most carefully reserves for the conservation of the individual, whose preservation she more heedfully regardeth than the propagating of the species, and multiplication of human kind. Whence it is that Diana is said to be chaste, because she is never idle, but always busied about her hunting. For the same reason was a camp, or leaguer, of old called *castrum,* as if they would have said *castum;* because the soldiers, wrestlers, runners, throwers of the bar, and other such like athletic champions as are usually seen in a military circumvallation, incessantly travel and turmoil, and are in a perpetual stir and agitation. To this purpose Hippocrates also writeth in his book, *De Aëre, Aqua, et Locis,* that in his time there were people in Scythia as impotent as eunuchs in the discharge of a venereal exploit; because that, without any cessation, pause, or respite, they were never from off horseback, or otherways assiduously employed in some troublesome and molesting drudgery. On the other part, in opposition and repugnance hereto, the philosophers say, *that idleness is the mother of lechery.* When it was asked Ovid why Ægystus became an adulterer, he made no answer but this, *because he was idle.* Who were able to rid the world of loitering and laziness might easily frustrate and disappoint *Cupid* in all his designs, aims, engines, and devices, and so disable and appal him, that his bow, quiver, and darts, should from thenceforth be a mere needless load and burthen to him; for that it could not then lie in his

365

power to strike or wound any of either sex with all the arms he had. He is not, I believe, so expert an archer, as that he can hit the cranes flying in the air, or yet the young stags skipping through the thickets, as the Parthians knew well how to do; that is to say, people moiling, stirring, and hurrying up and down, restless and without repose. He must have those hushed, still, quiet, lying at stay, lither, and full of ease, whom he is able, though his mother help him, to touch, much less to pierce with all his arrows. In confirmation hereof, Theophrastus being asked, on a time, what kind of beast or thing he judged a toyish, wanton love to be? he made answer, *that it was a passion of idle and sluggish spirits.* From which pretty description of tickling love-tricks that of Diogenes's hatching was not very discrepant, when he defined lechery. *Occupation of folks destitute of all other occupation.* For this cause, the Sicyonian sculptor, Canachus, being desirous to give to understand that sloth, drowsiness, negligence and laziness, were the prime guardians and governesses of ribaldry, made the statue of *Venus* (not standing, as other sculptors used to do, but) sitting.

"Fourthly, The tickling pricks of incontinency are blunted by an eager study; for thence proceedeth an incredible resolution of the spirits, that oftentimes there do not remain so many behind as may suffice to push and thrust forwards the generative resudation to the places thereto appropriated, and therewithal inflate the cavernous nerve, whose office is to ejaculate the moisture for the propagation of human progeny. Lest you should think it is not so, be pleased but to contemplate a little the form, fashion, and carriage of a man, exceeding earnestly set upon some learned meditation, and deeply plunged therein, and you shall see how all the arteries of his brains are stretched forth, and bent like the string of a cross-bow, the more promptly, dexterously, and copiously, to suppeditate, furnish, and supply him with store of spirits, sufficient to replenish and fill up the ventricles, seats, tunnels, mansions, receptacles, and cellules of the common sense; of the imagination, apprehension, and fancy; of the ratiocination, arguing, and resolution; as likewise of the memory, recordation, and remembrance; and with great alacrity, nimbleness, and agility, to run, pass, and course, from the one to the other, through those pipes, windings, and conduits, which, to skilful anatomists, are perceivable at the end of the wonderful net, where all the arteries close in a terminating point; which arteries, taking their rise and origin from the left capsula of the heart, bring, through several circuits, ambages, and anfractuosities, the vital spirits, to subtilize and refine them to the æthereal purity of animal spirits. Nay, in such a studiously-musing person, you may espy so extravagant raptures of one, as it were out of himself, that all his natural faculties for that time will seem to be suspended from each their proper charge and office, and his exterior senses to be at a stand. In a word, you cannot otherwise choose than think that he is, by an extraordinary ecstacy, quite transported out of what he was or should be; and that Socrates did not speak improperly when he said, 'that philosophy was nothing else but a meditation upon death.' This possibly is the reason, why Democritus deprived himself of the sense of seeing; prizing at a much lower rate the loss of his sight than the diminution of his contemplations; which he frequently had found disturbed by the vagrant flying out strayings of his unsettled and roving eyes. Therefore is it that Pallas, the goddess of wisdom, tutoress and guardianess of such as are diligently studious and painfully industrious, is and hath been still accounted a virgin. The *Muses,* upon the same consideration, are esteemed perpetual *Maids;* and the *Graces,* for the like reason, have been held to continue in a sempiternal *pudicity.* I remember to have read, that Cupid, on a time, being asked of his mother Venus why he did not assault and set upon the Muses, his answer was, that he found them so fair, so sweet, so fine, so neat, so wise, so learned, so modest, so discreet, so courteous, so virtuous, and so continually busied and employed;—one in the speculation of the stars; another in the supputation of numbers; the third in the dimension of geometrical quantities; the fourth in the composition of heroic poems; the fifth in jovial interludes of a comic strain; the sixth in the stately gravity of a tragic vein; the seventh in the melodious disposition of musical airs; the eighth in the completest manner of writing histories and books on all sorts of subjects; and the ninth in the mysteries, secrets, and curiosities of all sciences, faculties, disciplines, and arts, whatsoever, whether liberal or mechanic;—that approaching near unto them, he unbended his bow, shut his quiver, and extinguished his torch, through mere shame, and fear, that by mischance he might do them some hurt or prejudice; which done, he thereafter put off the fillet wherewith his eyes were bound, to look them in the face, and to hear their melody and poetic odes. There took he the greatest pleasures in the world; that many times he was transported with their beauty and pretty behaviour, and charmed asleep by the harmony: so far was he from assaulting them or interrupting their studies. Under this article may be comprised what Hippocrates wrote in the afore-cited treatise concerning the Scythians; as also that in a book of his entitled, 'Of Breeding and Production'; where he hath affirmed all such men to be unfit for generation as have their *parotid* arter-ies cut, whose situation is beside the ears: for the reason given al-ready, when I was speaking of the resolution of the spirits, and of that spiritual blood whereof the arteries are the sole and proper re-ceptacles; and that likewise he doth maintain a large portion of the parastatic liquor, to issue and descend from the brains and back-bone.

"Fifthly, by the too frequent reiteration of the act of venery." "There did I wait for you," quoth Panurge, "and shall willingly apply it to myself, whilst any one that pleaseth may, for me, make use of any of the four preceding." "That is the very same thing," quoth friar John, "which father Scyllino, prior of Saint Victor, at Marseilles, calleth by the name of *maceration* (*mortification*) *and taming of the flesh.* I am of the same opinion; and so was the her-mit of Saint Radegonde, a little above Chinon: for quoth he, 'the hermits of Thebaide can no more aptly or expediently macerate and bring down the pride of their bodies, daunt and mortify their lech-erous sensuality, or depress and overcome the stubbornness and rebellion of the flesh, than by *dufling* and *fanferluching* it five-and-twenty or thirty times a day." "I see Panurge," quoth Rondibilis, "neatly featured, and proportioned in all the members of his body, of a good temperament in his humours, well complexioned in his spirits, of a competent age, in an opportune time, and of a reason-ably forward mind, to be married. Truly, if he encounter with a wife of the like nature, temperament, and constitution, he may beget upon her children worthy of some Transpontine monarchy; and, the sooner he marry it will be the better for him, and the more con-ducible for his profit, if he would see and have his children in his own time well provided for." "Sir, my worthy master," quoth Pan-urge, "I will do it, do not you doubt thereof; and that quickly enough, I warrant you. Nevertheless, whilst you were busied in the uttering of your learned discourse, this flea, which I have in mine ear, hath tickled me more than ever. I retain you in the number of my festival guests, and promise you that we shall not want for mirth and good cheer enough; yea, over and above the ordinary rate. And, if it may please you, desire your wife to come along with you, together with her she-friends, and neighbours, that is to be understood; and there shall be fair play."

CHAPTER XXXII

HOW RONDIBILIS DECLARETH CUCKOLDRY TO BE NATURALLY ONE OF THE APPENDANCES OF MARRIAGE

THERE remaineth as yet," quoth Panurge, going on in his discourse, "one small scruple to be cleared: you have seen heretofore, I doubt not, in the Roman standards, S. P. Q. R., *si, peu, que, rien: shall not I be a cuckold?*" "By the haven of safety," cried out Rondibilis, "what is this you ask of me? if you shall be a cuckold? My noble friend, I am married, and you are like to be so very speedily; therefore be pleased, from my experiment in the matter, to write in your brain, with a steel-pen, this subsequent ditton, *there is no married man who doth not run the hazard of being made a cuckold.* Cuckoldry naturally attendeth marriage; the shadow doth not more naturally follow the body than cuckoldry ensueth after marriage, to place fair horns upon the husband's head.

"And when you shall happen to hear any man pronounce these three words, *he is married,* if you then say he is, hath been, shall be, or may be, a cuckold, you will not be accounted an unskilful artist in framing of true consequences." "Tripes and bowels of all the devils," cried Panurge, "what do you tell me?" "My dear friend," answered Rondibilis, "as Hippocrates, on a time, was in the very nick of setting forwards from Lango to Polistillo, to visit the philosopher Democritus, he wrote a familiar letter to his friend Dionysius, wherein he desired him, that he would, during the interval of his absence, carry his wife to the house of her father and mother, who were an honourable couple, and of good repute; 'because I would not have her at my home,' said he, 'to make abode in solitude: yet, notwithstanding this her residence before her parents, do not fail,' quoth he, 'with a most heedful care and circumspection, to pry into her ways, and to espy what places she shall go to with her mother, and who those be that shall repair unto her: not,' quoth he, 'that I do mistrust her virtue, or that I seem to have any diffidence of her pudicity and chaste behaviour, for of that I have frequently had good and real proofs; but I must freely tell you, *she is a woman:* there lies the suspicion.'

369

"My worthy friend, the nature of women is set forth before our eyes, and represented to us by the *moon,* in divers other things as well as in this, that they squat, sculk, constrain their own inclinations, and, with all the cunning they can, dissemble and play the hypocrite in the sight and presence of their husbands; who come no sooner to be out of the way, but that forthwith they take their advantage, pass the time merrily, desist from all labour, frolic it, gad abroad, lay aside their counterfeit garb, and openly declare and manifest the interior of their dispositions; even as the *moon,* when she is in *conjunction* with the *sun,* is neither seen in the heavens nor on the earth, but, in her *opposition,* when remotest from him, shineth in her greatest fulness, and wholly appeareth in her brightest splendour whilst it is night: *thus women are but women.*

"When I say, *womankind,* I speak of a sex so frail, so variable, so changeable, so fickle, inconstant, and imperfect, that, in my opinion, *Nature* (under favour nevertheless of the prime honour and reverence which is due unto her) did in a manner mistake the road which she had traced formerly, and stray exceedingly from that excellence of providential judgment by the which she had created and formed all other things, when she built, framed, and made up the *woman.* And, having thought upon it a hundred and five times, I know not what else to determine therein, save only that, in the devising, hammering, forging, and composing of the *woman,* she hath had a much tenderer regard, and by a great deal more respectful heed, to the delightful consortship and sociable delectation of the *man,* than to the perfection and accomplishment of the individual *womanishness,* or *muliebrity.* The divine philosopher Plato was doubtful in what rank of living creatures to place and collocate them, whether amongst the *rational animals,* by elevating them to an upper seat in the specifical classes of *humanity;* or with the *irrational,* by degrading them to a lower bench on the opposite side of a brutal kind, and mere *bestiality:* for nature hath posited, in a privy, secret, and intestine place of their bodies, a sort of member (by some not impertinently termed an *animal*) which is not to be found in men. Therein sometimes are engendered certain humours, so saltish, brackish, clammy, sharp, nipping, tearing, prickling, and most eagerly tickling, that, by their stinging acrimony, rending nitrosity, figging itch, wriggling mordicancy, and smarting salsitude (for the said member is altogether sinewy, and of a most quick and lively feeling), their whole body is shaken and ebrangled, their senses totally ravished and transported, the operations of their judgment and understanding utterly confounded, and all disordinate passions and perturbations of the mind thoroughly and absolutely allowed, admitted, and approved of; yea, in such sort, that, if nature had not been so favourable unto them as to have sprinkled their forehead with a little tincture of bashfulness and modesty, you should see them, in a frantic mood, run mad after lechery, and hie apace up and down with haste and lust, in quest of, and to fix some chamber-standard in, their Paphian ground, that never did the Proetides, Mimallonides, nor Lyæan Thyads, deport themselves, in the time of their Bacchanalian festivals, more shamelessly, or with so effronted and brazen-faced impudence; because this terrible *animal* is knit unto, and hath an union with, all the chief and most principal parts of the body, as to anatomists is evident. Let it not here be thought strange that I should call it an *animal,* seeing therein I do no otherwise than follow and adhere to the doctrine of the Academic and Peripatetic philosophers. For, if a proper motion be a certain mark and infallible token of the life and animation of the mover (as Aristotle writeth), and that any such thing as *moveth of itself* ought to be held *animated* and of a living *nature,* then assuredly Plato, with very good reason, did give it the denomination of an *animal;* for that he perceived and observed in it the proper and *self-stirring motion* of suffocation, precipitation, corrugation, and of indignation, so extremely violent, that oftentimes by them is taken and removed from the woman all other sense and moving whatsoever, as if she were in a swounding lipothymy, and benumming syncope, epileptic, apoplectic palsy, and true resemblance of a pale-faced death.

"Furthermore, in the said *member* there is a manifest discerning faculty of scents and odours very perceptible to women, who feel it fly from what is rank and unsavoury, and follow fragrant and aromatic smells. It is not unknown to me how Cl. Galen striveth, with might and main, to prove, that these are not proper and particular notions proceeding intrinsically from the thing itself, but accidentally and by chance. Nor hath it escaped my notice, how others of that sect have laboured hardly, yea, to the utmost of their abilities, to demonstrate that it is not a sensitive discerning or perception in it of the difference of wafts and smells, but merely a various manner of virtue and efficacy, passing forth and flowing from the diversity of odoriferous substances applied near unto it. Nevertheless, if you will studiously examine, and seriously ponder and weigh, in Critolaus's balance, the strength of their reasons and arguments, you shall find

371

that they, not only in this, but in several other matters also of the like nature, have spoken at random, and rather out of an ambitious envy to check and reprehend their betters, than for any design to make inquiry into the solid truth. I will not launch my little skiff any farther into the wide ocean of this dispute, only will I tell you, that the praise and commendation is not mean and slender which is due to those honest and good women, who, living chastely and without blame, have had the power and virtue to curb, range, and subdue, that unbridled, heady, and wild *animal*, to an obedient, submissive, and obsequious yielding unto reason. Therefore here will I make an end of my discourse thereon, when I shall have told you, that the said *animal*, being once satiated (if it be possible that it can be contented or satisfied) by that aliment which nature hath provided for it out of the epididymal store-house of man, all its former irregular and disordered motions are at an end laid, and assuaged; all its vehement and unruly longings lulled, pacified, and quieted; and all the furious and raging lusts, appetites, and desires thereof appeased, suppressed, calmed, and extinguished. For this cause let it seem nothing strange unto you, if we be in a perpetual danger of being *cuckolds;* that is to say, such of us as have not wherewithal fully to satisfy the appetite and expectation of that voracious animal." "Odds fish!" quoth Panurge, "have you no preventive cure in all your medicinal art for hindering one's head to be horny-graffed at home, whilst his feet are plodding abroad?" "Yes, that I have, my gallant friend," answered Rondibilis, "and that which is a sovereign remedy, whereof I frequently make use myself; which, that you may the better relish, it is set down and written in the book of a most famous author, whose renown is of a standing of two thousand years. Hearken and take good heed." "You are," quoth Panurge, "by *cockshobby,* a right honest man, and I love you with all my heart; eat a little of this quince-pie, it is very proper and convenient for the shutting up the orifice of the ventricle of the stomach, because of a kind of astringent stypticity which is in that sort of fruit, and is helpful to the first concoction. But what? I think I speak *Latin* before *clerks.* Stay, fill, I give you somewhat to drink out of this Nestorian goblet. Will you have another draught of white *Hippocras?* be not afraid of the squinzy: no: there is neither squinanthum, ginger, nor grains, in it; only a little choice cinnamon, and some of the best refined sugar, with the delicious white-wine of the growth of that vine, which was set in the slips of the great Sorbapple, above the Walnut-tree."

372

CHAPTER XXXIII

"AT what time," quoth Rondibilis, "Jupiter took a view of the state of his Olympic house and family, and had made the Calendar of all the gods and goddesses, appointing unto the festival of every one of them its proper day and season, establishing certain fixed places and stations for the pronouncing of oracles, and relief of travelling pilgrims, and ordaining victims, immolations, and sacrifices, suitable and correspondent to the dignity and nature of the worshipped and adored Deity." "Did not he do," asked Panurge, "therein, as Tinteville, the bishop of Auxerre, is said once to have done? This noble prelate loved entirely the pure liquor of the grape, as every honest and judicious man doth; therefore was it that he had an especial care and regard to the *bud* of the vine-tree, as to the grandfather of Bacchus. But so it is, that for sundry years together he saw a most pitiful havock, desolation, and destruction, made among the sprouts, shootings, buds, blossoms, and scions of the vines, by hoary frosts, dank fogs, hot mists, and unseasonable colds, chill blasts, thick hail, and other calamitous chances of foul weather, happening, as he thought, by the dismal inauspiciousness of the holy days of St. George, St. Mary, St. Paul, St. Eutropius, Holy Rood, the Ascension, and other festivals, in that time when the sun passeth under the sign of Taurus; and thereupon harboured in his mind this opinion, that the afore-named *saints* were *Saint* Hail-fingers, *Saint* Frost-senders, *Saint* Fogmongers, and *Saint* Spoilers of the vine-buds; for which cause he went about to have transferred their feasts from the spring to the winter, to be celebrated between Christmas and Epiphany (so the *Mother of the three Kings* called it), allowing them, with all honour and reverence, the liberty then to freeze, hail, and rain, as much as they would; for that he knew that, at such a time, frost was rather profitable than hurtful to the vinebuds; and in their steads to have placed the festivals of St. Christopher, St. John the Baptist, St. Magdalene, St. Ann, St. Domingo, and St. Lawrence; yea, to have gone so far as to collocate and transpose the middle of August in, and to the beginning of May; because, during the whole space of their solemnity, there was so little danger of hoary frosts and cold mists, that no artificers are then held in greater request than the afforders of refrigerating inventions, makers of junkets, fit disposers of cooling shades, composers of green arbours, and refreshers of wine."

373

"Jupiter," said Rondibilis, "forgot the poor devil *Cuckoldry,* who was then in the court at Paris, very eagerly soliciting a pedling suit at law for one of his vassals and tenants; within some few days thereafter (I have forgot how many), when he got full notice of the trick, which in his absence was done unto him, he instantly desisted from prosecuting legal processes, in the behalf of others, full of solicitude to pursue after his own business, lest he should be foreclosed: and thereupon he appeared personally at the tribunal of the great Jupiter, displayed before him the importance of his preceding merits, together with the acceptable services, which, in obedience to his commandments, he had formerly performed; and therefore, in all humility, begged of him, that he would be pleased not to leave him alone amongst all the sacred potentates, destitute and void of honour, reverence, sacrifices, and festival ceremonies. To this petition Jupiter's answer was excusatory, 'That all the places and offices of his house were bestowed.' Nevertheless, so importuned was he by the continual supplications of Monsieur Cuckoldry, that he, in fine, placed him in the rank, list, roll, rubric, and catalogue; and appointed honours, sacrifices, and festival rites, to be observed on earth in great devotion, and tendered to him with solemnity. His feast, because there was no void, empty, nor vacant place in the calendar, was to be celebrated jointly with and on the same day that had been consecrated to the goddess Jealousy: his power and dominion shall be over married folks, especially such as had handsome wives; his sacrifices were to be suspicion, diffidence, mistrust, a lowring, pouting sullenness, watchings, wardings, researchings, plyings, explorations, together with the way-layings, ambushes, narrow observations, and malicious doggings of the husband's scouts and espials of the most privy actions of their wives. Herewithal every married man was expressly and rigorously commanded to reverence, honour, and worship him; to celebrate and solemnize his festival with twice more respect than that of another saint or deity, and to immolate unto him, with all sincerity and alacrity of heart, the above-mentioned sacrifices and oblations, under pain of severe censures, threatenings, and comminations of these subsequent fines, mulcts, amerciaments, penalties, and punishments, to be inflicted on the delinquents— viz., That Monsieur Cuckoldry should never be favourable nor propitious to them: that he should never help, aid, supply, succour, nor grant them any subventitious furtherance, auxiliary suffrage, or adminiculary assistance: that he should never hold them in any reckoning, account, or estimation; that

374

he should never deign to enter within their houses, neither at the doors, windows, nor any other place thereof: that he should never haunt nor frequent their companies or conversations, how frequently soever they should invoke him, and call upon his name; and that not only he should leave and abandon them to rot alone with their wives in a sempiternal solitariness, without the benefit of the diversion of any copesmate or corival at all, but should withal shun and eschew them, fly from them, and eternally forsake and reject them, as impious heretics and sacrilegious persons, according to the accustomed manner of other gods, towards such as are too slack in offering up the duties and reverences which ought to be performed respectively to their divinities; as is evidently apparent in Bacchus towards negligent vine-dressers, in Ceres against idle plowmen and tillers of the ground; in Pomona to unworthy fruiterers and costermongers; in Neptune towards dissolute mariners and sea-faring men; in Vulcan towards loitering smiths and forge-men; and so throughout the rest.

"Now, on the contrary, this infallible promise was added: that unto all those who should make a *holy day* of the above recited festival, and cease from all manner of worldly work and negotiation, lay aside all their own most important occasions, and be so retchless, heedless, and careless of what might concern the management of their proper affairs, as to mind nothing else but a suspicious espying and prying into the secret deportments of their wives, and how to coop, shut up, hold at under, and deal cruelly and austerely with them, by all the harshness and hardships that an implacable and every way inexorable jealousy can devise and suggest, conformable to the sacred ordinances of the afore-mentioned sacrifices and oblations, he should be continually favourable to them, should love them, sociably converse with them, should be day and night in their houses, and never leave them destitute of his presence. Now I have said and you have heard my cure."

"Ha, ha, ha," quoth Carpalim, laughing, "this is a remedy yet more apt and proper than Hans Carvel's ring: the devil take me if I do not believe it. The humour, inclination, and nature of women, is like the thunder, whose force in its bolt, or otherways, burneth, bruiseth, and breaketh, only hard, massive, and resisting objects, without staying or stopping at soft, empty, and yielding matters; for it dasheth into pieces the steel sword, without doing any hurt to the velvet scabbard which insheatheth it; it rusheth also and consumeth the bones, without wounding or endamaging the flesh wherewith they are

375

veiled and covered; just so it is, that women, for the greater part, never bend the contention, subtility, and contradictory disposition of their spirits, unless it be to do what is prohibited and forbidden."

"Verily," quoth Hippothadeus, "some of our doctors aver for a truth, that the first woman of the world, whom the Hebrews call Eve, had hardly been induced or allured into the temptation of eating of the fruit of the *Tree of Life* if it had not been forbidden her so to do. And, that you may give the more credit to the validity of this opinion, consider how the cautelous and wily tempter did commemorate unto her, for an antecedent to his *Enthymeme,* the *prohibition* which was made to taste it, as being desirous to infer from thence, *It is forbidden thee; therefore thou shouldst eat of it, else thou canst not be a woman."*

CHAPTER XXXIV

HOW WOMEN ORDINARILY HAVE THE GREATEST LONGING
AFTER THINGS PROHIBITED

WHEN I was," quoth Carpalim, "a whoremaster, at Orleans, the whole art of rhetoric, in all its tropes and figures, was not able to afford unto me a colour or flourish of greater force and value; nor could I, by any other form or manner of elocution, pitch upon a more persuasive argument for bringing young beautiful married ladies into the snares of adultery, through alluring and enticing them to taste with me of amorous delights, than with a lively sprightfulness to tell them in downright terms, and to remonstrate to them (with a great show of detestation of a crime so horrid), how their husbands were jealous. This was none of my invention. It is written, and we have laws, examples, reasons, and daily experiences, confirmative of the same. If this belief once enter into their noddles, their husbands will infallibly be cuckolds, yea, by God, will they (without swearing), although they should do like Semiramis, Pasiphaë, Egesta, the women of the Isle Mandez in Egypt, and other such like queanish flirting harlots, mentioned in the writings of Herodotus, Strabo, and such like puppies."

"Truly," quoth Ponocrates, "I have heard it related, and it hath been told me for a verity, that Pope John XXII. passing on a day through the abbey of Toucherome, was in all humility required and besought by the abbess and other discreet mothers of the said convent, to grant them an indulgence, by means whereof they might confess themselves to one another, alledging, that *religious* women were subject to some petty secret slips and imperfections, which would be a foul and burning shame for them to discover and to reveal to men, how sacerdotal soever their function were; but that they would freelier, more familiarly, and with greater cheerfulness, open to each other their offences, faults, and escapes, under the seal of confession. 'There is not anything,' answered the pope, 'fitting for you to impetrate of me which I would not most willingly condescend unto; but I find one inconvenience; you know, *confession should be kept secret:* and you women are not able to do so.' 'Exceedingly well,' quoth they, 'most holy father, and much more closely than the best of men.' The holy father, on the very same day, gave them in keeping a pretty box, wherein he purposely caused a little linnet to be put, willing them very gently and cautiously to lock it up in some sure and hidden place; and promising them, by the *faith of a pope,* that he should yield to their request, if they would keep secret what was enclosed within that deposited box; enjoining them withal not to presume, one way nor other, directly or indirectly, to go about the opening thereof, under pain of the highest ecclesiastical censure, eternal excommunication. The prohibition was no sooner made, but that they did all of them boil with a most ardent desire to know and see what kind of thing it was that was within it: they thought it long already that the pope was not gone, to the end they might jointly, with the more leisure and ease, apply themselves to the box-opening curiosity. The holy father, after he had given them his benediction, retired and withdrew himself to the pontifical lodgings of his own palace; but he was hardly gone three steps from without the gates of their cloister, when the good ladies throngingly, and as in a huddled crowd, pressing hard on the backs of one another, ran thrusting and shoving who should be first at the setting open of the forbidden box, and descrying of the *quod latitat* within. On the very next day thereafter, the pope made them another visit, of a full design, purpose, and intention (as they imagined), to dispatch the grant of their sought and wished-for indulgence: but, before he would enter into a chat or communing with them, he commanded the casket to be brought unto him; it was done so accordingly; but, by your leave, the bird was no more there. Then was it that the pope did represent to their maternities, how hard a matter and difficult it was for them to keep secrets revealed to them in con-

377

fession, unmanifested to the ears of others; seeing for the space of four-and-twenty hours, they were not able to lay up in secret a box, which he had highly recommended to their discretion, charge, and custody."

"Welcome in good faith, my dear master, welcome; it did me good to hear you talk, the Lord be praised for all. I do not remember to have seen you, *before now,* since the last time that you acted at Montpellier with our ancient friends, Anthony Saporta, Guy Bour-guyer, Balthasar Noyer, Tollet, John Quentin, Francis Robinet, John Perdrier, and Francis Rabelais, the moral comedy of him who had espoused and married a *dumb wife."* "I was there," quoth Epis-temon; "the good honest man, her husband, was very earnestly urgent to have the fillet of her tongue untied, and would needs have her speak by any means: at his desire, some pains were taken on her, and, partly by the industry of the physician, other part by the expertness of the surgeon, the Encyliglotte, which she had under her tongue, being cut, she spoke, and spoke again; yea, within few hours, she spoke so loud, so fiercely, and so long, that her poor husband re-turned to the same physician for a recipe to make her hold her peace; 'There are,' quoth the physician, 'many proper remedies in our art to make dumb women speak, but there are none, that ever I could learn therein, to make them silent. The only cure, which I have found out, is their husband's *deafness.'* The wretch became within few weeks thereafter, by virtue of some drugs, charms, or enchant-ments, which the physician had prescribed unto him, so deaf that he could not have heard the thundering of nineteen hundred cannons at a *salvo.* His wife perceiving that indeed he was as deaf as a door-nail, and that her scolding was but in vain, sith that he heard her not, she grew stark mad. ....

"Some time after, the doctor asked for his fee of the husband; who answered, that truly he was deaf, and so was not able to understand what the tenour of his demand might be. Whereupon the leech be-dusted him with a little, I know not what, sort of powder, which rendered him a fool immediately: so great was the stultificating virtue of that strange kind of pulverized dose. Then did this fool of a hus-band and his mad wife join together, and, falling on the doctor and the surgeon, did so scratch, bethwack, and bang them, that they were left half dead upon the place, so furious were the blows which they received: I never in my lifetime laughed so much as at the acting of that buffoonery."

"Let us come to where we left off," quoth Panurge; "your words being translated from the clapper-dudgions (*Gypsy-language*) to plain English, do signify, that is not very inexpedient that I marry, and that I should not care for being a *cuckold*. You have hit the nail on the head. Rarely well! o' my word. I believe, master doctor, that on the day of my marriage you will be so much taken up with your patients, or otherwise so seriously employed, that we shall not enjoy your company: Sir, I will heartily excuse your absence.

> "'*Stercus et urina medici sunt prandia prima.*
> *Ex aliis paleas, ex istis collige grana.*'"

"You are mistaken," quoth Rondibilis, "in the second verse of our distich; for it ought to run thus:

> "'*Nobis sunt signa, vobis sunt prandia digna.*'

"If my wife at any time prove to be unwell and ill at ease—I will look upon the water which she shall have made in a urinal-glass," quoth Rondibilis, "grope her pulse, and see the disposition of her *hipogaster,* together with her umbilicary parts, according to the prescript rule of Hippocrates, 2 Aph. 35. before I proceed any farther in the cure of her distemper." "No, no," quoth Panurge, "that will be but to little purpose; such a feat is for the practice of us that are lawyers, who have the rubric, *De Ventre inspiciendo.* Do not therefore trouble yourself about it, master doctor, I will provide for her a plaster of warm guts. Do not neglect your more urgent occasions otherwhere for coming to my wedding. I will send you some supply of victuals to your own house, without putting you to the trouble of coming abroad, and you shall always be my special friend." With this, approaching somewhat nearer to him, he clapp'd into his hand, without the speaking of so much as one word, four rose-nobles; Rondibilis did shut his fist upon them right kindly; yet, as if it had displeased him to make acceptance of such golden presents, he, in a start, as if he had been wroth, said, "He, he, he, he, he, there was no need of anything, I thank you nevertheless: *from wicked folks I never get enough;* and *from honest people I refuse nothing.* I shall be always, Sir, at your command." "Provided that I pay you well," quoth Panurge. "That," quoth Rondibilis, "is to be understood."

CHAPTER XXXV

HOW THE PHILOSOPHER TROUILLOGAN HANDLETH THE DIFFICULTY OF MARRIAGE

WHEN this discourse was ended, Pantagruel said to the philosopher Trouillogan, "Our loyal, honest, true, and trusty friend, the lamp from hand to hand is come to you; it falleth to your turn to give an answer. Should Panurge, pray you, marry? yea, or no." "He should do both," quoth Trouillogan. "What say you?" asked Panurge. "That which you have heard," answered Trouillogan. "What have I heard?" replied Panurge. "That which I have said," replied Trouillogan. "Ha! ha! ha! are we come to that pass?" quoth Panurge. "Let it go nevertheless, I do not value it a rush, seeing we can make no better of the game. But howsoever tell me, should I marry or not?" "Neither the one nor the other," answered Trouillogan. "The devil take me," quoth Panurge, "if these odd answers do not make me dote, and may he snatch me presently away, if I do understand you. Stay awhile until I fasten these spectacles of mine on this left ear, that I may hear you better." With this Pantagruel perceived, at the door of the great hall (which was that day their dining-room), Gargantua's little dog, whose name was Kyne; for so was Toby's dog called, as is recorded. Then did he say to these who were there present, "Our king is not far off, let us all rise!" That word was scarcely sooner uttered, than that Gargantua with his royal presence graced that banqueting and stately hall. Each of their guests arose to do their king that reverence and duty which became them. After that Gargantua had most affably saluted all the gentlemen there present, he said, "Good friends, I beg this favour of you, and therein you will very much oblige me, that you leave not the places where you sate, nor quit the discourse you were upon.

"Let a chair be brought hither unto this end of the table, and reach me a cup full of the strongest and best wine you have, that I may drink to all the company. You are, in faith, all welcome [well-met], gentlemen. Now, let me know what talk you were about?" To this Pantagruel answered, "That at the beginning of the second service Panurge had proposed a problematic theme, to wit, *whether he should marry, or not marry?* That farther Hippothadeus and Doctor Rondibilis had already dispatched their resolutions thereupon; and that, just as his majesty was coming in, the faithful Trouillogan, in the delivery of his opinion, hath thus far proceeded, that, when Panurge asked whether he ought to *marry, yea or no,* at first he made this answer: *'Both together.'* When this same question was again propounded, the second answer was, *'Neither the one nor the other.'* Panurge exclaimeth, that those answers are full of repugnances and contradictions, protesting that he understands them not, nor what it is that can be meant by them." "If I be not mistaken," quoth Gargantua, "I understand it very well; the answer is not unlike to that which was once made by a philosopher in ancient times, who, being interrogated if he had a woman whom they named him to his wife; 'I have her,' quoth he, 'but she hath not me; possessing her, by her I am not possest.'" "Such another answer," quoth Pantagruel, "was once made by a certain bouncing wench of Sparta, who, being asked, if at any time she had had to do with a man? 'No,' quoth she, 'but sometimes men have had to do with me.'" "Well then," quoth Rondibilis, "let it be a *neuter* in physic; as when we say a body is *neuter* when it is neither sick nor healthful; and a mean in philosophy; *that* by an abnegation of both extremes, and *this* by the participation of the one and the other; even as when luke-warm water is said to be both hot and cold; or rather, as when time makes the partition, and equally divides betwixt the two, a while in the one, another while as long in the other opposite extremity." "The holy apostle," quoth Hippothadeus, "seemeth, as I conceive, to have more clearly explained this point, when he said, 'Those that are married, let them be as if they were not married; and those that have wives, let them be as if they had no wives at all.'" "I thus interpret," quoth Pantagruel, "the having and not having of a wife. To have a wife is to have the use of her in such a way as nature hath ordained, which is for the aid, society, and solace of man, and propagating of his race: to have no wife is not to be uxorious, play the coward, and be lazy about her, and not for her sake to disdain the lustre of that affection which man owes to God; nor yet for her, to leave those offices and duties which he owes unto his country, unto his friends, and kindred; nor on her account to abandon and forsake his precious studies, and other businesses, to wait still on her will, her beck, and her buttocks. If we be pleased in this sense to take the having and not having of a wife, we shall indeed find no repugnancy nor contradiction in the terms at all."

381

CHAPTER XXXVI

YOU speak wisely," quoth Panurge, "if the moon were green
cheese; such a tale once pissed my goose: I do not think but that
I am let down into that dark pit, in the lowermost bottom whereof
the truth was hid, according to the saying of Heraclitus. I see no whit
at all, I hear nothing, understand as little, my senses are altogether
dulled and blunted: truly I do very shrewdly suspect that I am enchanted. I will now alter the former style of my discourse, and talk
to him in another strain. Our trusty friend, stir not, nor imburse any;
but let us vary the chance, and speak without disjunctives: I see already that these loose and ill-joined members of an enunciation do
vex, trouble, and perplex you.

"Now go on, in the name of God, *Should I marry?*"

Trouil. "There is some likelihood therein."

Pan. "But if I do not marry?"

Trouil. "I see in that no inconvenience."

Pan. "You do not?"

Trouil. "None, truly, if my eyes deceive me not."

Pan. "Yea, but I find more than five hundred."

Trouil. "Reckon them."

Pan. "This is an impropriety of speech, I confess; for I do no more
thereby but take a certain for an uncertain number, and posite the
determinate term for what is indeterminate. When I say therefore
five hundred, my meaning is many."

Trouil. "I heard you."

Pan. "Is it possible for me to live without a wife, in the name of all
the subterranean devils?"

Trouil. "Away with these filthy beasts."

Pan. "Let it be then in the name of God; for my Salmigondinish
people used to say ,'*To lie alone, or without a wife, is certainly a brut-
ish life.*' And such a life also was it assevered to be by Dido in her
lamentations."

Trouil. "At your command."

Pan. "By the pody cody, I have fished fair; where are we now?
But will you tell me? Shall I marry?"

Trouil. "Perhaps."

Pan. "Shall I thrive or speed well with it?"

Trouil. "According to the encounter."

Pan. "But if in my adventure I encounter aright, as I hope to do, shall I be fortunate?"

Trouil. "Enough."

Pan. "Let us turn the clean contrary way, and brush our former words against the hair: what if I encounter ill?"

Trouil. "Then blame not me."

Pan. "But, of courtesy, be pleased to give me some advice; I heartily beseech you, what must I do?"

Trouil. "Even what thou wilt."

Pan. "Wishy, washy; trolly, lolly."

Trouil. "Do not invocate the name of anything, I pray you."

Pan. "In the name of God, let it be so. My actions shall be regulated by the rule and square of your counsel: what is it that you advise and counsel me to do?"

Trouil. "Nothing."

Pan. "Shall I marry?"

Trouil. "I have no hand in it."

Pan. "Then shall I not marry?"

Trouil. "I cannot help it."

Pan. "If I never marry, I shall never be a cuckold!"

Trouil. "I thought so."

Pan. "But put the case that I be married."

Trouil. "Where shall we put it?"

Pan. "Admit it to be so, then, and take my meaning in that sense."

Trouil. "I am otherways employed."

Pan. "By the death of a hog, and the mother of a toad, O Lord, if I durst hazard upon a little fling at the swearing game, though privily and under thumb, it would lighten the burthen of my heart, and ease my lights and reins exceedingly; a little patience nevertheless is requisite. Well then, if I marry, I shall be a cuckold?"

Trouil. "One would say so."

Pan. "Yet if my wife prove a virtuous, wise, discreet, and chaste woman, I shall never be cuckolded."

Trouil. "I think you speak congruously."

Pan. "Hearken."

Trouil. "As much as you will."

Pan. "Will she be discreet and chaste? This is the only point I would be resolved in."

Trouil. "I question it."

Pan. "You never saw her?"

Trouil. "Not that I know of."

Pan. "Why do you then doubt of that which you know not?"

Trouil. "For a cause."

Pan. "And if you should know her?"

Trouil. "Yet more."

Pan. "Page, my pretty little darling, take here my cap, I give it thee: have a care you do not break the spectacles that are in it; go down to the lower court: swear there half an hour for me, and I shall, in compensation of that favour, swear hereafter for thee as much as thou wilt. But who shall cuckold me?"

Trouil. "Somebody."

Pan. "By the belly of the wooden horse at Troy, Master Somebody, I shall bang, belam thee, and claw thee well for thy labour."

Trouil. "You say so."

Pan. "Nay, nay, that Nick in the dark cellar, who hath no white in his eye, carry me quite away with him, if, in that case, whensoever I go abroad from the palace of my domestic residence, I do not, with as much circumspection as they use to ring mares in our country to keep them from being sallied by stoned horses, clap a Bergamasco lock upon my wife."

Trouil. "Talk better."

Pan. "It is *bien chien, chié chanté,* well cacked and cackled, shitten and sung in matter of talk. Let us resolve on somewhat."

Trouil. "I do not gainsay it."

Pan. "Have a little patience. Seeing I cannot on this side draw any blood of you, I will try if, with the lancet of my judgment, I be able to bleed you in another vein. Are you married, or are you not?"

Trouil. "Neither the one nor the other, and both together."

Pan. "Oh! the good God help us! By the death of a buffle-ox I sweat with the toil and travel that I am put to, and find my digestion broke off, disturbed, and interrupted: for all my *phrenes, metaphrenes,* and *diaphragms,* my back, belly, midriff, muscles, veins, and sinews, are held in a suspense, and for a while discharged from their proper offices, to stretch forth their several powers and abilities, for *incornifistibulating,* and laying up into the hamper of my understanding your various sayings and answers."

Trouil. "I shall be no hinderer thereof."

384

Pan. "Tush, for shame: our faithful friend, speak; are you married?"

Trouil. "I think so."

Pan. "You were also married before you had this wife."

Trouil. "It is possible."

Pan. "Had you good luck in your first marriage?"

Trouil. "It is not impossible."

Pan. "How thrive you with this second wife of yours?"

Trouil. "Even as it pleaseth my fatal destiny."

Pan. "But what, in good earnest? Tell me; do you prosper well with her?"

Trouil. "It is likely."

Pan. "Come on, in the name of God: I vow, by the burthen of St. Christopher, that I had rather undertake the fetching of a fart forth of the belly of a dead ass than to draw out of you a positive and determinate resolution: yet shall I be sure at this time to have a snatch at you, and get my claws over you. Our trusty friend, let us shame the devil of hell, and confess the verity: were you ever a cuckold? I say, you who are here, and not that other you who playeth below in the Tennis-Court."

Trouil. "No; if it was not predestinated."

Pan. "By the flesh, blood, and body, I swear, reswear, forswear, abjure, and renounce: he evades and avoids, shifts and escapes me, and quite slips and winds himself out of my gripes and clutches."

At these words Gargantua arose, and said, "Praised be the good God in all things, but especially for bringing the world unto that height of refinedness, beyond what it was when I first came to be acquainted therewith, that now the learnedest and most prudent philosophers are not ashamed to be seen entering in at the porches and frontispieces of the schools of the *Pyrrhonian, Aporrhetic, Sceptic,* and *Ephectic sects.* Blessed be the holy name of God! Verily it is like henceforth to be found an enterprise of much more easy undertaking, to catch lions by the neck, horses by the mane, oxen by the horns, bulls by the muzzle, wolves by the tail, goats by the beard, and flying birds by the feet, than to entrap such philosophers in their words. Farewell, my worthy, dear and honest friends."

When he had done thus speaking, he withdrew himself from the company. Pantagruel and others with him, would have followed and accompanied him, but he would not permit them so to do. No sooner was Gargantua departed out of the banqueting-hall than that

Pantagruel said to the invited guests: "Plato's Timæus, at the *begin-ning* always of a solemn festival convention, was wont to count those that were called thereto; we, on the contrary, shall, at the closure and *end* of this treatment, reckon up our number; one, two, three. Where is the fourth? I miss my friend Bridlegoose: was not he sent for?" Epistemon answered, "That he had been at his house to bid and invite him, but could not meet with him; for that a messenger from the parliament of Myrelingois, in Myrelingues, was come from him, with a writ of summons, to cite and warn him personally to appear before the reverend senators of the high-court there, vindicate and justify himself at the bar, of the crimes of prevarication laid to his charge and to be peremptorily instanced against him in a certain decree, judgment, or sentence, lately awarded, given, and pronounced, by him: that therefore he had taken horse and departed in great haste from his own house, to the end that, without peril or danger of falling into a default or contumacy, he might be the better able to keep the prefixed and appointed time."

"I will," quoth Pantagruel, "understand how that matter goeth. It is now above forty years that he hath been constantly the judge of Fonsbeton; during which space of time he hath given upwards of four thousand definitive sentences; two thousand three hundred and nine whereof (although appeal was made, by the parties whom he had judicially condemned, from his inferior judicatory to the supreme court of the parliament of Myrelingois in Myrelingues) were all of them nevertheless confirmed, ratified, and approved of, by an order, decree, and final sentence of the said sovereign court, to the casting of the appellants, and utter overthrow of the suits wherein they had been foiled at law, for ever and a day: that now in his old age he should be personally summoned, who in all the foregoing time of his life hath demeaned himself so unblameably in the discharge of the office and vocation he had been called unto, it cannot assuredly be that such a change hath happened without some notorious misfortune and disaster. I am resolved to help and assist him, in equity and justice, to the utmost extent of my power and ability. I know the malice, despight, and wickedness of the world to be so much more now-a-days exasperated, increased, and aggravated, to what it was not long since, that the cause that is, how just and equitable soever it be, standeth in great need to be succoured, aided, and supported. Therefore presently, from this very instant, do I propose, till I see the event and closure thereof, most heedfully to attend and wait upon it, for fear of some underhand tricky surprisal, cavilling, petti-foggery, or fallacious quirks in law, to his detriment, hurt, or disadvantage."

Then dinner being done, and the tables drawn and removed, when Pantagruel had very cordially and affectionately thanked his invited guests for the favour which he had enjoyed of their company, he presented them with several rich and costly gifts, such as jewels, rings set with precious stones, gold and silver vessels, with a great deal of other sort of plate besides; and, lastly, taking of them all his leave, retired himself into an inner chamber.

CHAPTER XXXVII

HOW PANTAGRUEL PERSUADED PANURGE TO TAKE COUNSEL OF A FOOL

WHEN Pantagruel had withdrawn himself, he, by a little sloping window in one of the galleries, perceived Panurge in a lobby not far from thence, walking alone, with the gesture, carriage, and garb of a fond dotard, raving, wagging and shaking hands, dandling, lolling, and nodding with his head, like a cow bellowing for her calf; and having then called him nearer, spoke unto him thus: "You are at this present, as I think, not unlike to a mouse entangled in a snare, who, the more that she goeth about to rid and unwind herself out of the gin wherein she is caught, by endeavouring to clear and deliver her feet from the pitch whereto they stick, the foullier she is bewrayed with it, and the more strongly pestered therein: even so it is with you; for, the more that you labour, strive, and enforce yourself, to disencumber and extricate your thoughts out of the implicating involutions and fetterings of the grievous and lamentable gins and springs of anguish and perplexity, the greater difficulty there is in the relieving of you, and you remain faster bound than ever; nor do I know, for the removal of this inconveniency, any remedy but one.

"Take heed: I have often heard it said, in a vulgar proverb, *'The wise may be instructed by a fool.'* Seeing the answers and responses of sage and judicious men have in no manner of way satisfied you, take advice of some fool, and possibly, by so doing, you may come to get that counsel which will be agreeable to your own heart's desire and contentment. You know how, by the advice and counsel, and prediction of *fools,* many kings, princes, states, and commonwealths

387

have been preserved, several battles gained, and divers doubts of a most perplexed intricacy resolved. I am not so diffident of your memory as to hold it needful to refresh it with a quotation of examples; nor do I so far undervalue your judgment but that I think it will acquiesce in the reason of this my subsequent discourse.

"As he who narrowly takes heed to what concerns the dexterous management of his private affairs, domestic businesses, and those matters which are confined within the strait-laced compass of one family: who is attentive, vigilant, and active in the œconomic rule of his own house; whose frugal spirit never strays from home; who loseth no occasion whereby he may purchase to himself more riches, and build up new heaps of treasure on his former wealth, and who knows warily how to prevent the inconveniencies of poverty, is called a worldly-wise man, though perhaps, in the judgment of the intelligences which are above, he be esteemed a *fool;* so, on the contrary, is he most like (even in the thoughts of all celestial spirits) to be not only *sage,* but to *presage* events to come, by divine inspiration, who, laying quite aside those cares which are conducible to his body or his fortunes, and as it were departing from himself, rids all his senses of terrene affections, and clears his fancies of all those plodding studies which harbour in the minds of thriving men; all which neglects of sublunary things are vulgarly imputed to *folly.*

"After this manner, the son of Picus, king of the Latins, that great soothsayer Faunus, was called Fatuus by the witless rabble of the common people. The like we daily see practised amongst the comic players, whose dramatic rolls, in distribution of the personages, appoint the acting of the *fool* to him who is the wisest of the troop. In approbation also of this fashion, the mathematicians allow the very same horoscope to princes and to sots; whereof a right pregnant instance by them is given in the nativities of Æneas and Choræbus; the latter of which two is by Euphorion said to have been a *fool;* and yet had, with the former, the same aspects and heavenly genethliac influences.

"I shall not, I suppose, swerve much from the purpose in hand, if I relate unto you what John Andrew said, upon the return of a papal writ which was directed to the mayor of Rochelle and burgesses; after him, by Panormitanus upon the same pontifical canon, Barbatias on the *pandects,* and recently by Jason in his councils, concerning Seyny John, the noted fool of Paris, and great-grandfather to Caillete. The case is this:

388

"At Paris, in the roast-meat cookery of the Petit-Chastelet, before the cookshop of one of the roast-meat sellers of that lane, a certain hungry porter was eating his bread, after he had by parcels kept it awhile above the reek and steam of a fat goose on the spit turning at a great fire, and found it so besmoked with the vapour as to be savoury: which the cook observing, took no notice, till, after having ravined his penny-loaf (whereof no morsel had been unsmokified), he was about decamping and going away: but by your leave, as the fellow thought to have departed thence shot-free, the master-cook laid hold upon him by the gorget, demanding payment for the smoke of his roast-meat. The porter answered, that he had sustained no loss at all; that by what he had done, there was no diminution of the flesh; that he had taken nothing of his, and that therefore he was not indebted to him in anything: as for the smoke in question, that although he had not been there, it would howsoever have been evaporated: besides that, before that time it had never been seen nor heard that roast-meat smoke was sold upon the streets of Paris. The cook hereto replied, that he was not obliged, nor any way bound, to feed and nourish, for nought, a porter whom he had never seen before, with the smoke of his roast-meat: and thereupon swore, that, if he would not forthwith content and satisfy him with present payment for the repast which he had thereby got, he would take his crooked staves from off his back; which instead of having loads thereafter laid upon them, should serve for fuel to his kitchen-fires. Whilst he was going about so to do, and to have pulled them to him by one of the bottom rings which he had caught in his hand, the sturdy porter got out of his gripe, drew forth the knotty cudgel, and stood to his own defence. The altercation waxed hot in words; which moved the gaping hoydens of the sottish Parisians to run from all parts thereabouts, to see what the issue would be of that babbling strife and contention. In the interim of this dispute, to very good purpose, Seyny John, the *fool* and citizen of Paris, happened to be there; whom the cook, perceiving, said to the porter, 'Wilt thou refer and submit unto the noble Seyny John the decision of the difference and controversy which is betwixt us?' 'Yes, by the blood of a goose,' answered the porter, 'I am content.' Seyny John, the *fool,* finding that the cook and porter had compromised the determination of their variance and debate to the discretion of his award and arbitrament, after that the reasons on either side, whereupon was grounded the mutual fierceness of their brawling jar, had been to the full displayed and laid open

389

before him, commanded the porter to draw, out of the fob of his belt, a piece of money, if he had it. Whereupon the porter immediately, without delay, in reference to the authority of such a judicious umpire, put the tenth part of a silver philip into his hand. This little philip Seyny John took; then set it on his left shoulder, to try, by feeling, if it was of a sufficient weight: after that laying it on the palm of his hand, he made it ring and tingle, to understand by the ear if it was of a good alloy in the metal whereof it was composed: thereafter he put it to the ball or apple of his left eye, to explore by the sight if it was well stamped and marked. All which being done, in a profound silence of the whole doltish people who were there spectators of this pageantry, to the great hope of the cook's and despair of the porter's prevalency in the suit that was in agitation, he finally caused the porter to make it sound several times upon the stall of the cook's-shop. Then with a *presidential majesty,* holding his bauble (scepter-like) in his hand, muffling his head with a hood of martern-skins, each side whereof had the resemblance of an ape's face, sprucified up with ears of pasted paper, and having about his neck a bucked ruff, raised, furrowed, and ridged, with ponting-sticks of the shape and fashion of small organ-pipes, he first, with all the force of his lungs, coughed two or three times, and then with an audible voice pronounced the following sentence: 'The court declareth, that the porter, who ate his bread at the smoke of the roast meat, hath civilly paid the cook with the sound of his money: and the said court ordaineth that everyone return to his own home, and attend his proper business, without cost and charges, and for a cause.' This verdict, award, and arbitrament of the Parisian *fool,* did appear so equitable, yea, so admirable, to the aforesaid doctors, that they very much doubted, if the matter had been brought before the sessions for justice of the said place, or that the judges of the Rota at Rome had been umpires therein, or yet that the Areopagites themselves had been the deciders thereof, if by any one part, or all of them together, it had been so judicially sententiated and awarded. Therefore consider if you will be counselled by a *fool.*"

CHAPTER XXXVIII

BY my soul," quoth Panurge, "that overture pleaseth me exceedingly well: I will therefore lay hold thereon and embrace it. At the very motioning thereof my right entrail seemeth to be widened and enlarged, which was but just now hard-bound, contracted, and costive: but, as we have hitherto made choice of the purest and most refined cream of wisdom and sapience for our council, so would I now have, to preside and bear the prime sway in our consultation, as very a *fool* in the supreme degree." "Triboulet," quoth Pantagruel, "is completely *foolish,* as I conceive." "Yes truly," answered Panurge, "he is properly and totally a *fool,* a

Pantagruel.

Fatal f.
Natural f.
Celestial f.
Erratic f.
Eccentric f.
Ætherial and Junonian f.
Arctic f.
Heroic f.
Genial f.
Inconstant f.
Earthly f.
Salacious and sporting f.
Jocund and wanton f.
Pimpled f.
Freckled f.
Bell-tinging f.
Laughing and lecherous f.
Nimming and filching f.
Unpressed f.
First-broached f.
Augustal f.

Panurge.

Jovial f.

Mercurial f.
Lunatic f.
Ducal f.
Common f.
Lordly f.
Palatin f.
Principal f.
Pretorian f.
Elected f.
Courtly f.
Primipilary f.
Triumphant f.
Vulgar f.
Domestic f.
Civil f.
Popular f.
Familiar f.
Notable f.
Favourized f.
Latinized f.

Pantagruel.

Cesarine f.
Imperial f.
Royal f.

Patriarchal f.
Original f.
Loyal f.
Episcopal f.
Doctoral f.
Monachal f.
Fiscal f.
Extravagant f.
Writhed f.
Canonical f.
Such another f.
Graduated f.
Commensal f.
Primolicentiated f.
Trainbearing f.
Supererogating f.
Collateral f.
Haunch and Side f.
Nestling, Ninny and Young-
    ling f.
Exemplary f.
Rare outlandish f.
Satrapal f.
Predicamental and categoric f.
Decumane and superlative f.
Algebraical f.
Talmudical f.
Compendious f.
Hyperbolical f.
Allegorical f.
Solemn f.
Capital f.
Cordial f.
Hepatic f.
Splenetic f.
Windy f.
Almicantarized f.
Chinnified f.
Overcockrilifedlid and fied f.
Sublime f.
Ingrained f.

Basely accoutred f.
Modal f.
Well-fed f.
Heteroclite f.

Panurge.

Ordinary f.
Transcendent f.
Rising f.
Papal f.
Consistorian f.
Conclavist f.
Bullist f.
Synodal f.
Theatrical f.
Flitting, giddy, and unsteady f.
Brancher, novice, and cockney f.
Haggard, cross, and froward f.
Gentle, mild, and tractable f.
Mail-coated f.
Pilfering and purloining f.
Tail-grown f.
Grey-peckled f.
Crimson or ingrain f.
Doating and raving f.
Singular and surpassing f.
Special and excelling f.
Metaphysical f.
Ecstatical f.
Predicable and enunciatory f.
Dutiful and officious f.
Optical and perspective f.
Cabalistical and Masoretical f.
Algamalized f.
Abbreviated f.
Anatomostical f.
Tropological f.
Pleonasmical f.
Hare-brained f.
Intimate f.
Cupshotten and swilling f.
Legitimate f.

Proportioned f.
Swollen and puffed up f.
Corallery f.
Eastern f.
Crimson f.
City f.
Mast-headed f.
Second notial f.
Micher pinch-crust f.
          Pantagruel.
Abridging f.
Leaden-sealed f.
Compassionate f.
Crooching, showking, ducking f.
Well-hung and timbered f.
Crabbed and unpleasing f.
Lofty and stately f.
Architrave f.
Tetragonal f.
Cheerful and buxom f.
Solemn f.
Annual f.
Festival f.
Recreative f.
Boorish and counterfeit f.
Pleasant f.
Privileged f.
Rustical f.
Proper and peculiar f.
Ever ready f.
Diapasonal f.
Resolute f.
Hieroglyphical f.
Authentic f.
Worthy f.
Precious f.
Fanatic f.
Fantastical f.
Symphatic f.
Panic f.
Limbicked and distilled f.

Comportable f.
Wretched and heartless f.
Fooded f.
Thick and threefold f.
Damasked f.
Fearny f.
Unleavened f.
Barytonant f.
Pink and spot-powdered f.
Musket-proof f.
Pedantic f.
Strouting f.
Wood f.
Greedy f.
Senseless f.
Godderlich f.
Obstinate f.
          Panurge.
Summist f.
Morish f.
Mandatory f.
Titulary f.
Grim, stern, harsh, and way-
     ward f.
Ill-clawed, pounced and azy-
     mathallel f.
Winded and tainted f.
Kitchen-haunting f.
Spitrack f.
Pedestal f.
Renowned f.
Rheumatic f.
Flaunting and braggadochio f.
Egregious f.
Humorous and capricious f.
Rude, gross, and absurd f.
Large-measured f.
Babble f.
Down-right f.
Broad-listed f.
Downsical-bearing f.

Stale and over-worn f.
Saucy and swaggering f.
Full-bulked f.
Gallant and vain-glorious f.
Gorgeous and gaudy f.
Continual and intermitting f.
Rebasing and roundling f.
Prototypal and precedenting f.
Prating f.
Catechetic f.
Cacodoxical f.
Meridional f.
Nocturnal f.
Occidental f.
Trifling f.
Astrological and figure-flinging f.
Genethliac and horoscopal f.
Knavish f.
Idiot f.
Blockish f.

Beetle-headed f.
Grotesque f.
Impertinent f.

Pantagruel.

Contradictory f.
Pedagogical f.
Daft f.
Drunken f.
Peevish f.
Prodigal f.
Rash f.
Plodding f.

Panurge.

Quarrelsome f.
Unmannerly f.
Captious and sophistical f.
Soritic f.
Catholoproton f.
Hoti and dioti f.
Alphos and catati f.

Pantagruel. "If there was any reason why, at Rome, the Quirinal holidays of old were called the feasts of *fools,* I know not why we may not, for the like cause, institute, in France, the tribouletic festivals, to be celebrated and solemnized over all the land."

Panurge. "If all fools carried cruppers."

Pantagruel. "If he were the god Fatuus, of whom we have already made mention, the husband of the goddess of Fatua, his father would be *good day* and his grandmother *good even.*"

Panurge. "If all fools paced, albeit he be somewhat wry-legged, he would overlay at least a fathom at every rake. Let us go toward him without any further lingering or delay; we shall have, no doubt, some fine resolution of him. I am ready to go, and long for the issue of our progress impatiently." "I must needs," quoth Pantagruel, "according to my former resolution therein, be present at Bridlegoose's trial: nevertheless, whilst I shall be upon my journey towards Mirelingues, which is on the other side of the river of Loire, I will dispatch Carpalim, to bring hither with him, from Blois, the fool Triboulet." Then was Carpalim instantly sent away, and Pantagruel, at the same time, attended by his domestics, Panurge, Epistemon, Ponocrates, Friar John, Gymnast, Ryzotomus, and others, marched forward on the high road to Mirelingues.

CHAPTER XXXIX

HOW PANTAGRUEL WAS PRESENT AT THE TRIAL OF JUDGE BRIDLEGOOSE, WHO DECIDED CAUSES AND CONTROVERSIES IN LAW BY THE CHANCE AND FORTUNE OF THE DICE

ON the day following, precisely at the hour appointed, Pantagruel came to Mirelingues. At his arrival the presidents, senators, and counsellors prayed him to do them the honour to enter in with them, to hear the decision of all the causes, arguments, and reasons, which Bridlegoose, in his own defence, would produce, why he had pronounced a certain sentence against the subsidy-assessor Toucheronde; which did not seem very equitable to that centumviral court. Pantagruel very willingly condescended to their desire and accordingly, entering in, found Bridlegoose sitting within the middle of the inclosure of the said court of justice; who immediately, upon the coming of Pantagruel, accompanied with the senatorian members of that worshipful judicatory, arose, went to the bar, had his indictment read, and, for all his reasons, defences, and excuses, answered nothing else but that he was become old, and that his sight of late was very much failed and become dimmer than it was wont to be; instancing therewithal many miseries and calamities which old age bringeth along with it and are concomitant to wrinkled elders; which *not. per Archil. D. 86. C. tanta.* By reason of which infirmity he was not able so distinctly and clearly to discern the *points* of the *dice* as formerly he had been accustomed to do: whence it might very well have happened, said he, as old dim-sighted Isaac took Jacob for Esau, that after the same manner, at the decision of causes and controversies in law, he might have been mistaken in taking a *quatre* for a *cinque,* or a *tre* for a *deuce.* "This I beseech your worships," quoth he, "to take into your serious consideration, and to have the more favourable opinion of my uprightness (notwithstanding the prevarication whereof I am accused in the matter of Toucheronde's sentence), that at the time of that decree's pronouncing I only had made use of my small dice; and your worships," said he, "know very well how, by the most authentic rules of the law, it is provided, that the imperfections of

395

nature should never be imputed unto any for crimes and transgressions; as appeareth, *ff. de Re Milit. L. qui cum uno. ff. de Reg. Jur. L. fere. ff. de œdil. edict. per totum, ff. de term. Mod. L. Divus Adrianus,* resolved by *LUD. RO. in L. Si Vero. ff. Sol. Matr.* And who would offer to do otherways should not thereby accuse the man, but nature and the all-seeing providence of God, as is evident in *L. Maximum' Vitium C. de Lib. prœter."*

"What kind of dice" (quoth Trinquamelle, grand president of the said court) "do you mean, my friend Bridlegoose?" "The dice," quoth Bridlegoose, "of sentences at law, decrees, and peremptory judgments, *Alea Judiciorum,* whereof is written, *Per Doct. 26. qu. 2 Cap. Sort. L. nec. emptio. ff. de contrahend. empt. L. quod debetur. ff. de pecul. & ibi Bartol.* And which your worships do, as well as I use, in this glorious sovereign court of yours, so do all other righteous judges, in their decision of processes and final determination of legal differences; observing that which hath been said thereof by D. Henri Ferrandat. *& not. Gl. in m. G. fin. de sortil. & L. sed cum ambo ff. de jud. ubi Doc.* Where mark, that chance and fortune are good, honest, profitable, and necessary, for ending of, and putting a final closure to, dissensions and debates in suits of law. The same hath more clearly been declared by *Bald. Bartold & Alex. C. communia de Leg. Si duo."* "But how is it that you do these things?" asked Trinquamelle. "I very briefly," quoth Bridlegoose, "shall answer you according to the doctrine and instructions of *Leg. ampliorem § in refutatoriis. C. de Appell.* Which is conformable to what is said in *Gloss L. I. ff. quod met. caus. gaudent brevitate moderni.* My practice is therein the same with that of your other worships, and as the custom of the judicatory requires, unto which our law commandeth us to have regard, and by the rule thereof still to direct and regulate our actions and procedures: *un. not. extra. de consuet. C. ex. literis, & ibi Innoc.* for having well and exactly seen, surveyed, overlooked, reviewed, recognised, read, and read over again, turned, and tossed over, seriously perused and examined, the bills of complaint, accusations, impeachments, indictments, warnings, citations, summonings, comparitions, appearances, mandates, commissions, delegations, instructions, information, inquests, preparatories, productions, evidences, proofs, allegations, depositions, cross speeches, contradictions, supplications, requests, petitions, enquiries, instruments of the deposition of witnesses, rejoinders, replies, confirmations of former assertions, duplies, triplies, answers to rejoinders, writings, deeds, reproaches, disabling of exceptions taken, grievances, salvation-bulls, re-examination of witnesses, confronting of them together, declarations, denunciations, libels, certificates, royal missives, letters of appeal, letters of attorney, instruments of compulsion, delinatories, anticipatories, evocations, messages, dimissions, issues, exceptions, dilatory pleas, demurs, compositions, injunctions, reliefs, reports, returns, confessions, acknowledgments, exploits, executions, and other such-like confects and spiceries, both at the one and the other side, as a good judge ought to do, conform to what has been noted thereupon. *Spec. de ordination. Paragr. 3. & Tit. de Offi. omn. jud. Paragr. fin. & de rescriptis Præsent. Parag. 1.* I posite, on the end of a table in my closet, all the pokes and bags of the defendant, and then allow unto him the first hazard of the dice, according to the usual manner of your other worships. And it is mentioned, *L. Favorabiliores ff. de Reg. Jur. & in cap. cum sunt eod. Tit. Lib.* 6. which saith, *Quum sunt partium jura obscura, reo potius favendum est quam actori.* That being done, I thereafter lay down, upon the other end of the same table, the bags and satchels of the plaintiff (as your worships are accustomed to do), *Visum Visu,* just over-against one another; for, *Opposita juxta se posita clarius elucescunt: ut not. in L.* 1. *Parag. Videamus. F. de his qui sunt sui vel alieni juris & in L. munerum* § *Mixta F. de muner. & honor.* Then do I likeways and semblably throw the dice for him, and forthwith *livre* him his chance." "But," quoth Trinquamelle, "my friend, how came you to know, understand, and resolve, the obscurity of these various and seeming contrary passages in law, which are laid claim to by the suitors and pleading parties?" "Even just," quoth Bridlegoose, "after the fashion of your other worships; to wit, when there are many bags on the one side and on the other, I then use my little small dice (after the customary manner of your other worships), in obedience to the law, *semper in stipulationibus. f. de regulis juris,* and the law *versale* verifieth that, *eod. tit. semper in obscuris quod minimum est sequimur:* canonized in *c. in obscuris cod. tit. lib.* 6. I have other large dice, fair and goodly ones, which I employ on the fashion that your other worships use to do when the matter is more plain, clear, and liquid; that is to say, when there are fewer bags." "But, when you have done all these fine things," quoth Trinquamelle, "how do you, my friend, award your decrees and pronounce judgment?" "Even as your other worships," answered Bridlegoose; "for I give out sentence in his favour unto whom hath befallen the best chance by dice; judiciary, tribunian, pretorial, what comes first: so our laws command.

397

ff. qui pot. in pign. l. creditor c. de consul. i. & de regul. juris in 6.
Qui prior est jure."

CHAPTER XL

HOW BRIDLEGOOSE GIVETH REASONS WHY HE LOOKED OVER
THOSE LAW-PAPERS WHICH HE DECIDED BY THE CHANCE
OF THE DICE

YEA, but," quoth Trinquamelle, "my friend, seeing it is by the lot, chance, and throw of the dice, that you award your judgments and sentences, why do not you livre up these fair throws and chances, the very same day and hour, without any farther procrastination or delay, that the controverting party-pleaders appear before you? To what use can those writings serve you, those papers, and other procedures contained in the bags and pokes of the law-suitors?" "To the very same use," quoth Bridlegoose, "that they serve your other worships. They are behooful unto me, and serve my turn in three things very exquisite, requisite, and authentical. First, for formality sake; the omission whereof, that it maketh all whatever is done to be of no force nor value, is excellently well proved by *spec. i. tit. de instr. edit. & tit. de rescript. præsent.* Besides that it is not unknown to you, who have had many more experiments thereof than I, how oftentimes, in judicial proceedings, the formalities utterly destroy the materialities and substances of the causes and matters agitated; for *forma mutata, mutatur substantia. ff. ad exhib. l. julianus ff. ad leg. fals. l. si. is qui quadraginta. Et extra. de decim. c. ad audientiam. et de cel. miss. c. in quadam.*

"Secondly, they are useful and steadable to me (even as unto your other worships) in lieu of some other honest and healthful exercise. The late master Othoman Vadat, a prime physician, as you would say, *cod. de commit & archi. lib.* xii. hath frequently told me, that the lack and default of bodily exercise is the chief, if not the sole and only, cause of the little health and short lives of all officers of justice, such as your worships and I am. Which observation was singularly well, before him, noted and remarked by *Bartholus in lib.* i. *c. de sent. quæ pro eo quod:* therefore is it, that the practice of such like exercitations is appointed to be laid hold on by your other worships, and consequently not to be denied unto me, who am of the same profession:*Quia accessorium naturam sequitar principalis, de regul jur. l. 6.*

& l. cum principalis, & l. nihil dolo. f. eod. tit. ff. de fide juss. l. fide juss. & extra. de officio del. cap. i. Let certain honest and recreative sports and plays of corporeal exercises be allowed and approved of; and so far, *ut omnes obed. in princ. coll.* 7. *& f. de præscript, verò. l. si. gratuitam & l.* 1. *cod. de spect. l.* 11. Such also is the opinion of D. Thom, *in secunda, secundæ q.* 168. quoted to very good purpose, by D. Albert de Rosa, who, *fuit magnus practicus,* and a solemn doctor, as Barbaria attesteth in *principiis consil.* Wherefore the reason is evidently and clearly deduced, and set down before us, in *gloss. in proœmio f. ne autem tertii. Interpone tuis interdum gaudia curis.* In very deed, once, in the year a thousand four hundred fourscore and nine, having a business, concerning the portion and inheritance of a younger brother, depending in the court and chamber of the high treasurers of France, whereinto as soon as ever I got leave to enter, by a pecuniary permission of the usher thereof, as your other worships know very well, that *Pecunia obediunt omnia;* and there, says Baldus, in *l. singularia. f. si cert. pet. & salic. in l. receptitia. cod. de constit. pecuni. & card. in clem.* 1. *de baptism.* I found them all recreating and diverting themselves at the play called musse, either before or after dinner: to me, truly, it is a thing altogether indifferent whether of the two it was, provided that *hic not.* that the game of the musse is honest, healthful, ancient, and lawful, *a Muscho inventore, de quo cod. de petit. hæred. l. si post motam: & muscarii,* such as play and sport it at the musse, are excusable in and by law, *Lib.* 1. *c. de excus. artific. lib. x.* And at the very same time was master Tielman Picquet one of the players of that game of musse. There is nothing that I do better remember: for he laughed heartily when his fellow-members of the aforesaid judicial chamber spoiled their caps in swindging of his shoulders: he, nevertheless, did even then say unto them, that the banging and flapping of him, to the waste and havock of their caps, should not, at their return from the palace to their own houses, excuse them from their wives: *per. c. extra de præsum. & ibi gloss.* Now, *resoltoriè loquendo,* I should say, according to the style and phrase of your other worships, that there is no exercise, sport, game, play, nor recreation, in all this palatine, palacial, or parliamentary world, more aromatizing and fragrant then to empty and void bags and purses, turn over papers and writings, quote margins and backs of scrolls and rolls, fill panniers, and take inspection of causes: *ex Bart. & Joan. de prag. in l. falsa de condit. & demonst. ff.*

"Thirdly, I consider, as your own worships use to do, that time ripeneth and bringeth all things to maturity; that by time everything cometh to be made manifest and patent; and that time is the father of truth and virtue. *Gloss in l. cod. de servit. authent. de restit. & ea quœ pa. & spectat. de requis. cons.*—Therefore is it, that, after the manner and fashion of your other worships, I defer, protract, delay, prolong, intermit, surcease, pause, linger, suspend, prorogate, drive out, wire-draw, and shift off, the time of giving a definitive sentence, to the end that the suit, or process, being well vanned and winnowed, tost and canvassed to and fro; narrowly, precisely, and neatly garbelled, sifted, searched, and examined; and on all hands exactly argued, disputed, and debated, may, by success of time, come at last to its full ripeness and maturity; by means whereof, when the fatal hazard of the dice ensueth thereupon, the parties, cast or condemned by the said aleatory chance, will, with much greater patience, and more mildly and gently, endure, and bear up the disastrous load of their misfortune, than if they had been sentenced at their first arrival unto the court: as *not. gl. ff. de excus. tut. l. tria onera.*

> "*'Portatur leviter quod portat quisque libenter.'*

On the other part, to pass a decree or sentence, when the action is raw, crude, green, unripe, and unprepared, as at the beginning, a danger would ensue of a no less inconveniency than that which the physicians have been wont to say befalleth to him in whom an imposthume is pierced before it be ripe; or unto any other whose body is purged of a strong predominating humour before its digestion: for, as it is written, *in authent. hœc consist. in innoc. de constit. princip.* So is the same repeated, *in gloss. in c. cœterum extr. de juram. calum. quod medicamenta morbis exhibitent, hoc jura negotiis.* Nature furthermore admonisheth and teacheth us to gather and reap, eat and feed on fruits when they are ripe, and not before. *Instit. de rer. div. paragr. is ad quem & ff. de action. empt. l. Julianus.* To marry likeways our daughters when they are ripe, and no sooner, *ff. de donation. inter vir. & uxor. l. cum hic status parag. si quis sponsam, & 27. q. c. sicut dicii. gl.*

> "*'Jam matura thoro plenis adoleverat annis*
> *Virginitas.'*

"And, in a word, she instructeth us to do nothing of any considerable importance but in a full maturity and ripeness, 23. q. 2. paragr. ult. & 23. de. c. ultimo.*

CHAPTER XLI

I REMEMBER to the same purpose," quoth Bridlegoose, in continuing his discourse, "that in the time when at Poictiers I was a student of law under Crocadium Juris, there was at Semerua one Peter Dendin, a very honest man, careful labourer of the ground, fine singer in a church-desk, of good repute and credit, and older than the most aged of all your worships; who was wont to say, that he had seen the great good man, *council of lateran,* with his wide and broad-brimmed red hat; as also, that he had beheld and looked upon the fair, goodly, and gracious lady, pragmatical sanction, his wife, with her huge rosary or paternotrian chaplet of jetbeads, hanging at a large sky-coloured ribbon. This honest man compounded, attoned, and agreed more differences, controversies, and variances at law, than had been determined, voided, and finished, during his time, in the whole palace of Poictiers, in the auditory of Montmorillon, and in the town-house of the old Partenay. This amicable disposition of his rendered him venerable, and of great estimation, sway, power, and authority, throughout all the neighbouring places of Chauvigny, Nouaillé, Legugé, Vivonne, Mezeaux, Estables, and other bordering and circumjacent towns, villages, and hamlets: all their debates were pacified by him; he put an end to their brabling suits at law and wrangling differences. By his advice and counsels were accords and reconcilements no less firmly made than if the verdict of a sovereign judge had been interposed therein, although, in very deed, he was no judge at all, but a right honest man, as you may well conceive. *Arg. in l. si unius fl. de jure jur. & de verbis obligator. l. continuus.*

"There was not a hog killed, within three parishes of him, whereof he had not some part of the haslet and puddings. He was almost every day invited either to a marriage, banquet, christening-feast, an uprising, or woman-churching treatment, a birthday's anniversary-solemnity, a merry frolic gossiping, or otherways to some delicious entertainment in a tavern, to make some accord and agreement between persons at odds and in debate with one another. Remark what I say; for he never yet settled and compounded a difference, betwixt any two at variance, but he strait made the parties, agreed and pacified, to drink together, as a sure and infallible token and symbol of a perfect and completely well-cemented reconciliation, a sign of a sound and sincere amity, and proper mark of new joy and gladness to follow thereupon. *Ut not. per doc. ff. de peric. et com. rei. ven. l.* I. He had a son, whose name was Tenot Dendin, a lusty, young, sturdy, frisking royster, so help me God, who likewise (in imitation of his peace-making father) would have undertaken and meddled with the making-up of variances, and deciding controversies betwixt disagreeing and contentious party-leaders; as you know,

> " '*Sœpe solet similis filius esse patri.*
> *Et sequitur levitér filia matris iter.*'

"*Ut ait gloss. vi. quœst s. c. siquis g. de cons. dist. v. c.* 2, *fin. & est not. per doct. cod. de impub. & aliis substit. l. ult. & l. legitimœ. ff. de stat. hom. gloss. in l. quod si nolit, de œdil. edict. l. quisquis c. ad leg. Jul. majest. excipio filios à moniali susceptos ex monacho. per gloss. in c. impudicas* 27 *quœstione.* And such was his confidence, to have no worse success than his father, that he assumed unto himself the title of *law-strife-settler.* He was likeways in these pacificatory negotiations so active and vigilant; for *vigilantibus jura subveniunt, ex l. pupillus ff. quœ in fraud. cred. & ibid. l. non enim & instit. in proem.* that when he had smelt, heard, and understood; *ut ff. si quando paup. fec. l. agaso gloss. in verbo olfecit, id est, nasum ad culum posuit;* and found, that there was anywhere in the country a debatable matter at law, he would incontinently thrust in his advice, and so forwardly intrude his opinion in the business, that he made no bones of making offer and taking upon him to decide it, how difficult soever it might happen to be, to the full contentment and satisfaction of both parties: it is written, *qui non laborat non manducat.* And the said *gl. ff. de damn. infect. l. quamvis:* and *currere plus que lœ pas vetulam compellit egestas. gloss. ff. de lib. agnosco. l. si quis pro qua facit. l. si. plures, c. de cond. incert.* But, so huge great was his misfortune in this his undertaking, that he never composed any difference, how little soever you may imagine it might have been, but that, instead of reconciling the parties at odds, he did incense, irritate, and exasperate them to a higher point of dissension and enmity than ever they were at before. Your worships know, I doubt not, that,

> " '*Sermo datur cunctis, animi sapientia paucis.*'

"*Gl. ff. de alien. in mun. caus. fa. lib. ii.* This administered unto the tavern-keepers, wine-drawers. and vintners, of Semerua, an occasion to say, that under him they had not, in the space of a whole year, sold so much *reconciliation-wine* (for so were they pleased to call the good wine of Legugé) as under his father they had done in one half hour's time. It happened, a little while thereafter, that he made a most heavy lamentation to his father, attributing the causes of his bad success, in pacificatory enterprizes, to the perversity, stubbornness, froward, cross, and backward inclinations of the people of his time, roundly, boldly, and irreverently upbraiding, that if, but a score of years before, the world had been so wayward, obstinate, pervicacious, implacable, and out of all square, frame, and order, as it was then, his father had never attained to and acquired the honour and title of *strife-appeaser,* so irrefragably, inviolably, and irrevocably, as he hath done; in doing whereof Tenot did heinously transgress against the law which prohibited children to reproach the actions of their parents, *per gl. & Barth. l. iii. paragr. si quis ff. de cond. ob caus. & authent. de nupt. sed quod sancitum col. iv.* To this the honest old father answered thus: 'My son Dendin, when don oportet taketh place, this is the course which we must trace, *gl. c. de appel. l. eos etiam:* for the road that you went upon was not the way to the fuller's mill, nor in any part thereof was the form to be found wherein the hare did sit. Thou hast not the skill and dexterity of settling and composing differences. Why? Because thou takest them at the beginning, in the very infancy and bud as it were, when they are green, raw, and indigestible; yet I know, handsomely and featly, how to compose and settle them all. Why? Because I take them at their decadence, in their waining and when they are pretty well digested. So saith gloss.

> " 'Dulcior est fructus post multa pericula ductus.'

l. non moriturus c. de contrahend. & comit. stip. Didst thou ever hear the vulgar proverb, *Happy is the physician whose coming is desired at the declension of a disease?* For the sickness, being come to a crisis, is then upon the decreasing hand, and drawing towards an end, although the physicians should not repair thither for the cure thereof; whereby, though nature wholly do the work, he bears away the palm and praise thereof. My pleaders (clients), after the same manner thereof, before I did interpose my judgment in the reconciling of them, were waxing faint in their contestations; their altercation heat was much abated, and, in declining from their former strife, they, of themselves, inclined to a firm accommodation of their differences; because there wanted fuel to that fire of burning rancour, and despightful wrangling, whereof the lower sort of lawyers were the kindlers; that is to say, their purses were emptied of coin, they had not a win in their fob, nor penny in their bag, wherewith to solicit and present their actions.

" 'Deficiente pecu, deficit omne nia.'

"There wanted, then, nothing but some brother to supply the place of a paranymph, brawl-broker, proxenete, or mediator, who, acting his part dextrously, should be the first broacher of the motion of an agreement, for saving both the one and the other party from that hurtful and pernicious shame, whereof he could not have avoided the imputation, when it should have been said, that he was the first who yielded and spoke of a reconcilement; and that, therefore, his cause not being good, and being sensible where his shoe did pinch him, he was willing to break the ice, and make the greater haste to prepare the way for a condescendment to an amicable and friendly treaty. Then was it that I came in pudding-time (Dendin, my son), nor is the fat of bacon more relishing to boiled pease than was my verdict then agreeable to them: this was my luck, my profit, and good fortune. I tell thee, my jolly son Dendin, that, by this rule and method, I could settle a firm peace, or at least clap up a cessation of arms and truce, for many years to come, betwixt the great king and the Venetian state; the emperor and the cantons of Swisserland; the English and the Scots; and betwixt the pope and the Ferrarians. Shall I go yet farther? yea, as I would have God to help me, betwixt the Turk and the Sophy; the Tartars and the Muscovites. Remark well what I am to say unto thee; I would take them at that very instant nick of time, when both those of the one and the other side should be weary and tired of making war, when they had voided and emptied their own cashes and coffers of all treasure and coin, drained and exhausted the purses and bags of their subjects, sold and mortgaged their domains and proper inheritances, and totally wasted, spent, and consumed the munition, furniture, provision, and victuals, that were necessary for the continuance of a military expedition. There, I am sure, by God, or by his mother, that would they, would they, in spite of all their teeths, they should be forced to take a little respite and breathing-time, to moderate the fury and cruel rage of their ambitious aims. This is the doctrine in *gl. 37. d. c. si quando.*

" 'Odero, si potero; si non, invitus amabo.'

404

CHAPTER XLII

FOR this cause," quoth Bridlegoose, going on in his discourse, "I
temporise and apply myself to the times, as your other worships
used to do, waiting patiently for the maturity of the process, full
growth, and perfection therof in all its members; to wit, the writings
and bags. *Arg. in l. si major. c. commun. divid. & de cons. di i. c.
solemnitates, & ibi gloss.* A suit in law, at its production, birth, and
first beginning, seemeth to me, as unto your other worships, shapeless,
without form or fashion, incomplete, ugly, and imperfect, even as a
bear, at his first coming into the world, hath neither hands, skin, hair,
nor head, but is merely an infirm, rude, and ill-favoured, piece and
lump of flesh; and would remain still so, if his dam, out of the abundance of her affection to her hopeful cub, did not, with much licking,
put his members into that figure and shape which nature had provided for those of an arctic and ursinal kind, *ut not. doct. ff. ad l. aquil.
l. ii. in fin.* Just so do I see, as you other worships do, processes and
suits in law, at their first bringing-forth, to be numberless, without
shape, deformed, and disfigured; for that then they consist only of one
or two writings, or copies of instruments, through which defect they
appear unto me, as to your other worships, foul, loathsome, filthy, and
mis-shapen beasts; but, when there are heaps of these legiformal papers,
packed, piled, laid up together, impoked, insatcheled, and put up in
bags, then is it, that, with a good reason, we may term that suit, to
which, as pieces, parcels, parts, portions, and members, thereof, they
do pertain and belong, well-formed and fashioned, big-limbed, strong-
set, and in all and each of its dimensions most completely membered:
because *forma dat. esse rei. l. si is qui. ff. ad leg. falcid. in c. cum de-
lecta. de rescript. Barbaria consil. lib. ii.* And before him, *Balsus in c.
ult. extra decons. & l. Julianus exhib. & f. ad l. quæsitum f. de lege. 3.*
The manner is such as is set down *in gloss p. quæst. i. c. Paulus.*

"'*Dèbile principium melior fortuna sequitur.*'

"Like your other worships, also the serjeants, catchpoles, pur-
suivants, messengers, summoners, apparitors, ushers, door-keepers,
pettyfoggers, attornies, proctors, commissioners, justices of the peace,

judge-delegates, arbitrators, overseers, sequestrators, advocates, inquisitors, jurors, searchers, examiners, notaries, tabellions, scribes, scriveners, clerks, prenotaries, secondaries, and expedanean judges, *de quibus tit. est l. 3. c.* by sucking very much, and that exceeding forcibly, and licking at the purses of the pleading parties, they, to the suits already begot and engendered, form, fashion, and frame, head, feet, claws, talons, beaks, bills, teeth, hands, veins, sinews, arteries, muscles, humours, and so forth, through all the similary and dissimilary parts of the whole; which parts, particles, pendicles, and appurtenances, are the law pokes and bags, *gloss. de cons. d. 3. c. accepisti.*

> "'*Qualis vestis erit, talia corda gerit.*'

Hic notandum est, that, in this respect, the pleaders, litigants, and law-suitors are happier than the officers, ministers, and administrators, of justice: for *beatius est dare quam accipere. ff. com. l. 3. extra de celeb. miss. cum Marthœ & 24 quest. 1. cap. od. gloss.*

> "'*Affectum dantis pensat censura tonantis*':

Thus becometh the action, or process, by their care and industry, to be of a complete and goodly bulk, well shaped, framed, formed, and fashioned, according to the *canonical gloss.*

> "'*Accipe, sume, cape, sunt verba placentia papœ.*'

Which speech hath been more clearly explained by *Alb. de Ros. in verbo Roma.*

> "'*Roma manus rodit; quas rodere non valet, odit.*
> *Dantes custodit; non dantes spernit, & odit.*'

The reason whereof is thought to be this:

> "'*Ad prœsens ova, cras pullis sunt meliora.*'

Ut est gl. in l. quum h. ff. de transact. Nor is this all, for the inconvenience of the contrary is set down in *gloss. c. de allu. l. fin.*

> "'*Quum labor in damno est, crescit mortalis egestas.*'

In confirmation whereof, we find, that the true etymology and exposition of the word process is purchase—viz., of good store of money to the lawyers, and of many pokes, *id est,* prou-sacks, to the pleaders, upon which subject we have most cœlestial quips, gybes, and girds.

"'*Litigando jura crescunt, litigando jus acquiritur.*'

Item gl. in cap. illud extrem. de prœsumt. & c. de prob. l. instrum. l. non epistolis l. non nudis.

"'*Et si non prosunt singula, multa juvant.*'"

"Yea, but," asked Trinquamelle, "how do you proceed, my friend, in criminal causes, the culpable and guilty party being taken and seized upon, *flagrante crimine?*" "Even as your other worships use to do," answered Bridlegoose: "first, I permit the plaintiff to depart from the court, enjoining him not to presume to return thither till previously he should have taken a good, sound, and profound sleep, which is to serve for the prime entry and introduction to the legal carrying on of the business. In the next place, a formal report is to be made of his having slept. Thirdly, I issue forth a warrant to convent him before me. Fourthly, he is to produce a sufficient and authentic attestation of his having thoroughly and entirely sleeped, conform to the *gloss. 37. quœst. 7. siquis cum.*

"'*Quandoque bonus dormitat Homerus.*'

"Being thus far advanced in the formality of the process, I find that this consopiating act engendereth another act, whence ariseth the articulating of a member; that again produceth a third act, fashionative of another member; which third bringeth forth a fourth, procreative of another act; new members, in a greater number, are shaped and framed, one still breeding and begetting another (as, link after link, the coat of mail at length is made), till thus, piece after piece, by little and little, like information upon information, the process be completely well formed and perfect in all his members. Finally, having proceeded this length, I have recourse to my dice; nor is it to be thought, that this interruption, respite, or interpellation, is by me occasioned without very good reason inducing me thereunto, and a notable experience of a most convincing and irrefragable force.

407

"I remember, on a time, that in the camp at Stockholm there was a certain Gascon, named Gratianault, a native of the town of Saint Sever, who, having lost all his money at play, and consecutively being very angry thereat, as you know, *pecunia est alter sanguis, ut ait Anto. de Burtio, in accedens 2. extra ut lit. non contest. & Bald. in l. si tuis c. de op. lib. per not. in l. advocati. c. de advoc. div. jud. pecunia est vita hominis & optimus fide jussor in necessitatibus;* did at his coming forth of the gaming-house, in the presence of the whole company that was there, with very loud voice, speak, in his own language, these following words: '*Pap. cap. de bious nillots que maux depipes rous tresire: aresque de pergudes sont les mires bingt, & quavatre bagnelles, ta pla donne rien pies trucs & patacts, scy de gur de bons aulx, qui boille trequar ambe jou à belsambiz.*' Finding that none would make him any answer, he passed from thence to that part of the leaguer, where the huff-snuff, honder-sponder, swash-buckling, high Germans were, to whom he renewed these very terms, provoking them to fight with him; but all the return he had from them, to his stout challenge, was only, '*Der Gasconner thut schich, usz. mitt. cim. iedem zesclage aberer ist genegrer au stacleu darum liebem fram ve hend serg au inverm hausraut.*' Finding also, that none of that band of teutonic soldiers offered himself to the combat, he passed to that quarter of the leaguer where the French free-booting adventurers were encamped, and reiterating unto them, what he had before repeated to the Dutch warriors, challenged them likewise to fight him, and therewithal made pretty little gasconado frisking gambols, to oblige them the more cheerfully and gallantly to cope with him in the lists of a duellizing engagement; but no answer at all was made unto him. Whereupon the Gascon, despairing of meeting with any antagonists, departed from thence, and, laying himself down not far from the pavilions of the grand christian cavalier Cressie, fell fast asleep. When he had thoroughly sleeped an hour or two, another adventurous and all hazarding blade of the forlorn hope of the lavishingly-wasting gamesters, having also lost all his monies, sallied forth with a sword in his hand, in a firm resolution to fight with the aforesaid Gascon, seeing he had lost as well as he.

"'*Ploratur lachrymis amissa pecunia veris,*'

Saith the *gl. de penitent. distinct. 2. c. sunt plures.* To this effect having made enquiry and search for him throughout the whole camp, and in sequel thereof found him asleep, he said unto him, 'Up, ho, good fellow, in the name of all the devils of hell, rise up, rise up, get up; I have lost my money as well as thou hast done, let us, therefore, go fight lustily together, grapple and scuffle it to some purpose: thou may'st look and see my tuck is no longer than thy rapier.' The Gascon, altogether astonished at his unexpected provocation, without altering his former dialect, spoke thus: '*Cap. de Saint Arnault, qu'au segs tu qui me rebeillez? Que man de ta berne te gire; San Siobe cap de Gascoigne tapla dormy Jou, quand à quoest taquain me bingut estée.*' The venturous royster inviteth him again to the duel; but the Gascon, without condescending to his desire; said only this: '*Hepauvret jou squinerie ares, que son pla reposat; Vayne un pauque te posar comme jou, peusse-truqueren.*' Thus, in forgetting his loss, he forgot the eagerness which he had to fight. In conclusion, after that the other had likewise sleeped a little, they, instead of fighting, and possibly killing one another, went jointly to a sutler's tent, where they drank together very amicably, each upon the pawn of his sword. Thus, by a little sleep, was pacified the ardent fury of two warlike champions. There, gosip, comes the golden word of John Andrew *in cap. ult. de sent. & rejudic. l. sexto.* SEDENDO, ET DORMIENDO, FIT ANIMA PRUDENS."

CHAPTER XLIII

HOW PANTAGRUEL EXCUSETH BRIDLEGOOSE IN THE MATTER OF SENTENCING ACTIONS AT LAW BY THE CHANCE OF THE DICE

WITH this Bridlegoose held his peace. Whereupon Trinquamelle bade them withdraw from the court; which accordingly was done; and then directed his discourse to Pantagruel after this manner: "It is fitting (most illustrious prince), not only by reason of the deep obligations, wherein this present parliament, together with the whole marquisate of Mirelingues stand bound to your royal highness for the innumerable benefits, which, as effects of mere grace, they have received from your incomparable bounty, but for that excellent wit also, prime judgment, and admirable learning, wherewith Almighty God, the giver of all good things, hath most richly qualified and endowed you, that we tender and present unto you the decision of this new, strange, and paradoxical case of Bridlegoose; who, in your presence, to your both hearing and seeing, hath plainly confessed his final judging and determinating of suits of law by the mere chance and fortune of the dice: therefore do we beseech you that you would be pleased to give sentence therein, as unto you shall seem most just and equitable." To this Pantagruel answered; "Gentlemen, it is not unknown to you, how my condition is somewhat remote from the profession of deciding law-controversies; yet, seeing you are pleased to do me the honour to put that task upon me, instead of undergoing the office of a judge, I will become your humble supplicant. I observe, gentlemen, in this Bridlegoose, several things, which induce me to represent before you, that it is my opinion he should be pardoned. In the first place, his old age. Secondly, his simplicity. To both which qualities our statute and common laws, civil and municipal together, allow many excuses for any slips or escapes, which, through the invincible imperfection of either, have been inconsiderately stumbled upon by a person so qualified. Thirdly, gentlemen, I must needs display before you another case, which, in equity and justice, maketh much for the advantage of Bridlegoose; to wit, that this one, sole, and single, fault of his ought to be quite forgotten, abolished, and swallowed up, by that immense and vast ocean of just awards and sentences, which heretofore he hath given and pronounced: his demeanour, for these forty years and upwards, that he hath been a judge, having been so evenly balanced in the scales of uprightness, that envy itself, till now, could not have been so impudent as to accuse and twit him with any act worthy of a check or reprehension. As, if a drop of the sea were thrown into the Loire, none could perceive, or say, that, by this single drop, the whole river should be salt and brackish.

"Truly, it seemeth unto me, that, in the whole series of Bridlegoose's juridical decrees, there hath been I know not what of extraordinary savouring of the unspeakable benignity of God, that all those his preceding sentences, awards, and judgments, have been confirmed and approved of by yourselves, in this your own venerable and sovereign court; for it is usual (as you know well) with him, whose ways are inscrutable, to manifest his own ineffable glory in blunting the perspicacity of the eyes of the wise, in weakening the strength of potent oppressors, in depressing the pride of rich extortioners, and in erecting, comforting, protecting, supporting, upholding, and shoaring up, the poor, feeble, humble, silly, and foolish, ones of the earth. But, waving all these matters, I shall only beseech you, not by the obligations which you pretend to owe to my family, for which I thank you, but for that constant and unfeigned love and affection which you have always found in me, both on this and on the other side of Loire, for the maintenance and establishment of your places, offices, and dignities, that, for this one time, you would pardon and forgive him, upon these two conditions: first, that he satisfy, or put a sufficient surety for the satisfaction of the party wronged by the injustice of the sentence in question; for the fulfilment of this article I will provide sufficiently. And, secondly, that, for his subsidiary aid in the weighty charge of administrating justice, you would be pleased to appoint and assign unto him some pretty, little, virtuous, counsellor, younger, learneder, and wiser than he, by the square and rule of whose advice he may regulate, guide, temper, and moderate, in time coming, all his judiciary procedures; or otherways, if you intend totally to depose him from his office, and to deprive him altogether of the state and dignity of a judge, I shall cordially entreat you to make a present and free gift of him to me, who shall find in my kingdoms, charges and employments enough wherewith to imbusy him, for the bettering of his own fortunes and furtherance of my service. In the meantime, I implore the Creator, Saviour, and Sanctifier of all good things, in his grace, mercy, and kindness, to preserve you all, now and evermore, world without end."

These words thus spoken, Pantagruel vailing his cap, and making a leg with such majestic grace as became a person of his paramount degree and eminency, farewelled Trinquamelle, the president and master speaker of that Mirelinguesian parliament, took his leave of the whole court, and went out of the chamber; at the door whereof, finding Panurge, Epistemon, friar John, and others, he forthwith, attended by them, walked to the outer gate, where all of them immediately took horse to return towards Gargantua. Pantagruel, by the way, related to them, from point to point, the manner of Bridlegoose's sententiating differences of law. Friar John said, that he had seen Peter Dendin, and was acquainted with him at that time when he sojourned in the monastery of Fontaine le Conte, under the noble abbot Ardillon. Gymnast likewise affirmed, that he was in the tent of the grand christian cavalier de Cressie, when the Gascon, after his sleep, made answer to the adventurer. Panurge was somewhat incredulous in the matter of believing that it was morally possible Bridlegoose should have been for such a long space of time so continually fortunate in that aleatory way of deciding law-debates.

Epistemon said to Pantagruel, "Such another story, not much unlike to that, in all the circumstances thereof, is vulgarly reported of the provost of Montlehery. In good sooth, such a perpetuity of good luck is to be wondered at. To have hit right twice or thrice in a judgment so given by haphazard might have fallen out well enough, especially in controversies that were ambiguous, intricate, abstruse, perplexed, and obscure."

CHAPTER XLIV

HOW PANTAGRUEL RELATED A STRANGE HISTORY OF THE
PERPLEXITY OF HUMAN JUDGMENT

SEEING you talk," quoth Pantagruel, "of dark, difficult, hard, and knotty debates, I will tell you of one controverted before Cneius Dolabella, pro-consul in Asia. The case was this.

"A wife in Smyrna had of her first husband a child named Abecé; he dying, she, after the expiring of a year and a day, married again, and, to her second husband, bore a boy called Edege: a pretty long time thereafter, it happened (as you know the affection of step-fathers and step-dames is very rare towards the children of the first fathers and mothers deceased) that this husband, with the help of his son Effegé, secretly, wittingly, willingly, and treacherously, murthered Abecé. The woman came no sooner to get information of the fact, but, that it might not go unpunished, she had them both killed, to revenge the death of her first son. She was apprehended and carried before Cneius Dolabella, in whose presence, she, without dissembling anything, confessed all that was laid to her charge; yet alleged, that she had both right and reason on her side for the killing of them. Thus was the state of the question. He found the business so dubious and intricate, that he knew not what to determine therein, nor which of the parties to incline to. On the one hand, it was an execrable crime to cut off at once both her second husband and her son. On the other hand, the cause of the murder seemed to be so natural as to be grounded upon the law of nations and the rational instinct of all the people of the world; seeing they two together had feloniously and murderously destroyed her first son. Not that they had been in any manner of way wronged, outraged, or injured, by him, but out of an avaricious intent to possess his inheritance. In his doubtful quandary, and uncertainty what to pitch upon, he sent to the Areopagites, then sitting at Athens, to learn and obtain their advice and judgment. That judicious senate, very sagely perpending the reasons of his perplexity, sent him word to summon her personally to appear before him, a precise hundred years thereafter, to answer to some interrogatories touching certain points which were not contained in the verbal defence: which resolution of theirs did import, that it was, in their opinion, so difficult and inextricable a matter, that they knew not what to say or judge therein. Who had decided that plea by the chance and fortune of the dice could not have erred nor awarded amiss, on which side soever he had past his casting and condemnatory sentence: if against the woman, she deserved punishment for usurping sovereign authority, by taking that vengeance at her own hand, the inflicting whereof was only competent to the supreme power to administer justice in criminal cases: if for her, the just resentment of so atrocious an injury done unto her, in murdering her innocent son, did fully excuse and vindicate her of any trespass or offence about that particular committed by her. But this continuation of Bridlegoose, for so many years, still hitting the nail on the head, never missing the mark, and always judging aright by the mere throwing the dice and the chance thereof, is that which most astonisheth and amazeth me."

"To answer," quoth Epistemon, "categorically to that which you wonder at, I must ingenuously confess and avow that I cannot; yet, conjecturally to guess at the reason of it, I would refer the cause of that marvellously long continued happy success in the judiciary results of his definitive sentences to the favourable aspect of the heavens and benignity of the intelligences; who, out of their love to goodness, after having contemplated the pure simplicity and sincere unfeignedness of judge Bridlegoose in the acknowledgment of his inabilities, did regulate that for him by chance, which, by the profoundest act of his maturest deliberation, he was not able to reach unto. That likewise which possibly made him to diffide in his own skill and capacity, notwithstanding his being an expert and understanding lawyer, for anything that I know to the contrary, was the knowledge and experience which he had of the antinomies, contrarieties, antilogies, contradictions, traversings, and thwartings, of laws, customs, edicts, statutes, orders, and ordinances, in which dangerous opposition, equity, and justice, being structured and founded on either of the opposite terms, and a gap being thereby opened for the ushering in of injustice and iniquity, through the various interpretations of self-ended lawyers, being assuredly persuaded that the infernal calumniator, who frequently transformeth himself into the likeness of a messenger or angel of light, maketh use of these cross glosses and expositions in the mouths and pens of his ministers and servants, the perverse advocates, bribing judges, law-monging attornies, prevaricating counsellors, and other such like law-wresting members of a court of justice, to turn by those means black to white, green to grey, and what is straight to a crooked ply; for the more expedient doing whereof these diabolical ministers make both the pleading parties believe that their cause is just and righteous; for it is well known that there is no cause, how bad soever, which doth not find an advocate to patrocinate and defend it, else would there be no processes in the world, no suits at law, no pleadings at the bar. He did, in these extremities, as I conceive, most humbly recommend the direction of his judicial proceedings to the upright judge of judges, God Almighty; did submit himself to the conduct and guideship of the blessed Spirit in the hazard and perplexity of the definitive sentence; and, by this *aleatory* lot, did, as it were, implore the divine decree of his *goodwill* and pleasure, instead of that which we call the *final judgment of a court*. To this effect, for the better attaining to his purpose, which was to judge righteously, he did, in my opinion, throw and turn the dice, to the end, that, by the providence aforesaid, the best chance might fall to him whose action was uprightest, and backed with greatest reason; in doing whereof, he did not stray from the sense of the Talmudists, who say that there is so little harm in that manner of searching the truth, that, in the anxiety and perplexedness of human wits, God oftentimes manifesteth the secret pleasure of His divine will.

"Furthermore, I will neither think nor say, nor can I believe, that the unstraightness is so irregular, or the corruption so evident, of those of the parliament of Mirelingois in Mirelingues, before whom Bridlegoose was arraigned for prevarication, that they will maintain it to be a worse practice to have the decision of a suit at law referred to the chance and hazard of a throw of the dice hab-nab, or luck as it will, than to have it remitted to, and passed by, the determination of those whose hands are full of blood, and hearts of wry affections. Besides that their principal direction, in all law-matters, comes to their hands from one Tribonian, a wicked, miscreant, barbarous, faithless, and perfidious knave, so pernicious, unjust, avaricious, and perverse in his ways, that it was his ordinary custom to sell laws, edicts, declarations, constitutions, and ordinances, as at an outroop (public auction) of putsale, to him who offered most for them. Thus did he shape measures for the pleaders, and cut their morsels to them by and out of these little parcels, fragments, bits, scantlings, and shreds of the law now in use, altogether concealing, suppressing, disannulling, and abolishing the remainder, which did make for the total law; fearing that, if the whole law were made manifest and laid open to the knowledge of such as are interested in it, and the learned books of the ancient doctors of the law upon the exposition of the twelve tables and Prætorian edicts, his villainous pranks, naughtiness, and vile impiety should come to the public notice of the world. Therefore, were it better, in my conceit, that is to say, less inconvenient, that the parties at variance, in any juridicial case, should, in the dark, march upon caltrops, than to submit the determination of what is in their right to such unhallowed sentences and horrible decrees: as Cato, in his time, wished and advised, that every judiciary court should be paved with caltrops."

CHAPTER XLV

HOW PANURGE TAKETH ADVICE OF TRIBOULET

ON the sixth day thereafter, Pantagruel was returned home, at the very same hour that Triboulet was by water come from Blois. Panurge, at his arrival, gave him a hog's bladder, puffed with wind, and resounding because of the hard pease that were within it: moreover he did present him with a gilt wooden sword, a small budget made of a tortoise-shell, an osier wattled wicker-bottle full of Breton wine, and five-and-twenty apples of the orchard of Blandureau.

"If he be such a fool," quoth Carpalim, "as to be won with apples, there is no more wit in his pate than in the head of an ordinary cabbage." Triboulet girded the sword and scrip to his side, took the bladder in his hand, ate some few of the apples, and drank up all the wine. Panurge, very wistfully and heedfully looking upon him, said, "I never yet saw a fool (and I have seen ten thousand franks worth of that kind of cattle) who did not love to drink heartily, and by good long draughts." When Triboulet had done with his drinking, Panurge laid out before him and exposed the sum of the business wherein he was to require his advice, in eloquent, and choicely-sorted terms, adorned with flourishes of rhetoric. But, before he had altogether done, Triboulet, with his fist, gave him a bouncing whirret between the shoulders, rendered back into his hand again the empty bottle, flipped and flirted him on the nose with the hog's bladder; and, lastly, for a final resolution, shaking and wagging his head strongly and disorderly, he answered nothing else but this: *"By God, God; mad fool; beware the monk, Buzansay hornpipe."* These words thus finished, he slipped himself out of the company, went aside, and, rattling the bladder, took a huge delight in the melody of the rickling crackling noise of the pease: after which time it lay not in the power of them all to draw out of his chaps the articulate sound of one syllable; insomuch that, when Panurge went about to interrogate him farther, Triboulet drew his wooden sword, and would have stuck him therewith. "I have fished fair now," quoth Panurge, "and brought my pigs to a fine market. Have I not got a brave determination of all my doubts, and a response in all things agreeable to the oracle that gave it? He is a great fool; that is not to be denied; yet is he a greater fool who brought him hither to me; and myself the greatest of all for imparting my thought to him." "The second bolt," quoth Carpalim, "levels point blank at me."

"Without putting ourselves to any stir or trouble in the least," quoth Pantagruel, "let us maturely and seriously consider and prepend the gestures and speech which he hath made and uttered: in them veritably," quoth he, "have I remarked and observed some excellent and notable mysteries; yea, of such important worth and weight, that I shall never henceforth be astonished, nor think strange, why the Turks, with a great deal of worship and reverence, honour and respect natural fools equally with their primest doctors, mufties, divines, and prophets. Did not you take heed," quoth he, "a little before he opened his mouth to speak, what a shogging, shaking, and wagging his head did keep? By the approved doctrine of the ancient philosophers, the customary ceremonies of the most expert magi, and the received opinions of the learnedest lawyers, such a brangling agitation and moving should by us all be judged to proceed from, and be quickened and suscitated by, the coming and inspiration of the prophetizing and fatidical spirit, which, entering briskly, and on a sudden, into a shallow receptacle of a debil substance (for, as you know, and as the proverb shews it, *a little head containeth not much brains*), was the cause of that commotion. This is conform to what is avouched by the most skilful physicians, when they affirm, that shakings and tremblings fall upon the members of a human body, partly because

416

of the heaviness and violent impetuosity of the burthen and load that is carried, and, other parts by reason of the weakness and imbecility that is in the virtue of the bearing organ: a manifest example whereof appeareth in those, who, fasting, are not able to carry to their head a goblet full of wine without a trembling and a shaking in the hand that holds it. This, of old, was accounted a prefiguration and mystical pointing-out of the Pythian divineress, who used always, before the uttering of a response from the oracle, to shake a branch of her domestic laurel. Lampridius also testifieth, that the Emperor Heliogabalus, to acquire unto himself the reputation of a soothsayer, did, on several holy days of prime solemnity, in the presence of the fanatic rabble, make the head of his idol, by some slight within the body thereof, publicly to shake. Plautus, in his Asserie, declareth likewise that Saurius, whithersoever he walked, like one quite distracted of his wits, kept such a furious lolling and mad-like shaking of his head, that he commonly affrighted those who casually met with him in his way. The said author, in another place, shewing a reason why Charmides shook and brangled his head, assevered that he was transported and in an ecstasy. Catullus, after the same manner, maketh mention, in his Berecynthia and Atys, of the place wherein the Mænades, Bacchical women, she-priests of the Lyæan god, and demented prophetesses, carrying ivy-boughs in their hands, did shake their heads. As in the like case amongst the Gauls, the gelded priests of Cybele were wont to do in the celebrating of some festivals, which, according to the sense of the ancient Theologues, have from thence had their denomination; for κύθεσθαι signifies to *turn round,* whirl about, shake the head, and play the part of one that is wry-necked.

"Likewise Titus Livy writeth, that, in the solemnization-time of the Bacchanalian fobedays at Rome, both men and women seemed to prophetize and vaticinate, because of an affected kind of wagging of the head, shrugging of the shoulders, and jectigation of the whole body, which they used then punctually. For the common voice of the philosophers, together with the opinion of the people, asserteth, for an irrefragable truth, that vaticination is seldom by the heavens bestowed on any, without the concomitancy of a little phrenzy, and a head-shaking, not only when the said presaging virtue is infused, but when the person also, therewith inspired, declareth and manifesteth it unto others. The learned lawyer Julian, being asked, on a time, if that slave might be truly esteemed to be healthful and in a good plight, who had not only conversed with some furious maniac and enraged people, but in their company had also prophesied, yet without a noddle-shaking concussion, answered, 'That, seeing there was no head-wagging at the time of his predictions, he might be held for sound and competent enough.' Is it not daily seen how school-masters, teachers, tutors, and instructors of children, shake the heads of their disciples (as one would do a pot in holding it by the lugs), that by this erection, vellication, stretching, and pulling their ears (which, according to the doctrine of the sage Egyptians, is a member consecrated to the *memory*), they may stir them up to recollect their scattered thoughts, bring home those fancies of theirs which perhaps have been extravagantly roaming abroad upon strange and uncouth objects, and totally range their judgments, which possibly by disordinate affections have been made wild, to the rule and pattern of a wise, discreet, virtuous, and philosophical discipline? All which Virgil acknowledgeth to be true, in the branglement of Apollo Cynthius."

CHAPTER XLVI

HOW PANTAGRUEL AND PANURGE DIVERSELY INTERPRET THE WORDS OF TRIBOULET

HE says you are a *fool;* and what kind of *fool? a mad* fool, who in your old age would enslave yourself to the bondage of matrimony, and shut your pleasures up within a wedlock, whose key some ruffian carries in his codpiece. He says farthermore, *beware* of the *monk*. Upon mine honour it gives me in my mind that you will be cuckolded by a *monk*. Nay, I will engage mine honour, which is the most precious pawn I could have in my possession, although I were sole and peaceable dominator over all Europe, Asia, and Afric, that, if you marry, you will surely be one of the horned brotherhood of Vulcan. Hereby may you perceive how much I do attribute to the wise *foolery* of our morosoph Triboulet. The other oracles and responses did, in the general, prognosticate you a cuckold, without descending so near to the point of particular determination as to pitch upon what vocation, amongst the several sorts of men, he should profess who is to be the copesmate of your wife and hornifier of your proper self. Thus noble Triboulet tells us plainly; from whose words we may gather, with all ease imaginable, that your cuckoldry is to be infamous, and so much the more scandalous, that your conjugal bed will be incestuously contaminated with the filthiness of *monkery*. Moreover he says, that you will be the *hornpipe of Buzansay:* that is to say, well horned, hornified, and cornuted: and, as Triboulet's uncle asked from Louis the Twelfth, for a brother of his who lived at Blois, the *hornpipes of Buzansay,* for the organ pipes, through the mistake of one word for another; even so, whilst you think to marry a wise, humble, calm, discreet, and honest wife, you shall unhappily stumble upon one witless, proud, loud, obstreperous, bawling, clamorous, and more unpleasant than any *Buzansay-hornpipe.* Consider withal, how he flirted you on the nose with the *bladder,* and gave you a sound thumping blow with his fist upon the ridge of the back. This denotes and presageth, that you shall be banged, beaten, and filipped by her; and that she will also steal of your goods from you, as you stole the hog's bladder from the little boys of Vaubreton." "Flat contrary," quoth Panurge, "not that I would impudently exempt myself from being a vassal in the territory of *folly;* I hold of that jurisdiction, and am subject thereto, I confess it; and why should I not? for the whole world is *foolish.* In the old Lorrain Language (*fou* for *oou*) *all* and *fool* were the same thing. Besides, it is avouched by Solomon, that infinite is the number of *fools:* from an infinity nothing can be deducted or abated; nor yet, by the testimony of Aristotle, can anything thereto be added or subjoined. Therefore were I a *mad fool,* if, being a *fool,* I should not hold myself a fool. After the same manner of speaking, we may aver the number of the mad and enraged folks to be infinite. Avicenne maketh no bones to assert, that the several kinds of *madness* are infinite.

"Though this much of Triboulet's words tend little to my advantage, howbeit the prejudice which I sustain thereby be common with me to all other men, yet the rest of his talk and gesture maketh altogether for me. He said to my wife, *'Be weary of the monkey';* that is as much as if she should be cheery, and take as much delight in a monkey as ever did the Lesbia of Catullus in her sparrow; who will, for his recreation, pass his time no less joyfully, at the snatching of flies, than heretofore did the merciless fly-catcher Domitian. Withal he meant, by another part of his discourse, that she should be of a jovial country-like humour, as gay and pleasing as an harmonious *hornpipe* of Saulieu or Buzansay. The veridical Triboulet did therein hint at what I liked well, as perfectly knowing the inclinations and propensions of my mind, my natural disposition, and the bias of my interior passions and affections; for you may be assured that my humour is much better satisfied and contented with the pretty, frolic, rural, and dishevelled shepherdesses whose bums, through their coarse canvas smocks, smell of the claver-grass of the field, than with those great ladies, in magnific courts, with their flandan, top-knots, and sultanas, their polvil, postillos, and cosmetics. The homely sound likewise of a rustical *hornpipe* is more agreeable to my ears than the curious warbling and musical quavering of lutes, teorbes, viols, rebecs, and violins. He gave me a lusty rapping thwack on my back. What then? Let it pass, in the name and for the love of God, as an abatement of, and deduction from, so much of my future pains in *purgatory*. He did it not out of any evil intent: he thought, belike, to have hit some of the pages: he is an honest *fool* and an innocent changeling. It is a sin to harbour in the heart any bad conceit of him. As for myself, I heartily pardon him. He flirted me on the nose: in that there is no harm! for it importeth nothing else but that, betwixt my wife and me, there will occur some toyish wanton tricks, which usually happen to all new-married folks."

CHAPTER XLVII

HOW PANTAGRUEL AND PANURGE RESOLVED TO MAKE A
VISIT TO THE ORACLE OF THE HOLY BOTTLE

THERE is yet another point," quoth Panurge, "which you have not at all considered on, although it be the chief and principal head of the matter. He put the bottle in my hand, and restored it me again. How interpret you that passage? What is the meaning of that?" "He possibly," quoth Pantagruel, "signifieth thereby that your wife will be such a drunkard as shall daily take in her liquor kindly, and ply the pots and bottles apace." "Quite otherways," quoth Panurge; "for the bottle was empty. I swear to you, by the pricking bramble thorn of St. Fiacre in Brie, that our unique morosoph, whom I formerly termed the lunatic Triboulet, referreth me, for attaining to the final resolution of my scruple, to the response-giving bottle: therefore do I renew afresh the first vow which I made, and here, in your presence, protest and make oath, by Styx and Acheron, to carry still spectacles in my cap, and never to wear a codpiece in my breeches, until upon the enterprise in hand of my nuptial undertaking, I shall have obtained an answer from the *holy bottle*. I am acquainted with a prudent, understanding, and discreet gentleman, and besides a very good friend of mine, who knoweth the land, country, and place where its temple and oracle are built and posited: he will guide and conduct us thither sure and safely. Let us go thither: I beseech you, deny me not, and say not, nay; reject not the suit I make unto you, I entreat you. I will be to you an Achates, a Damis [Apollonius's companion], and heartily accompany you all along in the whole voyage, both in your going forth and coming back. I have of a long time known you to be a great lover of peregrination, desirous still to learn new things, and still to see what you had never seen before. We shall see wonderful things; take my word for it."

"Very willingly," quoth Pantagruel, "I condescend to your request: but, before we enter in upon our progress towards the accomplishment of so far a journey, replenished and fraught with eminent perils, full of innumerable hazards, and every way stored with evident and manifest dangers—" "What dangers?" quoth Panurge, interrupting him: "dangers fly back, run from, and shun me, whithersoever I go, seven leagues around; as in the presence of the sovereign, sub-magistracy ceases; [see Bodin Rep.] or as clouds and darkness quite vanish at the bright coming of a radiant sun; or as all sores and sicknesses did suddenly depart at the approach of the body of St. Matin à Quande." "Nevertheless," quoth Pantagruel, "before we adventure to set forwards on the road of our projected and intended voyage, some few points are to be discussed, expedited, and dispatched. First, let us send back Triboulet to Blois" (which was instantly done, after that Pantagruel had given him a frize coat). "Secondly, our design must be backed with the advice and counsel of the king my father. And, lastly, it is most needful and expedient for us that we search for and find out some Sibyl to serve us for a guide, truchman, and interpreter." To this Panurge made answer, "That his friend Xenomanes would abundantly suffice for the plenary discharge and performance of the sibyl's office; and that, farthermore, in passing through the lanternatory country, they should take along with them a learned and profitable lanternesse, who would be no less useful to them, in their voyage, than was the Sibyl to Æneas in his descent to the Elysian fields." Carpalim, in the interim, as he was upon the conducting away of Triboulet, in his passing by, hearkened a little to the discourse they were upon; then spoke out saying, "Ho! Panurge, master freeman, take my lord Debitis at Calais along with you; for he is *goud-fallot,* a good fellow: he will not forget those who are *debitors:* these are *lanterns:* thus shall you not lack for both *fallot* and *lantern.*" "I may safely, with the little skill I have," quoth Pantagruel, "prognosticate that by the way we shall engender no melancholy; I clearly perceive it already: the only thing that vexeth me is, that I cannot speak the *lantern* language." "I shall," answered Panurge, "speak for you all: I understand it every whit as well as I do my own maternal tongue: I have been no less used to it than to the vulgar French.

> "'Brisz marg dalgotbric nubstznezos,
> Isquefez prusq albork, crinqs zacbac.
> Mizbe dilbarsks morp nipp stanch bos,
> Strombtz, Panurge, walmap quost gruszbac.'*

"Now guess, friend Epistemon, what this is." "They are," quoth Epistemon, "names of arrant devils, passant devils, and rampant devils." "These words of thine, dear friend of mine, are true," quoth Panurge; "yet are they terms used in the language of the court of the lanternish people. By the way, as we go upon our journey, I will make to thee a pretty little dictionary; which, notwithstanding, shall not last you much longer than a pair of new shoes: thou shalt have learned it sooner than thou canst perceive the dawning of the next subsequent morning. What I have said, in the foregoing *tetrastic,* is thus translated out of the lanternish tongue in our vulgar dialect.

> "'All miseries attended me, whilst I
> A lover was, and had no good thereby:
> Of better luck the married people tell;
> Panurge is one of those, and knows it well.'"

"There is little more then," quoth Pantagruel, "to be done, but that we understand what the will of the king my father will be therein, and obtain his consent."

CHAPTER XLVIII

HOW GARGANTUA SHEWETH THAT CHILDREN OUGHT NOT TO MARRY WITHOUT THE SPECIAL KNOWLEDGE AND ADVICE OF THEIR FATHERS AND MOTHERS

NO sooner had Pantagruel entered in at the door of the great hall of the castle than that he encountered full but with the good honest Gargantua coming forth from the council-board; unto whom he made a succinct and summary narrative of what had passed and occurred, worthy of his observation, in his travels abroad, since their last interview: then, acquainting him with the design he had in hand, besought him that it might stand with his good will and pleasure to grant him leave to prosecute and go through-stitch with the enterprise which he had undertaken. The good man Gargantua, having, in one hand, two great bundles of petitions, indorsed and answered; and in the other, some remembrancing notes and bills, to put him in mind of such other requests of supplicants, which, albeit presented, had nevertheless been neither read nor heard, he gave both to Ulrich Gallet, his ancient and faithful master of requests; then drew aside Pantagruel, and with a countenance more serene and jovial than customary, spoke to him thus: "I praise God, and have great reason so to do, my most dear son, that he hath been pleased to entertain in you a constant inclination to virtuous actions. I am well content that the voyage which you have motioned to me be by you accomplished; but withal I could wish you would have a mind and desire to marry, for that I see you are of competent years." [Panurge in the meanwhile was in a readiness of preparing and providing for remedies, salves, and cures, against all such lets, obstacles, and impediments, as he could, in the height of his fancy, conceive might, by Gargantua, be cast in the way of their itinerary design.] "Most dear father," answered Pantagruel, "I have not yet thought upon it. In all this affair I wholly submit and rest in your good liking and paternal authority; for I shall rather pray unto God that he would throw me down stark dead at your feet in your pleasure, than that, against your pleasure, I should be found married alive. I never yet heard that, by any law, whether sacred or profane (yea, amongst the rudest and most barbarous nations in the world), it was allowed and approved of that children may be suffered and tolerated to marry at their own good will and pleasure, without the knowledge, advice, or consent, asked and had thereto, of their fathers, mothers, and nearest kindred. All legislators, everywhere upon the face of the whole earth have taken away and removed this licentious liberty from children, and totally reserved it to the discretion of the parents."

"My dearly-beloved son," quoth Gargantua, "I believe you, and from my heart thank God for having endowed you with the grace of having both a perfect notice of, and entire liking to, laudable and praiseworthy things; and that, through the windows of your exterior

423

senses, he hath vouchsafed to transmit, unto the interior faculties of your mind, nothing but what is good and virtuous. For in my time there hath been found on the continent a certain country, wherein are I know not what kind of *pastophorian* mole-catching priests, who, albeit averse from engaging their proper persons into a matrimonial duty, like the pontifical flamens of Cybele in Phrygia, as if they were capons and not cocks, full of lasciviousness, salacity, and wantonness, who yet have nevertheless, in the matter of conjugal affairs, taken upon them to prescribe laws and ordinances to married folks. I cannot goodly determine what I should most abhor, detest, loath, and abominate whether the tyrannical presumption of those dreadful sacerdotal *mole-catchers* who, not being willing to contain and coop up themselves within the grates and treillices of their own mysterious temples, do deal in, meddle with, obtrude upon, and thrust their sickles into, harvests of secular businesses, quite contrary and diametrically opposite to the quality, state, and condition, of their callings, professions, and vocations; or the superstitious stupidity and senseless scrupulousness of married folks, who have yielded obedience, and submitted their bodies, fortunes, and estates, to the discretion and authority of such odious, perverse, barbarous, and unreasonable laws. Nor do they see that which is clearer than the light and splendour of the morning star, how all these nuptial and connubial sanctions, statutes, and ordinances, have been decreed, made, and instituted for the sole benefit, profit, and advantage, of the *flaminal mysts* and mysterious *flamens,* and nothing at all for the good, utility, or emolument of the silly hood-winked married people: which administereth unto others a sufficient cause for rendering these church-men suspicious of iniquity, and of an unjust and fraudulent manner of dealing, no more to be connived at nor countenanced, after that it be well weighed in the scales of reason, than if, with a reciprocal temerity, the *laics,* by way of compensation, would impose laws to be followed and observed by those *mysts* and *flamens,* how they should behave themselves in the making and performance of their rites and ceremonies, and after what manner they ought to proceed in the offering up and immolating of their various oblations, victims, and sacrifices; seeing that, besides the edicimation and tithehaling of their goods, they cut off and take parings, shreddings, and clippings of the gain, proceeding from the labour of their hands and sweat of their brows, therewith to entertain themselves the better. Upon which consideration, in my opinion, their injunctions and commands would not prove so pernicious and impertinent as those of the ecclesiastic power, unto which they had tendered their blind obedience.

"For, as you have very well said, there is no place in the world where legally a licence is granted to the children to marry without the advice and consent of their parents and kindred. Nevertheless, by those wicked laws and *mole-catching* customs, whereat there is a little hinted in what I have already spoken to you, there is no scurvy, measly, leprous, or pocky ruffian, pander, knave, rogue, skelm, robber, or thief, pilloried, whipped, and burn-marked, in his own country, for his crimes and felonies, who may not violently snatch away and ravish what maid soever he had a mind to pitch upon, how noble, how fair, how rich, honest, and chaste soever she be, and that out of the house of her own father, in his own presence, from the bosom of her mother, and in the sight and despite of her friends and kindred looking on a so woful spectacle, provided that the rascally villain be so cunning as to associate unto himself some *mystical flamen,* who, according to the covenant made betwixt them two, shall be in hope some day to participate of the prey. Could the Goths, the Scyths, or Messagets, do a worse or more cruel act to any of the inhabitants of a hostile city, when, after the loss of many of their most considerable commanders, the expense of a great deal of money, and a long siege, they shall have stormed and taken it by a violent and impetuous assault? May not these fathers and mothers (think you) be sorrowful and heavy-hearted, when they see an unknown fellow, a vagabond, stranger, a barbarous lout, a rude cur, rotten, fleshless, putrified, scraggy, boily, botchy, poor, a forlorn caitiff and miserable snake, by an open rapt, snatch away before their own eyes their so fair, delicate, neat, well-behavioured, richly provided-for, and healthful daughters, on whose breeding and education they had spared no cost nor charges, by bringing them up in an honest discipline, to all the honourable and virtuous employments becoming one of their sex, descended of a noble parentage; hoping by those commendable and industrious means, in an opportune and convenient time, to bestow them on the worthy sons of their well-deserving neighbours and ancient friends, who had nourished, entertained, taught, instructed and schooled their children with the same care and solicitude, to make them matches fit to attain to the felicity of a so happy marriage; that from them might issue an offspring and progeny, no less heirs to the laudable endowments and exquisite qualifications of their parents, whom they every way resemble, than to their personal and real estates, moveables and inheritances? How doleful, trist and plangorous would such a sight and pageantry prove unto them? You shall not need to think that the collachrymation of the Romans, and their confederates, at the decease of Germanicus Drusus, was comparable to this lamentation of theirs. Neither would I have you to believe, that the discomfort and anxiety of the Lacedemonians, when the Greek Helen, by the perfidiousness of the adulterous Trojan Paris, was privily stolen away out of their country, was greater or more pitiful than this ruthful and deplorable collugency of theirs. You may very well imagine that Ceres, at the ravishment of her daughter Proserpina, was not more attristed, sad, nor mournful than they. Trust me, and your own reason, that the loss of Osyris was not so regretable to Isis; nor did Venus so deplore the death of Adonis; nor yet did Hercules so bewail the straying of Hylas; nor was the rapt of Polyxena more throbbingly resented and condoled by Priamus and Hecuba, than this aforesaid accident would be sympathetically bemoaned, grievous, ruthful and anxious to the wofully desolate and disconsolate parents. Notwithstanding all this, the greater part of so vilely abused parents, are so timorous and afraid of devils and hobgoblins, and so deeply plunged in superstition, that they dare not gainsay nor contradict, much less oppose and resist those unnatural and impious actions, when the *mole-catcher* hath been present at the perpetrating of the fact, and a party contractor and covenanter in that detestable bargain. What do they do then? they wretchedly stay at their own miserable homes, destitute of their well-beloved daughters; the fathers cursing the days and the hours wherein they were married; and the mothers howling and crying that it was not their fortune to have brought forth abortive issues, when they happened to be delivered of such unfortunate girls; and in this pitiful plight spend at best the remainder of their time, with tears and weeping for those their children, of and from whom they expected (and with good reason should have obtained and reaped) in these latter days of theirs, joy and comfort. Other parents there have been, so impatient of that affront and indignity put upon them and their families, that, transported with the extremity of passion, in a mad and frantic mood, through the vehemency of a grievous fury and raging sorrow, they have drowned, hanged, killed, and otherways put violent hands on themselves. Others again, of that parental relation, have, upon the reception of that like injury, been of a more magnanimous and heroic spirit, who (in imitation, and at the example of the children of Jacob, revenging upon the Sichemites the rapt of

426

their sister Dina) having found the rascally ruffian in the association of his mystical *mole-catcher*, closely and in hugger-mugger conferring, and parlying with their daughters, for the suborning, corrupting, depraving, perverting, and enticing these innocent, unexperienced maids unto filthy lewdnesses, have, without any further advisement on the matter, cut them instantly into pieces, and thereupon forthwith thrown out upon the fields their so dismembered bodies to serve for food unto the wolves and ravens. Upon the chivalrous, bold and courageous achievement of a so valiant, stout and manlike act, the other mole-catching symmists have been so highly incensed, and have so chaffed, fretted and fumed thereat, that bills of complaint and accusations have been in a most odious and detestable manner put in before the competent judges; the *arm of secular authority* hath with much importunity and impetuosity been by them implored and required; they proudly contending, that the *servants of God* would become contemptible, if exemplary punishment were not speedily taken upon the persons of the perpetrators of such an enormous, horrid, sacrilegious, crying, heinous and execrable Crime.

"Yet neither by natural equity, by the law of nations, nor by any imperial law whatsoever, hath there been found so much as one rubric, paragraph, point or tittle, by the which any kind of chastisement or correction hath been adjudged due to be inflicted upon any for their delinquency in that kind. Reason opposeth, and nature is repugnant: for there is no virtuous man in the world, who both naturally and with good reason will not be more hugely troubled in mind, hearing of the news of the rapt, disgrace, ignominy and dishonour of his daughter, than of her death. Now any man finding, in hot blood, one who with a fore-thought felony hath murdered his daughter, may, without tying himself to the formalities and circumstances of a legal proceeding, kill him on a sudden, and out of hand, without incurring any hazard of being attainted and apprehended by the officers of justice for so doing. What wonder is it then, or how little strange should it appear to any rational man, if a lechering rogue, together with his mole-catching abettor, be entrapped in the flagrant act of suborning his daughter, and stealing her out of his house, (though herself consent thereto) that the father, in such a case of stain and infamy by them brought upon his family, should put them both to a shameful death, and cast their carcasses upon dunghills, to be devoured and eaten up by dogs and swine; or otherwise fling them a little farther off, to the direption, tearing and rending asunder of their joints and members by the wild beasts of the field?

"Dearly beloved son, have an especial care, that after my decease none of these laws be received in any of your kingdoms: for whilst I breathe, by the grace and assistance of God, I shall give good order.

"Seeing therefore you have totally referred unto my discretion the disposure of you in marriage, I am fully of an opinion, that I shall provide sufficiently well for you in that point. Make ready and prepare yourself for Panurge's voyage: take along with you Epistemon, Friar John, and such others as you will chuse. Do with my treasures what unto yourself shall seem most expedient: none of your actions, I promise you, can in any manner of way displease me. Take out of my arsenal Thalasse whatsoever equipage, furniture, or provision you please, together with such pilots, mariners, and truchmen, as you have a mind to; and with the first fair and favourable wind set sail and make out to sea, in the name of God our Saviour. In the meanwhile, during your absence, I shall not be neglective of providing a wife for you; nor of those preparations, which are requisite to be made for the more sumptuous solemnizing of your nuptials with a most splendid feast, if ever there was any in the world, since the days of Assuerus."

CHAPTER XLIX

HOW PANTAGRUEL DID PUT HIMSELF IN A READINESS TO GO TO SEA, AND OF THE HERB NAMED PANTAGRUELION

WITHIN very few days after that Pantagruel had taken his leave of the good Gargantua, who devoutly prayed for his son's happy voyage, he arrived at the sea-port, near to Sammalo, accompanied with Panurge, Epistemon, Friar John of the funnels, abbot of Theleme, and others of the royal house, especially with Xenomanes, the great traveller, and crosser of dangerous ways, who was come at the bidding and appointment of Panurge, of whose castlewick of Salmigondin he did hold some petty inheritance by the tenure of a mesne fee. Pantagruel, being come thither, prepared and made ready for launching a fleet of ships, to the number of those which Ajax of Salamine had of old equipped, in convoy of the Grecian soldiery against the Trojan state. He likewise picked out for his use so many mariners, pilots, sailors, interpreters, artificers, officers and soldiers, as he thought fitting; and therewithal made provision of so much victuals of all sorts, artillery, munition of divers kind, cloaths, moneys, and other such luggage, stuff, baggage, chaffer, and furniture, as he deemed needful for carrying on the design of so tedious, long, and perilous a voyage. Amongst other things, it was observed how he caused some of the vessels to be fraught and loaded with a great quantity of an herb of his called pantagruelion, not only of the green and raw sort of it, but of the confected also, and of that which was notably well befitted for present use, after the fashion of conserves. The herb pantagruelion hath a little root, somewhat hard and rough, roundish, terminating in an obtuse and very blunt point, and having some of its veins, strings, or filaments coloured with some spots of white, never fixeth itself into the ground above the profoundness almost of a cubit, or foot and a half. From the root thereof proceedeth the one only stalk, orbicular, canelike, green without, whitish within, and hollow like the stem of *smyrnium, olus atrum,* beans and gentian: full of long threads, straight, easy to be broken, jagged, snipped, nicked, and notched a little, after the manner of pillars and columns, slightly furrowed, chamfered, guttered, and channelled, and full of fibres, or hair-like strings: in which consisteth the chief value and dignity of the herb, especially in that part thereof, which is termed *mesa,* as one would say the mean; and in that other which hath got the denomination of *mylasea.* Its height is commonly of five or six foot; yet sometimes it is of such a tall growth, as doth surpass the length of a lance: but that is only when it meeteth with a sweet, easy, warm, wet, and well-soaked soil (as is the ground of the territory of Olone, and that of Rosea, near to Preneste in Sabinia) and that it want not for rain enough about the season of the *fishers' holidays,* and the *œstival solstice.* There are many trees whose height is by it very far exceeded; and you may call it *dendromalache* by the authority of Theophrastus. The plant every year perisheth; the tree, neither in the trunk, root, bark, or boughs, being durable. From the stalk of this pantagruelion plant there issue forth several large and great branches, whose leaves have thrice as much length as breadth, always green, roughish and rugged like the orcanette, or Spanish buglose, hardish, slit round about like unto a sickle, or as the saxifragum, as betony, and finally ending as it were in the points of a Macedonian spear, or of such a lancet as surgeons commonly make use of in their phlebotomizing tiltings. The figure and shape of the leaves thereof is not much different from that of those of the ash-tree, or of agrimony; the herb itself being so like the eupatorian plant, that many skilful herbalists have called it the domestic eupator, and the eupator the wild pantagruelion. These leaves are in equal and parallel distances spread around the stalk, by the number in every rank either of five or seven; nature having so highly favoured and cherished this plant, that she hath adorned it with these two odd, divine, and mysterious numbers. The smell thereof is somewhat strong, and not very pleasing to nice, tender and delicate noses: the seed inclosed therein mounteth up to the very top of its stalk, and a little above it. This is a numerous herb; for there is no less abundance of it than of any other whatsoever. Some of these plants are spheric; some rhomboid, and some of an oblong shape; and all of those either black, bright-coloured, or tawny, rude to the touch, and mantled with a quickly-blasted-away coat; yet such an one as is of a delicious taste and savour to all shrill and sweetly singing birds, such as linnets, goldfinches, larks, canary birds, yellow-hammers, and other of that airy chirping quire: but it would quite extinguish the natural heat and procreative virtue of the semence of any man, who would eat much and often of it. And although that, of old, amongst the Greeks there were certain kinds of fritters, pancakes, buns and tarts made thereof, which commonly for a liquorish daintiness were presented on the table after supper, to delight the palate, and make the wine relish the better; yet is it of a difficult concoction, and offensive to the stomach; for it engendereth bad and unwholesome blood, and with its exorbitant heat woundeth the brain with grievous hurtful smart, and noisome vapours. And as in divers plants and trees there are two sexes, male and female, which is perceptible in laurels, palms, cypresses, oaks, holmes, the daffadil, mandrake, fern, the agaric, mushroom, birth-wort, turpentine, penny-royal, peony, rose of the mount, and many other such like, even so, in this herb there is a male, which beareth no flower at all, yet it is very copious of, and abundant in seed; there is likewise in it a female, which hath great store and plenty of whitish flowers, serviceable to little or no purpose; nor doth it carry in it seed of any worth at all, at least comparable to that of the male. It hath also a larger leaf, and much softer than the male; nor doth it altogether grow to so great a height. This pantagruelion is to be sown at the first coming of the swallows, and is to be plucked out of the ground when the grasshoppers begin to be a little hoarse.

CHAPTER L

THE herb pantagruelion, in September, under the autumnal equinox, is dressed and prepared several ways, according to the various fancies of the people, and diversity of the climates wherein it groweth. The first instruction which Pantagruel gave concerning it, was to divest and dispoil the stalk and stem thereof of all its flowers and seeds, to macerate or mortify it in pond, pool, or lake-water, which is to be made run a little for five days together, if the season be dry, and the water hot; or for full nine or twelve days, if the weather be cloudish, and the water cold: then must it be parched before the sun, till it be drained of its moisture: after this it is in the shadow, where the sun shines not, to be peeled, and its rind pulled off: then are the fibres and strings thereof to be parted (wherein, as we have already said, consisteth its prime virtue, price and efficacy) and severed from the woody part thereof, which is unprofitable, and serveth hardly to any other use, than to make a clear and glistering blaze, to kindle the fire, and for the play, pastime and disport of little children, to blow up hog's bladders, and make them rattle. Many times some use is made thereof by tippling, sweet-lipped bibbers, who out of it frame quills and pipes, through which they with their liquor-attractive breath suck up the new dainty wine from the bung of the barrel. Some modern pantagruelists, to shun and avoid that manual labour, which such a separating and partitional work would of necessity require, employ certain cataractic instruments, composed and formed after the same manner that the froward, pettish and angry Juno did hold the fingers of both her hands interwovenly clinched together, when she would have hindered the child-birth delivery of Alcmena, at the nativity of Hercules; and athwart those cataracts, they break and bruise to very trash the woody parcels, thereby to preserve the better the fibres, which are the precious and excellent parts. In and with this sole operation do these acquiesce and are contented, who, contrary to the received opinion of the whole earth, and in a manner paradoxical to all philosophers, gain their livelihoods backwards, and by recoiling. But those that love to hold it at a higher rate, and prize it according to its value, for their own greater profit do the very same which is told us of the recreation of the three fatal sisters, the Parcæ;

431

or of the nocturnal exercise of the noble Circe; or yet of the excuse which Penelope made to her fond wooing youngsters and effeminate courtiers, during the long absence of her husband Ulysses.

By these means is this herb put into a way to display its inestimable virtues, whereof I will discover a part (for to relate all is a thing impossible to do). I have already interpreted and exposed before you the denomination thereof. I find that plants have their names given and bestowed upon them after several ways. Some got the name of him who first found them out, knew them, sowed them, improved them by culture, qualified them to a tractability, and appropriated them to the uses and subserviencies they were fit for: as the mercurialis, from Mercury; panacea, from Panance the daughter of Esculapius; armois, from Artemis, who is Diana; eupatoria, from the king Eupator; telephion, from Telephus; euphorbium, from Euphorbus, king Juba's physician; climenos, from Clymenus; alcibiadium, from Alcibiades; gentian, from Gentius king of Sclavonia; and so forth, through a great many other herbs or plants. Truly, in ancient times, this prerogative of imposing the inventor's name upon an herb found out by him, was held in so great account and estimation, that as a controversy arose between Neptune and Pallas, from which of them two that land should receive its denomination, which had been equally found out by them both together, thereafter it was called and had the appellation of Athens, from Athene, which is Minerva: just so would Lyncus, king of Scythia, have treacherously slain the young Triptolemus, whom Ceres had sent to shew unto mankind the invention of corn, which until then had been utterly unknown, to the end, that after the murder of the messenger (whose death he made account to have kept secret) he might by imposing, with the less suspicion of false dealing, his own name upon the said found-out seed, acquire unto himself an immortal honour and glory, for having been the inventor of a grain so profitable and necessary, to and for the use of human life. For the wickedness of which treasonable attempt, he was by Ceres transformed into that wild beast, which by some is called a lynx, and by others an ounce. Such also was the ambition of others upon the like occasion, as it appeareth by that very sharp wars, and of a long continuance, have been made of old betwixt some residentiary kings in Cappadocia, upon this only debate, of whose name a certain herb should have the appellation: by reason of which difference, so troublesome and expensive to them all, it was by them

432

called polemonion, or polemonia; and by us, for the same cause, termed make-bate.

Other herbs and plants there are, which retain the names of the countries from whence they were transported: as the median apples, from Media, where they first grew; punic apples, from Punicia, that is to say, Carthage: ligusticum, which we call louage from Liguria, the coast of Genoua; rheubarb, from a flood in Barbary, as Ammianus attesteth, called Rhua; santonica, from a region of that name; fenugreek, from Greece; castanes, from a country so called; persicaria, from Persia; sabine, from a territory of that appellation; stæchas, from the Stæchad islands; spica celtica, from the land of the Celtic Gauls; and so throughout a great many others, which were tedious to enumerate. Some others again have obtained their denominations by way of anti-phrases, or contrariety: as absinth, because it is contrary to ψίντος; for it is bitter to the taste in drinking. Holosteon means all bones; whilst on the contrary there is no frailer, tenderer, nor brittler herb in the whole production of nature than it.

There are some other sorts of herbs, which have got their names from their virtues and operations; as aristolochia, because it helpeth women in childbirth; lichen, for that it cureth the disease of that name; mallow, because it mollifieth; callithricum, because it maketh the hair of a bright colour; alyssum, ephemerum, bachium, nasturtium, hen-bane, and so forth through many more.

Other some there are which have obtained their names from the admirable qualities that are found to be in them; as heliotropium (which is the marigold) because it followeth the sun; so that at the sun rising it displayeth and spreads itself out, at his ascending it mounteth, at his declining it waineth, and when he is set it is close shut; adianton, because although it grow near unto watery places, and albeit you should let it lie in water a long time, it will nevertheless retain no moisture nor humidity; hieracia, eringium, and so throughout a great many more. There are also a great many herbs and plants, which have retained the very same names of the men and women who have been metamorphosed and transformed in them: as from Daphne, the laurel is called also; myrrh, from Myrrha the daughter of Cynaras; pythis, from Pythis; cinara, which is the artichoke, from one of that name; narcissus, saffron, smilax, and divers others.

Many herbs likewise have got their names of those things which they seem to have some resemblance of; as hippuris, because it hath the likeness of a horse's tail; alopecuris, because it representeth in similitude the tail of a fox; psyllion, from a flea, which it resembleth; delphinium, for that it is like a dolphin fish; buglosse is so called, because it is a herb like an ox's tongue; iris, so called, because in its flowers it hath some resemblance of the rainbow; myosota, because it is like the ear of a mouse; coronopus, for that it is of the likeness of a crow's foot: a great many other such there are, which here to recite were needless. Furthermore, as there are herbs and plants which had their names from those of men; so by a reciprocal denomination, have the surnames of many families taken their origin from them: as the Fabii, à fabis, beans; the Pisons, à pisis, pease; the Lentuli, from lentils; the Cicerons, a ciceribus, vel ciceris, a sort of pulse called chick-pease; and so forth. In some plants or herbs the resemblance and likeness hath been taken from a higher mark or object; as when we say Venus' navel, Venus' hair, Venus' tub, Jupiter's beard, Jupiter's eye, Mars's blood, the hermodactyl or Mercury's fingers, which are all of them names of herbs, as there are a great many more of the like appellation. Others again have received their denomination from their forms; such as trefoil, because it is three leaved; pentaphylon, for having five leaves; serpolet, because it creepeth along the ground; helxine, petasites, myrobolans, which the Arabians call been, as if you would say an acorn; for it hath a kind of resemblance thereto, and withal is very oily.

CHAPTER LI

WHY IT IS CALLED PANTAGRUELION, AND OF THE ADMIRABLE VIRTUES THEREOF

BY such like means of attaining to a denomination (the fabulous ways being only from thence expected; for the Lord forbid that we should make use of any fables in this a so venerable history) is this herb called pantagruelion; for Pantagruel was the inventor thereof; I do not say of the plant itself, but of a certain use which it serves for, exceeding odious and hateful to thieves and robbers, unto whom it is more contrarious and hurtful than the strangle-weed and choke-fitch is to the flax, the cat's-tail to brakes, the sheavegrass to the mowers of hay, the fitches to the chickny pease, the darnel to barley, the hatchet-fitch to the lentil purse, the antramium to the beans, tares to

434

wheat, ivy to walls, the water lily to lecherous monks, the birchen rod to the scholars of the college of Navarre in Paris, colewort to the vine-tree, garlic to the load stone, onions to the sight, fern-seed to women with child, willow grain to vicious nuns, the yew-tree shade to those that sleep under it, wolfsbane to wolves and libbards, the smell of the fig-tree to mad bulls, hemlock to goslings, purslane to the teeth, or oil to trees: for we have seen many of those rogues, by virtue and right application of this herb, finish their lives, short and long, after the manner of Phillis queen of Thracia, of Bonosus emperor of Rome, of Amata king Latinus's wife, of Iphis, Autolicus, Lycambes, Arachne, Phædra, Leda, Achius king of Lydia, and many thousands more; who were chiefly angry and vexed at this disaster therein, that without being otherways sick, or evil disposed in their bodies, by a touch only of the pantagruelion, they came on a sudden to have the passage obstructed, and their pipes (thro' which were wont to bolt so many jolly sayings, and to enter so many luscious morsels) stopped, more cleverly than ever could have done the squinancy.

Others have been heard most wofully to lament, at the very instant when Atropos was about to cut the thread of their life, that Pantagruel held them by the gorge. But (well-a-day) it was not Pantagruel; he never was an executioner: it was the pantagruelion, manufactured and fashioned into an halter, and serving in the place and office of a cravat. In that verily they solæcized, and spoke improperly; unless you would excuse them by a trope, which alloweth us to posit the inventor in the place of the thing invented; as when Ceres is taken for bread, and Bacchus put instead of wine. I swear to you here, by the good and frolic words which are to issue out of that wine-bottle, which is a cooling below in the copper vessel full of fountain water, that the noble Pantagruel never snatched any man by the throat; unless it was such an one as was altogether careless and neglective of those obviating remedies, which were preventive of the thirst to come.

It is also termed pantagruelion by similitude: for Pantagruel, at the very first minute of his birth, was no less tall than this herb is long, whereof I speak unto you; his measure having been then taken the more easy, that he was born in the season of the great drought, when they were busiest in the gathering the said herb; to wit, at that time when Icarus's dog, with his fiery bawling and barking at the sun, maketh the whole world troglodytic, and enforceth people everywhere to hide themselves in the dens and subterranean caves. It is likeways called pantagruelion, because of the notable and singular qualities, virtues, and properties thereof: for as Pantagruel hath been the idea, pattern, prototype and exemplar of all jovial perfection and accomplishment (in the truth whereof I believe there is none of you, gentlemen drinkers, that putteth any question); so in this pantagruelion have I found so much efficacy and energy, so much compleatness and excellency, so much exquisiteness and rarity, and so many admirable effects and operations of a transcendent nature, that if the worth and virtue thereof had been known, when those trees, by the relation of the prophet, made election of a wooden king, to rule and govern over them, it without all doubt would have carried away from all the rest the plurality of votes and suffrages.

Shall I yet say more? If Oxylus the son of Orius had begotten this plant upon his sister Hamadryas, he had taken more delight in the value and perfection of it alone, than in all his eight children, so highly renowned by our ablest mythologians, that they have sedulously recommended their names to the never-failing tuition of an eternal remembrance. The eldest child was a daughter, whose name was Vine; the next born was a boy, and his name was Fig-tree; the third was called Walnut tree; the fourth, Oak; the fifth, Sorbapple-tree; the sixth, Ash; the seventh, Poplar; and the last had the name of Elm, who was the greatest surgeon in his time. I shall forbear to tell you, how the juice or sap thereof, being poured and distilled within the ears, killeth every kind of vermin, that by any manner of putrefaction cometh to be bred and engendered there: and destroyeth also any whatsoever other animal that shall have entered thereat. If likewise you put a little of the said juice within a pail or bucket full of water, you shall see the water instantly turn and grow thick therewith, as if it were milk curds; whereof the virtue is so great, that the water thus curdled is a present remedy for horses subject to the cholic, and such as strike at their own belly. The root thereof, well boiled, mollifieth the joints, softeneth the hardness of shrunk sinews, is every way comfortable to the nerves and good against all cramps and convulsions, as likewise all cold and knotty gouts. If you would speedily heal a burning, whether occasioned by water or fire, apply thereto a little raw pantagruelion; that is to say, take it so as it cometh out of the ground, without bestowing any other preparation or composition upon it; but have a special care to change it for some fresher, in lieu thereof, as soon as you shall find it waxing dry upon the sore.

Without this herb kitchens would be detested, the tables of dining rooms abhorred, although there were great plenty and variety of most dainty and sumptuous dishes of meat set down upon them; and the choicest beds also, how richly soever adorned with gold, silver, amber, ivory, porphyry, and the mixture of most precious metals, would without it yield no delight or pleasure to the reposers in them. Without it millers could neither carry wheat, nor any other kind of corn, to the mill; nor would they be able to bring back from thence flour, or any other sort of meal whatsoever. Without it, how could the papers and writs of lawyers' clients be brought to the bar? Seldom is the mortar, lime or plaister brought to the workhouse without it. Without it how should the water be got out of a draw-well? In what case would tabellions, notaries, copyists, makers of counterparts, writers, clerks, secretaries, scriveners, and such like persons be without it? Were it not for it, what would become of the toll-rates and rent-rolls? Would not the noble art of printing perish without it? Whereof could the chassis or paper windows be made? How should the bells be rung? The altars of Isis are adorned therewith: the pastophorian priests are therewith clad and accoutred; and whole human nature covered and wrapped therein, at its first position and production in, and into this world: all the lanific trees of Seres, the bumbast and cotton bushes in the territories near the Persian sea, and gulph of Bengala; the Arabian swans, together with the plants of Maltha, do not all of them cloath, attire, and apparel so many persons as this one herb alone. Soldiers are now-a-days much better sheltered under it, than they were in former times, when they lay in tents covered with skins. It overshadows the theatres and amphitheatres from the heat of a scorching sun: it begirdeth and encompasseth forests, chases, parks, copses and groves, for the pleasure of hunters: it descendeth into the salt and fresh of both sea and river waters, for the profit of fishers: by it are boots of all sizes, buskins, gamashes, brodkins, gambados, shoes, pumps, slippers, and every cobbled ware wrought and made steadable for the use of man: by it the butt and rover-bows are strung, the cross-bows bended, and the slings made fixed: and, as if it were an herb every whit as holy as the verveine, and reverenced by ghosts, spirits, hobgoblins, fiends and phantoms, the bodies of deceased men are never buried without it.

I will proceed yet further. By the means of this fine herb, the invisible substances are visibly stopped, arrested, taken, detained, and prisoner-like committed to their receptive gaols. Heavy and ponderous weights are by it heaved, lifted up, turned, veered, drawn, carried, and every way moved quickly, nimbly and easily, to the great profit and emolument of human kind. When I perpend with myself these and such like marvellous effects of this wonderful herb, it seemeth strange unto me, how the invention of so useful a practice did escape, through so many bypast ages, the knowledge of the ancient philosophers; considering the inestimable utility which from thence proceeded, and the immense labour, which, without it, they did undergo in their pristine elucubrations. By virtue thereof, through the retention of some aërial gusts, are the huge ramberges, mighty gallions, the large floyts, the chiliander, the myriander ships launched from their stations, and set a going at the pleasure and arbitrement of their rulers, conders and steersmen. By the help thereof those remote nations, whom nature seemed so unwilling to have discovered to us, and so desirous to have kept them still in abscondito, and hidden from us, that the ways through which their countries were to be reached unto, were not only totally unknown, but judged also to be altogether impermeable and inaccessible, are now arrived to us, and we to them.

Those voyages outreached the flights of birds, and far surpassed the scope of feathered fowls, how swift soever they had been on the wing, and notwithstanding that advantage which they have of us in swimming through the air. Taproban hath seen the heaths of Lapland, and both the Javas the Riphæan mountains; wide distant Phebol shall see Theleme, and the Islanders drink of the flood Euphrates: by it the chill-mouthed Boreas hath surveyed the parched mansions of the torrid Auster, and Eurus visited the regions which Zephyrus hath under his command: yea, in such sort have interviews been made, by the assistance of this sacred herb, that maugre longitudes and latitudes, and all the variations of the zones, the periæcian people, and antœcian, amphiscian, heteroscian, and periscian, have oft tendered and received mutual visits to, and from other, upon all the climates. These strange exploits bred such astonishment to the cœlestial intelligences, to all the marine and terrestrial gods, that they were on a sudden all afraid; from which amazement, which they saw how, by means of this blest pantagruelion, the arctic people looked upon the antarctic, scourd the atlantic ocean, passed the tropics, pushed through the torrid zone, measured all the zodiac, sported under the equinoctial, having both poles level with their horizon; they judged it high time to call a council, for their own safety and preservation.

The Olympic gods, being all and each of them affrighted at the sight of such achievements, said, "Pantagruel hath shapen work enough for us, and put us more to a plunge, and nearer our wit's end, by this sole herb of his, than did of old the Aloidæ by overturning mountains. He very speedily is to be married, and shall have many children by his wife: it lies not in our power to oppose this destiny; for it hath passed through the hands and spindles of the fatal sisters, necessity's inexorable daughters. Who knows but by his sons may be found out an herb of such another virtue and prodigious energy, as that by the aid thereof, in using it aright, according to their father's skill, they may contrive a way for human kind to pierce into the high aërian clouds, get up into the spring-head of the hail, take an inspection of the snowy sources, and shut and open as they please the sluices from whence proceed the flood-gates of the rain? Then prosecuting their æthereal voyage, they may step in unto the lightning work-house and shop, where all the thunderbolts are forged, where seizing on the magazine of heaven, and store-house of our warlike fire munition, they may discharge a bounding peal or two of thundering ordnance, for joy of their arrival to these new supernal places; and charging those tonitrual guns afresh, turn the whole force of that artillery against ourselves, wherein we most confided: then it is like they will set forward to invade the territories of the moon, whence passing thro' both Mercury and Venus, the sun will serve them for a torch, to shew the way from Mars to Jupiter and Saturn. We shall not then be able to resist the impetuosity of their intrusion, nor put a stoppage to their entering in at all whatever regions, domiciles, or mansions of the spangled firmament they shall have any mind to see, to stay in, or to travel through for their recreation: all the cœlestial signs together, with the constellations of the fixed stars, will jointly be at their devotion then: some will take up their lodgings at the ram, some at the bull, and others at the twins; some at the crab, some at the lion inn, and others at the sign of the virgin; some at the balance, others at the scorpion, and others will be quartered at the archer; some will be harboured at the goat, some at the water-pourer's sign, some at the fishes; some will lie at the crown, some at the harp, some at the golden eagle and the dolphin; some at the flying horse, some at the ship, some at the great, some at the little bear; and so throughout the glistning hostleries of the whole twinkling asteristic welkin. There will be sojourners come from the earth, who longing after the taste of the sweet cream, of their own scumming off, from the best

439

milk of all the dairy of the galaxy, will set themselves at the table down with us, drink of our nectar and ambrosia, and take to their own beds at night, for wives and concubines, our fairest goddesses, the only means whereby they can be deified." A junto hereupon being convocated, the better to consult upon the manner of obviating so dreadful a danger, Jove, sitting in the presidential throne, asked the votes of all the other gods: which after a profound deliberation amongst themselves on all contingencies, they freely gave at last, and then resolved unanimously to withstand the shock of all whatsoever sublunary assaults.

CHAPTER LII

HOW A CERTAIN KIND OF PANTAGRUELION IS OF THAT NATURE, THAT THE FIRE IS NOT ABLE TO CONSUME IT

I HAVE already related to you great and admirable things: but if you might be induced to adventure upon the hazard of believing some other divinity of this sacred pantagruelion, I very willingly would tell it you. Believe it if you will, or otherways believe it not, I care not which of them you do, they are both alike to me; it shall be sufficient for my purpose to have told you the truth, and the truth I will tell you. But to enter in thereat, because it is of a craggy, difficult and rugged access, this is the question which I ask of you: If I had put within this bottle two pints, the one of wine and the other of water, thoroughly and exactly mingled together, how would you unmix them? After what manner would you go about to sever them, and separate the one liquor from the other, in such sort, that you render me the water apart, free from the wine, and the wine also pure, without the intermixture of one drop of water; and both of them in the same measure, quantity, and taste that I had embottled them? Or, to state the question otherways, if your carmen and mariners, entrusted, for the provision of your houses, with the bringing of a certain considerable number of tuns, puncheons, pipes, barrels, and hogsheads of Graves wine, or of the wine of Orleans, Beaune, and Mirevaux, should drink out the half, and afterwards with water fill up the other empty halves of the vessels as full as before; as the Limosins use to do in their carriages by wains and carts, of the wines of Argenton and Sangaultier: after that, how would you part the water from the wine, and purify them both in such a case? I understand you well enough; your meaning is, that I must do it with an ivy funnel. That is written, it is true, and the verity thereof explored by a thousand experiments: you have learned to do this feat before; I see it: but those that have never known it, nor at any time have seen the like, would hardly believe that it were possible. Let us nevertheless proceed.

But put the case we were now living in the age of Sylla, Marius, Cæsar, and other Roman emperors; or that we were in the time of our ancient Druids, whose custom was to burn and calcine the dead bodies of their parents and lords, and that you had a mind to drink the ashes or cinders of your wives or fathers, in the infused liquor of some good white wine, as Artemisia drunk the dust and ashes of her husband Mausolus; or otherways, that you did determine to have them reserved in some fine urn, or reliquary pot; How would you save the ashes apart, and separate them from those other cinders and ashes into which the fuel of the funeral and bustuary fire hath been converted? Answer if you can: by my figgins, I believe it will trouble you so to do.

Well, I will dispatch and tell you, that if you take of this celestial pantagruelion so much as is needful to cover the body of the defunct, and after that you shall have inwrapped and bound therein as hard and closely as you can the corpse of the said deceased persons, and sowed up the folding-sheet with thread of the same stuff; throw it into the fire, how great or ardent soever it be, it matters not a straw; the fire through this pantagruelion will burn the body, and reduce to ashes the bones thereof, and the pantagruelion shall be not only not consumed nor burnt, but also shall neither lose one atom of the ashes enclosed within it, nor receive one atom of the huge bustuary heap of ashes resulting from the blazing conflagration of things combustible laid round about it, but shall at last, when taken out of the fire, be fairer, whiter, and much cleaner than when you did put it in at first. Therefore it is called asbeston, which is as much as to say incombustible. Great plenty is to be found thereof in Carpasia, as likewise in the climate Diasyene, at very easy rates. O how rare and admirable a thing it is that the fire which devoureth, consumeth and destroyeth all things else, should cleanse, purge and whiten this sole pantagruelion carpasian asbeston! If you mistrust the verity of this relation, and demand, for further confirmation of my assertion a visible sign, as the Jews, and such incredulous infidels use to do, take a fresh egg, and orbicularly (or rather ovally) infold it within this divine pantagruelion: when it is so wrapped up, put it into the hot embers of a fire, how great or ardent soever it be, and having left it there as long as you will, you shall at last, at your taking it out of the fire, find the egg roasted hard, and as it were burnt, without any alteration, change, mutation, or so much as a calefaction of the sacred pantagruelion: for less than a million pounds sterling, modified, taken down and amoderated to the twelfth part of one fourth part of fourpence halfpenny farthing, you are able to put it to a trial, and make proof thereof.

Do not think to over-match me here, by paragoning with it, in the way of a more eminent comparison, the salamander. That is a fib; for albeit a little ordinary fire, such as is used in dining-rooms and chambers, gladden, cheer up, exhilarate and quicken it; yet may I warrantably enough assure, that in the flaming fire of a furnace, it will, like any other animated creature, be quickly suffocated, choaked, consumed and destroyed. We have seen the experiment thereof, and Galen many ages ago hath clearly demonstrated and confirmed it, lib. 3. de temperamentis. And Dioscorides maintaineth the same doctrine, lib. 2. Do not here instance in competition with this sacred herb the feather allum, or the wooden tower of Pireum, which L. Sylla was never able to get burnt; for that Archelaus, governor of the town for Mithridates king of Pontus, had plaistered it all over on the outside with the said allum. Nor would I have you to compare therewith the herb, which Cornelius Alexander called fonem, and said that it had some resemblance with that oak which bears the misselto; and that it could neither be consumed, nor receive any manner of prejudice by fire, nor water, no more than the misselto, of which was built, said he, the so renowned ship Argos. Search where you please for those that will believe it. I in that point desire to be excused. Neither would I wish you to parallel therewith (although I cannot deny but that it is of a very marvellous nature) that sort of tree which groweth along the mountains of Brianson and Ambrun, which produceth out of its root the good agaric: from its body it yieldeth unto us a so excellent rosin, that Galen hath been bold to equal it to the turpentine: upon the delicate leaves thereof it retaineth for our use that sweet heavenly honey, which is called the manna: and although it be of a gummy, oily, fat, and greasy substance, it is notwithstanding unconsumable by fire. It is in the Greek and Latin called larix. The Alpenise name is melze. The Antenorides and Venetians term it larege; which gave occasion to that castle in Piedmont to receive the denomination of

Larignum by putting Julius Cæsar to a stand at his return from amongst the Gauls.

Julius Cæsar had commanded all the yeomen, boors, hinds, and other inhabitants in, near unto, and about the Alps and Piedmont, to bring all manner of victuals and provision for an army to those places, which on the military road he had appointed to receive them for the use of his marching soldiery: to which ordinance all of them were obedient, save only those that were within the garrison of Larignum; who, trusting in the natural strength of the place, would not pay their contribution. The emperor, proposing to chastise them for their refusal, caused his whole army to march straight towards that castle, before the gate whereof was erected a tower, built of huge big spars and rafters of the larch tree, fast bound together with pins and pegs of the same wood, and interchangeably laid on one another, after the fashion of a pile or stack of timber, set up in the fabrick thereof to such an apt and convenient height, that from the parapet above the portcullis, they thought with stones and leavers to beat off and drive away such as should approach thereto.

When Cæsar had understood the chief defence of those within the castle did consist in stones and clubs, and that it was not an easy matter to sling, hurl, dart, throw, or cast them so far as to hinder the approaches, he forthwith commanded his men to throw great store of bavins, faggots, and fascines round about the castle, and when they had made the heap of a competent height, to put them all in a fair fire; which was thereupon incontinently done. The fire was so great and so high, that it covered the whole castle, that they might well imagine the tower would thereby be altogether burnt to dust and demolished. Nevertheless, contrary to all their hopes and expectations, when the flame ceased, and that the faggots were quite burnt and and consumed, the tower appeared as whole, sound and entire as ever. Cæsar, after a serious consideration had thereof, commanded a compass to be taken, without the distance of a stone cast from the castle round about it; there, with ditches and entrenchments, to form a blockade: which when the Larignans understood, they rendered themselves upon terms; and then, by a relation from them, it was that Cæsar learned the admirable nature and virtue of this wood; which, of itself, produceth neither fire, flame, nor coal; and would therefore, in regard to that rare quality of incombustibility, have been admitted into this rank and degree of a true pantagruelional plant; and that so much the rather, for that Pantagruel directed that all the gates, doors, angiports, windows, gutters, frettized and embowed cielings, cans, and other whatsoever wooden furniture in the abbey of Theleme, should be all materiated of this kind of timber; that he likewise caused to cover therewith the sterns, stems, cook-rooms or laps, hatches, decks, coursies, bends and walls of his carricks, ships, gallions, galays, brigantins, foysts, frigates, crears, barks, floyts, pinks, pinnaces, hoys, catches, capers, and other vessels of his Thalassian arsenal; were it not the wood or timber of the larch-tree, being put within a large and ample furnace full of huge vehemently flaming fire, proceeding from the fuel of other sorts and kinds of wood, cometh at last to be corrupted, consumed, dissipated and destroyed, as are stones in a lime-kiln. But this pantagruelion asbeston is rather by the fire renewed and cleansed, than by the flames thereof consumed or changed. Therefore,

> "Arabians, Indians, Sabæans,
> Sing not, in hymns and io pæans,
> Your incense, myrrh, or ebony:
> Come here, a nobler plant to see;
> And carry home, at any rate,
> Some seed, that you may propagate.
> If in your soil it takes, to heaven
> A thousand thousand thanks be given;
> And say, with France, it goodly goes
> Where the pantagruelion grows!"

THE
AUTHOR'S EPISTLE DEDICATORY,

OF THIS

FOURTH BOOK,

TO THE

MOST ILLUSTRIOUS PRINCE,

AND

MOST REVEREND LORD, ODET,

CARDINAL DE CHASTILLION

YOU are not unacquainted, most illustrious prince, how often I have been, and am daily pressed and required, by great numbers of eminent persons, to proceed in the Pantagruelian fables: they tell me that many languishing, sick, and disconsolate persons perusing them, have deceived their grief, passed their time merrily, and been inspired with new joy and comfort. I commonly answer, that I aimed not at glory and applause, when I diverted myself with writing; but only designed to give by my pen, to the absent who labour under affliction, that little help which at all times I willingly strive to give to the present that stand in need of my art and service. Sometimes I at large relate to them, how Hippocrates in several places, and particularly in lib. 6. epidem. describing the institution of the physician his disciple, and also Soranus of Ephesus, Oribasius, Galen, Hali Abbas, and other authors, have descended to particulars, in the prescription of his motions, deportment, looks, countenance, gracefulness, civility, cleanliness of face, cloaths, beard, hair, hands, mouth, even his very nails; as if he were to play the part of a lover in some comedy or enter the lists to fight some potent enemy. And indeed the practice of physic is properly enough compared by Hippocrates to a fight, and also to a farce acted between three persons, the patient, the physician, and the disease. Which passage has sometimes put me in mind of Julia's saying to Augustus her father. One day she came before him in a very gorgeous, loose, lascivious dress, which very much displeased him, though he did

445

not much discover his discontent. The next day she put on another, and in a modest garb, such as the chaste Roman ladies wore, came into his presence. The kind father could not then forbear expressing the pleasure which he took to see her so much altered, and said to her: "Oh! how much more this garb becomes, and is commendable in the daughter of Augustus." But, she, having her excuse ready, answered: "This day, sir, I dressed myself to please my father's eye; yesterday, to gratify that of my husband." Thus disguised in looks and garb, nay even, as formerly was the fashion, with a rich and pleasant gown with four sleeves, which was called philomium, according to Petrus Alexandrinus in 6. Epidem. a physician might answer to such as might find the metamorphosis indecent: "Thus have I accoutred myself, not that I am proud of appearing in such a dress; but for the sake of my patient, whom alone I wholly design to please, and no ways offend or dissatisfy. There is also a passage in our father Hippocrates, in the book I have named, which causes some to sweat, dispute, and labour: not indeed to know whether the physician's frowning, discontented and morose Catonian look render the patient sad, and his joyful, serene, and pleasing counteance rejoice him; for experience teaches us that this is most certain: but whether such sensations of grief, or pleasure, are produced by the apprehension of the patient observing his motions and qualities in his physician, and drawing from thence conjectures of the end and catastrophe of his disease; as, by his pleasing look, joyful and desirable events, and by his sorrowful and unpleasing air, sad and dismal consequences; and whether those sensations be produced by a transfusion of the serene or gloomy, ærial or terrestrial, joyful or melancholic spirits of the physician, into the person of the patient, as is the opinion of Plato and Averroes.

Above all things, the fore-cited authors have given particular directions to physicians about the words, discourse, and converse, which they ought to have with their patients; every one aiming at one point, that is, to rejoice them without offending God, and in no ways whatsoever to vex or displease them. Which causes Herophilus much to blame the physician Callianax, who, being asked by a patient of his, "Shall I die?" impudently made him this answer:

"Patroclus died, whom all allow,
By much a better man than you."

Another, who had a mind to know the state of his distemper, ask-

446

ing him, after our merry Patelin's way; "Well, doctor, does not my water tell you I shall die?" He foolishly answered, "No; if Latona, the mother of those lovely twins, Phœbus and Diana, begot thee." Galen, lib. 4. comment. 6. epidem. blames much also Quintus his tutor, who a certain nobleman of Rome, his patient, saying to him, "You have been at breakfast, my master, your breath smells of wine"; answered arrogantly, "Yours smells of fever: which is the better smell of the two, wine, or a putrid fever?" But the calumny of certain cannibals, misanthropes, perpetual eaves-dropers, has been so foul and excessive against me, that it had conquered my patience, and I had resolved not to write one jot more. For the least of their detractions were, that my books are all stuffed with various heresies, of which, nevertheless, they could not shew one single instance: much indeed of comical and facetious fooleries, neither offending God nor the king (and truly I own they are the only subject, and only theme of these books); but of heresy, not a word, unless they interpreted wrong, and against all use of reason, and common language, what I had rather suffer a thousand deaths, if it were possible, than have thought: as who should make bread to be *stone,* a fish to be a *serpent,* and an egg to be a *scorpion.* This, my lord, emboldened me at once to tell you, as I was complaining of it in your presence, that if I did not esteem myself a better christian, than they show themselves towards me, and if my life, writings, words, nay thoughts, betrayed to me one single spark of heresy, or I should in a detestable manner fall into the snares crimes against me; I would then, like the phœnix, gather dry wood, of the spirit of detraction, Διάβολος, who, by their means, raises such kindle a fire, and burn myself in the midst of it. You were then pleased to say to me, that king Francis, of eternal memory, had been made sensible of those false accusations; and that having caused my books (mine, I say, because several false and infamous have been wickedly laid to me) to be carefully and distinctly read to him by the most learned and faithful anagnost in this kingdom, he had not found any passage suspicious; and that he abhorred a certain envious, ignorant, hypocritical informer, who grounded a mortal heresy on an n put instead of an m by the carelessness of the printers.

As much was done by his son, our most gracious, virtuous, and blessed sovereign, Henry, whom heaven long preserve: so that he granted you his royal privilege, and particular protection for me, against my slandering adversaries.

You kindly condescended since, to confirm me these happy news at

Paris; and also lately, when you visited my lord cardinal du Bellay, who, for the benefit of his health, after a lingering distemper, was retired to St. Maur, that place (or rather paradise) of salubrity, serenity, conveniency, and all desirable country pleasures.

Thus, my lord, under so glorious a patronage, I am emboldened once more to draw my pen, undaunted now and secure; with hopes that you will still prove to me, against the power of detraction, a second Gallic Hercules in learning, prudence, and eloquence; an Alexicacos in virtue, power, and authority: you, of whom I may truly say what the wise monarch Solomon saith of Moses, that great prophet and captain of Israel, Ecclesiast. 45. "A man fearing and loving God, who found favour in the sight of all flesh, well-beloved both of God and man; whose memorial is blessed. God made him like to the glorious saints, and magnified him so, that his enemies stood in fear of him: and for him made wonders; made him glorious in the sight of kings, gave him a commandment for his people, and by him shewed his light: he sanctified him in his faithfulness, and meekness, and chose him out of all men. By him he made us to hear his voice, and caused by him the law of life and knowledge to be given."

Accordingly, if I shall be so happy as to hear any one commend those merry composures, they shall be adjured by me to be obliged, and pay their thanks to you alone, as also to offer their prayers to heaven, for the continuance and increase of your greatness; and to attribute no more to me, than my humble and ready obedience to your commands: for by your most honourable encouragement, you at once have inspired me with spirit, and with invention; and without you my heart had failed me, and the fountain-head of my animal spirits had been dry. May the lord keep you in his blessed mercy.

My lord, your most humble, and most devoted servant,

FRANCIS RABELAIS, Physician.

Paris, this 28th of January, MDLII.

THE AUTHOR'S PROLOGUE

TO

THE FOURTH BOOK.

GOOD people. God save and keep you! Where are you? I can't
see you: stay—I'll saddle my nose with spectacles—oh, oh! 'twill
be fair anon, I see you. Well, you have had a good vintage, they say:
this is no bad news to Frank, you may swear. You have got an infallible cure against thirst: rarely performed of you, my friends! You,
your wives, children, friends, and families are in as good case as hearts
can wish; 'tis well, 'tis as I'd have it: God be praised for it, and if such
be his will, may you long be so. For my part, I am thereabouts, thanks
to his blessed goodness; and by the means of a little pantagruelism
(which you know is a certain jollity of mind, pickled in the scorn of
fortune) you see me now hale and cheery, as sound as a bell, and ready
to drink, if you will. Would you know why I'm thus, good people?
I'll e'en give you a positive answer—Such is the Lord's will, which I
obey and revere; it being said in his word, in great derision to the
physician, neglectful of his own health, "Physician, heal thyself."

Galen had some knowledge of the bible, and had conversed with
the christians of his time, as appears *lib.* ii. *de usu partium: lib.* 2. *de
differentiis pulsuum, cap.* 3. and *ibid. lib.* 3. *cap.* 2. *and lib. de rerum
affectibus* (if it be Galen's). Yet 'twas not for any such veneration
of holy-writ that he took care of his own health. No, 'twas for fear of
being twitted with the saying so well known among physicians.

> "He boasts of healing poor and rich,
> Yet is himself all over itch."

This made him boldly say, that he did not desire to be esteemed a
physician, if from his twenty-eighth year to his old age he had not
lived in perfect health, except some ephemerous fevers, of which he
soon rid himself: yet he was not naturally of the soundest temper, his
stomach being evidently bad. Indeed, as he saith, *lib.* 5. *de sanitate
tuenda,* that physician will hardly be thought very careful of the health
of others, who neglects his own. Asclepiades boasted yet more than
this: for he said that he had articled with fortune not to be reputed a

449

physician, if he could be said to have been sick, since he began to practise physic, to his latter age, which he reached, lusty in all his members, and victorious over fortune; till at last the old gentleman unluckily tumbled down from the top of a certain ill-propt and rotten staircase, and so there was an end of him.

If by some disaster health is fled from your worships to the right or to the left, above or below, before or behind, within or without, far or near, on this side or t'other side, wheresoever it be, may you presently, with the help of the Lord, meet with it. Having found it, may you immediately claim it, seize it, and secure it. The law allows it: the king would have it so: nay, you have my advice for it. Neither more nor less than the law-makers of old did fully impower a master to claim and seize his run-a-way servant, wherever he might be found. Ods-bodikins, is it not written and warranted by the ancient customs of this so noble, so rich, so flourishing realm of France, that the dead seizes the quick? See what has been declared very lately in that point by that learned, wise, courteous, humane, and just civilian, Andrew Tiraqueau, counsellor of the great, victorious, and triumphant Henry II. in the most honourable court of parliament at Paris. Health is our life, as Ariphron the Sicyonian wisely has it: without health, life is no life, 'tis not living life: 'ABI'OΣ BI'OΣ, BI'OΣ ABI'ΩTOΣ. Without health life is only a languishment, and an image of death. Therefore, you that want your health, that is to say, *that are dead, seize the quick;* secure life to yourselves, that is to say, health.

I have this hope in the Lord, that he will hear our supplications, considering with what faith and zeal we pray, and that he will grant this our wish, because 'tis moderate and mean. Mediocrity was held by the ancient sages to be golden, that is to say, precious, praised by all men, and pleasing in all places. Read the sacred bible, you'll find the prayers of those who asked moderately were never unanswered. For example, little dapper Zaccheus, whose body and reliques the monks of St. Garlick near Orleans boast of having, and nick-named him St. Sylvanus; he only wished to see our blessed Saviour near Jerusalem. 'Twas but a small request, and no more than anybody then might pretend to. But alas! he was but low built; and one of so diminutive a size among the crowd, could not so much as get a glimpse of him. Well then he struts, stands on tip-toes, bustles and bestirs his stumps, shoves and makes way, and with much ado clambers up a sycamore. Upon this, the Lord, who knew his sincere affection, presented himself to his sight, and was not only seen by him, but heard also: nay, what's more, he came to his house, and blessed his family.

One of the sons of the prophets in Israel felling wood near the river Jordan, his hatchet forsook the helve, and fell to the bottom of the river: so he prayed to have it again ('twas but a small request, mark ye me) and having a strong faith, he did not throw the hatchet after the helve, as some spirits of contradiction say by way of scandalous blunder, but the helve after the hatchet, as you all properly have it. Presently two great miracles were seen: up springs the hatchet from the bottom of the water, and fixes itself to its old acquaintance the helve. Now had he wished to coach it to heaven in a fiery chariot like Elias, to multiply in seed like Abraham, be as rich as Job, strong as Sampson, and beautiful as Absalom, would he have obtained it, d'ye think? I'troth, my friends, I question it very much.

Now I talk of moderate wishes in point of hatchet (but harkee me, be sure you don't forget when we ought to drink) I'll tell you what is written among the apologues of wise Æsop the Frenchman, I mean the Phrygian and Trojan, as Max. Planudes makes him; from which people, according to the most faithful chroniclers, the noble French are descended. Ælian writes that he was of Thrace; and Agathias, after Herodotus, that he was of Samos: 'tis all one to Frank.

In his time lived a poor honest country fellow of Gravot, Tom Wellhung by name, a wood-cleaver by trade, who in that low drudgery made shift so to pick up a sorry livelihood. It happened that he lost his hatchet. Now tell me who ever had more cause to be vexed than poor Tom? Alas, his whole estate and life depended on his hatchet: by his hatchet he earned many a fair penny of the best woodmongers or log merchants, among whom he went a jobbing: for want of his hatchet he was like to starve; and had death but met him six days after without a hatchet, the grim fiend would have mowed him down in the twinkling of a bed-staff. In this sad case he began to be in a heavy taking, and called upon Jupiter with the most eloquent prayers (for you know, necessity was the mother of eloquence). With the whites of his eyes turned up towards heaven, down on his marrowbones, his arms reared high, his fingers stretched wide, and his head bare, the poor wretch without ceasing was roaring out, by way of litany, at every repetition of his supplications, "My hatchet, lord Jupiter, my hatchet! my hatchet! only my hatchet, O Jupiter, or money to buy another, and nothing else! alas, my poor hatchet!"

Jupiter happened then to be holding a grand council about certain

451

urgent affairs, and old gammer Cybele was just giving her opinion, or, if you had rather have it so, it was young Phœbus, the beau; but in short, Tom's outcries and lamentations were so loud, that they were heard with no small amazement at the council-board, by the whole consistory of the gods. "What a devil have we below," quoth Jupiter, "that howls so horridly? By the mud of Styx, have not we had all along, and have not we here still enough to do, to set to rights a world of damned puzzling businesses of consequence? We made an end of the fray between Prestan, king of Persia, and Soliman, the Turkish emperor: we have stopped up the passages between the Tartars and the Muscovites; answered the Xeriff's petition; done the same to that of Golgots Rays; the state of Parma's dispatched; so is that of Maydemburg, that of Mirandola, and that of Africa, that town on the Mediterranean which we call Aphrodisium: Tripoli by carelessness has got a new master; her hour was come.

"Here are the Gascons cursing and damning, demanding the restitution of their bells.

"In yonder are the Saxons, Easterlings, Ostrogoths, and Germans, nations formerly invincible, but now aberkeids, bridled, curbed, and brought under by a paultry diminutive crippled fellow: they ask us revenge, relief, restitution of their former good sense and ancient liberty.

"But what shall we do with this same Ramus and this Galland, with a pox to 'em, who, surrounded with a swarm of their scullions, blackguard ragamuffins, sizers, vouchers and stipulators, set together by the ears the whole university of Paris? I am in a sad quandary about it, and for the heart's blood of me cannot tell yet with whom of the two to side.

"Both seem to me notable fellows, and as true cods as ever pissed. The one has rose-nobles, I say fine and weighty ones; the other would gladly have some too. The one knows something; the other's no dunce. The one loves the better sort of men: the other's beloved by them. The one is an old cunning fox; the other, with tongue and pen, tooth and nail, falls foul on the ancient orators and philosophers, and barks at them like a cur.

"What thinkest thou of it, say, thou bawdy Priapus? I have found thy council just before now, *et habet tua mentula mentem.*"

"King Jupiter" (answered Priapus, standing up and taking off his cowl, his snout uncased and reared up, fiercely and stifly propt), "since you compare the one to a yelping snarling cur, and the other to sly Reynard the fox, my advice is, with submission, that without fretting or puzzling your brains any farther about them, without any more ado, even serve them both as in the days of yore, you did the dog and the fox." "How?" asked Jupiter; "when? who were they? where was it?" "You have a rare memory, for ought I see!" returned Priapus. "This right worshipful father Bacchus, whom we have here nodding with his crimson phiz, to be revenged on the Thebans, had got a fairy fox, who, whatever mischief he did, was never to be caught or wronged by any beast that wore a head.

"The noble Vulcan here present had framed a dog of Monesian brass, and with long puffing and blowing, put the spirits of life into him: he gave it you, you gave it your Miss Europa, Miss Europa gave it Minos, Minos gave it Procris, Procris gave it Cephalus. He was also of the fairy kind; so that, like the lawyers of our age, he was too hard for all other sorts of creatures, nothing could scape the dog. Now who should happen to meet but these two? What do you think they did? Dog by his destiny was to take fox, and fox by his fate was not to be taken.

"The case was brought before your council: you protested that you would not act against the fates; and the fates were contradictory. In short, the end and result of the matter was, that to reconcile two contradictions was an impossibility in nature. The very pang put you into a sweat; some drops of which happening to light on the earth, produceth what the mortals call cabbage. All our noble consistory, for want of a categorical resolution, were seized with such a horrid thirst, that above seventy-eight hogsheads of nectar were swilled down at that sitting. At last you took my advice, and transmogriphied them into stones; and immediately got rid of your perplexity, and a truce with thirst was proclaimed through this vast Olympus. This was the year of flabby cods, near Teumessus, between Thebes and Chalcis.

"After this manner, it is my opinion, that you should petrify this dog and this fox. The metamorphosis will not be incongruous: for they both bear the name of peter. And because, according to the Limosin proverb, to make an oven's mouth there must be three stones, you may associate them with master Peter du Coignet, whom you formerly petrified for the same cause. Then those three dead pieces shall be put in an equilateral trigone, somewhere in the great temple at Paris; in the middle of the porch, if you will; there to perform the office of extinguishers, and with their noses put out the lighted candles, torches, tapers, and flambeaux; since, while they lived, they still lighted,

453

ballock-like, the fire of faction, division, ballock sects, and wrangling among those idle bearded boys, the students. And this will be an everlasting monument to shew, that those puny self-conceited pedants, ballock-framers, were rather contemned than condemned by you. Dixi, I have said my say."

"You deal too kindly by them," said Jupiter, "for ought I see, monsieur Priapus. You don't use to be so kind to everybody, let me tell you: for as they seek to eternize their names, it would be much better for them to be thus changed into hard stones, than to return to earth and putrefaction. But now to other matters. Yonder behind us, towards the Tuscan sea, and the neighborhood of Mount Appennin, do you see what tragedies are stirred up by certain topping ecclesiastical bullies? This hot fit will last its time, like the Limosin's ovens, and then will be cooled, but not so fast.

"We shall have sport enough with it; but I foresee one inconveniency: for methinks we have but little store of thunder-ammunition, since the time that you, my fellow gods, for your pastime, lavished them away to bombard new Antioch, by my particular permission; as since, after your example, the stout champions, who had undertaken to hold the fortress of Dindenarois against all comers, fairly wasted their powder with shooting at sparrows; and then not having wherewith to defend themselves in time of need, valiantly surrendered to the enemy, who were already packing up their awls, full of madness and despair, and thought on nothing but a shameful retreat. Take care this be remedied, son Vulcan; rouse up your drowsy cyclops, Asteropes, Brontes, Arges, Polyphemus, Steropes, Pyracmon, and so forth; set them at work, and make them drink as they ought.

"Never spare liquor to such as are at hot work. Now let us dispatch this bawling fellow below. You, Mercury, go see who it is, and know what he wants." Mercury looked out at heaven's trap door, through which, as I am told, they hear what's said here below. By the way, one might well enough mistake it for the scuttle of a ship; though Icaromenippus said it was like the mouth of a well. The light-heeled deity saw that it was honest Tom, who asked for his lost hatchet; and accordingly he made his report to the synod. "Marry," said Jupiter, "we are finely helped up; as if we had now nothing else to do here but to restore lost hatchets. Well, he must have it then for all this, for so it is written in the book of fate (do you hear?), as well as if it was worth the whole dutchy of Milan. The truth is, the fellow's

454

hatchet is as much to him as a kingdom to a king. Come, come, let no more words be scattered about it, let him have his hatchet again.

"Now, let us make an end of the difference betwixt the levites and mole-catchers of Landerousse. Whereabouts were we?" Priapus was standing in the chimney-corner, and having heard what Mercury had reported, said in a most courteous and jovial manner: "King Jupiter, while by your order and particular favour, I was garden-keeper-general on earth, I observed that this word hatchet is equivocal to many things: for it signifies a certain instrument, by the means of which men fell and cleave timber. It also signifies (at least I am sure it did formerly) a female soundly and frequently thumpthumpriggletickletwiddle-tobyed. Thus I perceived that every cock of the game used to call his doxy his hatchet; for with that same tool (this he said lugging out and exhibiting his nine inch knocker) they so strongly and resolutely shove and drive in their helves, that the females remain free from a fear epidemical amongst their sex—viz., that from the bottom of the male's belly the instrument should dangle at his heel for want of such feminine props. And I remember (for I have a member, and a memory too, ay, and a fine memory, large enough to fill a butter-fir-kin): I remember, I say, that one day of tubilustre [horn-fair] at the festivals of good-man Vulcan in May, I heard Josquin Des prez, Ol-kegan, Hobreths, Agricola, Brumel, Camelin, Vigoris, de la Fage, Bruyor, Prioris, Seguin, de la Rue, Midy, Moulu, Mouton, Gascoigne, Loiset, Compere, Penet, Fevin, Rousée, Richard Fort, Rousseau, Con-silion, Constantio Festi, Jacquet Bercan, melodiously singing the fol-lowing catch on a pleasant green:—

> "'Long John to bed went to his bride,
> And laid a mallet by his side:
> 'What means this mallet, John,' saith she?
> 'Why! 'tis to wedge thee home,' quoth he.
> 'Alas!' cry'd she, 'the man's a fool:
> What need you use a wooden tool?
> When lusty John does to me come,
> He never shoves but with his bum.'

"Nine olympiads, and an intercalary year after (I have a rare mem-ber, I would say memory; but I often make blunders in the symboliz-ation and colligance of those two words) I heard Adrian Villard, Gombert, Janequin, Arcadet, Claudin, Certon, Manchicourt, Auxerre, Villiers, Sandrin, Sobier, Hesdin, Morales, Passereau, Maille, Maillart,

Jacotin, Hurteur, Verdelot, Carpentras, l'Heritier, Cadeac, Doublet, Vermont, Bouteiller, Loupi, Pagnier, Millet, du Moulin, Alaire, Maraut, Morpin, Gendre, and other merry lovers of music, in a private garden, under some fine shady trees, round about a bulwark of flaggons, gammons, pasties, with several coated quails, and laced mutton, waggishly singing:

> "'Since tools without their hafts are useless lumber,
> And hatchets without helves are of that number;
> That one may go in t'other, and may match it,
> I'll be the helve, and thou shalt be the hatchet.'

"Now would I know what kind of hatchet this bawling **Tom** wants?" This threw all the venerable gods and goddesses into a fit of laughter, like any microcosm of flies; and even set limping Vulcan a hopping and jumping smoothly three or four times for the sake of his dear. "Come, come," said Jupiter to Mercury, "run down immediately, and cast at the poor fellow's feet three hatchets; his own, another of gold, and a third of massy silver, all of one size: then having left it to his will to take his choice, if he take his own, and be satisfied with it, give him the other two; if he take another, chop his head off with his own: and henceforth serve me all those losers of hatchets after that manner." Having said this, Jupiter, with an aukward turn of his head, like a jackanapes swallowing of pills, made so dreadful a phiz, that all the vast Olympus quaked again. Heaven's foot-messenger, thanks to his low-crowned narrow-brimmed hat, his plume of feathers, heel-pieces, and running stick with pigeon's wings, flings himself out at heaven's wicket, through the empty deserts of the air, and in a trice nimbly alights on the earth and throws at friend Tom's feet the three hatchets, saying unto him: "Thou hast bawled long enough to be a-dry: thy prayers and request are granted by Jupiter: see which of these three is thy hatchet, and take it away with thee." Wellhung lifts up the golden hatchet, peeps upon it, and finds it very heavy: then staring on Mercury, crys, "Codszouks this is none of mine; I will not have it": the same he did with the silver one, and said, "It is not this neither, you may even take them again." At last, he takes up his own hatchet, examines the end of the helve, and finds his mark there: then, ravished with joy, like a fox that meets some straggling poultry, and sneering from the tip of the nose, he cryed, "By the mass, this is my hatchet, master god; if you will leave it me, I will sacrifice to you a very good and huge pot of milk, brim full, covered with fine strawberries, next ides, i. e., the 15th of May."

"Honest fellow," said Mercury, "I leave it thee; take it; and because thou hast wished and chosen moderately, in point of hatchet, by Jupiter's command, I give thee these two others: thou hast now wherewith to make thyself rich: be honest." Honest Tom gave Mercury a whole cartload of thanks, and revered the most great Jupiter. His old hatchet he fastens close to his leathern girdle, and girds it above his breech like Martin of Cambray: the two others, being more heavy, he lays on his shoulder. Thus he plods on trudging over the fields keeping a good countenance amongst his neighbours and fellow-parishioners, with one merry saying or other after Patelin's way. The next day, having put on a clean white jacket, he takes on his back the two precious hatchets, and comes to Chinon, the famous city, noble city, ancient city, yea the first city in the world, according to the judgment and assertion of the most learned massoreths. At Chinon he turned his silver hatchet into fine testons, crown-pieces, and other white cash; his golden hatchet into fine angels, curious ducats, substantial ridders, spankers, and rose nobles: then with them purchases a good number of farms, barns, houses, out-houses, thatched-houses, stables, meadows, orchards, fields, vineyards, woods, arable lands, pastures, ponds, mills, gardens, nurseries, oxen, cows, sheep, goats, swine, hogs, asses, horses, hens, cocks, capons, chickens, geese, ganders, ducks, drakes, and a world of all other necessaries, and in a short time became the richest man in the country, nay even richer than that limping scrape-good Maulevrier. His brother bumpkins, and the other yeoman and country-puts thereabouts, perceiving his good fortune, were not a little amazed, insomuch that their former pity of Tom was soon changed into an envy of his so great and unexpected rise: and as thy could not for their souls devise how this came about, they made it their business to pry up and down, and lay their heads together, to enquire, seek, and inform themselves by what means, in what place, on what day, what hour, how, why, and wherefore, he had come by this great treasure.

At last, hearing it was by losing his hatchet, "Ha, ha!" said they, "was there no more to do, but to lose a hatchet, to make us rich? Bum for that; it is as easy as pissing abed, and will cost but little. Are then at this time the revolutions of the heavens, the constellations of the firmament, and aspects of the planets such, that whosoever shall lose a hatchet, shall immediately grow rich? Ha, ha, ha! by Jove, you shall even be lost, and it please you, my dear hatchet." With this they all fairly lost their hatchets out of hand. The devil of one that had a hatchet left: he was not his mother's son, that did not lose his hatchet.

457

No more was wood felled or cleaved in that country, through want of hatchets. Nay, the Æsopian apologue even saith, that certain petty country gents, of the lower class, who had sold Wellhung their little mill and little field, to have wherewithal to make a figure at the next muster, having been told that this treasure was come to him by this only means, sold the only badge of their gentility, their swords, to purchase hatchets to go to lose them, as the silly clodpates did, in hopes to gain store of chink by that loss.

You would have truly sworn they had been a parcel of your petty spiritual usurers, Rome-bound, selling their all, and borrowing of others to buy store of mandates, a penny-worth of a new-made pope.

Now they cried out and brayed, and prayed and bawled, and invoked Jupiter: "My hatchet! my hatchet! Jupiter, my hatchet!" on this side, "My hatchet!" on that side, "My hatchet! ho, ho, ho, ho, Jupiter, my hatchet!" The air round about rung again with the cries and howlings of these rascally losers of hatchets.

Mercury was nimble in bringing them hatchets; to each offering that which he had lost, as also another of gold, and a third of silver.

Every he still was for that of gold, giving thanks in abundance to the great giver Jupiter: but in the very nick of time, that they bowed and stooped to take it from the ground, whip, in a trice, Mercury lopped off their heads, as Jupiter had commanded; and of heads, thus cut off, the number was just equal to that of the lost hatchets.

You see how it is now; you see how it goes with those, who in the simplicity of their hearts wish and desire with moderation. Take warning by this, all you greedy, fresh-water shirks, who scorn to wish for anything under ten thousand pounds: and do not for the future run on impudently, as I have sometimes heard you wishing, "Would to God, I had now one hundred seventy-eight millions of gold! Oh! how I should tickle it off." The deuce on you, what more might a king, an emperor, or a pope wish for? For that reason, indeed, you see that after you have made such hopeful wishes, all the good that comes to you of it is the itch or the scabe, and not a cross in your breeches to scare the devil that tempts you to make these wishes: no more than those two mumpers, wishers after the custom of Paris; one of whom only wished to have in good old gold as much as hath been spent, bought and sold in Paris, since its first foundations were laid, to this hour; all of it valued at the price, sale, and rate of the dearest year in all that space of time. Do you think the fellow was bashful? Had he eaten sour plums unpeeled? Were his teeth on edge, I pray

458

you? The other wished our lady's church brim-full of steel needles, from the floor to the top of the roof, and to have as many ducats as might be crammed into as many bags as might be sowed with each and every one of these needles, till they were all either broke at the point or eye. This is to wish with a vengeance! What think you of it? What did they get by it, in your opinion? Why, at night both my gentlemen had kybed-heels, a tetter in the chin, a church-yard cough in the lungs, a catarrh in the throat, a swinging boil at the rump, and the devil of one musty crust of a brown george the poor dogs had to scour their grinders with. Wish therefore for mediocrity, and it shall be given unto you, and over and above yet; that is to say, provided you bestir yourselves manfully, and do your best in the meantime.

Ay, but, say you, God might as soon have given me seventy-eight thousand as the thirteenth part of one-half: for he is omnipotent, and a million of gold is no more to him than one farthing. Oh, oh! pray tell me who taught you to talk at this rate of the power and predestination of God, poor silly people? Peace, tush, st, st, st! fall down before his sacred face, and own the nothingness of your nothing.

Upon this, O ye that labour under the affliction of the gout, I ground my hopes; firmly believing, that if so it pleases the divine goodness, you shall obtain health; since you wish and ask for nothing else, at least for the present. Well, stay yet a little longer with half an ounce of patience.

The Genouese do not use, like you, to be satisfied with wishing health alone, when after they have all the live-long morning been in a brown-study, talked, pondered, ruminated, and resolved in the counting-houses, of whom and how they may squeeze the ready, and who by their craft must be hooked in, wheedled, bubbled, sharped, over-reached and choused; and they go to the exchange, and greet one another with a Sanità & guadagno, messer; health and gain to you, sir. Health alone will not go down with the greedy curmudgeons: they over and above must wish for gain, with a pox to them; ay, and for the fine crowns or scudi di Guadaigne: whence, heaven be praised, it happens many a time, that the silly wishers and woulders are baulked, and get neither.

Now, my lads, as you hope for good health, cough once aloud with lungs of leather; take me off three swinging bumpers; prick up your ears; and you shall hear me tell wonders of the noble and good Pantagruel.

THE FOURTH BOOK

OF

RABELAIS'S WORKS

CHAPTER I

HOW PANTAGRUEL WENT TO SEA, TO VISIT THE ORACLE OF BACBUC, ALIAS THE HOLY BOTTLE

IN the month of June, on Vesta's holiday, the very numerical day on which Brutus, conquering Spain, taught its strutting dons to truckle under him, and that niggardly miser Crassus was routed and knocked on the head by the Parthians, Pantagruel took his leave of the good Gargantua, his royal father. The old gentleman, according to the laudable custom of the primitive christians, devoutly prayed for the happy voyage of his son and his whole company, and then they took shipping at the port of Thalassa. Pantagruel had with him Panurge, Friar John des Entomeures, alias, of the funnels, Epistemon, Gymnast, Eusthenes, Rhizotomus, Carpalim, *cum multis aliis,* his ancient servants and domestics: also Xenomanes, the great traveller, who had crossed so many dangerous roads, dikes, ponds, seas, and so forth, and was come some time before, having been sent for by Panurge.

For certain good causes and considerations him thereunto moving, he had left with Gargantua, and marked out, in his great and universal hydrographical chart, the course which they were to steer to visit the oracle of the holy bottle Bacbuc. The number of ships were such as I described in the third book, convoyed by a like number of triremes, men of war, gallions and feluccas, well rigged, caulked, and stored with good quantity of pantagruelion.

All the officers, droggerman (interpreters), pilots, captains, mates, boatswains, midshipmen, quartermasters and sailors, met in the Thalamege, Pantagruel's principal flag-ship, which had in her stern, for her ensign, a huge large bottle, half silver, well polished, the other half gold, enameled with carnation; whereby it was easy to guess that white and red were the colours of the noble travellers, and that they went for the word of the bottle.

On the stern of the second was a lantern, like those of the ancients, industriously made with diaphanous stone, implying that they were to pass by Lanternland. The third ship had for her device a fine deep china ewer. The fourth, a double-handed jar, of gold, much like an ancient urn. The fifth, a famous can made of sperm of emerald. The sixth, a monk's mumping bottle made of the four metals together. The seventh, an ebony funnel, all imbossed and wrought with gold after the tauchic manner. The eighth, an ivy goblet very precious, inlaid with gold. The ninth, a cup of fine obriz gold. The tenth, a tumbler of aromatic agoloch (you call it lignum aloes) edged with cyprian gold, after the azemine make. The eleventh, a golden vine-tub of mosaic work. The twelfth, a runlet of unpolished gold, covered with a small vine of large Indian pearl of topiarian work. Insomuch that there was no man, however in the dumps, musty, sour-looked, or melancholic he were, not even excepting that blubbering whiner Heraclitus, had he been there, but, seeing this noble convoy of ships and their devices, must have been seized with present gladness of heart, and smiling at the conceit, have said, that the travellers were all honest topers, true pitcher-men; and have judged by a most sure prognostication, that their voyage, both outward and homeward bound, would be performed in mirth and perfect health.

In the Thalamege, where was the general meeting, Pantagruel made a short but sweet exhortation, wholly backed with authorities from Scripture upon navigation; which being ended, with an audible voice prayers were said in the presence and hearing of all the burghers of Thalassa, who had flocked to the mole to see them take shipping. After the prayers, was melodiously sung a psalm of the holy king David, which begins, *When Israel went out of Egypt;* and that being ended, tables were placed upon deck, and a feast speedily served up. The Thalassians, who had also borne a chorus in the *psalm,* caused store of belly-timber and vinegar to be brought out of their houses. All drank to them: they drank to all: which was the cause that none of the whole company gave up what they had eaten, nor were sea-sick, with a pain at the head and stomach; which inconveniency they could not so easily have prevented by drinking, for some time before, salt water, either alone or mixed with wine; using quinces, citron-peel, juice of pomegranates, sourish sweetmeats, fasting a long time, covering their stomachs with paper, or following such other idle remedies, as foolish physicians prescribe to those that go to sea.

Having often renewed their tipplings, each mother's son retired on board his own ship, and set sail all so fast with a merry gale at southeast; to which point of the compass the chief pilot, James Brayer by name, had shaped his course, and fixed all things accordingly. For seeing that the oracle of the holy bottle lay near Catay, in the Upper India, his advice, and that of Xenomanes also, was not to steer the course which the Portuguese use, while sailing through the torrid zone, and cape Bona speranza at the south point of Afric, beyond the equinoctial line, and losing sight of the northern pole, their guide, they make a prodigious long voyage; but rather to keep as near the parallel of the said India as possible, and to tack to the westward of the said pole, so that winding under the north, they might find themselves in the latitude of the port of Olone, without coming nearer it for fear of being shut up in the frozen sea; whereas following this canonical turn, by the said parallel, they must have that on the right to the eastward, which at their departure was on their left.

This proved a much shorter cut: for without shipwreck, danger, or loss of men, with uninterrupted good weather, except one day near the island of the Macreons, they performed in less than four months the voyage of Upper India; which the Portuguese, with a thousand inconveniences and innumerable dangers, can hardly complete in three years. And it is my opinion, with submission to better judgments, that this course was perhaps steered by those Indians who sailed to Germany, and were honourably received by the king of the Swedes, while Quintus Metellus Celer was proconsul of the Gauls; as Corn. Nepos, Pomponius Mela, and Pliny after them tell us.

CHAPTER II

HOW PANTAGRUEL BOUGHT MANY RARITIES IN THE ISLAND OF MEDAMOTHY

THAT day and the two following, they neither discovered land nor anything new; for they had formally sailed that way: but on the fourth they made an island called Medamothy, of a fine and delightful prospect, by reason of the vast number of light-houses, and high marble towers in its circuit, which is not less than that of Canada. Pantagruel, enquiring who governed there, heard that it was king Philophanes, absent at that time upon account of the marriage of his brother Philotheamon with the infanta of the kingdom of Engys.

Hearing this he went ashore in the harbour, and while every ship's crew watered, passed his time in viewing divers pictures, pieces of tapestry, animals, fishes, birds, and other exotic and foreign merchandises, which were along the walks of the mole, and in the markets of the port. For it was the third day of the great and famous fair of the place, to which the chief merchants of Africa and Asia resorted. Out of these Friar John bought him two rare pictures; in one of which the face of a man that brings in an appeal (or that calls out to another), was drawn to the life; and in the other a servant that wants a master, with every needful particular, action, countenance, look, gait, feature and deportment, being an original, by master Charles Charmois, principal painter to king Megistus; and he paid for them in the court fashion, with congé and grimace. Panurge bought a large picture, copied and done from the needle-work formerly wrought by Philomela, shewing to her sister Progne how her brother-in-law Tereus had by force hanselled her copyhold, and then cut out her tongue, that she might not (as women will) tell tales. I vow and swear by the handle of my paper lantern, that it was a gallant, a mirific, nay, a most admirable piece. Nor do you think, I pray you, that in it was the picture of a man playing the beast with two backs with a female; this had been too silly and gross: no, no; it was another-guise thing, and much plainer. You may, if you please, see it at Theleme, on the left hand, as you go into the high gallery. Epistemon bought another, wherein were painted to the life, the ideas of Plato and the atoms of Epicurus. Rhizotomus purchased another, wherein echo was drawn to the life. Pantagruel caused to be bought, by Gymnast, the life and deeds of Achilles, in seventy-eight pieces of tapestry, four fathoms long and three fathoms broad, all of Phrygian silk, imbossed with gold and silver; the work beginning at the nuptials of Peleus and Thetis, continuing to the birth of Achilles: his youth, described by Statius Papinius; his warlike achievements, celebrated by Homer; his death and exequies, written by Ovid and Quintus Calabar; and ending at the appearance of his ghost, and Polyxena's sacrifice, rehearsed by Euripides.

He also caused to be bought three fine young unicorns; one of them a male of a chestnut colour, and two grey dappled females; also a tarand, whom he bought of a Scythian of the Gelone's country.

A tarand is an animal as big as a bullock, having a head like a stag, or a little bigger, two stately horns with large branches, cloven feet, hair long like that of a furred Muscovite, I mean a bear, and a skin almost as hard as steel armour. The Scythian said that there are but few tarands to be found in Scythia, because it varieth its colour according to the diversity of the places where it grazes and abides, and represents the colour of the grass, plants, trees, shrubs, flowers, meadows, rocks, and generally of all things near which it comes. It hath this common with the sea-pulp, or polypus, with the thoes, with the wolves of India, and with the chamælion; which is a kind of a lizard so wonderful, that Democritus hath written a whole book of its figure, and anatomy, as also of its virtue and property in magic. This I can affirm, that I have seen it change its colour not only at the approach of things that have a colour, but by its own voluntary impulse, according to its fear or other affections: as for example, upon a great carpet, I have seen it certainly become green; but having remained there some time, it turned yellow, blue, tanned, and purple in course, in the same manner as you see a turkey-cock's comb change colour according to its passions. But what we find most surprising in this tarand is, that not only its face and skin, but also its hair could take whatever colour was about it. Near Panurge, with his kersy coat, its hair used to turn grey: near Pantagruel, with his scarlet mantle, its hair and skin grew red; near the pilot, dressed after the fashion of the isiacs of Anubis in Ægypt, its hair seemed all white; which two last colours the chamælion cannot borrow.

When the creature was free from any fear or affection, the colour of its hair was just as you see that of the asses of Meung.

CHAPTER III

HOW PANTAGRUEL RECEIVED A LETTER FROM HIS FATHER GARGANTUA, AND OF THE STRANGE WAY TO HAVE SPEEDY NEWS FROM FAR DISTANT PLACES

WHILE Pantagruel was taken up with the purchase of those foreign animals, the noise of ten guns and culverins, together with a loud and joyful cheer of all the fleet, was heard from the mole. Pantagruel looked towards the haven, and perceived that this was occasioned by the arrival of one of his father Gargantua's celoces, or advice-boats, named the Chelidonia; because on the stern of it was carved in Corinthian brass, a sea swallow; which is a fish as large as a dare-fish of Loire, all flesh, without scale, with cartilaginous wings (like a bat's) very long and broad, by the means of which I have seen them fly a fathom above water, about a bow-shot. At Marseilles this flying fish is called lendole. And indeed that ship was as light as a swallow; so that it rather seemed to fly on the sea than to sail. Malicorne, Gargantua's esquire carver, was come in her, being sent expressly by his master to have an account of his son's health and circumstances, and to bring him credentials. When Malicorne had saluted Pantagruel, and the prince had embraced him about the neck, and shewed him a little of the cap-courtesy, before he opened the letters, the first thing he said to him was, "Have you heard the Gozal, the heavenly messenger?" "Yes, sir," said he; "here it is swaddled up in this basket." It was a grey pigeon, taken out of Gargantua's dove-house, whose young ones were just hatched when the advice-boat was going off.

If any ill fortune had befallen Pantagruel, he would have fastened some black ribband to his feet; but because all things had succeeded happily hitherto, having caused it to be undressed, he tied to its feet a white ribband, and, without any further delay, let it loose. The pigeon presently flew away, cutting the air with an incredible speed; as you know that there is no flight like a pigeon's especially when it hath eggs or young ones, through the extreme care which nature hath fixed in it to relieve and be with its young; insomuch, that in less than two hours it compassed in the air the long tract which the advice-boat, with all her diligence, with oars and sails, and a fair wind, could not go through in less than three days and three nights, and was seen as it was going into the dove-house to its nest. Whereupon the worthy Gargantua, hearing that it had the white ribband on, was joyful and secure of his son's welfare. This was the custom of the noble Gargantua and Pantagruel, when they would have speedy news of something of great concern; as the event of some battle, either by sea or land; the surrendering or holding out of some strong place; the determination of some difference of moment; the safe or unhappy delivery of some queen or great lady; the death or recovery of their sick friends or allies, and so forth. They used to take the gozal, and had it carried from one to another by the post; to the places whence they desired to have news. The gozal, bearing either a black or white ribband, according to the occurrences and accidents, used to remove their doubts at its return, making, in the space of one hour, more way through the air than thirty post-boys could have done in one natural day. May not this be said to redeem and gain time with a vengeance, think you? For the like service, therefore, you may believe, as a most true thing, that, in the dove-houses of their farms, there were to be found, all the year long, store of pigeons hatching eggs, or rearing their young. Which may be easily done in aviaries and voleries, by the help of saltpetre and the sacred herb vervain.

The gozal being let fly, Pantagruel perused his father Gargantua's letter, the contents of which were as followeth:

"MY DEAREST SON,

"The affection that naturally a father bears to a beloved son, is so much increased in me by reflecting on the particular gifts which by the divine goodness have been heaped on thee, that since thy departure it hath often banished all other thoughts out of my mind; leaving my heart wholly possessed with fear, lest some misfortune has attended thy voyage: for thou knowest that fear was ever the attendant of true and sincere love. Now because (as Hesiod saith) *a good beginning of anything is the half of it;* or, *well begun's half done,* according to the old saying; to free my mind from this anxiety, I have expressly dispatched Malicorne, that he may give me a true account of thy health at the beginning of thy voyage. For if it be good, and such as I wish it, I shall easily foresee the rest.

"I have met with some diverting books, which the bearer will deliver thee: thou mayst read them when thou wantest to unbend and ease thy mind from thy better studies. He will also give thee at large the news at court. The peace of the Lord be with thee. Remember me to Panurge, Friar John, Epistemon, Xenomanes, Gymnast, and thy other principal domestics, my good friends. Dated at our paternal seat, this 13th day of June.

"Thy father and friend,

"GARGANTUA."

CHAPTER IV

HOW PANTAGRUEL WRIT TO HIS FATHER GARGANTUA, AND SENT HIM SEVERAL CURIOSITIES

PANTAGRUEL, having perused the letter, had a long conference with the esquire Malicorne; insomuch, that Panurge at last interrupting them, asked him, "Pray, sir, when do you design to drink; when shall we drink? When shall the worshipful esquire drink?

466

What a devil! have you not talked long enough to drink?" " 'Tis a good motion," answered Pantagruel; "go, get us something ready at the next inn; I think it is the satyr on horse-back." In the meantime he writ to Gargantua as followeth, to be sent by the aforesaid esquire.

"MOST GRACIOUS FATHER,

"As our senses and animal faculties are more discomposed at the news of events unexpected, though desired (even to an immediate dissolution of the soul from the body), than if those accidents had been foreseen; so the coming of Malicorne hath much surprised and disordered me. For I had no hopes to see any of your servants, or to hear from you, before I had finished our voyage; and contented myself with the dear remembrance of your august majesty, deeply impressed in the hindmost ventricle of my brain, often representing you to my mind.

"But since you have made me happy beyond expectation, by the perusal of your gracious letter, and the faith I have in your esquire hath revived my spirits by the news of your welfare; I am, as it were, compelled to do what formerly I did freely, that is, first to praise the Blessed Redeemer, who by His divine goodness preserves you in this long enjoyment of perfect health; then to return you eternal thanks for the fervent affection which you have for me your most humble son and unprofitable servant.

"Formerly a Roman, named Fernius, said to Augustus, who had received his father into favour, and pardoned him after he had sided with Anthony, that by that action the emperor had reduced him to this extremity, that for want of power to be grateful, both while he lived and after it, he should be obliged to be taxed with ingratitude. So I may say, that the excess of your fatherly affection drives me into such a straight, that I should be forced to live and die ungrateful; unless that crime be redressed by the sentence of the stoics, who say, that there are three parts in a benefit, the one of the giver, the other of the receiver, the third of the remunerator; and that the receiver rewards the giver, when he freely receives the benefit, and always remembers it; as on the contrary, that man is most ungrateful who despises and forgets a benefit. Therefore, being overwhelmed with infinite favours, all proceeding from your extreme goodness, and on the other side wholly incapable of making the smallest return, I hope, at least, to free myself from the imputation of ingratitude, since they can never be blotted out of my mind; and my tongue shall never cease to own, that, to thank you as I ought, transcends my capacity.

467

"As for us, I have this assurance in the Lord's mercy and help, that the end of our voyage will be answerable to its beginning, and so it will be entirely performed in health and mirth. I will not fail to set down in a journal a full account of our navigation, that, at our return, you may have an exact relation of the whole.

"I have found here a Scythian tarand, an animal strange and wonderful for the variations of colour on its skin and hair, according to the distinction of neighbouring things: it is as tractable and easily kept as a lamp; be pleased to accept of it.

"I also send you three young unicorns, which are the tamest of creatures.

"I have conferred with the esquire, and taught him how they must be fed. These cannot graze on the ground, by reason of the long horn on their forehead, but are forced to brouze on fruit trees, or on proper racks, or to be fed by hand, with herbs, sheaves, apples, pears, barley, rye, and other fruits, and roots, being placed before them.

"I am amazed that ancient writers should report them to be so wild, furious, and dangerous, and never seen alive: far from it, you will find that they are the mildest things in the world, provided they are not maliciously offended. Likewise I send you the life and deeds of Achilles, in curious tapestry; assuring you whatever rarities of animals, plants, birds, or precious stones, and others, I shall be able to find and purchase in our travels, shall be brought to you, God willing, whom I beseech, by His blessed grace, to preserve you.

"From Medamothy, this 15th of June. Panurge, Friar John, Epistemon, Xenomanes, Gymnast, Eusthenes, Rhizotomus, and Carpalim, having most humbly kissed your hand, return your salute a thousand times.

"Your most dutiful son and servant,

"PANTAGRUEL."

While Pantagruel was writing this letter, Malicorne was made welcome by all with a thousand goodly good-morrows and howd'ye's: they clung about him so, that I cannot tell you how much they made of him, how many humble services, how many from my love and to my love were sent with him. Pantagruel, having writ his letters, sat down at table with him, and afterwards presented him with a large chain of gold, weighing eight hundred crowns; between whose septenary links, some large diamonds, rubies, emeralds, turky stones, and unions were alternatively set in. To each of his bark's crew, he ordered to be given five hundred crowns. To Gargantua, his father, he sent the

468

tarand covered with a cloth of satin, brocaded with gold; and the tapestry containing the life and deeds of Achilles, with the three unicorns in frized cloth of gold trappings: and so they left Medamothy; Malicorne, to return to Gargantua; and Pantagruel, to proceed in his voyage: during which, Epistemon read to him the books which the esquire had brought: and because he found them jovial and pleasant, I shall give you an account of them, if you earnestly desire it.

CHAPTER V

HOW PANTAGRUEL MET A SHIP WITH PASSENGERS RETURNING FROM LANTERNLAND

ON the fifth day, beginning already to wind by little and little about the *pole,* going still farther from the *equinoctial-line,* we discovered a merchant-man to the windward of us. The joy for this was not small on both sides; we in hopes to hear news from sea, and those in the merchant-man from land. So we bore upon them, and coming up with them, we hailed them: and finding them to be Frenchmen of Xaintonge, backed our sails and lay by to talk to them. Pantagruel heard that they came from *Lanternland;* which added to his joy, and that of the whole fleet. We enquired about the state of that country, and the way of living of the *Lanterns:* and were told, that about the latter end of the following July, was the time prefixed for the meeting of the general chapter of the *Lanterns;* and that if we arrived there at that time, as we might easily, we should see a handsome, honourable, and jolly company of *Lanterns;* and that great preparations were making, as if they intended to *lanternise* there to the purpose. We were told also, that if we touched at the great kingdom of Gebarim, we should be honourably received, and treated by the sovereign of that country, king Ohabe, who, as well as all his subjects, speaks Touraine French.

While we were listening to this news, Panurge fell out with one Dingdong, a drover or sheep merchant of Taillebourg. The occasion of the fray was thus.

This same Dingdong, seeing Panurge without a cod-piece, with his spectacles fastened to his cap, said to one of his comrades, "Prithee, look, is not there a fine medal of a cuckold?" Panurge, by reason of his spectacles, as you may well think, heard more plainly by half with his ears than usually; which caused him (hearing this) to say to the saucy dealer in mutton, in a kind of a pet:

"How the devil should I be one of the hornified fraternity, since I am not yet a brother of the marriage-noose, as thou art; as I guess by thy ill-favoured phiz?"

"Yea, verily," quoth the grazier, "I am married, and would not be otherwise for all the pairs of spectacles in Europe; nay, not for all the magnifying gim-cracks in Africa; for I have got me the cleverest, prettiest, handsomest, properest, neatest, tightest, honestest, and soberest piece of woman's flesh for my wife, that is in all the whole country of Xaintonge; I'll say that for her, and a fart for all the rest. I bring her home a fine eleven-inch-long branch of red coral *for her christmas-box:* what hast thou to do with it? what is that to thee? who art thou? whence comest thou, O dark lanthorn of antichrist? Answer, if thou art of God." "I ask thee, *by the way of question,*" said Panurge to him very seriously, "if with the consent and countenance of all the elements, I had gingumbobed, cod-pieced, and thumpthumpriggledtickledtwidled thy so clever, so pretty, so handsome, so proper, so neat, so tight, so honest, and so sober female importance, insomuch that the stiff deity that has no forecast, Priapus (who dwells here at liberty, all subjection of fastened cod-pieces, or bolts, bars, and locks, abdicated), remained sticking in her natural *christmas-box* in such a lamentable manner, that it were never to come out, but eternally should stick there, unless thou didst pull it out with thy teeth; what wouldst thou do? Wouldst thou everlastingly leave it there, or wouldst thou pluck it out with thy grinders? Answer me, O thou ram of Mahomet, since thou art one of the devil's gang." "I would," replied the sheepmonger, "take thee such a woundy cut on this spectacle-bearing lug of thine, with my trusty bilbo, as would smite thee dead as a herring." Thus having taken pepper in the nose, he was lugging out his sword: but alas! cursed cows have short horns; it stuck in the scabbard; as you know that at sea, cold iron will easily take rust, by reason of the excessive and nitrous moistness. Panurge, so smitten with terror, that his heart sunk down to his midriff, scoured off to Pantagruel for help: but Friar John laid hand on his flashing scymitar that was new-ground, and would certainly have dispatched Dingdong to rights, had not the skipper, and some of his passengers, beseeched Pantagruel not to suffer such an outrage to be committed on board his ship. So the matter was made up, and Panurge and his antagonist shaked fists, and drank in course to one another, in token of a perfect reconciliation.

CHAPTER VI

THIS quarrel being hushed, Panurge tipped the wink upon Epistemon and Friar John, and taking them aside "Stand at some
distance out of the way," said he, "and take your share of the following scene of mirth: you shall have rare sport anon, if my cake be
not dough, and my plot do but take." Then addressing himself to
the drover, he took off to him a bumper of good *lantern* wine. The
other pledged him briskly and courteously. This done, Panurge
earnestly entreated him to sell him one of his sheep.

But the other answered him, "Is it come to that, friend and neighbour? Would you put tricks upon travellers? Alas, how finely
you love to play upon poor folk! Nay, you seem a rare chapman,
that is the truth on't. Oh what a mighty sheep-merchant you are! In
good faith, you look liker one of the diving trade, than a buyer of
sheep. Adzookers, what a blessing it would be to have one's purse,
well lined with chink, near your worship at a tripe-house, when it
begins to thaw! Humph, humph, did not we know you well, you
might serve one a slippery trick! Pray do but see, good people,
what a mighty conjuror the fellow would be reckoned." "Patience,"
said Panurge: "but waving that, be so kind as to sell me one of your
sheep. Come, how much!" "What do you mean, master of mine?"
answered the other. "They are long wooled sheep: from these did
Jason take his *golden fleece*. The order of the house of Burgundy
was drawn from them. Zwoons, man, they are oriental sheep, topping
sheep, fatted sheep, sheep of quality." "Be it so," said Panurge: "but
sell me one of them, I beseech you, and that for a cause, paying you
ready money upon the nail, in good and lawful occidental current
cash. Wilt say how much?" "Friend, neighbour," answered the
seller of mutton, "hark ye me a little, on the ear."

Panurge. "On which side you please; I hear you."

Ding. "You are going to *Lanternland,* they say."

Panurge. "Yea, verily."

Ding. "To see fashions?"

Panurge. "Yea, verily."

Ding. "And be merry?"

Panurge. "Yea, verily."

Ding. "Your name is, as I take it, Robin Mutton?"

Panurge. "As you please for that, sweet sir."

Ding. "Nay, without offence."

Panurge. "So I understand it."

Ding. "You are, as I take it, the king's jester; are not you?"

Panurge. "Yea, verily."

Ding. "Give me your hand,—humph, humph, you go to see fashions, you are the king's jester, your name is Robin Mutton! Do you see this same ram? His name too is Robin. Here Robin, Robin, Robin! Baea, baea, baea. Hath he not a rare voice?"

Panurge. "Ay, marry has he, a very fine and harmonious voice."

Ding. "Well, this bargain shall be made between you and me, friend and neighbour; we will get a pair of scales, then you, Robin Mutton, shall be put into one of them, and Tup Robin into the other. Now I'll hold you a peck of Busch oysters, that in weight, value, and price, he shall outdo you, and you shall be found light in the very numerical manner, as when you shall be hanged and suspended."

"Patience," said Panurge: "but you would do much for me, and your whole posterity, if you would chaffer with me for him, or some other of his inferiors. I beg it of you; good your worship, be so kind." "Hark ye, friend of mine," answered the other, "with the fleece of these, your fine Roan cloth is to be made; your Lemster superfine wool is mine arse to it; mere flock in comparison. Of their skins the best cordivant will be made, which shall be sold for Turkey and montelimart, or for Spanish leather at least. Of the guts shall be made fiddle and harp strings, that will sell as dear as if they came from Munican or Aquileia. What do you think on't, hah?" "If you please, sell me one of them," said Panurge, "and I will be yours for ever. Look, here is ready cash. What's the price?" This he said, exhibiting his purse stuffed with new henricuses.

CHAPTER VII

WHICH IF YOU READ, YOU WILL FIND HOW PANURGE
BARGAINED WITH DINGDONG

NEIGHBOUR, my friend," answered Dingdong, "they are meat for none but kings and princes: their flesh is so delicate, so savoury, and so dainty, that one would swear it melted in the mouth. I bring them out of a country where the very hogs, God be with us, live on nothing but myrobalans. The sows in their styes, when they lie-in (saving the honour of this good company) are fed only with orange-flowers." "But," said Panurge, "drive a bargain with me for one of them, and I will pay you for it like a king, upon the honest word of a true Trojan: come, come, what do you ask?" "Not so fast, Robin," answered the trader; "these sheep are lineally descended from the very family of the ram that wafted Phryxus and Helle over the sea, since called the Hellespont." "A pox on it," said Panurge, "you are *clericus vel addiscens!*" "*Ità* is a cabbage, and *verè* a leek," answered the merchant. "But rr, rrr, rrrr, rrrrr, hoh Robin, rr, rrrrrrr, you do not understand that gibberish, do you? Now I think on't, over all the fields, where they piss, corn grows as fast as if the Lord had pissed there; they need neither be tilled nor dunged. Besides, man, your chymists extract the best saltpetre in the world out of their urine. Nay, with their very dung (with reverence be it spoken) the doctors in our country make pills that cure seventy-eight kinds of diseases, the least of which is the evil of St. Eutropius of Xaintes, from which good Lord deliver us! Now what do you think on't, neighbour, my friend? The truth is, they cost me money, that they do." "Cost what they will," cried Panurge, "trade with me for one of them, paying you well." Our friend," quoth the quack-like sheep-man, "do but mind the wonders of nature that are found in those animals, even in a member which one would think were of no use. Take me but these horns, and bray them a little with an iron pestle, or with an andiron, which you please, it is all one to me; then bury them wherever you will, provided it be where the sun may shine, and water them frequently; in a few months I'll engage you will have the best asparagus in the world, not even excepting those of Ravenna. Now, come and tell me whether the horns of you other knights of the bull's feather have such a virtue and wonderful propriety?"

"Patience," said Panurge. "I do not know whether you be a scholar or no," pursued Dingdong: "I have seen a world of scholars, I say great scholars, that were cuckolds, I'll assure you. But hark you me, if you were a scholar, you should know that in the most inferior members of those animals (which are the feet) there is a bone (which is the heel) the astragalus, if you will have it so, wherewith, and with that of no other creature breathing, except the Indian ass and the dorcades of Libya, they used in old times to play at the royal game of dice, whereat Augustus the emperor won above fifty thousand crowns one evening. Now such cuckolds as you will be hanged ere

473

you get half so much at it." "Patience," said Panurge; "but let us dispatch." "And when, my friend and neighbour," continued the canting sheep-seller, "shall I have duly praised the inward members, the shoulders, the legs, the knuckles, the neck, the breast, the liver, the spleen, the tripes, the kidneys, the bladder, wherewith they make foot-balls; the ribs, which serve in Pigmy-land to make little cross-bows, to pelt the cranes with cherry-stones; the head, which with a little brimstone serves to make a miraculous decoction to loosen and ease the belly of costive dogs? "A turd on it," said the skipper to his preaching passenger, "what a fiddle-faddle have we here? There is too long a lecture by half: sell him one if thou wilt; if thou wilt not, do not let the man lose more time. I hate a gibble-gabble and a rimble-ramble talk; I am for a man of brevity." "I will, for your sake," replied the holder forth: "but then he shall give me three livres French money for each, pick and chuse." " 'Tis a woundy price," cried Panurge; "in our country I could have five, nay six for the money: see that you do not overreach me, master. You are not the first man whom I have known to have fallen, even sometimes to the endangering, if not breaking of his own neck, for endeavour-ing to rise all at once." "A murrain seize thee for a blockheaded booby," cried the angry seller of sheep; "by the worthy vow of our lady of Charroux, the worst in this flock is four times better than those which in days of yore the Coraxians in Tuditania, a country of Spain, used to sell for a good talent each; and how much doest thou think, thou Hibernian fool, that a talent of gold was worth?" "Sweet sir, you fall into a passion, I see," returned Panurge: "well hold, here is your money." Panurge, having paid his money, chose him out of all the flock a fine topping ram; and as he was hauling it along, crying out and bleating, all the rest, hearing and bleating in concert, stared, to see whither their brother ram should be carried. In the meanwhile the drover was saying to his shepherds: "Ah! how well the knave could chuse him out a ram; the whore-son has skill in cattle. On my honest word, I reserved that very piece of flesh for the lord of Cancale, well knowing his disposition: for the good man naturally is overjoyed when he holds a good sized handsome shoulder of mutton, instead of a left-handed racket, in one hand, with a good sharp carver in the other; got wot how he bestirs himself then."

CHAPTER VIII

HOW PANURGE CAUSED DINGDONG AND HIS SHEEP TO BE
DROWNED IN THE SEA

ON a sudden, you would wonder how the thing was so soon done;
for my part I cannot tell you, for I had not leisure to mind it;
our friend Panurge, without any further tittle-tattle, throws you his
ram overboard into the middle of the sea, bleating and making a
sad noise. Upon this all the other sheep in the ship, crying and
bleating in the same tone, made all the haste they could to leap
nimbly into the sea one after another; and great was the throng
who should leap in first after their leader. It was impossible to hinder
them: for you know that it is the nature of sheep always to follow
the first, wheresoever it goes; which makes Aristotle, lib. 9. de hist.
animal. mark them for the most silly and foolish animals in the world.
Dingdong, at his wit's end, and stark staring mad, as a man who
saw his sheep destroy and drown themselves before his face, strove
to hinder and keep them back by might and main; but all in vain:
they all one after the other frisked and jumped into the sea, and were
lost. At last he laid hold on a huge sturdy one by the fleece upon the
deck of the ship, hoping to keep it back, and so to save that and the
rest: but the ram was so strong that it proved too hard for him, and
carried its master into the herring pond, in spite of his teeth; where
it is supposed he drank somewhat more than his fill: so that he was
drowned, in the same manner as one-eyed Polyphemus's sheep carried
out of the den Ulysses and his companions. The like happened to
the shepherds and all their gang, some laying hold on their beloved
tup, this by the horns, the other by the legs, a third by the rump, and
others by the fleece; till in fine they were all of them forced to sea,
and drowned like so many rats. Panurge, on the gunnel of the ship,
with an oar in his hand, not to help them, you may swear, but to
keep them from swimming to the ship, and saving themselves from
drowning, preached and canted to them all the while like any little
friar Maillard, or another Friar John Burgess; laying before them
rhetorical common places concerning the miseries of this life, and the
blessings and felicity of the next; assuring them that the dead were
much happier than the living in this vale of misery, and promising to
erect a stately cenotaph and honorary tomb to every one of them on
the highest summit of mount Cenis, at his return from *Lantern-land;*

wishing them, nevertheless, in case they were not yet disposed to shake hands with this life, and did not like their salt liquor, they might have the good luck to meet with some kind whale which might set them ashore safe and sound, on some blessed land of Gotham, after a famous example.

The ship being cleared of Dingdong and his tups: "Is there ever another sheepish soul left lurking on board?" cried Panurge. "Where are those of Toby Lamb, and Robin Ram, that sleep whilst the rest are a feeding? Faith, I cannot tell myself. This was an old coaster's trick: what thinkest of it, Friar John, hah?" "Rarely performed," answered Friar John: "only methinks that as formerly in war, on the day of battle, a double pay was commonly promised the soldiers for that day: for if they overcome, there was enough to pay them; and if they lost, it would have been shameful for them to demand it, as the cowadly foresters did after the battle of Cerizoles: so likewise, my friend, you ought not to have paid your man, and the money had been saved." "A fart for the money," said Panurge: "have I not had above fifty thousand pounds worth of sport? Come now, let us be gone; the wind is fair. Hark you me, my friend John: never did man do me a good turn, but I returned, or at least acknowledged it: no, I scorn to be ungrateful; I never was, nor ever will be: never did man do me an ill one without ruing the day that he did it, either in this world or the next. I am not yet so much a fool neither." "Thou damnest thyself like any old devil," quoth Friar John: "it is written, *Mihi vindictam, &c.* Matter of breviary, mark ye me; *that's holy stuff.*"

CHAPTER IX

WE had still the wind at south south west, and had been a whole day without making land. On the 3rd day, at the flies up-rising [*which, you know, is some two or three hours after the sun's*] we got sight of a triangular island, very much like Sicily for its form and situation. It was called the island of alliances.

The people there are much like your carrot-pated Poitevins, save only that all of them, men, women, and children, have their noses

476

shaped like an ace of clubs. For that reason the ancient name of the country was Ennasin. They were all akin, as the mayor of the place told us, at least they boasted so.

You people of the other world esteem it a wonderful thing, that, out of the family of the Fabii at Rome, on a certain day, which was the 13th of February, at a certain gate, which was the porta carmentalis, since named scelerata, formerly situated at the foot of the capitol, between the Tarpeian rock and the Tyber, marched out against the Veientes of Etruria, three hundred and six men bearing arms, all related to each other, with five thousand other soldiers, every one of them their vassals, who were all slain near the river Cremera that comes out of the lake of Beccano. Now from this same country of Ennasin, in case of need, above three hundred thousand, all relations, and of one family, might march out. Their degrees of consanguinity and alliance are very strange; for being thus akin and allied to one another, we found that none was either father or mother, brother or sister, uncle or aunt, nephew or niece, son-in-law or daughter-in-law, god-father or god-mother, to the other; unless truly, a tall flat-nosed old fellow, who, as I perceived, called a little shitten-arsed girl, of three or four years old, father, and the child called him daughter.

Their distinction of degrees of kindred was thus: a man used to call a woman, my *lean bit;* the woman called him, my *porpus.* "Those," said Friar John, "must needs stink damnably of fish, when they have rubbed their bacon one with the other." One smiling on a young buxom baggage, said "Good morrow, dear *curry-comb.*" She, to return him his civility, said, "The like to you, my *Steed.*" "Hah! hah! hah!" said Panurge, "that is prettty well i'faith; for indeed it stands her in good stead to curry-comb this steed." Another greeted his buttock with a "Farwel, *my case.*" She replied, "Adieu, *trial.*" "By St. Winifred's placket," cried Gymnast, "this case has been often tried." Another asked a she-friend of his, "How is it, *hatchet?*" She answered him, "At your service, dear *helve.*" "Odds belly," saith Carpalim, "this *helve* and this *hatchet* are well matched." As we went on, I saw one who, calling his she-relation, styled her my *crum,* and she called him, my *crust.*

Quoth one to a brisk, plump, juicy female, "I am glad to see you, dear *tap.*" "So am I to find you so merry, sweet *spigot,*" replied she. One called a wench, his *shovel;* she called him, her *peal:* one named his, my *slipper;* and she him, my *foot:* another, my *boot;* she, my *shasoon.*

477

In the same degree of kindred, one called his, my *butter;* she called him, my *eggs;* and they were akin, just like a dish of buttered eggs. I heard one call his, my *tripe,* and she him, my *faggot.* Now I could not, for the heart's blood of me, pick out or discover what parentage, alliance, affinity, or consanguinity was between them, with reference to our custom: only they told us that she was faggot's tripe. [*Tripe de fagot,* means the smallest sticks in a faggot.] Another complementing his convenient, said, "Yours, my *shell":* she replied, "I was yours before, sweet *oyster."* "I reckon," said Carpalim, "she hath gutted his oyster." Another long-shanked, ugly rogue, mounted on a pair of high-heeled wooden slippers, meeting a strapping fusty squobbed dowdy, says he to her, "How is't, my *top?"* She was short upon him, and arrogantly replied, "Never the better for you, my *whip."* "By St. Anthony's hog," said Xenomanes, "I believe so; for how can this whip be sufficient to lash this top?"

A college professor well provided with cod, and powdered and prinked up, having a while discoursed with a great lady, taking his leave, with these words, "Thank you, *sweet-meat";* she cried, "There needs no thanks, *sour-sauce."* Saith Pantagruel, "This is not altogether incongruous, for sweet meat must have sour-sauce." A wooden loggerhead said to a young wench, "It is long since I saw you, *bag."* "All the better," cried she, *"pipe."* "Set them together," said Panurge, "then blow in their arses, it will be a bag-pipe." We saw, after that, a diminutive hump-backed gallant, pretty near us, taking leave of a she-relation of his, thus; "Fare thee well, friend *hole":* she reparteed, "Save thee, friend *peg."* Quoth Friar John, "What could they say more, were he all peg and she all hole? But now would I give something to know if every cranny of the hole can be stopped up with that same peg."

A bawdy bachelor, talking with an old trout, was saying, "Remember, *rusty gun."* "I will not fail," said she, *"scowerer."* "Do you reckon these two to be akin?" said Pantagruel to the mayor: "I rather take them to be foes: in our country a woman would take this as a mortal affront." "Good people of the other world," replied the mayor, "you have few such and so near relations as this gun and scowerer are to one another: for they both came out of one shop." "What, was the shop their mother?" quoth Panurge. "What mother," said the mayor, "does the man mean? That must be some of your world's affinity: we have here neither father nor mother: your little paultry fellows, that live on the other side the water, poor rogues,

booted with whisps of hay, may indeed have such; but we scorn it."
The good Pantagruel stood gazing and listening; but at those words
he had like to have lost all patience.

Having very exactly viewed the situation of the island, and the way
of living of the ennased nation, we went to take a cup of the creature
at a tavern, where there happened to be a wedding after the manner
of the country. Bating that shocking custom, there was special good
cheer.

While we were there, a pleasant match was struck up betwixt a female called *pear* (a tight thing, as we thought, but by some who
knew better things, said to be quaggy and flabby) and a young soft
male, called *cheese,* somewhat sandy. [Many such matches have been,
and they were formerly much commended.] In our country we say,
Il ne fut onc tel mariage, qu'est de la poire & du fromage; there is no
match like that made between the pear and the cheese: and in many
other places good store of such bargains have been driven. Besides,
when the women are at their last prayers, it is to this day a noted saying, that after cheese comes nothing.

In another room I saw them marrying an old greasy boot to a
young pliable buskin. Pantagruel was told that young buskin took
old boot *to have and to hold,* because she was of special leather, in
good case, and waxed, seared, liquored and greased to the purpose,
even though it had been for the fisherman that went to bed with his
boots on. In another room below I saw a young brogue taking a
young slipper *for better for worse:* which, they told us, was neither for
the sake of her piety, parts, or person, but for the fourth comprehen-
sive p, portion; the spankers, spur-royals, rose-nobles, and other cori-
ander seed with which she was quilted all over.

CHAPTER X

WE sailed right before the wind, which we had at west, leaving
those odd *alliancers* with their ace-of-club snouts, and having
taken height by the sun, stood in for Chely, a large, fruitful, wealthy
and well peopled island. King St. Panigon, first of the name, reigned
there, and, attended by the princes his sons, and the nobles of his

court, came as far as the port to receive Pantagruel, and conducted him to his palace: near the gate of which, the queen, attended by the princesses her daughters, and the court ladies, received us. Panigon directed her and all her retinue to salute Pantagruel and his men with a kiss; for such was the civil custom of the country; and they were all fairly bussed accordingly, except Friar John, who stept aside, and sneaked off among the king's officers. Panigon used all the entreaties imaginable, to persuade Pantagruel to tarry there that day and the next: but he would needs be gone, and excused himself upon the opportunity of wind and weather, which being oftener desired than enjoyed, ought not to be neglected when it comes. Panigon, having heard these reasons, let us go, but first made us take off some five and twenty or thirty bumpers each.

Pantagruel, returning to the port, missed Friar John, and asked why he was not with the rest of the company? Panurge could not tell how to excuse him, and would have gone back to the palace to call him, when Friar John overtook them, and merrily cried, "Long live the noble Panigon? As I love my belly, he minds good eating, and keeps a noble house and a dainty kitchen. I have been there, boys. Everything goes about by dozens: I was in good hopes to have stuffed my puddings there like a monk." "What! always in a kitchen, friend?" said Pantagruel. "By the belly of St. Cramcapon," quoth the Friar, "I understand the customs and ceremonies which are used there, much better than all the formal stuff, antic postures, and nonsensical fiddle-faddle that must be used with those women, *magni, magna, shittencumshita,* cringes, grimaces, scrapes, bows, and congées; double honours this way, triple salutes that way, the embrace, the grasp, the squeeze, the hug, the leer, the smack, *baso las manos de vostra mercé, de vostra maestá.* You are most *tarabin, tarabas Stront;* that is downright Dutch. Why all this ado? I do not say but a man might be for a bit by the bye and away, to be doing as well as his neighbours: but this little nasty cringing and courtesying made me as mad as any *March-devil.* You talk of kissing ladies: by the worthy and sacred frock I wear, I seldom venture upon it, lest I be served as was the lord of Guyercharois." "What was it?" said Pantagruel: "I know him; he is one of the best friends I have."

"He was invited to a sumptuous feast," said Friar John, "by a relation and neighbour of his, together with all the gentlemen and ladies in the neighbourhood. Now some of the latter [the ladies] expecting his coming, dressed the pages in women's cloathes, and *finified* them like any babies: then ordered them to meet my lord at his coming near the draw-bridge: so the *complimenting monsieur* came, and there kissed the petticoated lads with great formality. At last the ladies, who minded passages in the gallery, burst out with laughing, and made signs to the pages to take off their dress: which the good lord having observed, the devil a bit he durst make up to the true ladies to kiss them, but said, that since they had disguised the pages, by his great grandfather's helmet, these were certainly the very footmen and grooms still more cunningly disguised. Odds fish, *da jurandi,* why do not we rather remove our humanities into some good warm kitchen of God, that noble laboratory; and there admire the turning of the spits, the harmonious rattling of the jacks and fenders, criticise on the position of the lard, the temperature of the pottages, the preparation for the dessert, and the order of the wine service? *Beati immaculati in via.* Matter of breviary, my masters."

CHAPTER XI

WHY MONKS LOVE TO BE IN KITCHENS

THIS," said Epistemon, "is spoke like a true monk; I mean like a right *monking monk* not a *bemonked* monastical *monkling.* Truly you put me in mind of some passages that happened at Florence, some twenty years ago, in a company of studious travellers, fond of visiting the learned, and seeing the antiquities of Italy, among whom I was. As we viewed the situation and beauty of Florence, the structure of the dome, the magnificence of the churches and palaces, we strove to outdo one another in giving them their due; when a certain monk of Amiens, Bernard Lardon by name, quite angry, scandalized and out of all patience, told us, 'I do not know what the devil you can find in this same town, that is so much cried up: for my part I have looked and pored and stared as well as the best of you; I think my eyesight's as clear as another body's; and what can one see after all? There are fine houses indeed, and that's all. But the cage does not feed the birds. God and monsieur St. Bernard, our good patron, be with us! in all this same town I have not seen one poor lane of roasting cooks; and yet I have not a little looked about, and sought for so necessary a part of a commonwealth: ay, and I dare assure you that I have pried up and down with the exactness of an informer; as ready to number both to the right and left, how many, and on what side we might find most roasting cooks, as a spy would be to reckon the bastions of a town. Now at Amiens, in four, nay five times less ground than we have trod in our contemplations, I could have shewn you above fourteen streets of roasting cooks, most ancient, savoury, and aromatic. I cannot imagine what kind of pleasure you can have taken in gazing on the lions, and Africans (so methinks you call their tigers) near the belfry; or in ogling the porcupines and ostriches, in the lord Philip Strozzi's palace. Faith and troth, I had rather see a good fat goose at the spit. This porphyry, those marbles are fine; I say nothing to the contrary: but our cheesecakes at Amiens are far better in my mind. These ancient statues are well made; I am willing to believe it: but, by St. Ferreol of Abbeville, we have young wenches in our country which please me better a thousand times.' "

"What is the reason," asked Friar John, "that monks are always to be found in kitchens; and kings, emperors, and popes are never there?" "Is there not," said Rhizotomus, "some latent virtue and specific property hid in the kettles and pans, which, as the lode-stone attracts iron, draws the monks there, and cannot attract emperors, popes, or kings? Or is it a natural induction and inclination, fixed in the frocks and cowls, which of itself leads and forceth those good religious men into kitchens, whether they will or no?" "He means, forms following matter, as Averoës calls them," answered Epistemon. "Right," said Friar John.

"I'll not offer to solve this problem," said Pantagruel; "for it is somewhat ticklish, and you can hardly handle it without coming off scurvily: but I'll tell you what I have heard.

"Antigonus, king of Macedon, one day coming into one of the tents, where his cooks use to dress his meat, and finding there poet Antagoras frying a conger, and holding the pan himself, merrily asked him, 'Pray, Mr. Poet, was Homer frying congers when he writ the deeds of Agamemnon?' Antagoras readily answered: 'But do you think, sir, that when Agamemnon did them, he made it his business to know if any in his camp were frying congers?' The king thought it an indecency that a poet should be thus a frying in a kitchen; and the poet let the king know, that it was a more indecent thing for a king to be found in such a place." "I'll clap another story upon the neck of this," quoth Panurge, "and will tell you what Breton Villandry answered one day to the Duke of Guise.

"They were saying that at a certain battle of king Francis, against the emperor Charles the Fifth, Breton, armed capapé to the teeth, and mounted like St. George; yet sneaked off, and played least in sight during the engagement. 'Blood and oons,' answered Breton, 'I was there, and can prove it easily; nay, even where you, my lord, dared not have been.' The duke began to resent this as too rash and saucy: but Breton easily appeased him, and set them all a laughing. 'I gad, my lord,' quoth he, 'I kept out of harm's way; I was all the while with your page Jack, sculking in a certain place where you had not dared hide your head, as I did.'" Thus discoursing, they got to their ships, and left the island of Chely.

CHAPTER XII

HOW PANTAGRUEL PASSED THROUGH THE LAND OF PETTIFOGGING, AND OF
THE STRANGE WAY OF LIVING AMONG THE CATCHPOLES

STEERING our course forwards the next day, we passed through Pettifogging, a country all blurred and blotted, so that I could hardly tell what to make on't. There we saw some pettifoggers and catchpoles, rogues that will hang their father for a groat. They neither invited us to eat or drink; but, with a multiplied train of scrapes and cringes, said they were all at our service, for the *legem pone*.

One of our interpreters related to Pantagruel their strange way of living, diametrically opposite to that of our modern Romans: for at Rome a world of folks get an honest livelihood by poisoning, drubbing, lambasting, stabbing and murthering; but the catchpoles earn theirs by being thrashed; so that if they were long without a tight lambasting, the poor dogs with their wives and children would be starved. "This is just," quoth Panurge, "like those who, as Galen tells us, cannot erect the cavernous nerve towards the equinoctial circle, unless they are soundly flogged. By St. Patrick's slipper, whoever should jirk me so, would soon, instead of setting me right, throw me off the saddle, in the devil's name."

"The way is this," said the interpreter. "When a monk, levite, close-fisted usurer, or lawyer, owes a grudge to some neighbouring gentleman, he sends to him one of those catchpoles or apparitors, who nabs, or at least cites him, serves a writ or warrant upon him, thumps, abuses and affronts him impudently by natural instinct, and according to his

483

pious instructions; insomuch, that if the gentleman hath but any guts in his brains, and is not more stupid than a gyrin frog, he will find himself obliged either to apply a faggot-stick or his sword to the rascal's jobbernol, give him the gentle lash, or make him cut a caper out at the window, by way of correction. This done, catchpole is rich for four months at least, as if bastinadoes were his real harvest: for the monk, levite, usurer, or lawyer, will reward him roundly; and my gentleman must pay him such swinging damages, that his acres may bleed for it, and he be in danger of miserably rotting within a stone doublet, as if he had struck the king."

Quoth Panurge, "I know an excellent remedy against this; used by the lord of Basché." "What is it?" said Pantagruel. "The lord of Basché," said Panurge, "was a brave honest noble-spirited gentleman, who, at his return from the long war, in which the duke of Ferrara, with the help of the French, bravely defended himself against the fury of pope Julius the second, was every day cited, warned, and prosecuted at the suit, and for the sport and fancy of the fat prior of St. Louant.

"One morning, as he was at breakfast with some of his domestics (for he loved to be sometimes among them) he sent for one Loire his baker, and his spouse, and for one Oudart the vicar of his parish, who was also his butler, as the custom was then in France; then said to them before his gentleman and other servants: 'You all see how I am daily plagued with these rascally catchpoles: truly if you do not lend me your helping hand, I am finally resolved to leave the country, and go fight for the sultan, or the devil, rather than be thus eternally teased. Therefore to be rid of their damned visits, hereafter, when any of them come here, be ready, you baker and your wife, to make your personal appearance in my great hall, in your wedding cloaths, as if you were going to be affianced. Here, take these ducats, which I give you to keep you in a fitting garb. As for you, Sir Oudart, be sure you make your personal appearance there in your fine surplice and stole, not forgetting your holy water, as if you were to wed them. Be you there also, Trudon,' said he to his drummer, 'with your pipe and tabor. The form of matrimony must be read, and the bride kissed at the beat of the tabor: then all of you, as the witnesses use to do in this country, shall give one another the remembrance of the wedding (which you know is to be a blow with your fist, bidding the party struck, remember the nuptials by that token). This will but make you have the better stomach to your supper: but when you come to the catchpole's turn, thrash him thrice and threefold, as you would a sheaf of green corn: do not spare him; maul him, drub him, lambast him, swinge him off, I pray you. Here, take these steel gauntlets, covered with kid. Head, back, belly, and sides, give him blows innumerable: he that gives him most, shall be my best friend. Fear not to be called to an account about it; I'll stand by you: for the blows must seem to be given in jest, as it is customary among us at all weddings.'

" 'Ay, but how shall we know the catchpole,' said the man of God? 'All sorts of people daily resort to this castle.' 'I have taken care of that,' replied the lord. 'When some fellow, either on foot, or on a scurvy jade, with a large broad silver ring on his thumb, comes to the door, he is certainly a catchpole: the porter, having civilly let him in, shall ring the bell; then be all ready, and come into the hall to act the tragi-comedy, whose plot I have now laid for you.'

"That numerical day, as chance would have it, came an old fat ruddy catchpole. Having knocked at the gate, and then pissed, as most men will do, the porter soon found him out, by his large greasy spatterdashes, his jaded hollow flanked mare, his bag full of writs and informations dangling at his girdle, but, above all, by the large silver hoop on his left thumb.

"The porter was civil to him, admitted him in kindly, and rung the bell briskly. As soon as the baker and his wife heard it, they clapt on their best cloaths, and made their personal appearance in the hall, keeping their gravities like a new-made judge. The domine put on his surplice and stole, and as he came out of his office, met the catchpole, had him in there, and made him suck his face a good while, while the gauntlets were drawing on all hands; and then told him, 'You are come just in pudding-time; my lord is in his right cue: we shall feast like kings anon, here is to be swinging doings: we have a wedding in the house; here, drink and cheer up; pull away.'

"While these two were at it hand to fist, Basché, seeing all his people in the hall in their proper equipage, sends for the vicar. Oudart comes with the holy water pot, followed by the catchpole, who, as he came into the hall, did not forget to make good store of awkward cringes, and then served Basché with a writ. Basché gave him grimace for grimace, slipt an angel into his mutton fist, and prayed him to assist at the contract and ceremony; which he did. When it was ended, thumps and fisticuffs began to fly about among the assistants; but when it came to the catchpole's turn they all laid on him so unmercifully with their gauntlets, that they at last settled him, all stunned and battered, bruised and mortified, with one of his eyes black and blue, eight ribs bruised, his brisket sunk in, his omoplates in four quarters, his under jawbone in three pieces; and all this in jest, and no harm done. God wot how the levite belaboured him, hiding within the long sleeve of his canonical shirt his huge steel gauntlet lined with ermine: for he was a strong built *ball,* and an old dog at fisticuffs. The catchpole, all of a bloody tiger-like hue, with much ado, crawled home to l'isle Bouchart, well pleased and edified however with Basché's kind reception; and, with the help of the good surgeons of the place, lived as long as you'd have him. From that time to this not a word of the business: the memory of it was lost with the sound of the bells that rung for joy at his funeral.

CHAPTER XIII

HOW, LIKE MASTER FRANCIS VILLON, THE LORD OF BASCHÉ COMMENDED HIS SERVANTS

THE catchpole being packed off on blind Sorrel (so he called his one-eyed mare) Basché sent for his lady, her women, and all his servants, into the arbour of his garden; had wine brought, attended with good store of pasties, hams, fruit, and other table-ammunition for a nunchion; drank with them joyfully, and then told them this story.

" 'Master Francis Villon, in his old age, retired to St. Maixent, in Poitou, under the patronage of a good honest abbot of the place. There, to make sport for the mob, he undertook to get the *passion* acted after the way and in the dialect of the country. The parts being distributed, the play having been rehearsed, and the stage prepared, he told the mayor and aldermen that the mystery would be ready after Niort fair, and that there only wanted properties and necessaries, but chiefly cloaths fit for the parts: so the mayor and his brethren took care to get them.

" 'Villon, to dress an old clownish father grey-beard, who was to represent G—d the father, begged of Friar Stephen Tickletoby, sacristan to the franciscan friars of the place, to lend him a cope and a stole. Tickletoby refused him, alleging, that by their provincial statutes, it was rigorously forbidden to give or lend anything to players. Villon replied, that the statute reached no farther than farces, drolls, antics, loose and dissolute games, and that he asked no more than what he had seen allowed at Brussels and other places. Tickle-toby, notwithstanding, peremptorily bid him provide himself elsewhere if he would, and not to hope for anything out of his monastical ward-robe. Villon gave an account of this to the players, as of a most abominable action; adding, that God would shortly revenge himself, and make an example of Tickletoby.

" 'The Saturday following he had notice given him that Tickletoby, upon the filly of the convent (so they call a young mare that was never leaped yet), was gone a mumping to St. Ligarius, and would be back about two in the afternoon. Knowing this, he made a caval-cade of his devils of the passion through the town. They were all rigged with wolves, calves, and rams' skins, laced and trimmed with sheep's heads, bulls' feathers, and large kitchen tenter hooks, girt with broad leathern girdles; whereat hang'd dangling huge cow-bells and horse-bells, which made a horrid din. Some held in their claws black sticks full of squibs and crackers; others had long lighted pieces of wood, upon which, at the corner of every street, they flung whole handfuls of rosin-dust, that made a terrible fire and smoak. Having thus led them about to the great diversion of the mob, and the dread-ful fear of little children, he finally carried them to an entertainment at a summer-house, without the gate that leads to St. Ligarius.

" 'As they came near the place, he spied Tickletoby afar off, com-ing home from mumping, and told them in macaronic verse,

" 'Hic est mumpator natus de gente cucowli,
Qui solet antiquo scrappas portare bisacco.'

" 'A plague on his friarship,' said the devils then; 'the lousy beggar would not lend a poor cope to the fatherly father; let us fright him.' 'Well said,' cried Villon: 'but let us hide ourselves till he comes by, and then charge him home briskly with your squibs and burning sticks.' Tickletoby being come to the place, they all rushed on a sudden into the road to meet him, and in a frightful manner threw fire from all sides upon him and his filly foal, ringing and tingling their bells, and howling like so many real devils, 'Hho, hho, hho, hho, brrou, rrou, rrourrs, rrrourrs, hoo, hou, hou, hho, hho, hhoi. Friar Stephen, don't we play the devils rarely?' The filly was soon scared out of her seven senses, and began to start, to funk it, to squirt it, to trot it, to fart it, to bound it, to gallop it, to kick it, to spurn it, to calci-trate it, to wince it, to frisk it, to leap it, to curvet it, with double jirks, and bum-motions; insomuch that she threw down Tickletoby, though he held fast by the tree of the pack-saddle with might and main. Now his straps and stirrups were of cord; and on the right side his sandal was so entangled and twisted, that he could not for the heart's blood of him get out his foot. Thus he was dragged about by the filly through the road, scratching his bare breech all the way; she still multiplying her kicks against him, and straying for fear over hedge and ditch; insomuch that she trepanned his thick skull so, that his cockle brains were dashed out near the osanna or high-cross. Then his arms fell to pieces, one this way and the other that way; and even so were his legs served at the same time. Then she made a bloody havock with his puddings; and being got to the convent, brought back only his right foot and twisted sandal, leaving them to guess what was become of the rest.

"'Villon seeing that things had succeeded as he intended, said to his devils, 'You will act rarely, gentlemen devils, you will act rarely; I dare engage you will top your parts. I defy the devils of Saumur, Douay, Montmorillion, Langez, St. Espain, Angers; nay, by gad, even those of Poictiers, for all their bragging and vapouring, to match you.'

"'Thus, friends,' said Basché, 'I foresee that hereafter you will act rarely this tragical farce, since the very first time you have so skilfully hampered, bethwacked, belammed, and bebumped the catchpole. From this day I double your wages. As for you, my dear,' said he to his lady, 'make your gratifications as you please; you are my treasurer, you know. For my part, first and foremost, I drink to you all. Come on, box it about, it is good and cool. In the second place, you, Mr. Steward, take this silver bason, I give it you freely. Then you, my gentleman of the horse, take these two silver gilt cups, and let not the pages be horse-whipped these three months. My dear, let them have my best white plumes of feathers, with the gold buckles to them. Sir Oudart, this silver flaggon falls to your share; this other I give to the cooks. To the valets de chambre I give this silver basket; to the grooms, this silver gilt boat; to the porter, these two plates; to the hostlers, these ten porringers. Trudon, take you these silver spoons and this sugar box. You, footman, take this large salt. Serve me well, and I will remember you. For on the word of a gentleman, I had rather bear in war one hundred blows on my helmet in the service of my country, than be once cited by these knavish catchpoles, merely to humour this same gorbellied prior.'

CHAPTER XIV

A FURTHER ACCOUNT OF CATCHPOLES WHO WERE DRUBBED AT BASCHÉ'S HOUSE

FOUR days after, another, young, long-shanked, raw-boned catch-pole, coming to serve Basché with a writ at the fat prior's request, was no sooner at the gate, but the porter smelt him out, and rung the bell; at whose second pull, all the family understood the mystery. Loire was kneading his dough; his wife was sifting meal; Oudart was toping in his office; the gentlemen were playing at tennis; the lord Basché at in and out with my lady; the waiting-men and gentle-women at push-pin; the officers at lanterlue, and the pages at hot-cockles, giving one another smart bangs. They were all immediately informed that a catchpole was housed.

"Upon this Oudart put on his sacerdotal, and Loire and his wife their nuptial badges: Trudon piped it, and then tabered it like mad: all made haste to get ready, not forgetting the gauntlets. Basché went into the outward yard: there the catchpole meeting him, fell on his marrow-bones, begged of him not to take it ill, if he served him with a writ at the suit of the fat prior; and in a pathetic speech, let him know that he was a public person, a servant to the monking tribe, ap-paritor to the abbatial mitre, ready to do as much for him, nay, for the least of his servants, whensoever he would employ and use him.

"'Nay, truly,' said the lord, 'you shall not serve your writ till you have tasted some of my good quinquenays wine, and been a witness to a wedding which we are to have this very minute. Let him drink and refresh himself,' added he, turning towards the levitical butler, 'and then bring him into the hall.' After which, catchpole, well stuffed and moistened, came with Oudart to the place where all the actors in the farce stood ready to begin. The sight of their game set them a laughing, and the messenger of mischief grinned also for company's sake. Then the mysterious words were muttered to and by the couple, their hands joined, the bride bussed, and all besprinkled with holy water. While they were bringing wine and kickshaws, thumps began to trot about by dozens. The catchpole gave the levite several blows. Oudart, who had his gauntlet hid under his canonical shirt, draws it on like a mitten, and then, with his clenched fist, souse he fell on the catchpole, and mauled him like a devil: the junior gauntlets dropt on him likewise like so many battering rams. 'Remember the wedding by this, by that, by these blows,' said they. In short they stroaked him so to the purpose, that he pissed blood out at mouth, nose, ears, and eyes, and was bruised, thwackt, battered, be-bumped, and crippled at the back, neck, breast, arms, and so forth. Never did the batchelors at Avignon, in carnival time, play more melodiously at raphe, than was then played on the catchpole's micro-cosm: at last down he fell.

"They threw a great deal of wine on his snout, tied around the sleeve of his doublet a fine yellow and green favour, and got him upon his snotty beast, and God knows how he got to l'isle Bouchart; where I cannot truly tell you whether he was dressed and looked after or no, both by his spouse and the able doctors of the country; for the thing never came to my ears.

"The next day they had a third part to the same tune, because it did not appear by the lean catchpole's bag, that he had served his writ. So the fat prior sent a new catchpole, at the head of a brace of bums, for his guard du corps, to summon my lord. The porter ringing the bell, the whole family was overjoyed, knowing that it was another rogue. Basché was at dinner with his lady and the gentlemen; so he sent for the catchpole, made him sit by him, and the bums by the women, and made them eat till their bellies cracked with their breeches unbuttoned. The fruit served, the catchpole arose from table, and before the bums cited Basché. Basché kindly asked him for a copy of the warrant, which the other had got ready: he then takes witness, and a copy of the summons. To the catchpole and his bums he ordered four ducats for civility money. In the meantime all were withdrawn for the farce. So Trudon gave the alarm with his tabor. Basché desired the catchpole to stay and see one of his servants married, and witness the contract of marriage, paying him his fee. The catchpole slap dash was ready, took out his ink-horn, got paper immediately, and his bums by him.

"Then Loire came into the hall at one door, and his wife with the gentlewomen at another, in nuptial accoutrements. Oudart, in ponti-ficalibus, takes them both by their hands, asketh them their will, giveth them the matrimonial blessing, and was very liberal of holy water. The contract written, signed, and registered, on one side was brought wine and comfits; on the other, white and orange-tawny-coloured favours were distributed: on another, gauntlets privately handed about.

490

CHAPTER XV

HOW THE ANCIENT CUSTOM AT NUPTIALS IS RENEWED
BY THE CATCHPOLE

THE catchpole, having made shift to get down a swinging sneaker of Breton wine, said to Basché, 'Pray, sir, what do you mean? You do not give one another the memento of the wedding. By St. Joseph's wooden shoe all good customs are forgot. We find the form, but the hare's scampered; and the nest, but the birds are flown. There are no true friends now-a-days. You see how, in several churches, the ancient laudable custom of tippling on account of the blessed saints O O, at christmas, is come to nothing. The world is in its dotage, and doomsday is certainly coming all so fast. Now come on; the wedding, the wedding, the wedding; remember it by this.' This he said, striking Basché and his lady; then her women and the levite. Then the tabor beat a point of war, and the gauntlets began to do their duty; insomuch that the catchpole had his crown cracked in no less than nine places. One of the bums had his right arm put out of joint, and the other his upper jaw-bone or mandibule dislocated; so that it hid half his chin, with a denudation of the uvula, and sad loss of the molar, masticatory, and canine teeth. Then the tabor beat a retreat; the gauntlets were carefully hid in a trice, and sweet-meats afresh distributed to renew the mirth of the company. So they all drank to one another, and especially to the catchpole and his bums. But Oudart cursed and damned the wedding to the pit of hell, complaining that one of the bums had utterly disincornifistibulated his nether shoulder-blade. Nevertheless, he scorned to be thought a flincher, and made shift to tope to him on the square.

"The jawless bum shrugged up his shoulders, joined his hands, and by signs begged his pardon; for speak he could not. The sham bridegroom made his moan, that the crippled bum had struck him such a horrid thump with his shoulder-of-mutton first on the nether elbow, that he was grown quite esperruquanchuzelubelouzerireliced down to his very heel, to the no small loss of mistress bride.

"'But what harm had poor I done?' (cried Trudon, hiding his left eye with his kerchief, and shewing his tabor cracked on one side:) 'they were not satisfied with thus poaching, black and bluing, and morrambouzevezengouzequoquemorgasacbaquevezinemaffreliding my poor eyes, but they have also broke my harmless drum. Drums indeed are commonly beaten at weddings (and it is fit they should); but drummers are well entertained, and never beaten. Now let Belzebub e'en take the drum, to make his devilship a night-cap.' 'Brother,' said the lame catchpole, 'never fret thyself; I will make thee a present of a fine, large, old patent, which I have here in my bag, to patch up thy drum, and for madam St. Ann's sake I pray thee forgive us. By'r lady of Riviere, the blessed dame, I meant no more harm than the child unborn.' One of the querries, who, hopping and halting like a mumping cripple, mimicked the good limping lord de la Roche Posay, directed his discourse to the bum with the pouting jaw, and told him, 'What, Mr. Manhound, was it not enough thus to have morcrocaste-bezasteverestegrigeligoscopapopondrillated us all in our upper members with your botched mittens, but you must also apply such morderegripippiatabirofreluchamburelurecaquelurintimpaniments on our shin-bones with the hard tops and extremities of your cobbled shoes? Do you call this children's play? By the mass, it is no jest.' The bum, wringing his hands, seemed to beg his pardon, muttering with his tongue, 'Mon, mon, mon, vrelon, von, von,' like a dumb man. The bride crying laughed, and laughing cried, because the catchpole was not satisfied with drubbing her without choice or distinction of members, but had also rudely roused and toused her; pulled off her topping, and not having the fear of her husband before his eyes, treacherously trepignemanpenillorifrizonoufresterfumbledtumbled and squeezed her lower parts. 'The devil go with it,' said Basché; 'there was much need indeed that this same master King (this was the catchpole's name) should thus break my wife's back: however, I forgive him now; these are little nuptial caresses. But this I plain perceive, that he cited me like an angel, and drubbed me like a devil. He hath something in him of friar Thumpwell. Come, for all this, I must drink to him, and to you likewise his trusty esquires.' 'But,' said his lady, 'why hath he been so very liberal of his manual kindness to me, without the least provocation? I assure you, I by no means like it: but this I dare say for him, that he hath the hardest knuckles that ever I felt on my shoulders.' The steward held his left arm in a scarf, as if it had been rent and torn in twain: 'I think it was the devil,' said he, 'that moved me to assist at these nuptials; shame on ill luck; I must needs be meddling, with a pox, and now see what I have got by the bargain, both my arms are wretchedly engoulevezinemassed and bruised. Do you call this a wedding? By St. Briget's tooth, I had rather be at that of a Tom t——d-man. This is, o' my word, even just such another feast as was that of the Lapithæ, described by the philosopher of Samosate.' One of the bums had lost his tongue. The two other, though they had more need to complain, made their excuse as well as they could, protesting that they had no ill design in this dumbfounding; begging that, for goodness sake, they would forgive them; and so, though they could hardly budge a foot, or wag along, away they crawled. About a mile from Basché's seat, the catchpole found himself somewhat out of sorts. The bums got to l'isle Bouchard, publicly saying, that since they were born, they had never seen an honester gentleman than the lord of Basché, or civiller people than his, and that they had never been at the like wedding (which I verily believe); but that it was their own faults if they had been tickled off, and tossed about from post to pillar, since themselves had began the beating. So they lived I cannot exactly tell you how many days after this. But from that time to this it was held for a certain truth, that Basché's money was more pestilential, mortal, and pernicious to the catchpoles and bums, than were formerly the aurum tholosanum and the sejan horse to those that possessed them. Ever since this, he lived quietly, and Basché's wedding grew into a common proverb."

CHAPTER XVI

HOW FRIAR JOHN MADE TRIAL OF THE NATURE OF THE CATCHPOLES

THIS story would seem pleasant enough," said Pantagruel, "were we not to have always the fear of God before our eyes." "It had been better," said Epistemon, "if those gauntlets had fallen upon the fat prior. Since he took a pleasure in spending his money partly to vex Basché, partly to see those catchpoles banged, good lusty thumps would have done well on his shaved crown, considering the horrid concussions now-a-days among those puny judges. What harm had done those poor devils the catchpoles?" "This puts me in mind," said Pantagruel, "of an ancient Roman named L. Veratius. He was of noble blood, and for some time was rich; but had this tyrannical inclination, that whenever he went out of doors, he caused his servants to fill their pockets with gold and silver, and meeting in the streets your spruce gallants and better sort of beaux, without the least provocation, for his fancy, he used to strike them hard on the face with his fist, and immediately after that, to appease them, and hinder them from complaining to the magistrates, he would give them as much money as satisfied them according to the law of the twelve tables. Thus he used to spend his revenue, beating people for the price of his money." "By St. Bennet's sacred boot," quoth Friar John, "I will know the truth of it presently."

This said, he went on shore, put his hand in his fob, and took out twenty ducats; then said with a loud voice, in the hearing of a shoal of the nation of catchpoles, "Who will earn twenty ducats, for being beaten like the devil?" "Io, Io, Io," said they all: "you will cripple us for ever, sir, that is most certain; but the money is tempting." With this they were all thronging who should be first, to be thus preciously beaten. Friar John singled him out of the whole knot of these rogues in grain, a red-snouted catchpole, who upon his right thumb wore a thick broad silver hoop, wherein was set a good large toad-stone. He had sooner picked him out from the rest, but I perceived that they all muttered and grumbled; and I heard a young thin-jawed catchpole, a notable scholar, a pretty fellow at his pen, and, according to public report, much cried up for his honesty at Doctors-commons, making his complaint, and muttering, because this same crimson phyz carried away all the practice; and that if there were but a score and a half of bastinadoes to be got, he would certainly run away with eight and twenty of them. But all this was looked upon to be nothing but mere envy.

Friar John so unmercifully thrashed, thumped, and belaboured Red-snout, back and belly, sides, legs and arms, head, feet, and so forth, with the home and frequently repeated application of one of the best members of a faggot, that I took him to be a dead man: then he gave him the twenty ducats; which made the dog get on his legs, pleased like a little king or two. The rest were saying to Friar John, "Sir, sir, brother devil, if it please you to do us the favour to beat some of us for less money, we are all at your devilship's command, bags, papers, pens and all." Red-snout cried out against them, saying, with a loud voice, "Body of me, you little prigs, will you offer to take the bread out of my mouth? will you take my bargain over my head? would you draw and inveigle from me my clients and customers? Take notice, I summon you before the official this day sevennight; I will law and claw you like any old devil, that I will——" Then turning himself towards Friar John, with a smiling and joyful look, he said to him, "Reverend father in the devil, if you have found me a good hide, and

494

have a mind to divert yourself once more, by beating your humble servant, I will bate you half in half this time, rather than lose your custom: do not spare me, I beseech you; I am all, and more than all yours, good Mr. Devil; head, lungs, tripes, guts and garbage; and that at a pennyworth, I'll assure you." Friar John never heeded his proffers, but even left them. The other catchpoles were making addresses to Panurge, Epistemon, Gymnast and others, entreating them charitably to bestow upon their carcasses a small beating, for otherwise they were in danger of keeping a long fast: but none of them had a stomach to it. Some time after, seeking fresh water for the ship's company, we met a couple of old female catchpoles of the place, miserably howling and weeping in consort. Pantagruel had kept on board, and already had caused a retreat to be sounded. Thinking they might be related to the catchpole that was bastinadoed, we asked them the occasion of their grief. They replied, that they had too much cause to weep; for that very hour, from an exalted triple tree, two of the honestest gentlemen in Catchpoleland had been made to cut a caper on nothing. "Cut a caper on nothing?" said Gymnast: "my pages use to cut capers on the ground: to cut a caper on nothing, should be hanging and choaking, or I am out." "Ay, ay," said Friar John, "you speak of it like St. John de la Palisse."

We asked them why they treated these worthy persons with such a choaking hempen sallad. They told us they had only borrowed, alias stolen, the tools of the mass, and hid them under the handle of the parish. "This is a very allegorical way of speaking," said Epistemon.

CHAPTER XVII

HOW PANTAGRUEL CAME TO THE ISLANDS OF TOHU AND BOHU; AND OF THE
STRANGE DEATH OF WIDENOSTRILS, THE SWALLOWER OF WINDMILLS

THAT day Pantagruel came to two islands of Tohu and Bohu, where the devil a bit we could find anything to fry with. For one Widenostrils, a huge giant, had swallowed every individual pan, skillet, kettle, frying-pan, dripping-pan, and brass and iron pot in the land, for want of windmills, which were his daily food. Whence it happened, that somewhat before day, about the hour of his digestion, the greedy churl was taken very ill, with a kind of a surfeit, or crudity of stomach, occasioned, as the physicians said, by the weakness of the concocting faculty of his stomach, naturally disposed to digest whole windmills at a gust, yet unable to consume perfectly the pans and skillets; though it had indeed pretty well digested the kettles and pots; as, they said, they knew by the hypostases and encormes of four tubs of second-hand drink, which he had evacuated at two different times that morning. They made use of divers remedies, according to art, to give him ease: but all would not do; the distemper prevailed over the remedies, insomuch that the famous Widenostrils died that morning of so strange a death, that, I think, you ought no longer to wonder at that of the poet Æschylus. It had been foretold him by the soothsayers, that he would die on a certain day, by the ruin of something that should fall on him. That fatal day being come in its turn, he removed himself out of town, far from all houses, trees, rocks, or any other things that can fall, and endanger by their ruin; and strayed in a large field, trusting himself to the open sky; there very secure, as he thought, unless indeed the sky should happen to fall, which he held to be impossible. Yet, they say, that the larks are much afraid of it; for if it should fall, they must all be taken.

The Celtes that once lived near the Rhine (they are our noble valiant French) in ancient times were also afraid of the sky's falling: for being asked by Alexander the Great, what they feared most in the world, hoping well they would say that they feared none but him, considering his great achievements; they made answer, that they feared nothing but the sky's falling: however, not refusing to enter into a confederacy with so brave a king: if you believe Strabo, lib. 7, and Arrian, lib. 1.

Plutarch also, in his book of the face that appears on the body of the moon, speaks of one Phenaces, who very much feared the moon should fall on the earth, and pitied those that live under that planet, as the Æthiopians and Taprobanians, if so heavy a mass ever happened to fall on them; and would have feared the like of heaven and earth, had they not been duly propped up and borne by the atlantic pillars as the ancients believed, according to Aristotle's testimony, lib. 5, metaphys. Notwithstanding all this poor Æschylus was killed by the fall of the shell of a tortoise, which falling from betwixt the claws of an eagle high in the air, just on his head, dashed out his brains.

Neither ought you to wonder at the death of another poet, I mean old jolly Anacreon, who was choaked with a grape-stone. Nor at that of Fabius the Roman prætor, who was choaked with a single goat's hair, as he was supping up a porringer of milk. Nor at the death of that bashful fool, who by holding in his wind, and for want of letting out a bum-gunshot, died suddenly in the presence of the emperor Claudius. Nor at that of the Italian, buried on the Via Flaminia at Rome, who, in his epitaph, complains that the bite of a she puss on his little finger was the cause of his death. Nor of that of Q. Lecanius Bassus, who died suddenly of so small a prick with a needle on his left thumb. that it could hardly be discerned. Nor of Quenelault, a Norman physician, who died suddenly at Montpellier, merely for having side-ways took a worm out of his hand with a pen-knife. Nor of Philomenes, whose servant having got him some new figs for the first course of his dinner, whilst he went to fetch wine, a straggling well-hung ass got into the house, and seeing the figs on the table, without further invitation, soberly fell to: Philomenes coming into the room, and nicely observing with what gravity the ass eat its dinner, said to his man, who was come back, "Since thou hast set figs here for this reverend guest of ours to eat, methinks it is but reason thou also give him some of this wine to drink." He had no sooner said this, but he was so excessively pleased, and fell into so exorbitant a fit of laughter, that the use of his spleen took that of his breath utterly away, and he immediately died. Nor of Spurius Saufeius, who died supping up a soft boiled egg as he came out of a bath. Nor of him who, as Boccace tells us, died suddenly by picking his grinders with a sage-stalk. Nor of Philipot Placut, who being brisk and hale, fell dead as he was paying an old debt; which causes, perhaps, many not to pay theirs, for fear of the like accident. Nor of the painter Zeuxis, who killed himself with laughing at the sight of the antic jobbernol of an old hag drawn by him. Nor, in short, of a thousand more of which authors write; as Verrius, Pliny, Valerius, J. Baptista, Fulgosus, and Bacabery the elder. In short, gaffer Widenostrils choaked himself with eating a huge lump of fresh butter at the mouth of a hot oven, by the advice of physicians.

They likewise told us there, that the king of Cullan, in Bohu, had routed the grandees of king Mecloth, and made sad work with the fortresses of Belima.

After this we sailed by the islands of Nargues and Zargues; also by the islands of Teleniabin and Geleniabin, very fine and fruitful in ingredients for clysters; and then by the islands of Enig and Evig, on whose account formerly the landgrave of Hesse was swinged off with a vengeance.

CHAPTER XVIII

HOW PANTAGRUEL MET WITH A GREAT STORM AT SEA

THE next day we espied nine sail that came spooning before the wind: they were full of dominicans, jesuits, capuchins, hermits, austins, bernardins, celestins, theatins, egnatins, amadeans, cordeliers, carmelites, minims, and the devil and all of other holy monks and friars, who were going to the council of Chesil, to sift and garble some articles of faith against the new heretics. Panurge was overjoyed to see them, being most certain of good luck for that day, and a long train of others. So having courteously saluted the blessed fathers, and recommended the salvation of his precious soul to their devout prayers and private ejaculations, he caused seventy-eight dozen of Westphalia hams, units of pots of caviar, tens of Bolonia sausages, hundreds of botargoes, and thousands of fine angels, for the souls of the dead, to be thrown on board their ships. Pantagruel seemed metagrabolized, dozing, out of sorts, and as melancholic as a cat. Friar John, who soon perceived it, was enquiring of him whence should come this unusual sadness? when the master, whose watch it was, observing the fluttering of the ancient above the poop, and seeing that it began to overcast, judged that we should have wind; therefore he bid the boatswain call all hands upon deck, officers, sailors, foresmast men, swabbers, and cabin boys, and even the passengers; made them first settle their topsails, take in their sprit-sail; then he cried, "In with your top-sails, lower the foresail, tallow under the parrels, brade up close all them sails, strike your topmasts to the cap, make all sure with your sheepsfeet, lash your guns fast." All this was nimbly done. Immediately it blowed a storm; the sea began to roar, and swell mountain high: the rut of the sea was great, the waves breaking upon our ship's quarter; the northwest wind blustered and overblowed; boisterous gusts, dreadful clashing, and deadly scuds of wind whistled through our yards, and made our shrouds rattle again. The thunder grumbled so horridly, that you would have thought heaven had been tumbling about our ears: at the same time it lightened, rained, hailed; the sky lost its transparent hue, grew dusky, thick, and gloomy, so that we had no other light than that of the flashes of lightning, and rending of the clouds: the hurricanes, flaws, and sudden whirlwinds began to make a flame about us, by the lightnings, fiery vapours, and other aerial ejaculations. Oh, how our looks were full of amazement and trouble, while the saucy winds did rudely lift up above us the mountainous waves of the main! Believe me, it seemed to us a lively image of the chaos, where fire, air, sea, land, and all the elements were in a refractory confusion. Poor Panurge having, with the full contents of the inside of his doublet, plentifully fed the fish, greedy enough of such odious fare, sat on the deck all in a heap, with his nose and arse together, most sadly cast down, moping and half dead; invoked and called to his assistance all the blessed he and she saints he could muster up; swore and vowed to confess in time and place convenient, and then bawled out frightfully, "Steward, maistre d'hostel, see hoe! my friend, my father, my uncle, prithee let's have a piece of powdered beef or pork; we shall drink but too much anon, for ought I see. *Eat little, and drink the more,* will hereafter be my motto, I fear. Would to our dear Lord, and to our blessed, worthy, and sacred lady, I were now, I say, this very minute of an hour, well on shore, on terra firma, hale and easy. O twice and thrice happy those that plant cabbages! O destinies, why did you not *spin* me for a cabbage planter? O how few are there to whom Jupiter hath been so favourable, as to predestinate them to plant cabbages! They have always one foot on the ground, and the other not far from it. Dispute who will of felicity, and *summum bonum,* for my part, whosoever *plants* cabbage, is now, by my decree, proclaimed most happy; for as good a reason as the philosopher Pyrrho, being in the same danger, and seeing a hog near the shore eating some scattered oats, declared it happy in two respects, first, because it had plenty of oats, and besides that, was on shore. Hah, for a divine and princely habitation, commend me to the cow's floor.

"Murther! This wave will sweep us away, blessed Saviour! O my friends! a little vinegar. I sweat again with mere agony. Alas, the mizen sail's split, the gallery's washed away, the masts are sprung, the maintop-masthead dives into the sea; the keel is up to the sun; our shrouds are almost all broke, and blown away. Alas! alas! where is our main course? *Al is verlooren by Godt;* our top-mast is run adrift. Alas! who shall have this wreck? Friend, lend me here behind you one of these whales. Your lanthorn is fallen, my lads. Alas! don't let go the main tack nor the bowlin. I hear the block crack; is it broke? For the Lord's sake, let us save the hull, and let all the rigging be damned. Be, be, be, bous, bous, bous. Look to the needle of your compass, I beseech you, good sir Astrophil, and tell us, if you can, whence comes this storm. My heart's sunk down below my midriff. By my troth I am in a sad fright; bou, bou, bou, bous, I am lost for ever. I conskite myself for mere madness and fear. Bou, bou, bou, bou, Otto to to to to ti. Bou, bou, bou, ou, ou, ou, bou, bou, bous. I sink, I'm drown'd, I'm gone, good people, I'm drown'd."

CHAPTER XIX

WHAT COUNTENANCES PANURGE AND FRIAR JOHN KEPT DURING THE STORM

PANTAGRUEL, having first implored the help of the great and almighty Deliverer, and prayed publicly with fervent devotion, by the pilot's advice held tightly the mast of the ship. Friar John had stripped himself to his waistcoat, to help the seamen. Epistemon, Ponocrates, and the rest did as much. Panurge alone sat on his breech upon deck, weeping and howling. Friar John espied him going on the quarter-deck, and said to him: "Odzoons! Panurge the calf, Panurge the whiner, Panurge the brayer, would it not become thee much better to lend us here a helping hand, than to lie lowing like a cow, as thou dost, sitting on thy stones, like a bald-breech'd baboon?" "Be, be, be, bous, bous, bous," returned Panurge; "Friar John, my friend, my good father, I am drowning, my dear friend! I drown; I am a dead man, my dear father in God, I am a dead man, my friend: your cutting hanger cannot save me from this: alas! alas! we are above ela. Above the pitch, out of tune, and off the hinges. Be, be, be, bou, bous. Alas, we are now above *g sol re ut.* I sink, I sink, hah my father, my uncle, my all. The water is got into my shoes by the collar: bous, bous, bous, paisch, hu, hu, hu, he, he, he, ha, ha, I drown. Alas! alas! Hu, hu, hu, hu, hu, hu, hu, be be bous, bous, bobous, bobous, ho, ho, ho, ho, ho, alas! alas! Now am I like your tumblers, my feet stand higher than my head. Would to heaven I were now with those good, holy fathers bound for the council, whom we met this morning, so godly, so fat, so merry, so plump and comely. Holos, holos, holas, holas, alas. This devilish wave (*mea culpa Deus*) I mean this wave of God, will sink our vessel. Alas, Friar John, my father, my friend, confession. Here I am down on my knees; *confiteor;* your holy blessing." "Come hither and be damned, thou pitiful devil, and help us," said Friar John; who fell a swearing and cursing like a tinker: "in the name of thirty legions of black devils, come, will you come?" "Don't let us swear at this time," said Panurge: "holy father, my friend, don't swear, I beseech you; to-morrow as much as you please.

500

Holos, holos, alas, our ship leaks. I drown, alas, alas! I will give eighteen hundred thousand crowns to anyone that will set me on shore, all bewrayed, and bedawbed as I am now. If ever there was a man in my country in the like pickle. *Confiteor,* alas! a word or two of testament or codicil at least." "A thousand devils seize the cuckoldy, cow-hearted mungrel," cried Friar John. "Ods belly, art thou talking here of making thy will, now we are in danger, and it behoveth us to bestir our stumps lustily, or never? Wilt thou come, ho devil? Midshipman, my friend; O the rare lieutenant; here Gymnast, here on the poop. We are, by the mass, all beshit now, our light is out. This is hastening to the devil as fast as it can."—"Alas, bou, bou, bou, bou, bou, alas, alas, alas, alas," said Panurge, "was it here we were born to perish? Oh! hoh! good people, I drown, I die. *Consummatum est.* I am sped——" "*Magna gna, gna,*" said Friar John. "Fye upon him; how ugly the shitten howler looks.—Boy, younker, see hoyh.—Mind the pumps, or the devil choak thee.—Hast thou hurt thyself? Zoons, here fasten it to one of these blocks. On this side in the devil's name, hay, so my boy."—"Ah, Friar John," said Panurge, "good ghostly father, dear friend, don't let us swear, you sin. Oh ho, oh ho, be be be bous, bous, bhous, I sink, I die, my friends. I die in charity with all the world. Farewell, *in manus.* Bohous, bhous, bhousowwauswaus. St. Michael of Aure! St. Nicholas! now, now or never. I here make you a solemn vow, and to our Saviour, that if you stand by me but this time, I mean if you set me ashore out of this danger, I will build you a fine large little chapel or two, between Candé and Monsoreau, where neither cow nor calf shall feed. Oh ho, oh ho. Above eighteen pailfuls or two of it are got down my gullet; bous, bhous, bhous, bhous, how damned bitter and salt it is!"—"By the virtue," said Friar John, "of the blood, the flesh, the belly, the head, if I hear thee again howling, thou cuckoldly cur, I'll maul thee worse than any sea wolf. Ods fish, why don't we take him up by the lugs and throw him overboard to the bottom of the sea? Here, sailor, ho honest fellow. Thus, thus, my friend, hold fast above.—In truth here is a sad lightning and thundering; I think that all the devils are got loose; it is holiday with them; or else madam Proserpine is in child's labour: all the devils dance a morrice."

CHAPTER XX

"OH," said Panurge, "you sin, friar John, my former crony! Former, I say, for at this time I am no more, you are no more. It goes against my heart to tell it you; for I believe this swearing doth your spleen a great deal of good; as it is a great ease to a wood cleaver to cry hem at every blow; and as one who plays as nine-pins is wonderfully helped, if, when he hath not thrown his bowl right, and is like to make a bad cast, some *ingenious* stander-by leans, and screws his body half way about, on that side which the bowl should have took to hit the pin. Nevertheless you offend, my sweet friend. But what do you think of eating some kind of cabirotadoes? Would not this secure us from this storm? I have read, that in a storm at sea no harm ever befel the ministers of the gods Cabiri, so much celebrated by Orpheus, Apollonius, Pherecides, Strabo, Pausanias, and Herodotus." "He doats, he raves, the poor devil!" said friar John. "A thousand, a million, nay, a hundred million of devils seize the hornified doddipole. Lend's a hand here, hoh, tiger, wouldst thou? Here, on the starboard-side. Ods me, thou buffalo's head stuffed with relics, what ape's *paternoster* art thou muttering and chattering here between thy teeth? That devil of a sea-calf is the cause of all this storm, and is the only man who doth not lend a helping hand. By G—, if I come near thee, I'll fetch thee out by the head and ears with a vengeance, and chastise thee like any tempestative devil. Here mate, my lad, hold fast till I have made a double knot. O brave boy! would to heaven thou wert abbot of Talemouze, and that he that is were guardian of Croullay." "Hold! brother Ponocrates, you will hurt yourself, man. Epistemon, pr'ythee stand off out of the hatchway. Methinks I saw the thunder fall there but just now. Con the ship, so ho—Mind your steerage. Well said, thus, thus, steady, keep her thus, get the long-boat clear.—Steady. Ods fish, the beak-head is staved to pieces. Grumble, devils, fart, belch, shite a t—d o'the wave. If this be weather, the devil's a ram. Nay by G—, a little more would have wash'd me clear away into the current. I think all the legions of devils hold here their provincial chapter, or are polling, canvassing, and wrangling for the election of a new rector.—Starboard; well said. —Take heed; have a care of your noddle, lad, in the devil's name. So ho, starboard, starboard." "Be, be, be, bous, bous, bous," cried Panurge, "bous, bous, be, be, be, bous, bous, I am lost. I see neither heaven nor earth; of the four elements we have here only fire and water left. Bou, bou, bou, bous, bous, bous. Would it were the pleasure of the worthy divine bounty, that I were at this present hour in the close at Sevillé, or at Innocent's the pastrycook, over against the painted wine-vault at Chipon, though I were to strip to my doublet, and bake the petti-pasties myself.

"Honest man, could not you throw me ashore? you can do a world of good things, they say. I give you all Salmigondinois, and my large shore full of whilks, cockles, and periwinkles, if, by your industry, I ever set foot on firm ground. Alas! alas! I drown. Hark'ee, my friends, since we cannot get safe into port, let us come to an anchor into some road, no matter whither. Drop all your anchors; let us be out of danger, I beseech you. Here, honest tar, get you into the chains, and heave the lead, an't please you. Let us know how many fathom water we are in. Sound, friend, in the lord Harry's name. Let us know whether a man might here drink easily, without stooping. I am apt to believe one might." "Helm a lee, hoh!" cried the pilot. "Helm a lee; a hand or two at the helm; about ships with her; helm a lee, helm a lee.—Stand off from the leech of the sail.—Hoh!—belay, here make fast below; hoh, helm a lee, lash sure the helm a lee, and let her drive." "Is it come to that?" said Pantagruel: "our good Saviour then help us." "Let her lie under the sea,' cried James Brahier, our chief mate, "let her drive. To prayers, to prayers; let all think on their souls, and fall to prayers; nor hope to 'scape but by a miracle." "Let us," said Panurge, "make some good pious kind of vow: alas! alas! alas! bou, bou, be, be, be bous, bous, bous, oho, oho, oho, oho, let us make a pilgrim: come, come, let every man club his penny towards it, come on." "Here, here, on this side," said friar John, "in the devil's name. Let her drive, for the Lord's sake unhang the rudder: hoh, let her drive, let her drive, and let us drink, I say of the best and most cheering; d'ye hear, steward, produce, exhibit; for, d'ye see this, and all the rest will as well go the devil out of hand. A pox on that wind-broker Æolus, with his fluster-blusters. Sirrah, page, bring me here my drawer (for so he called his breviary); stay a little here, hawl, friend, thus. Odzoons! here's a deal of hail and thunder to no purpose. Hold fast above, I pray you. When have we all-saints day? I believe it is the unholy holiday of all the devil's crew." "Alas!" said Panurge, "friar John damns himself

503

here as black as buttermilk for the nonce. Oh what a good friend I lose in him. Alas, alas! this is anothergats bout than last year's. We are falling out of Scilla into Charybdis. Oho! I drown. Confiteor; one poor word or two by way of testament, friar John, my ghostly father; good Mr. Abstractor, my crony, my Achates, Xenomanes, my all. Alas! I drown; two words of testament here upon this ladder."

CHAPTER XXI

A CONTINUATION OF THE STORM, WITH A SHORT DISCOURSE ON THE SUBJECT OF MAKING TESTAMENTS AT SEA

TO make one's last will," said Epistemon, "at this time that we ought to bestir ourselves and help our seamen, on the penalty of being drowned, seems to me as idle and ridiculous a maggot as that of some of Cæsar's men, who, at their coming into the Gauls, were mightily busied in making wills and codicils; bemoaned their fortune, and the absence of their spouses and friends at Rome; when it was absolutely necessary for them to run to their arms, and use their utmost strength against Ariovistus their enemy.

"This also is to be as silly as that jolt-headed lob-lolly of a carter, who, having laid his waggon fast in a slough, down on his marrowbones, was calling on the strong-backed deity, Hercules, might and main, to help him at a dead lift, but all the while forgot to goad on his oxen, and lay his shoulder to the wheels, as it behoved him: as if *a Lord have mercy upon us,* alone, would have got his cart out of the mire.

"What will it signify to make your will now? for either we shall come off or drown for it. If we escape, it will not signify a straw to us; for testaments are of no value or authority, but by the death of the testators. If we are drowned, will it not be drowned too? Pr'ythee who will transmit it to the executors?" "Some kind wave will throw it ashore, like Ulysses," replied Panurge; "and some king's daughter, going to fetch a walk in the fresco, on the evening, will find it, and take care to have it proved and fulfilled; nay, and have some stately cenotaph erected to my memory, as Dido had to that of her good man Sichæus; Æneas to Deiphobus, upon the Trojan shore, near Rhœte; Andromache to Hector, in the city of Buthrotos; Aristotle to Hermias and Eubulus; the Athenians to the poet Euripides; the

504

Romans to Drusus in Germany, and to Alexander Severus, their emperor in the Gauls; Argentier to Callaischre; Xenocrates to Lysidices; Timares to his son Teleutagoras; Eupolis and Aristodice to their son Theotimus; Onestes to Timocles; Callimachus to Sopolis, the son of Dioclides; Catullus to his brother; Statius to his father; Germain of Brie to Hervé, the Breton tarpawlin." "Art thou mad?" said friar John, "to run on at this rate? Help here, in the name of five hundred thousand millions of cartloads of devils, help! May a shanker gnaw thy mustachios, and the three rows of pock-royals and colliflowers cover thy bum and turd-barrel, instead of breeches and codpiece. Codsooks! our ship is almost overset. Ods death! how shall we clear her? 'tis well if she don't founder. What a devilish sea there runs! She'll neither try nor hull; the sea will overtake her, so we shall never 'scape; the devil 'scape me." Then Pantagruel was heard to make a sad exclamation, saying with a loud voice, "Lord save us; we perish! yet not as we would have it, but thy holy will be done." "The Lord and the blessed virgin be with us," said Panurge. "Holos, alas! I drown; be be be bous, be bous, bous: in manus. Good heaven, send me some dolphin to carry me safe on shore, like a pretty little Arion. I shall make shift to sound the harp, if it be not unstrung." "Let nineteen legions of black devils seize me," said friar John ("The Lord be with us," whispered Panurge, between his chattering teeth). "If I come down to thee, I'll shew thee to some purpose, that the badge of thy humanity dangles at a calf's breech, thou ragged horned cuckoldy booby: mgna, mgnan, mgnan: come hither and help us, thou great weeping calf, or may thirty millions of devils leap on thee. Wilt thou come, sea-calf? Fie! how ugly the howling whelp looks. What, always the same ditty? Come on now, my bonny drawer." This he said, opening his breviary. "Come forward, thou and I must be somewhat serious for awhile; let me peruse thee stiffly. *Beatus vir qui non abiit.* Pshaw, I know all this by heart; let's see the legend of Mons. St. Nicholas.

" 'Horrida tempestas montem turbavit acutum.'

"Tempeste was a mighty flogger of lads, at Mountaigu college. If pedants be damned for whipping poor little innocent wretches their scholars, he is, upon my honour, by this time fixed within Ixion's wheel, lashing the crop-eared, bob-tailed cur that gives it motion. If they are saved for having whipped innocent lads, he ought to be above the—"

CHAPTER XXII

AN END OF THE STORM

SHORE! shore!" cried Pantagruel. "Land to, my friends, I see land! Pluck up a good spirit, boys, 'tis within a kenning. So! we are not far from a port.—I see the sky clearing up to the north-wards.—Look to the south-east!" "Courage, my hearts," said the pilot; "now she'll bear the hullock of a sail: the sea is much smoother; some hands aloft to the maintop.—Put the helm a'weather.—Steady! steady!—Hawl your after-mizen bowlings.—Hawl, hawl, hawl!—Thus, thus, and no near. Mind your steerage; bring your main tack aboard. —Clear your sheets; clear your bowlings; port, port,—Helm a lee.— Now to the sheet on the starboard side, thou son of a whore." "Thou art mightily pleased, honest fellow," quoth friar John, "with hearing him make mention of thy mother." "Loff, loff," cried the quarter-master that cuned the ship, "keep her full, loff the helm. Loff." "It is," answered the steersman. "Keep her thus.—Get the bonnets fixed. Steady, steady."

"That's well said," said friar John; "now, this is something like a tansey. Come, come, come, children, be nimble.—Good.—Loff, loff.— Thus.—Helm a weather.That's well said and thought on. Methinks the storm is almost over. It was high time, faith: however, the Lord be thanked.—Our devils begin to scamper.—Out with all your sails.— Hoist your sails.—Hoist.—That's spoke like a man, hoist, hoist. Here, a God's name, honest Ponocrates; thou'rt a lusty fornicator; the whore-son will get none but boys. Eusthenes, thou art a notable fellow. Run up to the fore-top sail.—Thus, thus.—Well said, I faith; thus, thus. I dare not fear anything all this while, for it is holiday. Vea, vea, vea! huzza! This shout of the seamen is not amiss, and pleases me, for it is holiday. Keep her full thus.—Good." "Cheer up, my merry mates all," cried out Epistemon; "I see already Castor on the right." "Be, be, bous, bous, bous," said Panurge; "I am much afraid it is the bitch Helen." " 'Tis truly Mixarchagenas," returned Episte-mon, "if thou likest better that denomination which the Argives give him. Ho, ho! I see land too: let her bear in with the harbour. I see a good many people on the beach; I see a light on an obeli-scolychny." "Shorten your sails," said the pilot; "fetch the sounding-line; we must double that point of land, and mind the sands." "We are clear of them," said the sailors. Soon after, "Away she goes," quoth the pilot, "and so doth the rest of our fleet: help came in good season."

"By St. John," said Panurge, "this is spoke somewhat like. O the sweet word! there's the soul of music in't." "Mgna, mgna, mgna," said friar John; "if ever thou taste a drop on't, let the devil's dam taste me, thou ballocky devil. Here, honest soul, here's a full sneaker of the very best. Bring the flagons: dost hear, Gymnast? and that same large pasty jambic, or gammonic, e'en as you will have it. Take heed you pilot her in right."

"Cheer up," cried out Pantagruel; "cheer up, my boys; let's be ourselves again. Do you see yonder, close by our ship, two barks, three sloops, five ships, eight pinks, four yawls, and six frigates, making towards us, sent by the good people of the neighbouring island to our relief? But who is this Ucalegon below, that cries and makes such a sad moan? Were it not that I hold the mast firmly with both my hands, and keep it straighter than two hundred tacklings, I'd——" "It is," said friar John, "that poor devil Panurge, who is troubled with a calf's ague; he quakes for fear when his belly's full." "If," said Pantagruel, "he hath been afraid during this dreadful hurricane and dangerous storm, provided he hath done his part like a man, I do not value him a jot the less for it. For as, to fear in all encounters, is the mark of a heavy and cowardly heart; as Agamemnon did, who, for that reason, is ignominiously taxed by Achilles with having dog's eyes, and a stag's heart: so, not to fear when the case is evidently dreadful, is a sign of want or smallness of judgment. Now, if anything ought to be feared in this life, next to offending God, I will not say it is death. I will not meddle with the disputes of Socrates and the academics, that death of itself is neither bad nor to be feared: but, I will affirm, that this kind of death by shipwreck is to be feared, or nothing is. For, as Homer saith, it is a grievous, dreadful, and unnatural thing to perish at sea. And, indeed, Æneas, in the storm that took his fleet near Sicily, was grieved that he had not died by the hand of the brave Diomedes; and said, that those were three, nay four times happy, who perished in the conflagration at Troy. No man here hath lost his life, the Lord our Saviour be eternally praised for it: but in truth, here is a ship sadly out of order. Well, we must take care to have the damage repaired. Take heed we do not run aground and bulge her."

CHAPTER XXIII

HOW PANURGE PLAYED THE GOOD FELLOW WHEN THE STORM WAS OVER

WHAT cheer, ho! fore and aft?" quoth Panurge. "Oh ho! all's well, the storm is over. I beseech ye, be so kind as to let me be the first that is set on shore; for I would by all means a little untruss a point.—Shall I help you still? Here, let me see, I'll coil this rope; I have plenty of courage, and of fear as little as may be. Give it me yonder, honest tar.—No, no, I have not a bit of fear. Indeed, that same decumane wave, that took us fore and aft, somewhat altered my pulse. Down with your sails; well said. How now, friar John? you do nothing. Is is time for us to drink now? Who can tell but St. Martin's running footman may still be hatching us some further mischief? shall I come and help you again? Pork and pease choak me, if I do not heartily repent, though too late, not having followed the doctrine of the good philosopher, who tells us that to walk by the sea, and to navigate by the shore, are very safe and pleasant things: just as it is to go on foot, when we hold our horse by the bridle.—Ha! ha! ha! by G— all goes well. Shall I help you here too? Let me see, I'll do this as it should be, or the devil's in't."

Epistemon (who had the inside of one of his hands all flead and bloody, having held a tackling with might and main), hearing what Pantagruel had said, told him: "You may believe, my lord, I had my share of fear as well as Panurge; yet I spared no pains in lending my helping hand. I considered, that since by fatal and unavoidable necessity, we must all die, it is the blessed will of God that we die this or that hour, and this or that kind of death; nevertheless we ought to implore, invoke, pray, beseech, and supplicate him: but yet we must not stop there; it behoveth us also to use our endeavours on our side, and, as the Holy Writ saith, to co-operate with him.

"You know what C. Flaminius the consul said, when by Hannibal's policy he was penned up near the lake of Peruse, alias Thrasymene. 'Friends,' said he to his soldiers, 'You must not hope to get out of this place barely by vows or prayers to the gods; no, 'tis by fortitude and strength we must escape, and cut ourselves a way with the edge of our swords, through the midst of our enemies.'

"Sallust likewise makes M. Portius Cato say this: 'The help of the gods is not obtained by idle vows and womanish complaints; 'tis by vigilance, labour, and repeated endeavours, that all things succeed according to our wishes and designs. If a man, in time of need and danger, is negligent, heartless, and lazy, in vain he implores the gods; they are then justly angry and incensed against him.'" "The devil take me," said friar John ("I'll go his halves," quoth Panurge), "if the close of Sevillé had not been all gathered, vintaged, gleaned, and destroyed, if I had only sung *contra hostium insidias* (matter of breviary) like all the rest of the monkish devils, and had not bestirred myself to save the vineyard as I did, dispatching the truant piccaroons of Lerné with the staff of the cross."

"Let her sink or swim a God's name," said Panurge; "all's one to friar John; he doth nothing: his name is friar John Do-little; for all he sees me here sweating and puffing to help, with all my might, this honest tar, first of the name.—Hark you me, dear soul, a word with you;—but pray be not angry. How thick do you judge the planks of our ship to be?" "Some two good inches and upwards," returned the pilot; "don't fear." "Odskilderkins!" said Panurge, "it seems then we are within two fingers' breadth of damnation.

"Is this one of the nine comforts of matrimony? Ah! dear soul, you do well to measure the danger by the yard of fear. For my part I have none on't; my name is William Dreadnought. As for heart, I have more than enough on't; I mean none of your sheep's heart; but of wolf's heart; the courage of a bravo. By the pavilion of Mars I fear nothing but danger."

CHAPTER XXIV

HOW PANURGE WAS SAID TO HAVE BEEN AFRAID WITHOUT REASON, DURING THE STORM

GOOD morrow, gentlemen," said Panurge, "good morrow to you all: you are in very good health, thanks to heaven and yourselves: you are all heartily welcome, and in good time. Let us go on shore.—Here, coxen, get the ladder over the gunnel; man the sides; man the pinnace, and get her by the ship's side.—Shall I lend you a hand here? I am stark mad for want of business, and would work like any two yokes of oxen.—Truly this is a fine place, and these look like a very good people. Children, do you want me still in anything? do not spare the sweat of my body, for God's sake. Adam (that is man) was made to labour and work, as the birds were made to fly.

509

Our Lord's will is, that we get our bread with the sweat of our brows, not idling and doing nothing like this tatterdemallion of a monk here, this friar Jack, who is fain to drink to hearten himself up, and dies for fear.—Rare weather.—I now find the answer of Anacharsis, the noble philosopher, very proper: being asked what ship he reckoned the safest? he replied, 'That which is in the harbour.'"
"He made yet a better repartee," said Pantagruel, "when somebody inquiring which is greater, the number of the living or that of the dead? he asked them, amongst which of the two they reckoned those that are at sea? ingeniously implying that they are continually in danger of death, dying alive, and living die. Portius Cato also said, that there were but three things of which he would repent; that is, if ever he had trusted his wife with his secret, if he had idled away a day, and if he had ever gone by sea to a place which he could visit by land." "By this dignified frock of mine," said friar John to Panurge, "friend, thou hast been afraid during the storm without cause or reason; for thou wert not born to be drowned, but rather to be hanged and exalted in the air, or to be roasted in the midst of a jolly bonfire. My lord, would you have a good cloak for the rain; leave me off your wolf and badger-skin mantle; let Panurge but be flead, and cover yourself with his hide. But do not come near the fire, nor near your blacksmith's forges, a-God's name; for in a moment you will see it in ashes. Yet be as long as you please in the rain, snow, hail; nay, by the devil's maker, throw yourself, or dive down to the very bottom of the water, I'll engage you'll not be wet at all. Have some winter boots made of it, they'll never take in a drop of water: make bladders of it to lay under boys, to teach them to swim, instead of corks, and they will learn without the least danger." "His skin, then," said Pantagruel, "should be like the herb called true maiden's hair, which never takes wet nor moistness, but still keeps dry, though you lay it at the bottom of the water as long as you please; and for that reason is called adiantos."

"Friend Panurge," said friar John, "I pray thee never be afraid of water; thy life for mine thou art threatened with a contrary element." "Ay, ay," replied Panurge, "but the devil's cooks doat sometimes, and are apt to make horrid blunders as well as others: often putting to boil in water, what was designed to be roasted on the fire: like the head cooks of our kitchen, who often lard partridges, queests, and stock-doves, with intent to roast them, one would think; but it happens sometimes that they even turn the partridges into the pot, to

be boiled with cabbages, the queests with leek-pottage, and the stock-
doves with turnips. But hark you me, good friends, I protest before
this noble company that as for the chapel which I vowed to Mons.
St. Nicholas, between Candé and Monsoreau, I honestly mean that it
shall be a chapel of rose-water, which shall be where neither cow nor
calf shall be fed; for between you and I, I intend to throw it to the
bottom of the water." "Here is a rare rogue for you," said Eusthenes;
"here is a pure rogue, a rogue in grain, a rogue enough, a rogue and
a half. He is resolved to make good the Italian proverb, *Passato il
pericolo, è gabato il santo.*

"'The devil was sick, the devil a monk would be:
The devil was well, the devil a monk was he.'"

CHAPTER XXV

HOW, AFTER THE STORM, PANTAGRUEL WENT ON SHORE IN THE ISLANDS
OF THE MACREONS

IMMEDIATELY after, we went ashore at the port of an island,
which they called the island of the Macreons. The good people
of the place received us very honourably. An old Macrobius (so
they called their eldest elderman) desired Pantagruel to come to
the town-house to refresh himself, and eat something: but he would
not budge a foot from the mole till all his men were landed. After
he had seen them, he gave order they should all change cloaths, and
that some of all the stores in the fleet should be brought on shore, that
every ship's crew might live well: which was accordingly done, and
God wot how they all toped and carouzed. The people of the place
brought them provisions in abundance. The Pantagruelists returned
them more: as the truth is, theirs were somewhat damaged by the
late storm. When they had well stuffed the insides of their doublets,
Pantagruel desired every one to lend their help to repair the damage;
which they readily did. It was easy enough to refit there; for all the
inhabitants of the island were carpenters, and all such handicrafts as
are seen in the arsenal at Venice. None but the largest island was
inhabited, having three ports, and ten parishes; the rest being over-
run with wood, and desert, much like the forest of Arden. We entreated the old Macrobius to shew us what was worth seeing in the
island; which he did; and in the desert and dark forest we discovered
several old ruined temples, obelisks, pyramids, monuments, and ancient

tombs, with divers inscriptions and epitaphs; some of them in hiero-glyphic characters; others in the gothic dialect; some in the arabic, agarenian, sclavonian, and other tongues; of which Epistemon took an exact account. In the interim, Panurge said to Friar John, "Is this the island of the Macreons? Macreon signifies in Greek an old man, or one much stricken in years." "What's that to me," said Friar John, "how can I help it? I was not in the country when they christened it." "Now I think on it," quoth Panurge, "I believe the name of mackarel (that is a bawd in French) was derived from it: for procuring is the province of the old, as buttock-riggling is that of the young. Therefore I do not know but this may be the bawdy or mackarel island, the original and prototype of the island of that name at Paris. Let us go and drudge for cock-oysters." Old Macrobius asked in the ionic tongue, how, and by what industry and labour Pantagruel got to their port that day, there having been such bluster-ing weather, and such a dreadful storm at sea. Pantagruel told him, "That the almighty preserver of mankind had regarded the sim-plicity and sincere affection of his servants, who did not travel for gain or sordid profit; the sole design of their voyage being a studious desire to know, see, and visit the oracle of Bacbuc, and take the word of the bottle upon some difficulties offered by one of the company: nevertheless this had not been without great affliction, and evident danger of shipwreck." After that, he asked him what he judged to be the cause of that terrible tempest, and if the adjacent seas were thus frequently subject to storms; as in the ocean are the Ratz of Sammaieu, Maumusson, and in the Mediterranean sea the gulph of Sataly, Mont-argentan, Piombino, Capo Melio in Laconia, the Straits of Gibraltar, Faro di Messina, and others.

CHAPTER XXVI

HOW THE GOOD MACROBIUS GAVE US AN ACCOUNT OF THE MANSION AND DECEASE OF THE HEROES

THE good Macrobius then answered; "Friendly strangers, this island is one of the Sporades; not of your Sporades that lie in the Carpathian sea, but one of the Sporades of the ocean: in former times rich, frequented, wealthy, populous, full of traffic, and in the dominions of the rulers of Britain, but now, by course of time, and in these latter ages of the world, poor and desolate, as you see. In this dark forest, above seventy-eight thousand Persian leagues in compass, is the dwelling-place of the dæmons and heroes, that are grown old, and we believe that some one of them died yesterday; since the comet, which we saw for three days before together, shines no more: and now it is likely, that at his death there arose this horrible storm; for while they are alive, all happiness attends both this and the adjacent islands, and a settled calm and serenity. At the death of every one of them, we commonly hear in the forest loud and mournful groans, and the whole land is infested with pestilence, earthquakes, inundations, and other calamities; the air with fogs and obscurity, and the sea with storms and hurricanes." "What you tell us, seems to be likely enough," said Pantagruel. "For, as a torch or candle, as long as it hath life enough and is lighted, shines round about, disperses its light, delights those that are near it, yields them its service and clearness, and never causes any pain or displeasure; but as soon as it is extinguished, its smoke and evaporation infects the air, offends the bystanders, and is noisome to all: so, as long as those noble and renowned souls inhabit their bodies, peace, profit, pleasure, and honour never leave the places where they abide; but as soon as they leave them, both the continent and adjacent islands are annoyed with great commotions; in the air, fogs, darkness, thunder, hail; tremblings, pulsations, agitations of the earth; storms and hurricanes at sea; together with sad complaints amongst the people, broaching of religions, changes in governments, and ruins of commonwealths."

"We had a sad instance of this lately," said Epistemon, "at the death of that valiant and learned knight, William du Bellay; during whose life France enjoyed so much happiness, that all the rest of the world looked upon it with envy, sought friendship with it, and stood in awe of its power; but now, after his decease, it hath for a considerable time been the scorn of the rest of the world."

"Thus," said Pantagruel, "Anchises being dead at Drepani, in Sicily, Æneas was dreadfully tossed and endangered by a storm; and perhaps for the same reason, Herod, that tyrant and cruel king of Judea, finding himself near the pangs of a horrid kind of death (for he died of a phthiriasis, devoured by vermin and lice; as before him died L. Sylla, Pherecydes the Syrian, the preceptor of Pythagoras, the Greek poet Alcmæon, and others) and foreseeing that the Jews would make bonfires at his death, caused all the nobles and magistrates to be summoned to his seraglio, out of all the cities, towns, and castles of Judea,

513

fraudulently pretending that he had some things of moment to impart to them. They made their personal appearance; whereupon he caused them all to be shut up in the hippodrome of the seraglio; then said to his sister Salome, and Alexander her husband: 'I am certain that the Jews will rejoice at my death; but, if you will observe and perform what I tell you, my funeral shall be honoured, and there will be a general mourning. As soon as you see me dead, let my guards, to whom I have already given strict commission to that purpose, kill all the noblemen and magistrates that are secured in the hippodrome. By these means, all Jewry shall, in spite of themselves, be obliged to mourn and lament, and foreigners will imagine it to be for my death, as if some heroic soul had left her body.' A desperate tyrant wished as much, when he said, '*When I die, let earth and fire be mixed together*'; which was as good as to say, let the whole world perish. Which saying the tyrant Nero altered, saying, '*While I live*,' as Suetonius affirms it. This detestable saying, of which Cicero, lib. 3, de finib. and Seneca, lib. 2, de clementia, make mention, is ascribed to the emperor Tiberius, by Dion Nicæus and Suidas.

CHAPTER XXVII

PANTAGRUEL'S DISCOURSE OF THE DECEASE OF HEROIC SOULS; AND OF THE DREADFUL PRODIGIES THAT HAPPENED BEFORE THE DEATH OF THE LATE LORD DE LANGEY

I WOULD not," continued Pantagruel, "have missed the storm that hath thus disordered us, were I also to have missed the relation of these things told us by this good Macrobius. Neither am I unwilling to believe what he said of a comet that appears in the sky some days before such a decease. For some of those souls are so noble, so precious. and so heroic, that heaven gives us notice of their departing, some days before it happens. And as a prudent physician, seeing by some symptoms that his patient draws towards his end, some days before, gives notice of it to his wife, children, kindred, and friends, that, in that little time he hath yet to live, they may admonish him to settle all things in his family, to tutor and instruct his children as much as he can, recommend his relict to his friends in her widowhood, and declare what he knows to be necessary about a provision for the orphans; that he may not be surprised by death without making his will, and may take care of his soul and family: in the same manner the heavens, as it were, joyful for the approaching reception of those blessed souls, seem to make bonfires by those comets and blazing meteors, which they at the same time kindly design should prognosticate to us here, that in a few days one of those venerable souls is to leave her body, and this terrestrial globe. Not altogether unlike this was what was formerly done at Athens, by the judges of the areopagus. For when they gave their verdict to cast or clear the culprits that were tried before them, they used certain notes according to the substance of the sentences; by O, signifying condemnation to death; by T, absolution; by A, ampliation or a demur, when the case was not sufficiently examined. Thus having publicly set up those letters, they eased the relations and friends of the prisoners, and such others as desired to know their doom, of their doubts. Likewise by these comets, as in ætherial characters, the heavens silently say to us, 'Make haste, mortals, if you would know or learn of the blessed souls anything concerning the public good, or your private interest; for their catastrophe is near, which being past, you will vainly wish for them afterwards.'

"The good-natured heavens still do more; and that mankind may be declared unworthy of the enjoyment of those renowned souls, they fright and astonish us with prodigies, monsters, and other foreboding sings, that thwart the order of nature.

"Of this we had an instance several days before the decease of the heroic soul of the learned and valiant chevalier de Langey, of whom you have already spoken." "I remember it," said Epistemon; "and my heart still trembles within me, when I think on the many dreadful prodigies that we saw five or six days before he died. For the lords D'Assier, Chemant, one-eyed Mailly, St. Ayl, Villeneufue-la-Guyart, master Gabriel, physician of Savillan, Rabelais, Cohuau, Massuau, Majorici, Bullou, Cercu alias Bourgmaistre, Francis Proust, Ferron, Charles Girard, Francis Bourré, and many other friends and servants to the deceased, all dismayed, gazed on each other without uttering one word; yet not without foreseeing that France would in a short time be deprived of a knight so accomplished, and necessary for its glory and protection, and that heaven claimed him again as its due." "By the tufted tip of my cowl," cried Friar John, "I am even resolved to become a scholar before I die. I have a pretty good head-piece of my own, you must confess. Now pray give me leave to ask you a civil question. Can these same heroes and demigods you talk of, die?

515

May I never be damned, if I was not so much a lobcock as to believe they had been immortal, like so many fine angels. Heaven forgive me! but this most reverend father, Macrobius, tells us, *they die at last.*" "We all must," returned Pantagruel.

"The stoics held them all to be mortal, except one, who alone is immortal, impassible, invisible. Pindar plainly saith, that there is no more thread, that is to say, no more life spun from the distaff and flax of the hard-hearted fates for the goddesses hamadryades, than there is for those trees that are preserved by them, which are good, sturdy, downright oaks; whence they derived their original, according to the opinion of Callimachus, and Pausanias in Phoci. With whom concurs Martianus Capella. As for the demigods, fauns, satyrs, sylvans, hobgoblins, ægipanes, nymphs, heroes, and dæmons, several men have, from the total sum, which is the result of the divers ages calculated by Hesiod, reckoned their life to be 9720 years: that sum consisting of four special numbers orderly arising from one, the same added together, and multiplied by four every way, amounts to forty; these forties, being reduced into triangles by five times, make up the total of the aforesaid number. See Plutarch, in his book about the cessation of oracles."

"This," said Friar John, "is not matter of breviary; I may believe as little or as much of it as you and I please." "I believe," said Pantagruel, "that all intellectual souls are exempted from Atropos's scissars. They are all immortal, whether they be of angels, of dæmons, or human: yet I will tell you a story concerning this, that is very strange, but is written and affirmed by several learned historians.

CHAPTER XXVIII

HOW PANTAGRUEL RELATED A VERY SAD STORY OF THE DEATH OF THE HEROES

EPITHERSES, the father of Æmilian the rhetorician, sailing from Greece to Italy, in a ship freighted with divers goods and passengers, at night the wind failed them near the Echinades, some islands that lie between the Morea and Tunis, and the vessel was driven near Paxos. When they were got thither, some of the passengers being asleep, others awake, the rest eating and drinking, a voice was heard that called aloud, 'Thamous!' which cry surprised them all. This same Thamous was their pilot, an Egyptian by birth, but known by name only to some few travellers. The voice was heard a second time, calling Thamous, in a frightful tone; and none making answer, but trembling, and remaining silent, the voice was heard a third time, more dreadful than before.

"This caused Thamous to answer; 'Here am I, what dost thou call me for? What wilt thou have me do?' Then the voice, louder than before, bid him publish, when he should come to Paloda, that the great god Pan was dead.

"Epitherses related, that all the mariners and passengers having heard this, were extremely amazed and frighted; and that consulting among themselves, whether they had best conceal or divulge what the voice had enjoined; Thamous said, his advice was, that if they happened to have a fair wind, they should proceed without mentioning a word of it, but if they chanced to be becalmed, he would publish what he had heard. Now when they were near Paloda, they had no wind, neither were they in any current. Thamous then getting up on the top of the ship's forecastle, and casting his eyes on the shore, said that he had been commanded to proclaim that the great god Pan was dead. The words were hardly out of his mouth, when deep groans, great lamentations, and doleful shrieks, not of one person, but of many together, were heard from the land.

"The news of this (many being present then) was soon spread at Rome; insomuch that Tiberius, who was then emperor, sent for this Thamous, and having heard him, gave credit to his words. And enquiring of the learned in his court, and at Rome, who was that Pan? he found by their relation that he was the son of Mercury and Penelope, as Herodotus and Cicero in his third book of the nature of the gods had written before.

"For my part, I understand it of that great Saviour of the faithful, who was shamefully put to death at Jerusalem, by the envy and wickedness of the doctors, priests, and monks of the Mosaic law. And methinks, my interpretation is not improper: for he may lawfully be said in the Greek tongue to be *Pan,* since he is our all. For all that we are, all that we live, all that we have, all that we hope, is him, by him, from him, and in him. He is the good Pan, the great shepherd, who, as the loving shepherd Corydon affirms, hath not only a tender love and affection for his sheep, but also for their shepherds. At his death, complaints, sighs, fears, and lamentations were spread through the whole fabric of the universe, whether heavens, land, sea, or hell.

517

"The time also concurs with this interpretation of mine; for this most good, most mighty Pan, our only Saviour, died near Jerusalem, during the reign of Tiberius Cæsar."

Pantagruel, having ended this discourse, remained silent, and full of contemplation. A little while after we saw the tears flow out of his eyes as big as ostrich's eggs. God take me presently, if I tell you one single syllable of a lye in the matter.

CHAPTER XXIX

HOW PANTAGRUEL SAILED BY THE SNEAKING ISLAND, WHERE SHROVETIDE REIGNED

THE jovial fleet being refitted and repaired, new stores taken in, the Macreons over and above satisfied, and pleased with the money spent there by Pantagruel, our men, in better humour yet than they used to be, if possible, we merrily put to sea the next day near sunset, with a delicious fresh gale.

Xenomanes shewed us afar off the Sneaking island, where reigned Shrovetide of whom Pantagruel had heard much talk formerly: for that reason he would gladly have seen him in person, had not Xenomanes advised him to the contrary: first, because this would have been much out of our way; and then for the lean cheer [*manger maigre*] which, he told us, was to be found at that prince's court, and indeed all over the island.

"You can see nothing there for your money," said he, "but a huge greedy guts: a tall woundy swallower of hot wardens and muscles; a long-shanked mole catcher; an overgrown bottler of hay; a mossy-chinned demy giant, with a double shaven crown, of lantern breed; a very great loitering noddy-peaked youngster, banner-bearer to the fish-eating tribe, dictator of mustard-land, flogger of little children, calciner of ashes, father and foster-father to physicians; swarming with pardons, indulgences, and stations; a very honest man; a good catholic, and as brimful of devotion as ever he can hold.

"He weeps the three-fourth parts of the day, and never assists at any weddings; but, give the devil his due, he is the most industrious larding-stick and skewer-maker in forty kingdoms.

"About six years ago, as I passed through Sneakingland, I brought home a large skewer from thence, and made a present of it to the butchers of Quande, who set a great value upon them, and that for a cause. Some time or other, if ever we live to come back to our own country, I will shew you two of them fastened on the great church-porch. His usual food is pickled coats of mail, salt helmets and head pieces, and salt sallads; which sometimes makes him piss pins and needles. As for his cloathing, it is comical enough o'conscience, both for make and colour; for he wears grey and cold, nothing before, and nought behind, with the sleeves of the same."

"You will do me a kindness," said Pantagruel, "if, as you have described his cloaths, food, actions, and pastimes, you will also give me an account of his shape and disposition in all its parts." "Prithee do, dear cod," said Friar John; "for I have found him in my breviary, and then follow the moveable holydays." "With all my heart," answered Xenomanes; "we may chance to hear more of him as we touch at the Wild Island, the dominions of the squob Chitterlings, his enemies; against whom he is eternally at odds: and, were it not for the help of the noble Carnival, their protector, and good neighbour, this meagre-looked Shrovetide would long before this have made sad work among them, and rooted them out of their habitation." "Are these same Chitterlings," said Friar John, "male or female, angels or mortals, women or maids?" "They are," replied Xenomanes, "female in sex, mortal in condition, some of them maids, others not." "The devil have me," said Friar John, "if I been't for them. What a shameful disorder in nature, is it not, to make war against women? Let's go back, and hack the villain to pieces."—"What! meddle with Shrovetide?" cried Panurge: "in the name of Belzebub, I am not yet so weary of my life. No, I am not yet so mad as that comes to. *Quid juris?* Suppose we should find ourselves pent up between the Chitterlings and Shrovetide? between the anvil and the hammers? Shankers and buboes! stand off! godzooks, let us make the best of our way. I bid you good night, sweet Mr. Shrovetide; I recommend to you the Chitterlings, and pray don't forget the puddings."

CHAPTER XXX

HOW SHROVETIDE IS ANATOMIZED AND DESCRIBED BY
XENOMANES

A S for the inward parts of Shrovetide," said Xenomanes; "his brain is (at least it was in my time) in bigness, colour, substance, and strength, much like the left cod of a he hand-worm.

"The ventricles of his said brain, like an auger.

The worm-like excrescence, like a christmas-box.

The membranes, like a monk's cowl.

The funnel, like a mason's chissel.

The fornix, like a casket.

The glandula pinealis, like a bagpipe.

The rete admirabile, like a gutter.

The dug-like processus, like a patch.

The tympanums, like a whirly-gig.

The rocky bones, like a goose-wing.

The nape of the neck, like a paper lanthorn.

The nerves, like a pipkin.

The uvula, like a sackbut.

The palate, like a mittain.

The spittle, like a shuttle.

The almonds, like a telescope.

The bridge of his nose, like a wheelbarrow.

The head of the larynx, like a vintage-basket.

The stomach, like a belt.

The pylorus, like a pitchfork.

The wind-pipe, like an oyster knife.

The throat, like a pincushion stuffed with oakham.

The lungs, like a prebend's fur gown.

The heart, like a cope.

The mediastin, like an earthen cup.

The pleura, like a crow's bill.

The arteries, like a watch-coat.

The midriff, like a mounteer-cap.

The liver, like a double-tongu'd mattock.

The veins, like a sash-window.

The spleen, like a catcal.

The guts, like a trammel.

The gall, like a cooper's adz.
The entrails, like a gantlet.
The mesentery, like an abbot's mitre.
The hungry gut, like a button.
The blind gut, like a breast-plate.
The colon, like a bridle.
The arse-gut, like a monk's leathern bottle.
The kidnies, like a trowel.
The loins, like a padlock.
The ureters, like a pot-hook.
The emulgent veins, like two gilly-flowers.
The spermatic vessels, like a cully-mully-puff.
The parastatas, like an ink-pot.
The bladder, like a stone-bow.
The neck, like a mill-clapper.
The mirach, or lower parts of the belly, like a high-crown'd hat.
The siphach, or its inner rind, like a wooden cuff.
The muscles, like a pair of bellows.
The tendons, like a hawking-glove.
The ligaments, like a tinker's budget.
The bones, like three-corner'd cheese-cakes.
The marrow, like a wallet.
The cartilages, like a field tortoise, alias a mole.
The glandules in the mouth, like a pruning-knife.
The animal spirits, like swinging fisty-cuffs.
The blood fermenting, like a multiplication of flirts on the nose.
The urine, like a fig-pecker.
The sperm, like a hundred of ten-penny nails.
"And his nurse told me, that being married to Mid-lent, he only
begot a good number of local adverbs, and certain double fasts.
His memory he had like a scarf.
His common sense, like a buzzing of bees.
His imagination, like the chime of a set of bells.
His thoughts, like a flight of starlings.
His conscience, like the unnestling of a parcel of young herns.
His deliberations, like a set of organs.
His repentance, like the carriage of a double cannon.
His undertakings, like the ballast of a gallion.
His understanding, like a torn breviary.
His notions, like snails crawling out of strawberries.

His will, like three filberts in a porringer.

His desire, like six trusses of hay.

His judgment, like a shoeing horn.

His discretion, like the truckle of a pully.

His reason, like a cricket stool.

CHAPTER XXXI

SHROVETIDE'S OUTWARD PARTS ANATOMIZED

SHROVETIDE," continued Xenomanes, "is somewhat better pro-portioned in his outward parts, excepting the seven ribs which he had over and above the common shape of men.

"His toes, were like a virginal on an organ.

His nails, like a gimblet.

His feet, like a guitar.

His heels, like a club.

The soles of his feet, like a crucible.

His legs, like a hawk's lure.

His knees, like a joint-stool.

His thighs, like a steel cap.

His hips, like a wimble.

His belly as big as a tun, button'd after the old fashion, with a girdle riding over the middle of his bosom.

His navel, like a cymbal.

His groin, like a minced pie.

His member, like a slipper.

His purse, like an oil cruet.

His genitals, like a joiner's plainer.

Their erecting muscles, like a racket.

The perineum, like a flageolet.

His arse-hole, like a crystal looking-glass.

His bum, like a harrow.

His loins, like a butter-pot.

The peritonæum, or caul, wherein his bowels were wrapped, like a billiard-table.

His back, like an overgrown rack-bent cross-bow.

The vertebræ, or joints of his back-bone, like a bag-pipe.

His ribs, like a spinning-wheel.

His brisket, like a canopy.
His shoulder-blades, like a mortar.
His breast, like a game at nine-pins.
His paps, like a hornpipe.
His arm-pits, like a chequer.
His shoulders, like a hand-barrow.
His arms, like a riding-hood.
His fingers, like a brotherhood's andirons.
The fibulæ, or lesser bones of his legs, like a pair of stilts.
His shin-bones, like sickles.
His elbows, like a mouse-trap.
His hands, like a curry-comb.
His neck, like a talboy.
His throat, like a felt to distil hippocras.
The knob in his throat, like a barrel, where hanged two brazen wens,
    very fine and harmonious, in the shape of an hour-glass.
His beard, like a lantern.
His chin, like a mushroom.
His ears, like a pair of gloves.
His nose, like a buskin.
His nostrils, like a forehead cloth.
His eyebrows, like a dripping-pan.
On his left brow was a mark of the shape and bigness of an urinal.
His eyelids, like a fiddle.
His eyes, like a comb-box.
His optic nerves, like a tinder-box.
His forehead, like a false cup.
His temples, like the cock of a cistern.
His cheeks, like a pair of wooden shoes.
His jaws, like a caudle cup.
His teeth, like a hunter's staff. Of such colts' teeth as his, you will
    find one at Colonges les royaux in Poictou, and two at la Brosse
    in Xaintonge, on the cellar door.
His tongue, like a jew's-harp.
His mouth, like a horse-cloth.
His face embroidered like a mule's pack-saddle.
His head contrived like a still.
His skull, like a pouch.
The suturæ, or seams of his skull, like the annulus piscatories, or the
    fisher's signet.

His skin, like a gabardine.

His epidermis, or outward skin, like a boulting-cloth.

His hair, like a scrubbing-brush.

His fur, such as above said.

CHAPTER XXXII

A CONTINUATION OF SHROVETIDE'S COUNTENANCE, POSTURES, AND WAY OF BEHAVING

'TIS a wonderful thing," continued Xenomanes, "to hear and see the state of Shrovetide.

"If he chanc'd to spit, it was whole baskets full of goldfinches.

If he blow'd his nose, it was pickled grigs.

When he wept, it was ducks with onion sauce.

When he trembled, it was large venison pasties.

When he did sweat, it was old ling with butter sauce.

When he belched, it was bushels of oysters.

When he sneezed, it was whole tubs full of mustard.

When he coughed, it was boxes of marmalade.

When he sobbed, it was water-cresses.

When he yawned, it was pots full of pickled pease.

When he sighed, it was dried neat's tongues.

When he whistled, it was a whole scuttle full of green apes.

When he snored, it was a whole pan full of fried beans.

When he frowned, it was sowsed hog's feet.

When he spoke, it was coarse brown russet cloth; so little it was like crimson silk, with which Parisatis desired that the words of such as spoke to her son Cyrus, king of Persia, should be interwoven.

When he blowed, it was indulgence money-boxes.

When he winked, it was buttered buns.

When he grumbled, it was March cats.

When he nodded, it was iron-bound waggons.

When he made mouths, it was broken staves.

When he muttered, it was lawyers' revels.

When he hopped about, it was letters of licence and protections.

When he stepped back, it was sea cockle-shells.

When he slabbered, it was common ovens.

When he was hoarse, it was an entry of morrice-dancers.

When he broke wind, it was dun cows' leather spatterdashes.

When he funked, it was washed-leather boots.

When he scratched himself, it was new proclamations.

When he sung, it was peas in cods.

When he evacuated, it was mushrooms and morilles.

When he puffed, it was cabbages with oil, alias caules ambolif.

When he talked, it was the last year's snow.

When he dreamt, it was of a cock and a bull.

When he gave nothing, so much for the bearer.

If he thought to himself, it was whimsies and maggots.

If he dozed, it was leases of lands.

"What is yet more strange, he used to work doing nothing, and did nothing though he worked; caroused sleeping, and slept carousing, with his eyes open, like the hares in our country, for fear of being taken napping by the Chitterlings, his inveterate enemies; biting he laughed, and laughing bit; eat nothing fasting, and fasted eating nothing; mumbled upon suspicion, drank by imagination, swam on the tops of high steeples, dried his clothes in ponds and rivers, fished in the air, and there used to catch decumane lobsters; hunted at the bottom of the herring-pond, and caught there ibices, stamboucs, chamois, and other wild goats; used to put out the eyes of all the crows which he took sneakingly; feared nothing but his own shadow, and the cries of fat kids; used to gad abroad some days, like a truant school-boy; played with the ropes of bells on festival days of saints; made a mallet of his fist, and writ on hairy parchment prognostications and almanacks with his huge pin-case."

"Is that the gentleman?" said Friar John: "he is my man: this is the very fellow I looked for; I'll send him a challenge immediately."

"This is," said Pantagruel, "a strange and monstrous sort of a man, if I may call him a man. You put me in mind of the form and looks of Amodunt and Dissonance." "How were they made," said Friar John? "May I be peeled like a raw onion, if ever I heard a word of them." "I'll tell you what I read of them in some ancient apologues," replied Pantagruel.

"Physis (that is to say Nature) at her first burthen begat Beauty and Harmony, without carnal copulation, being of herself very fruitful and prolific. Antiphysis, who ever was the counterpart of nature, immediately, out of a malicious spight against her for beautiful and honourable productions, in opposition begot Amodunt and Dissonance,

525

by copulation with Tellumon. Their heads were round like a football, and not gently flatted on both sides, like the common shape of men. Their ears stood pricked up like those of asses; their eyes, as hard as those of crabs, and without brows, stared out of their heads, fixed on bones like those of our heels; their feet were round like tennis-balls; their arms and hands turned backwards towards the shoulders; and they walked on their heads, continually turning round like a ball, topsy-turvy, heels over head.

"Yet (as you know that apes esteem their young the handsomest in the world) Antiphysis extolled her offspring, and strove to prove that their shape was handsomer and neater than that of the children of Physis; saying, that thus to have spherical heads and feet, and walk in a circular manner, wheeling round, had something in it of the perfection of the divine power, which makes all beings eternally turn in that fashion; and that to have our feet uppermost, and the head below them, was to imitate the Creator of the universe; the hair being like the roots, and the legs like the branches of man: for trees are better planted by their roots, than they could be by their branches. By this demonstration she implied, that her children were much more to be praised for being like a standing tree, than those of Physis, that made a figure of a tree upside down. As for the arms and hands, she pretended to prove that they were more justly turned towards the shoulders, because that part of the body ought not to be without defence, while the fore-part is duly fenced with teeth, which a man cannot only use to chew, but also to defend himself against those things that offend him. Thus, by the testimony and astipulation of the brute beasts, she drew all the witless herd and mob of fools into her opinion, and was admired by all brainless and nonsensical people.

"Since that, she begot the hypocritical tribes of eves-dropping dissemblers, superstitious pope-mongers, and priest-hidden bigots, the frantic pistolets, the scrapers of benefices, apparitors with the devil in them, and other grinders and squeezers of livings, your mad herb-stinking hermits, gulligutted dunces of the cowl, church vermin, false zealots, devourers of the substance of men, and many more other deformed and ill-favoured monsters, made in spite of nature."

CHAPTER XXXIII

HOW PANTAGRUEL DISCOVERED A MONSTROUS PHYSETERE, OR WHIRLPOOL, NEAR THE WILD ISLAND

ABOUT sun-set, coming near the Wild Island, Pantagruel spied afar off a huge monstrous physetere (a sort of a whale, which some call a whirlpool) that came right upon us neighing, snorting, raised above the waves higher than our maintops, and spouting water all the way into the air, before itself, like a huge river falling from a mountain: Pantagruel shewed it to the pilot, and to Xenomanes.

By the pilot's advice, the trumpets of the Thalamege were sounded, to warn all the fleet to stand close and look to themselves. This alarm being given, all the ships, gallions, frigates, brigantines (according to their naval discipline) placed themselves in the order and figure of a Greek upsilon (Y), the letter of Pythagoras, as cranes do in their flight; and like an acute angle, in whose cone and basis the Thalamege placed herself ready to fight smartly. Friar John, with the grenadiers, got on the forecastle.

Poor Panurge began to cry and howl worse than ever: "Babille-babou" (said he, shrugging up his shoulders, quivering all over with fear) "there will be the devil upon dun. This is a worse business than that t'other day. Let us fly, let us fly; old Nick take me if it is not Leviathan, described by the noble prophet Moses, in the life of patient Job. It will swallow us all, ships and men, shag, rag, and bob-tail, like a dose of pills. Alas, it will make no more of us, and we shall hold no more room in its hellish jaws, than a sugar plum in an ass's throat. Look, look, 'tis upon us; let's wheel off, whip it away, and get ashore. I believe 'tis the very individual sea monster, that was formerly designed to devour Andromeda: we are all undone. Oh! for some valiant Perseus here now to kill the dog."

"I'll do its business presently," said Pantagruel; "fear nothing." "'Ods-belly," said Panurge, "remove the cause of my fear then. When the devil would you have a man be afraid, but when there is so much cause?" "If your destiny be such, as Friar John was saying a while ago," replied Pantagruel, "you ought to be afraid of Pyrois, Eous, Æthon, and Phlegon, the sun's coach horses, that breathe fire at the nostrils; and not of physeteres, that spout nothing but water at the snout and mouth. Their water will not endanger your life; and that element will rather save and preserve than hurt or endanger you."

527

"Ay, ay, trust to that, and hang me," quoth Panurge: "yours is a very pretty fancy. Odd's fish! did I not give you a sufficient account of the elements' transmutation, and the blunders that are made of roast for boiled, and boiled for roast? Alas, here 'tis; I'll go hide myself below. We are dead men, every mother's son of us: I see upon our maintop that merciless hag Atropos, with her scissars new ground, ready to cut our threads all at one snip. Oh! how dreadful and abominable thou art; thou hast drowned a good many besides us, who never made their brags of it. Did it but spout good, brisk, dainty, delicious white-wine, instead of this damned bitter salt water, one might better bear with it, and there would be some cause to be patient; like that English lord, who being doomed to die, and had leave to chuse what kind of death he would, chose to be drowned in a butt of malmsy. Here it is.—Oh! oh! devil! Sathanas! Leviathan! I can't abide to look upon thee, thou are so abominably ugly.—Go to the bar, go take the pettifoggers."

CHAPTER XXXIV

HOW THE MONSTROUS PHYSETERE WAS SLAIN BY PANTAGRUEL

THE physetere, coming between the ships and the gallions, threw water by whole tuns upon them, as if it had been the catadupes of the Nile in Ethiopia. On the other side, arrows, darts, gleaves, javelins, spears, harping-irons, and partizans flew upon it like hail. Friar John did not spare himself in it. Panurge was half dead for fear. The artillery roared and thundered like mad, and seemed to gaul it in good earnest, but did but little good: for the great iron and brass cannon-shot, entering its skin, seemed to melt like tiles in the sun.

Pantagruel then, considering the weight and exigency of the matter, stretched out his arms, and shewed what he could do. You tell us, and it is recorded, that Commodus, the Roman emperor, could shoot with a bow so dexterously, that at a good distance he would let fly an arrow through a child's fingers, and never touch them. You also tell us of an Indian archer, who lived when Alexander the great conquered India, and was so skilful in drawing the bow, that at a considerable distance he would shoot his arrows through a ring,

528

though they were three cubits long, and their iron so large and weighty, that with them he used to pierce steel cutlasses, thick shields, steel breast-plates, and generally what he did hit, how firm, resisting, hard and strong soever it were. You also tell us wonders of the industry of the ancient Franks, who were preferred to all others in point of archery; and when they hunted either black or dun beasts, used to rub the head of their arrows with hellebore, because the flesh of the venison, struck with such an arrow, was more tender, dainty, wholesome, and delicious (paring off, nevertheless, the part that was touched round about). You also talk of the Parthians, who used to shoot backwards more dexterously than other nations forwards; and also celebrate the skill of the Scythians in that art, who sent once to Darius king of Persia an ambassador, that made him a present of a bird, a frog, a mouse, and five arrows, without speaking one word; and being asked what those presents meant, and if he had commission to say anything, answered, that he had not: which puzzled and gravelled Darius very much, till Gobrias, one of the seven captains that had killed the magi, explained it, saying to Darius: "By these gifts and offerings the Scythians silently tell you, that except the Persians, like birds, fly up to heaven, or, like mice, hide themselves near the centre of the earth, or, like frogs, dive to the very bottom of ponds and lakes, they shall be destroyed by the power and arrows of the Scythians."

The noble Pantagruel was, without comparison, more admirable yet in the art of shooting and darting: for with his dreadful piles and darts, nearly resembling the huge beams that support the bridges of Nantes, Saumur, Bergerac, and at Paris the millers and the changers bridges, in length, size, weight, and iron-work, he, at a mile's distance, would open an oyster, and never touch the edges; he would snuff a candle, without putting it out; would shoot a magpye in the eye; take off a boot's under-sole, or a riding-hood's lining, without soiling them a bit; turn over every leaf of Friar John's breviary, one after another, and not tear one.

With such darts, of which there was good store in the ship, at the first blow he ran the physetere in at the forehead so furiously, that he pierced both its jaws and tongue; so that from that time to this it no more opened its guttural trap-door, nor drew and spouted water. At the second blow he put out its right eye, and at the third its left: and we had all the pleasure to see the physetere bearing those three horns in its forehead, somewhat leaning forwards in an equilateral triangle.

Meanwhile it turned about to and fro, staggering and straying like one stunned, blinded, and taking his leave of the world. Pantagruel, not satisfied with this, let fly another dart, which took the monster under the tail likewise sloping; and then with three other on the chine in a perpendicular line, divided its flank from the tail to the snout at an equal distance: then he larded it with fifty on one side, and after that, to make even work, he darted as many on its other side: so that the body of the physetere seemed like the hulk of a gallion with three masts, joined by a competent dimension of its beams, as if they had been the ribs and chain-wales of the keel; which was a pleasant sight. The physetere then giving up the ghost, turned itself upon its back, as all dead fishes do; and being thus overturned, with the beams and darts upside down in the sea, it seemed a scolopendra or centipede, as that serpent is described by the ancient sage Nicander.

CHAPTER XXXV

HOW PANTAGRUEL WENT ON SHORE IN THE WILD ISLAND, THE ANCIENT ABODE OF THE CHITTERLINGS

THE boat's crew of the ship Lantern towed the physetere ashore on the neighbouring shore (which happened to be the Wild Island) to make an anatomical dissection of its body, and save the fat of its kidnies, which, they said, was very useful and necessary for the cure of a certain distemper, which they called want of money. As for Pantagruel, he took no manner of notice of the monster; for he had seen many such, nay bigger, in the Gallic ocean. Yet he condescended to land in the Wild Island, to dry and refresh some of his men (whom the physetere had wetted and bedawbed) at a small desert seaport towards the south, seated near a fine pleasant grove, out of which flowed a delicious brook of fresh, clear, and purling water. Here they pitched their tents, and set up their kitchens; nor did they spare fuel.

Every one having shifted, as they thought fit, friar John rang the bell, and the cloth was immediately laid, and supper brought in. Pantagruel eating cheerfully with his men, much about the second course, perceived certain little sly Chitterlings clambering up a high tree near the pantry, as still as so many mice. Which made him ask Xenomanes, what kind of creatures these were; taking them for squirrels, weasels, martins, or hermins. "They are Chitterlings," replied Xenomanes. "This is the Wild Island, of which I spoke to you this morning: there hath been an irreconcilable war, this long time, between them and Shrovetide, their malicious and ancient enemy. I believe that the noise of the guns, which we fired at the physetere, hath alarmed them, and made them fear their enemy was come with his forces to surprise them, or lay the island waste; as he hath often attempted to do, though he still came off but bluely; by reason of the care and vigilance of the Chitterlings, who (as Dido said to Æneas's companions, that would have landed at Carthage without her leave or knowledge) were forced to watch and stand upon their guard, considering the malice of their enemy, and the neighbourhood of his territories."

"Pray, dear friend," said Pantagruel, "if you find that by some honest means we may bring this war to an end, and reconcile them together, give me notice of it; I will use my endeavours in it, with all my heart, and spare nothing on my side to moderate and accommodate the points in dispute between both parties."

"That's impossible at this time," answered Xenomanes. "About four years ago, passing incognito by this country, I endeavoured to make a peace, or at least a long truce among them; and I certainly had brought them to be good friends and neighbours, if both one and the other parties would have yielded to one single article. Shrovetide would not include in the treaty of peace, the wild puddings, nor the highland sausages, their ancient gossips and confederates. The Chitterlings demanded, that the fort of Caques might be under their government, as is the castle of Sullouoir, and that a parcel of I don't know what stinking villains, murderers, robbers, that held it then, should be expelled. But they could not agree in this, and the terms that were offered seemed too hard to either party. So the treaty broke off, and nothing was done. Nevertheless, they became less severe, and gentler enemies than they were before: but since the denunciation of the national council of Chesil, whereby they (the Chitterlings) were roughly handled, hampered, and cited; whereby also Shrovetide was declared filthy, beshitten, and bewrayed, in case he made any league, or agreement with them; they are grown wonderfully inveterate, incensed, and obstinate against one another, and there is no way to remedy it. You might sooner reconcile cats and rats, or hounds and hares together."

531

CHAPTER XXXVI

HOW THE WILD CHITTERLINGS LAID AN AMBUSCADE FOR PANTAGRUEL

WHILE Xenomanes was saying this, friar John spied twenty or thirty young slender-shaped Chitterlings, posting as fast as they could towards their town, citadel, castle, and fort of Chimney, and said to Pantagruel, "I smell a rat: there will be here the devil upon two sticks, or I am much out. These worshipful Chitterlings may chance to mistake you for Shrovetide, though you are not a bit like him. Let us once in our lives leave our junketing for a while, and put ourselves in a posture to give them a belly full of fighting, if they would be at that sport." "There can be no false Latin in this," said Xenomanes; "Chitterlings are still Chitterlings, always double-hearted and treacherous."

Pantagruel then arose from table, to visit and scour the thicket, and returned presently; having discovered, on the left, an ambuscade of squab Chitterlings; and on the right, about half a league from thence, a large body of huge giant-like armed Chitterlings, ranged in battalia along a little hill, and marching furiously towards us at the sound of bag-pipes, sheep's paunches, and bladders, the merry fifes and drums, trumpets, and clarions, hoping to catch us as Moss caught his mare. By the conjecture of seventy-eight standards, which we told, we guessed their number to be two and forty thousand, at a modest computation.

Their order, proud gait, and resolute looks, made us judge that they were none of your raw, paultry links, but old warlike Chitterlings and Sausages. From the foremost ranks of the colours they were all armed cap-à-pié with small arms, as we reckoned them at a distance: yet, very sharp, and case-hardened. Their right and left wings were lined with a great number of forest puddings, heavy patti-pans, and horse sausages, all of them tall and proper islanders, banditti, and wild.

Pantagruel was very much daunted, and not without cause; though Epistemon told him that it might be the use and custom of the Chit-terlingonians to welcome and receive thus in arms their foreign friends, as the noble kings of France are received and saluted at their first coming into the chief cities of the kingdom, after their advance-ment to the crown. "Perhaps," said he, "it may be the usual guard of the queen of the place; who, having notice given her, by the junior Chitterlings of the forlorn hope, whom you saw on the tree, of the arrival of your fine and pompous fleet, hath judged that it was, without doubt, some rich and potent prince, and is come to visit you in person."

Pantagruel, little trusting to this, called a council, to have their advice at large in this doubtful case. He briefly shewed them how this way of reception, with arms, had often, under colour of compliment and friendship, been fatal. "Thus," said he, "the emperor Antonius Caracalla, at one time, destroyed the citizens of Alexandria, and at another time, cut off the attendants of Artabanus king of Persia, under colour of marrying his daughter: which, by the way, did not pass unpunished; for, a while after, this cost him his life.

"Thus Jacob's children destroyed the Sichemites, to revenge the rape of their sister Dina. By such another hypocritical trick, Gallienus the Roman emperor put to death the military men in Constantinople. Thus, under colour of friendship, Antonius inticed Artavasdes king of Armenia; then having caused him to be bound in heavy chains, and shackled, at last put him to death.

"We find a thousand such instances in history; and king Charles VI. is justly commended for his prudence to this day, in that, coming back victorious over the Ghenters and other Flemmings, to his good city of Paris, and when he came to Bourget (a league from thence) hearing that the citizens with their mallets (whence they got the name of Maillotins) were marched out of town in battalia, twenty thousand strong, he would not go into the town till they had laid down their arms, and retired to their respective homes; though they protested to him, that they had taken arms with no other design than to receive him with the greater demonstration of honour and respect."

CHAPTER XXXVII

HOW PANTAGRUEL SENT FOR COLONEL MAUL-CHITTERLING
AND COLONEL CUT-PUDDING; WITH A DISCOURSE WELL
WORTH YOUR HEARING, ABOUT THE NAMES OF PLACES
AND PERSONS

THE resolution of the council was, that, let things be how they would, it behoved the Pantagruelists to stand upon their guard.

Therefore Carpalim and Gymnast were ordered, by Pantagruel, to go for the soldiers that were on board the Cup gally, under the command of colonel Maul-chitterling, and those on board the Vine-tub frigate, under the command of colonel Cut-pudding the younger. "I will ease Gymnast of that trouble," said Panurge who wanted to be upon the run: "you may have occasion for him here." "By this worthy frock of mine," quoth friar John, "thou hast a mind to slip thy neck out of the collar, and absent thyself from the fight, thou white-livered son of a dunghill! upon my virginity thou wilt never come back. Well, there can be no great loss in thee: for thou wouldst do nothing here but howl, bray, weep, and dishearten the good soldiers." "I will certainly come back," said Panurge, "friar John, my ghostly father, and speedily too: do but take care that these plaguy Chitterlings don't board our ships. All the while you'll be a fighting, I'll pray heartily for your victory, after the example of the valiant captain and guide of the people of Israel, Moses." Having said this, he wheeled off.

Then said Epistemon to Pantagruel, "The denomination of these two colonels of yours, Maul-chitterling and Cut-pudding, promiseth us assurance, success, and victory, if those Chitterlings should chance to set upon us." "You take it rightly," said Pantagruel, "and it pleaseth me to see you foresee and prognosticate our victory by the name of our colonels.

"This way of foretelling by names is not new; it was in old times celebrated, and religiously observed by the Pythagoreans. Several great princes and emperors have formerly made use of it. Octavianus Augustus, second emperor of the Romans, meeting on a day a country fellow named Eutychius (that is, fortunate), driving an ass named Nicon (that is, in Greek, victorious), moved by the signification of the ass's and ass-driver's names, remained assured of all prosperity and victory.

"The emperor Vespasian, being once all alone at prayers, in the temple of Serapis, at the sight and unexpected coming of a certain servant of his, named Basilides (that is, royal) whom he had left sick a great way behind, took hopes and assurance of obtaining the empire of the Romans. Regilian was chosen emperor, by the soldiers, for no other reason but the signification of his name. See the Cratylus of the divine Plato." ("By my thirst I will read him," said Rhizotomus: "I hear you so often quote him.") "See how the Pythagoreans, by reason of the names and numbers, conclude that Patroclus was to fall

534

by the hand of Hector; Hector by Achilles; Achilles by Paris; Paris by Philoctetes. I am quite lost in my understanding when I reflect upon the admirable invention of Pythagoras, who by the number, either even or odd, of the syllables of every name, would tell you of what side a man was lame, hulch-backed, blind, gouty, troubled with the palsy, pleurisy, or any other distemper incident to human kind; allotting even numbers to the left, and odd ones to the right side of the body."

"Indeed," said Epistemon, "I saw this way of syllabising tried at Xaintes, at a general procession, in the presence of that good, virtuous, learned, and just president, Brian Vallée, lord of Douhait. When there went by a man or woman that was either lame, blind of one eye, or hump-backed, he had an account brought him of his or her name; and if the syllables of the name were of an odd number, immediately, without seeing the person, he declared them to be deformed, blind, lame, or crooked of the right side; and of the left, if they were even in number: and such indeed we ever found them."

"By this syllabical invention," said Pantagruel, "the learned have affirmed, that Achilles kneeling, was wounded by the arrow of Paris in the right heel; for his name is of odd syllables (here we ought to observe that the ancients used to kneel the right foot), and that Venus was also wounded before Troy in the left hand; for her name in Greek is ἀφροδίτη of four syllables; Vulcan lamed of his left foot for the same reason; Philip king of Macedon, and Hannibal, blind of the right eye; not to speak of sciaticas, broken bellies, and hemicranias, which may be distinguished by this Pythagorean reason.

"But returning to names; do but consider how Alexander the Great, son to king Philip, of whom we spoke just now, compassed his undertaking, merely by the interpretation of a name. He had besieged the strong city of Tyre, and for several weeks battered it with all his power: but all in vain; his engines and attempts were still baffled by the Tyrians, which made him finally resolve to raise the siege, to his great grief; foreseeing the great stain, which such a shameful retreat would be to his reputation. In this anxiety and agitation of mind he fell asleep, and dreamed that a satyr was come into his tent, capering, skipping, and tripping it up and down, with his goatish hoofs, and that he strove to lay hold on him. But the satyr still slipt from him, till at last, having penn'd him up into a corner, he took him. With this he awoke, and telling his dream to the philosophers and sages of his court, they let him know that it was a promise of victory from the gods, and that he should soon be master of Tyre; the word satyros, divided in two, being sa Tyros, and signifying Tyre is thine; and in truth, at the next onset, he took the town by storm, and, by a complete victory, reduced that stubborn people to subjection.

"On the other hand, see how, by the signification of one word, Pompey fell into despair. Being overcome by Cæsar at the battle of Pharsalia, he had no other way left to escape, but by flight; which, attempting by sea, he arrived near the island of Cyprus, and perceived on the shore, near the city of Paphos, a beautiful and stately palace: now asking the pilot what was the name of it, he told him, that it was called κακοβασιλέα, that is, evil king; which struck such a dread and terror in him, that he fell into despair, as being assured of losing shortly his life; insomuch that his complaints, sighs, and groans were heard by the mariners and other passengers. And indeed, a while after, a certain strange peasant, called Achillas, cut off his head.

"To all these examples might be added what happened to L. Paulus Emilius, when the senate elected him imperator, that is, chief of the army which they sent against Perses king of Macedon. That evening returning home to prepare for his expedition, and kissing a little daughter of his called Trasia, she seemed somewhat sad to him. "What is the matter," said he, "my chicken? Why is my Trasia thus sad and melancholy?" "Daddy," replied the child, "Persa is dead." This was the name of a little bitch, which she loved mightily. Hearing this, Paulus took assurance of a victory over Perses.

"If time would permit us to discourse of the sacred Hebrew writ, we might find a hundred noted passages, evidently shewing how religiously they observed proper names and their significations."

He had hardly ended this discourse, when the two colonels arrived with their soldiers, all well armed and resolute. Pantagruel made them a short speech, entreating them to behave themselves bravely, in case they were attacked; for he could not yet believe that the Chitterlings were so treacherous: but he bade them by no means to give the first offence; giving them carnival for the watch-word.

536

CHAPTER XXXVIII

HOW CHITTERLINGS ARE NOT TO BE SLIGHTED BY MEN

YOU shake your empty noddles now, jolly topers, and do not believe what I tell you here, any more than if it were some tale of
a tub. Well, well, I cannot help it. Believe it if you will; if you will
not, let it alone. For my part I very well know what I saw. It was in
the Wild Island, in our voyage to the holy bottle: I tell you the time
and place; what would you have more? I would have you call to
mind the strength of the ancient giants, that undertook to lay the high
mountain Pelion on the top of Ossa, and set among those the shady
Olympus, to dash out the gods' brains, unnestle them, and scour their
heavenly lodgings. Theirs was no small strength, you may well
think: and yet they were nothing but Chitterlings from the waste
downwards, or at least, serpents, not to tell a lie for the matter.

The serpent that tempted Eve too, was of the chitterling kind; and
yet it is recorded of him, that he was more subtle than any beast of
the field. Even so are Chitterlings. Nay, to this very hour they hold
in some universities, that this same tempter was the Chitterling called
Ithyphallus, into which was transformed bawdy Priapus, arch-seducer
of females in paradise; that is, a garden in Greek.

Pray now tell me, who can tell but that the Switzers, now so bold and
warlike, were formerly Chitterlings? For my part I would not take
my oath to the contrary. The Himantopodes, a nation very famous
in Ethiopia, according to Pliny's description, are Chitterlings, and
nothing else. If all this will not satisfy your worships, or remove
your incredulity, I would have you forthwith (I mean drinking first,
that nothing be done rashly) visit Lusignan, Parthenay, Vouant,
Mervant, and Ponzauges in Poictou. There you will find a cloud of
witnesses, not of your affidavit-men of the right stamp, but credible,
time out of mind, that will take their corporal oath, on Rigome's
knuckle-bone, that Melusina, their founder, or foundress, which you
please, was woman from the head to the prick-purse, and thence
downwards was a serpentine chitterling, or if you'll have it otherwise, a chitterlingdized serpent. She nevertheless had a genteel and
noble gait, imitated to this very day by your hop-merchants of Britanny, in their paspié and country dances.

What do you think was the cause of Erichthonius's being the first
inventor of coaches, litters, and chariots? Nothing but because Vul-

can had begot him with chitterlingdized legs; which to hide, he chose to ride in a litter, rather than on horseback: for Chitterlings were not yet in esteem at that time.

The Scythian nymph, Ora, was likewise half woman and half chitterling; and yet seemed so beautiful to Jupiter, that nothing could serve him but he must give her a touch of his godship's kindness; and accordingly he had a brave boy by her, called Colaxes: and therefore I would have you leave off shaking your empty noddles at this, as if it were a story, and firmly believe that nothing is truer than the gospel.

CHAPTER XXXIX

HOW FRIAR JOHN JOINED WITH THE COOKS TO FIGHT THE CHITTERLINGS

FRIAR JOHN, seeing these furious Chitterlings thus boldly march up, said to Pantagruel; "Here will be a rare battle of hobby-horses, a pretty kind of puppet-show fight, for ought I see. Oh! what mighty honour and wonderful glory will attend our victory! I would have you only be a bare spectator of this fight, and for anything else, leave me and my men to deal with them." "What men?" said Pantagruel. "Matter of breviary," replied friar John. "How come Potiphar, who was head cook of Pharaoh's kitchens, he that bought Joseph, and whom the said Joseph might have made a cuckold, if he had not been a Joseph; how came he, I say, to be made general of all the horse in the kingdom of Egypt? Why was Nabuzardan, king Nebuchadnezzar's head cook, chosen, to the exclusion of all other captains, to besiege and destroy Jerusalem?" "I hear you," replied Pantagruel. "By St. Christopher's whiskers," said friar John, "I dare lay a wager that it was because they had formerly engaged Chitterlings, or men as little valued; whom to rout, conquer, and destroy, cooks are, without comparison, more fit than cuirassiers and gens de armes armed at all points, or all the horse and foot in the world."

"You put me in mind," said Pantagruel, "of what is written amongst the facetious and merry sayings of Cicero. During the *more than civil wars* between Cæsar and Pompey, though he was much courted by the first, he naturally leaned more to the side of the latter. Now, one day, hearing that the Pompeians, in a certain rencontre, had lost a great many men, he took a fancy to visit their camp. There he perceived little strength, less courage, but much disorder. From that time, foreseeing that things would go ill with them, as it since happened, he began to banter now one and then another, and be very free of his cutting jests: so some of Pompey's captains, playing the good fellows, to shew their assurance, told him, 'Do you see how many eagles we have yet?' (They were then the device of the Romans in war.) 'They might be of use to you,' replied Cicero, 'if you had to do with magpies.'

"Thus seeing we are to fight Chitterlings," pursued Pantagruel, "you infer thence that it is a culinary war, and have a mind to join with the cooks. Well, do as you please. I'll stay here in the meantime, and wait for the event of the battle."

Friar John went that very moment among the sutlers, into the cooks' tents, and told them in a pleasing manner; "I must see you crowned with honour and triumph this day, my lads: to your arms are reserved such achievements, as never yet were performed within the memory of man. Odd's belly, do they make nothing of the valiant cooks? let us go fight yonder fornicating Chitterlings! I will be your captain. But first let us drink, boys—come on—let us be of good cheer." "Noble captain," returned the kitchen tribe, "this was spoken like yourself; bravely offered: huzza! we are all at your excellency's command, and will live and die by you." "Live, live," said friar John, "a God's name: but die by no means. That is the Chitterlings' lot; they shall have their belly fully on't: come on then, let us put ourselves in order; Nabuzardan's the word."

CHAPTER XL

HOW FRIAR JOHN FITTED UP THE SOW; AND OF THE VALIANT COOKS THAT WENT INTO IT

THEN, by friar John's order, the engineers and their workmen fitted up the great sow that was in the ship Leathern-bottle. It was a wonderful machine, so contrived, that, by means of large engines that were round about in rows, it threw forked iron bars, and foursquare steel bolts; and in its hold two hundred men at least could easily fight, and be sheltered. It was made after the model of the sow of Riole, by the means of which Bergerac was retaken from the English, in the reign of Charles the Sixth.

Here are the names of the noble and valiant cooks who went into the sow, as the Greeks did into the Trojan horse.

Sour-sauce.	Crisp-pig.	Carbonadoe.
Sweet-meat.	Greasy-slouch.	Sop-in-pan.
Greedy-gut.	Fat-gut.	Pick-fowl.
Liquorice-chops.	Bray-mortar.	Mustard-pot.
Sows'd-pork.	Lick-sauce.	Hog's-haslet.
Slap-sauce.	Hog's-foot.	Chopt-phiz.
Cock-broth.	Hodge-podge.	Gallimaufrey.
Slipslop.		

All these noble cooks, in their coat of arms, did bear, in a field gules, a larding-pin vert, charged with a chevron argent.

Lard, hog's-lard.	Pinch-lard.	Snatch-lard.
Nibble-lard.	Top-lard.	Gnaw-lard.
Filch-lard.	Pick-lard.	Scrape-lard.
Fat-lard.	Save-lard.	Chew-lard.

Gaillard (by syncope) born near Rambouillet. The said culinary doctor's name was Gaillardlardon, in the same manner as you use to say idolatrous for idololatrous.

Stiff-lard.	Cut-lard.	Waste-lard.
Watch-lard.	Mince-lard.	Ogle-lard.
Sweet-lard.	Dainty-lard.	Weigh-lard.
Eat-lard.	Fresh-lard.	Gulch-lard.
Snap-lard.	Rusty-lard.	Eye-lard.
Catch-lard.		

Names unknown among the Marranes and Jews.

Ballocky.	Monsieur-ragoust.	Kitchen-stuff.
Pick sallad.	Crack-pipkin.	Verjuice.
Broil-rasher.	Scrape-pot.	Salt-gullet.
Cony-skin.	Porridge-pot.	Snail-dresser.
Dainty-chops.	Lick-dish.	Soup-monger.
Pye-wright.	Toss-pot.	Brouis-belly.
Pudding-pan.	Mustard-sauce.	Chine-picker.
Save-dripping.	Claret-sauce.	Suck-gravy.
Water-creese.	Swill-broth.	Macaroon.
Scrape-turnip.	Thirsty.	Skewer-maker.
Trivet.		

Smell-smock; he was afterwards taken from the kitchen, and removed to chamber-practice, for the service of the noble cardinal Hunt venison.

Rot Roast.	Hog's-gullet.	Fox-tail.
Dish-clout.	Sirloin.	Fly-flap.
Save-suet.	Spit-mutton.	Old-Grizzle.
Fire-fumbler.	Fritter-fryer.	Ruff-belly.
Pillicock.	Flesh-smith.	Saffron-sauce.
Long-tool.	Cram-gut.	Strutting-Tom.
Prick-pride.	Tuzzymussy.	Slashed-snout.
Prick-madam.	Jacket-liner.	Smutty-face.
Pricket.	Guzzle-drink.	

Mondam, that first invented madam's sauce, and for that discovery, was thus called in the Scotch-French dialect.

Loblolly.	Sloven.	Trencher-man.
Slabber-chops.	Swallow-pitcher.	Goodman Goosecap.
Scum-pot.	Wafer-monger.	Munch-turnip.
Gully-guts.	Snap-gobbet.	Pudding-bag.
Rinse-pot.	Scurvy-phiz.	Pig-sticker.
Drink-spiller.		

Robert: he invented Robert's sauce, so good and necessary for roasted conies, ducks, fresh pork, poached eggs, salt fish, and a thousand other such dishes.

Cold-eel.	Fryingpan.	Big-snout.
Thornback.	Man of dough.	Lick-finger.
Gurnard.	Sauce doctor.	Tit-bit.
Grumbling-gut.	Waste-butter.	Sauce-box.
Alms-scrip.	Shitbreech.	All-fours.
Taste-all.	Thick-brawn.	Whimwham.
Scrap-merchant.	Tom T—d.	Baste-Roast.
Belly-timberman.	Mouldy-crust.	Gaping Hoyden.
Hashee.	Hasty.	Calf's-pluck.
Frig-palate.	Red-herring.	Leather-breeches.
Powdering-tub.	Cheesecake.	

All these noble cooks went into the sow, merry, cheery, hale, brisk, old dogs at mischief, and ready to fight stoutly. Friar John, ever and anon waving his huge scimitar, brought up the rear, and double-locked the doors on the inside.

CHAPTER XLI

THE Chitterlings advanced so near, that Pantagruel perceived that they stretched their arms and already began to charge their lances; which caused him to send Gymnast to know what they meant, and why they thus, without the least provocation, came to fall upon their old trusty friends, who had neither said nor done the least ill thing to them. Gymnast being advanced near their front, bowed very low, and said to them, as loud as ever he could: "We are friends, we are friends; all, all of us your friends, yours, and at your command: we are for carnival, your old confederate." Some have since told me, that he mistook, and said cavernal instead of carnival.

Whatever it was, the word was no sooner out of his mouth, but a huge wild squab Sausage, starting out of the front of their main body, would have griped him by the collar. "By the helmet of Mars," said Gymnast, "I'll swallow thee; but thou shalt only come in in chips and slices; for, big as thou art, thou could'st never come in whole." This spoke, he lugs out his trusty sword, kiss-mine-arse (so he called it) with both his fists, and cut the sausage in twain. Bless me, how fat the foul thief was! it puts me in mind of the huge bull of Berne, that was slain at Marignan, when the drunken Switzers were so mauled there. Believe me, it had little less than four inches lard on its paunch.

The Sausage's job being done, a crowd of others flew upon Gymnast, and had most scurvily dragged him down, when Pantagruel with his men came up to his relief. Then began the martial fray, higledy-pigledy. Maul-chitterling did maul chitterlings; Cut-pudding did cut puddings; Pantagruel did break the chitterlings at the knees; friar John played at least in sight within his sow, viewing and observing all things; when the patty-pans, that lay in ambuscade, most furiously sallied out upon Pantagruel.

Friar John, who lay snug all this while, by that time perceiving the rout and hurly-burly, set open the doors of his sow, and sallied out with his merry Greeks, some of them arm'd with iron-spits, others with andirons, racks, fire-shovels, frying-pans, kettles, gridirons, oven forks, tongs, dripping pans, brooms, iron pots, mortars, pestles, all in battle array, like so many housebreakers, hallowing and roaring out altogether most frightfully, "Nabuzardan, Nabuzardan, Nabuzardan." Thus shouting and hooting, they fought like dragons, and charged through the patty-pans and sausages. The Chitterlings, perceiving this fresh reinforcement, and that the others would be too hard for 'em, betook themselves to their heels, scampering off with full speed, as if the devil had been come for them. Friar John, with an iron crow, knocked them down as fast as hops: his men too were not sparing on their side. O! what a woful sight it was! the field was all over strewed with heaps of dead or wounded Chitterlings: and history relates, that had not heaven had a hand in it, the Chitterling tribe had been totally routed out of the world, by the culinary champions. But there happened a wonderful thing, you may believe as little or as much of it as you please.

From the north flew towards us a huge, fat, thick, grizzly swine, with long and large wings, like those of a windmill; its plumes red crimson, like those of a phenicoptere (which in Languedoc they call flaman); its eyes were red, and flaming like a carbuncle: its ears green like a Prasin emerald; its teeth like a topaz; its tail long and black like jet; its feet white, diaphanous, and transparent like a diamond, somewhat broad, and of the splay kind, like those of geese, and as queen Dick's used to be at Thoulouse, in the days of yore. About its neck it wore a gold collar, round which were some Ionian characters, whereof I could pick out but two words, ΣΥΣ ΑΘΗΝΑΝ ; hog teaching Minerva.

The sky was clear before; but at that monster's appearance, it changed so mightily for the worse that we were all amazed at it. As soon as the Chitterlings perceived the flying hog, down they all threw their weapons, and fell on their knees, lifting up their hands, joined together, without speaking one word, in a posture of adoration. Friar John and his party kept on mincing, felling, braining, mangling, and spitting the Chitterlings like mad: but Pantagruel sounded a retreat, and all hostility ceased.

The monster having several times hovered backwards and forwards between the two armies, with a tail-shot voided above twenty-seven buts of mustard on the ground; then flew away through the air, crying all the while "Carnival, carnival, carnival."

CHAPTER XLII

HOW PANTAGRUEL HELD A TREATY WITH NIPHLESETH,
QUEEN OF THE CHITTERLINGS

THE monster being out of sight, and the two armies remaining silent, Pantagruel demanded a parley with the lady Niphleseth, queen of the Chitterlings, who was in her chariot by the standards; and it was easily granted. The queen alighted, courteously received Pantagruel, and was glad to see him. Pantagruel complained to her of this breach of peace: but she civilly made her excuse, telling him that a false information had caused all this mischief; her spies having brought her word, that Shrovetide, their mortal foe, was landed, and spent his time in examining the urine of physeteres.

She, therefore, entreated him to pardon them their offence; telling him that sir-reverence was sooner found in Chitterlings than gall; and offering, for herself and all her successors, to hold of him, and his, the whole island and country; to obey him in all his commands, be friends to his friends, and foes to his foes; and also to send every year, as an acknowledgment of their homage, a tribute of seventy-eight thousand royal chitterlings, to serve him at his first course at table, six months in the year; which was punctually performed. For the next day she sent the aforesaid quantity of royal chitterlings to the good Gargantua, under the conduct of young Niphleseth, infanta of the island.

The good Gargantua made a present of them to the great king of Paris. But by change of air, and for want of mustard (the natural balsam and restorer of chitterlings), most of them died. By the great king's particular grant, they were buried in heaps in a part of Paris, to this day called, *La Rue pavée d'Andouilles;* the street paved with chitterlings. At the request of the ladies at his court, young Niphleseth was preserved, honourably used, and since that married to her heart's content; and was the mother of many children, for which heaven be praised.

Pantagruel civilly thanked the queen, forgave all offences, refused the offer she had made of her country, and gave her a pretty little knife. After that he asked her several nice questions concerning the apparition of that flying hog. She answered, that it was the idea of carnival, their tutelary god in time of war, first founder, and original of all the chitterling race; for which reason he resembled a hog; for chitterlings drew their extraction from hogs.

Pantagruel asking to what purpose, and curative indication, he had voided so much mustard on the earth, the queen replied, that mustard was their sang-real, and celestial balsam, of which, laying but a little in the wounds of the fallen Chitterlings, in a very short time the wounded were healed, and the dead restored to life. Pantagruel held no further discourse with the queen, but retired on shipboard. The like did all the boon companions, with their implements of destruction, and their huge sow.

CHAPTER XLIII

HOW PANTAGRUEL WENT INTO THE ISLAND OF RUACH

TWO days after we arrived at the island of Ruach; and I swear to you, by the celestial hen and chickens, that I found the way of living of the people so strange and wonderful, that I can't, for the heart's-blood of me, half tell it you. They live on nothing but wind, eat nothing but wind, and drink nothing but wind. They have no other houses but weathercocks. They sow no other seeds but the three sorts of wind flowers, rue, and herbs that make one break wind to the purpose: these scour them off charmingly. The common sort of people, to feed themselves, make use of feather, paper, or linen fans, according to their abilities. As for the rich, they live by the means of windmills.

When they would have some noble treat, the tables are spread under one or two windmills. There they feast as merry as beggars, and, during the meal, their whole talk is commonly of the goodness, excellency, salubrity, and rarity of winds; as you, jolly topers, in your cups, philosophize and argue upon wines. The one praises the south east, the other the south west, this the west and by south, and this the east and by north: another the west, and another the east; and so of the rest. As for lovers and amorous sparks, no gale for them like a smock-gale. For the sick they use bellows, as we use clysters among us.

"O!" (said to me a little diminutive swoln bubble) "that I had now but a bladder-full of that same Languedoc wind, which they call cierce. The famous physician, Scurron, passing one day by this country, was telling us, that it is so strong, that it will make nothing of

545

overturning a loaded waggon. Oh! what good would it not do my oedipodic leg." "The biggest are not the best: but," said Panurge, "rather would I had here a large butt of that same good Languedoc wine, that grows at Mirevaux, Canteperdrix, and Frontignan."

I saw a good likely sort of a man there, much resembling Ventrose, tearing and fuming in a grievous fret, with a tall burly groom, and a pimping little page of his, laying them on like the devil with a buskin. Not knowing the cause of his anger, at first I thought that all this was by the doctor's advice, as being a thing very healthy to the master to be in a passion, and to his man to be bang'd for't. But at last I heard him taxing his man with stealing from him, like a rogue as he was, the better half of a large leathern bag of an excellent southerly wind, which he had carefully laid up, like a hidden reserve, against the cold weather.

They neither exonerate, dung, piss, nor spit in that island; but, to make amends, they belch, fizzle, funk, and give tail shots in abundance. They are troubled with all manner of distempers; and, indeed, all distempers are engendered, and proceed from ventosities, as Hippocrates demonstrates, lib. de flatibus. But the most epidemical among them is the wind-cholic. The remedies which they use are large blisters, whereby they void store of windiness. They all die of dropsies and tympanies; the men farting, and the women fizzling: so that their soul takes her leave at the back door.

Some time after, walking in the island, we met three hair-brained airy fellows, who seemed mightily puffed up, and went to take their pastime, and view the pluvers, who live on the same diet as themselves and abound in the island. I observed that as you true topers, when you travel, carry flasks, leathern bottles, and small runlets along with you, so each of them had at his girdle a pretty little pair of bellows. If they happened to want wind, by the help of those pretty bellows they immediately drew some fresh and cool, by attraction and reciprocal expulsion: for, as you well know, wind, essentially defined, is nothing but fluctuating and agitated air.

Awhile after we were commanded, in the king's name, not to receive for three hours, any man or woman of the country, on board our ships; some having stolen from him a rouzing fart, of the very individual wind which old goodman Æolus, the snorer, gave Ulysses to conduct his ship, whenever it should happen to be becalmed. Which fart the king kept religiously, like another sangreal, and performed a world of wonderful cures with it, in many dangerous diseases, letting loose, and distributing to the patient, only as much of it as might frame a virginal fart; which is, if you must know, what our sanctimonials, alias nuns, in their dialect, call ringing backwards.

CHAPTER XLIV

HOW A SMALL RAIN LAYS A HIGH WIND

PANTAGRUEL commended their government and way of living, and said to their hypemenian mayor, "If you approve Epicurus's opinion, placing the *summum bonum* in pleasure (I mean pleasure that's easy and free from toil) I esteem you happy; for your food being wind, costs you little or nothing, since you need but blow." "True, sir," returned the mayor; "but, alas! nothing is perfect here below: for too often, when we are at table, feeding on some good blessed wind of God, as on celestial manna, merry as so many friars, down drops on a sudden some small rain, which lays our wind, and so robs us of it. Thus many a meal is lost for want of meat."

"Just so," quoth Panurge, "Jenin Toss-pot, of Quinquenois, evacuating some wine of his own burning on his wife's posteriors, laid the ill-fumed wind that blowed out of their centre, as out of some magisterial æolipyle. Here's a kind of a whim on that subject, which I made formerly:

> " 'One evening when Toss-pot had been at his butts,
> And Joan, his fat spouse, cramm'd with turnips her guts,
> Together they pigg'd, nor did drink so besot him,
> But he did what was done when his daddy begot him.
> Now when, to recruit, he'd fain have been snoring,
> Joan's back-door was filthily puffing and roaring:
> So, for spite he bepiss'd her, and quickly did find
> That a small rain lays a very high wind.' "

"We are also plagued yearly with a very great calamity," cried the mayor; "for a giant, called Widenostrils, who lives in the island of Tohu, comes hither every spring to purge, by the advice of his physicians, and swallows us like so many pills, a great number of windmills, and of bellows, also, at which his mouth waters exceedingly.

"Now this is a sad mortification to us here, who are fain to fast over

547

three or four whole lents every year for this, besides certain petty lents, ember weeks, and other orison and starving tides." "And have you no remedy for this?" asked Pantagruel. "By the advice of our mez-arims," replied the mayor, "about the time that he uses to give us a visit, we garrison our windmills with good store of cock and hens. So the first time that the greedy thief swallowed them, they had like to have done his business at once: for they crowed and cackled in his maw, and fluttered up and down athwart and along in his stomach, which threw the glutton into a lipothymy cardiac passion, and dreadful and dangerous convulsions, as if some serpent, creeping in at his mouth, had been frisking in his stomach."

"Here is a comparative, as altogether incongruous and impertinent," cried friar John, interrupting them, "for I have formerly heard, that if a serpent chance to get into a man's stomach, it will not do him the least hurt, but will immediately get out, if you do but hang the patient by the heels, and lay a pan full of warm milk near his mouth." "You were told this," said Pantagruel, "and so were those who gave you this account; but none ever saw or read of such a cure. On the contrary, Hippocrates, in his fifth book of Epidem, writes, that such a case happening in his time, the patient presently died of a spasm and convulsion."

"Besides the cocks and hens," said the mayor, continuing his story, "all the foxes in the country whipped into Widenostrils' mouth, posting after the poultry; which made such a stir with Reynard at their heels, that he grievously fell into fits each minute of an hour.

"At last, by the advice of a Baden enchanter, at the time of the paroxysm, he used to flea a fox by way of antidote and counter poison. Since that he took better advice, and eases himself with taking a clyster made with a decoction of wheat and barley corns, and of livers of goslings; to the first of which the poultry run, and the foxes to the latter. Besides, he swallows some of your badgers or foxdogs, by the way of pills and boluses. This is our misfortune."

"Cease to fear, good people," cried Pantagruel, "this huge Widenostrils, this same swallower of windmills, is no more, I'll assure you: he died, being stifled and choked with eating a lump of fresh butter at the mouth of a hot oven, by the advice of his physicians."

CHAPTER XLV

THE next morning we arrived at the island of Popefigs; formerly
a rich and free people, called the Gaillardets; but now, alas! miserably poor, and under the yoke of the Papimen. The occasion of it
was this.

On a certain yearly high holiday, the burgermaster, syndics and
topping rabbies of the Gaillardets, chanced to go into the neighbouring island of Papimany to see the festival, and pass away the time.
Now one of them having espied the pope's picture (with the sight
of which, according to a laudable custom, the people were blessed on
high-offering holidays) made mouths at it, and cried, "a fig for't!" as
a sign of manifest contempt and derision. To be revenged of this affront, the Papimen, some days after, without giving the others the least
warning, took arms, and surprised, destroyed, and ruined the whole
island of the Gaillardets; putting the men to the sword, and sparing
none but the women and children; and those too only on condition
to do what the inhabitants of Milan were condemned to by the emperor Frederic Barbarossa.

These had rebelled against him in his absence, and ignominiously
turned the empress out of the city, mounting her a horseback on a
mule called Thacor, with her breech foremost towards the old jaded
mule's head, and her face turned towards the crupper. Now Frederic
being returned, mastered them, and caused so careful a search to be
made, that he found out and got the famous mule Thacor. Then the
hangman, by his order, clapped a fig into the mule's jim-crack, in the
presence of the enslaved cits that were brought into the middle of the
great market-place, and proclaimed, in the emperor's name, with
trumpets, that whosoever of them would save his own life, should
publicly pull the fig out with his teeth, and after that, put it in again
in the very individual cranny whence he had drawed it, without using his hands, and that whoever refused to do this should presently
swing for't, and die in his shoes. Some sturdy fools, standing upon
their punctilio, chose honourably to be hanged, rather than submit to
so shameful and abominable a disgrace; and others, less nice in point
of ceremony, took heart of grace, and even resolved to have at the fig,
and a fig for't, rather than make a worse figure with a hempen col-

549

lar, and die in the air, at so short warning: accordingly when they had neatly picked out the fig with their teeth from old Thacor's snatch-blatch, they plainly showed it the headsman, saying, *"ecco lo fico,"* behold the fig.

By the same ignominy the rest of these poor distressed Gaillardets saved their bacon, becoming tributaries and slaves; and the name of Pope-figs was given them, because they said, *"a fig for the pope's image."* Since this the poor wretches never prospered, but every year the devil was at their doors, and they were plagued with hail, storms, famine, and all manner of woes, as an everlasting punishment for the sin of their ancestors and relations. Perceiving the misery and calamity of that generation, we did not care to go further up into the country; contenting ourselves with going into a little chapel near the haven to take some holy water. It was dilapidated and ruined, wanting also a cover (like St. Peter at Rome). When we were in, as we dipped our fingers in the sanctified cistern, we spied in the middle of that holy pickle, a fellow muffled up with stoles, all under water, like a diving duck, except the tip of his snout to draw his breath. About him stood three priests, true shavelings, clean shorn and polled, who were muttering strange words to the devils out of a conjuring book.

Pantagruel was not a little amazed at this; and, inquiring what kind of sport these were at, was told that for three years last past, the plague had so dreadfully raged in the island, that the better half of it had been utterly depopulated, and the lands lay fallow and unoccupied. Now, the mortality being over, this same fellow, who had crept into the holy tub, having a large piece of ground, chanced to be sowing it with white winter wheat, at the very minute of an hour that a kind of a silly sucking devil, who could not yet write or read, or hail and thunder, unless it were on parsly or colworts, had got leave of his master Lucifer to go into this island of Pope-figs, where the devils were very familiar with the men and women, and often went to take their pastime.

This same devil being got thither, directed his discourse to the husbandman, and asked him what he was doing. The poor man told him, that he was sowing the ground with corn, to help him to subsist the next year. "Ay, but the ground is none of thine, Mr. Plough-jobber," cried the devil, "but mine; for since the time that you mocked the pope, all this land has been proscribed, adjudged and abandoned to us. However, to sow corn is not my province: therefore I will give thee leave to sow the field; that is to say, provided we share the profit." "I will," replied the farmer. "I mean," said the devil, "that of what the land shall bear, two lots shall be made, one of what shall grow above ground, the other of what shall be covered with earth: the right of chusing belongs to me; for I am a devil of noble and ancient race; thou art a base clown. I therefore chuse what shall lie under ground, take thou what shall be above. When dost thou reckon to reap, hah?" "About the middle of July," quoth the farmer. "Well," said the devil, "I'll not fail thee then; in the meantime, slave as thou oughtest. Work, clown, work: I am going to tempt to the pleasing sin of whoring, the nuns of dryfart, the sham saints of the cowl, and the gluttonish crew; I am more than sure of these. They need but meet, and the job is done: true fire and tinder, touch and take; down falls nun, and up gets friar."

CHAPTER XLVI

HOW A JUNIOR DEVIL WAS FOOLED BY A HUSBANDMAN OF POPE-FIGLAND

IN the middle of July, the devil came to the place aforesaid, with all his crew at his heels, a whole choir of the younger fry of hell; and having met the farmer, said to him; "Well, clodpate, how hast thou done, since I went? Thou and I must now share the concern." "Ay, master devil," quoth the clown, "it is but reason we should." Then he and his men began to cut and reap the corn: and on the other side, the devil's imps fell to work, grubbing up, and pulling out the stubble by the root.

The countryman had his corn threshed, winnowed it, put it into sacks, and went with it to market. The same did the devil's servants, and sat them down there by the man, to sell their straw. The countryman sold off his corn at a good rate, and with the money filled an old kind of a demi-buskin, which was fastened to his girdle. But the devil a sous the devils took: far from taking hansel, they were flouted and jeered by the country louts.

Market being over, quoth the devil to the farmer, "Well, clown, thou hast choused me once, it is thy fault; chouse me twice, it will be mine." "Nay, good sir devil," replied the farmer, "how can I be said to have choused you, since it was your worship that chose first? The truth is, that, by this trick, you thought to cheat me, hoping that nothing would spring out of the earth for my share, and that you should find whole under ground the corn which I had sowed, and with it tempt the poor and needy, the close hypocrite, or the covetous griper; thus making them fall into your snares. But troth, you must e'en go to school yet: you are no conjurer, for ought I see: for the corn that was sowed is dead and rotten, its corruption having caused the generation of that which you saw me sell: so you chose the worst, and therefore are cursed in the gospel." "Well, talk no more of it," quoth the devil: "what canst thou sow our field with for next year?" "If a man would make the best of it," answered the ploughman, "it were fit he sow it with radishes." "Now," cried the devil, "thou talkest like an honest fellow, bumkin: well, sow me good store of radishes, I will see and keep them safe from storms, and will not hail a bit on them. But harkye me, this time I bespeak for my share what shall be above ground; what is under shall be thine. Drudge on, looby, drudge on. I am going to tempt heretics; their souls are dainty victuals, when boiled in rashers and well powdered. My lord Lucifer has the griping in the guts; they will make a dainty warm dish for his honour's maw."

When the season of radishes was come, our devil failed not to meet in the field, with a train of rascally underlings, all waiting devils, and finding there the farmer and his men, he began to cut and gather the leaves of the radishes. After him the farmer with his spade dug up the radishes, and clapped them up into pouches. This done, the devil, the farmer, and their gangs, hied them to market, and there the farmer presently made good money of his radishes: but the poor devil took nothing; nay, what was worse, he was made a common laughing-stock by the gaping hoydons. "I see thou hast played me a scurvy trick, thou villainous fellow," cried the angry devil: "at last I am fully resolved even to make an end of the business betwixt thee and myself, about the ground, and these shall be the terms; we'll clapperclaw each other, and whoever of us two shall first cry, *hold*, shall quit his share of the field, which shall wholly belong to the conqueror. I fix the time for this trial of skill, on this day se'nnight: assure thyself that I will claw thee off like a devil. I was going to tempt your fornicators, bailiffs, perplexers of causes, scriveners, forgers of deeds, two-handed counsellors, prevaricating solicitors, and other such vermin; but they were so civil as to send me word by an interpreter, that they are all mine already. Besides our master Lucifer is so cloyed with their souls, that he often sends them back to the smutty scullions, and slovenly devils of his kitchen, and they scarce go down with them, unless now and then, when they are high-seasoned.

"Some say there is no breakfast like a student's, no dinner like a lawyer's, no afternoon's nunchion like a vintner's, no supper like a tradesman's, no second supper like a serving wench's, and none of these meals equal to a frockified hobgoblin's. All this is true enough. Accordingly, at my lord Lucifer's first course, hobgoblins, alias imps in cowls, are a standish dish. He willingly used to breakfast on students: but, alas, I do not know by what ill luck, they have of late years joined the holy Bible to their studies: so the devil a one we can get down among us; and I verily believe that unless the hypocrites of the tribe of Levi help us, in it, taking from the enlightened book-mongers their St. Paul, either by threats, revilings, force, violence, fire and faggot, we shall not be able to hook-in any more of them, to nibble at below. He dines commonly on counsellors, mischief-mongers, multipliers of law-suits such as wrest and pervert right and law, and grind and fleece the poor: he never fears to want any of these. But who can endure to be wedded to a dish?

"He said the other day, at a full chapter, that he had a great mind to eat the soul of one of the fraternity of the cowl, that had forgot to speak for himself in his sermon; and he promised double pay, and a large pension, to any one that should bring him such a tit-bit piping hot. We all went a hunting after such a rarity, but came home without the prey: for they all admonish the good women to remember their convent. As for afternoon nuncheons, he has left them off, since he was so wofully griped with the cholic; his fosterers, sutlers, charcoal men, and boiling cooks having been sadly mawled and peppered off in the northern countries.

"His high devilship sups very well on tradesmen, usurers, apothecaries, cheats, coiners, and adulterers of wares. Now and then when he is on the merry pin, his second supper is of serving wenches; who, after they have, by stealth, soaked their faces with their master's good liquor, fill up the vessel with it at second hand, or with other stinking water.

"Well, drudge on, boor, drudge on: I am going to tempt the students of Trebisonde, to leave father and mother, forego for ever the established and common rule of living. disclaim and free themselves from obeying their lawful sovereign's edicts, live in absolute liberty, proudly despise every one, laugh at all mankind, and taking the fine jovial little cap of poetic licence, become so many pretty hobgoblins."

553

THE country lob trudged home very much concerned and thoughtful, you may swear; insomuch that his good woman, seeing him thus look moping, weened that something had been stolen from him at market: but when she had heard the cause of his affliction, and seen his budget well lined with coin, she bade him be of good cheer, assuring him that he'd be never the worse for the scratching bout in question; wishing him only to leave her to manage that business, and not trouble his head about it; for she had already contrived how to bring him off cleverly. "Let the worst come to the worst," said the husbandman, "it will be but a scratch; for I'll yield at the first stroke, and quit the field." "Quit a fart," replied the wife; "he shall have none of the field: rely upon me, and be quiet, let me alone to deal with him. You say he's a pimping little devil, that's enough; I'll soon make him give up the field, I'll warrant you. Indeed, had he been a great devil, it had been somewhat."

The day that we landed in the island happened to be that which the devil had fixed for the combat. Now the countryman, having, like a good catholic, very fairly confessed himself, and received, betimes in the morning, by the advice of the vicar, had hid himself, all but the snout, in the holy water-pot, in the posture in which we found him; and just as they were telling us this story, news came that the old woman had fooled the devil, and gained the field. You may not be sorry, perhaps, to hear how this happened.

The devil, you must know, came to the poor man's door, and rapping there, cried, "So ho! ho the house! ho, clod-pate! where art thou? Come out with a vengeance; come out with a wannion; come out and be damn'd: now for clawing." Then briskly and resolutely entering the house, and not finding the countryman there, he spied his wife lying on the ground, piteously weeping and howling. "What's the matter?" asked the devil. "Where is he? What does he?" "Oh! that I knew where he is," replied threescore and five, "the wicked rogue, the butcherly dog, the murderer! He has spoiled me; I am undone; I die of what he has done to me." "How," cried the devil, "what is it? I'll tickle him off for you by and by." "Alas," cried the old dissembler, "he told me, the butcher, the tyrant, the tearer of devils, told me that he had made a match to scratch with you this day, and to try his claws, he did but just touch me with his little finger, here betwixt the legs, and has spoiled me for ever. Oh! I am a dead woman! I shall never be myself again: do but see! Nay, and besides, he talked of going to the smith's, to have his pounces sharpened and pointed. Alas, you are undone, Mr. Devil; good sir, scamper quickly, I am sure he won't stay; save yourself, I beseech you." While she said this, she uncovered herself up to the chin, after the manner in which the Persian women met their children who fled from the fight, and plainly shewed her what d'ye call it. The frightened devil, seeing the enormous solution of the continuity in all its dimensions, blessed himself, and cried out, "Mahon, Demiourgon, Megæra, Alecto, Persephone; s'life, catch me here when he comes! I am gone: s'death, what a gash! I resign him the field."

Having heard the catastrophe of the story, we retired a shipboard, not being willing to stay there any longer. Pantagruel gave to the poor's-box of the fabric of the church, eighteen thousand gold royals, in commiseration of the poverty of the people, and the calamity of the place.

CHAPTER XLVIII

HOW PANTAGRUEL WENT ASHORE AT THE ISLAND OF PAPIMANY

HAVING left the desolate island of the Popefigs, we sailed, for the space of a day, very fairly and merrily, and made the blessed island of Papimany. As soon as we had dropped anchor in the road, before we had well moored our ship with ground-tackle, four persons, in different garbs, rowed towards us in a skiff. One of them was dressed like a monk in his frock, draggle-tailed, and booted; the other like a falconer, with a lure, and a long-winged hawk on his fist: the third like a solicitor, with a large bag, full of informations, subpœnas, breviates, bills, writs, cases, and other implements of pettifogging. The fourth looked like one of your vine barbers about Orleans, with a jantee pair of canvass trowsers, a dosser, and a pruning knife at his girdle.

As soon as the boat had clapped them on board, they all with one voice asked, "Have you seen him, good passengers, have you seen him?"—"Who?" asked Pantagruel. "You know who," answered they. "Who is it?" asked friar John. "Sblood and oonds, I'll thrash him thick and threefold." This he said, thinking that they enquired after some robber, murderer, or church-breaker. "Oh wonderful," cried the four, "do not you foreign people know the one?" "Sirs," replied Epistemon, "we do not understand those terms: but if you will be pleased to let us know who you mean, we'll tell you truth of the matter without any more ado." "We mean," said they, "He that is. Did you ever see him?" "He that is," returned Pantagruel, "according to our theological doctrine, is God, who said to Moses, 'I am that I am.' We never saw him, nor can he be beheld by mortal eyes." "We mean nothing less than that supreme God, who rules in heaven," replied they; "we mean the God on earth. Did you ever see him?" "Upon my honour," cried Carpalim, "they mean the pope." "Ay, ay," answered Panurge; "yea verily, gentlemen, I have seen three of them, whose sight has not much bettered me." "How!" cried they, "our sacred decretals inform us, that there never is more than one living." "I mean successively, one after the other," returned Panurge; "otherwise I never saw more than one at a time."

"O thrice and four times happy people!" cried they, "you are welcome, and more than double welcome!" They then kneeled down before us, and would have kissed our feet, but we would not suffer it, telling them that, should the pope come thither in his own person, 'tis all they could do to him. "No, certainly," answered they, "for we have already resolved upon the matter. We would kiss his bare arse, without boggling at it, and eke his two pounders: for he has a pair of them, the holy father, that he has; we find it so by our fine decretals, otherwise he could not be pope. So that, according to our subtile decretalin philosophy, this is a necessary consequence: he is pope; therefore, he has genitories (genitals) and should genitories no more be found in the world, the world could no more have a pope."

While they were talking thus, Pantagruel enquired of one of the coxswain's crew, who those persons were? he answered, "That they were the four estates of the island": and added, that we should be made as welcome as princes, since we had seen the pope. Panurge having been acquainted with this by Pantagruel, said to him in his ear, "I swear and vow, sir, 'tis even so; he that has patience may compass anything. Our seeing the pope hath done us no good: now, in the devil's name, 'twill do us a great deal." We then went ashore, and the whole country, men, women, and children, came to meet us as in a solemn procession. Our four estates cried out to them with a loud voice, "They have seen him! they have seen him! they have seen him!"

That proclamation being made, all the mob kneeled down before us, lifting up their hands towards heaven, and crying, "O happy men! O most happy!" and this acclamation lasted above a quarter of an hour.

Then came the Busby of the place, with all his pedagogues, ushers, and school-boys, whom he magisterially flogged, as they used to whip children in our country formerly, when some criminal was hanged, that they might remember it. This displeased Pantagruel, who said to them, "Gentlemen, if you do not leave off whipping these poor children, I'm gone." The people were amazed, hearing his Stentorean voice; and I saw a little hump with long fingers, say to the hypodidascal, "What! in the name of wonder do all those that see the pope grow as tall as yon huge fellow that threatens us! Ah! how I shall think time long till I have seen him too, that I may grow and look as big." In short, the acclamations were so great, that Homenas (so they called their bishop) hastened thither, on an unbridled mule, with green trappings, attended by his aposts (as they said) and his supposts, or officers, bearing crosses, banners, standards, canopies, torches, holy water-pots, &c. He too wanted to kiss our feet (as the good Christian Valfinien did to Pope Clement) saying, that one of their hypothetes, that's one of the scavengers, scowerers, and commentators of their holy decretals, had written, that, in the same manner as the Messiah, so long and so much expected by the Jews, at last appeared among them; so, on some happy day of God, the pope would come into that island; and that, while they waited for that blessed time, if any who had seen him at Rome, or elsewhere, chanced to come among them, they should be sure to make much of them, feast them plentifully, and treat them with a great deal of reverence. However, we civilly desired to be excused.

CHAPTER XLIX

HOW HOMENAS, BISHOP OF PAPIMANY, SHEWED US THE URANOPET DECRETALS

HOMENAS then said to us: " 'Tis enjoined us by our holy decretals to visit churches first, and taverns after. Therefore, not to decline that fine institution, let us go to church; we will afterwards go and feast ourselves." "Man of God," quoth friar John, "do you go before, we'll follow you: you spoke in the matter properly, and like a good Christian; 'tis long since we saw any such. For my part this rejoices my mind very much, and I verily believe that I shall have the better stomach after it. Well, 'tis a happy thing to meet with good men!" Being come near the gate of the church, we spied a huge thick book, gilt, and covered all over with precious stones, as rubies, emeralds, diamonds, and pearls, more, or at least as valuable as those which Augustus consecrated to Jupiter Capitolinus. This book hanged in the air, being fastened with two thick chains of gold to the zoophore of the porch. We looked on it, and admired it. As for Pantagruel, he handled it, and dandled it, and turned it as he pleased, for he could reach it without straining; and he protested that whenever he touched it, he was seized with a pleasant tickling at his fingers' end, new life and activity in his arms, and a violent temptation in his mind to beat one or two serjeants, or such officers, provided they were not of the shaveling kind. Homenas then said to us, "The law was formerly given to the Jews by Moses, written by God himself. At Delphos, before the portal of Apollo's temple, this sentence, ΓΝΩΘΙ ΣΕΑΥΤΟΝ, was found written with a divine hand. And some time after it, E I was also seen, and as divinely written and transmitted from heaven. Cybele's image was brought out of heaven, into a field called Pesinunt, in Phrygia; so was that of Diana to Tauris, if you will believe Euripides; the oriflambe, or holy standard, was transmitted out of heaven to the noble and most Christian kings of France, to fight against the unbelievers. In the reign of Numa Pompilius, second king of the Romans, the famous copper buckler, called Ancile, was seen to descend from heaven. At Acropolis, near Athens, Minerva's statue formerly fell from the empyreal heaven. In like manner the sacred decretals, which you see, were written with the hand of an angel, of the cherubim kind. You outlandish people will hardly believe this, I fear." "Little enough of conscience," said Panurge.—"And then," continued Homenas, "they were miraculously transmitted to us here from the very heaven of heavens; in the same manner as the river Nile is called Diipetes, by Homer, the father of all philosophy (the holy decretals always excepted). Now, because you have seen the pope, their evangelist and everlasting protector, we will give you leave to see and kiss them on the inside, if you think it meet. But then you must fast, three days before, and canonically confess; nicely and strictly mustering up, and inventorising your sins, great and small, so thick that one single circumstance of them may not 'scape you; as our holy decretals, which you see, direct. This will take up some time." "Man of God," answered Panurge, "we have seen and descried decrees, and eke decretals enough o' conscience; some on paper, others on parchment, fine and gay like any painted paper lantern, some on vellum, some in manuscript, and others in print: so you need not take half this pains to shew us these. We'll take the good-will for the deed, and thank you as much as if we had." "Ay, marry," said Homenas; "but you never saw these that are angelically written. Those in your country are only transcripts from ours; as we find it written by one of our old decretaline scholiasts. For me, do not spare me; I do not value the labour, so I may serve you: do but tell me whether you will be confessed, and fast only three short little days of God?" "As for confessing," answered Panurge, "there can be no great harm in it; but this same fasting, master of mine, will hardly down with us at this time, for we have so very much overfasted ourselves at sea, that the spiders have spun their cobwebs over our grinders. Do but look on this good friar John des Entomeures" (Homenas then courteously demy-clipped him about the neck): "some moss is growing in his throat, for want of bestirring and exercising his chaps." "He speaks the truth," vouched friar John; "I have so much fasted that I'm almost grown hump-shouldered." "Come then, let's go into the church," said Homenas; "and pray forgive us if for the present we do not sing you a fine high mass. The hour of mid-day is past, and after it our sacred decretals forbid us to sing mass, I mean your high and lawful mass. But I'll say a low and dry one for you." "I had rather have one moistened with some good Anjou wine," cried Panurge; "fall to, fall to your low mass, and dispatch." "Od's-boddikins!" quoth friar John, "it frets me to the guts that I must have an empty stomach at this time of day. For had I eaten a good breakfast, and fed like a monk, if he should chance to sing us the *requiem æternam dona eis domine,* I had then brought thither bread and wine for the traits passez (those that are gone before). Well, patience; pull away, and save tide: short and sweet, I pray you, and this for a cause."

CHAPTER L

HOW HOMENAS SHEWED US THE ARCH-TYPE, OR REPRESENTATION OF A POPE

MASS being mumbled over, Homenas took a huge bundle of keys out of a trunk near the head altar, and put thirty-two of them

559

into so many key-holes; put back so many springs; then with four-teen more master'd so many padlocks, and at last opened an iron window strongly barr'd above the said altar. This being done, in token of great mystery, he covered himself with wet sack-cloth, and drawing a curtain of crimson satin, showed us an image daubed over coarsely enough, to my thinking: then he touched it with a pretty long stick, and made us all kiss the part of the stick that had touched the image. After this he said unto us, "What think you of this image?" "It is the likeness of a pope," answered Pantagruel: "I know it by the triple crown, his furred aumusse, his rochet, and his slipper." "You are in the right," said Homenas; "it is the idea of that same good God on earth, whose coming we devoutly await, and whom we hope one day to see in this country. O happy, wished for, and much expected day! and happy, most happy you, whose propitious stars have so far favoured you as to let you see the living and real face of this good God on earth! by the single sight of whose picture we ob-tain full remission of all the sins which we remember that we have committed, as also a third part, and eighteen quarantaines of the sins which we have forgot: and indeed we only see it on high annual holidays."

This caused Pantagruel to say, that it was a work like those which Dædalus used to make: since, though it were deformed and ill drawn, nevertheless some divine energy, in point of pardons, lay hid and con-cealed in it. "Thus," said Friar John, "at Sevillé, the rascally beggars being one evening on a solemn holiday at supper in the spittle, one bragged of having got six blancs, or two-pence half-penny; another, eight liards, or two-pence; a third, seven carolus's, or six-pence: but an old mumper made his vaunts of having got three testons, or five shillings. 'Ah, but,' cried his comrades, 'thou hast a leg of God'; as if," continued Friar John, "some divine virtue could lie hid in a stench-ing ulcerated rotten shank." "Pray," said Pantagruel, "when you are for telling us some such nauseous tale, be so kind as not to forget to provide a bason, Friar John: I'll assure you, I had much ado to forbear bringing up my breakfast. Fie! I wonder a man of your coat is not asham'd to use thus the sacred name of God, in speaking of things so filthy and abominable; fie! I say. If among your monking tribes such an abuse of words is allowed, I beseech you leave it there, and do not let it come out of the cloisters." "Physicians," said Epistemon, "thus attribute a kind of divinity to some diseases: Nero also extolled mush-rooms, and, in a Greek proverb, termed them divine food, because with them he had poisoned Claudius his predecessor. But methinks, gentlemen, this same picture is not over-like our late popes. For I have seen them, not with their pallium, aumusse, or rochet on, but with helmets on their heads, more like the top of a Persian turbant; and while the christian commonwealth was in peace, they alone were most furiously and cruelly making war." "This must have been then," returned Homenas, "against the rebellious, heretical protestants; reprobates, who are disobedient to the holiness of this good God on earth. 'Tis not only lawful for him to do so, but it is enjoined him by the sacred decretals; and if any dare transgress one single iota against their commands, whether they be emperors, kings, dukes, princes, or commonwealths, he is immediately to pursue them with fire and sword, strip them of all their goods, take their kingdoms from them, proscribe them, anathematize them, and destroy not only their bodies, those of their children, relations, and others, but damn also their souls to the very bottom of the most hot and burning cauldron in hell." "Here, in the devil's name," said Panurge, "the people are no heretics; such as was our Raminagrobis, and as they are in Germany and England. You are christians of the best edition, all picked and culled for ought I see." "Ay, marry are we," returned Homenas, "and for that reason we shall all be saved. Now let us go and bless ourselves with holy-water, and then to dinner."

CHAPTER LI

TABLE-TALK IN PRAISE OF THE DECRETALS

NOW, topers, pray observe that while Homenas was saying his dry mass, three collectors, or licensed beggars of the church, each of them with a large basin, went round among the people, saying, with a loud voice, "Pray remember the blessed men who have seen his face." As we came out of the temple, they brought their basins brim full of papimany chink to Homenas, who told us that it was plentifully to feast with; and that, of this contribution and voluntary tax, one part should be laid out in good drinking, another in good eating, and the remainder in both: according to an admirable exposition hidden in a corner of their holy decretals: which was performed to a T, and that at a noted tavern not much unlike that of Will's at Amiens. Believe me, we tickled it off there with copious cramming, and numerous swilling.

561

I made two notable observations at that dinner: the one, that there was not one dish served up, whether of cabrittas, capons, hogs (of which latter there is great plenty in Papimany), pigeons, conies, leverets, turkies, or others, without abundance of magistral stuffing: the other, that every course, and the fruit also, were served up by unmarried females of the place, tight lasses, I'll assure you, waggish, fair, good-conditioned and comely, spruce and fit for business. They were clad all in fine long white albes, with two girts; their hair interwoven with narrow tape and purple ribbond, stuck with roses, gilly-flowers, marjoram, daffidown-dillies, thyme, and other sweet flowers.

At every cadence, they invited us to drink and bang it about, dropping us neat and genteel courtsies: nor was the sight of them unwelcome to all the company; and as for Friar John, he leered on them side-ways, like a cur that steals a capon. When the first course was taken off, the females melodiously sung as an epode in the praise of the sacrosanct decretals; and then the second course being served up, Homenas, joyful and cheery, said to one of the she-butlers, "Light here, Clerica." Immediately one of the girls brought him a tall-boy brim-full of extravagant wine. He took fast hold of it, and fetching a deep sigh, said to Pantagruel; "My lord, and you my good friends, here's t'ye, with all my heart: you are all very welcome." When he had tipped that off, and given the tall-boy to the pretty creature, he lifted up his voice and said; "Oh most holy decretals, how good is good wine found through your means!" "This is the best jest we have had yet," observed Panurge. "But it would still be a better," said Pantagruel, "if they could turn bad wine into good."

"O seraphic sextum!" (continued Homenas) "how necessary are you not to the salvation of poor mortals! O cherubic clementinæ! how perfectly the perfect institution of a true christian is contained and described in you! Oh angelical extravagants! how many poor souls that wander up and down in mortal bodies, through this vale of misery, would perish, were it not for you! When, ha! when shall this special gift of grace be bestowed on mankind, as to lay aside all other studies and concerns, to use you, to peruse you, to understand you, to know you by heart, to practise you, to incorporate you, to turn you into blood, and incentre you into the deepest ventricles of their brains, the inmost marrow of their bones, and most intricate labyrinth of their arteries? Then, ha then! and no sooner than then, nor otherwise than thus, shall the world be happy!" While the old man was thus running on, Epistemon arose and softly said to Panurge;

"For want of a close stool, I must e'en leave you for a moment or two: this stuff has unbunged the orifice of my mustard-barrel; but I'll not tarry long."

"Then, ah then!" continued Homenas, "no hail, frost, ice, snow, overflowing, or vis major: then plenty of all earthly goods here below. Then uninterrupted and eternal peace through the universe, an end of all wars, plunderings, drudgeries, robbing, assassinates, unless it be to destroy these cursed rebels the heretics. Oh, then, rejoicing, cheerfulness, jollity, solace, sports, and delicious pleasures, over the face of the earth. Oh! what great learning, inestimable erudition, and godlike precepts, are knit, linked, rivetted and morticed in the divine chapters of these eternal decretals!

"Oh! how wonderfully, if you read but one demy canon, short paragraph, or single observation of these sacrosanct decretals, how wonderfully, I say, do you not perceive to kindle in your hearts, a furnace of divine love, charity towards your neighbour, provided he be no heretic, bold contempt of all casual and sublunary things, firm content in all your affections, and extatic elevation of soul even to the third heaven."

CHAPTER LII

A CONTINUATION OF THE MIRACLES CAUSED BY THE DECRETALS

WISELY, brother Timothy," quoth Panurge; "did 'em, did 'em? He says blew: but for my part, I believe as little of it as I can. For, one day by chance I happened to read a chapter of them at Poictiers, at the most decretalipotent Scotch doctor's, and old Nick turn me into bumfodder, if this did not make me so hide-bound and costive, that for four or five days I hardly scumbered one poor butt of sir-reverence; and that too was full as dry and hard, I protest, as Catullus tells us were those of his neighbour Furius:

> " 'Nec toto decies cacas in anno,
>   Atque id durius est fabâ, & lapillis:
>   Quod tu si manibus teras, fricesque,
>   Non unquam digitum inquinare posses.' "

"Oh, ho," cry'd Homenas, "by'r lady, it may be you were then in the state of mortal sin, my friend." "Well turned," cried Panurge; "this was a new strain, egad."

"One day," said Friar John, "at Sevillé I had applied to my posteriors, by way of hind-towel, a leaf of an old clementinæ, which our rent-gatherer John Guimard, had thrown out into the green of our cloyster: now the devil broil me like a black pudding, if I was not so abominably plagued with chaps, chawns, and piles at the fundament, that the orifice of my poor nockandroe was in a most woeful pickle for I don't know how long." "By'r lady," cry'd Homenas, " 'twas a plain punishment of God, for the sin that you had committed in bewraying that sacred book, which you ought rather to have kissed and adored; I say with an adoration of latria, or of hyperdulia at least: the Panormitan never told a lie in the matter."

Saith Ponocrates; "At Montpelier, John Choüart having bought of the monks of St. Olary a delicate set of decretals, written on fine large parchment of Lamballe, to beat gold between the leaves, not so much as a piece that was beaten in them came to good, but all were dilacerated and spoiled." "Mark this," cried Homenas; " 'twas a divine punishment and vengeance."

"At Mans," said Eudemon, "Francis Cornu, apothecary, had turned an old set of extravagantes into waste paper: may I never stir, if whatever was lapt up in them was not immediately corrupted, rotten, and spoiled: incense, pepper, cloves, cinnamon, saffron, wax, cassia, rhubarb, tamarinds, all, drugs and spices, were lost without exception." "Mark, mark," quoth Homenas, "an effect of divine justice! This comes of putting the sacred scriptures to such profane uses."

"At Paris," said Carpalim, "Snip Groignet the taylor had turned an old clementinæ into patterns and measures, and all the clothes that were cut on them were utterly spoiled and lost; gowns, hoods, cloaks, cassocks, jerkins, jackets, waistcoats, capes, doublets, petticoats, corps de robes, vardingals, and so forth. Snip, thinking to cut a hood would cut you out a codpiece; instead of a cassock, he'd make you a high crown'd hat; for a waistcoat, he'd shape you out a rochet; on the pattern of a doublet, he'd make you a thing like a frying-pan; then his journeymen having stitched it up, did jag it and pink it at the bottom, and so it looked like a pan to fry chestnuts. Instead of a cape, he made a buskin; for a vardingal, he shaped a montero cap; and thinking to make a cloak, he'd cut out a pair of your big out-stroutting Switzers breeches, with panes like the outside of a tabor. Insomuch that Snip was condemned to make good the stuffs to all his customers;

and to this day poor cabbage's hair grows through his hood, and his arse through his pocket-holes." "Mark an effect of heavenly wrath and vengeance! cried Homenas.

"At Cahusac," said Gymnast, "a match being made by the lords of Estissac and viscount Lausun to shoot at a mark, Perotou had taken to pieces a set of decretals, and set one of the leaves for the white to shoot at: now I sell, nay I give and bequeath for ever and aye, the mould of my doublet to fifteen hundred hampers full of black devils, if ever any archer in the country (though they are singular marksmen in Guienne) could hit the white. Not the least bit of the holy scribble was contaminated or touched: nay, and Sansornin the elder, who held stakes, swore to us, figues dioures, hard figs (his greatest oath) that he had openly, visibly, and manifestly seen the bolt of Carquelin moving right to the round circle in the middle of the white; and that just on the point, when it was going to hit and enter, it had gone aside about seven foot and four inches wide of it towards the bakehouse."

"Miracle!" cry'd Homenas, "miracle! miracle! Clerica, come wench, light, light here. Here's to you all, gentlemen; I vow you seem to me very sound christians." While he said this, the maidens began to snicker at his elbow, grinning, giggling, and twittering among themselves. Friar John began to paw, neigh, and whinney at the snout's end, as one ready to leap, or at least to play the ass, and get up and ride tantivy to the devil, like a beggar on horseback.

"Methinks," said Pantagruel, " a man might have been more out of danger near the white of which Gymnast spoke, than was formerly Diogenes near another." "How's that?" asked Homenas; "what was it? Was he one of our decretalists?" "Rarely fallen in again egad," said Epistemon, returning from stool; "I see he will hook his decretals in, though by the head and shoulders."

"Diogenes," said Pantagruel, "one day, for pastime, went to see some archers that shot at butts, one of whom was so unskilful, that, when it was his turn to shoot, all the by-standers went aside, lest he should mistake them for the mark. Diogenes had seen him shoot extremely wide of it: so when the other was taking aim a second time, and the people removed at a great distance to the right and left of the white, he placed himself close by the mark; holding that place to be the safest, and that so bad an archer would certainly rather hit any other."

"One of the lord d'Estissac's pages at last found out the charm," pursued Gymnast, "and by his advice Perotou put in another white,

565

made up of some papers of Pouillac's lawsuit, and then every one shot cleverly."

"At Landerousse," said Rhizotomus, "at John Delif's wedding were very great doings, as 'twas then the custom of the country. After supper, several farces, interludes, and comical scenes were acted: they had also several morrice-dancers, with bells and tabors; and divers sorts of masks and mummers were let in. My schoolfellows, and I, to grace the festival to the best of our power (for, fine white and purple liveries had been given to all of us in the morning) contrived a merry mask with store of cockle-shells, shells of snails, periwinkles, and such other. Then for want of cuckoe-pint or priest pintle, lousebur, clote and paper, we made ourselves false faces with the leaves of an old sextum, that had been thrown by, and lay there for any one that would take it up; cutting out holes for the eyes, nose, and mouth. Now, did you ever hear the like since you were born? when we had played our little boyish antic tricks, and came to take off our sham faces, we appeared more hideous and ugly than the little devils that acted the passion at Douay: for our faces were utterly spoiled at the places which had been touched by those leaves: one had there the small pox; another, God's token, or the plague spot; a third, the crinckums; a fourth, the measles; a fifth, botches, pushes, and carbuncles; in short, he came off the least hurt, who only lost his teeth by the bargain." "Miracle!" bawled out Homenas, "miracle!"

"Hold, hold," cried Rhizotomus, " 'tisn't yet time to clap. My sister Kate, and my sister Ren, had put the crepines of their hoods, their ruffles, snuffekins, and neck-ruffs new washed, starched, and ironed, into that very book of decretals; for, you must know, it was covered with thick boards, and had strong clasps. Now by the virtue of God—" "Hold," interrupted Homenas, "what God do you mean?" "There is but one," answered Rhizotomus. "In heaven, I grant," replied Homenas, 'but we have another here on earth, d'ysee." "Ay, marry have we," said Rhizotomus; "but on my soul I protest I had quite forgot it.—Well then, by the virtue of God the Pope, their pinners, neck-ruffs, bibs, coifs, and other linen, turned as black as a charcoal-man's sack." "Miracle!" cried Homenas. "Here, Clerica, light me here; and prithee, girl, observe these rare stories." "How comes it to pass then," asked Friar John, "that people say,

" ' Ever since decrees had tails,
And gens d'arms lugg'd heavy mails,

566

Since each monk would have a horse,
All went here from bad to worse.' "

" ' *Depuis que decrets eurent ales,*
Et gens-d'armes porterent males,
Moines allerent à cheval,
En ce monde abonda tout mal.' "

"I understand you," answered Homenas: "this is one of the quirks and little satires of the new-fangled heretics."

CHAPTER LIII

HOW, BY THE VIRTUE OF THE DECRETALS, GOLD IS SUBTILLY DRAWN OUT OF FRANCE TO ROME

I WOULD," said Epistemon, "it had cost me a pint of the best tripe that ever can enter into gut, so we had but compared with the original the dreadful chapters, *execrabilis: de multa: si plures: de annatis per totum: nisi essent: cum ad monasterium: quod dilectio: mandatum;* and certain others, that draw every year out of France to Rome, four hundred thousand ducats and more."

"Do you make nothing of this?" asked Homenas. "Though methinks, after all, 'tis but little, if we consider that France, *the most christian,* is the only nurse the see of Rome has. However, find me in the whole world a book, whether of philosophy, physic, law, mathematics, or other human learning, nay, even, by my God, of the holy scripture itself, that will draw as much money thence? None, none, pshaw, tush, blurt, pish; none can. You may look till your eyes drop out of your head, nay, till doomsday in the afternoon, before you can find another of that energy; I'll pass my word for that.

"Yet these devilish heretics refuse to learn and know it. Burn 'em, tear 'em, nip 'em with hot pincers, drown 'em, hang 'em, spit 'em at the bunghole, pelt 'em, paut 'em, bruise 'em, beat 'em, cripple 'em, dismember 'em, cut 'em, gut 'em, bowell 'em, paunch 'em, thrash 'em, slash 'em, gash 'em, chop 'em, slice 'em, slit 'em, carve 'em, saw 'em, bethwack 'em, pare 'em, hack 'em, hew 'em, mince 'em, flea 'em, boil 'em, broil 'em, roast 'em, toast 'em, bake 'em, fry 'em, crucify 'em, crush 'em, squeeze 'em, grind 'em, batter 'em, burst 'em, quarter 'em, unlimb 'em, behump 'em, bethump 'em, belump 'em,

belabour 'em, pepper 'em, spitchcock 'em, and carbonade 'em on gridirons, these wicked heretics! decretalifuges, decretalicides, worse than
homicides, worse than patricides, decretalictiones of the devil of hell!

"As for you other good people, I must earnestly pray and beseech
you to believe no other thing, to think on, say, undertake, or do no
other thing than what's contained in our sacred decretals, and their
corollaries, this fine sextum, these fine clementinæ, these fine extravagantes. O deific books! So shall you enjoy glory, honour, exaltation,
wealth, dignities, and preferments in this world; be revered and
dreaded by all, preferred, elected, and chosen above all men.

"For, there is not under the cope of heaven a condition of men, out
of which you'll find persons fitter to do and handle all things, than
those who by divine prescience, eternal predestination, have applied
themselves to the study of the holy decretals.

"Would you chuse a worthy emperor, a good captain, a fit general
in time of war, one that can well foresee all inconveniences, avoid
all dangers, briskly and bravely bring his men on to a breach or at-
tack, still be on sure grounds, always overcome without loss of his
men, and know how to make a good use of his victory? Take me a
decretist.—No, no, I mean a decretalist." "Ho, the foul blunder,"
whisper'd Epistemon.

"Would you, in time of peace, find a man capable of wisely governing the state of a commonwealth, of a kingdom, of an empire, of a
monarchy; sufficient to maintain the clergy, nobility, senate and com-
mons in wealth, friendship, unity, obedience, virtue, and honesty?
Take a decretalist.

"Would you find a man who, by his exemplary life, eloquence, and
pious admonitions, may, in a short time, without effusion of human
blood, conquer the holy land, and bring over to the holy church the
mis-believing Turks, Jews, Tartars, Muscovites, Mammelucs, and Sar-
rabonites? Take me a decretalist.

"What makes, in many countries, the people rebellious and depraved,
pages saucy and mischievous, students sottish and duncical? Nothing
but that their governors, esquires, and tutors were not decretalists.

"But what, on your conscience, was it, d'ye think, that established,
confirmed and authorized those fine religious orders, with whom you
see the christian world everywhere adorned, graced, and illustrated,
as the firmament is with its glorious stars? The holy decretals.

"What was it that founded, underpropped, and fixed, and now
maintains, nourishes and feeds the devout monks and friars in convents,

monasteries, and abbies; so that did they not daily and mightily pray without ceasing, the world would be in evident danger of returning to its primitive chaos? The sacred decretals.

"What makes and daily increases the famous and celebrated patrimony of St. Peter in plenty of all temporal, corporeal, and spiritual blessings? The holy decretals.

"What made the holy apostolic see and pope of Rome, in all times, and at this present, so dreadful in the universe, that all kings, emperors, potentates, and lords, willing, nilling, must depend on him, hold of him, be crowned, confirmed, and authorized by him, come thither to strike sail, buckle, and fall down before his holy slipper, whose picture you have seen? The mighty decretals of God.

"I will discover you a great secret. The universities of your world have commonly a book, either open or shut, in their arms and devices: what book do you think it is?" "Truly, I do not know," answered Pantagruel; "I never read it." "It is the decretals," said Homenas, "without which the privileges of all universities would soon be lost. You must own, I have taught you this; ha, ha, ha, ha, ha!"

Here Homenas began to belch, to fart, to funk, to laugh, to slaver, and to sweat; and then he gave his huge greasy four-corner'd cap to one of the lasses, who clapt it on her pretty head with a great deal of joy, after she had lovingly buss'd it, a sure token that she should be first married. *"Vivat,"* cry'd Epistemon, *"fifat, bibat, pipat."*

"O apocalyptic secret!" continued Homenas, "light, light, Clerica, light here with double lanterns. Now for the fruit, virgins.

"I was saying then, that giving yourselves thus wholly to the study of the holy decretals, you'll gain wealth and honour in this world: I add, that in the next you'll infallibly be saved in the blessed kingdom of heaven, whose keys are given to our good God and decretaliarch. O my good God, whom I adore and never saw, by thy special grace open unto us, at the point of death at least, this most sacred treasure of our holy mother church, whose protector, preserver, butler, chief larder, administrator, and disposer thou art; and take care, I beseech thee, O Lord, that the precious works of supererogation, the goodly pardons, do not fail us in time of need: so that the devils may not find an opportunity to gripe our precious souls, and the dreadful jaws of hell may not swallow us. If we must pass through purgatory, thy will be done. It is in thy power to draw us out of it when thou pleasest." Here Homenas began to shed huge hot briny tears, to beat his breast, and kiss his thumbs in the shape of a cross.

569

CHAPTER LIV

HOW HOMENAS GAVE PANTAGRUEL SOME BON-CHRISTIAN
PEARS

EPISTEMON, Friar John, and Panurge, seeing his doleful catastrophe, began, under the cover of their napkins, to cry, meeow, meeow, meeow; feigning to wipe their eyes all the while as if they had wept. The wenches were doubly diligent, and brought brimmers of clementine wine to every one, besides store of sweetmeats; and thus the feasting was revived.

Before we arose from table, Homenas gave us a great quantity of fair large pears; saying, "Here, my good friends, these are singular good pears; you'll find none such anywhere else, I dare warrant. Every soil bears not everything, you know; India alone boasts black ebony; the best incense is produced in Sabæa; the sphragitid earth at Lemnos: so this island is the only place where such fine pears grow. You may, if you please, make seminaries with their kernels in your country."

"I like their taste extremely," said Pantagruel. "If they were sliced, and put into a pan on the fire with wine and sugar, I fancy they would be very wholesome meat for the sick, as well as for the healthy. Pray, what do you call them?" "No otherwise than you have heard," replied Homenas. "We are a plain downright sort of people, as God would have it, and call figs, figs; plums, plums; and pears, pears." "Truly," said Pantagruel, "if I live to go home (which I hope will be speedily, God willing), I'll set and graff some in my garden in Touraine, by the banks of the Loire, and will call them bon-christian or good-christian pears; for I never saw better christians than are these good papimans." "I'd like him two to one better yet," said Friar John, "would he but give us two or three cart-loads of yon buxom lasses." "Why, what would you do with them?" cried Homenas. Quoth Friar John, "No harm, only bleed the kind-hearted souls straight between the two great toes, with certain clever lancets of the right stamp: by which operation good-christian children would be inoculated upon them, and the breed be multiplied in our country, in which there are not many over good, the more's the pity."

"Nay, verily," replied Homenas, "we cannot do this; for you would make them tread their shoes awry, crack their pipkins, and spoil their shapes: you love mutton I see, you'll run at sheep; I know you by that same nose and hair of yours, though I never saw your face before. Alas! alas! how kind you are! And would you indeed damn your precious soul? Our decretals forbid this. Ah, I wish you had them at your fingers'-end." "Patience," said Friar John: "but, *si tu non vis dare, prœsta, quœsumus.* Matter of breviary. As for that, I defy all the world, and I fear no man that wears a head and a hood, though he were a chrystallin, I mean a decretalin doctor."

Dinner being over, we took our leave of the right reverend Homenas, and of all the good people, humbly giving thanks; and, to make them amends for their kind entertainment, promised them that, at our coming to Rome, we would make our applications so effectually to the pope, that he would speedily be sure to come to visit them in person. After this we went o'board.

Pantagruel, by an act of generosity, and as an acknowledgment of the sight of the pope's picture, gave Homenas nine pieces of double frized cloth of gold, to be set before the grates of the window. He also caused the church box, for its repairs and fabric, to be quite filled with double crowns of gold; and ordered nine hundred and fourteen angels to be delivered to each of the lasses, who had waited at table, to buy them husbands when they could get them.

CHAPTER LV

HOW PANTAGRUEL, BEING AT SEA, HEARD VARIOUS UNFROZEN WORDS

WHEN we were at sea, junketting, tippling, discoursing, and telling stories, Pantagruel rose and stood up to look out: then asked us, "Do you hear nothing, gentlemen? Methink I hear some people talking in the air, yet I can see nobody. Hark!" According to his command we listened, and with full ears sucked in the air, as some of you suck oysters, to find if we could hear some sound scattered through the sky; and to lose none of it, like the emperor Antoninus, some of us laid their hands hollow next to their ears: but all this would not do, nor could we hear any voice. Yet Pantagruel continued to assure us he heard various voices in the air, some of men and some of women.

At last we began to fancy that we also heard something, or at least that our ears tingled; and the more we listened, the plainer we discerned the voices, so as to distinguish articulate sounds. This mightily frightened us, and not without cause; since we could see nothing, yet heard such various sounds and voices of men, women, children, horses, &c., insomuch that Panurge cried out, "Cod's belly, there's no fooling with the devil; we are all beshit, let's fly. There's some ambuscade hereabouts. Friar John, art thou here, my love? I pr'ythee stay by me, old boy. Hast thou got thy swinging tool? See that it do not stick in the scabbard; thou never scourest it half as it should be. We are undone. Hark! They are guns, gad judge me; let's fly, I do not say with hands and feet, as Brutus said at the battle of Pharsalia; I say, with sails and oars: let's whip it away: I never find myself to have a bit of courage at sea; in cellars, and elsewhere, I have more than enough. Let's fly and save our bacon. I do not say this for any fear that I have; for I dread nothing but danger, that I don't; I always say it, that should not. The free archer of Baignolet said as much. Let's hazard nothing therefore, I say, lest we come off bluely. Tack about, helm a lee, thou son of a bachelor. Would I were now well in Quinquenois, tho' I were never to marry. Haste away, let's make all the sail we can; they'll be too hard for us; we are not able to cope with them; they are ten to our one, I'll warrant you; nay, and they are on their dunghill, while we do not know the country. They'll be the death of us. We'll lose no honour by flying: Demosthenes saith, that the man that runs away, may fight another day. At least, let us retreat to the leeward. Helm a lee; bring the main tack aboard, haul the bowlins, hoist the top-gallants; we are all dead men; get off, in the devil's name, get off."

Pantagruel, hearing the sad outcry which Panurge made, said, "Who talks of flying? Let's first see who they are; perhaps they may be friends: I can discover nobody yet, tho' I can see a hundred miles around me. But let's consider a little: I have read that a philosopher, named Perron, was of opinion that there were several worlds that touched each other in an equilateral triangle; in whose centre, he said, was the dwelling of truth: and that the words, ideas, copies, and images of all things past, and to come, resided there; round which was the age; and that with success of time part of them used to fall on mankind like rheums and mildews; just as the dew fell on Gideon's fleece, till the age was fulfilled.

"I also remember," continued he, "that Aristotle affirms Homer's words to be flying, moving, and consequently animated. Besides, Antiphanes said, that Plato's philosophy was like words, which, being

572

spoken in some country during a hard winter, are immediately congealed, frozen up, and not heard; for what Plato taught young lads could hardly be understood by them when they were grown old. Now," continued he, "we should philosophize and search whether this be not the place where those word are thawed.

"You'd wonder very much, should this be the head and lyre of Orpheus. When the Thracian women had torn him to pieces, they threw his head and lyre into the river Hebrus; down which they floated to the Euxine sea, as far as the island of Lesbos; the head continually uttering a doleful song, as it were, lamenting the death of Orpheus, and the lyre, with the wind's impulse, moving its strings, and harmoniously accompanying the voice. Let's see if we cannot discover them hereabouts."

CHAPTER LVI

HOW AMONG THE FROZEN WORDS PANTAGRUEL FOUND SOME ODD ONES

THE skipper made answer: "Be not afraid, my lord, we are on the confines of the Frozen Sea, on which, about the beginning of last winter, happened a great and bloody fight between the Arimaspians and the Nephelibates. Then the words and cries of men and women, the hacking, slashing, and hewing of battle-axes, the shocking, knocking, and jolting of armours and harnesses, the neighing of horses, and all other martial din and noise, froze in the air; and now the rigour of the winter being over, by the succeeding serenity and warmth of the weather, they melt and are heard."

"By jingo," quoth Panurge, "the man talks somewhat like; I believe him; but cou'dn't we see some of 'em? I think I have read, that, on the edge of the mountain on which Moses received the Judaic law, the people saw the voices sensibly."—"Here, here," said Pantagruel, "here are some that are not yet thawed." He then throwed us on the deck whole handfuls of frozen words, which seemed to us like your rough sugar plums, of many colours, like those used in heraldry; some words gules (this means also jests and merry sayings), some vert, some azur, some black, some or (this means fine fair words); and when we had somewhat warmed them between our hands, they melted like snow, and we really heard them, but could not understand them, for it was a barbarous gibberish. One of them only,

573

that was pretty big, having been warmed between friar John's hands, gave a sound much like that of chestnuts when they are thrown into the fire, without being first cut, which made us all start. "This was the report of a field-piece in its time," cried friar John.

Panurge prayed Pantagruel to give him some more: but Pantagruel told him, that to give words was the part of a lover. "Sell me some then, I pray you," cried Panurge. "That's the part of a lawyer," returned Pantagruel. "I would sooner sell you silence, though at a dearer rate; as Demosthenes formerly sold it by the means of his *arguentangina,* or silver squinsey."

However, he threw three or four handfuls of them on the deck; among which I perceived some very sharp words, and some bloody words, which, the pilot said, used sometimes to go back, and recoil to the place whence they came, but 'twas with a slit weesand: we also saw some terrible words, and some others not very pleasant to the eye.

When they had been all melted together, we heard a strange noise, hin, hin, hin, hin, his, tick, tock, taack, brededin, brededack, frr, frr, frr, bou, bou, bou, bou, bou, bou, bou, bou, track, track, trr, trr, trr, trrr, trrrrrr; on, on, on, on, on, on, ououououon, gog, magog, and I do not know what other barbarous words; which, the pilot said, were the noise made by the charging squadrons, the shock and neighing of horses.

Then we heard some large ones go off like drums and fifes, and others like clarions and trumpets. Believe me we had very good sport with them. I would fain have saved some merry odd words, and have preserved them in oil, as ice and snow are kept, and between clean straw. But Pantagruel would not let me saying, that 'tis a folly to hoard up what we are never like to want, or have always at hand, odd, quaint, merry, and fat words of gules, never being scarce among all good and jovial Pantagruelists.

Panurge somewhat vexed Friar John, and put him in the pouts; for he took him at his word, while he dreamt of nothing less. This caused the friar to threaten him with such a piece of revenge as was put upon G. Jousseaume, who having taken the merry Patelin at his word, when he had overbid himself in some cloth, was afterwards fairly taken by the horns like a bullock, by his jovial chapman, whom he took at his word like a man. Panurge, well knowing that threatened folks live long, bobbed, and made mouths at him, in token of derision, then cried, "Would I had here the word of the holy bottle, without being thus obliged to go further in pilgrimage to her."

CHAPTER LVII

HOW PANTAGRUEL WENT ASHORE AT THE DWELLING OF GASTER, THE FIRST MASTER OF ARTS IN THE WORLD

THAT day Pantagruel went ashore in an island, which, for situation and governor, may be said not to have its fellow. When you just come into it, you find it rugged, craggy, barren, unpleasant to the eye, painful to the feet, and almost as inaccessible as the mountain of Dauphiné, which is somewhat like a toad-stool, and was never climbed, as any can remember, by any but Doyac, who had the charge of king Charles the VIIIth's train of artillery.

This same Doyac, with strange tools and engines, gained that mountain's top, and there he found an old ram. It puzzled many a wise head to guess how it got thither. Some said that some eagle, or great horn-coot, having carried it thither, while 'twas yet a lambkin, it had got away, and saved itself among the bushes.

As for us, having with much toil and sweat overcome the difficult ways at the entrance, we found the top of the mountain so fertile, healthful, and pleasant, that I thought I was then in the true garden of Eden, or earthly paradise, about whose situation our good theologues are in such a quandary, and keep such a pother.

As for Pantagruel, he said, that there was the seat of Arete (that's as much as to say, virtue) described by Hesiod. This, however, with submission to better judgments. The ruler of this place was one master Gaster, the first master of arts in the world. For, if you believe that fire is the great master of arts, as Tully writes, you very much wrong him and yourself: alas, Tully never believed this. On the other side, if you fancy Mercury to be the first inventor of arts, as our ancient druids believed of old, you are mightily beside the mark. The satirist's sentence, that affirms master Gaster to be master of all arts, is true. With him peacefully resided old goody Penia, alias Poverty, the mother of the ninety-nine Muses, on whom Porus, the lord of Plenty, formerly begot Love, that noble child, the mediator of heaven and earth, as Plato affirms in Symposio.

We were all obliged to pay our homage and swear allegiance to that mighty soverign; for he is imperious, severe, blunt, hard, uneasy, inflexible: you cannot make him believe, represent to him, or persuade him anything.

He does not hear: and, as the Egyptians said that Harpocrates, the god of silence, named Sigalion in Greek, was astomé, that is, without a mouth; so Gasta was created without ears, even like the image of Jupiter in Candia.

He only speaks by signs: but those signs are more readily obeyed by every one, than the statutes of senates, or commands of monarchs; neither will he admit the least let or delay in his summons. You say, that when a lion roars, all the beasts at a considerable distance round about, as far as his roar can be heard, are seized with a shivering. This is written, 'tis true; I have seen it. I assure you, that at master Gaster's command, the very heavens tremble, and all the earth shakes: his command is called, Do this or die. Needs must when the devil drives; there's no gainsaying of it.

The pilot was telling us how, on a certain time, after the manner of the members that mutinied against the belly, as Æsop describes it, the whole kingdom of the Somates went off into a direct faction against Gaster, resolving to throw off his yoke: but they soon found their mistake, and most humbly submitted; for otherwise they had all been famished.

What company soever he is in, none dispute with him for precedence or superiority; he still goes first, though kings, emperors, or even the pope, were there. So he held the first place at the council of Basle; though some will tell you, that the council was tumultuous, by the contentions and ambition of many for priority.

Every one is busied, and labours to serve him; and indeed, to make amends for this, he does this good to mankind, as to invent for them all arts, machines, trades, engines, and crafts: he even instructs brutes in arts which are against their nature, making poets of ravens, jack-daws, chattering jays, parrots and starlings, and poetresses of magpies, teaching them to utter human languages, speak and sing; and all for the gut. He reclaims and tames eagles, gerfaulcons, faulcons gentle, sakers, lanniers, gosse-hawks, spar-hawks, merlins, hagards, passengers, wild rapacious birds; so that setting them free in the air, whenever he thinks fit, as high and as long as he pleases, he keeps them suspended, straying, flying, hovering and courting him above the clouds: then on a sudden he makes them stoop, and come down amain from heaven next to the ground; and all for the gut.

Elephants, lions, rhinocerotes, bears, horses, mares, and dogs, he teaches to dance, prance, vault, fight, swim, hide themselves, fetch and carry what he pleases; and all for the gut.

Salt and fresh-water fish, whales and the monsters of the main, he brings up from the bottom of the deep; wolves he forces out of the woods, bears out of the rocks, foxes out of their holes, and serpents out of the ground; and all for the gut.

In short, he is so unruly, that in his rage he devours all men and beasts; as was seen among the Vascons, when Q. Metellus besieged them in the Sertorian wars; among the Saguntines besieged by Hannibal; among the Jews besieged by the Romans, and six hundred more; and all for the gut. When his regent Penia takes a progress, wherever she moves, all senates are shut up, all statutes repealed, all orders and proclamations vain: she knows, obeys, and has no law. All shun her, in every place chusing rather to expose themselves to shipwrecks at sea, and venture through fire, rocks, caves, and precipices, than be seized by that most dreadful tormentor.

CHAPTER LVIII

HOW, AT THE COURT OF THE MASTER OF INGENUITY, PAN- TAGRUEL DETESTED THE ENGASTRIMYTHES AND THE GASTROLATERS

AT the court of that great master of ingenuity, Pantagruel observed two sorts of troublesome and too officious apparitors, whom he very much detested. The first were called Engastrimythes; the others, Gastrolaters.

The first pretended to be descended of the ancient race of Eurycles; and for this brought the authority of Aristophanes, in his comedy called The Wasps; whence of old they were called Euryclians, as Plato writes, and Plutarch in his book of the cessation of oracles. In the holy decrees, 26 qu. 3, they are styled Ventriloqui; and the same name is given them in Ionian by Hippocrates, in his fifth book of epid. as men who speak from the belly. Sophocles calls them Sternomantes. These were soothsayers, enchanters, cheats, who gulled the mob, and seemed not to speak and give answers from the mouth, but from the belly.

Such a one, about the year of our Lord 1513, was Jacoba Rodogina, an Italian woman of mean extract; from whose belly we, as well as an infinite number of others at Ferrara, and elsewhere, have often heard the voice of the evil spirit speak; low, feeble, and small indeed, but yet very distinct, articulate and intelligible, when she was sent for, out of curiosity, by the lords and princes of the Cisalpine Gaul. To remove all manner of doubt, and be assured that this was not a trick, they used to have her stripped stark naked, and caused her mouth and nose to be stopped. This evil spirit would be called Curled-pate, or Cincinnatulo, seeming pleased when any called him by that name; at which he was always ready to answer. If any spoke to him of things past or present, he gave pertinent answers, sometimes to the amazement of the hearers: but if of things to come, then the devil was gravelled, and used to lie as fast as a dog can trot. Nay, sometimes he seemed to own his ignorance; instead of an answer, letting out a rousing fart, or muttering some words with barbarous and uncouth inflexions, and not to be understood.

As for the Gastrolaters, they stuck close to one another in knots and gangs. Some of them merry, wanton, and soft as so many milksops; others louring, grim, dogged, demure and crabbed; all idle, mortal foes to business, spending half their time in sleeping, and the rest in doing nothing, a rent-charge and dead unnecessary weight on the earth, as Hesiod saith; afraid, as we judged, of offending or lessening their paunch. Others were masked, disguised, and so oddly dressed, that it would have done you good to have seen them.

There's a saying, and several ancient sages write, that the skill of nature appears wonderful in the pleasure which she seems to have taken in the configuration of sea-shells, so great is their variety in figures, colours, streaks, and imitable shapes. I protest the variety we perceived in the dresses of the gastrolatrous coquillons was not less. They all owned Gaster for their supreme God, adored him as a God, offered him sacrifices as to their omnipotent Deity, owned no other God, served, loved, and honoured him above all things.

You would have thought that the holy apostle spoke of this, when he said, Phil. chap. 3. "Many walk, of whom I have told you often, and now tell you even weeping, that they are enemies of the cross of Christ; whose end is destruction, whose God is their belly." Pantagruel compared them to the cyclops Polyphemus, whom Euripides brings in speaking thus: "I only sacrifice to myself (not to the gods) and to this belly of mine, the greatest of all the gods."

CHAPTER LIX

OF THE RIDICULOUS STATUE MANDUCE; AND HOW, AND
WHAT THE GASTROLATERS SACRIFICE TO THEIR VENTRI-
POTENT GOD

WHILE we fed our eyes with the sight of the phyzzes and actions of these lounging gulli-gutted Gastrolaters, we on a sudden heard the sound of a musical instrument called a bell; at which all of them placed themselves in rank and file, as for some mighty battle, every one according to his office, degree and seniority.

In this order, they moved towards master Gaster, after a plump, young, lusty gorbellied fellow, who, on a long staff, fairly gilt, carried a wooden statue grossly carved, and as scurvily daubed over with paint; such a one as Plautus, Juvenal, and Pomp. Festus describe it. At Lyons, during the carnival, 'tis called Maschecrouste, or Gnaw crust; they call this Manduce.

It was a monstrous, ridiculous, hideous figure, fit to fright little children: its eyes were bigger than its belly, and its head larger than all the rest of its body; well mouth-cloven, however, having a goodly pair of wide, broad jaws, lined with two rows of teeth, upper tier and under tier, which by the magic of a small twine hid in the hollow part of the golden staff, were made to clash, clatter, and rattle dreadfully one against another; as they do at Metz with St. Clement's dragon.

Coming near the Gastrolaters, I saw they were followed by a great number of fat waiters and tenders, laden with baskets, dossers, hampers, dishes, wallets, pots and kettles. Then under the conduct of Manduce, and singing I don't know what dithyrambics, crepalocomes, and epenons, opening their baskets and pots, they offered to their God,

White hippocras, with dry toasts.	Soft bread.
White bread.	Household bread.
Brown bread.	Capirotadoes.
Carbonadoes, six sorts.	Cold loins of veal, with spice.
Brawn.	Zinziberine.
Sweet-breads.	Beatille pies.
Fricassees, nine sorts.	Brewess.
Monastical brewess.	Marrow-bones, toast and cabbage.
Gravy soupe.	Hashes.
Hotch-pots.	

Eternal drink intermixed. Brisk delicate white-wine led the van; claret and champaign followed, cool, nay, as cold as the very ice, I say; filled and offered in large silver cups. Then they offered,

Chitterlings garnished with mustard.
Sausages.
Neats' tongues.
Hung-beef.
Chines and pease.
Hogs' haslets.
Scotch-collops.
Puddings.
Carvelats.
Bolonia sausages.
Hams.
Brawn heads.
Powdered venison, with turnips.
Pickled olives.

All this associated with sempiternal liquor. Then they housed within his muzzle,

Legs of mutton with shallots.
Ollas.
Lumber pies, with hot sauce.
Ribs of pork with onion sauce.
Roast capons, basted with their own dripping.
Caponets.
Caviar and toast.
Fawns, deer.
Hares, leverets.
Partridges, and young partridges.
Plovers.
Dwarf-herons.
Teals.
Duckers.
Bitterns.
Shovelers.
Curlews.
Wood-hens.
Coots, with leeks.
Fat kids.
Shoulders of mutton, with capers.
Sirloins of beef.
Breasts of veal.
Phesants, and phesant poots.
Peacocks.
Storks.
Woodcocks.
Snipes.
Hortolans.
Turkey cocks, hen turkeys, and turkey poots.
Stock doves, and wood-culvers.
Pigs, with wine sauce.
Blackbirds, owsels, and rayles.
Moor-hens.
Bustards, and bustard poots.
Fig-peckers.
Young Guinea hens.
Flemmings.
Cignets.
A reinforcement of vinegar intermixt.
Venison pasties.
Lark-pies.
Dormice-pies.
Cabretto-pasties.
Roe-buck pasties.
Pigeon-pies.
Kid-pasties.
Capon-pies.

Bacon-pies.
Souced hogs'-feet.
Fry'd pasty-crust.
Forced capons.
Parmesan cheese.
Red and pale hippocras.
Gold-peaches.
Artichokes.
Dry and wet sweetmeats, 78 sorts.
Boiled hens, and fat capons marinated.
Pullets with eggs.
Chickens.
Rabbits, and sucking rabbits.
Quails, and young quails.
Pigeons, squobbs, and squeakers.
Herons, and young herons.
Fieldfares.
Olives.
Thrushes.
Young sea-ravens.
Geese, goslins.
Queests.
Widgeons.

Mavises.
Grouses.
Turtles.
Doe-conies.
Hedge-hogs.
Snytes.
Then large puffs.
Thistle-finches.
Whore's farts.
Fritters.
Cakes, sixteen sorts.
Crisp wafers.
Quince tarts.
Curds and cream.
Whipp'd cream.
Preserv'd myrabolans.
Gellies.
Welch barrapyclids.
Macaroons.
Tarts, twenty sorts.
Lemon-cream, Rasberry-cream, &c.
Comfits, 100 colours.
Cream-wafers.
Cream-cheese.

Vinegar brought up the rear to wash the mouth, and for fear of the squinsy: also toasts to scower the grinders.

CHAPTER LX

WHAT THE GASTROLATERS SACRIFICED TO THEIR GOD ON INTERLARDED FISH-DAYS

PANTAGRUEL did not like this pack of rascally scoundrels, with their manifold kitchen sacrifices, and would have been gone, had not Epistemon prevailed with him to stay and see the end of the farce. He then asked the skipper, what the idle lob-cocks used to sacrifice to their gorbellied god on interlarded fish-days? "For his first course," said the skipper, "they give him:

581

Caviar.
Botargoes.
Fresh butter.
Pease soup.
Spinage.
Fresh herrings, full roed.
Sallads, a hundred varieties, of cresses, sodden hop-tops, bishops-cods, cellery, sives, rampions, jew's ears (a sort of mushrooms that sprout out of old elders), asparagus, woodbind, and a world of others.
Red herrings.
Pilchards.
Anchovies.
Fry of tunny.
Cauliflowers.
Beans.
Salt salmon.
Pickled griggs.
Oysters in the shell.

"Then he must drink, or the devil would gripe him at the throat: this therefore they take care to prevent, and nothing's wanting. Which being done, they give him lampreys with hippocras sauce:

Gurnards.
Salmon trouts.
Barbels, great and small.
Roaches.
Cockrells.
Minews.
Thornbacks.
Sleeves.
Sturgeons.
Sheath-fish.
Mackerels.
Maids.
Plaice.
Fry'd oysters.
Cockles.
Prawns.
Smelts.
Rock-fish.
Gracious lords.
Sword-fish.
Skate-fish.
Lamprills.
Jegs.
Pickerells.

Golden carps.
Burbates.
Salmons.
Salmon-peels.
Dolphins.
Barn trouts.
Miller's thumbs.
Precks.
Bret-fish.
Flounders.
Sea-nettles.
Mullets.
Gudgeons.
Dabs and sandings.
Haddocks.
Carps.
Pykes.
Botitoes.
Rochets.
Sea-bears.
Sharplings.
Tunnies.
Silver eels.
Chevins.

Cray-fish.
Pallours.
Shrimps.
Congers.
Porpoises.
Bases.
Shads.
Murenes, a sort of lampreys.
Craylings.
Smys.
Turbots.
Trouts, not above a foot long.
Salmons.
Meagers.
Sea-breams.
Halibuts.
Soles.
Dog's tongue, or kind fool.
Muscles.
Lobsters.
Great prawns.
Dace.

Bleaks.	Fausens, and griggs.	Moor-game.
Tenches.	Eel pouts.	Pearches.
Ombers.	Tortoises.	Loaches.
Fresh-cods.	Serpents, *i.e.* wood-	Crab-fish.
Dried-melwells.	eels.	Snails and whelks.
Darefish.	Dorees.	Frogs.

"If, when he had crammed all this down his guttural trap-door, he did not immediately make the fish swim again in his paunch, death would pack him off in a trice. Special care is taken to antidote his godship with vine-tree sirup. Then is sacrificed to him, haberdines, poor-jack, minglemangled, mishmashed, &c.

Eggs   fry'd,   beaten,   butter'd, Green-fish.
   poach'd, harden'd, boil'd, broil'd, Sea-batts.
   stew'd, slic'd, roasted in the em- Cod's ounds.
   bers, toss'd in the chimney, &c. Sea-pikes.
Stock-fish.

"Which to concoct and digest the more easily, vinegar is multiplied. For the latter part of their sacrifies they offer,

Rice milk, and hasty pudding.	Skirret-root.
Butter'd wheat, and flummery.	White-pot.
Watergruel, and milk porridge.	Raisins.
Frumenty, and bony-claber.	Dates.
Stew'd prunes, and bak'd bullace.	Chestnuts and wallnuts.
Pistachoes, or fistic-nuts.	Filberts.
Figs.	Parsnips.
Almond-butter.	Artichokes.

Perpetuity of soaking with the whole.

" 'Twas none of their fault, I'll assure you, if this same god of theirs was not publicly, preciously, and plentifully served in his sacrifices, better yet than Heliogabalus's idol; nay, more than Bel and the Dragon in Babylon under king Belshazzar. Yet Gaster had the manners to own that he was no God, but a poor, vile, wretched creature. And as king Antigonus, first of the name, when one Hermodotus (as poets will flatter, especially princes), in some of his fustian dubbed him a God, and made the sun adopt him for his son, said to him; 'My lysanophore (or, in plain English, my groom of the close-stool), can give thee the lie'; so master Gaster very civilly used to send back his bigoted worshippers to his close-tool, to see, smell, taste, philosophise, and examine what kind of divinity they could pick out of his sir-reverence."

CHAPTER LXI

HOW GASTER INVENTED MEANS TO GET AND PRESERVE CORN

THOSE gastrolatrous hobgoblins being withdrawn, Pantagruel carefully minded the famous master of arts, Gaster. You know that, by the institution of nature, bread has been assigned him for provision and food; and that, as an addition to this blessing, he should never want the means to get bread.

Accordingly, from the beginning he invented the smith's art, and husbandry to manure the ground, that it might yield him corn: he invented arms, and the art of war, to defend corn; physic and astronomy, with other parts of mathematics, which might be useful to keep corn a great number of years in safety from the injuries of the air, beasts, robbers, and purloiners: he invented water, wind, and hand-mills, and a thousand other engines to grind corn, and turn it into meal; leaven to make the dough ferment, and the use of salt to give it a savour; for he knew that nothing bred more diseases than heavy, unleavened, unsavoury bread.

He found a way to get fire to bake it; hour-glasses, dials, and clocks to mark the time of its baking; and, as some countries wanted corn, he contrived means to convey it out of one country into another.

He had the wit to pimp for asses and mares, animals of different species, that they might copulate for the generation of a third, which we call mules, more strong and fit for hard service than the other two. He invented carts and waggons, to draw him along with greater ease; and, as seas and rivers hindered his progress, he devised boats, gallies, and ships (to the astonishment of the elements) to waft him over to barbarous, unknown, and far distant nations, thence to bring, or thither to carry corn.

Besides, seeing that, when he had tilled the ground, some years the corn perished in it for want of rain in due season, in others rotted, or was drowned by its excess, sometimes spoiled by hail, eat by worms in the ear, or beaten down by storms, and so his stock was destroyed on the ground; we were told that ever since the days of yore, he has found out a way to conjure the rain down from heaven only with cutting certain grass, common enough in the field, yet known to very few, some of which was then shewn us. I took it to be the same as the plant, one of whose boughs being dipped by Jove's priest into the Agrian fountain, on the Lycian mountain in Arcadia, in time of drought, raised vapours which gathered into clouds, and then dissolved into rain, that kindly moistened the whole country.

Our master of arts was also said to have found a way to keep the rain up in the air, and make it fall into the sea; also to annihilate the hail, suppress the winds, and remove storms as the Mathanensians of Trœzene used to do. And as in the fields thieves and plunderers sometimes stole, and took by force the corn and bread which others had toiled to get, he invented the art of building towns, forts, and castles, to hoard and secure that staff of life. On the other hand, finding none in the fields, and hearing that it was hoarded up and secured in towns, forts, and castles, and watched with more care than ever were the golden pippins of the Hesperides, he turned engineer, and found ways to beat, storm, and demolish forts and castles, with machines and warlike thunderbolts, battering rams, balists, and catapults, whose shapes were shown us, not over-well understood by our engineers, architects, and other disciples of Vitruvius; as master Philebert de l'Orme king Megistus's principal architect has owned to us.

And seeing that sometimes all these tools of destruction were baffled by the cunning subtilty or the subtle cunning (which you please) of fortifiers, he lately invented cannons, field-pieces, culverins, mortarpieces, basilisks, murdering instruments that dart iron, leaden and brazen balls, some of them out-weighing huge anvils. This by the means of a most dreadful powder, whose hellish compound and effect has even amazed nature, and made her own herself out-done by art; the Oxydracian thunders, hails, and storms, by which the people of that name immediately destroyed their enemies in the field, being but mere potguns to these. For, one of our great guns, when used is more dreadful, more terrible, more diabolical, and maims, tears, breaks, slays, mows down, sweeps away more men, and causes a greater consternation and destruction, than a hundred thunderbolts.

CHAPTER LXII

GASTER having secured himself with his corn within strongholds, has sometimes been attacked by enemies; his fortresses, by that thrice three-fold curst instrument, levelled and destroyed; his dearly beloved corn and bread snatched out of his mouth, and sacked by a tyrannic force: therefore he then sought means to preserve his walls, bastions, rampiers, and sconces from cannon shot, and to hinder the bullets from hitting him, stopping them in their flight, or at least from doing him or the besieged and walls any damage. He shewed us a trial of this, which has been since used by Fronton, and is now common among the pastimes and harmless recreations of the Thelemites. I'll tell you how he went to work, and pray for the future be a little more ready to believe what Plutarch affirms to have tried. Suppose a herd of goats were all scampering as if the devil drove 'em, do but put a bit of eringo into the mouth of the hindmost nanny, and they will all stop stock still, in the time you can tell three.

Thus Gaster, having caused a brass faulcon to be charged, with a sufficient quantity of gunpowder, well purged from its sulphur, and curiously made up with fine camphire; he then had a suitable ball put into the piece, with twenty-four little pellets like hail shot, some round, some pearl fashion: then taking his aim, and levelling it at a page of his, as if he would have hit him on the breast; about sixty strides off the piece, half way between it and the page in a right line, he hanged on a gibbet by a rope a very large siderite, or ironlike stone, otherwise called herculean, formerly found on Ida in Phrygia by one Magnes, as Nicander writes, and commonly called loadstone: then he gave fire to the prime on the piece's touch-hole, which in an instant consuming the powder, the ball and hail-shot were with incredible violence and swiftness hurried out of the gun at its muzzle, that the air might penetrate to its chamber, where otherwise would have been a vacuum; which nature abhors so much, that this universal machine, heaven, air, land, and sea, would sooner return to the primitive chaos, than admit the least void anywhere. Now the ball and small shot, which threatened the page with no less than quick destruction, lost their impetuosity, and remained suspended and hovering round the stone; nor did any of them, notwithstanding the fury with which they rushed, reach the page.

586

Master Gaster could do more than all this yet, if you'll believe me: for he invented a way how to cause bullets to fly backwards, and recoil on those that sent 'em, with as great a force, and in the very numerical parallel for which the guns were planted. And indeed, why should he have thought this difficult, seeing the herb ethiopis opens all locks whatsoever; and an echineis or remora, a silly weakly fish, in spite of all the winds that blow from the 32 points of the compass, will in the midst of a hurricane make you the biggest first rate remain stock still as if she were becalmed, or the blustering tribe had blown their last: nay, and with the flesh of that fish, preserved with salt, you may fish gold out of the deepest well that was ever sounded with a plummet; for it will certainly draw up the precious metal. Since, as Democritus affirmed, and Theophrastus believed and experienced, that there was an herb at whose single touch an iron wedge, tho' never so far driven into a huge log of the hardest wood that is, would presently come out: and 'tis this same herb your hickways, alias woodpeckers, use, when with some mighty ax any one stops up the hole of their nests, which they industriously dig and make in the trunk of some sturdy tree. Since stags and hinds, when deeply wounded with darts, arrows, and bolts, if they do but meet the herb called dittany, which is common in Candia, and eat a little of it, presently the shafts came out, and all's well again: even as kind Venus cured her beloved by-blow Æneas, when he was wounded on the right thigh with an arrow by Juturna, Turnus's sister. Since the very wind of laurels, fig-trees, or sea calves, makes the thunder sheer off, insomuch that it never strikes them. Since at the sight of a ram, mad elephants recover their former senses. Since mad bulls coming near wild fig-trees, called caprificii, grow tame, and will not budge a foot, as if they had the cramp. Since the venomous rage of vipers is assuaged if you but touch them with a beechen bough. Since also Euphorian writes, that in the isle of Samos, before Juno's temple was built there, he has seen some beasts called neades, whose voice made the neighbouring places gape and sink into a chasm and abyss. In short, since elders grow of a more pleasing sound, and fitter to make flutes, in such places where the crowing of cocks is not heard, as the ancient sages have writ, and Theophrastus relates: as if the crowing of a cock dulled, flattened, and perverted the wood of the elder, as it is said to astonish and stupefy with fear that strong and resolute animal, a lion. I know that some have understood this of wild elder, that grows so far from towns or villages, that the crowing of cocks cannot reach near it; and doubtless that sort ought to be preferred to the stenching common elder, that grows about decayed and ruined places: but others have understood this in a higher sense, not literal, but allegorical, according to the method of the Pythagoreans: as when it was said that Mercury's statue could not be made of every sort of wood; to which sentence they gave this sense; that God is not to be worshipped in a vulgar form, but in a chosen and religious manner. In the same manner by this elder, which grows far from places where cocks are heard, the ancients meant, that the wise and studious ought not to give their minds to trivial or vulgar music, but to that which is celestial, divine, angelical, more abstracted, and brought from remoter parts, that is, from a region where the crowing of cocks is not heard: for, to denote a solitary and unfrequented place, we say, cocks are never heard to crow there.

CHAPTER LXIII

HOW PANTAGRUEL FELL ASLEEP NEAR THE ISLAND OF CHANEPH, AND OF THE PROBLEMS PROPOSED TO BE SOLVED WHEN HE WAKED

THE next day merrily pursuing our voyage, we came in sight of the island of Chaneph, where Pantagruel's ship could not arrive, the wind chopping about, and then failing us so that we were becalmed, and could hardly get ahead, tacking about from starboard to larboard, and from larboard to starboard, though to our sails we had added drabblers.

With this accident we were all out of sorts, moping, drooping, metagrabolized, as dull as dun in the mire, in C sol fa ut flat, out of tune, off the hinges, and I don't know howish, without caring to speak one single syllable to each other.

Pantagruel was taking a nap, slumbering and nodding on the quarter deck, by the cuddy, with an Heliodorus in his hand; for still it was his custom to sleep better by book than by heart.

Epistemon was conjuring, with his astrolabe, to know what latitude we were in.

Friar John was got into the cook-room, examining, by the ascendant of the spits, and the horoscope of ragousts and fricassees, what time o'day it might then be.

Panurge (sweet baby!) held a stalk of pantagruelion, alias hemp, next his tongue, and with it made pretty bubbles and bladders.

Gymnast was making tooth pickers with lentisk.

Ponocrates, dozing, dozed, and dreaming, dreamed; tickled himself to make himself laugh, and with one finger scratched his noddle where it did not itch.

Carpalim, with a nut shell, and a trencher of verne [that't a card in Gascony] was making a pretty little merry windmill, cutting the card longways into four slips, and fastening them with a pin to the convex of the nut, and its concave to the tared side of the gunnel of the ship.

Eusthenes, bestriding one of the guns, was playing on it with his fingers, as if it had been a trump-marine.

Rhizotomus, with the soft coat of a field tortoise, alias ycleped a mole, was making himself a velvet purse.

Xenomanes was patching up an old weather-beaten lantern with a hawk's jesses.

Our pilot (good man!) was pulling maggots out of the seamen's noses.

At last Friar John, returning from the forecastle, perceived that Pantagruel was awake. Then breaking this obstinate silence, he briskly and cheerfully asked him how a man should kill time, and raise good weather during a calm at sea?

Panurge, whose belly thought his throat cut, backed the motion presently, and asked for a pill to purge melancholy.

Epistemon also came on, and asked how a man might be ready to bepiss himself with laughing, when he has no heart to be merry.

Gymnast, arising, demanded a remedy for a dimness of eyes?

Ponocrates, after he had a while rubbed his noddle and shaked his ears, asked, how one might avoid dog-sleep? "Hold," cried Pantagruel, "the peripatetics have wisely made a rule, that all problems, questions, and doubts, which are offered to be solved, ought to be certain, clear, and intelligible. What do you mean by dog's-sleep?" "I mean," answered Ponocrates, "to sleep fasting in the sun at noon-day, as the dogs do."

Rhizotomus, who lay stooping on the pump, raised his drowsy head, and lazily yawning, by natural sympathy, set almost every one in the ship a yawning too: then he asked for a remedy against oscitations and gapings.

Xenomanes, half puzzled and tired out with new vamping his antiquated lantern, asked, how the hold of the stomach might be so well ballasted and freighted from the keel to the main hatch, with stores well stowed, that our human vessels might not heel, or be walt, but well trimmed and stiff?

Carpalim, twirling his diminutive windmill, asked how many motions are to be felt in nature, before a gentleman may be said to be hungry?

Eusthenes, hearing them talk, came from between decks, and from the capstern called out to know why a man that's fasting, bit by a serpent also fasting, is in greater danger of death, than when man and serpent have eat their breakfasts? Why a man's fasting spittle is poisonous to serpents and venomous creatures?

"One single solution may serve for all your problems, gentlemen," answered Pantagruel, "and one single medicine for all such symptoms and accidents. My answer shall be short, not to tire you with a long needless train of pedantic cant. The belly has no ears, nor is it to be filled with fair words: you shall be answered to content by signs and gestures. As formerly at Rome, Tarquin, the proud, its last king, sent an answer by signs to his son Sextus, who was among the Gabii (at Gabii). (Saying this, he pulled the string of a little bell, and Friar John hurried away to the cook-room.) The son having sent his father a messenger, to know how he might bring the Gabii (Gabini) under a close subjection; the king, mistrusting the messenger, made him no answer, and only took him into his privy garden, and in his presence, with his sword, lopt off the heads of the tall poppies that were there. The express returned without any other dispatch: yet having related to the prince what he had seen his father do, he easily understood that by those signs he advised him to cut off the heads of the chief men in the town, the better to keep under the rest of the people."

CHAPTER LXIV

HOW PANTAGRUEL GAVE NO ANSWER TO THE PROBLEMS

PANTAGRUEL then asked, what sorts of people dwelled in that damn'd island? "They are," answered Xenomanes, "all hypocrites, holy mountebanks, tumblers of beads, mumblers of Ave Maries, spiritual comedians, sham saints, hermits, all of them poor rogues, who, like the hermit of Lormont, between Blaye and Bourdeaux, live wholly on alms given them by passengers." "Catch me there if you can," cried Panurge: "may the devil's head cook conjure my bum-gut into a pair of bellows, if ever you find me among them. Hermits, sham saints, living forms of mortification, holy mountebanks, avaunt, in the name of your father Satan, get out of my sight: when the devil's a hog, you shall eat bacon. I shall not forget yet a while our fat Concilipetes of Chesil. O that Beelzubub and Astaroth had counselled them to hang themselves out of the way, and they had don't! we had not then suffered so much by devilish storms as we did for having seen them. Hark'ee me, dear rogue, Xenomanes, my friend, I prithee are these hermits, hypocrites, and eves-droppers, maids or married? Is there anything of the feminine gender among them? Could a body hypocritically take there a small hypocritical touch? Will they lie backwards, and let out their fore-rooms?" "There's a fine question to be asked!" cried Pantagruel. "Yes, yes," answered Xenomanes; "you may find there many goodly hypocritesses, jolly spiritual actresses, kind hermitesses, women that have a plaguy deal of religion; then there's the copies of 'em, little hypocritillons, sham-sanctitos, and hermitillons." "Foh! away with them," cried friar John; "a young saint, an old devil!" (Mark this, an old saying, and as true a one as a young whore, an old saint.) "Were there not such," continued Xenomanes, "the isle of Chaneph, for want of a multiplication of progeny, had long ere this been desert and desolate."

Pantagruel sent them by Gymnast, in the pinnace, seventy-eight thousand fine pretty little gold half-crowns, of those that are marked with a lantern. After this he asked, "What's o'clock?" "Past nine," answered Epistemon. " 'Tis then the best time to go to dinner," said Pantagruel; "for the sacred line, so celebrated by Aristophanes in his play called Concionatores, is at hand, never failing when the shadow is decempedal.

"Formerly, among the Persians, dinner time was at a set hour only for kings: as for all others, their appetite and their belly was their clock; when that chimed, they thought it time to go to dinner. So we find in Plautus a certain parasite making a heavy do, and sadly railing at the inventors of hour-glasses and dials, as being unnecessary things, there being no clock more regular than the belly.

"Diogenes, being asked at what times a man ought to eat, answered, 'The rich when he is hungry, the poor when he has anything to eat.' Physicians more properly say, that the canonical hours are,

" 'To rise at five, to dine at nine,
To sup at five, to sleep at nine.' "

591

"The famous king Petosiris's magic was different."—Here the officers for the gut came in, and got ready the tables and cupboards; laid the cloth, whose sight and pleasant smell were very comfortable; and brought plates, napkins, salts, tankards, flaggons, tall-boys, ewers, tumblers, cups, goblets, basons, and cisterns.

Friar John, at the head of the stewards, sewers, yeomen of the pantry, and of the mouth, tasters, carvers, cup-bearers, and cupboard-keepers, brought four stately pasties, so huge, that they put me in mind of the four bastions at Turin. Odsfish, how manfully did they storm them! What havoc did they make with the long train of dishes that came after them! How bravely did they stand to their pan-puddings, and paid off their dust! How merrily did they soak their noses!

The fruit was not yet brought in, when a fresh gale at west and by north began to fill the main-course, mizen-sail, foresail, tops, and top-gallants: for which blessing they all sung divers hymns of thanks and praise.

When the fruit was on the table, Pantagruel asked; "Now tell me, gentlemen, are your doubts fully resolved or no?" "I gape and yawn no more," answered Rhizotomus. "I sleep no longer like a dog," said Ponocrates. "I have cleared my eyesight," said Gymnast. "I have broke my fast," said Eusthenes: "so that for this whole day I shall be secure from the danger of my spittle.

Asps.	Basilisks.	Cuhersks, two-tongued
Amphisbenes.	Fitches.	adders
Anerudutes.	Sucking water-snakes.	Amphibious serpents.
Abedissimons.	Black wag-legflies.	Cenchres.
Alhatrafs.	Spanish flies.	Cockatrices.
Ammobates.	Catoblepes.	Dipsades.
Apimaos.	Horn'd snakes.	Domeses.
Alhatabans.	Caterpillars.	Dryinades.
Aractes.	Crocodiles.	Dragons.
Asterions.	Toads.	Elopes.
Alcharates.	Night-mares.	Enhydrides.
Arges.	Mad dogs.	Falvises.
Spiders.	Colotes.	Galeotes.
Starry Lizards.	Cychriodes.	Harmenes.
Attelabes.	Cafezates.	Handons.
Ascalabotes.	Cauhares.	Icles.
Hæmorrhoids.	Snakes.	Jarraries.

Ilicines.	Phalangs.	Deaf-asps.
Pharao's mice.	Pemphedrons.	Horse-leeches.
Kedusudures.	Pine-tree-worms.	Salt-haters.
Sea-hares.	Rutulæ.	Rot-serpents.
Chalcidic newts.	Worms.	Stink-fish.
Footed serpents.	Rhagia.	Stuphes.
Manticores.	Rhaganes.	Sabrins.
Mulures.	Salamanders.	Blood-sucking flies.
Mouse-serpents.	Sloe-worms.	Hornfretters.
Shrew-mice.	Stellions.	Scolopendres.
Miliares.	Scorpones.	Tarantulas.
Megalaunes.	Scorpions.	Blind-worms.
Spitting-asps.	Horn-worms.	Tetragnathias.
Porphyri.	Scalavotins.	Teristals.
Parcades.	Solofruidars.	Vipers, &c"

CHAPTER LXV

HOW PANTAGRUEL PAST THE TIME WITH HIS SERVANTS

IN what hierarchy of such venomous creatures do you place Panurge's future spouse?" asked friar John. "Art thou speaking ill of women?" cried Panurge; "thou mangy scoundrel, thou sorry, noddy-peaked shaveling monk?" "By the cenomanic paunch and gixie," said Epistemon, "Euripides has written, and makes Andromache say it, that by industry, and the help of the gods, men had found remedies against all poisonous creatures; but none was yet found against a bad wife."

"This flaunting Euripides," cried Panurge, "was gabbling against women every foot, and therefore was devoured by dogs, as a judgment from above; as Aristophanes observes.—Let's go on. Let him speak that's next." "I can leak now like any stone-horse," said then Epistemon. "I am," said Xenomanes, "full as an egg and round as a hoop; my ship's hold can hold no more, and will now make shift to bear a steady sail." Said Carpalim, "A truce with thirst, a truce with hunger; they're strong, but wine and meat are stronger." "I'm no more in the dumps," cried Panurge; "my heart's a pound lighter. I'm in the right cue now, as brisk as a body-louse, and as merry as a beggar. For my part, I know what I do when I drink; and 'tis a true thing (though 'tis in your Euripides) that is said by that jolly toper Silenus of blessed memory, that

> " 'The man's emphatically mad
> Who drinks the best, yet can be sad.'

"We must not fail to return our humble and hearty thanks to the Being, who, with this good bread, this cool delicious wine, these good meats and rare dainties, removes from our bodies and minds these pains and perturbations, and at the same time fills us with pleasure and with food.

"But methinks, sir, you did not give an answer to friar John's question; which, as I take it, was, how to raise good weather?" "Since you ask no more than this easy question," answered Pantagruel, "I'll strive to give you satisfaction; and some other time we'll talk of the rest of the problems, if you will.

"Well then, friar John asked how good weather might be raised. Have we not raised it? Look up and see our full top-sails: Hark! how the wind whistles through the shrouds, what a stiff gale it blows; observe the rattling of the tacklings, and see the sheets that fasten the main-sail behind; the force of the wind puts them upon the stretch. While we passed our time merrily, the dull weather also passed away; and while we raised the glasses to our mouths, we also raised the wind by a secret sympathy in nature.

"Thus Atlas and Hercules clubbed to raise and underprop the falling sky, if you'll believe the wise mythologists; but they raised it some half an inch too high; Atlas, to entertain his guest Hercules more pleasantly, and Hercules to make himself amends for the thirst which sometimes before had tormented him in the deserts of Africa."— "Your good father," said friar John, interrupting him, "takes care to free many people from such an inconveniency: for I have been told by many venerable doctors that his chief butler, Turelupin, saves above eighteen hundred pipes of wine yearly, to make servants, and all comers and goers drink before they are dry."—"As the camels and dromedaries of a caravan," continued Pantagruel, "use to drink for the thirst that's past, for the present, and for that to come; so did Hercules: and being thus excessively raised, this gave new motion to the sky, which is that of *titubation and trepidation,* about which our crackbrain'd astrologers make such a pother." "This," said Panurge, "makes the saying good,

594

> " 'While jolly companions carouse it together
> A fig for the storm, it gives way to good weather.' "

"Nay," continued Pantagruel, "some will tell you, that we have not only shortened the time of the calm, but also much disburthened the ship; not like Æsop's basket, by easing it of the provisions, but by breaking our fasts; and that a man is more terrestrial and heavy when fasting, than when he has eaten and drank, even as they pretend that he weighs more dead than living. However it is, you'll grant they are in the right, who take their morning's draught, and breakfast before a long journey; then say that the horses will perform the better, and that a spur in the head, is worth two in the flank; or, in the same horse dialect,

> " 'That a cup in the pate
> Is a mile in the gate.'

"Don't you know that formerly the Amycleans worshipped the noble father Bacchus above all other gods, and gave him the name of Psila, which in the Doric dialect signifies wings: for, as the birds raise themselves by a towering flight with their wings above the clouds, so, with the help of soaring Bacchus, the powerful juice of the grape, our spirits are exalted to a pitch above themselves, our bodies are more sprightly, and their earthly parts become soft and pliant."

CHAPTER LXVI

HOW, BY PANTAGRUEL'S ORDER, THE MUSES WERE SALUTED NEAR THE ISLE OF GANABIM

THIS fair wind and as fine talk brought us in the sight of a high land, which Pantagruel discovering afar off, shewed it Xenomanes, and asked him, "Do you see yonder to the leeward a high rock, with two tops much like mount Parnassus in Phocis?" "I do plainly," answered Xenomanes; " 'tis the isle of Ganabim. Have you a mind to go ashore there?" "No," returned Pantagruel. "You do well indeed," said Xenomanes; "for there is nothing worth seeing in the place. The people are all thieves: yet there is the finest fountain in the world, and a very large forest towards the right top of the mountain. Your fleet may take in wood and water there."

"He that spoke last spoke well," quoth Panurge; "let us not by any means be so mad as to go among a parcel of thieves and sharpers. You make take my word for't, this place is just such another, as, to my knowledge, formerly were the islands of Sark and Herm, between the smaller and the greater Britain; such as were the Poncropolis of Philip in Thrace; islands of thieves, banditti, picaroons, robbers, ruffians, and murderers, worse than rawhead and bloody bones, and full as honest as the senior fellows of the college of iniquity, the very outcasts of the county-gaols common-side. As you love yourself, do not go among 'em; if you go, you'll come off but bluely, if you come off at all. If you will not believe me, at least believe what the good and wise Xenomanes tells you; for may I never stir if they are not worse than the very cannibals; they would certainly eat us alive. Do not go among 'em, I pray you; 'twere safer to take a journey to hell. Hark! by cod's body, I hear 'em ringing the alarm bell most dreadfully, as the Gascons about Bourdeaux used formerly to do against the commissaries and officers for the tax on salt, or my ears tingle. Let's shear off."

"Believe me, sir," said friar John, "let's rather land; we'll rid the world of that vermin, and inn there for nothing." "Old Nick go with thee for me," quoth Panurge. "This rash hare-brained devil of a friar fears nothing, but ventures and runs on like a mad devil as he is, and cares not a rush what becomes of others; as if every one was a monk, like his friarship. A pox on grinning honour, say I." "Go to," returned the friar, "thou mangy noddypeak! thou forlorn druggle-headed sneaksby! and may a million of black devils anatomize thy cockle brain. The hen-hearted rascal is so cowardly, that he bewrays himself for fear every day. If thou art so afraid, dunghill, don't go, stay here and be hanged, or go and hide thy loggerhead under madam Proserpine's petticoat."

Panurge hearing this, his breech began to make buttons; so he slunk in in an instant, and went to hide his head down in the breadroom among the musty biscuits, and the orts and scraps of broken bread.

Pantagruel in the meantime said to the rest, "I feel a pressing retraction in my soul, which like a voice admonishes me not to land there. Whenever I have felt such a motion within me, I have found myself happy in avoiding what it directed me to shun, or in undertaking what it prompted me to do! and never had occasion to repent following its dictates."

"As much," said Epistemon, "is related of the dæmon of Socrates,

596

so celebrated among the academics." "Well then, sir," said friar John, "while the ship's crew water, have you a find to have good sport? Panurge is got down somewhere in the hold, where he is crept into some corner, and lurks like a mouse in a cranny: let 'em give the word for the gunner to fire yon gun over the round-house on the poop; this will serve to salute the muses of this Antiparnassus; besides, the powder does but decay in it." "You are i'th' right," said Pantagruel; "here, give the word for the gunner."

The gunner immediately came, and was ordered by Pantagruel to fire that gun, and then charge it with fresh powder; which was soon done. The gunners of the other ships, frigates, gallions, and gallies of the fleet, hearing us fire, gave every one a gun to the island; which made such a horrid noise, that you'd have sworn heaven had been tumbling about our ears.

CHAPTER LXVII

HOW PANURGE BEWRAYED HIMSELF FOR FEAR; AND OF THE HUGE CAT RODILARDUS, WHICH HE TOOK FOR A PUNY DEVIL

PANURGE, like a wild, addle-pated, giddy goat, sallies out of the bread-room in his shirt, with nothing else about him but one of his stockings, half on half off, about his heel, like a rough-footed pigeon; his hair and beard all bepowdered with crums of bread, in which he had been over head and ears, and a huge and mighty puss partly wrapt up in his other stocking. In this equipage, his chops moving like a monkey's who's a louse-hunting, his eyes staring like a dead pig's, his teeth chattering, and his bum quivering, the poor dog fled to friar John, who was then sitting by the chain-wales of the starboard-side of the ship, and prayed him heartily to take pity on him, and keep him in the safeguard of his trusty bilbo; swearing by his share of Papimany, that he had seen all hell broke loose.

"Woe's me, my Jacky," cried he, "my dear Johnny, my old crony, my brother, my ghostly father! all the devils keep holiday, all the devils keep their feast to-day, man: pork and pease choke me, if ever thou sawest such preparations in thy life for an infernal feast. Dost thou see the smoke of hell's kitchens?" (This he said, showing him the smoke of the gunpowder above the ships.) "Thou never sawest so

597

many damned souls since thou wast born; and so fair, so bewitching they seem, that one would swear they are stygian ambrosia. I thought at first (God forgive me) that they had been English souls; and I don't know, but that this morning the isle of Horses, near Scotland, was sacked, with all the English who had surprised it, by the lords of Termes and Essay."

Friar John, at the approach of Panurge, was entertained with a kind of a smell that was not like that of gunpowder, nor altogether so sweet as musk; which made him turn Panurge about, and then he saw that his shirt was dismally bepawed and bewrayed, with fresh sir-reverence. The retentive faculty of the nerve, which restrains the muscle called sphincter ('tis the arse-hole, an't please you) was relaxated by the violence of the fear which he had been in during his fantastic visions. Add to this, the thundering noise of the shooting, which seems more dreadful between decks than above. Nor ought you to wonder at such a mishap; for one of the symptoms and accidents of fear is, that it often opens the wicket of the cupboard wherein second-hand meat is kept for a time. Let's illustrate this noble theme with some examples.

Messer Pantolfe de la Cassina, of Sienna, riding post from Rome, came to Chamberry, and alighting at honest Vinet's house, took one of the pitchforks in the stable; then turning to the inn-keeper, said to him, *"Da Roma in qua io non son andato del corpo. Di gratia piglia in mano questa forcha, & fa mi paura."* "I have not had a stool since I left Rome. I pray thee take this pitchfork, and fright me." Vinet took it, and made several offers, as if he would in good earnest have hit the signor; but did not: so the Sienese said to him, *"Si tu non fai altramente, tu non fai nulla: pero sforzati di adoperarli più guagliardamente."* "If thou dost not go another way to work, thou hadst as good do nothing: therefore try to bestir thyself more briskly." With this, Vinet lent him such a swinging stoater with the pitch-fork souce between the neck and the collar of his jerkin, that down fell signore on the ground arsyversy, with his spindle shanks wide straggling over his pole. Then mine host, sputtering, with a full-mouthed laugh, said to his guest, "By Belzebub's bum gut, much good may do you, signore Italiano. Take notice this is *datum Camberiaci,* given at Chamberry." 'Twas well the Sienese had untrussed his points, and let down his drawers: for this physic worked with him as soon as he took it; and as copious was the evacuation, as that of nine buffaloes and fourteen missificating arch-lubbers. Which operation being over, the mannerly Sienese courteously gave mine host a whole bushel of thanks, saying to him, *"Io ti ringratio, bel messere; cosi facendo tu m'ai esparmiata la speza d'un servitiale."* "I thank thee, good landlord; by this thou hast e'en saved me the expence of a clyster."

I'll give you another example of Edward the fifth, king of England. Master Francis Villon, being banished France, fled to him, and got so far into his favour, as to be privy to all his household affairs. One day the king, being on his close-stool, showed Villon the arms of France, and said to him, "Dost thou see what respect I have for thy French kings? I have none of their arms anywhere but in this back-side, near my close-stool." "Odd's life," said the buffoon, "how wise, prudent and careful of your health, your highness is! How carefully your learned doctor Thomas Linacer looks after you! He saw that, now you grow old, you are inclined to be somewhat costive, and every day were fain to have an apothecary; I mean, a suppository or clyster thrust into royal nockandroe: so he has, much to the purpose, induced you to place here the arms of France; for the very sight of them puts you into such a dreadful fright, that you immediately let fly, as much as would come from eighteen squattering *bonasi of Pœonia*. And if they were painted in other parts of your house, by jingo, you would presently conskite yourself wherever you saw them. Nay, had you but here a picture of the great oriflamb of France, odds bodikins, your tripes and bowels would be in no small danger of dropping out at the orifice of your posteriors.—But henh, henh, *atque iterum* henh.

> " 'A silly cockney am I not,
>   As ever did from Paris come?
> And with a rope and sliding knot
>   My neck shall know what weighs my bum.'

"A cockney of short reach, I say, shallow of judgment, and judging shallowly, to wonder, that you should cause your points to be untrussed in your chamber before you come into this closet. By'r lady, at first I thought your close-stool had stood behind the hangings of your bed! otherwise it seemed very odd to me you should untruss so far from the place of evacuation. But now I find I was a gull, a wittal, a woodcock, a mere ninny, a jolt-head, a noddy, a changeling, a calf-lolly, a doddipole. You do wisely, by the mass, you do wisely: for had not you been ready to clap your hind-face on the mustard-pot as soon as you came within sight of these arms, mark ye me, cop's body, the bottom of your breeches had supplied the office of a close-stool."

Friar John, stopping the handle of his face with his left hand, did, with the forefinger of the right, point out Panurge's shirt to Pantagruel; who, seeing him in this pickle, scared, appalled, shivering, raving, staring, bewrayed, and torn with the claws of the famous cat Rodilardus, could not chuse but laugh, and said to him; "Pr'ythee what wouldst thou do with this cat?" "With this cat," quoth Panurge, "the devil scratch me, if I did not think it had been a young soft-chined devil, which with this same stocking instead of mittain, I had snatched up in the great hutch of hell, as thievishly as any sizar of Montague college could have done. The devil take Tybert: I feel it has all bepinked my poor hide, and drawn on it to the life I don't know how many lobsters' whiskers." With this he threw his boar-cat down.

"Go, go," said Pantagruel, "be bathed and cleaned, calm your fears, put on a clean shirt, and then your cloaths." "What! do you think I am afraid?" cried Panurge. "Not I, I protest: by the testicles of Hercules, I am more hearty, bold, and stout, though I say it that should not, than if I had swallowed as many flies as are put into plumb-cakes, and other paste at Paris, from Mid-summer to Christmas.——But what's this? hah! oh, ho! how the devil came I by this? Do you call this what the cat left in the malt, filth, dirt, dung, dejection, fœcal matter, excrement, stercoration, sir-reverence, ordure, second-hand meats, fewmets, stronts, scybal or syparathe? 'Tis Hibernian saffron, I protest. Hah, hah, hah! it is Irish saffron, by shaint Pautrick, and so much for this time. Selah. Let us drink."

THE AUTHOR'S PROLOGUE

THE FIFTH BOOK

INDEFATIGABLE topers, and you thrice precious martyrs of the smock, give me leave to put a serious question to your worships, while you are idly stroking your cod-pieces, and I myself not much better employed: Pray, why is it that people say that men are not such sots now-a-days as they were in the days of yore? Sot is an old word, that signifies a dunce, dullard, jolthead, gull, wittal, or noddy, one without guts in his brains, whose cockloft is unfurnished, and, in short, a fool. Now would I know, whether you would have us understand by this same saying, as indeed you logically may, that formerly men were fools, and in this generation are grown wise? How many and what dispositions made them fools? How many and what dispositions were wanting to make 'em wise? Why were they fools? How should they be wise? Pray, how came you to know that men were formerly fools? How did you find that they are now wise? Who the devil made 'em fools? Who a God's name made 'em wise? Who d'ye think are most, those that loved mankind foolish, or those that love it wise? How long has it been wise? How long otherwise? Whence proceeded the foregoing folly? Whence the following wisdom? Why did the old folly end now, and no later? Why did the modern wisdom begin now, and no sooner? What were we the worse for the former folly? What the better for the succeeding wisdom? How should the ancient folly be come to nothing? How should this same new wisdom be started up and established?

Now answer me, an't please you: I dare not adjure you in stronger terms, reverend sirs, lest I make your pious fatherly worships in the least uneasy. Come, pluck up a good heart; speak the truth and shame the devil, that enemy to paradise, that enemy to truth: be cheery, my lads; and if you are for me, take me off three or five bumpers of the best, while I make an halt at the first part of the sermon; then answer my question. If you are not for me, avaunt! avoid Satan! for I swear by my great grandmother's placket, that if you don't help me to solve that puzzling problem, I will, nay, I already do repent having proposed it: for still I must remain nettled and gravelled, and the devil a bit I know how to get off. Well, what say you? I' faith, I begin to smell you out. You are not yet disposed to give me an answer; nor I neither, by these whiskers. Yet to give some light into the business, I'll e'en tell you what had been anciently foretold in the matter, by a venerable doc, who being moved by the spirit in a prophetic vein, wrote a book ycleped, the prelatical bagpipe. What do you think the old fornicator saith? Hearken, you old noddies, hearken now or never.

> "The jubilee's year, when all, like fools were shorn,
> Is about thirty [trente] supernumerary,
> O want of veneration! fools they seem'd,
> But, persevering, with long breves, at last
> No more they shall be gaping greedy fools:
> For they shall shell the shrub's delicious fruit,
> Whose flow'r they in the spring so much had fear'd."

Now you have it, what do you make on't? The seer is ancient, the style laconic, the sentences dark, like those of Scotus, though they treat of matters dark enough in themselves. The best commentators on that good father take the jubilee after the thirtieth, to be the years that are included in this present age till 1550, [there being but one jubilee every fifty years]. Men shall no longer be thought fools next green pease season.

The fools, whose number, as Solomon certifies, is infinite, shall go to pot like a parcel of mad bedlamites as they are: and all manner of folly shall have an end, that being also numberless, according to Avicenna, *maniæ infinitæ sunt species*. Folly having been driven back and hidden towards the centre, during the rigour of the winter, 'tis now to be seen on the surface, and buds out like the trees. This is as plain as a nose in a man's face: you know it by experience; you see it. And it was formerly found out by that great good man Hippocrates, Aphorism. *Veræ etenim maniæ,* &c. This world therefore, wisifying itself, shall no longer dread the flower and blossoms of beans every coming spring, that is, as you may piously believe, bumper in hand, and tears in eyes, in the woful time of lent, which used to keep them company.

Whole cartloads of books, that seemed florid, flourishing, and flowery, gay and gaudy, as so many butterflies; but in the main were tiresome, dull, soporiferous, irksome, mischievous, crabbed, knotty, puzzling, and dark as those of whining Heraclitus, as unintelligible as the numbers of Pythagoras, that king of the bean, according to l. 2. sat. 6, Horace: those books, I say, have seen their best days, and shall soon come to nothing, being delivered to the executing worms, and merciless petty-chandlers: such was their destiny, and to this they were predestinated.

In their stead beans in cod are started up; that is, these merry and fructifying Pantagruelian books, so much sought now-a-days, in expectation of the following jubilee's period; to the study of which writings all people have given their minds, and accordingly have gained the name of wise.

Now, I think I have fairly solved and resolved your problem: then reform, and be the better for it. Hem once or twice, like hearts of oak; stand to your pan-puddings, and take me off your bumpers, nine go-downs, and huzza! since we are like to have a good vintage, and misers hang themselves. Oh! they'll cost me an estate in hempen collars if fair weather hold. For I hereby promise to furnish them with twice as much as will do their business, on free-cost, as often as they will take the pains to dance at a rope's end, providently to save charges, to the no small disappointment of the finisher of the law.

Now, my friends, that you may put in for a share of this new wisdom, and shake off the antiquated folly this very moment, scratch me out of your scrolls, and quite discard the symbol of the old philosopher with the golden thigh, by which he has forbidden you to eat beans: for you may take it for a truth, granted among all professors in the science of good eating, that he enjoined you not to taste of them only with the same kind intent with the fresh water physician Amer, late lord of Camelotiere, kinsman to the lawyer of that name, who forbad his patients the wing of the partridge, the rump of the chicken, and the neck of the pigeon, saying, *"Ala mala, rumpum dubium, collum bonum, pelle remotâ."* For the dunsical dog-leech was so selfish as to reserve them for his own dainty chops, and allowed his poor patients little more than the bare bones to pick, lest they should overload their squeamish stomachs.

To the heathen philosopher succeeded a pack of capusions, monks, who forbid us the use of beans, that is, Pantagruel books. They seem to follow the example of Philoxenus and Gnatho, one of whom was a Sicilian, of fulsome memory, the ancient master-builders of their monastic cram-gut voluptuousness; who, when some dainty bit was served up at a feast, filthily used to spit on it, that none but their nasty selves might have the stomach to eat of it, though their liquorish chops watered never so much after it.

So those hideous, snotty, pthisicky, eves-dropping, musty, moving forms of mortification, both in public and private, curse those dainty books, and like toads spit their venom upon them.

Now, though we have in our mother-tongue several excellent works in verse and prose, and, heaven be praised, but little left of the trash and trumpery stuff of those dunsical mumblers of Ave Maries, and the barbarous foregoing Gothic age; I have made bold to chuse to chirrup and warble my plain ditty, or, as they say, to whistle like a goose among the swans, rather than be thought deaf among so many pretty poets and eloquent orators. And thus I am prouder of acting the clown, or any other under part, among the many ingenious actors in this noble play, than of herding among those mutes, who, like so many shadows and cyphers, only serve to fill up the house, and make up a number; gaping and yawning at the flies, and pricking up their lugs, like so many Arcadian asses, at the striking up of the music; thus silently giving to understand, that their fopships are tickled in the right place.

Having taken this resolution, I thought it would be amiss to move my Diogenical tub, that you might not accuse me of living without example. I see a swarm of our modern poets and orators, your Colinets, Marots, Herouets, Saint Gelias, Selels, Masuels, and many more; who having commenced masters in Apollo's academy on mount Parnassus, and drunk brimmers at the caballian fountain, among the nine merry muses, have raised our vulgar tongue, and made it a noble and everlasting structure. Their works are all Parian marble, alabaster, porphyry, and royal cement: they treat of nothing but heroic deeds, mighty things, grave and difficult matters; and this in a crimson, alamode, rhetorical style. Their writings are all divine nectar, rich, racy, sparkling, delicate and luscious wine. Nor does our sex wholly engross this honour; ladies have had their share of the glory: one of them, of the royal blood of France, whom it were a profanation but to name here, surprises the age at once by her transcendent and inventive genius in her writings, and the admirable graces of her style. Imitate those great examples, if you can; for my part, I cannot. Every one, you know, cannot go to Corinth. When Solomon built the temple, all could not give gold by handfuls; each offered a shekel of gold.

Since then 'tis not in my power to improve our architecture as much as they, I am e'en resolved to do like Renault of Montauban: I'll wait on the masons, set on the pot for the masons, cook for the stone-cutters; and since it was not my good luck to be cut out for one of them, I will live and die the admirer of their divine writings.

As for you, little envious prigs, snarling bastards, puny Zoiluses, you'll soon have railed your last: go hang yourselves, and chuse you out some well-spread oak, under whose shade you may swing in state, to the admiration of the gaping mob; you shall never want rope enough. While I here solemnly protest before my Helicon, in the presence of my nine mistresses the muses, that if I live yet the age of a dog, eked out with that of three crows, sound wind and limbs, like the old Hebrew captain Moses, Xenophilus the musician, and Demonax the philosopher, by arguments no ways impertinent, and reasons not to be disputed, I will prove, in the teeth of a parcel of brokers and retailers of ancient rhapsodies, and such mouldy trash, that our vulgar tongue is not so mean, silly, inept, poor, barren, and contemptible as they pretend. Nor ought I to be afraid of I know not what botchers of old threadbare stuff, a hundred and a hundred times clouted up, and pieced together; wretched bunglers, that can do nothing but new vamp old rusty saws; beggarly scavengers, that rake even the muddiest canals of antiquity for scraps and bits of Latin, as insignificant as they are often uncertain. Beseeching our grandees of Witland, that, as when formerly Apollo had distributed all the treasures of his poetical exchequer to his favourites, little hulch-backed Æsop got for himself the office of apologue-monger: in the same manner, since I do not aspire higher, they would not deny me that of puny rhyparographer, or riff-raff follower of Pyreicus.

I dare swear they will grant me this: for they are all so kind, so good-natured, and so generous, that they'll never boggle at so small a request. Therefore both dry and hungry souls, pot and trenchermen, fully enjoying those books, perusing, quoting them in their merry conventicles, and observing the great mysteries of which they treat, shall gain a singular profit and fame; as in the like case was done by Alexander the Great, with the books of prime philosophy composed by Aristotle.

O rare! belly on belly! what swillers, what twisters will there be!

Then be sure all you that take care not to die of the pip, be sure, I say, you take my advice, and stock yourselves with good store of such books, as soon as you meet with them at the booksellers; and do not only shell those beans, but even swallow them down like an opiate cordial, and let them be in you; I say, let them be within you: then you shall find, my beloved, what good they do to all clever shellers of beans.

Here is a good handsome basketful of them, which I here lay before your worships: they were gathered in the very individual garden whence the former came. So I beseech you, reverend sirs, with as much respect as ever was paid by dedicating author, to accept of the gift, in hopes of somewhat better against next visit the swallows give us.

THE FIFTH BOOK

OF

RABELAIS

TREATING OF THE HEROIC DEEDS AND SAYINGS

OF THE

GOOD PANTAGRUEL

CHAPTER I

HOW PANTAGRUEL ARRIVED AT THE RINGING ISLAND, AND OF THE NOISE THAT WE HEARD

PURSUING our voyage, we sailed three days without discovering anything, on the fourth we made land. Our pilot told us that it was the Ringing Island, and indeed we heard a kind of a confused and often repeated noise, that seemed to us, at a great distance, not unlike the sound of great, middle-sized, and little bells, rung all at once, as 'tis customary at Paris, Tours, Gergeau, Nantes, and elsewhere, on high holidays; and the nearer we came to the land, the louder we heard that jangling.

Some of us doubted that it was the Dodonian kettle, or the portico called Heptaphone, in Olympia, or the eternal humming of the colossus raised on Memnon's tomb, in Thebes of Egypt, or the horrid din that used formerly to be heard about a tomb at Lipara, one of the Æolian Islands. But this did not square with chorography.

"I don't know," said Pantagruel, "but that some swarms of bees hereabouts may be taking a ramble in the air, and so the neighbourhood make this dingle dangle with pans, kettles, and basons, the corybantine cymbals of Cybele, grandmother of the gods, to call them back. Let's hearken." When we were nearer, among the everlasting ringing of these indefatigable bells, we heard the singing, as we thought, of some men. For this reason, before we offered to land on the Ringing Island, Pantagruel was of opinion that we should go in the

607

pinnace to a small rock, near which we discovered an hermitage, and a little garden. There we found a diminutive old hermit, whose name was Braguibus, born at Glenay. He gave us a full account of all the jangling, and regaled us after a strange sort of fashion: four live-long days did he make us fast, assuring us that we should not be admitted into the Ringing Island otherwise, because it was then one of the four fasting, or ember weeks. "As I love my belly," quoth Panurge, "I by no means understand this riddle: methinks this should rather be one of the four windy weeks; for while we fast we are only puffed up with wind. Pray now, good father hermit, have not you here some other pastime besides fasting? Methings 'tis somewhat of the leanest: we might well enough be without so many palace holidays, and those fasting times of yours." "In my Donatus," quoth friar John, "I could find yet but three times or tenses, the preterit, the present, and the future, and therefore I make a donative of the fourth (*i.e.,* the fast of the quatre-tems) to be kept by my footman." "That time or tense," said Epistemon, "is aorist, derived from the preter-imperfect tense of the Greeks, admitted in variable and uncertain times. Patience per force is a remedy for a mad-dog." Saith the hermit, " 'Tis as I told you, fatal to go against this; whoever does it is a rank heretic, and wants nothing but fire and faggot, that's certain." "To deal plainly with you, my dear *pater,*" cried Panurge, "being at sea, I much more fear being wet than being warm, and being drowned than being burnt.

"Well, however, let us fast in God's name; yet I have fasted so long, that it has quite undermined my flesh, and I fear that at last the bastions of this bodily fort of mine will fall to ruin. Besides, I am much more afraid of vexing you in this same trade of fasting; for the devil a bit I understand anything in it, and it becomes me very scurvily, as several people have told me, and I am apt to believe them. For my part I don't much mind fasting: for alas! 'tis as easy as pissing a bed, and a trade of which anybody may set up: there needs no tools. I am much more inclined not to fast for the future: for to do so, there's some stock required, and some tools are set to work. No matter, since you are so stedfast, and have us fast, let us fast as fast as we can, and then breakfast in the name of famine. Now we are come to these esurial idle days. I vow I had quite put them out of my head long ago." "If we must fast," said Pantagruel, "I see no other remedy but to get rid of it as soon as we can, as we would out of a bad way. I'll in that space of time somewhat look over my papers, and examine whether the marine study be as good as ours at land. For Plato, to describe a silly, raw, ignorant fellow, compares him to those that are bred on shipboard, as we would do one bred up in a barrel, who never saw anything but through the bung-hole."

To tell you the short and long of the matter, our fasting was most hideous and terrible: for, the first day we fasted at fisticuffs, the second at cudgels, the third at sharps, and the fourth at blood and wounds: such was the order of the fairies.

CHAPTER II

HOW THE RINGING ISLAND HAD BEEN INHABITED BY THE SITICINES, WHO WERE BECOME BIRDS

HAVING fasted as aforesaid, the hermit gave us a letter from one whom he called Albian Camar, master Ædituus of the Ringing island: but Panurge greeting him, called him, master Antitius. He was a little queer old fellow, bald-pated, with a snout whereat you might easily have lighted a card match, and a phiz as red as a cardinal's cap. He made us all very welcome, upon the hermit's recommendation, hearing that we had fasted, as I have told you.

When we had well stuffed our puddings, he gave us an account of what was remarkable in the island; affirming, that it had been at first inhabited by the Siticines: but that, according to the course of nature, as all things, you know, are subject to change, they were become birds.

There I had a full account of all that Atteius, Capito, Pollux, Marcellus, A. Gellius, Athenæus, Suidas, Ammonius and others had writ of the Siticines; and then we thought we might as easily believe the transmutations of Nectymene, Progne, Itys, Alcyone, Antigone, Tereus, and other birds. Nor did we think it more reasonable to doubt of the transmogrification of the Macrobian children into swans, or that of the men of Pallene in Thrace into birds, as soon as they had bathed themselves in the Tritonic lake. After this the devil a word could we get out of him but of birds and cages.

The cages were spacious, costly, magnificent, and of an admirable architecture. The birds were large, fine, and neat accordingly; looking as like the men in my country, as one pea does like another: for they eat and drank like men, muted like men, digested like men, but stunk like devils; slept, billed and trod their females like men, but somewhat oftener: in short, had you seen and examined 'em from top to toe, you would have laid your head to a turnip that they had been mere men. However, they were nothing less, as master Ædituus told us; assuring us, at the same time, that they were neither secular nor laic: and 'truth is, the diversity of their feathers and plumes did not a little puzzle us,

Some of them were all over as white as swans, others as black as crows, many as grey as owls, others black and white like magpies, some all red like red-birds, and others purple and white like some pigeons. He called the males clerghawks, monkhawks, priesthawks, abbothawks, bishhawks, cardinhawks, and one popehawk, who is a species by himself. He called the females clergkites, nunkites, priest-kites, abbesskites, bishkites, cardinkites, and popekites.

"However," said he, "as hornets and drones will get among the bees, and there do nothing but buzz, eat, and spoil everything; so, for these last three hundred years, a vast swarm of bigottelloes flocked I don't know how among these goodly birds every fifth full moon, and have bemuted, bewrayed, and conskited the whole island. They are so hard favoured and monstrous, that none can abide 'em. For their wry necks make a figure like a crooked billet; their paws are hairy, like those of rough-footed pigeons; their claws and pounces, belly and breech, like those of the stymphalid harpies. Nor is it possible to root them out: for if you get rid of one, straight four and twenty new ones fly thither."

There had been need of another monster-hunter, such as was Hercules: for Friar John had like to have run distracted about it, so much he was nettled and puzzled in the matter. As for the good Pantagruel, he was e'en served as was messer Priapus, contemplating the sacrifices of Ceres, for want of skin.

CHAPTER III

WE then asked master Ædituus why there was but one popehawk among such numbers of venerable birds, multiplied in all their species? He answered, "That such was the first institution and fatal destiny of the stars: that the clerghawks begot the priesthawks and monkhawks, without carnal copulation, as some bees are born of a young bull: the priesthawks begat the bishhawks, the bishhawks the stately cardinhawks, and the stately cardinhawks, if they lived long enough, at last come to be popehawk.

"Of this last kind, there never is more than one at a time; as in a bee-hive there is but one king, and in the world but one sun.

"When the popehawk dies, another rises in his stead out of the whole brood of cardinhawks; that is, as you must understand it all along, without carnal copulation. So that there is in that species an individual unity, with a perpetuity of succession, neither more or less than in the Arabian phœnix.

" 'Tis true that about two thousand seven hundred and sixty moons ago, two popehawks were seen upon the face of the earth: but then you never saw in your lives such a woful rout and hurly-burly as was all over this island. For all these same birds did so peck, clapperclaw, and maul one another all that time, that there was the devil and all to do, and the island was in a fair way of being left without inhabitants. Some stood up for this popehawk, some for t'other. Some, struck with a dumbness, were as mute as so many fishes! the devil a note was to be got out of them: part of the merry bells here were as silent as if they had lost their tongues, I mean their clappers.

"During these troublesome times, they called to their assistance the emperors, kings, dukes, earls, barons, and commonwealths of the world that live on t'other side the water; nor was this schism and sedition at an end, till one of them died, and the plurality was reduced to a unity."

We then asked, what moved those birds to be thus continually chanting and singing? He answered, "that it was the bells that hang on the top of their cages." Then he said to us, "Will you have me make these monkhawks, whom you see bardocucullated with a bag, such as you use to strain Hippocras wine through, sing like any wood-larks?" "Pray do," said we. He then gave half a dozen pulls to a little rope, which caused a diminutive bell to give so many tingtangs; and presently a parcel of monkhawks ran to him, as if the devil had drove 'em, and fell a singing like mad.

"Pray, master," cried Panurge, "if I also rang this bell, could I make those other birds yonder, with redherring coloured feathers, sing?" "Ay, marry would you," returned Ædituus. With this Panurge hanged himself (by the hands, I mean) at the bell-rope's end, and no sooner made it speak, but those smoked birds hied them thither, and began to lift up their voices, and make a sort of untowardly hoarse noise, which I grudge to call singing. Ædituus indeed told us, that they fed on nothing but fish, like the herns and cormorants of the world, and that they were a fifth kind of cucullati newly stamped.

He added, that he had been told by Robert Valbringue, who lately passed that way in his return from Africa, that a sixth kind was to fly hither out of hand, which he called capushawks, more grum, vinegar-faced, brainsick, froward, and loathsome, than any kind whatsoever in the whole island. "Africa," said Pantagruel, "still uses to produce some new and monstrous thing."

CHAPTER IV

HOW THE BIRDS OF THE RINGING ISLAND WERE ALL PASSENGERS

"SINCE you have told us," said Pantagruel, "how the popehawk is begot by the cardinhawks, the cardinhawks by the bishhawks, and the bishhawks by the priesthawks, and the priesthawks by the clerghawks, I would gladly know whence you have these same clerghawks." "They are all passengers, or travelling birds," returned Ædituus, "and come hither from t'other world: part out of a vast country, called Want-o'-bread, the rest out of another toward the west, which they style, Too-many-of-'em. From these two countries flock hither, every year, whole legions of these clerghawks, leaving their fathers, mothers, friends and relations.

"This happens when there are too many children, whether male or female, in some good family of the latter country; insomuch that the house would come to nothing, if the paternal estate were shared among them all (as reason requires, nature directs, and God commands). For this cause parents used to rid themselves of that inconveniency, by packing off the younger fry, and forcing them to seek their fortune in this isle Bossart (or humpy island)." "I suppose he means l'isle Bouchart, near Chinon," cried Panurge. "No," replied t'other, "I mean Bossart (crooked), for there is not one in ten among them, but is either crooked, crippled, blinking, limping, ill-favoured, deformed, or an unprofitable load to the earth."

"'Twas quite otherwise among the heathens," said Pantagruel, "when they used to receive a maiden among the number of vestals: for Leo Antistius affirms, that it was absolutely forbidden to admit a virgin into that order, if she had any vice in her soul, or defect in her body, though it were but the smallest spot on any part of it." "I can hardly believe," continued Ædituus, "that their dams on t'other side the water go nine months with them; for they cannot endure them nine years, nay, scarce seven, sometimes in the house: but by putting only a shirt over the other clothes of the young urchins, and lopping off I don't well know how many hairs from their crowns, mumbling certain apostrophised and expiatory words, they visibly, openly, and plainly, by a Pythagorical metempsychosis, without the least hurt, transmogrify them into such birds as you now see; much after the fashion of the Egyptian heathens, who used to constitute their isiacs, by shaving them, and making them put on certain linostoles, or sur- plices. However, I don't know, my good friends, but that these she- things, whether clergkites, monkites, and abbesskites, instead of sing- ing pleasant motets and charisteres, such as used to be sung to Oro- masis by Zoroaster's institution, may be bellowing out such catarates and scythropys (cursed, lamentable, and wretched imprecations) as were usually offered to the Arimanian dæmon; being thus in con- tinual devotion for their kind friends and relations, that transformed them into birds, whether when they were maids, or thornbacks, in their prime, or at their last prayers.

"But the greatest number of our birds came out of Want-o'-bread, which, though a barren country, where the days are of a most tedious lingering length, overstocks this whole island with the lower class of birds. For hither fly the assaphis that inhabit that land, either when they are in danger of passing their time scurvily for want of belly-tim- ber, being unable, or, what's more likely, unwilling, to take heart of grace, and follow some honest lawful calling, or too proud hearted and lazy to go to service in some sober family. The same is done by your frantic inamoradoes, who, when crossed in their wild desires, grow stark-staring mad, and chuse this life suggested to them by their despair [too cowardly to make them swing, like their brother Iphis of doleful memory]. There is another sort, that is, your gaol birds, who having done some rogues' trick, or other heinous villainy, and being sought up and down to be trussed up, and made to ride the two or three-legged mare that groans for them, warily scour off, and come here to save their bacon: because all these sorts of birds are here provided for, and grow in an instant as fat as hogs, though they came as lean as rakes: for having the benefit of the clergy, they are as safe as thieves in a mill within this sanctuary."

"But," asked Pantagruel, "do these birds never return to the world where they were hatched?" "Some do," answered Ædituus; "formerly some few, but very late and very unwillingly: however, since some certain eclipses, by the virtue of the celestial constellations, a great crowd of them fled back to the world. Nor do wet fret or vex ourselves a jot about it: for those that stay, wisely sing, the fewer the better cheer; and all those that fly away first, cast off their feathers here among these nettles and briars."

Accordingly we found some thrown by there; and as we looked up and down, we chanced to light on what some people will hardly thank us for having discovered; and thereby hangs a tale.

CHAPTER V

OF THE DUMB KNIGHTHAWKS OF THE RINGING ISLAND

THESE words were scarce out of his mouth, when some five and twenty or thirty birds flew towards us: they were of a hue and feather like which we had not yet seen anything in the whole island. Their plumes were as changeable as the skin of the camelion, and the flower of *tripolion,* or *tencrion.* They had all under the left wing a mark, like two diameters dividing a circle into equal parts, or, if you had rather have it so, like a perpendicular line falling on a right line. The marks which each of them bore, were much of the same shape, but of different colours; for some were white, others green, some red, others purple, and some blue. "Who are those," asked Panurge, "and how do you call them?" "They are mongrels," quoth Ædituus.

"We call them knighthawks, and they have a great number of rich commanderies (fat livings) in your world." "Good your worship," said I, "make them give us a song, an't please you, that we may know how they sing." "They scorn your words," cried Ædituus, "they are none of your singing birds; but, to make amends, they feed as much as the best two of them all." "Pray, where are their hens? where are their females?" said I. "They have none," answered Ædituus. "How comes it to pass then," asked Panurge, "that they are thus bescabbed, bescurfed, all embroidered over the phiz with carbuncles, pushes, and pockroyals, some of which undermine the handles of their faces." "This same fashionable and illustrious disease," quoth Ædituus, "is common among that kind of birds, because they are pretty apt to be tossed on the salt deep."

He then acquainted us with the occasion of their coming. "This next to us," said he, "looks so wistfully upon you, to see whether he may not find among your company a stately gaudy kind of huge dreadful birds of prey, which yet are so untoward, that they never could be brought to the lure, nor to perch on the glove. They tell us that there are such in your world, and that some of them have goodly garters below the knee, with an inscription about them, which condemns him (*qui mal y pense*) who shall think ill of it, to be be-wrayed and conskitted. Others are said to wear the devil in a string before their paunches; and others a ram's skin." "All that's true enough, good master Ædituus," quoth Panurge; "but we have not the honour to be acquainted with their knightships."

"Come on," cried Ædituus in a merry mood, "we have had chat enough o'conscience! let's e'en go drink——" "And eat," quoth Pan-urge. "Eat," replied Ædituus, "and drink bravely, old boy; twist like plough jobbers, and swill like tinkers; pull away and save tide: for nothing is so dear and precious as time, therefore we'll be sure to put it to a good use."

He would fain have carried us first to bathe in the bagnios of the cardinhawks, which are goodly delicious places, and have us licked over with precious ointments by the alyptes, alias rubbers, as soon as we should come out of the bath. But Pantagruel told him, that he could drink but too much without that. He then led us into a spacious delicate refectuary, or fratrie-room, and told us: "Braguibus, the hermit, made you fast four days together; now, contrariwise, I'll make you eat and drink of the best four days through-stitch, before you budge from this place." "But hark-ye-me," cried Panurge, "mayn't we take a nap in the meantime?" "Ay, ay," answered Ædituus, "that's as you shall think good; for he that sleeps, drinks." Good Lord! how we lived! what good bub! what dainty cheer! O what an honest cod was this same Ædituus!

CHAPTER VI

HOW THE BIRDS ARE CRAMMED IN THE RINGING ISLAND

PANTAGRUEL looked I don't know howish, and seemed not very well pleased with the four days' junketing which Ædituus enjoined us. Ædituus, who soon found it out, said to him, "You know, sir, that seven days before winter, and seven days after, there is no storm at sea; for then the elements are still, out of respect for the halcions, or king-fishers, birds sacred to Thetis, which then lay their eggs, and hatch their young near the shore. Now here the sea makes itself amends for this long calm; and whenever any foreigners come hither, it grows boisterous and stormy for four days together. We can give no other reason for it, but that it is a piece of its civility, that those ꞌwho come among us may stay whether they will or no, and be copiously feasted all the while with the incomes of the ringing. Therefore, pray don't think your time lost; for, willing, nilling, you'll be forced to stay; unless you are resolved to encounter Juno, Neptune, Doris, Æolus, and his fluster-blusters; and, in short, all the pack of ill-natured left-handed godlings and vejoves. Do but resolve to be cheery, and fall to briskly."

After we had pretty well staid our stomachs with some tight snatches, friar John said to Ædituus, "For ought I see, you have none but a parcel of birds and cages in this island of yours, and the devil-a-bit of one of them all that sets his hand to the plough, or tills the land, whose fat he devours: their whole business is to be frolic, to chirp it, to whistle it, to warble it; tossing it, and roaring it merrily night and day: pray then, if I may be so bold, whence comes this plenty and overflowing of all dainty bits and good things, which we see among you?" "From all the other world," returned Ædituus, "if you except some part of the northern regions, who of late years have stirred up the jakes. Mum! they may chance e'er long to rue the day they did so; their cows shall have porridge, and their dogs oats; there will be work made among them, that there will: come, a fig for't, let's drink——But pray what countrymen are you?" "Tourain is our country," answered Panurge. "Cod so," cried Ædituus, "you were not then hatched of an ill bird, I'll say that for you, since the blessed Tourain is your mother: for from thence there comes hither every year such a vast store of good things, that we were told by some folks of the place, that happened to touch at this island, that your duke of Tourain's income will not afford him to eat his belly full of beans and bacon (a good dish spoiled between Moses and Pythagoras) because his predecessors have been more than liberal to these most holy birds of ours, that we might here munch it, twist it, cram it, gorge it, craw it, riot it, junket it, and tickle it off; stuffing our puddings with dainty pheasants, partridges, pullets with eggs, fat capons of Loudunois, and all sorts of venison and wild fowl. Come, box it about, tope on my friends: pray do you see yon jolly birds that are perched together, how fat, how plump, and in good case they look, with the income that Tourain yields us! And in faith they sing rarely for their good founders, that's the truth on't. You never saw any Arcadian birds mumble more fairly than they do over a dish, when they see these two gilt batoons, or when I ring for them those great bells that you see above their cages. Drink on, sirs, whip it away: verily, friends, 'tis very fine drinking today, and so 'tis every day o' the week; then drink on, toss it about, here's to you with all my soul; you are most heartily welcome: never spare it, I pray you; fear not we should ever want good bub, and belly-timber; for, look here, though the sky were of brass, and the earth of iron, we should not want wherewithal to stuff the gut, though they were to continue so seven or eight years longer than the famine in Egypt. Let us then, with brotherly love and charity, refresh ourselves here with the creature."

"Woons man," cried Panurge, "what a rare time you have on't in this world!" "Pshaw!" returned Ædituus, "this is nothing to what we shall have in t'other: the Elysian fields will be the least that can fall to our lot. Come, in the meantime let's drink here; come, here's to thee, old fuddlecap."

"Your first siticines," said I, "were superlatively wise, in devising thus a means for you to campass whatever all men naturally covet so much; and so few, or (to speak more properly) none can enjoy together; I mean a paradise in this life, and another in the next. Sure you were born wrapt in your mother's smickets! O happy creatures! O more than men! Would I had the luck to fare like you!"

CHAPTER VII

HOW PANURGE RELATED TO MASTER ÆDITUUS THE FABLE
OF THE HORSE AND THE ASS

WHEN we had crammed and crammed again, Ædituus took us into a chamber that was well furnished, hung with tapestry, and finely gilt. Thither he caused to be brought store of mirabolans, cashou, green ginger preserved, with plenty of hypocras and delicious wine. With those antidotes, that were like a sweeter Lethe, he invited us to forget the hardships of our voyage, and at the same time he sent plenty of provisions on board our ship that rid in the harbour. After this, we e'en jogged to bed for the night; but the devil a bit poor pilgarlic could sleep one wink; the everlasting jingle jangle of the bells kept me awake whether I would or no.

About midnight Ædituus came to wake us, that we might drink. He himself shewed us the way, saying, "You men of t'other world say that ignorance is the mother of all evil, and so far you are right: yet for all that, you don't take the least care to get rid of it, but still plod on, and live in it, with it, and by it; for which cause a plaguy deal of mischief lights on you every day, and you are right enough served: you are perpetually ailing somewhat, making a moan, and never right. 'Tis what I was ruminating upon just now. And, indeed, ignorance keeps you here fastened in bed, just as that bully-rock Mars was detained by Vulcan's art: for all the while you don't mind that you ought to spare some of your rest, and be as lavish as you can of the goods of this famous island. Come, come, you should have eaten three breakfasts already; and take this from me for a certain truth, That if you would consume the mouth-ammunition of this island, you must rise betimes; eat them, they multiply; spare them, they diminish.

"For example: mow a field in due season, and the grass will grow thicker and better; don't mow it, and in a short time 'twill be floored with moss. Let's drink, and drink again, my friends: come, let's all carouse it. The leanest of our birds are now singing to us all; we'll drink to them, if you please. Let's take off one, two, three, nine bumpers. *Non zelus, sed charitas.*"

When day, peeping in the east, made the sky turn from black to red, like a boiling lobster, he waked us again to take a dish of monastical brewess. From that time we made but one meal, that only lasted the whole day; so that I cannot well tell how I may call it, whether dinner, supper, nunchion, or after-supper; only to get a stomach, we took a turn or two in the island, to see and hear the blessed singing birds.

At night Panurge said to Ædituus, "Give me leave, sweet sir, to tell you a merry story of something that happened some three and twenty moons ago, in the country of Chastelleraud.

"One day in April, a certain gentleman's groom, Roger by name, was walking his master's horses in some fallow ground; there 'twas his good fortune to find a pretty shepherdess, feeding her bleating sheep and harmless lambkins, on the brow of a neighbouring mountain, in the shade of an adjacent grove: near her, some frisking kids tripped it o'er a green carpet of nature's own spreading: and, to complete the landskip, there stood an ass. Roger, who was a wag, had a dish of chat with her, and after some if's, and's, and but's, hem's, and heigh's on her side, got her in the mind to get up behind him, to go and see his stable, and there take a bit by the bye in a civil way. While they were holding a parley, the horse, directing his discourse to the ass (for all brute beasts spoke that year in divers places), whispered these words in his year: 'Poor ass, how I pity thee! thou slavest like any hack, I read it on thy crupper: thou dost well, however, since God has created thee to serve mankind; thou art a very honest ass; but not to be better rubbed down, curricombed, traped, and fed than thou art, seems to me indeed to be too hard a lot. Alas! thou art all rough-coated, in ill plight: jaded, foundered, crest-fallen, and drooping like a mooting duck, and feedest here on nothing but coarse grass, or briars and thistles; therefore do but pace it along with me, and thou shalt see how we noble steeds, made by nature for war, are treated. Come, thou'lt lose nothing by coming; I'll get thee a taste of my fare.' 'I' troth, sir, I can but love you and thank you,' returned the ass; 'I'll wait on you, good Mr. Steed.' 'Methinks, gaffer ass, you might as well have said, sir grandpaw steed.' 'O! cry mercy, good sir grandpaw,' returned the ass; 'we country clowns are somewhat gross, and apt to knock words out of joint. However, an't please you, I'll come after your worship at some distance, lest for taking this run, my side should chance to be firked and curried with a vengeance, as 'tis but too often, the more's my sorrow.'

"The shepherdess being got behind Roger, the ass followed, fully resolved to bait like a prince with Roger's steed; but when they got to the stable, the groom, who spied the grave animal, ordered one of his underlings to welcome him with a pitchfork, and curricomb him with a cudgel. The ass, who heard this, recommended himself mentally to the god Neptune, and was packing off, thinking and syllogising within himself thus: 'Had not I been an ass, I had not come here among great lords, when I must needs be sensible that I was only made for the use of the small vulgar. Æsop had given me a fair warning of this in one of his fables. Well, I must e'en scamper, or take what follows.' With this he fell a trotting, and wincing, and yerking, and calcitrating, alias kicking, and farting, and funking, and curvetting, and bounding, and springing, and galloping full drive, as if the devil had been come for him in *propriâ personâ*.

"The shepherdess, who saw her ass scour off, told Roger that 'twas her cattle, and desired he might be kindly used, or else she would not stir her foot over the threshold. Friend Roger no sooner knew this, but he ordered him to be fetched in, and that my master's horses should rather chop straw for a week together, than my mistress's beast should want his belly-full of corn.

"The most difficult point was to get him back; for in vain the youngsters complimented and coaxed him to come. 'I dare not,' said the ass, 'I am bashful.' And the more they strove by fair means to bring him with them, the more the stubborn thing was untoward, and flew out at heels; insomuch that they might have been there to this hour, had not his mistress advised them to toss oats in a sieve, or in a blanket, and call him; which was done, and made him wheel about, and say, 'Oats by mackins! oats shall go to pot. *Adveniat;* oats will do, there's evidence in the case; but none of the rubbing down, none of the firking.' Thus melodiously singing (for, as you know, that Arcadian bird's note is very harmonious) he came to the young gentleman of the horse, alias black garb, who brought him into the stable.

"When he was there, they placed him next to the great horse, his friend, rubbed him down, curricombed him, laid clean straw under him up to the chin, and there he lay at rack and manger; the first stuffed with sweet hay, the latter with oats; which when the horse's *valet-de-chambre* sifted, he clapped down his lugs, to tell them by signs that he could eat it but too well without sifting and that he did not deserve so great an honour.

"When they had well fed, quoth the horse to the ass, 'Well, poor ass, how is it with thee now? How dost thou like this fare? Thou wert so nice at first, a body had much ado to get thee hither.' 'By the fig,' answered the ass, 'which one of our ancestors eating, Philemon died laughing, this is all sheer ambrosia, good sir grandpaw: but what would you have an ass say? Methinks all this is yet but half cheer. Don't your worships here now and then use to take a leap?' 'What leaping dost thou mean?' asked the horse, 'the devil leap thee; dost thou take me for an ass?' 'I' troth, sir grandpaw,' quoth the ass, 'I am somewhat a blockhead, you know, and can't for the heart's blood of me learn so fast the court way of speaking of you gentlemen horses; I mean, don't you stallionize it sometimes here among your mettled fillies?' 'Tush!' whispered the horse, 'speak lower; for by Bucephalus, if the grooms but hear thee, they'll maul and be-lamb thee thrice and threefold; so that thou'lt have but little stomach to a leaping bout. Cod so, man, we dare not so much as grow stiff at the tip of the low-

ermorst snout, though 'twere but to leak or so, for fear of being jirked
and paid out of our lechery. As for anything else, we are as happy
as our master, and perhaps more.' 'By this pack-saddle, my old acquaintance,' quoth the ass, 'I have done with you; a fart for thy litter
and hay, and a fart for thy oats: give me the thistles of our fields,
since there we leap when we list: eat less, and leap more, I say; 'tis
meat, drink, and cloth to us. Ah! friend grandpaw, it would do thy
heart good to see us at fair, when we hold our provincial chapter!
Oh! how we leap it, while our mistresses are selling their goslins and
other poultry!' With this they parted. Dixi: I have done."

Panurge then held his peace. Pantagruel would have had him to have
gone on to the end of the chapter; but Ædituus said, "A word to the
wise is enough; I can pick out the meaning of that fable, and know
who is that ass, and who the horse; but you are a bashful youth, I
perceive. Well, know that there's nothing for you here; scatter no
words." "Yet," returned Panurge, "I saw but e'en now a pretty kind
of a cooing abbeykite as white as a dove, and her I had rather ride
than lead. May I never stir if she is not a dainty bit, and very well
worth a sin or two. Heaven forgive me! I meant no more harm
in it than you; may the harm I meant in it befal me presently."

CHAPTER VIII

HOW WITH MUCH ADO WE GOT A SIGHT OF THE POPEHAWK

OUR junketing and banqueting held on at the same rate the third
day, as the two former. Pantagruel then earnestly desired to see
the popehawk; but Ædituus told him, it was not such an easy matter
to get a sight of him. "How," asked Pantagruel, "has he Plato's
helmet on his crown, Gyges' ring on his pounces, or a cameleon on
his breast, to make him invisible when he pleases?" "No, sir," returned Ædituus; "but he is naturally of pretty difficult access: however, I will see and take care that you may see him, if possible." With
this he left us piddling: then within a quarter of an hour came back,
and told us the popehawk is now to be seen: so he led us, without the
least noise, directly to the cage wherein he sat, drooping with his
feathers staring about him, attended by a brace of little cardinhawks,
and six lusty fusty bishhawks.

Panurge stared at him like a dead pig, examining exactly his figure,
size and motions. Then with a loud voice he said, "A curse light

on the hatcher of the ill bird; o' my word this is a filthy whoophooper."
"Hush, speak softly," said Ædituus; "by G— he has a pair of ears,
as formerly Michael de Metiscome remarked." "What, then," returned Panurge, "so hath a whoopcat." "Whilst," said Ædituus, "if
he but hear you speak such another blasphemous word, you had as
good be damned: do you see that bason yonder in his cage? Out of it
shall sally thunderbolts and lightnings, storms, bulls, and the devil
and all, that will sink you down to Peg Trantum's, an hundred fathom
under ground." "It were better to drink and be merry," quoth friar
John.

Panurge was still feeding his eyes with the sight of the popehawk,
and his attendants, when somewhere under his cage he perceived a
madgehowlet. With this he cried out, "By the Devil's maker, master,
there is roguery in the case; they put tricks upon travellers here more
than anywhere else, and would make us believe that a t—d is a sugar-
loaf. What damned cozening, gulling, and cony-catching have we
here? Do you see this madgehowlet? By Minerva, we are all beshit."
"Odsoons," said Ædituus, "speak softly, I tell you: it is no madgehowlet, no she-thing, on my honest word; but a male, and a noble
bird."

"May we not hear the popehawk sing?" asked Pantagruel. "I dare
not promise that," returned Ædituus; "for he only sings and eats at his
own hours." "So don't I," quoth Panurge; "poor pilgarlic is fain to
make everybody's time his own: come then, let us go drink if you will."
"Now this is something like a tansy," said Ædituus; "you begin to
talk somewhat like: still speak in that fashion, and I will secure you
from being thought a heretic. Come on, I am of your mind."

As we went back to have the other fuddling-bout, we spied an old
green-headed bishhawk, who sat moping with his mate and three jolly
bittorn attendants, all snoring under an arbour. Near the old cuff
stood a buxom abbesskite, that sung like any linnet; and we were so
mightily tickled with her singing, that I vow and swear we could
have wished all our members but one turned into ears, to have had
more of the melody. Quoth Panurge, "This pretty cherubim of cherubims is here breaking her head with chanting to this huge, fat, ugly
face, who lies grunting all the while like a hog as he is. I will make
him change his note presently, in the devil's name." With this he
rang a bell that hung over the bishhawk's head; but though he rang
and rang again, the devil a bit bishhawk would hear; the louder the
sound, the louder his snoring. There was no making him sing. "By

622

G—," quoth Panurge, "you old buzzard, if you won't sing by fair means, you shall by foul." Having said this, he took up one of St. Stephen's loaves, alias a stone, and was going to hit him with it about the middle. But Ædituus cried to him, "Hold, hold, honest friend! strike, wound, poison, kill and murder all the kings and princes in the world, by treachery or how thou wilt, and as soon as thou wouldest, unnestle the angels from their cockloft; popehawk will pardon thee all this: but never be so mad as to meddle with these sacred birds, as much as thou lovest the profit, welfare, and life, not only of thyself, and thy friends and relations alive or dead, but also of those that may be born hereafter to the thousandth generation: for so long thou wouldest entail misery upon them. Do but look upon that bason." "Catso, let us rather drink then," quoth Panurge. "He that spoke last, spoke well, Mr. Antitus," quoth friar John: "while we are looking on these devilish birds, we do nothing but blaspheme; and while we are taking a cup, we do nothing but praise God. Come on then, let us go drink; how well that word sounds!"

The third day (after we had drank, as you must understand) Ædituus dismissed us. We made him a present of a pretty little Perguois knife, which he took more kindly than Artaxerxes did the cup of cold water that was given him by a clown. He most courteously thanked us, and sent all sorts of provisions aboard our ships, wished us a prosperous voyage, and success in our undertakings, and made us promise and swear by Jupiter of stone to come back by his territories. Finally he said to us, "Friends, pray note, that there are many more stones in the world than men; take care you don't forget it."

CHAPTER IX

HOW WE ARRIVED AT THE ISLAND OF TOOLS

HAVING well ballasted the holds of our human vessels, we weighed anchor, hoisted up sail, stowed the boats, set the land, and stood for the offing with a fair loom gale, and for more haste unparrelled the mizen-yard, and launched it and the sail over the lee-quarter, and fitted gyves to keep it steady, and boomed it out: so in three days we made the island of tools, that is altogether uninhabited. We saw there a great number of trees which bore mattocks, pick-axes, crows, weeding-hooks, scythes, sickles, spades, trowels, hatchets, hedging-bills, saws, adzes, bills, axes, sheers, pincers, bolts, piercers, augers and wimbles.

Others bore dags, daggers, poniards, bayonets, square bladed tucks, stillettoes, poinadoes, skenes, penknifes, puncheons, bodkins, swords, rapiers, backswords, cutlasses, scymeters, hangers, falchions, glaives, raillons, whittles and whinyards.

Whoever would have any of these, needed but to shake the tree, and immediately they dropped down as thick as hops, like so many ripe plums; nay, what is more, they fell on a kind of grass called scabbard, and sheathed themselves in it cleverly. But when they came down, there was need of taking care lest they happened to touch the head, feet, or other parts of the body. For they fell with the point downwards, and in they stuck, or slit the continuum of some member, or lopped it off like a twig: either of which generally was enough to have killed a man, though he were a hundred years old, and worth as many thousand spankers, spur-royals, and rose-nobles.

Under some other trees, whose names I can't justly tell you, I saw some certain sorts of weeds that grew and sprouted like pikes, lances, javelins, javelots, darts, dartlets, halberts, boarspears, eelspears, partisans, tridentes, prongs, troutstaves, spears, halfpikes and hunting staffs. As they sprouted up and chanced to touch the tree, strait they met with their heads, points, and blades, each suitable to its kind, made ready for them by the trees over them, as soon as every individual weed was grown up, fit for its steel: even like the children's coats, that are made for them as soon as they can wear them, and you wean them of their swaddling clothes. Nor do you mutter, I pray you, at what Plato, Anaxagoras, and Democritus have said: od's fish! they were none of your lower-form gimcracks; were they?

Those trees seemed to us terrestrial animals, in no wise so different from brute beasts as not to have skin, fat, flesh, veins, arteries, ligaments, nerves, cartilages, kernels, bones, marrow, humour, matrices, brains and articulations; for they certainly have some, since Theophrastus will have it so: but in this point they differed from other animals, that their heads, that is, the part of their trunks next to the root, are downwards; their hair, that is their roots, in the earth; and their feet, that is their branches, upside down: as if a man should stand on his head with outstretched legs. And as you, battered sinners, on whom Venus has bestowed something to remember her, feel the approach of rains, winds, cold, and every change of weather, at

624

your ischiatic legs, and your omoplates, by means of the perpetual almanack which she has fixed there: so these trees have notice given them, by certain sensations which they have at their roots, stocks, gums, paps, or marrow, of the growth of the staffs under them; and accordingly they prepare suitable points and blades for them beforehand. Yet as all things, except God, are sometimes subject to error, nature itself is not free from it, when it produceth monstrous things; likewise I observed something amiss in these trees. For a halfpike, that grew up high enough to reach the branches of one of these instrumentiferous trees, happened no sooner to touch them, but instead of being joined to an iron head, it impaled a stub broom at the fundament. Well, no matter, it will serve to sweep the chimney. Thus a pertusan met with a pair of garden shears. Come, all is good for something, it will serve to nip off these little twigs, and destroy caterpillars. The staff of a halbert got the blade of a scythe, which made it look like a hermaphrodite. Happy-be-lucky, it is all a case, it will serve for some mower. Oh it is a great blessing to put our trust in the Lord! As we went back to our ships, I spied behind I don't know what bush, I don't know what folks, doing I don't know what business, in I don't know what posture. scowering I don't know what tools, in I don't know what manner, and I don't know what place.

CHAPTER X

HOW PANTAGRUEL ARRIVED AT THE ISLAND OF SHARPING (OR GAMING)

WE left the island of tools to pursue our voyage, and the next day stood in for the island of sharping, the true image of Fontainbleau: for the land is so very lean, that the bones, that is, the rocks, shoot through its skin. Besides, it is sandy, barren, unhealthy, and unpleasant. Our pilot shewed us there two little square rocks, which had eight equal points in the shape of a cube. They were so white, that I might have mistaken them for alabaster or snow, had he not assured us they were made of bone.

He told us that twenty-one chance devils, very much feared in our country, dwelt there in six different stories, and that the biggest twins or braces of them were called sixes, and the smallest amb's-ace; the rest cinques, quaters, treys, and duces. When they were conjured up, otherwise coupled, they were called either sice cinque, sice quater, sice trey, sice duce, and sice ace; or cinque quater, cinque trey, and so forth. I made there a shrewd observation: would you know what it is, gamesters? It is, that there are very few of you in the world, but what call upon and invoke the devils. For the dice are no sooner thrown on the board, and the greedy gazing sparks have hardly said, ",Two sixes, Frank"; but "Six devils damn it!" cry as many of them. If amb's ace, then, "A brace of devils broil me," will they say. "Quater duce, ,Tom," "The duce take it," cries another. And so on to the end of the chapter. Nay, they don't forget sometimes to call the black cloven-footed gentlemen by their christian-names and sir-names; and what is stranger yet, they use them as the greatest cronies, and make them so often the executors of their wills; not only giving themselves, but everybody, and everything, to the devil, that there is no doubt but he takes care to seize, soon, or late, what is so zealously bequeathed him. Indeed, it is true, Lucifer does not always immediately appear by his lawful attornies: but, alas! it is not for want of good will: he is really to be excused for his delay; for what the devil would you have a devil do? He and his blackguards are then at some other places, according to the priority of the persons that call on them: therefore, pray let none be so venturesome as to think, that the devils are deaf and blind.

He then told us, that more wrecks had happened about those square-rocks, and a greater loss of body and goods, than about all the syrtes, Scyllas and Charibdes, sirens, Scrophades, and gulphs in the universe. I had not much ado to believe it, remembering that formerly, among the wise Egyptians, Neptune was described in hieroglyphics for the first cube, Apollo by an ace, Diana by a duce, Minerva by seven, and so forth.

He also told us that there was a phial of sanggreal, a most divine thing, and known to a few. Panurge did so sweeten up the syndics of the place, that they blessed us with the sight of it: but it was with three times more pother and ado, with more formalities and antic tricks, than they shew the pandects of Justinian at Florence, or the holy Veronica at Rome. I never saw such a sight of flambeaux, torches, and hagio's, and sanctified tapers, in my whole life. After all, that which was shewn us was only the ill-faced countenance of a roasted coney.

All that we saw there worth speaking of, was a good face set upon an ill game, and the shells of the two eggs formerly laid up and hatched by Leda, out of which came Castor and Pollux, fair Helen's brothers. These same syndics sold us a piece of them for a song, I mean, for a morsel of bread. Before we went, we bought a parcel of hats and caps of the manufacture of the place; which, I fear, will turn to no very good account: nor are those who shall take 'em off our hands, more likely to commend their wearing.

CHAPTER XI

HOW WE PASSED THROUGH THE WICKET, INHABITED BY GRIPE-MEN-ALL, ARCH-DUKE OF THE FURRED LAW-CATS

FROM thence Condemnation was passed by us. It is another damned barren island, whereat none for the world cared to touch. Then we went through the wicket; but Pantagruel had no mind to bear us company; and it was well he did not, for we were nabbed there, and clapped into lob's pound by order of Gripe-men-all, arch-duke of the furred law-cats, because one of our company would ha' put upon a serjeant some hats of the sharping island.

The furred law-cats are most terrible and dreadful monsters, that devour little children, and trample over marble stones. Pray tell me, noble topers, do they not deserve to have their snouts slit? The hair of their hides does not lie outwards; and every mother's son of them for his device wears a gaping pouch, but not all in the same manner: for some wear it tied to their neck scarf-wise, others upon the breech, some on the paunch, others on the side, and all for a cause, with reason and mystery. They have claws so very strong, long, and sharp, that nothing can get from them what is once fast between their clutches. Sometimes they cover their heads with mortar-like caps, at other times with mortified caparisons.

As we entered their den, said a common mumper, to whom we had given half a teston, "Worshipful culprits, God send you a good deliverance. Examine well," said he, "the countenance of these stout props and pillars of this catch-coin law and iniquity; and pray observe, that if you still live but six olympiads, and the age of two dogs more, you will see these furred law-cats lords of all Europe, and in peaceful possession of all the estates and dominions belonging to it: unless, by divine providence, what is got over the devil's back, is spent under his belly: or the goods which they unjustly get, perish with their prodigal heirs. Take this from an honest beggar.

"Among them reigns the sixth essence; by the means of which they gripe all, devour all, conskite all, burn all, draw all, hang all, quarter all, behead all, murder all, imprison all, waste all, and ruin all, without the least notice of right or wrong: for among them vice is called virtue; wickedness, piety; treason, loyalty; robbery, justice. Plunder is their motto, and when acted by them, is approved by all men, except the heretics: and all this they do because they dare; their authority is sovereign and irrefragable. For a sign of the truth of what I tell you, you will find, that there the mangers are above the racks. Remember hereafter, that a fool told you this; and if ever plague, famine, war, fire, earthquakes, inundations, or other judgments befal the world, do not attribute them to the aspects and conjunctions of the malevolent planets, to the abuses of the court of Romania, or the tyranny of secular kings and princes; to the impostures of the false zealots of the cowl, heretical bigots, false prophets and broachers of sects; to the villainy of griping usurers, clippers, and coiners; nor to the ignorance, impudence, and imprudence of physicians, surgeons, and apothecaries; nor to the lewdness of adulteresses, and destroyers of by-blows; but charge them all wholly and solely to the inexpressible, incredible, and inestimable wickedness and ruin, which is continually hatched, brewed, and practised in the den or shop of those furred law-cats. Yet it is no more known in the world than the cabala of the Jews; the more is the pity; and therefore it is not detested, chastised, and punished, as it is fit it should be. But should all their villany be once displayed in its true colours, and exposed to the people; there never was, is, nor will be any spokesman so sweet-mouthed, whose fine colloguing tongue could save them; nor any law so rigorous and draconic, that could punish them as they deserve; nor yet any magistrate so powerful, as to hinder their being burnt alive in their coney-burrows without mercy. Even their own furred kittlings, friends, and relations would abominate them.

"For this reason, as Hannibal was solemnly sworn by his father Amilcar to pursue the Romans with the utmost hatred, as long as ever he lived; so, my late father has enjoined me to remain here without, till God Almighty's thunder reduce them there within to ashes, like other presumptuous Titans, prophane wretches, and opposers of God; since mankind is so inured to their oppressions, that they either do not remember, foresee, or have a sense of the woes and miseries which they have caused; or if they have, either will not, dare not or cannot root them out."

"How," said Panurge, "say you so? Catch me there and hang me! Damme, let us march off! This noble beggar has scared me worse than thunder in autumn." Upon this we were filing off; but alas! we found ourselves trapped: the door was double locked and barricaded. Some messengers of ill news told us it was full as easy to get in there as into hell, and no less hard to get out. Ay, there indeed lay the difficulty, for there is no getting loose without a pass, and discharge in due course from the bench. This for no other reason than because folks go easier out of a church than out of a spunging-house, and because they could not have our company when they would. The worst on't was when we got through the wicket; for we were carried, to get out our pass or discharge, before a more dreadful monster than ever was read of in the legends of knight errantry. They called him Gripe-men-all. I can't tell what to compare it to, better than to a chimæra, a sphynx, a Cerberus; or to the image of Osiris, as the Egyptians represented him, with three heads, one of a roaring lion, the other of a fawning cur, and the last of a howling prowling wolf, twisted about with a dragon biting his tail, surrounded with fiery rays. His hands were full of gore, his talons like those of the harpies, his snout like a hawk's bill, his fangs or tusks like those of an overgrown brindled wild boar; his eyes were flaming, like the jaws of hell, all covered with mortars interlaced with pestles, and nothing of his arms was to be seen but his clutches. His hutch, and that of the warren-cats his collaterals, was a long, spick-and-span new rack, a-top of which (as the mumper told us) some large, stately mangers were fixed in the reverse. Over the chief seat was the picture of an old woman, holding the case or scabbard of a sickle in her right hand, a pair of scales in her left, with spectacles on her nose: the cups or scales of the balance were a pair of velvet pouches; the one full of bullion, which overpoised the other, empty and long, hoisted higher than the middle of the beam. I am of opinion it was the true effigies of justice Gripe-men-all; far different from the institution of the ancient Thebans, who set up the statues of their dicastes without hands, in marble, silver, or gold, according to their merit, even after their death.

When we made our personal appearance before him, a sort of I don't-know-what men, all cloathed with I don't-know-what bags and pouches, with long scrowls in their clutches, made us sit down upon a cricket [such as criminals sit on when tried in France]. Quoth Panurge to them, "Good my lords, I am very well as I am; I'd as lieve

629

stand, an't please you. Besides, this same stool is somewhat of the lowest for a man that has new breeches and a short doublet." "Sit you down," said Gripe-men-all again, "and look that you don't make the court bid you twice. Now," continued he, "the earth shall immediately open its jaws, and swallow you up to quick damnation, if you don't answer as you should."

CHAPTER XII

HOW GRIPE-MEN-ALL PROPOUNDED A RIDDLE TO US

WHEN we were sate, Gripe-men-all, in the middle of his furred cats, called to us in a hoarse dreadful voice, "Well, come on, give me presently—an answer." "Well, come on," muttered Panurge between his teeth, "give, give me presently—a comforting dram." "Hearken to the court," continued Gripe-men-all.

> "AN ENIGMA
> "A young tight thing, as fair as may be,
> Without a dad conceiv'd a baby;
> And brought him forth without the pother
> In labour made by teeming mother.
> Yet the curs'd brat fear'd not to gripe her,
> But gnaw'd, for haste, her sides, like viper.
> Then the black upstart boldly sallies,
> And walks and flies o'er hills and vallies.
> Many fantastic sons of wisdom,
> Amaz'd, foresaw their own in his doom;
> And thought, like an old Grecian noddy,
> A human spirit mov'd his body."

"Give, give me out of hand—an answer to this riddle," quoth Gripe-men-all. "Give, give me—leave to tell you, good, good my lord," answered Panurge, "that if I had but a sphinx at home, as Verres, one of your precursors had, I might then solve your enigma presently: but verily, good my lord, I was not there; and, as I hope to be saved, am as innocent in the matter as the child unborn." "Foh, give me—a better answer," cried Gripe-men-all; "or, by gold, this shall not serve your turn: I'll not be paid in such coin; if you have nothing better to offer, I'll let your rascalship know that it had been better for you to have fallen into Lucifer's own clutches, than into ours. Dost thou see 'em here, sirrah? hah? and dost thou prate here of thy being innocent, as if thou could'st be delivered from our racks and tortures for being so! Give me—Patience! thou widgeon. Our laws are like cobwebs: your silly little flies are stopped, caught, and destroyed therein; but your stronger ones break them, and force and carry them which way they please. Likewise, don't think we are so mad as to set up our nets to snap up your great robbers and tyrants; no, they are somewhat too hard for us, there's no meddling with them; for they would make no more of us than we make of the little ones: but you paltry, silly, innocent wretches, must make us amends; and, by gold, we will innocentise your fopship with a wannion, you never were so innocentised in your days; the devil shall sing mass among ye."

Friar John, hearing him run on at that mad rate, had no longer the power to remain silent, but cried to him, "High-day! Pr'ythee, Mr. Devil in a coif, wouldst thou have a man tell thee more than he knows? Has not the fellow told you he does not know a word of the business? His name's Twyford. A plague rot you, won't truth serve your turns?" "Why, how now, Mr. Prate-a-pace," cried Gripe-men-all, taking him short, "marry come up, who made you so saucy as to open your lips before you were spoken to? Give me—Patience! By gold! this is the first time since I've reigned that any one has had the impudence to speak before he was bidden. How came this mad fellow to break loose?" ("Villain, thou liest," said friar John, without stirring his lips.) "Sirrah! sirrah!" continued Gripe-men-all, "I doubt thou'lt have business enough on thy hands, when it comes to thy turn to answer." ("Damme, thou liest," said friar John, silently.) "Dost thou think," continued my lord, "thou'rt in the wilderness of your foolish university, wrangling and bawling among the idle, wandering searchers and hunters after truth? By gold, we have here other fish to fry; we go another gat's way to work, that we do. By gold, people here must give categorical answers to what they don't know. By gold, they must confess they have done those things which they have not, nor ought to have done. By gold, they must protest that they know what they never knew in their lives: and, after all, patience per force must be their only remedy, as well as a mad dog's. Here silly geese are plucked, yet cackle not. Sirrah, give me—an account, whether you had a letter of attorney, or whether you were feed, or no, that you offered to bawl in another man's cause? I see you had no authority to speak, and I may chance to have you wed to something you won't like." "Oh, you devils," cried friar John, "proto-devils, panto-devils, you would wed a monk, would you? Ho hu! ho hu! A heretic! a heretic! I'll give thee out for a rank heretic."

CHAPTER XIII

HOW PANURGE SOLVED GRIPE-MEN-ALL'S RIDDLE

GRIPE-MEN-ALL, as if he had not heard what friar John said, directed his discourse to Panurge, saying to him, "Well, what have you to say for yourself, Mr. Rogue-enough, hah? Give, give me out of hand—an answer." "Say!" quoth Panurge, "why what would you have me say? I say, that we are damnably beshit, since you give no heed at all to the equity of the plea, and the devil sings among you: let this answer serve for all, I beseech you, and let us go about our business; I am no longer able to hold out, as gad shall judge me."

"Go to, go to," cried Gripe-men-all; "when did you ever hear that, for these three hundred years last past, anybody ever got out of this weal without leaving something of his behind him? No, no, get out of the trap if you can without losing leather, life, or at least some hair, and you'll have done more than ever was done yet. For why, this would bring the wisdom of the court into question, as if we had took you up for nothing, and dealt wrongfully by you. Well, by hook or by crook we must have something out of you. Look ye, 'tis a folly to make a rout for a fart and ado: one word's as good as twenty; I have no more to say to thee, but that as thou likest thy former entertainment, thou'lt tell me more of the next; for 'twill go ten times worse with thee, unless, by gold, you give me—a solution to the riddle I propounded. Give, give—it, without any more ado."

"By gold," quoth Panurge, " 'tis a black mite or weevil, which is born of a white bean, and sallies out at the hole which he makes, gnawing it: the mite, being turned into a kind of fly, sometimes walks, and sometimes flies, over hills and dales. Now, Pythagoras the Greek sage, and his sect, beside many others, wondering at its birth in such a place (which makes some argue for equivocal generation), thought that by a metempsychosis the body of that insect was the lodging of an human soul. Now, were you men here, after your welcome death, according to his opinion, your souls would most certainly enter into

632

the body of mites or weevils; for as in your present state of life you are good for nothing in the world, but to gnaw, bite, eat, and devour all things; so in the next you'll e'en gnaw and devour your mother's very sides, as the vipers do. Now, by gold, I think I have fairly solved and resolved your riddle."

"May my bauble be turned into a nut-cracker," quoth friar John, "if I could not almost find in my heart to wish that what comes out at my bung-hole were beans, that these evil weevils might feed as they deserve."

Panurge then, without any more ado, threw a large leathern purse, stuffed with gold crowns (*escus au soleil*) among them. The furred law-cats no sooner heard the jingling of the chink, but they all began to bestir their claws, like a parcel of fiddlers running a division: and then fell to't, squimble, squamble, catch that catch can. They all said aloud, "These are the fees, these are the gloves; now this is somewhat like a tansy. Oh! 'twas a pretty trial, a sweet trial, a dainty trial. O' my word they did not starve the cause. These are none of your sniveling *forma pauperises:* no, they are noble clients, gentlemen every inch of them." "By gold, 'tis gold," quoth Panurge, "good old gold, I'll assure you."

Saith Gripe-men-all, "The court, upon a full hearing ("Of the gold," quoth Panurge) and weighty reasons given, finds the prisoners not guilty, and accordingly orders them to be discharged out of custody, paying their fees. Now, gentlemen, proceed, go forwards," said he to us: "we have not so much of the devil in us as we have of his hue; though we are stout, we are merciful."

As we came out at the wicket we were conducted to the port by a detachment of certain highland griffins, *scribere cum dashoes,* who advised us, before we came to our ships, not to offer to leave the place till we had made the usual presents, first to the lady Gripe-men-all, then to all the furred law-pusses; otherwise we must return to the place from whence we came. "Well, well," said Friar John, "we'll fumble in our fobs, examine every one of us his concern, and e'en give the women their due; we'll ne'er boggle nor stick out on that account; as we tickled the men in the palm, we'll tickle the women in the right place." "Pray, gentlemen," added they, "don't forget to leave somewhat behind you for us poor devils to drink your healths." "O lawd! never fear," answered Friar John, "I don't remember that I ever went anywhere yet, where the poor devils are not remembered and encouraged."

FRIAR John had hardly said those words, ere he perceived seventy-eight gallies and frigates just arriving at the port. So he hied him thither to learn some news; and as he asked what goods they had o' board, he soon found that their whole cargo was venison, hares, capons, turkeys, pigs, swine, bacon, kids, calves, hens, ducks, teal, geese, and other poultry and wild-fowl.

He also spied among these some pieces of velvet, satin, and damask. This made him ask the new-comers, "Whither, and to whom, they were going to carry those dainty goods?" They answered that they were for Gripe-men-all, and the furred law-cats.

"Pray," asked he, "what's the true name of all these things in your country language?" "Corruption," they replied. "If they live on corruption," said the friar, "they'll perish with their generation. May the devil be damned, I have it now: their fathers devoured the good gentlemen, who, according to their state of life, used to go much a hunting and hawking, to be the better inured to toil in time of war: for hunting is an image of a martial life; and Xenophon was much in the right on't, when he affirmed that hunting had yielded a great number of excellent warriors, as well as the Trojan horse. For my part I am no scholar, I have it but by hearsay, yet I believe it. Now the souls of those brave fellows according to Gripe-men-all's riddle, after their decease, enter into wild boars, stags, roebucks, herons, and such other creatures, which they loved, and in quest of which they went while they were men; and these furred law-cats, having first destroyed and devoured their castles, lands, demesnes, possessions, rents and revenues, are still seeking to have their blood and soul in another life. What an honest fellow was that same mumper, who had forewarned us of all these things, and bid us take notice of the mangers above the racks!"

"But," said Panurge to the new-comers, "how do you come by all this venison? Methinks the great king has issued out a proclamation, strictly inhibiting the destroying of stags, does, wild boars, roe-bucks, or other royal game, on pain of death." "All this is true enough," answered one for the rest; "but the great king is so good and gracious, you must know, and these furred law-cats so curst and cruel, so mad and thirsting after Christian blood, that we have less cause to fear in trespassing against that mighty sovereign's commands, than reason to hope to live, if we do not continually stop the mouths of these furred law-cats with such bribes and corruption. Besides," added he, "tomorrow Gripe-men-all marries a furred law-puss of his, to a high and mighty double-furred law-tibert. Formerly we used to call them chop-hay: but alas! they are not such clean creatures now as to eat any, or chew the cud. We call them chop-hares, chop-partridges, chop-woodcocks, chop-pheasants, chop-pullets, chop-venison, chop-conies, chop-pigs, for they scorn to feed on coarser meat." "A t—d for their chops," cried friar John, "next year we'll have 'em called chop-dung, chop-stront, chop-filth.

"Would you take my advice?" added he, to the company. "What is it?" answered we. "Let's do two things," returned he. "First, let's secure all this venison and wild fowl (I mean paying well for them): for my part, I am but too much tired already with our salt meat, it heats my flank so horribly. In the next place, let's go back to the wicket, and destroy all these devilish furred law-cats." "For my part," quoth Panurge, "I know better things: catch me there, and hang me: no. I am somewhat more inclined to be fearful than bold; I love to sleep in a whole skin."

CHAPTER XV

HOW FRIAR JOHN TALKS OF ROOTING OUT THE FURRED LAW-CATS

VERTUE of the frock," quoth friar John, "what kind of voyage are we making? A shitten one, o'my word: the devil of any thing we do, but fizzling, farting, funking, squattering, dozing, raving, and doing nothing. Odds belly, 'tis not in my nature to lie idle; I mortally hate it: unless I am doing some heroic deed every foot, I can't sleep one wink o' nights. Damn it, did you then take me along with you for your chaplain, to sing mass and shrive you? By Maunday-Thursday, the first of ye all that comes to me on such an account shall be fitted: for the only penance I'll enjoin shall be, that he immediately throw himself headlong overboard into the sea, like a base cow-hearted son of ten fathers. This in deduction of the pains of purgatory.

"What made Hercules such a famous fellow, d'ye think? Nothing, but that while he travelled, he still made it his business to rid the world of tyrannies, errors, dangers, and drudgeries: he still put to death all robbers, all monsters, all venomous serpents, and hurtful creatures. Why then do we not follow his example, doing as he did in the countries through which we pass? He destroyed the stymphalides, the lernæan hydra, Cacus, Antheus, the centaurs, and what not: I am no clericus, those that are such tell me so.

"In imitation of that noble by-blow, let us destroy and root out these wicked furred law-cats, that are a kind of ravenous devils: thus we shall remove all manner of tyranny out of the land. Mawmet's tutor swallow me body and soul, tripes and guts, if I would stay to ask your help or advice in the matter, were I but as strong as he was. Come, he that would be thought a gentleman, let him storm a town; well then, shall we go? I dare swear, we'll do their business for them with a wet finger: they'll bear it, never fear; since they could swallow down more foul language that came from us, than ten sows and their words, or dishonour in the world, at a rush, so they but get the coin babies could swill hogwash. Damn 'em, they don't value all the ill into their purses, though they were to have it in a shitten clout. Come, we may chance to kill 'em all, as Hercules would have done, had they lived in his time. We only want to be set to work by another Eurystheus, and nothing else for the present; unless it be what I heartily wish them, that Jupiter may give them a short visit, only some two or three hours long, and walk among their lordships in the same equipage that attended him when he came last to his Miss Semele, jolly Bacchus's mother."

" 'Tis a very great mercy," quoth Panurge, "that you have got out of their clutches: for my part I have no stomach to go there again; I'm hardly come to myself yet, so scared and appalled I was: my hair still stands up an end when I think on't; and most damnably troubled I was there, for three very weighty reasons. First, because I was troubled. Secondly, because I was troubled. Thirdly, and lastly, because I was troubled. Hearken to me a little on the right side, friar John, my left cod, since thou'lt not hear at the other: whenever the maggot bites thee, to take a journey down to hell, and visit the tribunal of Minos, Æacus, Rhadamantus, and Dis, do but tell me, and I'll be sure to bear thee company, and never leave thee, as long as my name's Panurge, but will wade over Acheron, Styx, and Cocytus, drink whole bumpers of Lethe's water (though I mortally hate that element) and even pay thy passage to that bawling cross-grain'd ferryman Charon. But as for the damned wicket, if thou art so weary of thy life as to go thither again, thou may'st e'en look for somebody else to bear thee company; for I'll not move one step that way: e'en rest satisfied with this positive answer. By my good will, I'll not stir a foot to go thither as long as I live, any more than Calpe will come over to Abyla. Was Ulysses so mad as to go back into the cyclop's cave to fetch his sword? No, marry was he not. Now, I have left nothing behind me at the wicket through forgetfulness; why then should I think of going thither?"

"Well," quoth friar John, "as good sit still as rise up and fall; what can't be cured, must be endured. But pr'ythee let's hear one another speak in turn. Come, wert thou not a wise doctor, to fling away a whole purse of gold on those mangy scoundrels? Ha? A squinzy choak thee, we were too rich, were we? Had it not been enough to have thrown the hell-hounds a few cropt pieces of white cash?"

"How could I help it?" returned Panurge. "Did you not see how Gripe-men-all held his gaping velvet-pouch, and every moment roared and bellowed, 'By gold, give me out of hand; by gold, give, give, give me presently?' Now thought I to myself, we shall never come off scot-free: I'll even stop their mouths with gold, that the wicket may be opened, and we may get out; the sooner the better. And I judged that lousy silver would not do the business: for, d'ye see, velvet-pouches don't use to gape for little paultry clipt silver and small cash: no, they are made for gold, my friend John, that they are, my dainty cod. Ah! when thou hast been larded, basted, and roasted, as I was, thou'lt hardly talk at this rate, I doubt. But now what's to be done?— We are enjoined by them to go forwards."

The scabby slabberdegulions still waited for us at the port, expecting to be greased in the fist as well as their masters. Now, when they perceived that we were ready to put to sea, they came to friar John, and begged that we would not forget to gratify the apparitors before we went off, according to the assessment for the fees at our discharge. "Hell and damnation," cried friar John, "are you here still, ye blood-hounds, ye citing, scribbling imps of Satan? Rot you, am I not vexed enough already, but you must have the impudence to come and plague me, ye scurvy fly-catchers you? By cod's-body I'll gratify your ruffian-ships as you deserve; I'll apparatorize you presently, with a wannion, that I will." With this he lugged out his slashing cutlas, and in a mighty heat, came out of the ship, to cut the cozening varlets into steaks; but they scampered away, and got out of sight in a trice.

However, there was somewhat more to do: for some of our sailors, having got leave of Pantagruel to go ashore, while we were had before Gripe-men-all, had been at a tavern near the haven to make much of themselves, and roar it, as seamen will do when they come into some port. Now I don't know whether they had paid their reckoning to the full, or no; but, however it was, an old fat hostess, meeting friar John on the quay, was making a woful complaint, before a serjeant, son-in-law to one of the furred law-cats, and a brace of bums, his assistants.

The friar, who did not much care to be tired with their impertinent prating, said to them, "Harkee me, ye lubberly gnat-snappers, do you presume to say, that our seamen are not honest men? I'll maintain they are, ye dotterells, and will prove it to your brazen faces, by justice; I mean, this trusty piece of cold iron by my side." With this he lugged it out, and flourished with it. The forlorn lobcocks soon shewed him their backs, betaking themselves to their heels: but the old fusty landlady kept her ground, swearing like any butter-whore, that the tarpawlins were very honest cods; but that they only forgot to pay for the bed on which they had lain after dinner, and she asked five-pence French money for the said bed. "May I never sup," said the friar, "if it be not dog-cheap: they are sorry guests, and unkind customers, that they are; they don't know when they have a pennyworth, and will not always meet with such bargains: come, I myself will pay you the money, but I would willingly see it first."

The hostess immediately took him home with her, and shewed him the bed, and having praised it for its good qualifications, said, that she thought, as times went, she was not out of the way, in asking five-pence for't. Friar John then gave her the five-pence; and she no sooner turned her back, but he presently began to rip up the ticking of the feather-bed and bolster, and throwed all the feathers out at the window. In the meantime the old hag came down, and roared out for help, crying out "Murder!" to set all the neighbourhood in an uproar. Yet she also fell to gathering the feathers that flew up and down in the air, being scattered by the wind. Friar John let her bawl on, and without any further ado, marched off with the blanket, quilt, and both the sheets, which he brought aboard undiscovered: for the air was darkened with the feathers, as it uses sometimes to be with snow. He gave them away to the sailors; then said to Pantagruel, that beds were much cheaper at that place than in Chinnonois, though we have there the famous geese of Pautilé; for the old beldam had asked him but five-pence for a bed, which in Chinnonois had been worth above twelve francs. As soon as friar John and the rest of the company were embarked, Pantagruel set sail. But here arose a south-east wind, which blew so vehemently they lost their way, and in a manner going back to the country of the furred law-cats, they entered into a huge gulph, where the sea run so high and terrible, that the ship-boy on the top of the mast cried out, he again saw the habitation of Gripe-men-all: upon which Panurge, frightened almost out of his wits, roared out, "Dear master, in spite of the wind and waves, change your course, and turn the ship's head about: O my friend! let's come no more into that cursed country where I left my purse." So the wind carried them near an island, where, however, they did not dare at first to land, but entered about a mile off.

CHAPTER XVI

HOW PANTAGRUEL CAME TO THE ISLAND OF THE APEDEFTS, OR IGNORAMUS'S WITH LONG CLAWS AND CROOKED PAWS, AND OF TERRIBLE ADVENTURES AND MONSTERS THERE

AS soon as we had cast anchor, and had moored the ship, the pinnace was put over the ship's side, and manned by the coxswain's crew. When the good Pantagruel had prayed publicly, and given thanks to the Lord that had delivered him from so great a danger, he stepped into the pinnace with his whole company, to go on shore, which was no ways difficult to do; for as the sea was calm, and the winds laid, they soon got to the cliffs. When they were set on shore, Epistemon, who was admiring the situation of the place, and the strange shape of the rocks, discovered some of the natives. The first he met, had on a short purple gown, a doublet cut in panes, like a Spanish leather jerkin; half sleeves of satin, and the upper part of them leather; a coif like a black pot tipped with tin. He was a good likely sort of a body, and his name, as we heard afterwards, was Double-fee. Epistemon asked him, "How they called those strange craggy rocks and deep valleys?" He told them it was a colony, brought out of Attorneyland, and called Process; and that if we forded the river somewhat further beyond the rocks, we should come into the island of the Apedefts. "By the sacred memory of the decretals," said friar John, "tell us, I pray you, what you honest men here live on? Could not a man take a chirping bottle with you, to taste your wine? I can see nothing among you but parchment, inkhorns, and pens." "We

639

live on nothing else," returned Double-fee; "and all who live in this place must come through my hands." "How," quoth Panurge, "are you a shaver then? Do you fleece them?" "Ay, ay, their purse," answered Double-fee, "nothing else." "By the foot of Pharaoh," cried Panurge, "the de'el a sous you will get of me. However, sweet sir, be so kind as to shew an honest man the way to those Apedefts, or ignorant people; for I come from the land of the learned, where I did not learn over much."

Still talking on, they got to the island of the Apedefts, for they were soon got over the ford. Pantagruel was not a little taken up with admiring the structure and habitation of the people of the place. For they live in a swinging wine-press, fifty steps up to it. You must know there are some of all sorts, little, great, private, middle-sized, and so forth. You go through a large peristyle, alias a long entry set about with pillars, in which you see, in a kind of landscape, the ruins of almost the whole world; besides so many gibbets for great robbers, so many gallows and racks, that it is enough to fright you out of your seven senses. Double-fee perceiving that Pantagruel was taken up with contemplating those things, "Let us go further, sir," said he to him, "all this is nothing yet." "Nothing, quotha," cried friar John; "by the soul of my overheated codpiece, friend Panurge and I here shake and quiver for mere hunger. I had rather be drinking, than staring on these ruins." "Pray come along, sir," said Double-fee. He then led us into a little wine-press, that lay backwards in a blind corner, and was called pithies in the language of the country. You need not ask whether master John and Panurge made much of their sweet selves there; it is enough that I tell you there was no want of Bolonia sausages, turkey-pouts, capons, bustards, malmsey-wine, and all other sorts of good belly-timber, very well drest.

A pimping son of ten fathers, who, for want of a better, did the office of a butler, seeing that friar John had cast a sheep's eye at a choice bottle that stood near a cupboard by itself, at some distance from the rest of the bottellic magazine, like a jack-in-an-office, said to Pantagruel, "Sir, I perceive that one of your men here is making love to this bottle: he ogles it, and would fain caress it: but I beg that none offer to meddle with it; for it is reserved for their worships." "How," cried Panurge, "there are some grandees here then, I see. It is vintage time with you, I perceive."

Then Double-fee led up to a private staircase, and shewed us into a room, whence, without being seen, out at a loop-hole, we could see their worships in the great wine-press, where none could be admitted without their leave. Their worships, as he called them, were about a score of fusty crack-ropes and gallow-clappers, or rather more, all posted before a bar, and staring at each other, like so many dead pigs: their paws or hands were as long as a crane's leg, and their claws or nails four and twenty inches long at least; for you must know they are enjoined never to pare off the least chip of them, so that they grow as crooked as a welch hook or a hedging-bill.

We saw a swinging bunch of grapes, that are gathered and squeezed in that country, brought in by them. As soon as it was laid down, they clapped it into the press, and there was not a bit of it out of which each of them did not squeeze some oil of gold. Insomuch that the poor grape was tried with a witness, and brought off so drained and picked, and so dry, that there was not the least moisture, juice, or substance left in it; for they had pressed out its very quintessence.

Double-fee told us they had not often such huge bunches; but, let the worst come to the worst, they were sure never to be without others in their press. "But hark you me, master of mine," asked Panurge, "have they not some of different growth?" "Ah, marry have they," quoth Double-fee. "Do you see here this little bunch, to which they are going to give t'other wrench? It is of tythe-growth, you must know; they crushed, wrung, squeezed and strained out the very heart's blood of it but t'other day: but it did not bleed freely; the oil came hard, and smelt of the priest's chest; so that they found there was not much good to be got out of it." "Why then," said Pantagruel, "do they put it again into the press?" "Only," answered Double-fee, "for fear there should still lulk some juice among the husks and hullings, in the mother of the grape." "The devil be damned!" cried friar John, "do you call these same folks illiterate lobcocks, and dunsical doddi-poles? May I be broiled like a red herring if I don't think they are wise enough to skin a flint, and draw oil out of a brick wall." "So they are," said Double-fee; "for they sometimes put castles, parks, and forests into the press, and out of them all extract *aurum potabile.*" "You mean *portabile,* I suppose," cried Epistemon, "such as may be borne." "I mean as I said," replied Double-fee, "*potabile* such as may be drunk; for it makes them drink many a good bottle more than otherwise they should.

"But I cannot better satisfy you as to the growth of the vine-tree syrup that is here squeezed out of grapes, than in desiring you to look yonder in that back-yard, where you will see above a thousand dif-

641

ferent growths that lie waiting to be squeezed every moment. Here are some of the public, and some of the private growth; some of the fortifications, loans, gifts, and gratuities, escheats, forfeitures, fines, and recoveries, penal statutes, crownlands, and demesne, privy-purse, post-offices, offerings, lordships of manors, and a world of other growths for which we want names." "Pray," quoth Epistemon, "tell me of what growth is that great one, with all those little grapelings about it." "Oh, oh!" returned Double-fee, "that plump one is of the treasury, the very best growth in the whole country. Whenever any one of that growth is squeezed, there is not one of their worships but gets juice enough out of it to soak his nose six months later." When their worships were up, Pantagruel desired Double-fee to take us into that great wine-press, which he readily did. As soon as we were in, Epistemon, who understood all sorts of tongues, began to show us many devices on the press, which was large and fine, and made of the wood of the cross (at least Double-fee told us so). On each part of it were names of everything in the language of the country. The spindle of the press was called receipt; the trough, costs and damages; the hole for the vice-pin, state; the sideboards, money paid into the office; the great beam, respite of homage; the branches, *radietur;* the side-beams, *recuperetur;* the fats, ignoramus; the two-handled baskets, the rolls; the treading-place, acquittance; the dossers, validation; the panniers, authentic decrees; the pailes, *potentials;* the funnel, *quietus est.*

"By the queen of the chitterlings," quoth Panurge, "all the hieroglyphics of Egypt are mine a—— to this jargon. Why! here is a parcel of words full as analogous as chalk and cheese, or a cat and a cartwheel! But why, pr'ythee, dear Double-fee, do they call these worshipful dons of yours ignorant fellows?" "Only," said Double-fee, "because they neither are, nor ought to be clerks, and all must be ignorant as to what they transact here: nor is there to be any reason given but, 'The court hath said it'; 'The court will have it so'; 'The court has decreed it.'" "Cop's Body," quoth Pantagruel, "they might full as well have called them necessity; for necessity has no law."

From thence, as he was leading us to see a thousand little puny presses, we spied another paltry bar, about which sat four or five ignorant waspish churls, of so testy fuming a temper, like an ass with squibs and crackers tied to its tail, and so ready to take pepper in the nose for yea and nay, that a dog would not have lived with them. They were hard at it with the lees and dregs of the grapes, which they griped over and over again, might and main, with their clenched fists. They were called contractors, in the language of the country. "These are the ugliest, misshapen, grim-looked scrubs," said friar John, "that ever were beheld with or without spectacles." Then we passed by an infinite number of little pimping wine-presses, all full of vintage-mongers, who were picking, examining, and raking the grapes with some instruments called bills of charge.

Finally, we came into a hall down stairs, where we saw an overgrown cursed mangy cur, with a pair of heads, a wolf's belly, and claws like the devil of hell. The son of a bitch was fed with costs; for he lived on a multiplicity of fine amonds, and amerciaments, by order of their worships, to each of whom the monster was worth more than the best farm in the land. In their tongue of ignorance they called him Twofold. His dam lay by him, and her hair and shape was like her whelps, only she had four heads, two male and two female, and her name was Fourfold. She was certainly the most cursed and dangerous creature of the place, except her grandam, which we saw, and had been kept locked up in a dungeon time out of mind, and her name was Refusing of fees.

Friar John, who had always twenty yards of gut ready empty, to swallow a gallimaufry of lawyers, began to be somewhat out of humour, and desired Pantagruel to remember he had not dined, and bring Double-fee along with him. So away we went, and as we marched out at the back-gate, whom should we meet but an old piece of mortality in chains. He was half ignorant, and half learned, like an hermaphrodite of Satan. The fellow was all caparisoned with spectacles, as a tortoise is with shells, and lived on nothing but a sort of food which, in their gibberish, was called appeals. Pantagruel asked Double-fee, of what breed was that prothonotary, and what name they gave him? Double-fee told us, that, time out of mind, he had been kept there in chains, to the great grief of their worships, who starved him, and his name was Review. "By the pope's sanctified two pounders," cried friar John, "I don't much wonder at the meagre cheer which this old chuff finds among their worships. Do but look a little on the weatherbeaten scratch-toby, friend Panurge: by the sacred tip of my cowl, I'll lay five pounds to a hazel nut, the foul thief has the very looks of Gripe-men-all. These same fellows here, ignorant as they be, are as sharp and knowing as other folks. But were it my case, I would send him packing with a squib in his breech, like a rogue as he is." "By my oriental barnacles," quoth Panurge, "honest

643

friar, thou art in the right: for if we but examine that treacherous Review's ill-favoured phiz, we find that the filthy snudge is yet more mischievous and ignorant than these ignorant wretches here, since they (honest dunces!) grapple and glean with as little harm and pother as they can, without any long fiddle-come-farts, or tantalizing in the case: nor do they dally and demur in your suit; but in two or three words, whip stitch, in a trice, they finish the vintage of the close, bating you all these damned tedious interlocutories, examinations and appointments, which fret to the heart's blood your furred law-cats."

CHAPTER XVII

HOW WE WENT FORWARDS, AND HOW PANURGE HAD LIKE TO HAVE BEEN KILLED

WE put to sea that very moment, steering our course forwards, and gave Pantagruel a full account of our adventures, which so deeply struck him with compassion, that he wrote some elegies on that subject, to divert himself during the voyage. When we were safe in the port, we took some refreshment, and took in fresh water and wood. The people of the place, who had the countenance of jolly fellows and boon companions, were all of them forward folks, bloated and puffed up with fat; and we saw some who slashed and pinked their skins, to open a passage to the fat, that it might swell out at the slits and gashes which they made: neither more nor less than the shit-breech fellows in our country bepink and cut open their breeches, that the taffety on the inside may stand out and be puffed up. They said, that what they did was not out of pride or ostentation, but because otherwise, their skins would not hold them without much pain. Having thus slashed their skin, they used to grow much bigger; like the young trees, on whose barks the gardeners make incisions, that they may grow the better.

Near the haven there was a tavern, which forwards seemed very fine and stately. We repaired thither, and found it filled with people of the forward nation, of all ages, sexes, and conditions; so that we thought some notable feast or other was getting ready: but we were told that all that throng were invited to the bursting of mine host, which caused all his friends and relations to hasten thither.

We did not understand that jargon, and therefore thought in that country, by that bursting they meant some merry meeting or other, as we do in ours by betrothing, wedding, groaning, christening, churching (of women), shearing (of sheep), reaping (of corn, or harvest-home), and many other junketing bouts that end in ing. But we soon heard that there was no such matter in hand.

The master of the house, you must know, had been a good fellow in his time, loved heartily to wind up his bottom, to bang the pitcher, and lick his dish: he used to be a very fair swallower of gravy soup, a notable accountant in matter of hours; and his whole life was one continual dinner, like mine host at Rouillac [in Perigord]. But now having farted out much fat for ten years together, according to the custom of the country, he was drawing towards the busting hour; for neither the inner thin caul wherewith the entrails are covered, nor his skin that had been jagged and mangled so many years, were able to hold and enclose his guts any longer, or hinder them from forcing their way out. "Pray," quoth Panurge, "is there no remedy, no help, for the poor man, good people? Why don't you swaddle him round with good tight girts, or secure his natural tub with a strong sorb-apple-tree hoop? Nay, why don't you iron-bind him, if needs be? This would keep the man from flying out and bursting." The word was not yet out of his mouth, when we heard something give a loud report, as if a huge sturdy oak had been split in two. Then some of the neighbours told us, that the bursting was over, and that the clap, or crack, which we heard, was the last fart: and so there was an end of mine host.

This made me call to mind a saying of the venerable abbot of Castilliers, the very same who never cared to hump his chamber-maids but when he was in pontificalibus. That pious person, being much dunned, teased and importuned by his relations to resign his abbey in his old age, said and professed, "That he would not strip till he was ready to go to bed; and that the last fart which his reverend paternity was to utter, should be the fart of an abbot."

CHAPTER XVIII

HOW OUR SHIPS WERE STRANDED, AND WE WERE RELIEVED BY SOME PEOPLE
THAT WERE SUBJECT TO QUEEN WHIMS (QUI TENOIENT DE LA QUINTE)

WE weighed and set sail with a merry westerly gale, when about seven leagues off (twenty-two miles) some gusts, or scuds of wind, suddenly arose, and the wind veering and shifting from point to point, was, as they say, like an old woman's breech, at no certainty; so we first got our starboard tacks aboard, and hauled off our lee-sheets. Then the gusts increased, and by fits blowed all at once from several quarters: yet we neither settled nor braded up close our sails, but only let fly the sheets, not to go against the master of the ship's direction; and thus having let go amain, lest we should spend our topsails, or the ship's quick-side should lie in the water, and she be overset, we lay by and run adrift, that is, in a landloper's phrase, we temporised it. For he assured us, that, as these gusts and whirlwinds would not do us much good, so they could not do us much harm, considering their easiness and pleasant strife, as also the clearness of the sky, and calmness of the current. So that we were to observe the philosopher's rule, bear and forbear: that is, trim, or go according to the time.

However, these whirlwinds and gusts lasted so long, that we persuaded the master to let us go and lie at trie with our main course; that is, to haul the tack aboard, the sheet close aft, the bowline set up, and the helm tied close aboard: so after a stormy gale of wind, we broke through the whirlwind. But 'twas like falling into Scylla to avoid Charybdis (out of the frying pan into the fire). For we had not sailed a league, e'er our ships were stranded upon some sands, such as are the flats of St. Maixant.

All our company seemed mightily disturbed, except friar John, who was not a jot daunted, and with sweet sugar-plum words comforted now one, and then another, giving them hopes of speedy assistance from above, and telling them that he had seen Castor at the main-yard arm. "Oh! that I were but now ashore," cried Panurge, "that's all I wish for myself at present, and that you, who like the sea so well, had each man of you two hundred thousand crowns! I would fairly let you set up shop on these sands, and would get a fat calf dressed, and 100 of faggots cooled for you against you come ashore. I freely consent never to mount a wife, so you but set me ashore, and mount me on a horse that I may go home: no matter for a servant, I'll be contented to serve myself; I am never better treated than when I'm without a man. Faith old Plautus was in the right on't when he said, the more servants the more crosses: for such they are, even supposing they could want what they all have but too much of, a tongue, that most busy, dangerous, and pernicious member of servants: accordingly 'twas for their sakes alone, that the racks and tortures for confession were invented; though some foreign civilians in our time have drawn alogical and unreasonable consequences from it."

That very moment we spied a sail, that made towards us. When it was close by us, we soon knew what was the lading of the ship, and who was aboard of her. She was full freighted with drums: I was acquainted with many of the passengers that came in her, who were most of 'em of good families: among the rest Harry Cottiral, the chymist, an old toast, who had got a swinging ass's touchtripe (penis) fastened to his waist, as the good women's beads are to their girdle. In his left hand he held an old overgrown greasy foul cap, such as your scaldpated fellows wear, and in the right, a huge cabbage stump.

As soon as he saw me he was overjoyed, and bawled out to me, "What cheer ho! How dost like me now? Behold the true algamana" (this he said, shewing me the ass's ticklegizzard). "This doctor's cap is my true elixo; and this" (continued he, shaking the cabbage stump in his fist) "is *lunaria major:* I have it, old boy, I have it; we'll blow the coal when thou'rt come back." "But pray, father," said I, "whence come you? Whither go you? What's your lading? Have you smelt the salt deep?" To these four questions he answered, "From queen Whims; for Touraine; alchymy; to the very bottom."

"Whom have you got on board?" said I. Said he, "Astrologers, fortune-tellers, alchymists, rhymers, poets, painters, projectors, mathematicians, watchmakers, sing-songs, musicianers, and the devil and all of others that are subject to queen Whims. They have very fair legible patents to shew for't, as anybody may see." Panurge had no sooner heard this, but he was upon the high rope, and began to rail at them like mad. "What o' devil d'ye mean," cried he, "to sit idly here, like a pack of loitering sneaksbies, and see us stranded, while you may help us, and tow us off into the current! A plague o' your whims; you can make all things whatsoever, they say, so much as good weather and little children; yet won't make haste to fasten some hawsers and cables, and get us off." "I was coming to set you afloat," quoth Harry Cottiral, "by Trismegistus, I'll clear you in a trice." With this he caused 7532810 huge drums to be unheaded on one side, and

647

set that open side so, that it faced the end of the streamers and pendants; and having fastened them to good tacklings, and our ship's head to the stern of theirs, with cables fastened to the bits abaft the manger in the ship's loof, they towed us off ground at one pull; so easily and pleasantly, that you'd have wondered at it, had you been there. For the dub-o-dub rattling of the drums, with the soft noise of the gravel, which murmuring disputed us our way, and the merry cheers and huzzas of the sailors, made an harmony almost as good as that of the heavenly bodies when they roll and are whirled round their spheres, which rattling of the celestial wheels Plato said he heard some nights in his sleep.

We scorned to be behind-hand with 'em in civility, and gratefully gave them store of our sausages and chitterlings, with which we filled their drums; and we were just a hoisting two and sixty hogsheads of wine out of the hold, when two huge whirlpools (physeteres) with great fury made towards their ship; spouting more water than is in the river Vienne (Vigenne), from Chinon to Saumur: to make short, all their drums, all their sails, their concerns, and themselves were soused, and their very hose were watered by the collar.

Panurge was so overjoyed, seeing this, and laughed so heartily, that he was forced to hold his sides, and it set him into a fit of the cholic for two hours and more. "I had a mind," quoth he, "to make the dogs drink, and those honest whirlpools, egad, have saved me that labour and that cost. There's sauce for them; ἄριστον μέν ὕδωρ. Water's good, saith a poet; let 'em pindarise upon it: they never cared for fresh water, but to wash their hands or their glasses. This good salt water will stand 'em in good stead, for want of sal-ammoniac and nitre in Geber's kitchen."

We could not hold any further discourse with 'em; for the former whirlwind hindered our ship from feeling the helm. The pilot advised us henceforwards to let her run adrift, and follow the stream, not busying ourselves with anything, but making much of our carcasses. For our only way to arrive safe at the queendom of Whims was to trust to the whirlwind, and be led by the current.

CHAPTER XIX

HOW WE ARRIVED AT THE (QUEENDOM OF WHIMS, OR) KINGDOM OF QUINTESSENCE, CALLED ELTELECHY

WE did as he directed us for about twelve hours, and on the third day the sky seemed to us somewhat clearer, and we happily arrived at the port of Mateotechny, not far distant from the palace of Quintessence.

We met full-but on the quay a great number of guards and other military men that garrisoned the arsenal; and we were somewhat frighted at first, because they made us all lay down our arms, and, in a haughty manner, asked us whence we came?

"Cousin," quoth Panurge to him that asked the question, "we are of Touraine, and come from France, being ambitious of paying our respects to the lady Quintessence, and visit this famous realm of Entelechy."

"What do you say?" cried they; "do you call it Entelechy or Endelechy?" "Truly, truly, sweet cousins," quoth Panurge, "we are a silly sort of grout-headed lobcocks, an't please you; be so kind as to forgive us if we chance to knock words out of joint: as for anything else, we are down-right honest fellows, and true hearts."

"We haven't asked you this question without a cause," said they: "for a great number of others, who have passed this way from your country of Touraine, seemed as meer joltheaded doddipoles as ever were scored over the coxcomb, yet spoke as correct as other folks. But there has been here from other countries a pack of I know not what over-weening self-conceited prigs, as moody as so many mules, and as stout as any Scotch lairds, and nothing would serve these, forsooth, but they must wilfully wrangle and stand out against us at their coming; and much they got by it after all. Troth, we e'en fitted them, and clawed 'em off with a vengeance, for all they looked so big and so grum.

"Pray tell me, does your time lie so heavy upon you in your world, that you don't know how to bestow it better than in thus impudently talking, disputing, and writing of our sovereign lady? There was much need that your Tully, the consul, should go and leave the care of his commonwealth to busy himself idly about her; and after him, your Diogenes Laertius, the biographer, and your Theodorus Gazar, the philosopher, and your Argiropilus, the emperor, and your Bes-

649

sario, the cardinal, and your Politian, the pedant, and your Budæus, the judge, and your Lascaris, the embassador, and the devil and all of those you call lovers of wisdom; whose number, it seems, was not thought great enough already, but lately your Scaliger, Bigot, Chambrier, Francis Fleury, and I can't tell how many such other junior sneaking fly-blows, must take upon them to increase it.

"A squincy gripe the cods-headed changlings at the swallow, and eke at the cover-weesel; we shall make 'em—But the deuce take 'em." ("They flatter the devil here, and smoothify his name," quoth Panurge, "between their teeth.") "You don't come here," continued the captain, "to uphold 'em in their folly, you have no commission from 'em to this effect; well then, we'll talk no more on't.

"Aristotle, that first of men, and peerless pattern of all philosophy, was our sovereign lady's godfather; and wisely and properly gave her the name of Entelechy. Her true name then is Entelechy, and may he be in tail beshit, and entail a shit-a-bed faculty, and nothing else on his family, who dares call her by any other name: for whoever he is, he does her wrong, and is a very impudent person. You are heartily welcome, gentlemen." With this they colled and clipt us about the neck, which was no small comfort to us, I'll assure you.

Panurge then whispered me: "Fellow-traveller," quoth he, "hast thou not been somewhat afraid this bout?" "A little," said I. "To tell you the truth of it," quoth he, "never were the Ephraimites in a greater fear and quandary, when the Gileadites killed and drowned them for saying sibboleth instead of shibboleth; and among friends, let me tell you, that perhaps there is not a man in the whole country of Beauce, but might easily have stopt my bunghole with a cart-load of hay."

The captain afterwards took us to the queen's palace, leading us silently with great formality. Pantagruel would have said something to him; but the other, not being able to come up to his height, wished for a ladder, or a very long pair of stilts; then said, "Patience, if it were our sovereign lady's will, we'd be as tall as you; well, we shall, when she pleases."

In the first galleries we saw great numbers of sick persons, differently placed according to their maladies. The leprous were apart; those that were poisoned on one side; those that had got the plague, alias the pox, in the first rank, accordingly.

CHAPTER XX

THE captain shewed us the queen, attended with her ladies and
gentlemen in the second gallery. She looked young, though
she was at least eighteen hundred years old: and was handsome, slender, and as fine as a queen, that is, as hands could make her. He then
said to us, " 'Tis not yet a fit time to speak to the queen; be you but
mindful of her doings in the meanwhile.

"You have kings in your world, that fantastically pretend to cure
some certain diseases; as for example scrofula or wens, swelled throats,
nick-named the king's evil, and quartan agues, only with a touch:
now our queen cures all manner of diseases without so much as touching the sick, but barely with a song, according to the nature of the
distemper." He then shewed us a set of organs, and said, that when
it was touched by her, those miraculous cures were performed. The
organ was indeed the strangest that ever eyes beheld: for the pipes
were of cassia fistula in the cod; the top and cornice of guaiacum; the
bellows of rhubard; the pedas of turbith, and the clavier or keys of
scammony.

While we were examining this wonderful new make of an organ,
the leprous were brought in by her abstractors, spodizators, masticators, pregustics, tabachins, chachanins, neemanins, rabrebans, nercins,
rozuins, nebidins, tearins, segamions, perarons, chasinins, sarins, sot-
eins, aboth, enilins, archasdarpenins, mebins, chabourins, and other
officers, for whom I want names; so she played 'em I don't know what
sort of a tune or song, and they were all immediately cured.

Then those who were poisoned were had in, and she had no sooner
given them a song, but they began to find a use for their legs, and up
they got. Then came on the deaf, the blind and the dumb, and they
too were restored to their lost faculties and senses with the same remedy; which did so strangely amaze us (and not without reason, I
think) that down we fell on our faces, remaining prostrate, like men
ravished in ecstacy, and were not able to utter one word through the
excess of our admiration, till she came, and having touched Pantagruel
with a fine fragrant nosegay of red roses, which she held in her hand,
thus made us recover our senses and get up. Then she made us the
following speech in Byssin words, such as Parisatis desired should be
spoken to her son Cyrus, or at least of crimson alamode.

"The probity that scintillizes in the superficies of your persons, informs my ratiocinating faculty, in a most stupendous manner, of the radiant virtues, latent within the precious caskets and ventricles of your minds. For, contemplating the mellifluous suavity of your thrice discreet reverences, 'tis impossible not to be persuaded with facility, that neither your affections nor your intellects are vitiated with any defect, or privation of liberal and exalted sciences; far from it, all must judge that in you are lodged a cornucopia, and encyclopedia, an unmeasurable profundity of knowledge in the most peregrine and sublime disciplines, so frequently the admiration, and so rarely the concomitants of the imperite vulgar. This gently compels me, who in preceding times indefatigably kept my private affections absolutely subjugated, to condescend to make my application to you in the trivial phrase of the plebeian world; and assure you, that you are well, most well, most hearty well, more than most heartily welcome."

"I have no hand at making of speeches," quoth Panurge to me privately: "pr'ythee, man, make answer to her for us, if thou canst." This would not work with me however, neither did Pantagruel return a word, so that queen Whims, or queen Quintessence (which you please) perceiving that we stood as mute as fishes, said: "Your taciturnity speaks you not only disciples of Pythagoras, from whom the venerable antiquity of my progenitors, in successive propagation was emaned and derives its original; but also discovers, that through the revolution of many retrograde moons, you have in Egypt pressed the extremities of your fingers, with the hard tenants of your mouths, and scalptized your heads with frequent application of your unguicules. In the school of Pythagoras, taciturnity was the symbol of abstracted and superlative knowledge; and the silence of the Egyptians was agnited as an expressive manner of divine adoration: this caused the pontiffs of Hierapolis to sacrifice to the great deity in silence, impercussively, without any vociferous or obstreperous sound. My design is not to enter into a privation of gratitude towards you; but by a vivacious formality, though matter were to abstract itself from me, excentricate to you my cogitations."

Having spoken this, she only said to her officers, "Tabachins, A panacea"; and strait they desired us not to take it amiss, if the queen did not invite us to dine with her: for she never eat anything at dinner but some categories, jecabots, emnins, dimions, abstractions, harborins, chelimins, second intentions, caradoths, antitheses, metempsychoses, transcendent prolepsies, and such other light food.

Then they took us into a little closet, lined through with alarums, where we were treated God knows how. 'Tis said that Jupiter writes whatever is transacted in the world, on the diphthera or skin of the Amalthæan goat that suckled him in Crete, which pelt served him instead of a shield against the Titans, whence he was nick-named Ægiochos. Now, as I hate to drink water, brother topers, I protest, it would be impossible to make eighteen goat-skins hold the description of all the good meat they brought before us; though it were written in characters as small as those in which were penned Homer's Iliads, which Tully tells us he saw enclosed in a nutshell.

For my part, had I one hundred mouths, as many tongues, a voice of iron, a heart of oak, and lungs of leather, together with the melliffuous abundance of Plato; yet I never could give you a full account of a third part of a second of the whole.

Pantagruel was telling me, that he believed the queen had given the symbolic word used among her subjects to denote sovereign good cheer, when she said to her tabachins, "A panacea": just as Lucullus used to say, "In Apollo," when he designed to give his friends a singular treat; though sometimes they took him at unawares, as, among the rest, Cicero and Hortensius sometimes used to do.

CHAPTER XXI

HOW THE QUEEN PASSED HER TIME AFTER DINNER

WHEN we had dined, a chachanin led us into the queen's hall, and there we saw how, after dinner, with the ladies and princes of her court, she used to sift, searse, boult, range, and pass away time with a fine large white and blue silk sieve. We also perceived how they revived ancient sports, diverting themselves together at,

1. Cordax.	6. Phrygia.	11. Monogas.
2. Emmelia.	7. Thracia.	12. Terminalia.
3. Sicinnia.	8. Calabrisme.	13. Floralia.
4. Jambics.	9. Molossia.	14. Pyrrhice.
5. Persica.	10. Cernophorum.	15. Nicatism.

And a thousand other dances.

Afterwards she gave orders that they should shew us the apartments and curiosities in her palace: accordingly we saw there such new, strange, and wonderful things, that I am still ravished in admiration every time I think on't. However, nothing surprised us more than what was done by the gentlemen of her household, abstractors, parazons, nebidins, spodizators, and others, who freely, and without the least dissembling, told us, that the queen their mistress did all impossible things, and cured men of incurable diseases; and they, her officers, used to do the rest.

I saw there a young parazon cure many of the new consumption, I mean the pox, though they were never so peppered: had it been the rankest Roan ague [anglicè, the Covent Garden gout], 'twas all one with him; touching only their dentiform vertebra thrice with a piece of a wooden shoe, he made them as wholesome as so many sucking pigs.

Another did thoroughly cure folks of dropsies, tympanies, ascites, and hyposarcides, striking them on the belly nine times with a Tenedian satchel, without any solution of the continuum.

Another cured all manner of fevers and agues, on the spot, only with hanging a fox-tail on the left side of the patient's girdle.

One removed the tooth-ach only with washing the root of the aching tooth with elder-vinegar, and letting it dry half an hour in the sun.

Another, the gout, whether hot or cold, natural or accidental, by barely making the gouty person shut his mouth, and open his eyes.

I saw another ease nine good gentlemen of St. Francis's distemper, in a very short space of time, having clapped a rope about their necks, at the end of which hanged a box with ten thousand golden crowns in't.

One, with a wonderful engine, throwed the houses out at the windows, by which means they were purged of all pestilential air.

Another cured all the three kinds of hectics, the tabid, atrophes, and emaciated, without bathing, without tabian milk, dropax, alias depilatory, or other such medicaments: only turning the consumptive for three months into monks: and he assured me that if they did not grow fat and plump in a monastic way of living, they never would be fattened in this world, either by nature or by art.

I saw another surrounded with a crowd of two sorts of women. Some were young, quaint, clever, neat, pretty, juicy, tight, brisk, buxom, proper, kind-hearted, and as right as my leg, to any man's thinking. The rest were old, weather-beaten, over-ridden, toothless, blear-eyed, tough, wrinkled, shrivelled, tawny, mouldy, phthysicky, decrepid hags, beldams, and walking carcasses. We were told that his office was to cast anew those she-pieces of antiquity, and make them such as the pretty creatures whom we saw, who had been made young again that day, recovering at once the beauty, shape, size, and disposition, which they enjoyed at sixteen; except their heels, that were now much shorter than in their former youth.

This made them yet more apt to fall backwards, whenever any man happened to touch 'em, than they had been before. As for their counterparts, the old mother-scratch-tobies, they most devoutly waited for the blessed hour, when the batch that was in the oven was to be drawn, that they might have their turns, and in a mighty haste they were pulling and hauling the man like mad, telling him, that 'tis the most grievous and intolerable thing in nature for the tail to be o'fire, and the head to scare away those who should quench it.

The officer had his hands full, never wanting patients; neither did his place bring him in little, you may swear. Pantagruel asked him, whether he could also make old men young again? He said he could not. But the way to make them new men, was to get them to cohabit with a new-cast female: for thus they caught that fifth kind of crinckams, which some call pellade, in Greek ὀφίασις, that makes them cast off their old hair and skin, just as the serpents do; and thus their youth is renewed like the Arabian phœnix's. This is the true fountain of youth, for there the old and decrepid become young, active, and lusty.

Just so, as Euripides tells us, Iolaus was transmogrified; and thus Phaon, for whom kind-hearted Sappho run wild, grew young again for Venus's use: so Tithon by Aurora's means; so Æson by Medea, and Jason also, who, if you'll believe Pherecides and Simonides, was new-vamped and died by that witch; and so were the nurses of jolly Bacchus, and their husbands, as Eschylus relates.

CHAPTER XXII

HOW QUEEN WHIM'S OFFICERS WERE EMPLOYED; AND HOW THE SAID LADY RETAINED US AMONG HER ABSTRACTORS

I THEN saw a great number of the queen's officers, who made black-a-moors white as fast as hops, just rubbing their bellies with the bottom of a pannier.

Others, with three couples of foxes in one yoke, plowed a sandy shore, and did not lose their seed.

Others washed burnt tiles, and made them lose their colour.

Others extracted water out of pumice-stones; braying them a good while in a mortar, and changed their substance.

Others sheered asses, and thus got long fleece wool.

Others gathered off of thorns grapes, and figs off of thistles.

Others stroked he-goats, by the dugs, and saved their milk in a sieve; and much they got by it.

Others washed asses heads, without losing their soap.

Others taught cows to dance, and did not lose their fiddling.

Others pitched nets to catch the wind, and took cock lobsters in them.

I saw a young spodizator, who very artificially got farts out of a dead ass, and sold them for fivepence an ell.

Another did putrify beetles. O the dainty food!

Poor Panurge fairly cast up his accounts, and gave up his half-penny [*i.e.,* vomited] seeing an archasdarpenin, who laid a huge plenty of chamberlie to putrify in horse-dung, mish-mash'd, with abundance of christian sir-reverence. Pugh, fie upon him, nasty dog! However, he told us, that with this sacred distillation he watered kings and princes, and made their sweet lives a fathom or two the longer.

Others built churches to jump over the steeples.

Others set carts before the horses, and began to flay eels at the tail; neither did the eels cry before they were hurt, like those of Melun.

Others out of nothing made great things, and made great things return to nothing.

Others cut fire into steakes, with a knife, and drew water with a fish-net.

Others make chalk of cheese, and honey of a dog's t—d.

We saw a knot of others, about a baker's dozen in number, tippling under an arbour. They toped out of jolly bottomless cups, four sorts of cool, sparkling, ·pure, delicious vine-tree syrup, which went down like mother's milk; and healths and bumpers flew about like lightning. We were told that these true philosophers were fairly multiplying the stars by drinking till the seven were fourteen, as brawny Hercules did with Atlas.

Others made a virtue of necessity, and the best of a bad market, which seemed to me a very good piece of work.

Others made alchymy with their teeth, and clapping their hind retort to the recipient, made scurvy faces, and then squeezed.

Others, in a large grass-plat, exactly measured how far the fleas could go at a hop, a step, and a jump; and told us, that this was exceeding useful for the ruling of kingdoms, the conduct of armies, and the administration of commonwealths; and that Socrates, who first got philosophy out of heaven, and from idle and trifling, made it profitable and of moment, used to spend half his philosophizing time in measuring the leaps of fleas, as Aristophanes, the quintessential, affirms.

I saw two gibroins by themselves, keeping watch on the top of a tower; and we were told they guarded the moon from the wolves.

In a blind corner I met four more very hot at it, and ready to go to loggerheads. I asked what was the cause of the stir and ado, the mighty coil and pother they made? And I heard that for four or five live-long days, those over-wise roisters had been at it ding-dong, disputing on three high, more than metaphysical propositions, promising themselves mountains of gold by solving them: the first was concerning a he ass's shadow; the second, of the smoke of a lantern; and the third of goats' hair, whether it were wool or no? We heard that they did not think it a bit strange that two contradictions in mode, form, figure, and time should be true. Though I'll warrant the sophists of Paris had rather be unchristened than own so much.

While we were admiring all those men's wonderful doings, the evening star already twinkling; the queen (God bless her) appeared attended with her court, and again amazed and dazzled us. She perceived it, and said to us:

"What occasions the aberrations of human cogitations through the perplexing labyrinths and abysses of admiration, is not the source of the effects, which sagacious mortals visibly experience to be the consequential result of natural causes: 'tis the novelty of the experiment which makes impressions on their conceptive, cogitative faculties; that do not previse the facility of the operation adequately, with a subact and sedate intellection, associated with diligent and congruous study. Consequently let all manner of perturbation abdicate the ventricles of your brains, if any one has invaded them while they were contemplating what is transacted by my domestic ministers. Be spectators and auditors of every particular phænomenon, and every individual proposition, within the extent of my mansion; satiate yourselves with all that can fall here under the consideration of your visual or ascultating powers, and thus emancipate yourselves from the servitude of crassous ignorance. And that you may be induced to apprehend how sincerely I desire this, in consideration of the studious cupidity that so demonstratively emicates at your external organs, from this present particle of time, I retain you as my abstractors: Geber, my principal talachin, shall register and initiate you at your departing."

We humbly thanked her queenship, without saying a word, accepting of the noble office she conferred on us.

CHAPTER XXIII
HOW THE QUEEN WAS SERVED AT DINNER, AND OF HER
WAY OF EATING

QUEEN WHIMS, after this, said to her gentlemen: "The orifice of the ventricle, that ordinary embassador for the alimentation of all members, whether superior or inferior, importunes us to restore, by the apposition of idoneous sustenance, what was dissipated by the internal calidity's action on the radical humidity. Therefore spodizators, gesinins, memains, and parazons, be not culpable of dilatory protractions in the apposition of every re-roborating species, but rather let 'em pullulate and super-abound on the tables. As for you, nobilissim prægustators, and my gentilissim masticators, your frequently experimented industry, internected with perdiligent sedulity, and sedulous perdiligence, continually adjuvates you to perficiate all things in so expeditious a manner that there is a necessity of exciting in you a cupidity to consummate them. Therefore I can only suggest to you still to operate, as you are assuefacted indefatigably to operate."

Having made this fine speech, she retired for awhile with part of her women, and we were told that 'twas to bathe, as the ancients did more commonly than we use now-a-days to wash our hands before we eat. The tables were soon placed, the cloth spread, and then the queen sat down. She eat nothing but celestial ambrosia, and drank nothing but divine nectar. As for the lords and ladies that were there, they, as well as we, fared on as rare, costly, and dainty dishes as ever Apicius wot or dreamed of in his life.

When we were as round as hoops, and as full as eggs, with stuffing the gut, an olla podrida was set before us, to force hunger to come to terms with us, in case it had not granted us a truce; and such a huge vast thing it was, that the plate which Pythies Althius gave king Darius, would hardly have covered it. The olla consisted of several sorts of pottages, sallads, fricasees, saugrenees, cabirotadoes, roast and boiled meat, carbonadoes, swinging pieces of powdered beef, good old hams, dainty deifical somates, cakes, tarts, a world of curds after the morisk way, fresh cheese, jellies, and fruit of all sorts. All this seemed to me good and dainty: however the sight of it made me sigh; for, alas, I could not taste a bit on't; so full I had filled my puddings before, and a bellyful's a bellyful, you know. Yet I must tell you what I saw, that seemed to me odd enough o'conscience: 'twas some pasties in paste; and what should those pasties in paste be, d'ye think, but pasties in pots? At the bottom I perceived store of dice, cards, tarots, luettes, chess-men and chequers, besides full bowls of gold crowns for those who have a mind to have a game or two, and try their chance. Under this I saw a jolly company of mules in stately trappings, with velvet foot-cloths, and a troop of ambling nags, some for men and some for women; besides I don't know how many litters all lined with velvet, and some coaches of Ferrara make: all this for those who had a mind to take the air.

This did not seem strange to me; but if anything did, 'twas certainly the queen's way of eating; and truly 'twas very new, and very odd; for she chewed nothing, the good lady; not but that she had good sound teeth, and her meat required to be masticated, but such was her highness's custom. When her prægustators had tasted the meat, her masticators took it and chewed it most nobly, for their dainty chops and gullets were lined through with crimson satin, with little welts and gold purls, and their teeth were of delicate white ivory. Thus, when they had chewed the meat ready for her highness's maw, they poured it down her throat through a funnel of fine gold, and so on to her craw. For that reason, they told us, she never visited a close-stool but by proxy.

CHAPTER XXIV

HOW THERE WAS A BALL IN THE MANNER OF A TOURNA-
MENT, AT WHICH QUEEN WHIMS WAS PRESENT

AFTER supper there was a ball in the form of a tilt or tournament, not only worth seeing, but also never to be forgotten. First, the floor of the hall was covered with a large piece of velveted white and yellow chequered tapestry, each chequer exactly square, and three full spans in breadth.

Then thirty-two young persons came into the hall, sixteen of them arrayed in cloth of gold; and of these, eight were young nymphs, such as the ancients described Diana's attendants: the other eight were a king, a queen, two wardens of the castle, two knights, and two archers. Those of the other band were clad in cloth of silver.

They posted themselves on the tapestry in the following manner: the kings on the last line of the fourth square; so that the golden king was on a white square, and the silvered king on a yellow square, and each queen by her king; the golden queen on a yellow square, and the silvered queen on a white one; and on each side stood the archers to guard their kings and queens; by the archers the knights, and the wardens by them. In the next row before 'em stood the eight nymphs; and between the two bands of nymphs four rows of squares stood empty.

Each band had its musicians, eight on each side, dressed in its livery; the one with orange-coloured damask, the other with white; and all played on different instruments most melodiously and harmoniously, still varying in time and measure as the figure of the dance required. This seemed to me an admirable thing, considering the numerous diversity of steps, back-steps, bounds, rebounds, jerts, paces, leaps, skips, turns, coupés, hops, leadings, risings, meetings, flights, ambuscadoes, moves, and re-moves.

I was also at a loss when I strove to comprehend how the dancers could so suddenly know what every different note mean; for they no sooner heard this or that sound, but they placed themselves in the place which was denoted by the music, though their motions were all different. For the nymphs that stood in the first file, as if they designed to begin the fight, marched straight forwards to their enemies from square to square, unless it were the first step, at which they were free to move over two steps at once. They alone never fall back [which is not very natural to other nymphs] and if any of them is so lucky as to advance to the opposite king's row, she is immediately crowned queen of her king, and after that, moves with the same state, and in the same manner as the queen; but till that happens, they never strike their enemies but forwards, and obliquely in a diagonal line. However, they make it not their chief business to take their foes; for if they did, they would leave their queen exposed to the adverse parties, who then might take her.

The kings move and take their enemies on all sides square-ways, and only step from a white square into a yellow one, and vice versa, except at their first step the rank should want other officers than the wardens; for then they can set 'em in their place, and retire by him.

The queens take a greater liberty than any of the rest; for they move backwards and forwards all manner of ways, in a straight line, as far as they please, provided the place be not filled with one of their own party, and diagonally also keeping to the colour on which they stand.

The archers move backwards or forwards, far and near, never changing the colour on which they stand.

The knights move, and take in a lineal manner, stepping over one square, though a friend or a foe stand upon it, posting themselves on the second square to the right or left, from one colour to another; which is very welcome to the adverse party, and ought to be carefully observed, for they take at unawares.

The wardens move, and take to the right or left, before or behind them, like the kings, and can advance as far as they find places empty; which liberty the kings take not.

The law which both sides observe, is, at the end of the fight, to besiege and enclose the king of either party, so that he may not be able to move; and being reduced to that extremity, the battle is over, and he loses the day.

Now, to avoid this, there is none of either sex of each party, but is willing to sacrifice his or her life, and they begin to take one another on all sides in time, as soon as the music strikes up. When anyone takes a prisoner, he makes his honours, and striking him gently in the hand, puts him out of the field and combat, and encamps where he stood.

If one of the kings chance to stand where he might be taken, it is not lawful for any of his adversaries that had discovered him, to lay hold on him: far from it, they are strictly enjoined humbly to pay him their respects, and give him notice, saying, "God preserve you, sir!" that his officers may relieve and cover him, or he may remove, if unhappily he could not be relieved. However, he is not to be taken, but greeted with a good-morrow, the others bending the knee; and thus the tournament uses to end.

CHAPTER XXV

HOW THE THIRTY-TWO PERSONS AT THE BALL FOUGHT

THE two companies having taken their stations, the music struck up, and with a martial sound, which had something of horrid in it, like a point of war, roused and alarmed both parties, who now began to shiver, and then soon were warmed with warlike rage; and having got in readiness to fight desperately, impatient of delay, stood waiting for the charge.

Then the music of the silvered band ceased playing, and the instruments of the golden side alone were heard, which denoted that the golden party attacked. Accordingly a new movement was played for the onset, and we saw the nymph, who stood before the queen, turn to the left towards her king, as it were to ask leave to fight; and thus saluting her company at the same time, she moved two squares forwards, and saluted the adverse party.

Now the music of the golden brigade ceased playing, and their antagonists began again. I ought to have told you, that the nymph, who began by saluting her company, had by that formality also given them to understand that they were to fall on. She was saluted by them in the same manner with a full turn to the left, except the queen, who went aside towards her king to the right; and the same manner of salutation was observed on both sides during the whole ball.

The silvered nymph that stood before her queen likewise moved, as soon as the music of her party sounded a charge: her salutations, and those of her side, were to the right, and her queen's to the left. She moved in the second square forwards, and saluted her antagonists, facing the first golden nymph: so that there was not any distance between them, and you would have thought they two had been going to fight; but they only strike sideways.

Their comrades, whether silvered or golden, followed 'em in an intercalary figure, and seemed to skirmish a while, till the golden nymph, who had first entered the lists, striking a silvered nymph in the hand on the right, put her out of the field, and set herself in her place. But soon the music playing a new measure, she was struck by a silvered archer, who after that was obliged himself to retire. A silvered knight then sallied out, and the golden queen posted herself before her king.

Then the silvered king, dreading the golden queen's fury, removed to the right, to the place where his warden stood, which seemed to him strong and well guarded.

The two knights on the left, whether golden or silvered, marched up, and on either side took up many nymphs, who could not retreat; principally the golden knight, who made this his whole business: but the silvered knight had greater designs, dissembling all along, and even sometimes not taking a nymph when he could have done it, still moving on till he was come up to the main body of the enemies, in such a manner, that he saluted their king with a "God save you, sir!"

The whole golden brigade quaked for fear and anger, those words giving notice of their king's danger: not but that they could soon relieve him, but because their king being thus saluted, they were to lose their warden on the right wing, without any hopes of a recovery. Then the golden king retired to the left, and the silvered knight took the golden warden, which was a mighty loss to that party. However, they resolved to be revenged, and surrounded the knight that he might not escape. He tried to get off, behaving himself with a great deal of gallantry, and his friends did what they could to save him; but at last he fell into the golden queen's hands, and was carried off.

Her forces, not yet satisfied, having lost one of her best men, with more fury than conduct moved about, and did much mischief among their enemies. The silvered party warily dissembled, watching their opportunity to be even with them, and presented one of their nymphs to the golden queen, having laid an ambuscado; so that the nymph being taken, a golden archer had like to have seized the silvered queen. Then the golden knight undertakes to take the silvered king and queen and says, "Good-morow." Then the silvered archer salutes them, and was taken by a golden nymph, and she herself by a silvered one.

The fight was obstinate and sharp. The wardens left their posts, and advanced to relieve their friends. The battle was doubtful, and victory hovered over both armies. Now the silvered host charge and break through their enemy's ranks, as far as the golden king's tent, and now they are beaten back: the golden queen distinguishes herself from the rest by her mighty achievements, still more than by her garb and dignity; for at once she takes an archer, and going sideways, seizes a silvered warden. Which thing the silvered queen per-

663

ceiving, she came forwards, and rushing on with equal bravery, takes the last golden warden and some nymphs. The two queens fought a long while hand to hand; now striving to take each other by surprise, then to save themselves, and sometimes to guard their kings. Finally, the golden queen took the silvered queen; but presently after she herself was taken by the silvered archer.

Then the silvered king had only three nymphs, an archer, and a warden left; and the golden only three nymphs and the right knight: which made them fight more slowly and warily than before. The two kings seemed to mourn for the loss of their loving queens, and only studied and endeavoured to get new ones out of all their nymphs, to be raised to that dignity, and thus be married to them. This made them excite those brave nymphs to strive to reach the farthest rank, where stood the king of the contrary party, promising them certainly to have them crowned if they could do this. The golden nymphs were beforehand with the others, and out of their number was created a queen, who was dressed in royal robes, and had a crown set on her head. You need not doubt the silvered nymphs made also what haste they could to be queens: one of them was within a step of the coronation place; but there the golden knight lay ready to intercept her, so that she could go no further.

The new golden queen, resolved to shew herself valiant, and worthy of her advancement to the crown, achieved great feats of arms. But, in the meantime, the silvered knight takes the golden warden who guarded the camp: and thus there was a new silvered queen, who, like the other, strove to excel in heroic deeds at the beginning of her reign. Thus the fight grew hotter than before. A thousand stratagems, charges, rallying, retreats and attacks were tried on both sides; till at last the silvered queen, having by stealth advanced as far as the golden king's tent, cried, "God save you, sir!" Now none but his new queen could relieve him: so she bravely came and exposed herself to the utmost extremity to deliver him out of it. Then the silvered warden, with his queen, reduced the golden king to such a stress, that to save himself, he was forced to lose his queen; but the golden king took him at last. However, the rest of the golden party were soon taken; and that king being left alone, the silvered party made him a low bow, crying, "Good-morrow, sir!" which denoted that the silvered king had got the day.

This being heard, the music of both parties loudly proclaimed the victory. And thus the first battle ended, to the unspeakable joy of all the spectators.

After this the two brigades took their former stations, and began to tilt a second time, much as they had done before; only the music played somewhat faster than at the first battle, and the motions were altogether different. I saw the golden queen sally out one of the first, with an archer and a knight, as it were angry at the former defeat, and she had like to have fallen upon the silvered king in his tent among his officers: but having been baulked in her attempt, she skirmished briskly, and overthrew so many silvered nymphs and officers, that it was a most amazing sight. You would have sworn she had been another Penthesilea: for she behaved herself with as much bravery as that Amazonian queen did at Troy.

But this havoc did not last long; for the silvered party, exasperated by their loss, resolved to perish, or stop her progress: and having posted an archer in ambuscado on a distant angle, together with a knight errant, her highness fell into their hands, and was carried out of the field. The rest were soon routed after the taking of their queen; who, without doubt, from that time resolved to be more wary, and keep near her king, without venturing so far amidst her enemies, unless with more force to defend her. Thus the silvered brigade once more got the victory.

This did not dishearten or deject the golden party: far from it, they soon appeared again in the field to face their enemies; and being posted as before, both the armies seemed more resolute and cheerful than ever. Now the martial concert began, and the music was above a hemiole the quicker, according to the warlike phrygian mode, such as was invented by Marsyas.

Then our combatants began to wheel about, and charge with such a swiftness, that in an instant they made four moves, besides the usual salutations. So that they were continually in action, flying, hovering, jumping, vaulting, curvetting, with petauristical turns and motions, and often intermingled.

Seeing them turn about on one foot after they had made their honours, we compared them to your tops or gigs, such as boys use to whip about; making them turn round so swiftly, that they sleep, as they call it, and motion cannot be perceived, but resembles rest, its contrary: so that if you make a point or mark on some part of one of those gigs, 'twill be perceived not as a point, but as a continual line, in a most divine manner, as Cusanus has wisely observed.

665

While they were thus warmly engaged, we heard continually the claps and episemapsises, which those of the two bands reiterated at the taking of their enemies; and this, joined to the variety of their motions and music, would have forced smiles out of the most severe Cato, the never-laughing Crassus, the Athenian man-hater Timon; nay, even whining Heraclitus, though he abhorred laughing, the action that's most peculiar to man. For who could have forborn? seeing those young warriors, with their nymphs and queens, so briskly and gracefully advance, retire, jump, leap, skip, spring, fly, vault, caper, move to the right, to the left, every way still in time, so swiftly, and yet so dexterously, that they never touched one another but methodically.

As the number of the combatants lessened, the pleasure of the spectators increased; for the stratagems and motions of the remaining forces were more singular. I shall only add, that this pleasing entertainment charmed us to such a degree, that our minds were ravished with admiration and delight; and the martial harmony moved our souls so powerfully, that we easily believed what is said of Ismenias's having excited Alexander to rise from table, and run to his arms, with such a warlike melody. At last the golden king remained master of the field: and while we were minding those dancers, queen Whims vanished, so that we saw her no more from that day to this.

Then Geber's michelots conducted us, and we were set down among her abstractors, as her queenship had commanded. After that, we returned to the port of Mateotechny, and thence straight aboard our ships: for the wind was fair, and had we not hoisted out o'hand, we could hardly have got off in three quarters of a moon in the wain.

CHAPTER XXVI

HOW WE CAME TO THE ISLAND OF ODES, WHERE THE WAYS GO UP AND DOWN

WE sailed before the wind, between a pair of courses, and in two days made the island of Odes, at which place we saw a very strange thing. The ways there are animals: so true is Aristotle's saying, that all self-moving things are animals. Now the ways walk there. Ergo, they are then animals. Some of them are strange unknown ways, like those of the planets; others are highways, cross-ways, and byways. I perceived that the travellers and inhabitants of that country asked, "Whither does this way go? Whither does that way go?" Some answered "Between Midy and Fevrolles, to the parish church, to the city, to the river," and so forth. Being thus in their right way, they used to reach their journey's end without any farther trouble, just like those who go by water from Lyons to Avignon or Arles.

Now, as you know that nothing is perfect here below, we heard there was a sort of people whom they called highwaymen, way-beaters, and makers of inroads in roads; and that the poor ways were sadly afraid of them, and shunned them as you do robbers. For these used to way-lay them, as people lay trains for wolves, and set gins for woodcocks. I saw one who was taken up with a lord chief justice's warrant, for having unjustly, and in spite of Pallas, taken the school-way, which is the longest. Another boasted that he had fairly taken the shortest, and that doing so, he first compassed his design. Thus Carpalim, meeting once Epistemon looking upon a wall with his fiddle-diddle, or live urinal, in his hand, to make a little maid's water, cried, "That he did not wonder now how the other came to be still the first at Pantagruel's levee, since he held his shortest, and least used."

I found Bourges highway among these. It went with the deliberation of an abbot, but was made to scamper at the approach of some waggoners, who threatened to have it trampled under their horses' feet, and make their waggons run over it, as Tullia's chariot did over her father's body.

I also espied there the old way between Peronne and St. Quentin, which seemed to me a very good, honest, plain way, as smooth as a carpet, and as good as ever was trod upon by shoe of leather.

Among the rocks I knew again the good old way to la Ferrare, mounted on a huge bear. This at a distance would have put me in mind of St. Jerome's picture, had but the bear been a lion; for the poor way was all mortified, and wore a long hoary beard uncombed and entangled, which looked like the picture of winter, or at least like a white-frosted bush.

On that way were store of beads or rosaries, coarsely made of wild pine tree; and it seemed kneeling, not standing, nor lying flat: but its sides and middle were beaten with huge stones; insomuch that it proved to us at once an object of fear and pity.

While we were examining it, a runner, bachelor of the place, took us aside, and shewing us a white smooth way, somewhat filled with straw, said "Henceforth, gentlemen, do not reject the opinion of Thales the Milesian, who said that water is the beginning of all things; nor that of Homer, who tells us, that all things derive their original from the ocean: for, this same way which you see here, had its beginning from water, and is to return whence she came before two months come to an end; now carts are driven here where boats used to be rowed."

"Truly," said Pantagruel, "you tell us no news; we see five hundred such changes, and more, every year in our world." Then reflecting on the different manner of going of those moving ways, he told us, he believed that Philolaus and Aristarchus had philosophized in this island, and that Saleucus indeed was of opinion, the earth turns round about its poles, and not the heavens, whatever we may think to the contrary: As when we are on the river Loire, we think the trees and the shore moves, though this is only an effect of our boat's motion.

As we went back to our ships, we saw three waylayers, who having been taken in ambuscado, were going to be broken on the wheel; and a huge fornicator was burned with a lingering fire, for beating away, and breaking one of its sides: we were told it was the way of the banks of the Nile in Egypt.

CHAPTER XXVII

HOW WE CAME TO THE ISLAND OF SANDALS; AND OF
THE ORDER OF SEMIQUAVER FRIARS

THENCE we went to the island of Sandals, whose inhabitants live on nothing but ling-broth. However, we were very kindly received and entertained by Benius the third, king of the island; who, after he had made us drink, took us with him to shew us a spick-and-span new monastery, which he had contrived for the semiquaver friars: so he called the religious men whom he had there. For he said, that on t'other side the water lived friars, who styled themselves her sweet ladyship's most humble servants. Item, the goodly friar-minors, who are semibreves of bulls; the smoaked-herring tribe of minim friars; then the crotchet friars. So that these diminutives could be no more than semiquavers. By the statutes, bulls, and patents of queen Whims, they were all dressed like so many house-burners; except that, as in

Anjou your tilers used to quilt their knees when they tile houses, so these holy friars had usually quilted bellies, and thick quilted paunches were among them in much repute. Their cod-pieces were cut slipper-fashion, and every monk of them wore two; one sewed before, and another behind; reporting that some certain dreadful mysteries were duly represented by this duplicity of cod-pieces.

They wore shoes as round as basons, in imitation of those who inhabit the sandy sea. Their chins were close shaved, and their feet iron-shod; and to shew they did not value fortune, Benius made them shave and poll the hind part of their poles, as bare as a bird's arse, from the crown to the shoulder-blades: but they had leave to let their hair grow before, from the two triangular bones in the upper part of the skull.

Thus they did not value fortune a button, and cared no more for the goods of this world, than you or I do for hanging. And to shew how much they defied that blind jilt, all of them wore, not in their hands like her, but at their waist, instead of beads, sharp razors, which they used to new grind twice a day, and set thrice a night.

Each of them had a round ball on their feet, because fortune is said to have one under hers.

The flap of their cowls hanged forward, and not backwards, like those of others: thus none could see their noses, and they laughed without fear both at fortune and the fortunate; neither more nor less than our ladies laugh at bare-faced trulls, when they have those mufflers on, which they call masks, and which were formerly much more properly called charity, because they cover a multitude of sins.

The hind part of their faces were always uncovered, as are our faces, which made them either go with the belly, or the arse foremost, which they pleased. When their hind face went forwards, you would have sworn this had been their natural gait; as well on account of their round shoes, as of the double cod-piece, and their face behind, which was as bare as the back of my hand, and coarsely daubed over with two eyes, and a mouth, such as you see on some Indian nuts. Now, if they offered to waddle along with their bellies forwards, you would have thought they were then playing at blindman's buff. May I never be hanged if it was not a comical sight.

Their way of living was thus. About owl-light they charitably began to boot and spur one another; this being done, the least thing they did was to sleep and snoar; and thus sleeping, they had barnacles on the handles of their faces, or spectacles at most.

You may swear, we did not a little wonder at this odd fancy; but they satisfied us presently, telling us that the day of judgment is to take mankind napping; therefore to shew they did not refuse to make their personal appearance, as fortune's darlings used to do, they were always thus booted and spurred, ready to mount whenever the trumpet should sound.

At noon, as soon as the clock struck, they used to awake. You must know that their clock-bell, church-bells, and refectuary-bells were all made according to the pontial device, that is, quilted with the finest down, and their clappers of fox-tails.

Having then made a shift to get up at noon, they pulled off their boots, and those that wanted to speak with a maid, alias piss, pissed; those that wanted to scumber, scumbered; and those that wanted to sneeze, sneezed. But all, whether they would or no (poor gentlemen!) were obliged largely and plentifully to yawn, and this was their first breakfast. (O rigorous statute!) Methought 'twas very comical to observe their transactions; for, having laid their boots and spurs on a rack, they went into the cloisters; there they curiously washed their hands and mouths, then sat them down on a long bench, and picked their teeth till the provost gave the signal, whistling through his fingers; then every he stretched out his jaws as much as he could, and they gaped and yawned for about half an hour, sometimes more, sometimes less, according as the prior judged the breakfast to be suitable to the day.

After that, they went in procession; two banners being carried before them, in one of which was the picture of virtue, and that of fortune in the other. The last went before, carried by a semiquavering friar, at whose heels was another with the shadow or image of virtue in one hand, and an holy-water sprinkle in the other; I mean of that holy mercurial-water, which Ovid describes in his de fastis. And as the preceding semiquaver rang a hand-bell, this shaked the sprinkle with his fist. With that, says Pantagruel, "This order contradicts the rule which Tully and the academics prescribed, that virtue ought to go before, and fortune follow." But they told us, they did as they ought, seeing their design was to breech, lash, and bethwack fortune.

During the processions, they trilled and quavered most melodiously betwixt their teeth I don't know what antiphonies, or chantings by turns: for my part, 'twas all Hebrew-Greek to me, the devil a word I could pick out on't; at last, pricking up my ears, and intensely listening, I perceived they only sang with the tip of theirs. Oh, what a rare harmony it was! How well 'twas tuned to the sound of their bells! You'll never find those to jar, that you won't. Pantagruel made a notable observation upon the processions: "For," says he, "have you seen and observed the policy of these semiquavers? To make an end of their procession, they went out at one of their church-doors, and came in at the other; they took a deal of care not to come in at the place whereat they went out." "On my honour, these are a subtle sort of people," quoth Panurge; "they have as much wit as three folks, two fools and a madman; they are as wise as the calf that ran nine miles to suck a bull, and when he came there t'was a steer." "This subtilty and wisdom of theirs," cried friar John, "is borrowed from the occult philosophy: may I be gutted like an oyster if I can tell what to make on't." "Then the more 'tis to be feared," said Pantagruel; "for subtilty suspected, subtilty foreseen, subtilty found out, loses the essence and very name of subtilty, and only gains that of blockishness. They are not such fools as you take them to be; they have more tricks than are good, I doubt."

After the procession, they went sluggingly into the fratry room by the way of walk and healthful exercise, and there kneeled under the tables, leaning their breasts on lanterns. While they were in that posture, in came a huge sandal, with a pitchfork in his hand, who used to baste, rib-roast, swaddle, and swinge them well favouredly, as they said, and in truth treated them after a fashion. They began their meal as you end yours, with cheese, and ended it with mustard and lettuce, as Martial tells us the ancients did. Afterwards a platter full of mustard was brought before every one of them; and thus they made good the proverb, "After meat comes mustard."

Their diet was this.

O' Sundays they stuffed their puddings with puddings, chitterlings, links, Bolonia sausages, forced-meats, liverings, hogs'-haslets, young quails, and teals: you must also always add cheese for the first course, and mustard for the last.

O' Mondays, they were crammed with peas and pork, cum commento, and interlineary glosses.

O' Tuesdays, they used to twist store of holy-bread, cakes, buns, puffs, lenten loaves, jumbals, and biscuits.

O' Wednesdays, my gentlemen had fine sheeps'-heads, calves'-heads, and brocks'-heads of which there's no want in that country.

O' Thursdays, they guzzled down seven sorts of porridge, not forgetting mustard.

O' Fridays, they maunched nothing but services or sorb-apples; neither were these full ripe, as I guessed by their complexion.

O' Saturdays, they gnawed bones; not that they were poor or needy, for every mother's son of 'em had a very good fat belly-benefice.

As for their drink, 'twas an antifortunal; thus they called I don't know what sort of a liquor of the place.

When they wanted to eat or drink, they turned down the back-points or flaps of their cowls forwards, below their chins, and that served 'em instead of gorgets or slabbering-bibs.

When they had well dined, they prayed rarely all in quavers and shakes; and the rest of the day, expecting the day of judgment, they were taken up with acts of charity, and particularly

O' Sundays, rubbers at cuffs.

O' Mondays, lending each other flirts and fillips on the nose.

O' Tuesdays, clapperclawing one another.

O' Wednesdays, sniting and fly-flapping.

O' Thursdays, worming and pumping.

O' Fridays, tickling.

O' Saturdays, jirking and firking one another.

Such was their diet when they resided in the convent, and if the prior of the monk-house sent any of them abroad, then they were strictly enjoined, neither to touch nor eat any manner of fish, as long as they were on sea or rivers; and to abstain from all manner of flesh whenever they were at land; that every one might be convinced, that while they enjoyed the object, they denied themselves the power, and even the desire, and were no more moved with it than the Marpesian rock.

All this was done with proper antiphones, still sung and chanted by ear, as we have already observed.

When the sun went to bed, they fairly booted and spurred each other as before, and having clapped on their barnacles, e'en jogged to bed too. At midnight the sandal came to them, and up they got, and having well whetted and set their razors, and been a processioning, they clapped the tables over themselves, and like wiredrawers under their work, fell to it as aforesaid.

Friar John des Entoumeures, having shrewdly observed these jolly semiquaver friars, and had full account of their statutes, lost all patience, and cried out aloud, "Bounce tail, and God ha' mercy guts; if every fool should wear a bauble, fuel would be dear. A plague rot it, we must know how many farts go to an ounce. Would Priapus were here, as he used to be at the nocturnal festivals in Crete, that I might see him play backwards, and wriggle and shake to the purpose. Ay, ay, this is the world and t'other is the country: may I never piss if this be not an antichthonian land, and our very antipodes. In Germany they pull down monasteries and unfrockify the monks; here they go quite kam, and act clean contrary to others, setting new ones up, against the hair."

CHAPTER XXVIII

HOW PANURGE ASKED A SEMIQUAVER FRIAR MANY QUESTIONS, AND WAS ONLY ANSWERED IN MONOSYLLABLES

PANURGE, who had since been wholly taken up with staring at these royal semiquavers, at last pulled one of them by the sleeve, who was as lean as a rake, and asked him,

"Hark'e me, friar quaver, semiquaver, demi-semiquavering quaver, where's the punk?"

The friar pointing downwards, answered, "There."

Pan. "Pray have you many?"

Fri. "Few."

Pan. "How many scores have you?"

Fri. "One."

Pan. "How many would you have?"

Fri. "Five."

Pan. "Where do you hide 'em?"

Fri. "Here."

Pan. "I suppose they are not all of one age; but pray how is their shape?"

Fri. "Straight."

Pan. "Their complexion?"

Fri. "Clear."

Pan. "Their hair?"

Fri. "Fair."

Pan. "Their eyes?"

Fri. "Black.

Pan. "Their features?"

Fri. "Good."

Pan. "Their brows?"

Fri. "Soft."

Pan. "Their graces?"

Fri. "Ripe."

Pan. "Their looks?"

Fri. "Free."

Pan. "Their feet?"

Fri. "Flat."

Pan. "Their heels?"

Fri. "Short."

Pan. "Their lower parts?"

Fri. "Rare."

Pan. "And their arms?"

Fri. "Long."

Pan. "What do they wear on their hands?"

Fri. "Gloves."

Pan. "What sort of rings on their fingers?"

Fri. "Gold."

Pan. "What rigging do you keep 'em in?"

Fri. "Cloth."

Pan. "What sort of cloth is it?"

Fri. "New."

Pan. "What colour?"

Fri. "Sky."

Pan. "What kind of cloth is it?"

Fri. "Fine."

Pan. "What caps do they wear?"

Fri. "Blue."

Pan. "What's the colour of their stockings?"

Fri. "Red."

Pan. "What wear they on their feet?"

Fri. "Pumps."

Pan. "How do they use to be?"

Fri. "Foul."

Pan. "How do they use to walk?"

Fri. "Fast."

Pan. "Now let's talk of the kitchen, I mean that of the harlots, and without going hand over head, let's a little examine things by particulars. What is in their kitchens?"

Fri. "Fire."

Pan. "What fuel feeds it?"

Fri. "Wood."

Pan. "What sort of wood is it?"

Fri. "Dry."

Pan. "And of what other trees?"

Fri. "Yews."

Pan. "What are the faggots and brushes of?"

Fri. "Holme."

Pan. "What wood do you burn in your chambers?"

Fri. "Pine."

Pan. "And of what other trees?"

Fri. "Line."

Pan. "Harkee me, as for the buttocks, I'll go your halves: pray, how do you feed 'em?"

Fri. "Well."

Pan. "First, what do they eat?"

Fri. "Bread."

Pan. "Of what complexion?"

Fri. "White."

Pan. "And what else?"

Fri. "Meat."

Pan. "How do they love it drest?"

Fri. "Roast."

Pan. "What sort of porridge?"

Fri. "None."

Pan. "Are they for pies and tarts?"

Fri. "Much."

Pan. "There I'm their man. Will fish go down with them?"

Fri. "Well."

Pan. "And what else?"

Fri. "Eggs."

Pan. "How do they like 'em?"

Fri. "Boiled."

Pan. "How must they be done?"

Fri. "Hard."

Pan. "Is this all they have?"

Fri. "No."

Pan. "What have they besides, then?"

Fri. "Beef."

Pan. "And what else?"
Fri. "Pork."
Pan. "And what more?"
Fri. "Geese."
Pan. "What then?"
Fri. "Ducks."
Pan. "And what besides?"
Fri. "Cocks."
Pan. "What do they season their meat with?"
Fri. "Salt."
Pan. "What sauce are they most dainty for?"
Fri. "Must."
Pan. "What's their last course?"
Fri. "Rice."
Pan. "And what else?"
Fri. "Milk."
Pan. "What besides?"
Fri. "Pease."
Pan. "What sort?"
Fri. "Green."
Pan. "What do they boil with 'em?"
Fri. "Pork."
Pan. "What fruit do they eat?"
Fri. "Good."
Pan. "How?"
Fri. "Raw."
Pan. "What do they end with?"
Fri. "Nuts."
Pan. "How do they drink?"
Fri. "Neat."
Pan. "What liquor?"
Fri. "Wine."
Pan. "What sort?"
Fri. "White."
Pan. "In winter?"
Fri. "Strong."
Pan. "In the spring?"
Fri. "Brisk."
Pan. "In summer?"
Fri. "Cool."

676

Pan. "In autumn?"

Fri. "New."

"Buttock of a monk!" cried friar John, "how plump these plaguy trulls, these arch semiquavering strumpets must be! That damned cattle are so high fed that they must needs be high-mettled, and ready to wince, and give two ups for one go-down, when any one offers to ride 'em below the crupper."

"Pr'ythee, friar John," quoth Panurge, "hold thy prating tongue, stay till I have done.

"Till what time do the doxies sit up?"

Fri. "Night."

Pan. "When do they get up?"

Fri. "Late."

Pan. "May I ride on a horse that was foaled of an acorn, if this be not as honest a cod as ever the ground went upon, and as grave as an old gate-post into the bargain. Would to the blessed St. Semiquaver, and the blessed worthy virgin St. Semiquavera, he were lord chief president [justice] of Paris. Odsbodikins, how he'd dispatch! With what expedition would he bring disputes to an upshot! What an abbreviator and clawer off of law-suits, reconciler of differences, examiner and fumbler of bags, peruser of bills, scribbler of rough-draughts, and an engrosser of deeds would he not make! Well, friar, spare your breath to cool your porridge: come, let's now talk with deliberation, fairly and softly, as lawyers go to heaven. Let's know how you victual the venereal camp.

"How is the snatchblatch?"

Fri. "Rough."

Pan. "How is the gate-way."

Fri. "Free."

Pan. "And how'st within?"

Fri. "Deep."

Pan. "I mean, what weather is it there?"

Fri. "Hot."

Pan. "What shadows the brooks?"

Fri. "Groves."

Pan. "Of what's the colour of the twigs?"

Fri. "Red."

Pan. "And what of the old?"

Fri. "Grey."

Pan. "How are you when you shake?"

Fri. "Brisk."

Pan. "How is their motion?"

Fri. "Quick."

Pan. "Would you have them vault or wriggle more?"

Fri. "Less."

Pan. "What kind of tools are yours?"

Fri. "Big."

Pan. "And in their helves?"

Fri. "Round."

Pan. "Of what colour's the tip?"

Fri. "Red."

Pan. "When they've been used, how are they?"

Fri. "Shrunk."

Pan. "How much weighs each bag of tools?"

Fri. "Pounds."

Pan. "How hang your pouches?"

Fri. "Tight."

Pan. "How are they when you have done?"

Fri. "Lank."

Pan. "Now, by the oath you have taken, tell me, when you have a mind to cohabit, how you throw 'em?"

Fri. "Down."

Pan. "And what do they say then?"

Fri. "Fie."

Pan. "However, like maids, they say nay, and take it; and speak the less, but think the more; minding the work in hand: do they not?"

Fri. "True."

Pan. "Do they get you bairns?"

Fri. "None."

Pan. "How do you pig together?"

Fri. "Bare."

Pan. "Remember you're upon your oath, and tell me justly, and bonâ fide, how many times a day you monk it?"

Fri. "Six."

Pan. "How many bouts o'nights?"

Fri. "Ten."

"Cat so," quoth friar John, "the poor fornicating brother's bashful, and sticks at sixteen, as if that were his stint." "Right," quoth Panurge, "but couldst thou keep pace with him, friar John, my dainty cod? May the devil's dam suck my teat, if he does not look as if he had got a blow over the nose with a Naples' cowl-staff.

Pan. "Pray, friar Shakewell, does your whole fraternity quaver and shake at that rate?"

Fri. "All."

Pan. "Who of them is the best cock o'the game?"

Fri. "I."

Pan. "Do you never commit dry bobs, or flashes in the pan?"

Fri. "None."

Pan. "I blush like any black dog, and could be as testy as an old cook, when I think on all this; it passes my understanding. But, pray, when you have been pumpt dry one day, what have you got the next?"

Fri. "More."

Pan. "By Priapus, they have the Indian herb, of which Theophrastus spoke, or I am much out. But harkee me, thou man of brevity, should some impediment honestly, or otherwise, impair your talents, and cause your benevolence to lessen, how would it fare with you then?"

Fri. "Ill."

Pan. "What would the wenches do?"

Fri. "Rail."

Pan. "What if you skipt, and let 'em fast a whole day?"

Fri. "Worse."

Pan. "What do you give 'em then?"

Fri. "Thwacks."

Pan. "What say they to this?"

Fri. "Bawl."

Pan. "And what else?"

Fri. "Curse."

Pan. "How do you correct 'em?"

Fri. "Hard."

Pan. "What do you get out of 'em then?"

Fri. "Blood."

Pan. "How's their complexion then?"

Fri. "Odd."

Pan. "What do they mend it with?"

Fri. "Paint."

Pan. "Then, what do they do?"

Fri. "Fawn."

Pan. "By the oath you have taken, tell me truly, what time of the year do you do it least in?"

Fri. "Now."

Pan. "What season do you do it best in?"

Fri. "March."

Pan. "How is your performance the rest of the year?"

Fri. "Brisk."

"Then," quoth Panurge, sneering, "of all, and of all, commend me to ball; this is the friar of the world for my money: you've heard how short, concise, and compendious he is in his answers? Nothing is to be got out of him but monosyllables? By jingo, I believe he would make three bites of a cherry."

"Damn him," cried friar John, "that's as true as I am his uncle: the dog yelps at another gat's rate when he is among his bitches; there he is polysyllable enough, my life for yours. You talk of making three bites of a cherry! God send fools more wit, and us more money: may I be doomed to fast a whole day, if I don't verily believe he would not make above two bites of a shoulder of mutton, and one swoop of a whole pottle of wine; zoons, do but see how down o' the mouth the cur looks! He's nothing but skin and bones; he has pissed his tallow."

"Truly, truly," quoth Epistemon, "this rascally monastical vermin all over the world mind nothing but their gut, and are as ravenous as any kites, and then, forsooth, they tell us they've nothing but food and raiment in this world: 'sdeath, what more have kings and princes?"

CHAPTER XXIX

HOW EPISTEMON DISLIKED THE INSTITUTION OF LENT

Pray did you observe," continued Epistemon, "how this damned ill-favoured semiquaver mentioned March as the best month for caterwauling." "True," said Pantagruel: "yet Lent and March always go together; and the first was instituted to macerate and bring down our pampered flesh, to weaken and subdue its lusts, and to curb and assuage the venereal rage."

"By this," said Epistemon, "you may guess what kind of a pope it was, who first enjoined it to be kept; since this filthy wooden-shoe'd semiquaver owns that his spoon is never oftener nor deeper in the porringer of lechery than in Lent. Add to this the evident reasons given by all good and learned physicians, affirming, that throughout the whole year no food is eaten, that can prompt mankind to lascivious acts, more than at that time.

"As, for example, beans, pease, phasels or long-peason, ciches, onions, nuts, oysters, herrings, salt-meats, garum (a kind of anchovy), and sallads, wholly made up of venereous herbs and fruits, as,

"Rocket,
Nose-smart,
Taragon,
Cresses,
Parsley,
Rampions,
Poppy,
Celery,
Hopbuds,
Figs,
Rice,
Raisins, and others."

" 'Twould not a little surprise you," said Pantagruel, "should a man tell you that the good pope, who first ordered the keeping of Lent, perceiving that that time o' year the natural heat (from the centre of the body, whither it was retired, during the winter's cold) diffuses itself as the sap does in trees, through the circumference of the members, did therefore in a manner prescribe that sort of diet to forward the propagation of mankind. What makes me think so is, that by the registers of christenings at Tours, it appears that more children are born in October and November, than in the other ten months of the year, and reckoning backwards, 'twill be easily found that they were all made, conceived, and begotten in Lent."

"I listen to you with both my ears," quoth friar John, "and that with no small pleasure, I'll assure you. But I must tell you, that the vicar of Jambert ascribed this copious prolification of the women, not to that sort of food that we chiefly eat in Lent, but to the little licensed stooping members, your little booted Lent-preachers, your little draggle-tailed father confessors; who, during all that time of their reign, damn all husbands that run astray, three fathoms and a half below the very lowest pit of hell. So the silly cod's-headed brothers of the noose dare not then stumble any more at the truckle-bed, to the no small discomfort of their maids, and are even forced, poor souls! to take up with their own bodily wives. Dixi, I have done."

"You may discant on the institution of Lent as much as you please," cried Epistemon; "so many men, so many minds: but certainly all the physicians will be against its being suppressed, though I think that time is at hand; I know they will, and have heard 'em say, were it not for Lent, their art would soon fall into contempt, and they'd get nothing, for hardly anybody would be sick.

"All distempers are sowed in Lent; 'tis the true seminary and native bed of all diseases: nor does it only weaken and putrefy bodies, but also maks souls mad and uneasy. For then the devils do their best, and drive a subtle trade, and the tribe of canting dissemblers come out of their holes. 'Tis then term-time with your cucullated pieces of formality, that have one face to God, and the other to the devil; and a wretched clutter they make with their sessions, stations, pardons, syntereses, confessions, whippings, anathematizations, and much prayer, with as little devotion. However, I'll not offer to infer from this that the Arimaspians are better than we are in that point; yet I speak to the purpose."

"Well," quoth Panurge to the semiquaver friar, who happened to be by, "dear bumbasting, shaking, trilling, quavering cod, what think'st thou of this fellow?—is he not a rank heretic?"

Fri. "Much."

Pan. "Ought he not to be singed?"

Fri. "Well."

Pan. "As soon as may be?"

Fri. "Right."

Pan. "Should not he be scalded first?"

Fri. "No."

Pan. "How then should he be roasted?"

Fri. "Quick."

Pan. "Till at last he be?"

Fri. "Dead."

Pan. "What has he made you?"

Fri. "Mad."

Pan. "What do you take him to be?"

Fri. "Damned."

Pan. "What place is he to go to?"

Fri. "Hell."

Pan. "But first, how would you have him served here?"

Fri. "Burnt."

Pan. "Some have been served so?"

682

Fri. "Store."

Pan. "That were heretics?"

Fri. "Less."

Pan. "And the number of those that are to be warmed thus here-after is?"

Fri. "Great."

Pan. "How many of 'em d'ye intend to save?"

Fri. "None."

Pan. "So you'd have them burnt?"

Fri. "All."

"I wonder," said Epistemon to Panurge, "what pleasure you can find in talking thus with this lousy tatterdemallion of a monk; I vow, did I not know you well, I might be ready to think you had no more wit in your head than he has in both his shoulders." "Come, come, scatter no words," returned Panurge, "every one as they like, as the woman said when she kissed her cow. I wish I might carry him to Gargantua; when I'm married he might be my wife's fool." "And make you one," cried Epistemon. "Well said," quoth friar John: "now poor Panurge, take that along with thee, thou'rt e'en fitted; 'tis a plain case thou'lt never scape wearing the bull's feather; thy wife will be as common as the highway, that's certain."

CHAPTER XXX

HOW WE CAME TO THE LAND OF SATIN

HAVING pleased ourselves with observing that new order of semi-quaver friars, we set sail, and in three days our skipper made the finest and most delightful island that ever was seen; he called it the island of Frize; for all the ways were of frize.

In that island is the land of Satin, so celebrated by our court pages. Its trees and herbage never lose their leaves or flowers, and are all damask and flowered velvet. As for the beasts and birds, they are all of tapestry work. There we saw many beasts, birds on trees, of the same colour, bigness, and shape, of those in our country; with this difference, however, that these did eat nothing, and never sung, or bit like ours: and we also saw there many sorts of creatures which we never had seen before.

Among the rest, several elephants in various postures: twelve of which were the six males and six females that were brought to Rome

683

by their governor in the time of Germanicus, Tiberius's nephew: some of them were learned elephants, some musicians, others philosophers, dancers, and shewers of tricks; and all sat down at table in good order, silently eating and drinking like so many fathers in a fratry-room.

With their snouts or proboscises, some two cubits long, they draw up water for their own drinking, and take hold of palm-leaves, plums, and all manner of edibles, using them offensively or defensively, as we do our fists; with them tossing men high into the air in fight, and making them burst with laughing when they come to the ground.

They have joints in their legs, whatever some men, who never saw any but painted, may have written to the contrary. Between their teeth they have two huge horns: thus Juba called 'em, and Pausanias tells us, they are not teeth, but horns: however, Philostratus will have 'em to be teeth, and not horns. 'Tis all one to me, provided you'll be pleased to own them to be true ivory. These are some three or four cubits long, and are fixed in the upper jaw-bone, and consequently not in the lowermost. If you hearken to those who will tell you the contrary, you'll find yourselves damnably mistaken, for that's a lie with a latchet: though 'twere Ælian that long-bow man that told you so, never believe him, for he lies as fast as a dog can trot. 'Twas in this very island that Pliny, his brother tell-truth, had seen some elephants dance on the rope with bells, and whip over the tables, presto, begone, while people were at feasts, without so much as touching the toping topers, or the topers toping.

I saw a rhinoceros there, just such a one as Harry Clerberg had formerly shewed me: methought it was not much unlike a certain boar which I had formerly seen at Limoges, except the sharp horn on its snout, that was about a cubit long; by the means of which that animal dares encounter with an elephant, that is sometimes killed with its point thrust into its belly, which is its most tender and defenceless part.

I saw there two and thirty unicorns. They are a curst sort of creatures, much resembling a fine horse, unless it be that their heads are like a stag's, their feet like an elephant's, their tails like a wild boar's, and out of each of their foreheads sprouts a sharp black horn, some six or seven foot long; commonly it dangles down like a turkey-cock's comb. When an unicorn has a mind to fight, or put it to any other use, what does he do but make it stand, and then 'tis as straight as an arrow.

I saw one of them, which was attended with a throng of other wild beasts, purify a fountain with its horn. With that Panurge told me, that his prancer, alias his nimble-wimble, was like the unicorn, not altogether in length indeed, but in virtue and propriety: for as the unicorn purified pools and fountains from filth and venom, so that other animals came and drank securely there afterwards; in the like manner, others might water their nags, and dabble after him without fear of shankers, carnosities, gonorrhæas, buboes, crinkams, and such other plagues, caught by those who venture to quench their amorous thirst in a common puddle; for with his nervous horn he removed all the infection that might be lurking in some blind cranny of the mephitic sweet-scented hole.

"Well," quoth friar John, "when you are sped, that is, when you are married, we'll make a trial of this on thy spouse, merely for charity-sake, since you are pleased to give us so beneficial an instruction."

"Aye, aye," returned Panurge, "and then immediately I'll give you a pretty gentle aggregrative pill of God, made up of two and twenty kind stabs with a dagger, after the Cæsarian way." "Cat so," cried friar John, "I had rather take off a bumper of good cool wine."

I saw there the golden fleece, formerly conquered by Jason, and can assure you on the word of an honest man, that those who have said it was not a fleece, but a golden pipin, because μῆλον signifies both an apple and a sheep, were utterly mistaken.

I saw also a cameleon, such as Aristotle describes it, and like that which had been formerly shewed me by Charles Maris, a famous physician of the noble city of Lyons on the Rhone: and the said cameleon lived on air, just as the other did.

I saw three hydras, like those I had formerly seen. They are a kind of a serpent, with seven different heads.

I saw also fourteen phœnixes. I had read in many authors that there was but one in the whole world in every century: but if I may presume to speak my mind, I declare, that those who said this, had never seen any, unless it were in the land of tapestry; though 'twere vouched by Lactantius Firmianus.

I saw the skin of Apuleius's golden ass.

I saw three hundred and nine pelicans.

Item, six thousand and sixteen Seleucid birds marching in battalia, and picking up straggling grasshoppers in corn-fields.

Item, some synamologi, argatiles, caprimulgi, thynnunculs, onocrotals, or bitterns, with their wide swallows, stymphalides, harpies, panthers, dorcas's, or bucks, cemas's, cynocephalis's, satyrs, cartasons, tarands, uri, monopses, pegasi, neades, cepes, marmosets, or monkeys, presteres, bugles, musimons, byturos's, ophyri, screech owls, goblins, fairies, and griffins.

I saw Mid-lent o'horseback, with Mid-august and Mid-march holding its stirrups.

I saw some mankind wolves, centaurs, tigers, leopards, hyænas, camelopardels, and orix's, or huge wild goats with sharp horns.

I saw a remora, a little fish called echineis by the Greeks, and near it a tall ship, that did not get o'head an inch, though she was in the offing with top and top-gallants spread before the wind. I am somewhat inclined to believe, that 'twas the very numerical ship in which Periander the tyrant happened to be, when it was stopt by such a little fish in spite of wind and tide. 'Twas in this land of Satin, and in no other, that Mutianus had seen one of them.

Friar John told us, that in the days of yore, two sorts of fishes used to abound in our courts of judicature, and rotted the bodies and tormented the souls of those who were at law, whether noble or of mean descent, high or low, rich or poor: the first were your April fish or mackerel [pimps, panders, and bawds]; the others your beneficial remoras, that is, the eternity of law-suits; the needless lets that keep 'em undecided.

I saw some sphynges, some raphes, some ounces, and some cepphi, whose fore-feet are like hands, and their hind-feet like man's feet.

Also some crocuta's and some eali as big as sea-horses, with elephant's tails, boars' jaws and tusks, and horns as pliant as an ass's ears.

The leucrocutes, most fleet animals, as big as our asses of Mirebalais, have necks, tails, and breasts like a lion's, legs like a stag's, the mouth up to the ears, and but two teeth, one above and one below; they speak with human voices, but when they do, they say nothing.

Some people say, that none ever saw an airy, or nest of sakers; if you'll believe me, I saw no less than eleven, and I'm sure I reckoned right.

I saw some left-handed halberts, which were the first that I had ever seen.

I saw some manticores, a most strange sort of creatures, which have of teeth which close together, as if you joined your hands with your fingers between each other: they have a sting in their tails like a scorpion's and a very melodious voice.

I saw some catablepas's, a sort of serpents, whose bodies are small, but their heads large without any proportion, so that they've much ado to lift them up; and their eyes are so infectious, that whoever sees 'em, dies upon the spot, as if he had seen a basilisk.

I saw some beasts with two backs, and those seemed to me the merriest creatures in the world: they were most nimble at wriggling the buttocks, and more diligent in tail-wagging than any water-wagtails, perpetually jogging and shaking their double rumps.

I saw there some milched craw-fish, creatures that I never heard of before in my life: these moved in very good order, and 'twould have done your heart good to have seen 'em.

CHAPTER XXXI

HOW IN THE LAND OF SATIN WE SAW HEAR-SAY, WHO KEPT A SCHOOL OF VOUCHING

WE went a little higher up into the country of Tapestry, and saw the Mediterranean sea open to the right and left down to the very bottom: just as the Red Sea very fairly left its bed at the Arabian gulph, to make a lane for the Jews, when they left Egypt.

There I found Triton winding his silver shell instead of a horn, and also Glaucus, Proteus, Nereus, and a thousand other godlings and sea monsters.

I also saw an infinite number of fish of all kinds, dancing, flying, vaulting, fighting, eating, breathing, billing, shoving, milting, spawning, hunting, fishing, skirmishing, lying in ambuscado, making truces, cheapening, bargaining, swearing, and sporting.

In a blind corner we saw Aristotle holding a lantern, in the posture in which the hermit uses to be drawn near St. Christopher, watching, prying, thinking, and setting everything down in writing.

Behind him stood a pack of other philosophers, like so many bums by a head bailiff: as Appian, Heliodorus, Athenæus, Porphyrius, Pancrates, Archadian, Numenius, Possidonius, Ovidius, Oppianus, Olypius, Seleucus, Leonides, Agathocles, Theophrastus, Damostratus, Mutianus, Nymphodorus, Ælian, and five hundred other such plodding dons, who were full of business, yet had little to do: like Chrysippus or Aristarchus of Soli, who for eight and fifty years together did nothing in the world but examine the state and concerns of bees.

I spied Peter Gilles among these, with an urinal in his hand, narrowly watching the water of those goodly fishes.

When we had long beheld everything in this land of Satin, Pantagruel said, "I have sufficiently fed my eyes, but my belly is empty all this while, and chimes to let me know it is time to go to dinner: let us take care of the body, lest the soul abdicate it; and to this effect, let us taste some of these anacampserotes that hang over our heads." "Pshaw," cried one, "they are mere trash, stark nought o' my word, they are good for nothing."

I then went to pluck some myrobolans off of a piece of tapestry, whereon they hung, but the devil a bit I could chew or swallow them; and had you had them betwixt your teeth, you would have sworn they had been thrown silk; there was no manner of savour in them.

One might be apt to think Heliogabalus had taken a hint from thence, to feast those whom he had caused to fast a long time, promising them a sumptuous, plentiful, and imperial feast after it: for all the treat used to amount to no more than several sorts of meat in wax, marble, earthenware, painted and figured tablecloths.

While we were looking up and down to find some more substantial food, we heard a loud various noise, like that of paper-mills, or women bucking of linen: so with all speed we went to the place whence the noise came, where we found a diminutive, monstrous, misshapen old fellow, called Hear-say. His mouth was slit up to his ears, and in it were seven tongues, each of them cleft into seven parts. However he chattered, tattled, and prated with all the seven at once, of different matters, and in divers languages.

He had as many ears all over his head and the rest of his body, as Argus formerly had eyes; and was as blind as a beetle, and had the palsy in his legs.

About him stood an innumerable number of men and women, gaping, listening, and hearing very intensely: among them I observed some who strutted like crows in a gutter, and principally a very handsome bodied man in the face, who held then a map of the world, and with little aphorisms compendiously explained everything to them; so that those men of happy memories grew learned in a trice, and would most fluently talk with you of a world of prodigious things, the hundredth part of which would take up a man's whole life to be fully known.

Among the rest, they descanted with great prolixity on the pyramids and hieroglyphics of Egypt, of the Nile, of Babylon, of the Troglodytes, the Hymantopodes, or crumpfooted nation, the Blemiæ, people that wear their heads in the middle of their breasts, the Pigmies, the Cannibals, the Hyperborei and their mountains, the Egypanes with their goat's-feet, and the devil and all of others: every individual word of it by hear-say.

I am much mistaken if I did not see among them Herodotus, Pliny, Solinus, Berosus, Philostratus, Pomponius, Mela, Strabo, and God knows how many other antiquaries.

Then Albert, the great Jacobin friar, Peter Tesmoin, alias Witness, Pope Pius the second, Volaterran, Paulus Jovius the valiant, Jemmy Cartier, Chaton the Armenian, Marco Paulo the Venetian, Ludovico Romano, Pedro Aliares, and forty cartloads of other modern historians, lurking behind a piece of tapestry, where they were at it ding-dong, privately scribbling the Lord knows what, and making rare work on't, and all by hear-say.

Behind another piece of tapestry [on which Naboth and Susanna's accusers were fairly represented] I saw close by Hear-say, good store of men of the country of Perche and Maine, notable students, and young enough.

I asked what sort of study they applied themselves to? and was told, that from their youth they learned to be evidences, affidavit men, and vouchers; and were instructed in the art of swearing: in which they soon became such proficients, that, when they left that country, and went back into their own, they set up for themselves, and very honestly lived by their trade of evidencing: positively giving their testimony of all things whatsoever, to those who feed them most roundly to do a job of journey-work for them; and all this by hear-say.

You may think what you will of it, but I can assure you, they gave some of us corners of their cakes, and we merrily helped to empty their hogsheads. Then in a friendly manner, they advised us to be as sparing of truth as possibly we could, if ever we had a mind to get court preferment.

CHAPTER XXXII

HOW WE CAME IN SIGHT OF LANTERN-LAND

HAVING been scurvily entertained in the land of Satin, we went o' board, and having set sail, in four days came near the coast of Lantern-land. We then saw certain little hovering fires on the sea.

For my part I did not take them to be lanterns, but rather thought they were fishes, which lolled their flaming tongues on the surface of the sea; or lampyrises, which some call cicindelas or glow-worms, shining there as ripe barley does o' nights in my country.

But the skipper satisfied us that they were the lanterns of the watch, or more properly light-houses, set up in many places round the precinct of the place to discover the land, and for the safe piloting in of some outlandish lanterns, which, like good franciscan and jacobin friars, were coming to make their personal appearance at the provincial chapter.

However, some of us were somewhat suspicious that these fires were the forerunners of some storm: but the skipper assured us again they were not.

CHAPTER XXXIII

HOW WE LANDED AT THE PORT OF THE LYCHNOBII,
AND CAME TO LANTERN-LAND

SOON after we arrived at the port of Lantern-land, where Pantagruel discovered, on a high tower, the lantern of Rochel, that stood us in good stead, for it cast a great light. We also saw the lantern of Pharos, that of Nauplion, and that of Acropolis, at Athens, sacred to Pallas.

Near the port, there is a little hamlet inhabited by the Lychnobii, that live by lanterns, as the gulligutted friars in our country live by nuns: they are studious people, and as honest men as ever shit in a trumpet. Demosthenes had formerly lanternised there.

We were conducted from that place to the palace by three obeliscolichnys, military guards of the port, with high-crowned hats, whom we acquainted with the cause of our voyage, and our design; which was to desire the queen of the country to grant us a lantern to light and conduct us, during our voyage to the oracle of the bottle.

They promised to assist us in this, and added, that we could never have come in a better time: for then the lanterns held their provincial chapter.

When we came to the royal palace, we had an audience of her highness, the queen of Lantern-land, being introduced by two lanterns of honour, that of Aristophanes, and that of Cleauthes. Panurge in few words acquainted her with the causes of our voyage, and she received us with great demonstrations of friendship; desiring us to come to her at supper-time, that we might more easily make choice of one to be our guide; which pleased us extremely. We did not fail to observe intensely everything we could see, as the garbs, motions and deportments of the queen's subjects, principally the manner after which she was served.

The bright queen was dressed in virgin crystal of Tutia, wrought damaskwise, and beset with large diamonds.

The lanterns of the royal blood were clad partly with bastard diamonds, partly with diaphanous stones; the rest with horn, paper, and oiled cloth.

The cresset-lights took place according to the antiquity and lustre of their families.

An earthen dark-lantern, shaped like a pot, notwithstanding this, took place of some of the first quality: at which I wondered much, till I was told it was that of Epictetus, for which three thousand drachmas had been formerly refused.

Martial's polymix lantern made a very good figure there: I took particular notice of its dress, and more yet of the icosimyx, formerly consecrated by Canopa, the daughter of Tisias.

I saw the pensile lantern, formerly taken out of the temple of Apollo Palatinus at Thebes, and afterwards by Alexander the Great, carried to the town of Cymos.

I saw another that distinguished itself from the rest by a bushy tuft of crimson silk on its head. I was told it was that of Bartolus, the lantern of the civilians.

Two others were very remarkable for glister-pouches that dangled at their waist. We were told, that one was the greater light, and the other the lesser light of the 'pothecaries.

When it was supper-time, the queen's highness first sat down, and then the rest, according to their rank and dignity.

For the first course, they were all served with large Christmas candles; except the queen, who was served with a hugeous, thick, stiff, flaming taper, of white wax, somewhat red towards the tip; and the royal family, as also the provincial lantern of Mirebalais, who were served with nut-lights; and the provincial of lower Poitou, with an armed candle.

After that, God-wot, what a glorious light they gave with their wicks: I do not say all; for you must except a parcel of junior lanterns, under the government of a high and mighty one. These did not cast a light like the rest, but seemed to me dimmer than any long-snuff farthing candle, whose tallow has been half melted away in a hot house.

After supper we withdrew to take some rest, and the next day the queen made us chuse one of the most illustrious lanterns to guide us: after which we took our leave.

CHAPTER XXXIV

HOW WE ARRIVED AT THE ORACLE OF THE BOTTLE

OUR glorious lantern lighting and directing us to our heart's content, we at last arrived at the desired island, where was the oracle of the bottle. As soon as friend Panurge landed, he nimbly cut a caper with one leg for joy, and cried to Pantagruel, "Now we are where we have wished ourselves long ago. This is the place we have been seeking with such toil and labour." He then made a compliment to our lantern, who desired us to be of good cheer, and not be daunted or dismayed, whatever we might chance to see.

To come to the temple of the holy bottle, we were to go through a large vineyard, in which were all sorts of vines, as the Falernian, Malvesian, the Muscadine, those of Taige, Beaune, Mirevaux, Orleans, Picardent, Arbois, Coussi, Anjou, Grave, Corsica, Vierron, Nerac, and others. This vineyard was formerly planted by the good Bacchus, with so great a blessing, that it yields leaves, flowers, and fruit all the year round, like the orange trees at Serene.

Our magnificent lantern ordered every one of us to eat three grapes, to put some vine-leaves in his shoes, and take a vine-branch in his left hand.

At the end of the close, we went under an arch built after the manner of those of the ancients. The trophies of a toper were curiously carved on it.

First, on one side, was to be seen a long train of flaggons, leathern bottles, flasks, cans, glass bottles, barrels, nipperkins, pint-pots, quart-pots, pottles, gallons, and old fashioned semaises [swinging wooden pots, such as those out of which the Germans fill their glasses]: these hung on a shady arbour.

On another side was store of garlic, onions, shallots, hams, botargos, caviar, biscuits, neat's tongues, old cheese, and such like comfits, very artificially interwoven, and packed together with vine-stocks.

On another were a hundred sorts of drinking glasses, cups, cisterns, ewers, false cups, tumblers, bowls, mazers, mugs, jugs, goblets, tal-boys, and such other bacchic artillery.

On the frontispiece of the triumphal arch, under the zoophore, was the following couplet:

> "You, who presume to move this way,
> Get a good lantern, lest you stray."

"We took special care of that," cried Pantagruel, when he read them: "for there is not a better or a more divine lantern than ours in all Lantern-land."

This arch ended at a fine large round alley, covered over with the interlaid branches of vines, loaded and adorned with clusters of five hundred different colours, and of as many various shapes, not natural, but due to the skill of agriculture: some were golden, other blueish, tawny, azure, white, black, green, purple, streaked with many colours, long, round, triangular, cod-like, hairy, great-headed and grassy. That pleasant alley ended at three old ivy trees, verdant, and all loaden with rings. Our most illustrious lantern directed us to make ourselves high-crowned hats with some of their leaves, and cover our heads wholly with them, which was immediately done.

"Jupiter's priestess," said Pantagruel, "in former days, would not, like us, have walked under this arbour." "There was a mystical reason," answered our most perspicuous lantern, "that would have hindered her. For had she gone under it, the wine, or the grapes of which it is made, that is the same thing, had been over her head, and then she would have seemed overtopt and mastered by wine. Which implies that priests, and all persons who devote themselves to the contemplation of divine things, ought to keep their minds sedate and calm, and avoid whatever may disturb and discompose their tranquillity; which nothing is more apt to do than drunkenness.

"You also," continued our lantern, "could not come into the holy bottle's presence, after you have gone through this arch, did not that noble priestess Bacbuc first see your shoes full of vine leaves: which action is diametrically opposite to the other, and signifies that you despise wine, and having mastered it, as it were, tread it underfoot."

"I am no scholar," quoth friar John, "for which I am heartily sorry; yet I find, by my breviary, that in the Revelation, a woman was seen with the moon under her feet, which was a most wonderful sight. Now, as Bigot explained it to me, this was to signify that she was not of the nature of other women; for they have all the moon at their heads, and consequently their brains are always troubled with a lunacy: this makes me willing to believe what you said, dear madam Lantern."

CHAPTER XXXV

HOW WE WENT UNDERGROUND TO COME TO THE TEMPLE OF THE HOLY BOTTLE; AND HOW CHINON IS THE OLDEST CITY IN THE WORLD

WE went underground through a plastered vault, on which was coarsely painted a dance of women and satyrs, waiting on old Silenus, who was grinning o' horseback on his ass. This made me say to Pantagruel, that this entry put me in mind of the painted cellar, in the oldest city in the world, where such paintings are to be seen, and in as cool a place.

"Which is the oldest city in the world?" asked Pantagruel. "It is Chinon, sir, or Cainon in Touraine," said I. "I know," returned Pantagruel, "where Chinon lies, and the painted cellar also, having myself drunk there many a glass of cool wine: neither do I doubt but that Chinon is an ancient town; witness its blazon. I own it is said twice or thrice,

> " 'Chinon,
> Little town,
> Great renown,
> On old stone
> Long has stood:
> There's the Vienne, if you look down;
> If you look up, there's the wood.'

"But how," continued he, "can you make it out that it is the oldest city in the world? Where did you find this written?" "I have found it in the Sacred Writ," said I, "that Cain was the first that built a town: we may then reasonably conjecture that from his name he gave it that of Cainon. Thus, after his example, most other founders of towns have given them their names: Athena, that is Minerva in Greek, to Athens; Alexander, to Alexandria; Constantine, to Constantinople; Pompey, to Pompeiopolis in Cilicia; Adrian, to Adrianople; Canaan, to the Canaanites; Saba, to the Sabæans; Assur, to the Assyrians; and so Ptolemais, Cæsara, Tiberias, and Herodium in Judæa got their names."

While we were thus talking, there came to us the great flask whom our lantern called the philosopher, her holiness the bottle's governor. He was attended with a troop of the temple-guards, all French bottles in wicker armour; and seeing us with our javelins wrapped with ivy, with our illustrious lantern, whom he knew, he desired us to come in with all manner of safety, and ordered we should be immediately conducted to the princess Bacbuc, the bottle's lady of honour, and priestess of all the mysteries; which was done.

CHAPTER XXXVI

HOW WE WENT DOWN THE TEDRATIC STEPS, AND OF PANURGE'S FEAR

WE went down one marble step underground, where there was a resting, or (as our workmen call it) a landing-place; then turning to the left, we went down two other steps, where there was another resting-place: after that we came to three other steps turning about, and met a third; and the like at four steps which we met afterwards. "There," quoth Panurge, "is it here?" "How many steps have you told?" asked our magnificent lantern. "One, two, three, four," answered Pantagruel. "How much is that?" asked she. "Ten," returned he. "Multiply that," said she, "according to the same pythagorical tètrad." "That is ten, twenty, thirty, forty," cried Pantagruel. "How much is the whole?" said she. "One hundred," answered Pantagruel. "Add," continued she, "the first cube, that is eight; at the end of that fatal number you will find the temple-gate; and pray observe, this is the true psychogony of Plato, so celebrated by the academics, yet so little understood; one moiety of which con-

695

sists of the unity of the two first numbers full of two square and two cubic numbers." We then went down those numerical stairs, all underground; and I can assure you in the first place that our legs stood us in good stead, for had it not been for them we had rolled just like so many hogsheads into a vault. Secondly, our radiant lantern gave us just so much light as is in Saint Patrick's hole in Ireland, or Trophonius's cavern in Bœotia; which caused Panurge to say to her, after we were got down some seventy-eight steps:

"Dear madam, with a sorrowful aching heart, I most humbly beseech your lanternship to lead us back. May I be led to hell if I be not half dead with fear; my heart is sunk down into my hose; I am afraid I shall make buttered eggs in my breeches. I freely consent never to marry. You have given yourself too much trouble on my account; the Lord shall reward you in his great rewarding-place; neither will I be ungrateful when I come out of this cave of Troglodytes. Let us go back, I pray you. I am very much afraid this is Tænarus, the low way to hell, and methinks I already hear Cerberus bark. Hark! I hear the cur, or my ears tingle: I have no manner of kindness for the dog, for there never is a greater tooth-ache than when dogs bite us by the shins: and if this be only Trophonius's pit, the lemures, hobthrushes and goblins will certainly swallow us alive; just as they devoured formerly one of Demetrius's halbardiers, for want of lunchions of bread. Art thou here, friar John? Pr'ythee, dear, dear cod, stay by me; I am almost dead with fear. Hast thou got thy bilbo? Alas! poor pilgarlic is defenceless: I am a naked man thou knowest: let us go back." "Zoons! fear nothing," cried friar John; "I am by thee, and have thee fast by the collar: eighteen devils shan't get thee out of my clutches, though I were unarmed. Never did a man yet want weapons who had a good arm with as stout a heart; heaven would sooner send down a shower of them; even as in Provence, in the fields of la Crau, near Mariane, there rained stones (they are there to this day) to help Hercules, who otherwise wanted wherewithal to fight Neptune's two bastards. But whither are we bound? Are we a going to the little children's limbo? By Pluto they will bepaw and conskite us all. Or are we going to hell for orders? By cob's body, I'll hamper, bethwack, and belabour all the devils, now I have some vine-leaves in my shoes. Thou shalt see me lay about me like mad, old boy. Which way? where the devil are they? I fear nothing but their damned horns: but cuckoldy Panurge's bull's feather will altogether secure me from them.

"Lo! in a prophetic spirit I already see him, like another Actæon, horned, horny, hornified." "Pr'ythee," quoth Panurge, "take heed thyself, dear frater, lest, till monks have leave to marry, thou wed'st something thou dost not like, as some quartan ague: if thou dost, may I never come safe and sound out of this hypogeum, this subterranean cave, if I don't tup and ram that disease merely for the sake of making thee a cornuted, a corniferous property: otherwise I fancy the quartan ague is but an indifferent bed-fellow, I remember Gripemen-all threatened to wed thee to some such thing, for which thou calledst him heretic."

Here our splendid lantern interrupted them, letting us know this was the place where we were to have a taste of the creature, and be silent; bidding us not despair of having the word of the bottle before we went back, since we had lined our shoes with vine-leaves.

"Come on, then," cried Panurge, "let's charge through and through all the devils of hell: we can but perish, and that's soon done: however, I thought to have reserved my life for some mighty battle. Move, move, move forwards; I am as stout as Hercules, my breeches are full of courage: my heart trembles a little, I own, but that's only an effect of the coldness and dampness of this vault; 'tis neither fear nor an ague. Come on, move on, piss, pish, push on. My name's William Dreadnought."

CHAPTER XXXVII

HOW THE TEMPLE GATES IN A WONDERFUL MANNER OPENED
OF THEMSELVES

AFTER we were got down the steps, we came to a portal of fine jasper, of Doric order, on whose front we read this sentence in the finest gold, EN 'OINΩ AΛHΘ EIA ; that is, "In wine, truth." The two folding doors of the gate were of Corinthian-like brass, massy, wrought with little vine-branches, finely embossed and engraven, and were equally joined and closed together in their mortaise without any padlock, key chain, or tie whatsoever. Where they joined, there hanged an Indian loadstone as big as an Egyptian bean, set in gold, having two points, hexagonal, in a right line; and on each side, towards the wall, hanged a handful of scordium.

There our noble lantern desired us not to take it amiss that she went no further with us, leaving us wholly to the conduct of the priestess Bacbuc: for she herself was not allowed to go in, for certain causes rather to be concealed than revealed to mortals. However, she advised us to be resolute and secure, and to trust to her for the return. She then pulled the loadstone that hanged at the folding of the gates, and throwed it into a silver box fixed for that purpose: which done, from the threshold of each gate she drew a twine of crimson silk about nine foot long, by which the scordium hanged, and having fastened it to two gold buckles that hanged at the sides, she withdrew.

Immediately the gates flew open without being touched: not with a creaking, or loud harsh noise, like that made by heavy brazen gates; but with a soft pleasing murmur that resounded through the arches of the temple.

Pantagruel soon knew the cause of it, having discovered a small cylinder or roller that joined the gates over the threshold, and, turning like them towards the wall on a hard well-polished ophites stone, with rubbing and rolling caused that harmonious murmur.

I wondered how the gates thus opened of themselves to the right and left, and after we were all got in, I cast my eye between the gates and the wall, to endeavour to know how this happened: for one would have thought our kind lantern had put between the gates the herb æthiopis, which they say opens some things that are shut: but I perceived that the parts of the gates that joined on the inside were covered with steel; and just where the said gates touched when they were opened, I saw two square Indian loadstones, of a blueish hue, well polished, and half a span broad, mortaised in the temple wall. Now, by the hidden and admirable power of the loadstones, the steel plates were put into motion, and consequently the gates were slowly drawn: however, not always, but when the said loadstone on the outside was removed, after which the steel was freed from its power, the two bunches of scordium being at the same time put at some distance, because it deadens the magnet, and robs it of its attractive virtue.

On the loadstone that was placed on the right side, the following iambic verse was curiously engraven in ancient Roman characters:

"Ducunt volentem fata, nolentem trahunt."
"Fate leads the willing, and th' unwilling draws."

The following sentence was neatly cut in the loadstone that was on the left:

"ALL THINGS TEND TO THEIR END."

CHAPTER XXXVIII

OF THE TEMPLE'S ADMIRABLE PAVEMENT

WHEN I had read those inscriptions, I admired the beauty of the temple, and particularly the disposition of its pavement, with which no work that is now, or has been under the cope of heaven, can justly be compared: not that of the temple of fortune at Præneste in Sylla's time; or the pavement of the Greeks, called asarotum, laid by Sosistratus in Pergamus. For this here was wholly in compartments of precious stones, all in their natural colours. One of red jasper, most charmingly spotted. Another of ophites. A third of porphyry. A fourth of lycophtalmy, a stone of four different colours, powdered with sparks of gold, as small as atoms. A fifth of agate, streaked here and there with small milk-coloured waves. A sixth of costly chalcedony. And another of green jasper, with certain red and yellowish veins. And all these were disposed in a diagonal line.

At the portico, some small stones were inlaid, and evenly joined on the floor, all in their native colours, to embellish the design of the figures; and they were ordered in such a manner, that you would have thought some vine-leaves and branches had been carelessly strewed on the pavement: for in some places they were thick, and thin in others. That inlaying was very wonderful everywhere: here were seen, as it were in the shade, some snails crawling on the grapes; there, little lizards, running on the branches: on this side, were grapes that seemed yet greenish; on another, some clusters that seemed full ripe, so like the true, that they could easily have deceived starlings, and other birds, as those which Zeuxis drew.

Nay, we ourselves were deceived; for where the artist seemed to have strewed the vine-branches thickest, we could not forbear walking with great strides, lest we should entangle our feet, just as people go over an unequal stony place.

I then cast my eyes on the roof and walls of the temple, that were all pargetted with porphyry and mosaic work; which from the left side at the coming in, most admirably represented the battle, in which the good Bacchus overthrew the Indians; as followeth.

CHAPTER XXXIX

AT the beginning, divers towns, hamlets, castles, fortresses and forests were seen in flames; and several mad and loose women, who furiously ripped up, and tore live calves, sheep, and lambs, limb from limb, and devoured their flesh. There we learned how Bacchus, at his coming into India, destroyed all things with fire and sword.

Notwithstanding this, he was so despised by the Indians, that they did not think it worth their while to stop his progress; having been certainly informed by their spies, that his camp was destitute of warriors, and that he had only with him a crew of drunken females, a low-built, old, effeminate, sottish fellow, continually addled, and as drunk as a wheel-barrow, with a pack of young clownish doddipoles, stark naked, always skipping and frisking up and down, with tails and horns like those of young kids.

For this reason the Indians had resolved to let them go through their country without the least opposition, esteeming a victory over such enemies more dishonourable than glorious.

In the meantime, Bacchus marched on, burning everything; for, as you know, fire and thunder are his paternal arms; Jupiter having saluted his mother Semele with his thunder; so that his maternal house was ruined by fire. Bacchus also caused a great deal of blood to be spilt; which, when he is roused and angered, principally in war, is as natural to him, as to make some in time of peace.

Thus the plains of the island of Samos, are called Panema, which signifies all bloody, because Bacchus there overtook the Amazons, who fled from the country of Ephesus, and there let them blood, so that they all died of phlebotomy. This may give you a better insight into the meaning of an ancient proverb, than Aristotle does in his problems; viz., Why 'twas formerly said, "Neither eat, nor sow any mint in time of war." The reason is, that blows are given in time of war without any distinction of parts or persons; and if a man that's wounded has that day handled or eaten any mint, 'tis impossible, or at least very hard, to staunch his blood.

After this, Bacchus was seen marching in battalia, riding in a stately chariot, drawn by six young leopards. He looked as young as a child, to shew that all good topers never grow old: he was as red as a cherry, or a cherub, which you please; and had no more hair on his chin than there is in the inside of my hand; his forehead was graced with pointed horns, above which he wore a fine crown or garland of vine-leaves and grapes, and a mitre of crimson velvet, having also gilt buskins on.

He had not one man with him, that looked like a man; his guards, and all his forces, consisted wholly of bassarides, evantes, euhyades, edonides, trietherides, ogygiæ, mimallonides, mænades, thyiades, and bacchides, frantic, raving, raging, furious, mad women begirt with live snakes and serpents, instead of girdles, their dishevelled hair flowing about their shoulders, with garlands of vine-branches instead of forehead-cloths, clad with stags or goats-skins, and armed with torches, javelins, spears, and halberts, whose ends were like pine-apples: besides, they had certain small light bucklers, that gave a loud sound if you touched them never so little, and these served them instead of drums: they were just seventy-nine thousand two hundred twenty-seven.

Silenus, who led the van, was one on whom Bacchus relied very much, having formerly had many proofs of his valour and conduct. He was a diminutive, stooping, palsied, plump, gorbellied, old fellow, with a swinging pair of stiff-standing lugs of his own, a sharp Roman nose, large, rough eyebrows, mounted on a well-hung ass: in his fist he held a staff to lean upon, and also bravely to fight, whenever he had occasion to alight; and he was dressed in a woman's yellow gown. His followers were all young, wild, clownish people, as hornified as so many kids, and as fell as so many tigers, naked, and perpetually singing and dancing country dances: they were called tityri and satyrs; and were in all eighty-five thousand one hundred and thirty-three.

Pan, who brought up the rear, was a monstrous sort of thing: for his lower parts were like a goat's, his thighs hairy, and his horns bolt upright; a crimson fiery phiz, and a beard that was none of the shortest. He was a bold, stout, daring, desperate fellow, very apt to take pepper in the nose for yea and nay.

In his left hand he held a pipe, and a crooked stick in his right. His forces consisted also wholly of satyrs, ægipanes, agripanes, sylvans, fauns, lemures, lares, elves, and hobgoblins; and their number was seventy-eight thousand one hundred and fourteen. The signal or word common to all the army, was "euohe."

CHAPTER XL

HOW THE BATTLE, IN WHICH THE GOOD BACCHUS OVERTHREW THE INDIANS, WAS REPRESENTED IN MOSAIC WORK

IN the next place we saw the representation of the good Bacchus's engagement with the Indians. Silenus, who led the van, was sweating, puffing, and blowing, belabouring his ass most grievously: the ass dreadfully opened its wide jaws, drove away the flies that plagued it, winced, flounced, went back, and bestirred itself in a most terrible manner, as if some damned gad-bee had stung it at the breech.

The satyrs, captains, serjeants, and corporals of companies, sounding the orgies with cornets, in a furious manner went round the army, skipping, capering, bounding, jerking, farting, flying out at heels, kicking and prancing like mad, encouraging their company to fight bravely; and all the delineated army cried out "Euohe!"

First the mænades charged the Indians with dreadful shouts, and a horrid din of their brazen drums and bucklers: the air rung again all-around, as the mosaic work well expressed it. And pray, for the future don't so much admire Apelles, Aristides the Theban, and others who drew claps of thunder, lightnings, winds, words, manners and spirits.

We then saw the Indian army, who had at last taken the field, to prevent the devastation of the rest of their country. In the front were the elephants, with castles well garrisoned on their backs. But the army and themselves were put into disorder; the dreadful cries of the bacchides having filled them with consternation, and those huge animals turned tail, and trampled on the men of their party.

There you might have seen gaffer Silenus on his ass, putting on as hard as he could, striking athwart and alongst, and laying about him lustily with his staff, after the old fashion of fencing. His ass was prancing and making after the elephants, gaping and martially braying, as it were to sound a charge, as he did when formerly in the bacchanalian feasts, he waked the nymph Lottis, when Priapus, full of priapism, had a mind to priapise, while the pretty creature was taking a nap.

There you might have seen Pan frisk it with his goatish shanks about the mænades, and with his rustic pipe excite them to behave themselves like mænades.

A little further you might have blessed your eyes with the sight of a young satyr who led seventeen kings his prisoners; and a Bacchis who, with her snakes, hauled along no less than two and forty captains; a little faun, who carried a whole dozen of standards taken on the enemy; and good man Bacchus on his chariot, riding to and fro fearless of danger, making much of his dear carcass, and cheerfully toping to all his merry friends.

Finally, we saw the representation of his triumph, which was thus. First, his chariot was wholly covered with ivy, gathered on the mountain Meros: this for its scarcity, which you know raises the price of everything, and principally of those leaves in India. In this Alexander the great follow his example at his Indian triumph. The chariot was drawn by elephants joined together. wherein he was imitated by Pompey the Great, at Rome, in his African triumph. In it the good Bacchus was seen, drinking out of a mighty urn, which action Marius aped after his victory over the Cimbri near Aix in Provence. All his army were crowned with ivy; their javelins, bucklers, and drums, were also wholly covered with it; there was not so much as Silenus's ass, but was betrapped with it.

The Indian kings were fastened with chains of gold close by the wheels of the chariot; all the company marched in pomp with unspeakable joy, loaded with an infinite number of trophies, pageants, and spoils, playing and singing merry epiniciums, songs of triumph, and also rural lays and dithyrambs.

At the farthest end was a prospect of the land of Egypt; the Nile with its crocodiles, marmosets, ibides, monkeys, trochilos's, or wrens, ichneumons, or Pharaoh's mice, hippopotami, or sea-horses, and other creatures, its guests and neighbours. Bacchus was moving towards that country under the conduct of a couple of horned beasts, on one of which was written in gold, Apis, and Osiris on the other; because no ox or cow had been seen in Egypt till Bacchus came thither.

CHAPTER XLI

HOW THE TEMPLE WAS ILLUMINATED WITH A WONDERFUL LAMP

BEFORE I proceed to the description of the bottle, I'll give you that of an admirable lamp, that dispensed so large a light over all the temple, that, though it lay under ground, we could distinguish every object as clearly as above it at noon-day.

In the middle of the roof was fixed a ring of massy gold, as thick as my clenched fist. Three chains somewhat less, most curiously wrought, hung about two foot and a half below it, and in a triangle supported a round plate of fine gold, whose diameter or breadth did not exceed two cubits and half a span. There were four holes in it, in each of which an empty ball was fastened, hollow within, and open o'top, like a little lamp; its circumference about two hands breadth: each ball was of precious stone; one an amethyst, another an African carbuncle, the third an opale, and the fourth an anthracites: they were full of burning water, five times distilled in a serpentine lymbeck, and inconsumptible, like the oil formerly put into Pallas's golden lamp at Acropolis of Athens by Callimachus. In each of them was a flaming wick, partly of asbestine flax, as of old in the temple of Jupiter Ammon, such as those which Cleombrotus, a most studious philosopher, saw, and partly of carpasian flax, which were rather renewed than consumed by the fire.

About two foot and a half below that gold plate, the three chains were fastened to three handles, that were fixed to a large round lamp of most pure crystal, whose diameter was a cubit and a half, and opened about two hands breadth o'top; by which open place a vessel of the same crystal, shaped somewhat like the lower part of a gourd-like lymbeck, or an urinal, was put at the bottom of the great lamp, with such a quantity of the afore-mentioned burning water, that the flame of asbestine wick reached the centre of the great lamp. This made all its spherical body seem to burn and be in a flame, because the fire was just at the centre and middle point: so that it was not more easy to fix the eye on it, than on the disk of the sun; the matter being wonderfully bright and shining, and the work most transparent and dazzling, by the reflection of the various colours of the precious stones, whereof the four small lamps above the main lamp were made, and their lustre was still variously glittering all over the temple. Then this wandering light being darted on the polished marble and agate, with which all the inside of the temple was pargetted, our eyes were entertained with a sight of all the admirable colours which the rainbow can boast, when the sun darts his fiery rays on some dropping clouds.

The design of the lamp was admirable in itself, but, in my opinion, what added much to the beauty of the whole, was, that round the body of the crystal lamp, there was carved in cataglyphic work, a lively and pleasant battle of naked boys, mounted on little hobby-horses, with little whirligig lances and shields, that seemed made of vine-branches with grapes on them: their postures generally were very different, and their childish strife and motions wre so ingeniously expressed, that art equalled nature in every proportion and action. Neither did this seem engraved, but rather hewed out and imbossed, in relief, or, at least like grotesque, which by the artist's skill has the appearance of the roundness of the object it represents: this was partly the effect of the various and most charming light, which flowing out of the lamp, filled the carved places with its glorious rays.

CHAPTER XLII

HOW THE PRIESTESS BACBUC SHEWED US A FANTASTIC FOUNTAIN
IN THE TEMPLE; AND HOW THE FOUNTAIN-WATER HAD THE
TASTE OF WINE, ACCORDING TO THE IMAGINATION OF
THOSE WHO DRANK OF IT

WHILE we were admiring this incomparable lamp, and the stupendous structure of the temple, the venerable priestess Bacbuc, and her attendants, came to us with jolly smiling looks, and seeing us duly accoutred, without the least difficulty took us into the middle of the temple, where, just under the aforesaid lamp, was the fine fantastic fountain. She then ordered some cups, goblets, and talboys of gold, silver, and crystal to be brought, and kindly invited us to drink of the liquor that sprung there, which we readily did: for to say the truth, this fantastic fountain was very inviting, and its materials and workmanship more precious, rare, and admirable than anything Plato ever dreamt of in limbo.

Its basis or ground work was of most pure and limpid alabaster, and its height somewhat more than three spans; being a regular heptagon on the outside, with its stylobates or footsteps, arulets, cymasults or blunt tops, and doric undulations about it. It was exactly round within. On the middle point of each angle brink stood a pillar orbiculated, in form of a circle of ivory or alabaster. These were seven in number, according to the number of the angles.

Each pillar's length, from the basis to the architraves, was near seven hands, taking an exact dimension of its diameter through the centre of its circumferences and inward roundness; and it was so disposed, that casting our eyes behind one of them, whatever its cube

705

might be, to view its opposite, we found that the pyramidal cone of our visual light ended at the said centre, and there, by the two opposites, formed an equilateral triangle, whose two lines divide the pillar into two equal parts.

That which we had a mind to measure, going from one side to another, two pillars over, at the first third part of the distance between them, was met by their lowermost and fundamental line, which in a consult line drawn as far as the universal centre, equally divided, gave, in a just partition, the distance of the seven opposite pillars in a right line; beginning at the obtuse angle on the brink: as you know that an angle is always found placed between two others in all angular figures odd in number.

This tacitly gives us to understand that seven semidiameters are in geometrical proportion, compass and distance, somewhat less than the circumference of a circle, from the figure of which they are extracted; that is to say, three whole parts, with an eighth and a half, a little more; or a seventh and a half, a little less; according to the instructions given us of old by Euclid, Aristotle, Archimedes, and others.

The first pillar, I mean that which faced the temple gate, was of azure, sky-coloured sapphire.

The second of hyacinth, a precious stone, exactly of the colour of the flower into which Ajax's choleric blood was transformed; the Greek letters A I, being seen on it in many places.

The third an anachite diamond, as bright and glittering as lightning.

The fourth a masculin ruby ballais (peach-coloured) amethystising, its flame and lustre ending in violet or purple, like an amethyst.

The fifth an emerald, above five hundred and fifty times more precious than that of Serapis in the labyrinth of the Egyptians, and more verdant and shining than those that were fixed instead of eyes in the marble lion's head, near king Hermias's tomb.

The sixth of agate, more admirable and various in the distinctions of its veins, clouds, and colours, than that which Pyrrhus, king of Epirus, so mightily esteemed.

The seventh of syenites, transparent, of the colour of a beril, and the clear hue of hymetian honey; and within it the moon was seen, such as we see in the sky, silent, full, new, and in the wain.

These stones were assigned to the seven heavenly planets by the ancient Chaldeans; and that the meanest capacities might be informed of this, just at the central perpendicular line, on the chapiter of the first pillar, which was of sapphire, stood the image of Saturn in elutian lead, with his scythe in his hand, and at his feet a crane of gold, very artfully enamelled according to the native hue of the saturnine bird.

On the second, which was hyacinth towards the left, Jupiter was seen in jovetian brass, and on his breast an eagle of gold enamelled to the life.

On the third was Phœbus in the purest gold, and a white cock in his right hand.

On the fourth was Mars in Corinthian brass, and a lion at his feet.

On the fifth was Venus in copper, the metal of which Aristonidas made Athamas's statue, that expressed in a blushing whiteness his confusion at the sight of his son, Learchus, who died at his feet of a fall.

On the sixth was Mercury in hydrargyre; I would have said quicksilver, had it not been fixed, malleable, and unmoveable: that nimble deity had a stork at his feet.

On the seventh was the moon in silver, with a greyhound at her feet.

The size of these statues was somewhat more than a third part of the pillars on which they stood; and they were so admirably wrought, according to mathematical proportion, that Polycletus's canon (or rule) could hardly have stood in competition with them.

The basis of the pillars, the chapiters, the architraves, zoophores and cornices, were Phrygian work of massy gold, purer and finer than any that is found in the river Leede near Montpellier, Ganges in India, Po in Italy, Hebrus in Thrace, Tagus in Spain, and Pactolus in Lydia.

The small arches between the pillars were of the same precious stone of which the pillars next to them were. Thus that arch was of sapphire which ended at the hyacinth pillar; and that was of hyacinth which went towards the diamond and so on.

Above the arches and chapiters of the pillars, on the inward front, a cupola was raised to cover the fountain: it was surrounded by the planetary statues, heptagonal at the bottom, and spherical o'top; and of crystal so pure, transparent, well-polished, whole and uniform in all its parts, without veins, clouds, flaws, or streaks, that Xenocrates never saw such a one in his life.

Within it were seen the twelve signs of the zodiac, the twelve months of the year, with their properties, the two equinoxes, the ecliptic line, with some of the most remarkable fixed stars about the antarctic pole, and elsewhere, so curiously engraven that I fancied them to be the workmanship of king Necepsus, or Petosiris the ancient mathematician.

On the top of the cupola, just over the centre of the fountain, were three noble long pearls, all of one size, pear fashion, perfectly imitating a tear, and so joined together as to represent a flower-de-lis or lily, each of the flowers seeming above a hand's breadth. A carbuncle jetted out of its calyx or cup, as big as an ostrich's egg, cut seven square (that number so beloved of nature) and so prodigiously glorious, that the sight of it had like to have made us blind; for the fiery sun, or the pointed lightning, are not more dazzling and unsufferably bright.

Now were some judicious appraisers to judge of the value of this incomparable fountain, and the lamp of which we have spoke, they would undoubtedly affirm, it exceeds that of all the treasures and curiosities in Europe, Asia, and Africa put together. For that carbuncle alone would have darkened the pantharb of Iarchas the Indian magician, with as much ease as the sun outshines and dims the stars with his meridian rays.

Now let Cleopatra, that Egyptian queen, boast of her pair of pendants, those two pearls, one of which she caused to be dissolved in vinegar in the presence of Anthony the triumvir, her gallant!

Or let Pompeia Plautina be proud of her dress covered all over with emeralds and pearls curiously intermixed, she who attracted the eyes of all Rome, and was said to be the grave-pit and magazine of the conquering robbers of the universe.

The fountain had three tubes or channels of right pearl, seated in three equilateral angles already mentioned, extended on the margin; and those channels proceeded in a snail-like line, winding equally on both sides.

We looked on them awhile, and had cast our eyes on another side, when Bacbuc directed us to watch the water: we then heard a most harmonious sound, yet somewhat stopped by starts, far distant and subterranean; by which means it was still more pleasing than if it had been free, uninterrupted, and near us; so that our minds were as agreeably entertained through our ears with that charming melody, as they were through the windows of our eyes, with those delightful objects.

Bacbuc then said, "Your philosophers will not allow that motion is begot by the power of figures; look here, and see the contrary. By that single snail-like motion, equally divided as you see, and a five-fold infoliature, moveable at every inward meeting, such as is the vena cava, where it enters into the right ventricle of the heart; just so is the flowing of this fountain, and by it an harmony ascends as high as your world's ocean.

She then ordered her attendants to make us drink; and to tell you the truth of the matter as near as possible, we are not, heaven be praised! of the nature of a drove of calf-lollies, who (as your sparrows can't feed unless you bob them on the tail) must be rib-roasted with tough crab-tree, and firked into a stomach, or at least into an humour to eat or drink: no, we know better things, and scorn to scorn any man's civility, who civilly invites us to a drinking bout. Bacbuc asked us then, how we liked our tiff. We answered, that it seemed to us good harmless sober Adam's liquor, fit to keep a man in the right way, and, in a word, mere element; more cool and clear than Argyrontes in Ætolia, Peneus in Thessaly, Axius in Mygdonia, or Cydnus in Cilicia, a tempting sight of whose cool silver stream caused Alexander to prefer the short-lived pleasure of bathing himself in it, to the inconveniences which he could not but foresee would attend so ill-timed an action.

"This," said Bacbuc, "comes of not considering with ourselves, or understanding the motions of the musculous tongue when the drink glides on it in its way to the stomach. Tell me, noble strangers, are your throats lined, paved, or enamelled, as formerly was that of Pithyllus, nick-named Theutes, that you can have missed the taste, relish, and flavour of this divine liquor? Here," said she, turning towards her gentlewomen, "bring my scrubbing brushes, you know which, to scrape, rake, cleanse and clear their palates."

They brought immediately some stately, swinging, jolly hams; fine, substantial neats-tongues; good hung beef, pure and delicate botargos, venison, sausages, and such other gullet-sweepers. And, to comply with her invitation, we crammed and twisted till we owned ourselves thoroughly cured of thirst, which before did damnably plague us.

"We are told," continued she, "that formerly a learned and valiant Hebrew chief leading his people through the deserts, where they were in danger of being famished, obtained of God some manna, whose taste was to them by imagination such as that of meat was to them before in reality: thus, drinking of this miraculous liquor, you'll find its taste like any wine that you shall fancy to drink. Come then, fancy and drink." We did so, and Panurge had no sooner whipped off his brimmer, but he cried, "By Noah's open shop, 'tis vin de Baulne, better than ever was yet tipped over tongue, or may ninety and sixteen devils swallow me. Oh! that to keep its taste the longer, we gentlemen topers had but necks some three cubits long, or so, as Philoxenus desired to have, or at least like a crane's, as Melanthius wished his."

"On the faith of true lanterners," quoth friar John, " 'tis gallant, sparkling Greek wine: now, for God's sake, sweetheart, do but teach me how the devil you make it." "It seems to me Mirevaux wine," said Pantagruel; "for before I drank I supposed it to be such. Nothing can be misliked in it, but that 'tis cold, colder, I say, than the very ice, colder than the water of Nonacris and Dircé or the Conthoporian spring at Corinth, that froze up the stomach and nutritive parts of those that drank of it."

"Drink once, twice, or thrice more," said Bacbuc, "still changing your imagination, and you shall find its taste and flavour to be exactly that on which you shall have pitched. Then never presume to say that anything is impossible to God." "We never offered to say such a thing," said I; "far from it, we maintain he is omnipotent."

CHAPTER XLIII

HOW THE PRIESTESS BACBUC EQUIPT PANURGE, IN ORDER TO HAVE THE WORD OF THE BOTTLE

WHEN we had thus chatted and tippled, Bacbuc asked, "Who of you here would have the word of the holy bottle?" "I, your most humble little funnel, an't please you," quoth Panurge. "Friend," saith she, "I have but one thing to tell you, which is, that when you come to the oracle, you take care to hearken and hear the word only with one ear." "This," cried friar John, "is wine of one ear, as Frenchmen call it."

She then wrapt him up in gaberdine, bound his noodle with a goodly clean biggin, clapt over it a felt, such as those through which hypocras is distilled, at the bottom of which, instead of a cowl, she put three obelisks; made him draw on a pair of old-fashioned codpieces instead of mittens, girded him about with three bagpipes bound together, bathed his jobbernol thrice in the fountain; then threw a handful of meal on his phiz, fixed three cock's feathers on the right side of the hypocratical felt, made him take a jaunt nine times round the fountain, caused him to take three little leaps, and to bump his a—— seven times against the ground, repeating I don't know what kind of conjurations all the while in the Tuscan tongue, and ever and anon reading in a ritual or book of ceremonies, carried after her by one of her mystagogues.

For my part, may I never stir, if I don't really believe, that neither Numa Pompilius the second king of the Romans, nor the Cerites of Tuscia, nor the old Hebrew captain, ever instituted so many ceremonies as I then saw performed; nor were ever half so many religious forms used by the soothsayers of Memphis in Egypt to Apis; or by the Euboians, at Rhamnus, to Rhamnusia; or to Jupiter Ammon, or to Feronia.

When she had thus accoutred my gentleman, she took him out of our company, and led him out of the temple through a golden gate on the right, into a round chapel made of transparent speculary stones, by whose solid clearness the sun's light shined there through the precipice of the rock without any windows or other entrance, and so easily and fully dispersed itself through the greater temple, that the light seemed rather to spring out of it than to flow into it.

The workmanship was not less rare than that of the sacred temple at Ravenna, or that in the island of Chemnis in Egypt. Nor must I forget to tell you, that the work of that round chapel was contrived with such a symmetry, that its diameter was just the height of the vault.

In the middle of it was an heptagonal fountain of fine alabaster most artfully wrought, full of water, which was so clear, that it might have passed for element in its purity and simplicity. The sacred bottle was in it to the middle, clad in pure fine crystal, of an oval shape, except its muzzle, which was somewhat wider than was consistent with that figure.

CHAPTER XLIV

HOW BACBUC, THE HIGH-PRIESTESS, BROUGHT PANURGE BEFORE THE HOLY BOTTLE

THERE the noble priestess Bacbuc made Panurge stoop and kiss the brink of the fountain; then bade him rise and dance three ithymbi. Which done, she ordered him to sit down, between two

711

stools placed there for that purpose, his arse upon the ground. Then she opened her ritual book, and, whispering in his left ear, made him sing an epileny, inserted here in the figure of the bottle.

Bottle! whose mysterious deep
　　Does ten thousand secrets keep,
　　　With attentive ear I wait;
　　　　Ease my mind, and speak my fate.
Soul of joy, like Bacchus, we
More than India gain by thee.
Truths unborn thy juice reveals,
Which futurity conceals.
Antidote to frauds and lies,
Wine, that mounts us to the skies,
May thy father Noah's brood
Like him drown, but in thy flood.
Speak, so may the liquid mine
Of rubies or of diamonds, shine.
　　Bottle! whose mysterious deep,
　　　Does ten thousand secrets keep,
　　　　With attentive ear I wait;
　　　　　Ease my mind, and speak my fate.

When Panurge had sung, Bacbuc throwed I don't know what into the fountain, and straight its water began to boil in good earnest, just for the world as doth the great monastical pot at Bourgueil, when 'tis high holiday there. Friend Panurge was listening with one ear, and Bacbuc kneeled by him, when such a kind of humming was heard out of the bottle, as is made by a swarm of bees bred in the flesh of a young bull killed and dressed according to Aristæus's art, or such as is made when a bolt flies out of a cross-bow, or when a shower falls on a sudden in summer. Immediately after this was heard the word TRINC. "By cob's body," cried Panurge, "'tis broken, or cracked at least, not to tell a lie for the matter; for, even so do crystal bottles speak in our country, when they burst near the fire."

Bacbuc arose, and gently taking Panurge under the arms, said, "Friend, offer your thanks to indulgent heaven, as reason requires: you have soon had the word of the goddess-bottle; and the kindest, most favourable and certain word of an answer that I ever yet heard her give, since I officiated here at her most sacred oracle: rise, let us go to the chapter, in whose gloss that fine word is explained." "With all my heart," quoth Panurge; "by jingo, I'm just as wise as I was last year: light, where's the book? Turn it over, where's the chapter? Let's see this merry gloss."

CHAPTER XLV

HOW BACBUC EXPLAINED THE WORD OF THE GODDESS BOTTLE

BACBUC having thrown I don't know what into the fountain, straight the water ceased to boil; and then she took Panurge into the greater temple, in the central place, where was the enlivening fountain.

There she took out a hugeous silver book, in the shape of a half tierce, or hogshead, of sentences: and having filled it at the fountain, said to him; "The philosophers, preachers, and doctors of your world, feed you up with fine words and cant at the ears; now, here we really incorporate our precepts at the mouth. Therefore I'll not say to you, read this chapter, see this gloss: no, I say to you, taste me this fine chapter, swallow me this rare gloss. Formerly an ancient prophet of the Jewish nation eat a book, and became a clerk even to the very teeth! now will I have you drink one, that you may be a clerk to your very liver. Here, open your mandibules."

Panurge gaping as wide as his jaws would stretch, Bacbuc took the silver book, at least we took it for a real book, for it looked just for the world like a breviary; but, in truth, it was a breviary, or flask of right Falernian wine, as it came from the grape, which she made him swallow every drop.

"By Bacchus," quoth Panurge, "this was a notable chapter, a most authentic gloss, o' my word. Is this all that the trismegistian bottle's word means? I' troth I like it extremely, it went down like mother's milk." "Nothing more," returned Bacbuc: "for trinc is a panomphean word, that is, a word understood, used, and celebrated by all nations, and signifies, drink.

"Some say in your world, that sack is a word used in all tongues, and justly admitted in the same sense among all nations: for, as Æsop's fable hath it, all men are born with a sack at the neck, naturally needy, and begging of each other; neither can the most powerful king be without the help of other men, or can any one that's poor subsist without the rich, though he be never so proud and insolent; nay, even were it Hippias the philosopher, who boasted he could do everything. Much less can any one make shift without drink than without a sack. Therefore here we hold not that laughing, but that drinking is the distinguishing character of man. I don't say drinking, taking that word singly and absolutely in the strictest sense; no, beasts then might put in for a share; I mean drinking cool delicious wine. For you must know, my beloved, that by wine we become divine; neither can there be a surer argument, or a less deceitful divination. Your academics assert the same, when they make the etymology of wine, which the Greeks call ΟΙΝΟΣ, to be from vis, strength, virtue, and power; for 'tis in its power to fill the soul with all truth, learning, and philosophy.

"If you observe what is written in Ionian letters on the temple gate, you may have understood that truth is in wine. The goddess bottle therefore directs you to the divine liquor; be yourself the expounder of your undertaking."

" 'Tis impossible," said Pantagruel to Panurge, "to speak more to the purpose than does this true priestess: you may remember I told you as much when you first spoke to me about it.

"Trinc then: what says your heart, elevated by Bacchic enthusiasm?"

With this, quoth Panurge,

714

"Trinc, trinc; by Bacchus let us tope,
And tope again; for, now I hope
To see some brawny, juicy rump,
And tickle't with my carnal stump.
E'er long, my friends, I shall be wedded,
Sure as my trap-stick has a red head;
And my sweet wife shall hold the combat,
Long as my baws can on her bum beat.
O what a battle of a— fighting
Will there be! which I much delight in!
What pleasing pains then shall I take
To keep myself and spouse awake!
All heart and juice, I'll up and ride,
And make a duchess of my bride.
Sing Io pæan! loudly sing
To Hymen, who all joys will bring.
Well, friar John, I'll take my oath,
This oracle is full of troth;
Intelligible truth it bears,
More certain than the sieve and shears."

CHAPTER XLVI

HOW PANURGE AND THE REST RHYMED WITH POETIC FURY

WHAT a pox ails the fellow?" quoth friar John. "Stark staring
mad, or bewitched o' my word! Do but hear the chiming
dotterel gabble in rhyme. What o' devil has he swallowed? His
eyes roll in his logger-head, just for the world like a dying goat's.
Will the addle-pated wight have the grace to sheer off? Will he rid
us of his damned company, to go shite out his nasty rhyming balder-
dash in some boghouse? Will no body be so kind as to cram some
dog's-bur down the poor cur's gullet? or will he, monk-like, run his
fist up to the elbow into his throat to his very maw, to scour and
clear his flanks? Will he take a hair of the same dog?"
Pantagruel chid friar John, and said:

"Bold monk, forbear; this, I'll assure ye,
Proceeds all from poetic fury;

715

Warm'd by the God, inspired with wine,
His human soul is made divine.

For without jest,
His hallowed breast,
With wine possessed,
Could have no rest,
Till h'had expressed
Some thoughts at least
Of his great guest.
Then straight he flies
Above the skies,
And molifies,
With prophesies,
Our miseries.

And since divinely he's inspired,
Adore the soul by wine acquired,
And let the toss-pot be admired."

"How!" quoth the friar, "is the fit of rhyming upon you too? Is't come to that? Then we are all peppered, or the devil pepper me. What would I not give to have Gargantua see us while we are in this magotty crambo-vein! Now may I be curst with living on that damned empty food, if I can tell, whether I shall scape the catching distemper. The devil a bit do I understand which way to go about it: however, the spirit of fustain possesses us all, I find. Well, by St. John, I'll poetise, since everybody does; I find it coming. Stay, and pray pardon me, if I don't rhyme in crimson; 'tis my first essay.

"Thou, who canst water turn to wine,
Transform my bum by power divine
Into a lantern, that may light
My neighbour in the darkest night."

Panurge then proceeds in his rapture, and says:

"From Pythian Tripos ne'er were heard
More truths, nor more to be revered.
I think from Delphos to this spring,

Some wizard brought that conjuring thing.
Had honest Plutarch here been toping,
He then so long had ne'er been groping
To find according to his wishes,
Why oracles are mute as fishes
At Delphos: now the reason's clear,
No more at Delphos they're, but here.
Here is the tripos, out of which
Is spoke the doom of poor and rich.
For Athenæus does relate
This bottle is the womb of fate:
Prolific of mysterious wine,
And big with prescience divine:
It brings the truth with pleasure forth,
Besides you hav't a pennyworth.
So, friar John, I must exhort you
To wait a word that may import you,
And to enquire, while here we tarry,
If it shall be your luck to marry."

Friar John answers him in a rage, and says:

"How, marry! by St. Bennet's boot,
And his gambadoes, I'll ne'er do't.
No man that knows me e'er shall judge
I mean to make myself a drudge:
Or that pilgarlic e'er will doat
Upon a paltry petticoat.
I'll ne'er my liberty betray
All for a little leap-frog play;
And ever after wear a clog
Like monkey or like mastiff-dog:
No, I'd not have, upon my life,
Great Alexander for my wife,
Nor Pompey, nor his dad-in-law,
Who did each other clapper-claw.
Not the best he that wears a head,
Shall win me to his truckle-bed."

Panurge, pulling off his gaberdine and mystical accoutrements, replied:

717

"Wherefore thou shalt, thou filthy beast,
Be damned twelve fathoms deep at least;
While I shall reign in Paradise,
Whence on thy loggerhead I'll piss.
Now when that dreadful hour is come,
That thou in hell receiv'st thy doom,
E'en there, I know, thou'lt play some trick,
And Proserpine shan't scape a prick
Of the long pin within thy breeches.
But when thou'rt using these capriches,
And catterwauling in her cavern,
Send Pluto to the farthest tavern,
For the best wine that's to be had,
Lest he should see, and run horn mad:
She's kind, and ever did admire
A well-fed monk, or well-hung friar."

"Go to," quoth friar John, "thou old noddy, thou doddipoled ninny, go to the devil thou'rt prating of; I've done with rhyming; the rheum gripes me at the gullet. Let's talk of paying and going; come."

CHAPTER XLVII

HOW WE TOOK OUR LEAVE OF BACBUC, AND LEFT THE ORACLE OF THE HOLY BOTTLE

DO not trouble yourself about anything here," said the priestess to the friar; "if you be but satisfied, we are. Here below, in these circumcentral regions, we place the sovereign good not in taking and receiving, but in bestowing and giving; so that we esteem ourselves happy, not if we take and receive much of others, as perhaps the sects of teachers do in your world, but rather if we impart and give much. All I have to beg of you, is that you leave us here your names in writing, in this ritual." She then opened a fine large book, and as we gave our names, one of her (she) mystagogues, with a gold pin, drew some lines on it, as if she had been writing; but we could not see any characters.

This done, she filled three small leather vessels with fantastic water, and giving them into our hands, said, "Now, my friends, you may depart, and may that intellectual sphere, whose centre is everywhere, and circumference nowhere, whom we call GOD, keep you in his Almighty protection. When you come into your world, do not fail to affirm and witness that the greatest treasures, and most admirable things, are hidden under ground; and not without reason.

"Ceres was worshipped because she taught mankind the art of husbandry, and by the use of corn, which she invented, abolished that beastly way of feeding on acorns; and she grievously lamented her daughter's banishment into our subterranean regions, certainly foreseeing that Proserpine would meet with more excellent things, more desirable enjoyments, below, than she her mother could be blest with above.

"What do you think is become of the art of forcing the thunder and celestial fire down, which the wise Prometheus had formerly invented? 'Tis most certain you have lost it; 'tis no more on your hemisphere: but here below we have it. And, without a cause, you sometimes wonder to see whole towns burnt and destroyed by lightning and ethereal fire, and are at a loss about knowing from whom, by whom, and to what end, those dreadful mischiefs were sent. Now, they are familiar and usual to us; and you philosophers, who complain that the ancients have left them nothing to write of, or to invent, are very much mistaken. Those phænomena which you see in the sky; whatever the surface of the earth affords you, and the sea, and every river contains, it is not to be compared with what is hid within the bowels of the earth.

"For this reason the subterranean ruler has justly gained, in almost every language, the epithet of rich. Now, when your sages shall wholly apply their minds to a diligent and studious search after truth, humbly begging the assistance of the sovereign God, whom formerly the Egyptians in their language called The Hidden and the Concealed, and invoking him by that name, beseech him to reveal and make himself known to them, that almighty Being will, out of his infinite goodness, not only make his creatures, but even himself known to them.

"Thus will they be guided by good lanterns. For all the ancient philosophers and sages have held two things necessary, safely and pleasantly to arrive at the knowledge of God and true wisdom; first, God's gracious guidance, then man's assistance.

"So among the philosophers, Zoroaster took Arimaspes for the companion of his travels; Æsculapius, Mercury; Orpheus, Musæus; Pythagoras, Aglaophemus; and among princes and warriors, Hercules, in his most difficult achievements, had his singular friend Thesus; Ulysses, Diomedes; Æneas, Achates: you followed their examples, and came under the conduct of an illustrious lantern: now, in God's name depart, and may he go along with you!"

THE END OF THE FIFTH AND LAST BOOK OF THE HEROIC DEEDS AND SAYINGS OF THE NOBLE PANTAGRUEL

198